Brian Fern

Collected Writings

Contemporary Music Studies

A series of books edited by Peter Nelson and Nigel Osborne, University of Edinburgh, UK

Please see the back of this book for other titles in the Contemporary Music Studies series.

Brian Ferneyhough
Collected Writings

edited by

James Boros and Richard Toop

with a foreword by

Jonathan Harvey

Routledge
Taylor & Francis Group

LONDON AND NEW YORK

First published 1995
Second printing 1998

Reprinted 2003
By Routledge
11 New Fetter Lane, London EC4P 4EE

Transferred to Digital Printing 2003

Routledge is an imprint of the Taylor & Francis Group

British Library Cataloguing in Publication Data

Ferneyhough, Brian
    Collected Writings. — (Contemporary
    Music Studies, ISSN 0891-5415; Vol. 10)
    I. Title II. Boros, James III. Toop,
    Richard IV. Series
    780

    ISBN 3-7186-5577-2 (paperback)

CONTENTS

INTRODUCTION TO THE SERIES

The rapid expansion and diversification of contemporary music is explored in this international series of books for contemporary musicians. Leading experts and practitioners present composition today in all aspects – its techniques, aesthetics and technology, and its relationships with other disciplines and currents of thought – as well as using the series to communicate actual musical materials.

The series also features monographs on significant twentieth-century composers not extensively documented in the existing literature.

NIGEL OSBORNE

FOREWORD

To be asked to introduce a substantial collection of the writings of Brian Ferneyhough in his fiftieth year (1993) is both an honor and an ideological challenge. Despite his achievement of seniority, there is no doubt that he is not part of most people's 'establishment' pantheon, and that, if anything, the tide of musical aesthetics has turned against much of what he does and stands for. The importance of these writings and the importance of supporting and recommending them can therefore scarcely be underestimated. His name is widely known and spoken of, but too often as a token of some ill-defined and insufficiently known peripheral musical discourse. He is, for many, a bogeyman. It is to his credit that he has gone on his way unruffled by all this, preserving an integrity worthy of those Americans whose country he has chosen to share – Ives, Varèse, Carter, Cage and Babbitt. But of course there the resemblance ends (except for Varèse, whose work was one of his first models): he is quintessentially European in spirit, as claustrophobically distant from 'the wide-open spaces' as Adorno and Walter Benjamin are from Buckminster Fuller and Leonard B. Meyer. If we are to see him as standing for anything, rather than simply being a unique and individually powerful musical personality, it should be for the principles of evolution in music. He refuses to allow socio-economic pressures of rehearsal time, box-office viability, easy social-role messages and so on to dilute his push to ever greater musical development. He is as suspicious of the isolated expressive gesture which directly draws on well-established codes of signification, such as may be obtained through flirtations with tonality, as he is of dance-like body rhythms, rhythms which would be equally accepting of what has already been adequately developed by composers of earlier generations, in his view. He stands for the undeterred quest to go steadily beyond, taking the language of expressionist Schoenberg to an almost unbearably heightened pitch.

There was no 'jumping in' in Ferneyhough's career. Whereas many composers seem to jump from time to time onto a vehicle, little understanding how it got where it was, Ferneyhough evolved, and became progressively more sophisticated within the mainstream of central European thought – that of Schoenberg, Webern, Stockhausen, and Boulez.

There is a sense, by way of illustration, in which various composers' use of an objective aesthetic, whether it be minimalism, serialism or Zen aleatoricism, is arrived at by too short a cut. Objectivity is often authentically arrived at after a lengthy refinement of an intense subjectivity. Beethoven is, of course, the classic example. But it is equally true of Debussy, Webern, Stravinsky and Messiaen. To leap into the posture of objectivity, without having come there by way of refining and making less gross one's subjectivity, often seems like a heuristic fantasy. Or a suppression of honesty.

Ferneyhough's subjectivity is palpably present: the music is emotional. But it is sometimes developed to a point where it seems to go beyond itself. The speed with which different expressivenesses follow each other, and the density with which they superimpose vertically, are so great that a sort of overload can occur, one which transcends the restlessness of arousal, like a film run through at ten times the proper speed. The occasional passage where a more normal rate of invention happens can, in context, seem almost banal – a measure of the distance we have travelled in the music.

What is so good about the writings collected here is that we get a strong sense of the musical thought itself, as well as of its more usually discussed aesthetic aura. In the interviews, the questions on general aesthetic considerations are often answered within a shift of focus to purely musical preoccupations, and one sees the complexity of a mind deeply engaged with fundamentals of sonic structure. There are technical essays on such matters as rhythm, explaining the very difficult interrelationship between speed-ratios within a measure and the length of the measure itself; these are vital to any deeper analysis of the music, with its legendary complexity of bracketing and time signature. Fully brought out also is the polyphony of the parameter development. The integral serialists elevated all the parameters to self-sufficient form-making status, but none of them, except Ferneyhough, went on to develop the gestural, expressive independence of the parameters to such a high degree. Ferneyhough, I think, does not counterpoint his dynamics and timbres (for instance) to articulate quasi-serial patterns; they are polyphonically employed in more basic intuitive developments. They have a life and history of their own, yet they are born of gesture and they reform to make new gestures. An aspect (parameter) of a coherent expressive gesture will split off and go its own way. Taking every aspect of a sonic object so seriously gives Ferneyhough's music an extraordinary richness, where every line seems to have the significance of three, and we can move in and out of focus from the microscopic to the macroscopic with equal reward. Because these atoms of structure are constantly developing in clashing counterpoint with each other – perhaps the mode of playing is changing rapidly while the dynamics (or pitches or vibrato or register . . .) are slowing down their rate of change – the perception one has is of a world in constant flux – a Heraclitean cosmos – or a lumpy universe in which matter congeals and disperses. Yet it is, overall, a consistent order.

The extraordinary creative ferment collides violently with the grid of measure-structure which contains it. Sitting next to Brian at a lecture once, I witnessed him shifting restlessly on his seat for a few minutes, then getting out a scrap of paper which he rapidly covered with complex notations encrusting one another like a coral reef for the next fifty minutes. When he talks, a torrent of ideas pours from his mind, often hard to follow because their rapid sequence has the character of sparks shot off white-hot metal rather than cool linear argument. The intuitive molten metal clearly has to meet a rational crucible of strong build. That can occur on many levels: ratio-bracket structure, measure-length structure, sonority-structure (how the sound is layered), timbre-structure (how the timbres are grouped in families, seating disposition, etc.) and sectional structure. Aspects (parameters) of the sound communities get eliminated or transformed, but something of consistent identity moves between micro and macro levels. On the simplest level, there are always big moments in dramatic places giving a crucible of formal strength: the brass climax at the end of **Transit,** the suddenly unmuted explosion a third of the way through **Funérailles II,** after which everything decays, the rhythmic unisons from which the **Second Quartet** starts out, the ever-clearer sectioning of the **Fourth Quartet** with soprano, the high shrieking eruption of the final song of **Etudes transcendantales,** with its much greater length and silence-infected end, contrasting radically with what went before, and so on. Most listeners are rarely totally lost, despite the difficulties on the micro level.

At fifty, Ferneyhough has already redefined instrumental virtuosity. The phenomenally difficult notation, once laboriously mastered, brings the player to the energy of a hot improvisation, yet with every detail purposefully directed. For those who accept it, and they are the important ones, a new standard is born, a new speed of thinking and feeling where hyper-intellectual meets manic raver. They experience an energy born of rapid switching, for all humans are monophonic in consciousness and only learn to be multiphonic by activating an energized unconscious. New delicacy is born too: listen to the performances of the quartets by the Ardittis – fleeting gettatos, spectral glissando harmonics, wispy ponticellos – the colors are almost transparent.

It seems to me that Ferneyhough mirrors a consciousness that is at the heart of contemporary living, particularly for the thoughtful. There is in his 'perpetual variation', a reflection of the view that everything is questionable; that, since Freud and Marx, there is known to be a hidden agenda behind every assertion, every establishment of 'fact', every respected value. Motives and influences are secretly supporting thoughts and actions from behind, whether springing from the unconscious or from the pressuring environment of socio-economic forces. The further back one goes to unravel the root cause, the more questions and hidden expanses come to light, in infinite and spiralling regress. The simplest belief, assertion, value is revealed as uncomfortably lacking in innocence. As critical theory has exemplified, this constitutes something of a spiritual crisis, a profound anxiety engendered by the nihilism of circularity. There is no getting out. Trapped in the imprisoned arguments that do not let us escape our location in history, we sense only the darkness beyond. Inevitably, anything less than a multi-faceted model is inadequate as a response. Hence complexity. Hence ambiguity, polyphony, perpetual flux. Ferneyhough's music is uniquely valuable in having the courage to hold the mirror up to that sensibility without flinching. We may not agree, as I do not, that it is the only model, but it is certainly the most widespread in the Western world today.

Ferneyhough's illumination of that crisis, through his music, his teaching, his painting and now his collected writings, is an important cultural moment; we only save ourselves if we know ourselves.

JONATHAN HARVEY (U.K.)

EDITORS' INTRODUCTION

The present collection brings together the majority of Brian Ferneyhough's extant writings, many of them here appearing in English for the first time, along with some edited transcripts of informal talks, and a number of major interviews. Given the amount of material in these categories, we decided against the inclusion of some shorter program notes which were not, at the same time, discussions of broader issues.

It will be noted that there are, strictly speaking, no 'early writings' from the period of the **Sonatas for String Quartet**; the early days are dealt with largely anecdotally, in the course of various interviews. Apart from a Webern analysis dating from 1972, coverage effectively begins in the late 1970s, in the wake of the **Time and Motion Studies** cycle. Thereafter, Ferneyhough's work is covered from almost every angle, from broad aesthetic considerations to technical *minutiae*. Although the vast majority of the texts deal with Ferneyhough's compositions – an output which we would unhesitatingly regard as one of the most significant of the last quarter-century – there are others which reflect his activities as a highly influential composition teacher, and some (notably the interview with Jeffrey Stadelman) which touch on his recent work as a poet. Somewhat to our regret, there is no extant text dealing with his highly accomplished painting.[1]

The grouping of the various texts into four categories, each chronologically ordered, involved some slightly arbitrary decisions, since there is not always a clear line of demarcation between categories. However, we feel that the present arrangement gives a more cohesive result than the simple presentation of all texts in a single chronological sequence. It seemed to us that the essays, as Ferneyhough's most obviously 'formalised' statements, should have pride of place. Yet, as the most introspective, and in some respects most 'specialised' of the texts, they are not necessarily the ideal starting point for a reader who is relatively unfamiliar with Ferneyhough's work, and for whom the interviews, especially the wide-ranging one with Philippe Albèra, may perhaps provide the best introduction to the composer's music and thought.

The considerable space accorded to interviews may seem in need of justification, the interview being, traditionally, a somewhat ephemeral and

---

[1] An example of which can be seen on the cover of the Etcetera recording of recent chamber works (KTC 1070); see discography.

anecdotal genre. We believe the reader will soon gain a very different impression of the 'Ferneyhough interviews' genre; though more volatile, and more mercurial than the essays, they are no less intense. In passing, readers may also get some insight into the difference between the composer's European and American interlocutors, the former of whom are more inclined to enter into dispute with their subject, while the latter are more likely to seek amplifications of statements made previously in other contexts.

The reader will doubtless be struck by the individuality of Ferneyhough's English usage – potentially the despair of any house editor – and also, more importantly, by the range and richness of metaphors and references in his verbal discourse; French semiotics and literary criticism, the new physics, philosophies as diverse as those of Ayers and Adorno, and any number of other strands of contemporary intellectual endeavour have clearly left their mark on his vocabulary, without his having become enslaved by any of them. Given the sheer number of key concepts that permeate these pages, we decided to append a separate subject index which, without claiming to be exhaustive, will certainly be of use to any reader seeking to compare the composer's aesthetic and technical preoccupations at various points in time. As for orthography, Ferneyhough's originals employ both English and American usage, depending on the date and origins of the material; we have decided – with the composer's approval – to standardize the spelling to American.

In their original form, many of these essays and interviews included footnotes or endnotes. We have treated all of these as endnotes, and in addition have inserted further comments _as footnotes_ when this seemed necessary to clarify the text. However, we have sought to keep these editorial additions to a minimum.

Because of the striking visual appearance of Ferneyhough's scores, it has become something of a convention for publications concerning his work to be interleaved with scores pages, often of dubious relevance to the text. After considering the total number of musical examples legitimately called for by the articles in their original forms, it seemed to us useful to add a few more – sometimes to facilitate understanding of the text, and sometimes because particular periods of the composer's output seemed to be unrepresented. These editorially inserted score examples are indicated by letters (_Example A_) instead of by the customary numbers. The reader will now be able to see excerpts from most of the major scores, although certain large-format works such as **Firecycle Beta** and **La terre est un homme** had to be omitted on practical grounds.

Our thanks are due above all to Brian Ferneyhough for his patient assistance in excavating, revising, and even translating and retyping certain texts. Particular thanks also to Jonathan Harvey, always an eloquent advocate of Ferneyhough's work, for providing a foreword, and to Nancy Boros, for her constant patience and support. Thanks go to Peters Edition (London) for permission to reproduce numerous score pages from Ferneyhough's works, to Associated Music Publishers and Theodor Presser for permission to reproduce the excerpts from works by Ruggles, and to Universal Edition (London) and Edition Modern (Munich) for similar permission in relation to works by Finnissy and Webern. Acknowledgements of permission to reprint various items are included in the Sources section at the end of the volume. Thanks are also due to Lyn Osman and Dr Tom Hughes (Sydney) for wrestling with various problems posed by Mac/IBM diskette conversions.

Reprint 1998: Though the selection of writings in this reprint is the same as in the initial print run, the List of Compositions and Discography have been updated. It was possible to provide better-quality copies of some score examples, and various typing errors have been corrected; particular thanks to Jim Gardner for spotting some of the latter.

JAMES BOROS (Dumont, NJ)
RICHARD TOOP (Sydney)

I Essays

ASPECTS OF NOTATIONAL AND COMPOSITIONAL PRACTICE
(1978)

No discussion of one particular aspect of compositional practice can penetrate to the heart of its subject while failing to accord due regard to the very specific esthetic attitudes of the artistic personality whose formulations form the objective foundation of the discourse. As with techniques of material manipulation, so with types of notation. Since there are certainly no value-free systems (particularly those with pretensions to being such) one must necessarily begin with certain axioms which, while in no way intended (or expected) to be prescriptive in respect of details of realization, nevertheless seem to me sufficiently general in application as to suggest the likelihood of coherence in detail.

Notation (*particularly* notation) shows us two faces: traceable and analyzable in terms of historic development as it doubtless is, it is nevertheless hardly to be separated, even in principle, from the actual goals which a particular artist has set himself. It is far from accidental that so many works of the last three decades are perhaps more immediately categorizable in terms of their visual rather than their aural characteristics.

Thus: it is scarcely feasible to make exceptions - any and every attempt to undertake a tentative re-integration of music into a wider cultural frame (the most pressing task facing us) must surely commence at the most basic (but by no means most primitive) level possible, must illuminate the hierarchy of its own concealed internal ideologies; must, via recourse to an extended ritual of musical self-reflection, aim at putting its own house in order. Notation, as an explicit ideological vehicle (whether intended as such or not from the point of view of the composer), would seem to have a vital role to play in any strategy directed towards the accomplishment of such a program, or, at the very least, towards a comprehensive presentation of the type and disposition of the problems involved. It is probably inevitable that the preliminary mapping-out of this terrain will tend to generate more confusion than it manages to eliminate but, in any case, it seems to me that one of the principal characteristics of an authentic work consists in exactly this: to recognize the endless continuum of complexity uniting all things.

The attractions of musical notation (occupying a strange ontological position: a sign constellation referring directly to a further such constellation of a completely different perceptual order) are always qualified by the presence of corresponding dangers. The constraints placed upon, and the potential for action contained in the specific matrix which each self-consistent notational system (as represented in a particular compositional context) offers are not, in themselves, to be separated from the value which the written necessarily incorporates. Naturally enough, the emphasis will always be the adequacy of such systems as methods of specifying *sounds*: at the same time any such system must be judged inadequate whose premises do not reflect a concern for the sound *after its production*. The sound (the totality of sonic phenomena defined in an individual instance as constituting a realization of the score) cannot, via the force of its reaching out towards emancipation, be permitted to expand into a vacuum, but must be curved back inside the space which the original organizational characteristics of the score (as reflection of the final stage of the *act* of composition, its *record*) should have assumed the task of defining. Both - score and sound - are sign systems whose primary fields of signification must always remain their respective opposites.

No notation, of whatever iconically representational status, can presume to record information encompassing all aspects of the sonic phenomenon for which it stands. It may be argued that this is a state of affairs not to be regretted (the argument seeking to decry exactitude because of its supposed limitation of the freedom of the performer's interpretation being one example of a thoroughgoing misunderstanding of the role of notation in general), but there seems, on the face of it, no convincing reason why the musical effects of as near an approach as possible to this unreachable ideal should not be investigated. The nearer we come to this 'absolute zero' of realization, the more likely it becomes that the *essential* components of the relationship between the various modes of existence of a composition will emerge, freed from irrelevancies and uncertainties such as serve to disguise their 'otherness' in more compromising circumstances. The unity of expression which a successful work evokes is surely a function of the play of incompatibilities which these modes represent.

Perhaps the single most important task facing the composer in his confrontation with the various aspects of his *own* activity is the postulation of a universe within which these extremes be enabled to *speak* to one another and, in so doing, point out a path towards overcoming the endless proliferation of barriers compartmentalizing the realm of the senses.

One point of departure for an iconology of compositional activity: the representation of the act of composition as a polyphonic membrane, whose scale of resonance encompasses and reflects the common ground linking the several interlocking connotational complexes making up the nature of composition as signifying action in the widest sense of the term.

As the most immediate and natural iconic vehicle, notation seems to be the key to one possible area of musical auto-introspection. In particular, it seems at least conceivable that a thoroughly reformulated approach to notation / realization might be in a position to throw some light on the essential nature of the 'work' (its preconditions, situational validity etc.) as such and, in so doing, allow the very concept of closed form in present-day compositional practice to acquire a renewed esthetic foundation.

The essential presuppositions for such a capability are three in number:

(1) an adequate notation must demonstrate its ability to offer a *sound-picture* of the events for which it stands. Without this direct link in terms of a specified, decodable repertoire one is forced to abandon one of the most essential tools of the analytic function to the arbitrary orchestration of external factors.

(2) an adequate notation must be in a position to offer all essential (as defined by the *a priori* given sign systems in which every notational statement is embedded) instructions for a *valid reproduction* (i.e. what is to count as such) of those sounds / actions defined as constituting (as ensemble) the 'text' of the work. This aspect does not concern itself directly with the matter of influences upon performer psychology, although the common boundaries are naturally fluid in the extreme.

(3) an adequate notation must (should) incorporate, in and through the conflation and mutual resonance of the two elements already mentioned, an *implied ideology of its own process of creation.*

Although the third aspect is, to some extent, a facet of all notational conventions (present in the form, more often than not, of vague inherited 'performance traditions' lurking in the darker corners of conservatoires), it has only seldom been so consistently incorporated into the visual mode of a work that one would be justified in speaking of it as being 'part of' the piece in question. Perhaps it is considered indecent?

An important qualification: whilst being present in an *unambiguous* notational formulation, this ideological trace or spoor must, in order to be suggestive and not prescriptive, be *non-specific*. This unordered field of consequences must, at all costs, remain specific to the performer, since it is performers who engage in feeding back into the work / audience connex the record of their own personal path through the array of possibilities offered.

The goal here, I think, is, therefore, a notation which demands of the performer the formulation of a conscious selection-procedure in respect of the order in which the units of interpretational information contained in the score are surveyed and, as an extension of this choice, a determination of the combination of elements (strata) which are to be assigned preferential status at any given stage of the realization process. The choice made here colors in the most fundamental manner the rehearsal hierarchy of which, in performance, the composition itself is a token.

An extreme example of this approach: a notation which deliberately sets out to offer a *practical surfeit of information* at any particular juncture, thus underlining in an even more radical fashion the indissoluble links binding hierarchically (ideologically) grounded selection procedures with the ultimate sonic result. Omitting information (whether voluntarily or involuntarily): is this not the ultimate recognition of *priorities*?

A consequence of the increased emphasis on the unstable interface: performer / notation, the deeply artificial and fragile nature of this often naively unquestioned link, is the constant stressing of the 'fictionality' of the work ('work') as a graspable, invariant entity, as something that can be *directly transmitted*. That this is no longer the case has been recognized ever since indeterminacy assumed the mantle of progress; here, however, where the 'work' is posited at least to the degree that an attempt has been made to correlate the topologies of sound and notation, directionality in both physical and temporal dimensions, the *notation* (its depth of perspective) must incorporate, via the mediation of the performer (his personal 'approach'), the destruction (secondary encoding) which it seems to be the task of most music to brush impatiently aside. The object of music thus becomes its conditions of realization, as these are made manifest in and through the encapsulated real-time structuration of composition / rehearsal / listening. There is simply one illusion less to contend with.

Projected outwards: the parallelism of work and world. The social role of notation as point of intersection of disparate fields of interest (*a common denominator*). Notation as *fuse*.

To notate is already to be engaged in analysis: to analyze is to move at once beyond the proper boundaries of the discrete, self-identical work. To notate the work is at one and the same time to listen to its echo. There can be no compromise in the search for origins, the tracing-back of notational conventions to the unformed 'material' (itself a supreme fiction), shot-through as it is with *self-notation* as precondition of its thinkability. This is where a work (the work), in all its specificity, begins.

In order to make more concrete some of the speculations engaged in above, I append examples from several of my own compositions in which the matter of notation and its effects has received particular attention.

(1) Notation as intermediary, connecting border areas of representation.

In **Cassandra's Dream Song** (1970) (Ex. 1) for solo flute, the material has been intentionally so slanted as to present, at times, a literally 'unplayable' image. The boundary separating the playable from the unplayable has not been defined by resorting to pitches lying outside the range of the flute, or other, equally obvious subterfuges, but has been left undefined, depending for its precise location on the specific abilities of the individual performer, whose interpretational endowment forms a relativizing 'filter'. In the introductory notes I wrote, at the time:

> "...the audible (and visual) degree of difficulty is to be drawn, as an integral structural element, into the fabric of the composition itself."

Ex. 1: Cassandra's Dream Song

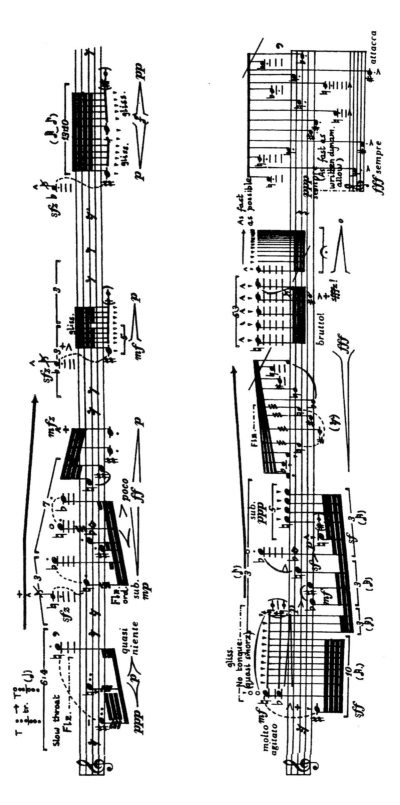

(2) I have always been attracted to the ideal possibility of total textural homogeneity when viewed in depth: a notation of such analicity that, no matter how far one penetrates into detail at a given reading, the density of information remains relatively constant until the smallest compositionally meaningful unit of articulation has been attained. The implication here is of a total freedom on the part of the listener to move at will inside and through the textures, transferring from level to level with a minimum of difficulty and adapting a maximum of previous structural categories to articulate the new context. These same qualities afford performers precisely analogous ideological trace echoes, thus enabling them to transform the score into a personal exercitium, a ritual practice of living reconstitution. The largely spontaneous and intuitive mobility of the attentive ear is thus shadowed by a suggestion of temporal articulation embodied in the accumulated residual evidence of the rehearsal process, transcribed into the 'real time' by being manifest forth in the local incarnation of a particular interpretational act. The psychologizing of virtuosity (its effective transcendence) as medium of communication. Works of mine in which this particular aspect of notational practice have been particularly exposed are: **Unity Capsule** (1975) for solo flute (Ex. 2); **Time & Motion Study II** (1976-7) for cello and electronics (Ex. 3) and **Time & Motion Study III** (1974) for voices and electronic amplification (Ex. 4).

It is in these works that I felt myself to have most nearly approached and defined the outer limits of a potential self-critical formalism, and to have demonstrated this fact in the specific notational models employed.

(3) In several other compositions I have adopted notational conventions which are designed to effect (in terms of an ideal performance) no audible differentiation of sound texture whatever, by reason of being directed solely at the 'internal polyphony' called up in the mind of the interpreting musician. In **Sieben Sterne** (1970) for organ, for example, several sections (Ex. 5) are notated in extremely complex, but otherwise rather conventional ways, while yet other passages (Ex. 6) are presented to the eye (the critical reasoning faculty) in such a fashion as to allow the performer practically unlimited scope in shaping the basic material according to his own wishes and needs. The instructions applying to these latter passages specify solely that: "it is vital that the ambiguity of these sections in the overall scheme be expressed by striving to make the resultant interpretations resemble the fully written-out passages as nearly as possible."

While it may be a platitude to observe that no notation, whatever its degree of complexity, can aspire to approach the reality of the audible phenomenon as reconstituted within the individual frame of reference of the individual, there seems, to my mind, to reside no inherent contradiction in the situation. What can a specific notation, under favorable conditions, hope to achieve?

Ex. 2: Unity Capsule

Ex. 3: **Time and Motion Study II**

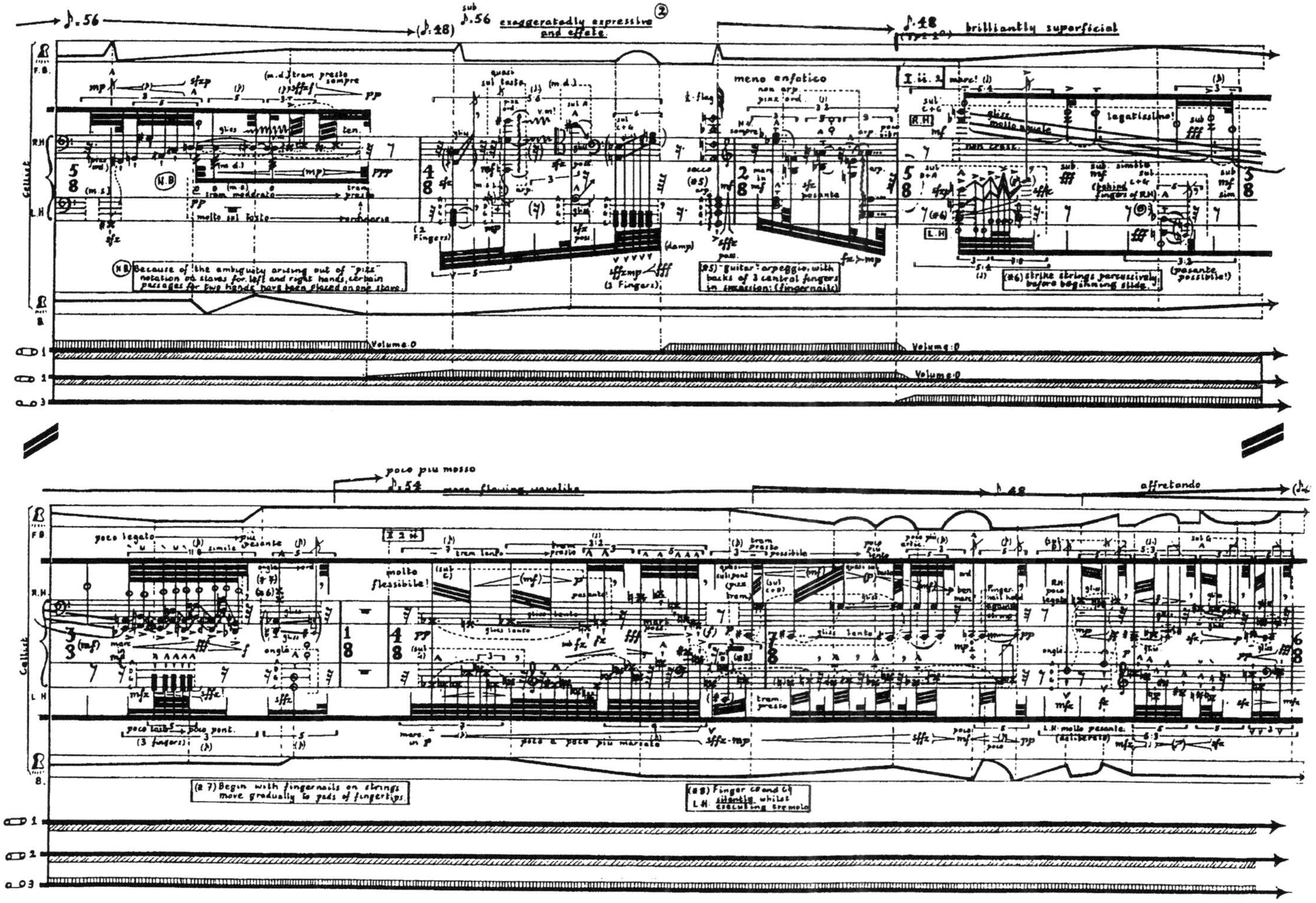

Ex. 4: **Time and Motion Study III**

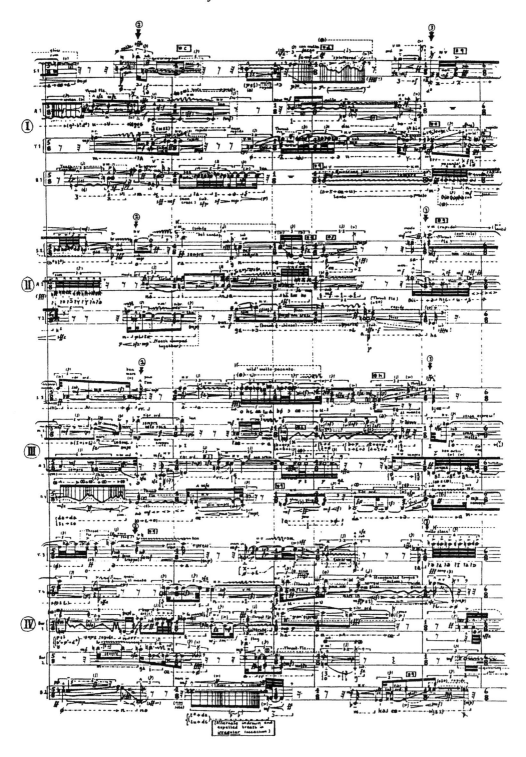

Ex. 5: Sieben Sterne

Ex. 6: **Sieben Sterne**

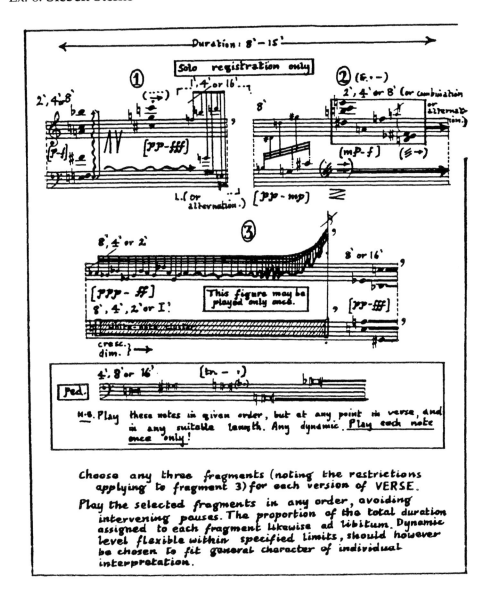

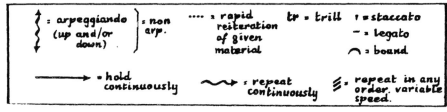

Perhaps simply this: a *dialogue* with the composition of which it is a token such that the realm of non-equivalence separating the two (where, perhaps the 'work' might be said to be ultimately located?) be sounded out, articulating the inchoate, outlining the way from the conceptual to the experiential and back. (The 'encapsulation of unity'.)

COMPOSER – COMPUTER – ACTIVE FORM
(1980)

Perhaps the most immediately striking double image encountered in a first approach to the outer boundaries of computer composition by a composer unversed in the practicalities of the medium is that offered by the (possibly rather vague) vision of a *conjunctio oppositorum*[1] between, on the one hand, unexampled freedom of decision-making and, on the other, extreme rigor of conception, formulation and realization. It may, of course, be platitudinous to affirm that this vision is usually summarily dismissed upon closer acquaintance with the state of present-day research as applied to concrete compositional practice: it is certainly plausible to assume that the type of freedom envisaged by some is the product of an all too imprecise concept of what the medium does and does not permit if it is to be deployed to best advantage. Nevertheless, it is within the area enclosed by these two (however darkly defined) limits that an increasingly significant number of composers is anxious to locate its personal investigations. The seemingly absolutized confrontation engineered in the computer studio between these imagined limits of the world seems to these artists potentially fruitful as a 'coordinate system' within and through which their creative concerns can be paradigmatically realized. Certainly, if Nietzsche's concept of 'creative misunderstanding' is to find wider application on this most recent of aesthetic battlefields, some form of *modus vivendi* will have to be reached, some production strategy via which these seemingly unrelenting extremes can, in reality, be induced to enter into a dialogue on a more thoroughly reflected compositional level. It is by no means obvious, as yet, whether the aesthetic criteria of computer music (as they are, at present, constituted) allow this sort of cross-fertilization. The attraction of unfettered freedom and absolute rigor are limited, unless and until this can be achieved.

For a composer equipped with a certain amount of experience in the world of analog procedures or (like myself) live electronic transformation, first contacts with computer conventions inevitably prove highly disorientating. While the absorption of the initially overwhelming quantity of information opens up new and often agonizing paths through one's long-established frames of

---

[1]*Conjunctio oppositorum*: in alchemy, the "synthesis of psychic opposites" (cf. C.G. Jung, *Mysterium coniunctionis*, Collected Works Vol. 14, Princeton University Press, New Jersey 1977).

intellectual reference, there remains the urgent necessity of forcibly establishing some degree of *distance* between these comfortably established channels and the new input. Often, the creation and maintenance of this awareness of an individualized 'interface' will remain the primary task at hand, acting as a valve regulating the flow of information at an acceptable level long before this latter has crystallized into the active formulation of personally-contoured projects. Holding off the threatening chaos can, to be sure, provide a creative drive all its own; mapping out, as accurately as possible, the fluctuating neutral zones separating rigorous pre-ordering from more obviously spontaneous reactions to (against) the resultant pressure seems, in any case, to be one of the more immediately pressing tasks offering themselves at this juncture - particularly in view of the sometimes astonishing discrepancy to be observed in much present-day practice between the powerful and systematically coherent tools available and the musical forms arising from them. Nowhere in contemporary music, in fact, has this gap managed to assume such dimensions as here; even if conventional instrumental composition has taken shelter under a primitive polemic smokescreen, in which the various parties vie with one another for the honor of distorting and castrating most efficiently the vast and rich potential of quotidian expressive means, this has come about primarily for cultural-tactical reasons rather than because of some inherent structural fault of the 'system'. Investigating this interface, and building bridges connecting one side to the other, are tasks which composers from outside the medium proper might well be in a favorable position to undertake, providing they be furnished with means enabling them to critically reflect on the state of affairs encountered. If this happens, such individuals would appear to be at least as likely as anyone else to manage the transformation of their own creative sensibilities into the outlines of a pattern of wider application in the sense sketched out above.

At first sight it might appear paradoxical that a composer relying in large measure on the specific characteristics of performer capacity in the face of a musical text of great complexity should find interest in computer music *sui generis*. In fact, many of my own works have applied themselves to that constellation of problems clustered about the concept of *efficiency* i.e. the relationship pertaining between effort and its result in the context of goal-directed activity, but also the partially-concealed ideological positions concerning value-judgement processes, upon which the assessment of levels of efficiency are frequently based. The application, in particular, of technologically-conditioned evaluative scales to various areas in which human perception and sensibility are central factors (as in the arts), and the ever-present peril of excessive anthropomorphization (concealment of the quality of *otherness*) of any given medium, based largely on principles not specifically anthropocentric seem, in particular, to be perfectly valid objects of investigation and dissection in musical terms, since 'performance adequacy', there, is always a topic of immediate concern. One of the most significant areas of investigation in live instrumental music - that pertaining to the degree of approximation attained in any given realization of a particular type of musical text - offers itself most directly for transference into the computer studio, by reason of the obviously significant extent to which the concept of efficiency (in both human and computer terms) is (at least in real time) self-contradictory. However, the observed discrepancy between means and ends attained (however these values are measured) characterizing computer music production is only one step in this particular chain: the eventual goal would be to delineate a 'creative environment', a 'body language', of the areas of discourse in which value frameworks of computer (technician) and composer would allow themselves to be articulated in such a fashion that both extremes would be mutually illuminated.

Thus, a confrontation in the initial stages may be composed-out into a synthesis of more than merely subjective, anecdotal import. This synthesis itself, on the other hand, does not at all rest content with being the vehicle for the most 'efficient' production of artworks, since this would, again, reduce it to the status of transparent supportive structure, which, like Wittgenstein's ladder, could be thrown away after climbing up it. Efficiency in aesthetic terms does not, I think, consist of presenting the finished work as if the mode of production were a mere contingency. As in my recent instrumental and instrumental/ electronic music, I have primarily been concerned with allowing all aspects of production (notational explicitness, duration and intensity of precompositional and compositional activity, rehearsal method, realizational capacity of the performer and variability of reception mode) to leave structures and structuring traces to the final work fabric. I would like to extend these investigations into the domain of digitally-organized formal complexes. The opportunities offered by computer technology seem, in fact, to be uniquely suited to the discovery and exposure of certain hitherto obscure corners of Western musical tradition; my own approach to the computer presupposes, therefore, the possibility (at this preliminary stage, the necessity) of outlining a sphere in which noncongruent concepts of efficiency can be superimposed. This would be accomplished by coupling various types and intensities of real time interaction between performer and computer such as to generate conditions in which the common ground between the two will be firm enough to permit the articulation of complex musical forms. My aim thereby is not to eliminate all elements of the accidental or eradicate supposed imperfections standing in the way of an 'ideal' presentation of the argument: in a certain sense, the imperfections, and consequent system-immanent reactions to them *are* the piece, in that the course of development of the musical materials is determined to a large extent (although perhaps by not much more than might be the case for a composition involving more 'normal' media) by the unforeseen and its subjective consequences. The aim is to reorganize the perceptual contextuality of a specific realization in such a manner as to incorporate it, reflexively, into the course of the composition, somewhat as if a silent polyphonic strand were nevertheless to make its effect felt on every level of the discourse.

    The goal of such an undertaking would not be the creation of an 'open' work such as was typical of a certain period some twenty years ago.[¶¶] We need to move on to a deeper awareness of the consequences of form than would have perhaps been entirely possible at that juncture. Rather, the informational texture would be continually enriched, to the extent that a particular performer succeeded in establishing a personal rapport with the exigencies and constraints constituting the environment within which he is to move. A fixed form allowing for mobile realization seems the approach best able to meet these demands at this time. One would, indeed, suppose that the computer would be particularly adept at registering and storing such arrays of predetermined situational alternatives called for by this sort of project. The essential aim, in any event, would be to explore, on as many levels as currently practicable, and in the context of a rigorous stylistic consistency, the ramified implications of a pluriform information evaluation and storage system of potentially endless scope. Basic to this end would be the development of equipment capable of providing this sort of real time support in an interactive field characterized by rapid selection among a number of alternative courses of action branching off at predetermined points. Certainly for a composer who does not see himself as continually occupied in this area, I would envisage such research, undertaken in a spirit of robust pragmatism, as one valid means of inserting this as yet perhaps rather self-regarding area into a more generally accessible context, while at the same time pursuing those concomitant advantages which increasing sophistication concerning the ultimate elements of 'molecular music' brings in its train.

    The ultimate goal of the project which forms the substance of my collaboration with IRCAM at this time is, in connection with some of the considerations outlined above, a work in which a single performer is counterpoised against a series of units of computer generated sonic material in the dual role of signal-transmitting and reacting focus.[¶¶¶] Its aim is not only to allow for a flexible flow of decision-making in real time (selection from predetermined arrays of structurally equivalent elements at structural bifurcation points) but also to be open to precisely the sort of feedback process in which mistakes are not necessarily to be corrected or ignored, but are themselves incorporated as data of reference into later modifications of the material. While this has already

---

[¶¶]The reference here is to works of the late fifties and early sixties such as Boulez's *Third Piano Sonata*, and Stockhausen's *Zyklus*.

[¶¶¶]The work in question was never completed. Cf. p. 394.

been attempted in a comparatively simple fashion in **Time and Motion Study II** for cello and electronics, by requiring not only the generation of certain categories of signal, but also immediate reactions to those same signals in varying states of transformation and diffusion on the part of the performer, I envisage a more thoroughgoing and complex form, each step of which is determined by (and, in turn, determines future states of) analogous principles. In an ideally realized version, performer and computer would thus function at their appropriate respective levels and categories of 'efficiency', even though no two such 'optimized' versions would be likely to reproduce exactly the same formal path through the precompositional maze. Not only would this layout ensure a high level of practical flexibility, it would also fulfil the important task of removing the burdensome responsibility of living out his interpretation in 'tape time' (the continual distortion or modification of subjectively experienced time which coordinating with the fixed proportions of prerecorded materials involves) from the shoulders of the performer, thus freeing him for the execution of more essential and less mechanically foreordained decision-making procedures.

Two specific obstacles would appear, at present, to stand in the way of an adequate realization of such ideas. The first of these concerns the amount of computer memory available to the composer at any given juncture - something which limits immensely the complexity and duration of event groups which the composer may realistically prescribe. Particularly in a work in which each and every decision is seen as a real time reaction (by either performer or computer) to a specific prior signal, the implication is that, somewhat in the manner of a flow diagram, several alternative courses of action are simultaneously available for instant recall. In all likelihood, the composer could find some way of accommodating his ideas to present limitations; on the other hand, there is perhaps an upper limit to the extent to which basic concepts should be diluted in the name of realism (itself a form of ideology, signifying, as it does, a particular attitude towards the hierarchy within which conceptualization and production are located). Certainly, there will be strategies for productively incorporating even these problems into the auto-reflexive work-fabric to the extent that the underlying principles governing such considerations become clear in the course of intensive compositional research. The second handicap is one inhering in the relationship of the composer to the equipment at hand, rather than expressive of a particular attitude towards the generational capacity possibilities of computers as a medium i.e. the present lack of tangible correlates, in and through which his musical ideas offer themselves to him in a concretely manipulable (quasi-analog) fashion. The concentration on the expression of such notions in, and projection through, one or another form of notation has become an obvious and uncritically acclaimed *sine qua non* of most forms of organized activity, so that the absence of any comparable mediatory conjunction can cause the inexperienced composer either to modify his methods of working to an unacceptable degree, or else to resort to one or other form of 'improvisatory' juggling with relatively unfocused or vaguely conceptualized sonic materials. Neither solution (if such they be) can be said to be ideal, since both assume some variety of absolutist attitude in the face of the increased variety of means now becoming available, and are likely to lead either to the grudging acceptance of second-best solutions or to an exaggerated reliance on uncritically exclusive criteria of technological competence. One essential service which the computer can, I think, render the composer is the opportunity to reconsider, on a very basic level, the relationship of elementary elements to their consequences, transposed onto some common plane of time-versus-analog space (whether visual or physical). Accordingly, two specific aspects of research strike me as being open to investigation at this juncture; on the one hand, the creation of some *basic visual notational conventions*, with which the composer can work more or less in the manner to which he is accustomed, and which permit him to work his way through (and perhaps past) some of the more labyrinthine convolutions of the medium; on the other hand (and, on one level at least, intersecting with the previous point as a form of 'space notation in real time'), the search for a method of correlating visual and spatial forms of information presentation with their equivalents in 'psycho-acoustic' space. Anyone familiar with analog studio techniques will be only too aware of the sometimes unexpected discrepancies which arise when (for example) linear spatial motion is translated into a notionally equivalent transformation of a given sonic object. The essential heterogeneity of perceived quality and quantity of transformation on each level is an elementary fact which demands to be investigated and - at least in outline - codified, before any serious claims can be made for the comprehensive exploitation of the undoubtedly sophisticated sound-generation technology now available.

It will be evident from the above that it is not my concern to make life easier for the composer who is neither willing nor able to face up to the demands which any but the most elementary exercise in digital composition procedures inevitably impose. On the contrary, it is precisely because the adequate means of translating information together with its attendant mode of thinking are, as yet, markedly underdeveloped that the means of production and depth of aesthetic position sometimes remain at such a striking distance from one another. Of course, each compositional project will demand its own, sometimes very specific notational and operational conventions; nevertheless, the realm opening up exponentially on one front will remain *de facto* inexploitable on others as long as some such 'compromise' (which, for its part, might eliminate the need for much more deadly compromises of a different sort) is not attempted.

My concern in the foregoing has been less with such intensely-researched fields as timbral definition and modification, since such aspects remain, for me, somewhat tangential to my own compositional interests. In any case, a larger-scale search for the sort of structural/processual synthesis suggested above would, by its very nature, be capable of accommodating any and all individual variants in whatever parametric dimension. My suggestions concern strategy, not the dictation of legitimate compositional ends.

FORM - FIGURE - STYLE:
AN INTERMEDIATE ASSESSMENT
(1982)

En art, et
en peinture comme en
musique, il ne s'agit pas de
reproduire ou d'inventer des
formes mais de capter des forces.

Gilles Deleuze

One of the most unfruitful arenas of confrontation in recent compositional aesthetics has been the question of style and its rationale. The more the general climate of opinion has tended towards embracing some version of pan-stylistic pluralism, the more mutual intolerance and virtuoso attitudinizing have come to obscure entire groups of central issues. The increasingly uncritical acceptance of any and all incidental stylistic usages has driven many composers into one or other of the currently flourishing ideological camps in which serious application to specific areas of difficulty has given way to the production of writings which are often little more than verbally-articulated body gesture, transmitting approval or opprobrium as the case may be, irrespective of the works themselves. By these means a clear-headed re-examination of the implications inherent in particular stylistic norms is conveniently diverted into satisfyingly primitive expressions of clan spirit. Most disturbing, perhaps, has been the phenomenon of deliberate re-mystification of musical expression: the following considerations will seek to underline the dangers of such a position at a time when the expressive potential of music is being eroded by continual resort to false forms of directness,[1] since it is this same supposed immediacy of transmission which engenders the self-congratulatory point of view that there can be such a thing as a global solution to the chronic dissolution of musical substance. One conceivable approach to a provisional resolution of the dilemma

---

[1]The primary reference is to the *Neue Romantik* tendency (Rihm, von Bose, von Schweinitz et al.) which assumed considerable prominence in Germany and Austria from c. 1975 onwards.

might be a renewed concentration on, and re-definition of, the term *style* itself: in particular, it seems vital to focus attention more intensively on the diachronic features of stylistic formation, since this alone promises a salutary counterbalance to views of style which concentrate on the simultaneity of diverse physiognomic features in some historically referential, but apparently extra-historically utopian subjectivism. The unholy alliance of period reference and formal organization often little more than noncommittal in nature, is founded, like many another flourishing aesthetic sectarianism, upon a falsified model of musical history. Being hypostatized into a massive totality (in however limited a real form), such model-building rapidly leads to a devaluation of the internal co-herence of the individual work and its own specific criteria of auto-historical signifying.

It should scarcely be necessary to emphasize that the carefully staged (but nonetheless supremely artificial) opposition of two equally untenable fictions - (1) a music distinguished and authenticated by either the rapidity and spontaneity of the associated creative act, or else by reason of some supposedly natural qualities innate to the gesturally discursive vocables employed and (2) one-dimensional distillations of abstract, material-bound strategies of generation such as are often purported to characterize that all-purpose scape-goat, Serialism - does not survive much detailed examination. All structuring systems are, to some extent, arbitrary and spontaneous, just as most spontane-ity is nothing but the final stage of a frequently lengthy and intense ritual of self-programming on the part of the composer. The ideology of the affective transparency of musical substance as an iconic trace of the creative volitional act is full of pitfalls. The increasing emphasis placed upon the direct expressive power of the musical gesture attempts to convince us that the internal rhetori-cal energy which it is said to generate is sufficient to supplant any secondary formative function which the constituent qualities of a 'formal continuum' might otherwise have been in a position to contribute.

This is a highly perilous doctrine, if only because any attempt to under-line still more clearly the immediate, holistic significance of a gestural unit leads, almost inevitably, to its assumption of effective self-sufficiency and formally passive encapsulation in a henceforth largely contingent context. Focusing on immediacy of expression - however that term may be defined - suggests that little else is required for the adequate appreciation of its specific vehicle than (a) its capacity to be categorized as to denotational intent and (b) the appercep-tion of its direct material presence. That such experientially isolationist tenden-cies have gained access to the heartlands of current musical thinking at the same time as the adoption of vocables derived relatively unmediatedly from earlier historical epochs is surely significant, and points to the destabilizing and diso-rientating factors which such seemingly unproblematic appeals to 'expressivity' conceal beneath the surface.

Although the relevant connotations of the term 'expression' have scarcely been defined except by reading between the lines of otherwise vacuous *ex cathedra* pronouncements,[11] the essence of the matter would seem to be this: that the musical sign or sign-constellation be, to a significant degree, *transparent to emotive intentionality.* According to this view, the sign would, in some respects, be analogous to a glass pane with variable degrees of translucency, through which the emotive object - the spiritual state, one assumes, of the composer in the act of composing (as transubstantiation of the act of self-observation) - is rendered palpable. The necessity and desirability of mediational artifice are either ignored or denied. But that is not all: such a doctrine suggests that there are categories of musical gesture which are somehow *naturally* permeable to particular emotional images, while offering corresponding resistance to others. Though it is clear that the human ear tends to react to various types of sound stimulus according to relatively constant somatic considerations, this would not, *prima facie,* be a sufficiently powerful interpretation of what such a doctrine must needs involve. Much recent music relies heavily on variants of a rather limited repertoire of gestural types calculated to energize the receptive and interpretational faculties of the listener in a culturally quite specific fashion.

It is especially disturbing that this species of 'Pavlovian' semanticism has succeeded in gaining so much ground at the expense of subtler and vastly more flexible views of expressive strategy - particularly when, in so doing, a number of larger-scale aspects of compositional organization grow thereby still more rigid, mechanically unaccommodating and divorced from the fundamental, vitalist energies which one assumes to be both their ultimate *raison d'être* and generator. In particular, it is this tendency's espousal of a form of 'expressive atomism' which vitiates most gravely the life force of its own devoutly-proclaimed program: the more efficiently the individual emotively denotational complex succeeds in transmitting its one-to-one correspondence with its triggering emotive state, the less it needs - or can allow itself to be compromised by - any form of functional interaction with its immediate surroundings in the work. Even if it were to be argued that this view be overly inflexible (in that, in practice, the various gestural/affective units merge into one another) the principle remains clear: expressive denotational monads negate their own potential internal power by evoking it in the act of signification itself.

At the very moment at which the gesture aspires to rise above its material presence it falls back into the mere historically-conditioned material state, since its aspiration to uniqueness empties it of the possibility of entering the

---

[11]See for instance *Fragen an junge Komponisten,* in *Musica* vol. 37/5 (September/ October 1983), p. 405ff. (statements by von Dadelsen, Febel, Müller-Siemens, Rihm, von Schweinitz and many others).

community of signifying acts as a subcategory in its own right. The energy required to create the gesture is consumed by the time its boundaries have been established, so that its ability to exercise an influence on the category pertinent to it is insignificant. Such gestures remain, like strangely visible black holes, at the still center of their own burnt-out identity. They exist solely on condition that they relinquish any claim to enter into more complexly fruitful formal associations except in the form of primitive chains or by a despairing reliance on the shaky mechanisms of the 'Contrast Principle'. By proclaiming their tendentially absolutist iconic pretensions they become, paradoxically, interchangeable, depersonalized tokens of generally (but only generally) recognizable categories of communicational activity, since it is principally by means of some degree of porousness that a gestural unit attains access to any viable framework of articulative possibilities. The sense of the arbitrariness of a gesture increases in direct proportion to its fundamental isolation. The barriers erected against large-scale argument by this body of principles can be only partially surmounted by the acting-out of a state of affirmative monolithicity by the composing individual; even then, the degree of strained self-awareness demanded by such a role bears eloquent witness to the extent to which the creed of spontaneity remains distinctly fragile, reflecting the insistently subversive contradictions at its very core. The last available counter to this formal dislocation and inconsequentiality seems to be a version of programmatic revanchism - the imposition of arbitrary, external formal principles upon a repertoire of sign categories incapable of developing its own grammar of continuity.

Thus, recent years have witnessed the re-emergence of textbook forms such as variations, passacaglia, rondo and the like: whilst there is nothing implausible *per se* in the employment of such molds it nevertheless seems likely that the current drive away from forms which are intimately interwoven with the expressive strategies of which they are composed represents a symptom of the abyss yawning between the immediate ideals and 'image' of neo-romantic aesthetic arguments and the forced unnaturalness of their reification through abstract forms which are, themselves, the most persuasive witnesses to the lacunae in the naturalist position. If semantically loaded elements are to be called upon to guarantee directness of communication, the dilution of these same elements as a result of their integration in organic formal patterns leads to them being called into question as functioning iconic signals: if, on the other hand, more arbitrary formal models be imposed, the gestural elements retain their monadic innocence only at the considerable cost of appearing in a condition of radically schizophrenic disassociation from their circumambient context, which latter itself pretends to a more conventional interlocking of levels than is, in fact, present. On a larger scale, then, the arguments of this school of thought against so-called 'Serial' music rebound upon its members with a vengeance. Forced inconsequentiality and a species of Neo-conservatism are the logical endpoints of this trend. Material which exhausts itself in the violent flare of its own emergence into the world can scarcely serve as the basis for a revised concept of stylistic integrity, be this pluralistically orientated or not. Perhaps, for some, a period of polemic reductionism has been a necessary prelude to the reconsideration of stylistic means. If so, it would be pleasant to be able to foresee a renewed concentration, not upon still further vistas of ready-made, found objects, but, by means of an intense investigation of the energy sources which invest gestural complexes with their propulsive drive towards the future, upon these lines of force themselves as *expression in waiting*.

The situation outlined above has not been selected as a convenient weapon with which to attack particular individuals. It is intended far more to serve as one of several possible illustrations through which the need for new perspectives on the question of style might usefully be demonstrated. Of equal pertinence would also have been a consideration of that approach to pluralism which attempts to integrate elements extracted from various disparate cultural sources into a single 'metastyle', since many of the arguments already offered would apply here in equal measure. It is not necessary to examine in very close detail the many works offering vast and fractured vistas of 'quantum leaps' from one prefabricated stylistic habitat to another. Where there is no conceivable answer to a problem, it appears likely that there is no problem. This would seem to be especially true in respect of stylistic plurality at the present time. In any case, it is at least very questionable if any single stylistic tendency could, by reason of creative *force majeure*, provide that substitute 'common language' whose present lack is loudly, if sometimes perfunctorily, lamented on all sides. Far more wide-reaching consequences would be achieved, not by praying for rain, but through a consequent and painstaking attempt to reconstruct the authenticity of a musical dialect - be it that of one or several composers - from the interstices out.

Faced with that interpretation of style which concentrates largely on the surface characteristics of given materials, it would appear necessary to affirm the importance of the cumulative, developmental aspects of the endeavor. Elements do not simply appear, they emerge imbued with history - not only that ubiquitous but vague shadow of the past, but also, more significantly, their very own 'autobiography', the scars of their own growth. Theories which depend on the exclusivity of the spontaneity/precalculation axis for their validation unwittingly depreciate the means in their own hands, since both postulated extremes presuppose channels of signification which remain imprisoned in the one-dimensional *suddenness of surface* which a more deeply, more differentiatedly oblique species of discourse would avoid. The re-integration of some form of depth perspective depends on re-establishing contact between the surface features of a work and its inner, subcutaneous drives. Like the beautiful illusion of perfection offered by many virtuoso performers, the compositional style which aspires implicitly to the status of natural object denies us entry into the crossplay of forces by which that very illusion is sustained. It is thus imperative that the ideology of the holistic gesture be dethroned in favor of a type of patterning which takes greater account of the transformative and energic potential of the subcomponents of which the gesture is composed. It is a question, in the first instance, of the conscious employment of perceptual categories in respect of the 'afterlife' of a gesture, since it is here, at the moment of dissolution, that the constrictive preforming of gestural material is able to be released as formal energy. A gesture whose component defining features - timbre, pitch contour, dynamic level etc. - display a tendency towards escaping from that specific context in order to become independently signifying radicals, free to recombine, to 'solidify' into further gestural forms may, for want of other nomenclature, be termed a *figure*. The deliberate enhancement of the separatist potential of specific parametric aspects of the figure produces a unit at one and the same time material presence, semantic sign and temporary focus of the lines of organizational force until the moment of their often violent release.

The concept of the parameter has become part of our communal creative experience. Whatever the pros and cons of aesthetic maneuvering as far as its original function is concerned, the term is surely indispensable if we wish to come to practical grips with the above-outlined notions. Regardless of the extent to which many composers might seek to persuade us that the analytical mobility of parametric inflection has been superseded by a return to the integral and indivisible nature of the emotive gesture, we should not permit ourselves to become confused: the power of such rhetorical assertions lies mainly in their undifferentiated substance, while the character of even minimally complex musical discourse is of quite another order. One of the most far-reaching consequences of the sometimes over-literal manipulations typical of the 'classical' serial period has been, not so much the flawless establishment of some materially egalitarian utopia of authorless creation, but, rather, the almost incidental demonstration that any form of sonic unit is the potential focus of many lines of directional energy.

The a-causally immobile quality of the parametric complexes in such compositions was not, in the first instance, a necessary consequence of parametric thinking as such but, rather, follows directly from the specific aesthetic positions adopted. The deepest doubts concerning serial thinking are related to the perception that total mobility of parametric deployment tended to generate a series of contextless monads, whose aural logic by no means obviously followed from the abstract rules of play to which they owed their existence. It was thus the overall decontextualization of parametric structuring which led inevitably to the decay of compositional credibility, not any particular inadequacy inhering in the view of a sonic event as being a momentary fixing of a number of independently moving streams of information. On the contrary, the resultant 'dematerialization' of the event, its radiation into, and illumination of its defining context, is an essential prerequisite for the establishment of those taut chains of mutually embedded perspectives without which the event must needs remain largely incommunicado in respect of larger formal concerns. In this fashion, the event experiences a return to itself as affective substance at the very moment at which the illusion of stable identity is processually transcended.

A realistic re-integration of parametrically defined perspectives suggests the need for a stylistic ambience in which an uninterrupted movement from level to level, from largest to smallest element of form, is an ever-present possibility. A mode of composition which enhances the affective gesture with the energy to productively dissolve itself in a quasi-analytical fashion suggests itself since, by adopting such a standpoint, the gesture is brought to function in several ways simultaneously, thus throwing its shadow beyond the limits set by its physical borders, while the strands of parametric information of which it is composed take on lives of their own - without, however, divorcing themselves from the concrete point of their common manifestation to such a degree that their independence on the processual level could ever pose a serious threat to the credibility or integrity of the gesture itself. The enhanced figure, being primarily a subclass of the gesture, partakes of the general 'speech resemblance' character of the latter, without at any point renouncing its essentially *synthetic* emphasis. Its very dependence on the material immediacy of the gestural manifestation guarantees that a return to the static inconsequentiality of neoserial hierarchies will be rendered improbable.

The present state of value-free pluralism demands resolution, not in the continued search for some Holy Grail of 'common language' (since this would also imply common purpose), but rather through the rigorous definition, both in the single work and in the work series, of a continuity of context in and through which particular vocables - whatever their incidental origins - may assume audible responsibility for the embodiment of a stylistic tradition in the making. The major prerequisite for such an undertaking, far from being the punctual selection of general types of surface feature, is the creation of a continuously evolving state of stylistic homogeneity. The current defeatist denunciation of 'progress' need not inhibit this quest, since there is always room for a language which offers the listener a rich panorama of life-forms in motion. Progress in this sense is surely attainable.

Only the conscious and systematic deconstruction of the gesture into semantically mobile figural constellations promises to overcome the former's inherent limitations, since it is the synthetic nature of the figure which permits the definition of the category through which it wishes to be heard, rather than vice-versa. Expressive energy derives, in large measure, from the impacting power of restriction; arrested motion has a peculiar force all its own, and it is precisely this impetus which informs the dissolution of the gesture into a cloud of liberated, form-building atoms. A musical element possesses radically different qualities, depending on whether it is presented as the evidential trace of a completed process, or as a concrete given, the result and goal of unmediated invention. Analogously, we can imagine a species of form in which all contributory sonic events would be so formulated as to permit the differentiated radiation of their particles into a governing corona of classificatory hierarchies: it is this articulatedly febrile world of forces which remains for us to secure.

Style is important as the vehicle for, and governing instance of, the expansion, diversification and combination of independently-steered streams of formal potential. The progressive accretion, from work to work, of that form of aura which only long-term evolution can provide will be the most effective guarantee for the proper exploitation of such possibilities, no matter what surface characteristics an individual composer's style may display. More than ever, it is likely to be the consistency of whatever stylistic means are adopted that, simultaneously resisting and encouraging invention, will prove most capable of validating a species of expressive vitality which, like the architectural fantasies of Piranesi,[111] does not content itself with remaining industriously imprisoned within the limits of the individual work.

---

[111]Piranesi's **Carceri d'Invenzione** engravings were shortly to provide the inspiration for a major cycle of works; cf. pp. 131, 290.

DIVINING RODS AND LIGHTNING CONDUCTORS:
A VIEW OF COMPOSITION TEACHING
(1983)

Is it possible to teach *composition*? Can composition be *taught*? Attempting to answer such questions appears to be a risky undertaking to the extent that composition teaching is more an *activity* - as Wittgenstein might have put it, a 'form of life' - than an unshakably monolithic construct of pre-packaged theories, facts or formulas. Practically all composers have negotiated one or another version of the pedagogic machine; nevertheless, a definitive response to these controversial questions has never seemed more distant. A glance at a few of the often mutually conflicting demands imposed by conservatory examinations for courses frequently offered concurrently serves to underline the current lack of professional unanimity. The difficulty is evident: as with certain schools of contemporary philosophy, composition teaching has become a subject in search of content. Much of what, at one time, was considered an integral part of composition studies has begun to be diverted to a number of adjacent disciplines (harmony and counterpoint, classical analysis, instrumentation...) so that the composition student might be forgiven for considering himself condemned to operate in that obscure no man's land where territorial conflicts between academically more robust subjects have not yet been amicably resolved. In contradistinction, for example, to rules appropriate to the construction of a fugal exposition, norms appropriate to the encouragement of autonomous creative activity can be neither prescriptive nor descriptive in nature; just as the highest level of knowledge in abstract technical matters cannot guarantee its meaningful employment, so the analysis of works by other contemporary composers - as profound as it may be - is in a position to give neither the teacher nor the pupil the *a priori* certainty that the latter will be in a position to resolve the infinite series of challenges posed by a personal integration of style and the received wisdom of the craft. It is precisely here, in the interstices of the creative act, that the composition teacher has a vital role to play. Expressed somewhat frivolously: he has to be able to function, at one and the same time, both as divining rod and lightning conductor. This demands the assumption of responsibility for a continual re-evaluation of methods - and the significance of those methods - at his disposal in the pedagogical situation. It is this strikingly vertiginous fluidity which ensures that any balanced and exhaustive exegesis of the contents of a composition course will give an impression which remains, at best, a half truth.

An understandable reaction to the state of things outlined above would, logically, be to not teach at all; another might be to insist on limiting the scope of instruction to a species of 'good handiwork' the goal of which being a facility in adequately reproducing styles of recent date (which are thus objectively comparable one with another). It seems to me that both these reactions are fundamentally faulted, in the sense that it is not at all clear that such standardized strategies as these approaches seem to require are really desirable. The present situation in music, characterized as it is by an extraordinary level of pluralism in both style and scales of value, demands, to be sure, the abandonment of the tempting mirage of some sort of *lingua franca* in favor of approaches to teaching which focus on those problems immediately arising from the creative efforts of the pupil, rather than on those rejoicing in the dubious *imprimatur* of a concrete normative consensus, by whatever means arrived at.

Effective composition teaching needs, above all, to be clear as to the nature and proper limits of its own objectives. Without doubt, one of the primary tasks is orientation. Because, today more than ever before, composers deprived of first-hand familiarity with as broad as possible a spectrum of contemporary artistic practice will find themselves in grave difficulties when attempting to realize their full potential, the teacher must see to it that pupils develop both their critical faculties and the necessary enthusiasm and curiosity to a level permitting them to evaluate and subjectively organize the experiences thus accumulated.

Traditional methods ally analysis to the imitation of selected models. While this approach may occasionally be appropriate, it is preferable to relegate it to a decidedly more peripheral status in the present situation, in which stylistic and procedural peculiarities are inseparable from the intentions specific to the creative biography of particular composers. It is not the acquisition of techniques as such which guarantees quality but, rather, the depth of the pupil's insight into those considerations which lead to their integration in a functioning organic unity. Concentrating on reproducing characteristic aspects of particular compositional dialects tends, it seems to me, to devalue these latter, coming dangerously close to mere epigonalism (something completely different from what is involved, for example, in the harmonizing of chorale melodies). In the same way, the evolving composer needs firm support in his attempt to forge tools in and through his own individual creative activity, since it is only along this path that technique can expand to attain a credible level of utility. Although set tasks and exercises of limited scope can sometimes be appropriate, these inevitably take the form of 'resistance', problematic situations in which the student has to maneuver, seeking answers making use of his own personal idiomatic vocabulary.

The more advanced the student, the more these tasks can assume a fundamental, general aspect. Not infrequently, compositions of genuine individual value can emerge; on the other hand, the results of such research can lead to a significantly wider scale of possibilities. At a certain point, the distinction between set tasks and regular discussion and encouragement is transcended - at the latest when students' independent composition projects have reached the level on which the development and maintenance of autodidactic capabilities becomes feasible (to the extent that a good composition tends to pose more questions than it answers?).

However composition courses are otherwise conceived, the central core of all activities is, almost invariably, the individual lesson. This weekly or bi-weekly encounter furnishes a focus for continuing evaluation of progress as well as for establishing the special personal rapport which is the *sine qua non* for fruitful collaboration. The almost ritualistic regularity of these lessons forms a stable framework within which virtually anything at all may be discussed; it also permits the gradual growth of a mutually comprehensible vocabulary - something of vital importance, but, in a few cases, surprisingly difficult to achieve.

One conclusion I have arrived at is that, in the long term, the role of the teacher is largely passive in nature. Clearly, he cannot renounce his ultimate responsibility; first and foremost, however, he is constrained to react to the problems and difficulties which pupils bring with them to their lessons. Because the students have to formulate and structure their needs in advance, they become active participants in their own instruction. The teacher's role is to function as a 'resonating body' through which the pupils' own ideas are reflected back at them, amplified and clarified. It is not the teacher's task to impose his own solutions; what is required is to assist to the surface those solutions already latent in the material and which - by reason of lack of conceptualizing experience, or else simply because of an inability to translate intuition into concrete processes - have eluded the best efforts of the pupil. Even if the imposition of stylistic guidelines is to be avoided as much as possible, the instructor has nevertheless the responsibility for seeing that the works produced under his tutelage demonstrate an adequate grasp of the consequences associated with the employment of particular stylistic conventions. Around this core of personally orientated attention, one might reasonably expect that a course contain informational and orientational activities, and one of its functions (not least in order of importance) is to ensure the establishment of a regular and intense contact among the course participants. These meetings can take the form of lectures (collective lessons) or, more usually, seminars, to which the students themselves actively contribute. As often as possible these activities should be complemented with visiting lecturers and outside performers, in order to guarantee a certain breadth of perspective. A further important provision is the establishment of close relationships with other areas of discipline in the conservatory. This has the double function of reducing the isolation suffered by composers ('exotic birds'...) and to create possibilities - often in the form of open workshops - for the presentation of students' works. The discussion, critique and practical rehearsal experience furnished via this route are of fundamental importance, in that they provide a counterbalance to purely theoretical (and, often enough, isolated) activities.

The above observations concern, for the most part, full-time courses of study at conservatories and similar institutions, since it is in such contexts that the majority of composers gain their first experience of composition lessons. Most of these opinions are also valid for alternative forms of teaching, such as summer courses or private lessons. Every sort of teaching has something unique to offer; the only didactic instruction which strikes me as futile, if not directly dangerous, is that which is either too long to be considered a 'refresher course' or, in contrast, too short to lead to the growth of a fruitful relationship on a more profound level, thus encouraging the illusion that composition consists of a mass of facts and universally recognized skills which are able to be 'taught'.

In my view, the ideal situation would be one in which the teacher, by unremittingly exemplifying creative renewal in his encounters with his pupils, would create the conditions in which composers are not made, but come into being.

IL TEMPO DELLA FIGURA
(1984)

In his poem *Self-portrait in a convex mirror*[1] John Ashbery says of dreams:

> They seemed strange only because we couldn't actually see them
> And we realized this only at a point where they lapse
> Like a wave breaking on a rock, giving up
> Its shape in a gesture that expresses that shape.

I propose to return to this haunting image later in my presentation as offering some hints as to possible resolutions of a whole succession of problems facing contemporary composition, especially in respect of the relationship between musical style and the perception of discursive, form-generating energy.

The term *figure* has been employed with a vast spectrum of nuance over the course of several centuries: on the one hand, this renders its useful present-day definition an all but impossible task; on the other, there would seem nothing inherently objectionable in adding one more definition to those already extant, especially since long searching has led me reluctantly to conclude that no better general term is available for the precise distinction I have in mind. In particular, I would like to avoid any examination of historically mediated usage at this point. What specifically interests me is the extent to which some form of clear distinction between (1) the global delineation of a musical shape and (2) its internal potential for assisting in the creation of musical states with which it is not co-extant is a prerequisite for achieving a more precise insight into the present problematic condition of compositional/formal thinking.

In the first instance, we are talking of a fundamental semantic/syntactic fissure; the gesture *means*, for the most part, by virtue of reference to specific hierarchies of symbolic convention - either artificially established ones or, more basically still, those deriving, by means of abstraction and analogy, from species of bodily comportment. It has been in this area, rather than in the field of musically immanent, synthetic meaning-generation, that the late Twentieth Century has wreaked many of its more offensive depredations, since very few

---

[1]In, John Ashbery, *Selected Poems* (Expanded Edition), Paladin, London 1987, p. 201.

generally-accepted gestural vocables have managed to withstand the storms of dissolution and renewal so characteristic of the last forty years. Response to this deprivation has been especially regressive of late, in that significant numbers of composers have taken to looking back towards a supposedly pristine and (crucial assumption!) somehow more 'natural' era of musical communication in which compositional means stood in an intimate and unproblematic relationship with whatever "content" (emotional states?) music was implicitly assumed to manifest. While it is clear that this attitude towards the cultural recycling of *disjecta membra* of previous epochs is not to be uncritically rejected as a means of assuring the "shock-effect" demanded by W. Benjamin, it seems equally plausible to assume that an increasingly marked preference for historically preformed elements will lead to a partial *disenfranchisement* of those same elements. Ripping such units out of the contexts which gave them being leads to a fatal debilitation of their innate expressive powers at the same time as their integration into new montage forms demands precisely this unimpaired semantic impact in order to support and bring out the envisaged innovatory impact of their juxtaposition. Denuded of their auratic mantles, such isolated elements present themselves, more often than not, as references to anterior worlds of sensibility rather than as their symbolic re-evocation. It must be admitted that music seems significantly more problematic in this respect than the visual arts, where conventions may be said to exist prior to any particular realization. In music, in contrast, it is difficult to envision semantic units entirely divorced from the specific succession of processes engendering them. It is perhaps for this reason that quotation has, in music, such a powerful capacity for undermining discursive identity. The same can be said, to a lesser extent, of more generalized stylistic reference.

One possible counter to this pervasive problem is the return to a semanticity largely dependent on information resistant to concretization in a 'super-contextual' manner. It is on the basis of this consideration that the *figure* is proposed as an element of musical signification composed entirely of details defined by their contextual disposition rather than their innate, stylistically defined referential capacity. The synchronic is replaced by diachronic successivity as the central mode of 'reading' musical states, for the reason that a progressive, accretional definition of musical vocables is indispensable if a counterweight to the suffocating presence of historically concrete stylistic triggers is to be created. In this presentation I will be examining various paths towards the isolation of figural significance and, in particular, will be focusing on the concepts of *musical energy* and *lines of force* as being of some utility in making more precise the envisioned relationship between musical objects (seen as morphologically discrete, self-consistently affective signals) and those formal perspectives suggested by the interaction of local, ancillary aspects of those same objects considered as free-floatingly mobile structural radicals possessing the potential to unfold and reproduce themselves in independently meaningful linear trajectories.

Returning to the Ashbery citation from the beginning: two main ideas seem to be inextricably entwined in those few lines. Firstly, the view that the present constitutes itself only as *sensed absence*; secondly, that our 'life-line' to reality might perhaps be interpreted as a special form of *motion*. What, after all, is 'expression' but a sort of passage from one state to another, in which neither the presumptive beginning and end points are primary, but rather the 'no longer' and 'not yet' whose *impressum* they bear. In this context, the image of the wave refers both to some natural, unformed undertow of creative potential, shaping events according to whatever form of dynamic law, and to the fleetingly insubstantial moment of perception, born along on the crest of the wave as an unrepeatable trace of being. The energy entrapped in the wave (which *is*, in a sense, the wave) being ejected into concrete form by the unyielding resistance of the rock, is instrumental in effecting the transition from the physical to the configurational, thereby becoming invested, as action, with symbolic stature. Force, as the liberation of entrapped energy, finds its counterpart in an energy definable as the application of force to a resistant object. The intersection of these trajectories in the musical discourse is the locus of the present, which is thus weighted, at any given juncture, by a unique balance of tensions, a unique 'fingerprint'. Thus: musical force and musical energy are not identical. Energy is invested in concrete musical objects to the extent that they are capable of rendering forces acting upon them visible. Lines of force arise in the space between objects - not space as a temporal lacuna, atopia, but at that moment of conceptual differentiation in which identity is born - and take as their vehicular object the connective impetus established in the act of moving from one discrete musical event to another.

There are objects which resist distortion by the forces directed at them; their damaged, violated integrity signals to us the measure of those same forces and energies deployed: it is their 'expressive history'. Just as some musical objects are comparatively more resilient, so the nature and power of the forces to which they are exposed need to be calculated with a view to gradual 'weathering', erosion, or their sudden omnidirectional 'dematerialization'. At such moments it is the line of force itself which, like a wave, assumes momentary physical shape as a spectral foreground projected onto the cloud of energized particles seeking opportunity to congeal into a further, gesturally coherent (delimited) object. The gesture is 'frozen force' to the extent that it stands for expressive sentiment, for an absent exchange of expressive energies. The gestural vocable is, in many ways, comparable to the individual word, in that it may be usefully recognized in radically diverse contexts and manifested through a vast variety of individual nuance. One may thus register the semantic component of a gesture without feeling constrained to follow-through the implications of the received information, thereby activating the inner structure and constitution of the gesture itself. To some extent, the affective content of the gesture is only loosely related to its apperceptible surface; the figural activity thus consists, in part, of devising means of ensuring that the latent volatility of the gesture burst through this contingent carapace in order to liberate that surplus of discursivity hitherto locked into the interstices of the sonic object.

In certain interpretations of tonal music, the gesture rises to figural status via the specificities of its harmonic embedding; it is individuated by its evident contextual utility. One readily appreciates why this type of figural energy was, in the final analysis, auto-destructive, in that increasingly extreme individuation led irreversibly to the dissolution of the activating framework - tonality - itself. It seems to me to be vital that the composer seek to establish broadly comparable relations between the quasi-denotational sense of the gesture and its less specific connotational import. If the individual gesture is perceived as the mere casual exemplification of, say, a particular rhetorical category, the individuation of its component elements degenerates to the status of incidental embellishment. If, on the other hand, this very same individuation assumes such particularized independence, the *topos* from which it emerges recedes beyond the 'recognition threshold'. The balancing of these aspects in a continual process of give-and-take is situated at the core of the figural enhancement issue: if, as I believe, the purpose of the figure in much recent music is situated parallel to the progressive decay of 'background' posited above, then the process is presently cycling through at a significantly more rapid rate of flow. At such velocities of figural dissolution and re-formation the gestural object itself threatens to break up, being replaced with a shimmering web of energy exchange. Thus it is that we sense a disturbing and fundamental fracture between the concrete presence of the sound object and any credible context-bound validation in terms of functional (figural) projection. The search, in recent decades, for ever more innovative sonic characteristics might, in this light, be seen as a dim reflection of the sense of unease which is provoked when the impotent, immobile object and an adequately autonomous structuring methodology fail to coincide. The idea of the figure as mediating instance assumes great constructive significance in such a situation, to the extent that emphasis is placed on the structurally mediating capacity of concrete gestural qualities. John Ashbery employs the image of consciousness as the crest of a wave, always changing the material of which it is composed, always driven forward by the sea's restless energy but, in a certain sense (like all wave forms) not really moving. The function and nature of the figure are closely allied to this image: musical consciousness is always the impingement of the past upon the array of possible futures to which (*pace* Derrida) it continually defers. The moment itself is defined, not by any constancy of material substratum, but by its motion; it is the projection of figural energies which *make the pointer visible* by means of which the motion is measured.

The idea of the figure is locked, for me, precisely at the intersection of the defined, concretely apperceptible gesture and the estimation of its 'critical mass', its energic volatility. Both aspects are generated by means of broadly equivalent means; if this were not so, a large-scale modulation, employable as a linguistic tool, would scarcely be conceivable. The figure delivers momentary perceptual frames - stage sets - capable of projecting particular hypothetical evaluational categories into the still-to-be perceived future of the discourse. To some extent, we recognize and locate the nature of such a frame while still physically living-through the decay and dissipation of one or more anterior frames, whereby the partial superincumbence or 'cross fading' of an indeterminate series of prior states comes to provide a significant, albeit necessarily fluid and evolutionary perspectival orientation.

The late German author Arno Schmidt employed the term 'löchriges Dasein' ('perforated Being') when attempting to come to grips with the structure of individual experience. He suggested that perception is characterized less by a hypothetical unbroken stream of consciousness, along which a sovereign subject moves, than by a series of relatively independent and uniquely specific experiential monads - favored instants of great depth and spiritual resonance. Between these brilliantly illuminated points, for him, lie indefinite quantities of instants distinguished by various degrees of flatter, duller sensibility, where time itself moves according to different laws. Thus, the composer needs to attain some degree of control over this perspectival fluctuation if he aspires to master his means in anything like their full formal and expressive potential. Means must be determined to generate distinguishable degrees of purposive depth which, in my view, the steady flow of gestural rhetoric is no longer (if indeed it ever was) capable of assuring.

To the extent that the present stage of compositional ideology tends to favor surface interaction of sometimes only primitively related emotive signifiers, it inevitably encourages the acceptance of an 'all-over', one-dimensional rationale of the perception/reception connex. I do not believe that this assumption can ever adequately do justice to the mind's need for insightful re-ordering of the experientially given, even though it naturally forms one link in the chain whereby significance is assigned. The subsuming of as many phenomena as possible to criteria of a dual nature - gestural as well as figural - allows for an infinity of intermediate steps, of contextually determinable and evaluable relationships between the crest of the wave and the hidden forces investing the marine deep.

It is not my intention to suggest a fundamental schism between the figure and all other vehicles of musical meaning. In reality, it is more fruitful to speak of *figural aspects* of this or that concretely extant vocable, constellation or formal unit. No figure is exclusively or merely a figure, just as no gesture is ever devoid of its proper aura of figural connotations to be activated at will. Our central concern will therefore be the establishment of criteria of intentionality: if parametric constituents of gestures are not to be more plausibly perceived as largely independent of their 'matrix' (in the sense of being consciously 'aimed' elsewhere) we will scarcely be able to speak of their particular *directional energies*.

The possibility of the analogical treatment of diverse sonic characteristics is certainly the conceptual pivot of figurally-orientated thinking and associated procedures. Without the ability to 'infiltrate' the structure of the work on various parallel levels composers would scarcely find themselves possessed of the capacity to trap, accumulate and strategically redirect the energies which the figural dissolution of the gesture calls forth. One way of achieving 'depth perspective' will be to seek procedural modalities amenable to being *transferred* at will from one point of observation in the field to one or more others. A single example will suffice to illustrate the general direction I have in mind. The following string of rhythmic values is capable of being modified and redeployed on multiple concurrently operative levels, for instance: (a) internal structural consistency (degrees of long-short relationship); (b) transformational potential (the sensing of a certain tendency or processuality in the progression from 'very long' to 'very short' within a group, as opposed to the progressive transformation of the two values into longer and shorter on a much subtler scale).

Ex. 1.

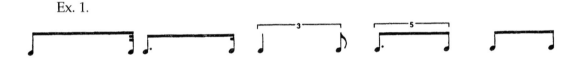

It will quickly become apparent that some lines of force are already at work: if these patterns are allowed to *submerge* in order to assume the role of ordering models, as opposed to concretely present sonic entities, we can sense the added depth of perspective which resorting to such analogical displacement renders possible. For instance, other materials or processes may be predicated onto these patterns of comportment in ways tending to confirm or deny patterns of sensation already promoted; the periodicity of the superimposed elements may be quite at odds with the predominantly linear tendency of the models, or else the two layers may conjoin in the production of a still more long-term, secondary periodicity, where tendencies owing their origins to distinct and diverse generational precepts coincide with a perceptible jolt after a span of independent deviation.

The energies released by these patterns on different levels can be longer or shorter term in nature - in the latter case it will be clear that processing the figural import is likely to occupy a significantly greater time span than the superficial registering of elements predominantly according to the weight of their gestural aspects. In fact, such considerations have little to do with neo-serial manias for order; rather, they reveal a path towards the redefinition of function through the context-bound deployment of local, informal parametric manipulation. The constant creation of 'fuzzy parameters' of this sort is the primary purpose of the figure, to the extent that it supports the deconstruction and subsequent opening-up of the self-enclosed organism in an indefinite number of possible directions. A few variations derived from the example already given will, I believe, be of more utility than lengthy commentary: it will be evident that 'lines of force' have a major role to play in situations of this genre.

Ex. 2(a)

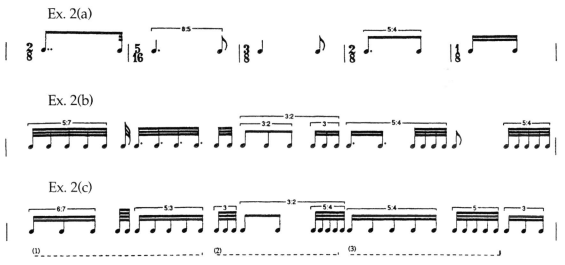

Ex. 2(b)

Ex. 2(c)

In Ex. 2(a) the tendency of the original example towards the elimination of longer values in each cell unit has been compromised by the distortion of these latter by means of the imposition of irregular measure lengths, in which an initial increase in duration is followed by a more rapid decrease. The line of force informing the basic linear formation has thus become partially obscured by an equally fundamental, but less immediately apperceivable tendency - a process which thus imposes two tendency-modifying operations on the individual components of the sequence instead of the single step of Ex. 1. In Ex. 2(b) the original relationship obtaining between the cells has been maintained (in that all durational pairs have identical global durations) but rendered still less evident by the combination of two opposing movements, that is to say, a reduction in the number of equidistant impulses contained in the total value of the first component of each cell, while the number of impulses dividing the second value increases. Even leaving out of consideration the measure length distortion it will be clear that this sort of energy redistribution is more perceptually problematic in a total process of relatively short duration by reason of the significantly increased amount of information to be evaluated. Ex. 2(c) illustrates the possibility of a superposition of two tendencies with different rates of change. Successive groups of three, two and five subdivisions have been mapped onto the durations furnished by our initial cell but, because there are now three subdivision values as against two global values in each basic cell unit, a progressive encroachment of the two figural levels occurs. If these techniques are repeated over the total duration of a fragment of whatever length, their homogeneity will tend to be registered, to a certain degree, as a subcutaneous phenomenon, as a regulator permitting other aspects of the discourse to be exposed more effectively. If, moreover, the other parametric variables, such as instrumentation, register, pitch, secondary articulation etc. are taken into account, there is clearly a vast scope for multiple stratification of formally significant linear, figurally-fuelled impetus. The more that individual aspects are reunited as concrete gestural elements, the more their contextual independence engineers rich conflicts between the thereby accumulated energy and its forceful dissolution.

The idea of a return to some form of rhetorically specific figural vocabulary in contemporary compositional practice would, *prima facie*, seem to presuppose a communality of language and intent such as to render the individual work (as expression of primarily subject-specific states of consciousness) more or less superfluous. The rejection of this self-defeating pseudo-option leads to the conclusion that some form of diachronic (linear, processual...) procedure of figural definition needs to be mobilized in the search for musical significance in the context of any given closed form. The fact that such relationships remain, at best, imprecisely quantifiable according to generally accepted evaluative criteria is by no means an insuperable obstacle, since the existence of such ubiquitous norms would be tantamount to a species of meta-language, fulfilling a similar role to that mentioned above in connection with rhetorical *topoi*. It is the glaring absence of such binding scales of value that, in the final analysis, renders the existence of the individual work necessary.

Acceptance of these hypotheses would seem to imply the possibility of direct interrelationship of figures by way of the selective interpenetration/exchange of common component elements, whereby it would be the progress of this informal processuality which would decisively dictate the relative power of specific instances of figural activity. The accumulation of several layers of such interpenetrational/amplificatory activity with respect to diverse parametric qualities would both increase the degree of in-binding of particular layers in the discourse and ensure that no layer would exhaust itself in the mere act of thrusting the discourse over the hurdle separating it from subsequent instances of figural deployment: a form of statistical 'safety net' would spread. The capacity of distinct aspects of the figure to create credible examples of powerful ordering categories along the lines sketched out above should be seen as one measure of its compositional utility, while its capacity for generating multiple (simultaneous and/or successive) streams of directionality (allowing time to flow not only horizontally but also 'vertically' and 'obliquely') in the sense of forcing the attention to accelerate or retard scanning operations according to the degree of interlocking - and thus resistance - of figural elements) promotes the onward-flowing projection of multiple or ambiguous perspectives, of 'depth effect' in the prioritization of the sonic objects themselves.

The search for a fixed definition of the term 'figure' is, in my view, an enterprise of at best doubtful utility. It will, I hope, have emerged from the above considerations that a figure does not exist, in material terms, in its own autonomous right; rather, it represents a way of perceiving, categorizing and mobilizing concrete gestural configurations, whatever the further purpose of these latter might be. It implies compositional attitudes, since it will be these attitudes which, by revealing themselves gradually, form the measure according to which we are enabled to perceptually ground the continuing flow of the discourse. Music is not dead material, nor yet abstract form. Still less is it meaningless maneuvering in an uncaring, arbitrary void. The idea of the figure seen as a constructive and purposive reformulation of the gesture should clear the path for aura, the visionary ideal of a work entering into conversation with the listener *as if it were another aware subject.* We, as composers, do not only manipulate material; it signals to us - by means of the ordered freeing-up and redisposing of figural energies - what it itself desires. If this concept seems unduly metaphorical: what is musical meaning, if not the revelation of new perspectives according to constantly mutating sets of (musically immanent) rules of play?

THE TACTILITY OF TIME
(1988)

In spite of the strange, portentous-seeming title, you should not think of this talk as being some sort of hermetically self-enclosed object. Some of you have, I suppose, attended Darmstadt in earlier years and will thus be aware of the virulent spread of the peculiarly aggressive assertion that one cannot really talk about music at all[1] - or at least, not in any meaningful way on matters of compositional intention and technique. However strange it may seem that many hours of lecture time have been consumed with verbalizing this thesis, this is not something that I want to overemphasize today: rather, I would like to talk, not so much theoretically (although there will be a little of that, perhaps), but speculatively, on the search for a possible language in which one central aspect of my own compositional concerns may be provisionally formulated, that is, the concept of time and the concrete sensation of its presence as manifest in one particular piece, **Mnemosyne** for bass flute and prerecorded tape. In pursuing this goal it may be that I will come a personal step further in re-establishing such topics as possible areas of practical/theoretical discourse in such contexts as this.

Mnemosyne (the eponymous Greek goddess of memory) forms the final part of the evening-filling **Carceri d'Invenzione** cycle after Piranesi given its first complete performance at the 1986 Donaueschinger Musiktage. The reason that I am presenting this piece today is that, when starting work on it, I adopted a new approach to processing the interaction between large-scale formal/variational structure and its temporal contiguity. The anamorphic, perforated 'motivicity' of the rhythmic patterning in the live bass flute part was locked into the linear expansion of primary and secondary pitch domains with a view to rendering immediate various degrees of temporal 'tactility' - that is to say, situations in which alterations in the flow of time through and around objects or states become sensually (consciously) palpable. I employ the term 'tactile' even though I am well aware of the problems attached to the uncritical transference of vocabulary from one area of discourse to another. Still, we have sufficiently frequent recourse to physical, bodily analogies when referring to musical events

---

[1]Cf. Ferneyhough's comments on talking about music in *String Quartet No. 4* (this volume, pp. 155).

for such an extension to have some inherent intuitive plausibility. If it would not be entirely inappropriate to classify musical events of, for instance, high amplitude according to criteria such as 'weight' then it would also seem legitimate to seek communally acceptable terms for the fluctuating balance between the identity of discrete event-objects and their temporal frames of reference. What, in Webern and after, could be said of silence as a 'contextually-defined empty class' can surely be extended to the larger empty class of time itself.

Even though, when talking about 'tactility' in musico-temporal terms, one is speaking with connotational rather than denotational intent, I still feel that the term serves to identify an experience most of us have occasionally had. When we listen intensively to a piece of music there are moments when our consciousness detaches itself from the immediate flow of events and comes to stand apart, measuring, scanning, aware of itself operating in a 'speculative time-space' of dimensions different from those appropriate to the musical discourse in and of itself. We become aware of the passing of time as something closely approaching a physical, objectivized *presence*. There have been occasions when I have had the experience of time 'sliding' across the inner surface of the brain with a certain impetus: it seems to be the weight and sequential ordering of *resistances* offered by whatever evaluational model the mind is currently attuned to, combined perhaps with some form of *inertial energy* generated by this encounter (and by the separate awareness that this is happening) which creates an irregular segmentation of experiential continuity and, hence, of the awareness of time as a distinct affective entity. One specific compositional problem I have recently been working on is: how can this 'objectivized' sense of time be invested with specific form-articulating qualities? One approach to this issue has been adopted, on a plurality of interreferential levels, in **Mnemosyne** and revolves around questions of meter as defining feature of experience-units.

There appears to me to be a major difficulty at the present juncture in assigning important areas of formal organization to abstract metric or rhythmic frames. Similarly, it seems doubtful if received conventions of 'speech-resemblance' are still widely applicable as tools for suggesting 'natural' or 'anti-natural' rates of flow for particular categories of musical event, even though it is clear that all involuntary and most voluntary bodily functions (heartbeat, rate of breathing, adrenalin flow etc.) ultimately contribute significantly to the *temporal perspective* adopted by the listener. It's a dual relationship: if we postulate a metric structure and we project against it musical objects we have one specific frame of reference; it must also be born in mind, however, that there is a parallel, more subtle frame at work i.e. the relationship established between the body's somatic condition and the mediating metric lattice. We perceive this latter as being itself 'fast' or 'slow' according to our bodily condition. Since there is a constant feedback between the two poles the position (perspective) of the listener is constantly in motion - for instance, in respect of the perceived density or rapidity of the surface of the music itself, the understanding of what is to count as an object at that point in the relationship.

This issue has sometimes been practically harnessed to musical expression - as, for example, in Holliger's **Cardiophonie** for oboe, in which the rapidity of execution progressively accelerates in proportion to the excitation of the physis as a direct result of the performative act. Something similar is found in the same composer's Hölderlin cycle,[11] in one of the vocal movements of which each singer takes an independent tempo from her own pulse rate, taken by holding a finger to the wrist. Here, the tempo diverges considerably from performer to performer as a function of personal temperament and the nature of the material to be sung. My own immediate interest in **Mnemosyne** and the **Third String Quartet** was the creation of fore-, middle- and background transformations which would evince different somatic densities. There seems to me to be only a rather small number of strategies according to which we can allow a musical discourse to manifest the feeling of time as something concretely present, as having, as it were, a specific gravity all its own - perhaps different from but certainly equal to that encountered in the materials employed. One of these strategies pertains specifically to the nature of the musical objects themselves: we perceive discrete events as being of a certain density, translucency, as moving with a greater or lesser degree of dynamicism relative to the amount of information contained. If the perceived potential for informational substance is rather high, the time frame required for the efficient reception and absorption of that information is usually more expansive, so that if the time frame is deliberately compressed a sense of pressure, of 'too little time', emerges as a major factor conditioning reception - something which leads the listener to categorize the musical flow as 'fast'. Thus, when listeners to my music say that it is 'too fast' they tend to mean, not that the momentary density of events is excessive, but rather that there is a sort of 'time lag' zone located in the wake of the event itself which is the real arena of temporal sensation. Sometimes, to be sure, there is a certain resentment caused by the feeling of being pushed somehow beyond the 'normal' threshold of temporal tolerance, into an area in which provisionally erected frameworks are continually being violated by current events which invade them. The challenge, of course, is to specify objects which suggest such a high degree of internal coherence that the listening ear is necessarily twisted at an angle towards a structured awareness of the *insufficiency* built into the dimensions of the time-space within which the object is located. As a result, the

---

[11]Heinz Holliger, **Scardanelli-Zyklus** (Scardanelli is the name with which Hölderlin signs many of his later poems). The pieces in question are **Der Sommer I-III** from the subcycle **Die Jahreszeiten** (1975-78).

time frame itself becomes rather 'gluey'; it stands apart and offers relentless resistance to linear energies. I suppose that all of us have occasionally had dreams of attempted escape from some unnameable fear in which our feet are caught in some substance such as glue or molasses, so that it's a tremendous, step-by-step effort to keep moving. That is but one basic example of the sort of experience I'm talking about.

The more the internal integrity of a musical event suggests its autonomy, the less the capacity of the 'time arrow' to traverse it with impunity; it is 'bent' by the contact. By the same token, however, the impact of the time vector 'damages' the event-object, thus forcing it to reveal its own generative history, the texturation of its successivity: its perceptual potential has been redefined by the collision. As the piece progresses we are continually stumbling across further stages in this catastrophic obstacle race. The energy accumulation and expenditure across and between these confrontational moments is perceived as a form of internalized metronome, and in fact it is a version of this procedure which most clearly fuels the expressive world of **Mnemosyne**: the retardational and catastrophic timeline modifiers are employed equally to focus temporal awareness through the lens of material. The means employed derive, for the most part, from the varied 'filtering' (erasure or conflation of rhythmic impulses) of a highly rationalized set of precomposed metric/rhythmic models. The choice of medium (solo instrument and prerecorded tape) is a direct reflection of my basic concept: how can 'transparency' and 'resistance' of musical materials with respect to temporal perspective be foregrounded as expressive energy?

The problem was addressed on three fronts simultaneously (1) the manifestation of background metric-spatio/temporal co-ordinates on the eight-track tape (where only the *down beat* of each and every measure of the piece is attacked); (2) the 'interference patterns' created by the partial erasure of the subsurface rhythmic models (their degree of *explicit* representation) and (3) the prevailing level of explicit interruptive activity in the solo part, whereby each of the three lines of independently calculated rhythmic patterns is able to cut off already present actions on one or both other levels. (In a monophonic instrument, it is clear that the entry of material on a second level necessarily causes that on the first level to be broken off, regardless of its written duration). These three aspects thus have the interruptive strategy in common, since even the metric structures of the tape material are based on continual cross-cutting between measures employing eighth-note beats and those characterized by particular fractions (usually quintuplet or triplet values) of those beats, whereby the 'feel' of the relationship between surface gesture and (for the audience inaudible) click track is constantly changing. In addition, what is true between measure and measure is also valid for the tempi relationships between adjacent sections. It is important that the performer come to creative terms with this pyramid structure of conventions: a note begun *as if* it were going to continue for its full written length, for instance, is going to have a considerably different effect when interrupted than a note written as having an *identical real duration* (even supposing that, in context, to be possible). Performative shaping energy will be distributed according to quite other criteria, other mental trajectories.

It's clear that, if we have several musical objects following-on from one another, we will perceive the flow of time differently according to whether (e.g.) these objects are obviously cross-related, whether they are connected by gradualistic transformations in one or more parameters, whether there exist codifiable consistencies in intervening 'buffer materials', and so on. If, for instance, we move through a piece entirely on the basis of quasi-instantaneous modulations ('film cuts') then the irregular weighting of the temporal dimension is magnified by the parallel disposition of material identity and exclusivity of temporal container. Concomitantly, the tempo flow within any one of those same units becomes somewhat less constitutive. If, on the other hand, we postulate a music whose structural extremes, whilst equally powerful, are less obvious, relegated to a set of subsurface ordering mechanisms (like predicting the length of a measure in the density of impulses in the immediately preceding measure), then our ears naturally adopt other assumptions of priority, of grouping in time, even where general density and stylistic ductus are directly comparable. I actually used identical rhythmic substructures to **Mnemosyne** in **Intermedio**,[¶¶¶] a piece for solo violin whose end effect was very different precisely because I deliberately chose other conventions of immediate and mediated 'causality', different assemblages of density units within distended metric frames. At least for the performer, the overlaying of fluctuating metric frames on essentially homogeneous materials provides important clues as to the latter's structural segmentation characteristics. At the same time, one can imagine manipulating actual sonic density within this model in ways supportive of or subverting the information gleaned from the metric patterning. The aperiodic cycling with respect to one another of these two levels permits the projection of further macro-periodicities of great utility as regards large-scale formal articulation. In each instance we encounter 'threshold' values (of duration and/or density) beyond which the experiential function of that value trajectory - its status as active formal marker - undergoes radical transformation (e.g. from field to event-object or from primary process to secondary intervention).

In this particular composition there is the added aspect of the click track. It was suggested to me by a number of performers that, ultimately, they would be sufficiently familiar with the temporal proportioning (its 'contextual naturalness') to be able to dispense with the click altogether; I am not in favor of

---

[¶¶¶]The third piece of the **Carceri d'Invenzione** cycle, though the last to be composed.

this, though, since the mental interference patterns set up by (say) attempting to weave 'x' number of regular impulses into a measure broken up in the performer's ear into 'y' clicks contributes a lot, I think, to the moment-to-moment flow of expressive tension. The clicks, in such cases, provide 'micro-measures' serving to divide up the material in a way analogous to the role of measures in a given section. If the flautist were to abandon the click track, it seems likely that he would expend significantly more energy in 'phrasing' the material more traditionally, weakening the interaction of the specifics of rhythmic detailing and larger aspects of temporal organization.

So this is the first aspect of what I shall term metric contextualization. The second might be called that of interruptive polyphony (both ultimately subsumable to the larger category of interference form). You will notice that the bass flute part is written out on between one and three staves.

Ex. 1: **Mnemosyne** (measures 12-15)

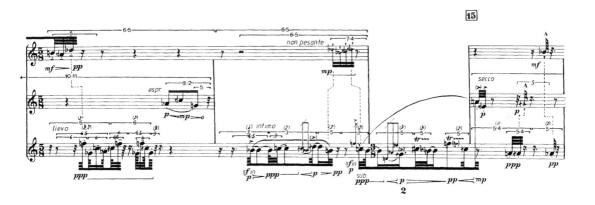

The number of staves employed is, in fact, one of the factors delineating the overall formal progression. What is happening is this: each stave employed represents the results of an independent rhythmic process. Since these run concurrently and are, in part, not mutually (grammatically) compatible in terms of reduction to one particular common denominator it is clear that no monophonic instrument is going to be able to perform all materials on all three lines. With a piano this doesn't matter: there's the possibility of distributing three voices among two hands. It is interesting that what comes naturally to a keyboard player encounters tremendous resistance in the minds of (say) woodwind soloists, who are not accustomed to freeing-up the 'natural' relationship between hands, or hand and embouchure. In this instance, however, I am not (always) notating partial aspects of single sounds, but distinct musical processes. What happens is that each of the three lines has its own typical materials in any given section; hence, there is always a particular priority pattern characteristic of the lines among themselves - one is always dominant, the others accompanimental, interjectional or otherwise subordinate. Similarly, particular tone colors, registral distributions or degree of relative density contribute to the sense of separation of essences between simultaneous layers of linear unfolding. Since the monophonic capability of the instrument comes into continual conflict with the highly polyphonic nature of the superincumbent materials, events or event chains are always being *interrupted* by the beginning of new events on other levels. For the most part, events are not held for their full durations before being broken into by reminders of the claims of other, 'suppressed' tendencies. The degree of 'tactility' emerging from this subversion is dictated in large measure, firstly, by the amount of perceptible regularity or consistency set up in the predominant layer and, secondly, by the degree of explicitness with which the interruptive functions themselves assume a certain measure of predictability. How the layers interact in detail is left to the performer to determine, since it is he who assigns relative hierarchical values to the intersecting or colliding linear tendencies. When notating the piece I had to determine a method of precisely locating the commencement of each sound, together with the point at which it is interrupted by an event elsewhere: for this I selected the convention of a continuous horizontal line drawn from the notehead on the first level to just above or below the interrupting event, connecting the two with a vertical line.

Ex. 2: **Mnemosyne** (measures 24-27)

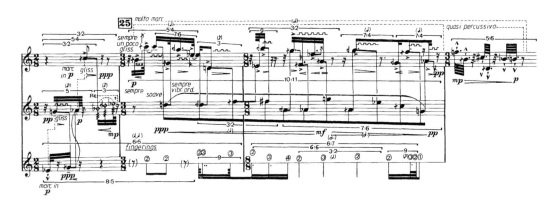

So far we have covered four major facets of time-flow control in **Mnemosyne**: (1) the relative duration of measures as 'constellation spaces'; (2) the density of material presented within each space; (3) the interaction of click track with the distribution of materials and (4) the intensity and explicitness of interruptive function with which the effective simultaneity of vectorial tendencies is exposed. There are obvious parallels and intersections of these classes: I am always concerned with providing as many structural bridges as possible between categorically distinct levels of listening. Analogous but not identical principles of ordering and listening are the goal.

A further essential perspective is given by the tape - something I briefly mentioned earlier. There, I described how the 'micro metronome' of the click track is 'resonated' by, and counterpoised to, the 'macro metronome' marked by the succession of downbeat impulses provided by the taped bass flutes. Several further essential functions are served by the tape, among which are: the provision of an essentially cumulative formal drive (against the solo instrument's more nonlinear tendencies); the sonic definition of 'constellation spaces' as given by the bar proportions; the signaling of new sections by heavy eight-note chords and, not least, the increasingly emphatic imprisoning of the bass flute in a complex web of reference pitches - something which provides more clear orientation but also undermines his gesturally directional autonomy. Since the soloist is permitted to play only (a) pitches already sounding in the tape or (b) secondary pitches articulating a specific (and ever-reducing) repertoire of intervals around those primary pitches, the reliance of the bass flute's pitch material on that simultaneously sounding on tape becomes more and more constricting. By allowing the accretive tendencies in chordal density of the tape (starting with a single pitch, moving gradually up to eight pitches) to intersect with these reductive tendencies in the solo line, large scale patterns of tendential flow are established against which specific conjunctions may momentarily give rise to non-linearly perceived events. It is the pendulum-like motion between various degrees of background flow criteria and the sudden emergence of such relatively unpredictable events which serves as the vehicle of 'temporal tactility'. At the beginning and end of the piece the functional dichotomy is very clear, the hierarchies distinct; the specifically transgressional aspect of the two levels is at a minimum. At the beginning you will hear only a single note in the tape counterpoised against a great variety of intervals and movement in the bass flute. At the end, precisely the opposite is the case, that is, a high density of pitches in the tape has reduced the solo line to a mere demonstrative horizontalization of that verticality, exhausting thereby its linear energic potential, its ability to penetrate the opaque time screen of tape chords. Clearly, all sorts of games can be played with directional and intervallic consistency when relating secondary intervals to primary pitch identities: various consistencies of explicitness in processual attachment can aid or hinder the general prevailing degree of linear consistency. It is only in the interstices of these 'grey zones' of destabilization that the instantaneous shift in perspectival assessment underlying the entire 'tactile' dimension of temporal flow becomes dominant; *oblique* temporal scanning is predominant - the mental distance to be traversed having been increased, the 'speed' at which perceptual assessment mechanisms must move in relation to the density of material unfolding is constantly changing, is being compressed or attenuated.

In all this I have said nothing specific about the function of tempo and meter proportioning. Suffice it to say here that, just as all tempi relate directly back in a limited number of ratios either to the base tempo or to immediately preceding tempi, so metric structure within the groups so formed utilizes 'irrational beats' relating to the prevailing beat speed in similarly derived proportions. From section to section there are also gradual modifications (of a linear additive or subtractive sort) in bar length, but I would need a much lengthier presentation to lay out the precise paths taken by these various vectors in their dance of approach and avoidance. It is my view in general that the awareness of temporal flow as a sensually palpable and thus relatively independent given is in large part dependent on *both* the communal resonantial capabilities of these several levels of organization *and* the disruptive astonishment generated in the wake of their occasional intersection, collision and mutual subversion. This seems to me a major compositional resource.

DURATION AND RHYTHM AS
COMPOSITIONAL RESOURCES
(1989)

The issue of rhythmic structuring in contemporary music has long remained vexed, in spite of many significant attempts to free it from the lingering residues of superseded affective vocabularies and general over-reliance on the more commonplace aspects of speech-resemblance. It has frequently been conceded that the de-coupling of rhythmic articulation from larger considerations of formal ordering, such as harmonic flow, has seriously inhibited its ability to offer powerful context-defining tools to the composer. Rhythm is not simply - or even largely - a matter of temporal extension *per se*, nor do the received wisdoms of agogic pattern-making (metric emphasis, iterative impulse chains and the like) apply to the same degree as hitherto. On the contrary; when no longer applied to specifics of larger-scale articulation in other domains, meter is at best anecdotal, at worst an actively debilitating factor. As always in the discussion of matters artistic, it is not the clear-cut cases which prove most pertinent, but the ill-defined and fluctuating 'grey zones' where a given rhythmic phenomenon may be called on to assume multiple functional roles.

My purpose in what follows is, therefore, not to specifically define the liminal instances of my aesthetic treatment of rhythmic issues, but rather to explore, albeit punctually, some of the infinitude of possible points along the network of lines through which these defining conceptual instances are conjoined.

There is arguably little point in retaining regular iterative rhythmic structures in a stylistic context devoid of tonal (or tonal-type) harmonic patterns. Very often, the presence of such patterns is a negative feature (comparable to the residual patterns in some Schoenberg, for instance), and fails to fulfill higher-level referential functions. Parallel to this, we confirm that metric structuring has been largely forced to cede its agogic orientational role and, in consequence, has been downgraded to a 'time-keeping' function. Some composers have attempted to overcome these problems by recourse to more or less complex species of proportional relationship (as evinced in Carter's metric modulation techniques, for instance), and there is no doubt that much can be done to extend this form of *mise en perspective* into still further-developed areas. In my own music I have concentrated on the issue of interrelating iterative rhythm and metric structure through ratio relationships which are individually quantifiable, and thus open to interaction in many diverse and complex ways.

In particular, I start from the standpoint that a measure is not primarily a unit of emphasis, of agogic priorities, but a space, serving to delimit the field of operations or presence of specific sound qualities, of musical processes. The consistency of iterative impulses serves primarily to set off the limits, operative boundaries between one such space and another. Whilst the impulse-structure and its audibility are clearly variably perceptible in concrete compositional situations, I maintain that enough of a correspondence is maintained in the middle to long term to enable the flow of space/density ratios demonstrated capable of carrying the main weight of formal organization. According to this principle, degrees of compression, distortion, convergence or mutual interference are calculable in respect of the degree to which the sense of clock time is supported or subverted by the specific tactility of impulse density setting the 'inner clock' of a particular metric space. Expressions of ratio relationships and proportionally-related structures are, in essence, expressed by means of different categories of perceptual mechanism. While it might be argued that the mental association of durational ratios with impulse-density ratios may not be intuitively immediate, it would seem that a careful integration and contextualization of these informational strands can lead to a clear sense of structural inter-reference.

I start with the assumption that the ratio '4:5' (to take an arbitrary example) is expressible in terms of both *absolute duration* and *quantity of discrete impulses in a given time-space*. In the former instance, a group of four basic beat-units is succeeded by one comprising five equivalent units; in the latter case, four equidistant impulses (of whatever duration) are succeeded by five equidistant units (however, as we shall see, not necessarily exhibiting the same basic unit-duration).

Ex. 1

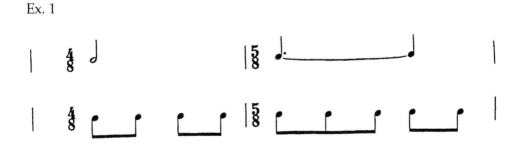

We are familiar with this situation in polymetric musics, where basic units remain constant from measure to measure, whereby the quantity of units moves in parallel with (is coupled to) the respective lengths of the measures themselves (e.g. the concluding section of **Le Sacre**, or the 'additive' metric techniques employed in the early postwar period by Boris Blacher). Interesting 'curvatures of perceptual space' occur, however, when this situation no longer pertains, that is to say when absolute metrical duration and impulse density are decoupled. In a music in which the meter remains relatively constant (4/8) the ratio 4:5 can be expressed only in terms of either four or five impulses per measure (assuming the measure to contain only one density-expression).

Ex. 2

In such cases, the greater density is invariably associated with increased rapidity of impulse presentation. Where the measure duration is also mobile, on the other hand, many more and variously related ratio expressions are conceivable; a case in point would be alternating measures of 4/8 and 5/8 where density values of 'four in four', 'five in five', 'four in five' and 'five in four' are realizable.

Ex. 3

Here, the 'five in four' utilizes impulse durations considerably faster than the 'four in five', whereby a new ratio of 16/25 arises. Hence it is possible to maintain the coherent presentation of a basic proportional scheme whilst continually modifying the actual clock duration of the individual impulses generated. This has been an extremely basic example for the sake of immediate clarity; richness and variety increase exponentially with the addition of remarkably small numbers of extra values. The immediate goal of this initial presentation has been to suggest the inextricable interlocking of meter and subdivisional impulse as correlatable strands of sonic information. I have found that many other macro- and microformal consequences of these principles are derivable - and (more importantly) are audible, particularly if and when series of these basic manipulations are organized to act in concert on a more general formal plane.

An immediate consequence in my own work has been the basing of compositional-formal structures on cycles of recurring (and thereby progressively transforming) measure durations. Such cycles perform a significant function in that they are able - depending on number of measures and the consistency of their developing relationships - to furnish us with relatively clearly graspable orientational tools. The longer such patterns become, the more complex and unpredictable their modificatory strategies, the greater is their tendency to abandon the heights of surface coherence. This enables them, among other things, to mediate usefully between immediate contingent detail of texturing and very large-scale organizational concepts. Conversely, the shorter their relative lengths, the more their values remain identifiably consistent; the greater the degree of consistency in moment-to-moment association with particular impulse quantification, the more marked will be their explication power in terms of 'expressive mechanics', of figural/generative alliances.

Let me take another straightforward example. Here, the cycle of measures comprises merely three values - 3/8, 4/8 and 5/8. In contrast to this, the impulse density matrix contains 4 values: 4, 5, 6 and 7. Simply setting these two chains in motion against each other will create a wealth of contextual relationships i.e. (beginning) 3:4; 4:5; 5:6; 3:7; 4:4....

Ex. 4

Further, a 'macro-phase' is created at the common ending-point of both cycles (after 12 values) which may itself be emphasized by other compositional markers. While it will clearly take some time for the mechanics of the relationship to become reasonably apparent, this is not to be seen as a negative quality, unless one posits a 'steady-state' theory of musical information as an essential prerequisite for coherence. Since I myself tend to regard processes as 'oblique objects' (in the sense that, by definition, their full identity only becomes clear with the elapse of time) the ever-changing quality of partial clarification is an extremely valuable aspect of the basic 'stuff' of composition.

The above example utilized only partially intersecting ratio series; it may be that compositional desiderata demand a total coincidence, so that the predictive power of the system be enhanced (whereby the density of impulses in measure 'a' might be organized with a view to reflecting the length in basic units of the immediately subsequent measure 'b', as in the following example).

Ex. 5

Many other direct or derived interactive relationships of this sort are conceivable: I have investigated many of them in my works of the last fifteen years. On the other hand, it may be that totally different value scales and diverging variational vectors would need to be applied in order to create a notional quanta-interchangeability between the two dimensions. The basic concept is very open in this regard; it is relatively value-free in its implications for style and vocabulary.

It will be immediately obvious how flexible this approach may be in practice. For example, imagine a series of measures with a common duration - say, (again) 4/8: these may be assigned internal, equidistant subdivisions with densities of 2, 3, 4 and 5 respectively.

Ex. 6

The linear effect is of an *accelerando*, a progressive increase in density. Alternatively; if we create a measure pattern with decreasing duration for successive measures, but retaining an identical density pattern (5/8, 4/8, 3/8, 2/8, each subdivided into 4) there is still a sense of *accelerando*, but with very different ratios obtaining between the four units (4:5; 4:4; 4:3 and 4:2 in the latter case as opposed to 2:4; 3:4; 4:4 and 5:4 in the former).

Ex. 7

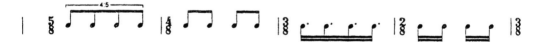

In the latter case, too, the obvious compartmentalization into groups of four contributes much to the sense of time being palpably manipulated, almost like a physical object.

Following-on from these examples, it is naturally possible to modify both levels independently. Taking a measure structure of 2/8, 4/8, 3/8, and 5/8 and applying a linearly increasing density pattern we arrive at the following conjunction: 2:2; 3:4; 4:3 and 5:5.

Ex. 8

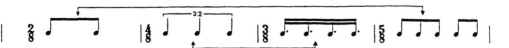

This process has several interesting features, not least of which are: correspondence between length of beat and impulse in the outer two measures and mirror reversal of impulse density and measure length ratios in the two inner units. Much can be made of such formal correspondences, particularly in cases where one or other dimension exhibits symmetrical characteristics, whilst the other follows a more linearly developmental, asymmetrical course of action. In any event, the total applicability of any set of quanta to both levels of articulation indifferently opens a number of avenues of organizational perspective, in particular concerning the suggestion of middle-ground interactive perceptual hierarchies.

The most complex and formally most extended essays in the elaboration of these techniques that I have yet attempted have been undertaken whilst creating a stereophonic click track for the purpose of coordinating two groups of live performers in **Morte Subite** (1990). Example 9 shows the two layers of metric activity, each of which is followed by two players.

During the first two phases the upper line remains, for the sake of initial clarity, constant in measure length, relationship to basic eighth beat, and emphasis of down beat. During the first phase, line 2 follows an identical plan, but compressing five basic cycles into the space of four, thus finding itself at variance with the initial 5/8 meter. In order to obviate the necessity of extending irrational groups over bar lines, a measure duration of 5/10 has been selected i.e. groups moving in the ratio of 4/5 with line 1 (thus having the value of quintuplet eighths in that latter's tempo). In Phase II the situation begins similarly, but rapidly becomes more complex, in that the 5/10 measure is maintained for only one measure, thereafter reducing progressively down to 1/10 slightly after the mid-point of the phrase. At this moment the basic value changes from 4/5ths of line 1's value to 2/3rds (i.e. triplet eighths). To this is applied the same process of measure length modification, but in reverse: 1/12 increments to 4/12, leaving the phase to be 'filled-out' by a single 2/12 measure. Note where the coincidences occur between line 1 and line 2. The concept of 'macro-rhythm' is becoming fleshed out (even though the points of coincidence do not always occur at moments of maximum agogic emphasis in line 2). In this passage we can observe the 'disturbance' effect of a second essentially linear process being superimposed on a primary, even more basic discoordination.

Phase III brings in still another slight modification, albeit one with which the ear has already become familiar in the preceding section. Line 1 takes over the incremental tactics of line 2, reducing from 5/8 through 2/8, thereafter increasing to 3/8, with a further measure of 3/8 filling in the total section length. Some of you will already have remarked that considerable efforts have been made to maintain some aural orientational possibility in that each of the lines 1 & 2 remains invariant during two successive phases.

Ex. 9: From **Morte Subite**

Thus, here, we see that line 2 is repeating note-for-note its material from phase II.

Up until this point the upper line has exercised something of a reference function, in that - whatever the metric variability - the eighth beat has remained constant. The same (at one variational remove) has been true of the lower line, except that the basic unit of counting has assumed various, proportionally derived, values. From Phase IV on, we encounter values foreign to the lower line (1st measure, 4 impulses in place of 5): the measures are divided up into between 1 and 5 impulses. Note that the first group has been so selected that it coincides exactly with the first five impulses of the upper line, thereafter deviating widely. As can be seen by comparison with Phases III and V, the metric pattern of the lower line remains constant, regardless of the impulse densities imposed. The second half of Phase IV offers several 'encounter points' between the two levels, thus calling forth much rhythmic 'punning', one of the core techniques involved in rendering rhythmic conjunctions - and thus the sensation of time underpinning them - 'tactile'.

Phases V and VI, in contrast, have exceptionally few subphase-creating intersections of this type. The boundary between Phases V and VI is characterized by massive contrasts in (a) metric structure of both voices and (b) the density of subdivisions (including irrational values) employed. The disorientation caused by this sudden change of pace is striking; it serves once more to underline the permeability of the membrane separating perceived articulate order from the levelling tendencies of chaos.

Although the example comes to an end at this point, it could have easily been extended - for example, by retaining the strongly differentiated internal structures of the two lines whilst calculating-in many more points of coincidence, or by making the transformations more emphatically directional in outline - and, even though this material has been presented here as a structure sufficient unto itself, it should not be forgotten that it forms the basic coordinational skeleton for more complex, 'second generation' rhythmic patternings and formal flow strategies.

Partitioning of given rhythmic patterns forms part of the composer's arsenal of tools for apportioning contextual meaning to the 'raw facts' of the initial structure. It is important to note that these secondary articulative techniques are themselves amenable to quantified distribution by means of precisely the same numerical models as were employed to determine the initial measure/subdivision ratios. Just as pitch-partitioning operations allow pitch-space to be traversed in many subtly nuanced ways, so different 'textural times' can be evoked by distributing available impulses according to hierarchically-preferential schemata, some emphasizing the fundamental beat relationships - the 'mechanics' of the operation - some perhaps bringing out specific peculiarities of density or direction.

Ex. 10: From **Morte Subite**

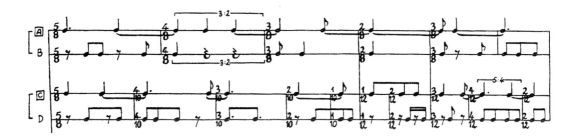

Example 10 takes Phase V of our model and distributes the available impulses between four voices (A-D): note that the impulses omitted in the main voices A and C are made up in B and D, this being, in fact, one of the two reasons for the latter voices' inclusion. The selection of impulses for A + C was made by means of so-called 'filter operations'; these dictate how many original impulses are to be added together, subsumed to a total duration which may (but need not) be expressed in continuous sound (the reason for this being that it is not, strictly speaking, the *duration* of the filtered impulse which counts, but the *placing of its attack* in the metric frame). To the extent that A + C are derived exclusively from respectively the upper and lower lines of Phase V the layout of the underlying model remains relatively clear: when, however, the filtered lines move back and forth at will it is clear that the immediacy of the relationship will be greatly obscured. The underlying metric scheme can, on the other hand, be procedurally emphasized in that, irrespective of further filtering decisions, the down-beat of every measure is allocated to *both* voices in each pair A-B, C-D. Just as there has been a ratio-relationship between (a) measure and measure, (b) impulse density and measure and (c) impulse density and impulse density, so ratio relationships can be established between each of these qualities and the dimensions of secondary filtering activity adopted. The consequent elimination of some reference impulses naturally tends to generate a sense of fluctuation, of irregularity of perspective which, while not as potentially powerful an instrument of prediction as the other relationships discussed above, can pave the way to a more comprehensive interlocking of all aspects of compositional technique on one and the same procedural basis.

As well as redistribution, two further extensions of the principles of measure subdivision discussed at the very outset have proven their utility. They are closely related, in the sense of being mirror images of each other. Both are primarily concerned with articulating the 'inside' of an already-extant basic formation (such as the 2-part click track study). While one furnishes extra information, however, the other's goal is to omit elements already present. The first is the application of a second level of subdivision operations which take as their field of operations the impulse unit(s) imposed upon the original measure structure, thus treating the former in a fashion precisely corresponding to that applied to the latter. If the same set of proportions are utilized a second time round, it is clear that a species of quasi-canonic relationships is generated, with the new level moving much faster than the old. A simple example will illustrate what I mean.

Ex. 11

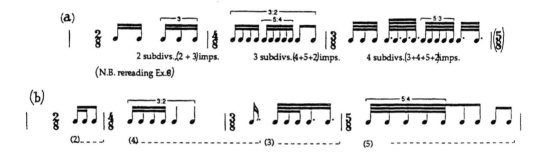

The measure durations having been translated into subdivision-pulses on the intra-metric level (themselves reflecting the beat-durations of the measures), the same relationships are predicated (a) on the individual impulses and (b) on groups of impulses corresponding (in terms of number of impulses of whatever length) to the ratios pertaining between the original measures. The effect (in the medium term at least) is one akin to the tensile strength of a chain-link fence, where each link is 'locked-into' the whole. In creating the above passage I have already resorted to the second of my pair of techniques, namely, *filtration*. Where, before, impulses were *added*, now they are *omitted* according to identical governing criteria. Example 12 (b) illustrates the application of a further layer of subdivision procedure to the substance of (a), whereby the sustained tones of this latter have been successively divided into 2, 4, 3 and 5 impulses. It will be noted that the sequential order in which these operations are carried out has a decisive effect on the details of the final result, in that the application of an eliminational procedure to the basic scheme is dealing with a far smaller number of impulses than when the 'densification' process has already been invoked.

Ex. 12(a)

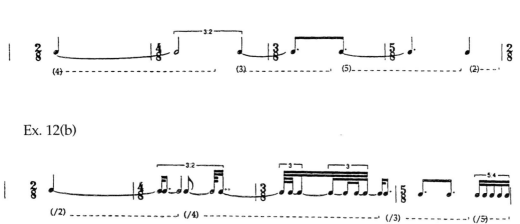

Ex. 12(b)

It has often been argued that reliance on numerically-based operations of this type is essentially flawed as a compositional strategy, the implicit or explicit assumption being that the superincumbence of correlated layers of definition is not adequately assimilable by the ear. To this one might reply: it all depends - it depends, above all, on accepting that some species of musical information are immediately accessible, as momentarily grasped, holistic events with clearly delimited borders, whilst others are, by their very nature, relational, i.e. assume formal potential in consequence of their embedding in a particular musical situation. Still other forms of awareness are stimulated, I maintain, via accretional ploys, the *gradual* coming into focus of shape and function. Not all levels of the discourse, in order to be ultimately effective, are necessarily assimilated simultaneously, as if projected onto a flat screen. Musical perspective (in the absence of external reference) is best suggested by means of the making audible of hierarchies of compositional articulation - something often reached as the result of actual successive applications of technique to an increasingly rich substrate. One final example of such perspectival play might be taken from my **Trittico per G.S.** for solo double bass (1989). (Example 13)

There, I composed the basic rhythmic densities on two distinct but concurrent levels. As the form developed, values for these densities are incremented by one, section by section. One consequence of this operation is that simultaneous values from the beginning of the piece which are relatively distinct (say 5 : 9) arrive at a level of high 'dissonance' when incremented to a ratio of 12 : 13. At the same time, the secondary densities encountered are progressively reduced in value, again by one per seven-measure form-unit. The result here is, I think, clear, namely an increasing approximation, both of the two main densities *and* their concomitant secondary modifications. An increasing level of confluence

Ex. 13: From **Trittico per G.S.**

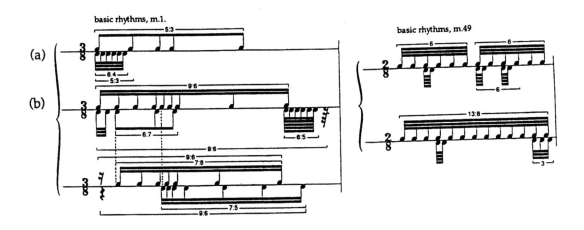

on the macro-level is thus mirrored and complemented by greater indifference of status on the micro-level. What began as a very clear perspectival distinction has, in the course of some 49 measures, become a state in which the mutual interference of operative levels has become the primary perceptual quality. Whilst moment-to-moment interaction of levels (and more are obviously operating than I have mentioned here) remains less than explicit, I believe that the long-term tendencies and tensions generated provide a powerful contextual frame within and through which, for example, surface texturing and registral movement are assimilated.

To conclude, examples from two other works. The **Fanfare for Klaus Huber** for two percussionists was written for the sixtieth birthday of my composition teacher, and responds to the demand for a work contained entirely on one page. (Example 14)

As you can see, I have recurred to the basic principles outlined in this presentation in respect of the density proportions employed. One innovation perhaps worthy of mention here is the utilization of ratio relationships in respect of the speed of beat (see 1/12, 2/10 time signatures) as employed in the click-track example, serving to define the actual speed of impulse set up in each successive measure to be carried across into the next measure, regardless of the time signature employed (see the notation in perc. 2, mm. 2-3). This is a principle continued throughout and causes continual 'changing of gears' by alternating performers. The duration of this carry-over, as well as its relationship to the

Ex. 14: FANFARE for Klaus Huber

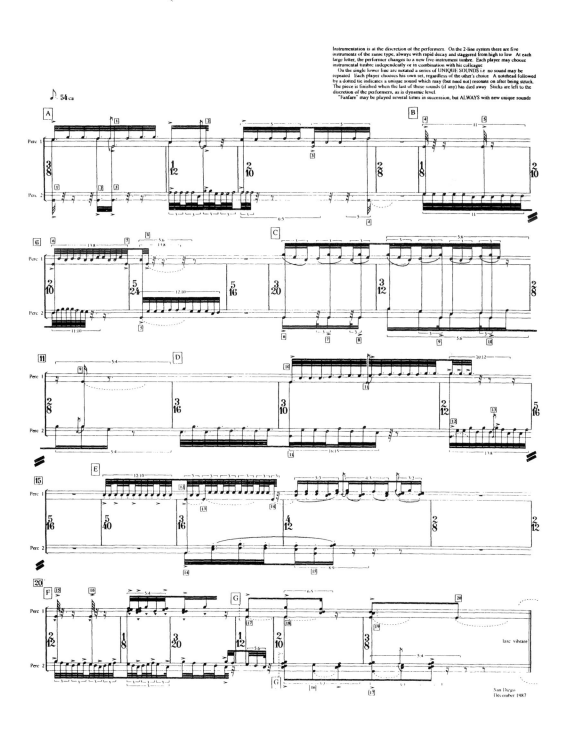

Instrumentation is at the discretion of the performers. On the 2-line system there are five instruments of the same type, always with rapid decay and staggered from high to low. At each large letter, the performer changes to a new five-instrument timbre. Each player may choose instrumental timbre independently or in combination with his colleague.

On the single lower line are notated a series of UNIQUE SOUNDS i.e. no sound may be repeated. Each player chooses his own set, regardless of the other's choice. A notehead followed by a dotted tie indicates a unique sound which may (but need not) resonate on after being struck. The piece is finished when the last of these sounds (if any) has died away. Sticks are left to the discretion of the performers, as is dynamic level.

"Fanfare" may be played several times in succession, but ALWAYS with new unique sounds

San Diego
December 1987

new unit of measurement are the main operative variables. Elsewhere, for example, I have inserted such elements into textures with simultaneous but asynchronous metric schemes, thus providing high levels of variability with regard to the entry points of subsequent units. A larger, much more irregular pulse system is generated by the 'unique sounds' called for a total of 37 times. The distance separating each of these (undefined) sonorities is itself a function of a proportion series imposed upon the final impulse grid as a final articulative modification. It should perhaps be added that some of these sonorities resonate-on over pauses, and that the individual choice of sonorities (richness; amplitude; relative continuity/similarity...) affects considerably the perceived rhythmic flow of the whole.

As a conclusion to this in no way exhaustive survey of some aspects of my approach to rhythm, let me mention a composition for wind and three percussion, **Carceri d'Invenzione III,**[1] which forms part of an evening-filling cycle of seven compositions premiered in the Donaueschingen Festival in 1986. This work makes extensive use of percussion impulses to initiate and articulate the moment-to-moment flow of activity. In this respect it functions very much like the **Morte Subite** click track, in that the final result is based on the simultaneous unfolding of multiple tempo and meter relationships. Each new event is triggered by a percussion impulse. At first rather infrequent, these impulses become ever closer together until, at the end, they are close to articulating groups, becoming, that is, complex events in their own right. Rather like other examples I have offered to you, these impulses are based on three independent layers of proportional, filtered density patterns. Each player, in the first, primarily additive section of the work articulates the impulses originating with one of these layers. Particular textural qualities also serve to clarify this process - for example, the bass drum presents various durations of legato tremolo, whilst another layer works with complex iterated subgroupings. At the outset, individual percussionists are associated with particular timbres (solo clarinet, brass choir etc). In the middle part of the work the percussion serve to trigger the two antiphonally-placed, mixed timbre instrumental ensembles; in the final main part the impulses come so thick and fast that only solo instruments, duos (or infrequently, all instruments of an ensemble) are available to be set in motion. Just at the moment when the density of percussive activity grows towards becoming an independent layer of activity (i.e. at the point where filtering-out of impulses has been reduced to a minimum) the process is abruptly terminated. I hope that this single example of a macroformal utilization of my principles will serve to suggest where my thinking has of late

---

[1]cf. p. 136.

been moving. Another direction I have been investigating is the confrontation of multiple time and density streams in one and the same monophonic instrument,[11] so that continual interruptions and foreshortening of durational values occur as lines of activity intersect. But that belongs in a different lecture.

---

[11]cf. the discussion of **Mnemosyne** in *The Tactility of Time* (this volume, p. 42).

RESPONSES TO A QUESTIONNAIRE
ON 'COMPLEXITY'
(1990)

Q: What is meant by complexity in music?

A: As a term, 'complexity' pertains more to the relationships linking situations, tendencies or states than to the amount and type of sonic material defining a particular space. What may, on the local level, be perceived as chaotic or not amenable to useful prediction is often seen to be highly ordered when observed from a differently-scaled perspective. This sort of gradual transformational re-assessment capability is by definition complex in respect of the codification and transmission potential since it encourages the active contraposition of hypothetical formal models on the basis of momentary and incomplete information. While all art forms have a reliance on such 'back-and-forth' motion between sensual *concreta* and speculative pragmatics, it seems likely that, the more 'complex' the objects involved, the more a conscious effort has been made to involve the contextual structure in the evolution of new hypothetical models (rather than, for instance, the more usual practice of attempting to fit already-extant models on new experience). The principal defining features might be seen as: discrepancy, incommensurability and the consequent reliance upon ambiguity as mobile mediator between perceptual categories. The absence of generally accepted interpretational norms leads the 'complex' work (always understood here as a relative term, not a separate aesthetic domain!) towards the institutionalization of the Russellian 'Category Error' as a fundamental mode of address; the fluctuating relationships informing its inner life must themselves seek to suggest modes of re-ordering perceptual approaches, hierarchies, perspectives. The coming into being of the work necessarily occupies center stage; the performer (and, by extension, the listener) is led to share some sense of the anxiety-generating provisional, is continually being made productively aware of his own binding contribution.

A particularly vital quality of complex states is often their self-reflexivity. This is not an attempt to ground aesthetic positions in debased versions of fractal mathematics or the rapidly-developing theory of complex physical states: it is simply an observation based on experience with music which interests me, music often exploring the nature of limits, of extreme conditions in which 'normal' received rules of comportment are clearly not universally applicable. In reflecting on the history and conditions of its own creation and perception a work is already opening a window to the outside, no matter how refractory its substance may otherwise be.

Closely related to the above is my constant concern with the 'perspectival' quality of the art work i.e. the placement of its components both in various forms of time-space and in flexible webs of mutual interaction, common vocables for enunciating the formative power of energy. In my own work there is a constant concern with the perturbations created by the impingement (confluence/divergence; intersection/collision) of relatively simple vectorial tendencies - 'lines of force' - which are themselves held in check by successively more general networks of formal constraint. It seems to me important to get the sense, not only of simple superposition or multiplication of material, but also its functional differentiation, through which individuated activities ('textures', 'events', 'objects'...) are readable as both governing and governed. Whilst I attempt to realize this as far as possible inside the work and its systems, there are naturally other composers who deal with matters differently: everyone's perception of complexity is their own.

Q: What has led to the present complex tendencies in music?

A: It's more a matter of attitude than the programmatic adoption of this or that specific technique or stylistic characteristic. It would be nice to abandon the use of the term "complex" in the way that the title of this event[¶] and choice of compositional exemplifications has seemed to define it, since there is little communality of intent or aesthetic position discernable beyond the number of note-heads per page. In the past, that sort of pigeon-holing has led one to be excoriated, on the one hand for not being Elliott Carter, on the other hand for not being Iannis Xenakis. 'Complexity' needs to be seen more as a *terminus technicus* and less as a convenient blanket term for a style or school.

That said, perhaps one should dare to state one more time the rather obvious fact that ALL music is, in some respect and to some extent, complex. It's more a question of how far the composer needs to go in a particular direction in order to problematize particular issues of contemporary music which, although no longer resting on more than distinctly shaky foundations of received 'tradition', are often enough subject to a general conspiracy of silence. The less we are able to assume as given, the more it is necessary to compositionally integrate some of the subcutaneous tensions arising from this imbalance with a view to re-projecting them as overt themes or topics of discourse. This sometimes involves one in the pointing-up of what may well be perceived as uncomfortable

---

[¶]i.e. the *"Complexity?"* festival, which took place from March 8-10 1990, in Rotterdam.

situations - for instance, the frequently 'anti-natural' confrontation between the actual flow of events and the amount of time that would normally be understood to be 'appropriate' for their adequate reception. It is usually this quality of 'too fast-ness', in fact, which is seen as a major stumbling block to the absorption of my own works to the approved canon of normalcy. One spur to taking new directions is surely always the perceived inadequacy of current practice. It remains with the individual composer to settle on specific problem areas: one which always struck me with particular force was that of performative interpretation.

Closely allied to these considerations, at least for me, was what I saw to be a general decay of confidence in the cohesive power of musical languages (understood as formulations embedded in and derived from delimited stylistic domains). Perhaps this came about through the influence of Cage in Europe, perhaps because of the 'exhaustion of material' syndrome - I don't pretend to know. I never subscribed to that set of interpretations of history, nor yet to the despairing *volte face*, when confronted with the craggy barrier of the Adornoesque dictum that all that remains is absurdity or silence, which led to a multitude of alternate universes whose most obvious common trait was a retracing of 20th Century music around the Schoenbergian 'mistake'. It has always struck me as absolutely fundamental to continue to (differentiatedly) assert the validity of personal style as the guarantor of linguistic (diachronic) expansion, since it is only this continuum of concern and operative invention on the personal level which offers the prospect of a tentative objectivity. Perhaps this fragile prospect is ultimately untenable. We'll see.

Q: What about the relationship between 'complexity' and 'intricacy'?

A: There is no necessary and sufficient relationship between these two terms. Complexity is a resultant function of the interaction of allied but distinct aspects, while intricacy is, at best, one possible pointer towards certain sorts of alliance. Only if we were to assume the highly doubtful proposition that intricately-crafted objects evince necessarily complex internal regimes of reference might this be the case. On the other hand, certain levels of detailed working may well ultimately give rise to complex or ambiguous apperceptions: it all depends what the composer wants and how faithfully the operations carried out are made manifest in some fashion (although not necessarily in the same way as they were composed-in) through the final work.

Q: What is complex (or simple) about simplicity?

A: Simplicity seems to me to be characterized by its PASSIVE ambiguity of import (which is not intended as any form of value judgement on my part);

complex structures, on the other hand, tend towards an ACTIVE projection of multiplicity (in the sense of incorporating alternative and competing trajectories as constituent contradictions making out an essential element of their expressive substance). Clearly, one's reaction to reductive phenomena can end up by being highly differentiated; that evoked by complex constellations can, equally, be flat and undifferentiated. I'm talking more of the intention and nature of the composition rather than its contingent reception. One of the 'complex' things about 'complex' music is its quality of refusing to present a straightforward object (as for instance in much minimal sculpture): it is always perceived in the act of underlining its own ongoing and provisional nature. It doesn't present the illusion of not being an illusion — in large measure because of the continual problematization of the performance/interpretation context.

Some works appear 'simple' because we have assumed large portions of their generalizable structural ambience as so naturally 'given' that it becomes effectively transparent. Since this is not the case for much contemporary music we are clearly going to be confronted with some variety of 'overload' situation, if only by reason of the need to reconstruct speculative orientational models in *ad hoc*, work-specific circumstances. To skate over these issues does indeed lead to more digestible products in a rather banal sense, of course: but at what price?

Q: Is difficulty a mode of communication?

A: Clearly it is, at least to the extent that it is perceived as such, and is thus distinguished from alternative modes of organization. There is a particular texture or grain to the slowness of comprehension traversed by the mercurial scanning beam of speculation which is not reproducible in any other way. The disjunct nature of Mallarmé's sonnet structure is a good example of this, as are (in their very different ways) the energetic semantic weavings of Gertrude Stein's **Tender Buttons** or the endlessly drawn-out repetitions of her later texts, such as **Ida** or large parts of **The Making of Americans**. In Mallarmé, as in the more aphoristic Stein, complexity resides in the sensation of instantaneity provided by (unspoken) elision, the latter tendency pitting momentary flourishings of memory against the endlessly deferred expansion of semantic space. Both the aphoristic and discursive/permutational facets of Stein's writing deal explicitly with the notion of *speed* both in respect of the 'natural rate of unfolding' implied by particular materials and the means through which the author encourages the reader to significantly deviate from these implied norms. The same can be all the more true in music, and is one of my personal interests.

In any case, a distinction should be made between difficulty and obscurity. A text may be quite conventional in its structure (say, sonnet form) whilst resisting comprehension by reason of the lack of clear meaning in the terms employed. Or, the overt semantic content of the text may be obscure because serving to cover meanings on quite different levels (as, for instance, in "Mots d'heures; gousses, rames"[1] where all is clear but only when one gets the point - "Mother Goose Rhymes"!). The complexity of the situation lies outside the object in such cases, at least in part. It implies the partial interlocking of diverse fields of meaning production. (See the pseudo-learned academic glosses accompanying the texts in my last example.) Difficulty, for me, is something which is also essentially relational in nature, but arising out of the interaction of preponderantly work-immanent planes of ordering (which is not to say that the tendency is not amplified by other considerations).

Q: What are the limits of the playable? What is the sense of 'overnotation'? What does the word 'interpretation' mean in this context?

A: Playable by whom, to what purpose?
        The entire issue of 'exactitude' as principal criterion of performative excellence is riddled with half-articulated problems. Perhaps the concept of 'fidelity to the intentions of the text' is more appropriate because less exact? Let me offer a not-entirely-hypothetical example: given is a new string quartet whose original material is entirely derived from a well-known Mozart quartet. This material was subsequently filtered, distorted and re-ordered per computer with the goal of creating virtually seamless transitions from 'real' Mozart, via 'pseudo-Mozart', to passages in which little or no direct connection to the background models is present, in respect either of style or specific material. Leaving aside the success or failure of the composition itself, there remains the problem of adequacy of interpretation: do the performers attempt to interpret the identifiably Mozart materials according to the canon of received tradition? If so, at what point in the transformative process are they required to return to the (presumably more objectively sanitized) conventions of literal reproduction frequently applied to any and all varieties of contemporary music? Are they, alternatively, expected to play the Mozartian residua also according to these latter criteria? Or should they not rather attempt a transference of the Mozartian codex to textual situations in which extremes of distortion and dismemberment are the norm? This alternative would seem problematic at best, given the lack of obvious common values in vocabulary and continuity.
        My point is, that notation is always relative to intention, whereby it is up to the composer to adequately suggest appropriate forms of response. It is clear that no conceivable notation would ever be equal to the task of rendering every aspect of a work's physiognomy in a manner capable of performer reproduction; nor am I suggesting that this would even be desirable. Given the lack of externally given criteria (historical, cultural) the composer surely has the responsibility to reflect upon such problems and to come up with forms of notation and degrees of physical involvement on the part of the performer which would begin to suggest (and then stop!) possible avenues of fruitful approach

to the text. At least in solo works, or pieces for small groups of players, this is a valid and practicable ideal. The term 'overnotation' seems to me, in this light, a misnomer of a particularly pernicious kind. One chooses degrees and emphases of notational precision with the intention of suggesting appropriate interpretational approaches to the text at hand, not with the aim of eliminating performer autonomy. Quite the opposite!

I emphasize the above considerations rather than issues of performative difficulty in a mechanical sense, since in my view almost any music is likely to remain inaccessible (and therefore 'difficult') if manual and mental dexterity are not mobilized in the cause of articulating rich and rewarding contexts. No composer, whatever his persuasion, is invariably adequate to the challenge in the same degree.

Q: When do you qualify a performance as a reasonable attempt and when as a failure?

A: If the score may be understood as being a constant 'token' of the work of which it is the notated form, any and all performances which represent a conscious attempt to realize that score are valid interpretations. There is no difference here between Xenakis and Haydn. The criteria for aesthetically adequate performances lie in the extent to which the performer is technically and spiritually able to recognize and embody the demands of fidelity (NOT 'exactitude'!). It is not a question of 20% or 99% 'of the notes'; it all depends what is being asked for. The fake issue of 'unperformability' is really a red herring. While some composers may not be concerned with practicality, I think that I am not one of them, except (perhaps) in the inevitable but infrequent cases of crass composer error. Where literally impossible (or at least: unlikely) actions are called for, I specify this in context, so that the relevant indication forms part of the actual score. There is really a whole bundle of issues involved here: one of them is, to what extent does a particular style require precise notation of particular interpretational dimensions? Conventions differ, so that inevitably assumptions concerning supposedly 'natural' degrees of notational fixing of articulative nuance are quickly shown to be empty. The term 'overnotation' is really misleading if it implies the presence of sign complexes which have no real referent, or whose referent is so contextually obvious as to require no specific notation. It's true that the momentary conjunction of notational symbols may lead to a consistent problematization of the totalized musical 'image', but this is part of the point, if one imagines that the performer has to remain relatively conscious of the need to be always re-evaluating visual, contextual and sonic correlates.

Endnotes

1. *Luis d'Antin Van Rooten,* Mots d'heures: gousses, rames - The d'Antin Manuscript, *Angus & Robertson, Brighton 1968.*

PREFACE TO *CONTEMPORARY COMPOSERS*
(1992)

In recent years the situation of contemporary music has been undergoing sweeping change more rapidly, both socially and stylistically, than at perhaps any previous period in living memory. At the same time that composition has tended towards a greater internationality (thus becoming less the province of a smaller group of 'traditional' new music-producing nations) the accelerating revolution in the electronic media has come to make the world seem both more densely populated and more claustrophobic than hitherto. Most recently, the opening up of Eastern Europe has significantly increased contact and opportunities for interaction and will surely produce many as yet unpredictable changes in our perspective as to where contemporary compositional practice may be tending.

Given the complexity and multifariousness characteristic of the present juncture it would be invidious to attempt to simplify matters with the aid of a few prefabricated categories; nevertheless some central issues of great moment have become clear, not the least pressing of which is the issue of stylistic diversity. Musical style in the 20th Century has never been as conveniently monolithic - even in the 1950s - as many commentators would like to pretend; the current sea change may arguably reflect transformed modes of cultural perception rather than realities of stylistic hegemony. Much ink has nevertheless been spilled of late over the question of the 'total availability' of musical history as a valid object of compositional invention. It seems characteristic of our 'Alexandrine' epoch that such a de-historicising attitude towards material and context should walk hand in hand with the attempt to make new music more accessible to larger audiences by couching it in stylistic traits and aesthetic stances characteristic of a much earlier (and perhaps - at least when 'creatively misunderstood' - more simple) period. It is a sign of the social power of the newer media that we should have come to appreciate the past as a function of its symbolic transmission, thus robbing it of its perspectival potential. I suppose that many, if not most composers today on the threshold of their careers have come to contemporary music via popular, commercial music of one kind or another; this is certainly true on the North American continent. It is extremely interesting to see how such artists manage to grapple with the thicket of issues surrounding such 'crossover' phenomena, where 'History' is in any case an extremely relative concept.

The remarkable acceleration in the field of music technology has impinged directly on the current state of composing, not least the increasing isolation of composers from the organs of public reproduction, the rapid internationalization of research activity and a new focus beginning to emerge in the important area of musical perception and cognition. The instrumental palette, meanwhile, has been rejuvenated through the use of commercially developed electronic equipment (although much remains to be done to persuade the industry to take heed of the specific needs of the non-commercial artist) and major advances have been made in the combination of prerecorded tape materials and live instruments. Entire new perspectives are being opened with the application of most recent computer technology to real time manipulation of instrumental and vocal signals and there are signs that many composers are once more becoming actively involved with the performance of their own works on this basis. Whilst this may indeed represent one major trend it is disturbing to the extent that the gap between experimental art forms and those amenable to assimilation by existing vehicles (such as the symphony orchestra) may finally become unbridgeable.

Hand in hand with the progressive internationalization of contemporary music comes the notable increase in the number of women composers active in the mainstream. Many women now in their '30s and '40s have succeeded in establishing themselves as regular and integral parts of present day concert life and one notes with interest the significant proportion of them coming from countries until quite recently not particularly identified as centers of new music activity. Their contribution is certain to grow even more rapidly in the coming decade, in spite of the tendency of music publishers to abdicate from their traditional role in the dissemination of new works and artists. That this is an enforced abdication is clear, stemming as it does both from the economic marginality of new music and the sheer impossibility of keeping up with the expansion in the number of composers now active on the professional scene. Although a few major publishers do indeed maintain this traditional role as best they may, there is little hope for the vast majority of young composers to be adopted and supported in this fashion. One immediate result of this change has been the tendency of many individuals to set themselves up as the publishers of their own music - something that has become a practical possibility only in the last few years. Even major publishers are beginning to resort to electronic means of servicing large catalogues, thus eliminating the need to maintain costly storage space for products that typically sell very slowly. The primary advantage of this situation from the point of view of composers is that most income from the hire, sales and performance of works remains in their own hands. Problematic, on the other hand, is the sheer effort involved in publicizing oneself, in making individual voices heard to the degree necessary for a career to 'take off'. In part, it is the purpose of *Contemporary Composers* to address this issue by means of work lists and personal statements, not only by already established figures, but by many individuals having as yet insufficient access to broader avenues of professional communication.

Several pressing issues continue to concern those active, in whatever capacity, in new music circles. One of the most weighty of these is the tendency, already far advanced, for recent works to be eliminated from the programming of the majority of radio stations. To be sure, there are notable exceptions, especially in smaller countries, where the creative artist is often in more direct and active contact with those responsible for planning: unfortunately they remain exceptions, and the compact for mutual support that carried much new music programming since World War 2 has been eroded to the point where a thoroughgoing redefinition of goals and possibilities seems unavoidable. Another concern has been the parallel dilution of journals actively propagating contemporary issues, in particular those aimed at a non-specialist readership. Music, ephemeral by definition, is in great need of support by the written word to maintain a constant profile in the public eye.

On the positive side, official support for the young composer seems to be growing, if one is to judge by the plethora of competitions and scholarships on offer. At the same time, one cannot help but see the present juncture as extremely difficult for such individuals in view of the 'New Unclearness'[1] of both the aesthetic and economic situation. Composers from Eastern Europe will surely come to feel this in especially exacerbated measure when suddenly freed from socio-political constraints and exposed to the tender mercies of the market at large.

Few generally recognized 'hubs' of contemporary music pretend any longer to the sort of hegemony prevalent a decade or two ago. The major festivals of the '70's and early '80's have, by and large, made way for a decentralized network of lower-key events, often supported by local rather than national institutions. Although several names are still current - Donaueschingen, Darmstadt, Holland Festival, Metz, Warsaw, ISCM etc. - their status has come to be seen as increasingly problematic in a time of general belt-tightening and reduced expectations. It might be argued that this is a wholly positive phenomenon, insofar as the future belongs to a different species of internationalism (by implication more modest, realistic and egalitarian). My own feeling, though, is that the elimination of the sort of collision of resources and vision which such major events have often occasioned would ultimately prove a serious impoverishment, leaving the field of large-scale productions to opera and smorgasbords of 'personality cult'-influenced television spectacles, themselves often enough the instruments of political or industrial interests.

---

[1] In the sense of Jurgen Habermas's *Neue Unübersichtlichkeit.*

In spite of all these cavils, the scope of contemporary music making has never been wider, its role and its application never more open to negotiation in the public forum. This is surely all to the good. In any event, I wish this present attempt to map, however provisionally, the essential contours of current creative activity all the best. Something of these dimensions and scope has been a signal lack for all too long.

PARALLEL UNIVERSES
(1993)

*Chaos is not without its own
directional components, which
are its own ecstasies.*[1]

The paper that I am about to present[2] is in many ways a transitional and tentative document. It represents a stage of thinking still too closely entwined with the pleasures and difficulties of the compositional act and its possible futures for me to be able, with any security, to identify, let alone remedy, the plethora of inconsistencies and intellectual fault lines by which its arguments are doubtlessly riven. Perhaps, in some small way, that is even symptomatic of the necessarily provisional and self-subverting nature of any theoretical strategy in a period robbed of the nest-warmth of communally-accepted discursive value systems. The art of theory has become as destabilized as the theory of art. At best, we are still under way.

It has been increasingly stridently suggested that the "End of History" in the Hegelian/Adornoesque sense has finally made available any and all stylistic domains in a sort of desublimatized eternal equidistance. In his book, *The Human Province*, Elias Canetti went so far as to suggest that, at some specific but undecided moment in recent time, the human race dropped out of history and, in so doing, left reality behind it. So busy, indeed, are so many artists and theorists celebrating the resultant autistically featureless cultural void that the potential reinsertion of a critical (rather than purely ironic) self-reflexivity into the post-Historic pure contingency of the artwork by means of the dialectic historicization of the acting subject in and through the autobiographically linear elaboration of consistently evolving stylistic qualities has been rejected (if considered at all) out of hand. If the Dialectic of Enlightenment was primarily defined by the exhaustion and exposure of latency in artistic expression (thus inevitably instigating its own disappearance at the hand of that very aesthetic of autonomy to which it had given rise) so the concept of "personal style" can now be re-interpreted in terms of the unresolved tensions manifested in the individual work seen as a temporary and volatile confrontation of materials validated by linear consistency (from work to work) *from within*, and the

dissonantial energies residing in the dynamic interpenetration of the linguisti-
cally contingent and the "subjective history" of the composing intelligence. Thus,
while there can (and probably should) be no overarching ruling paradigm imbuing artistic discourse with intersubjective significance, there can (and surely
should) be a continuing intense intramural examination of means and expression, pitting tendencies and implications of material against the concretion of
specific subjective contexts with no pretension to an ultimate resolution of these
conflicting but co-extant perceptual domains. The insistent focusing-in on, and
arguing-out of, the consequences of such resistant vectorial incommensurabilities
works powerfully against the sort of levelling process initiated by treating style
as an essentially museal given, something beginning life already totally transparent, decelerated to objecthood. The critical subject is itself demonstratively
constituted as a conflictual relationship, rather than acting out its institutionalized absence on already-present codes (no matter how inventively this may be
carried out). *Complexity* (insofar as the term has any utility other than as a crude
form of involuntary trademark) might thus be seen as a specific characteristic
feature of artworks subsisting primarily on the particular type of subject-object
generative conflict outlined above. Complex perceptual states arise, not from
the quantity of discrete particles distinguishable therein (since this is depend-
ant on the means of observation employed), but by reason of the perspectival
causal energies with which they are invested as a result of the intersection, impingement and mutual transformation of linear processes in momentary successive or overlapping chaotic vortices of perturbation. I conceive of complex
forms of music primarily as examining and articulating such fluctuating bound-
ary-states as a continuing manifestation of revelatory "progress" and thus as
continuing the most indispensable authenticating strategies of the Modern into
the present less systematically differentiated, and differentiable, field.

It is on the basis of such considerations that I offer the following
comments on possible ways of reconfiguring the mental maps according to
which we view (and are viewed by) the current state of compositional activity
as reflected in my own work as a composer and teacher. Whatever picture that
may emerge is not intended as being universally applicable, but - at the very
least - exemplificatory of one individual's re-thinking of the communal task in
a notably complex and fluid situation.

My subject, in a sense, is the Subject, that most painfully ambiguous of
all social constructs. The time of the composition is a web of porous fractures
seeping subjective time into the evolving differentiation of social temporality.
The autobiography of the Subject, then, much like music, unfolds both linearly
and vertically, as both successive mutual annihilations of past and future, and
the sudden awareness of many-dimensioned, striatedly interdependent opaci-
ties, the ever-changing perspectives of which at one and the same time demand,
resist and, finally, contain as many Borgesian Gardens of Forked Paths of

perception as there are individuals to traverse them. New Music has - arguably with a greater faithfulness than any other art form - lived through and reflected the agony of the autonomous subject who, created as a golem from the clay of Instrumental Reason during the Enlightenment, has now been summarily banished by the inability of that same totalizing Reason to invest it with the vital breath of self-validational grounding. New Music has, above all, witnessed in its own body the catastrophic reversal wrought by increasing throughrationalization of means and the subsequent fetishization of material predicted by Adorno, realized first by rejection of the primarily form-generating aspects of the Modernist tradition in favor of non-directional chains of local invention and/or aleatoric strategies and, later, by the schizophrenic fragmentation of experience described by Deleuze and Guattari and others as the objectified free play of values on the dance floor of symbolic exchange. To be sure, Foucault, among others, celebrates this disappearance of the subject in its objects of exchange as a form of liberation from the pervasive images of imprisonment and observation which, in his writings, are embodiments of a repressive, omnipresent ratio imposing its specific forms of order on the naturally chaotic structure of impulsive desire. His entire oeuvre is haunted by the specter of this terrible, unblinking gaze in whose blinding surface of identity the Other, the Beyond Bounds Within Bounds, fades to nothing.

At the same time, though, other, more inherently hopeful, interpretations are possible. The aporia of the direct reaction to total serialism was, to my mind at least, the assumption that the increasingly threatening discrepancy between process and perception which lay at the heart of advanced serial practice could validly be annulled via recourse to the blatantly uncritical mimeticism of the aleatoric, in which the problematic nature of the fracture was naively celebrated rather than critically probed. If, as Canetti argues, there really was a fall from grace with history, then - at least in the besieged fortress of New Music - this was one moment where that unsuspected turning point might be located (or its impending arrival, in retrospect, was clearly enunciated). A further crucial moment (quite sudden in historical terms) was the denunciation of individual style as an anachronistic souvenir of a superseded and henceforth untenable icon of metadiscursive autonomy, and its widespread supersedence by various ideologies of the contingently depersonalized objective, as exemplified by the declaration of the empire of the total availability of previously historically validated musical sign constellations. The possibility is widely discounted, that the very presumptions of universality characterizing this massive reversal is itself a suspicious indication that a similar error may have been perpetrated as was diagnosed in the immediately preceding state of tense contradiction. Oversimplification, while understandable, even sympathetic to the puzzled participant in the unfolding drama, is of little long-term utility when a veritable renewal of aesthetic means and ends is the goal. The subject will not go away merely because its existence is an impossibility.

My essential premise is that there is a danger of allowing the very totalizing tendency of *soi-disant* "postmodern" thinking to emerge as the repressive "metadiscourse" of our time, without considering the necessarily more limited and prestructured perspective in and through which the individual composer faces the world, attempting to evoke and re-articulate aspects of it. "History" exists primarily within the intellectual universe of the reflecting and acting individual as a series of uneasily coexisting, interconnected frames or models: its defining essence is motion, its articulating paradigm, perspective. If there is to be any real liberating impetus emerging from the continuing debate on style and its scope, then, it will be vital to escape views tending to define positions by recourse to isolation and rigid dogma. The various comments I will be making are intended less as a self-consistent and exclusive 'theory' than as the scanning of different points along the line of my own recent creative activity, itself a single trace across the vast field of the possible. Since the Second World War, much has been made of the effect of scientific thinking and resultant cognitive models on a wide range of compositional enterprise. Anyone more than passingly familiar with relevant literature on and around music will be able to confirm that scientific terminology (however 'loosely' or 'poetically' employed) has powerfully fueled the debates of the last forty years; at the same time, it has been my experience (both in talking to other composers, students and, not least, in developing vehicular concepts in terms of my own work) that the least typical cases are those in which extra-musical theoretical models have been adapted wholesale to musical ends. Significantly more typical, in fact, have been instances of extremely selective adaptations of often remarkably superficially absorbed theories in a sort of patchwork quilt of intellectual images whose overall structure is almost aggressively deficient in terms of orthodox evaluative criteria of consistency. It would seem that one of the most powerful stimuli of creative reaction to ideas of the outside world has been the deliberate evocation of rifts, lacunae or incommensurabilities in what were originally intended as consistent bodies of theory. This effect is perhaps most strikingly in evidence in the field of artistic production, where appeal is frequently made to punctually selected evocative images or terms culled from various scientific, historical, philosophical or poetic zones of discourse in order to be rewoven, with all the tools of rhetoric, into sometimes notably involuted mantras of conceptual synesthesia. If, as Jürgen Habermas argues, the goal of the Enlightenment was attained in the demythificatory separation of knowledge into three mutually exclusive domains, those of science, morals and aesthetics, it is interesting to note insistent attempts on the part of artists to reclaim, if only by means of notionally illicit and inconsequent sorties across dimly defined common boundaries, at least some tattered remnant of concretely objectified subjective perception, some sense of self through transgression of the exclusional discursive integrity of the "body politic" of rationally sanctified domains. If I seem to be tendentiously overstating my case here, it is because I, too, have a goal whose interests are served by resorting to suggestive imagery of a similar sort - something for which I offer not even the semblance of an apology, since my own metaphors adapt elements of a number of otherwise independent theoretical constructs in ways not entirely licit, except as retrospectively supported by the suasion of the conclusions reached. With this cavil in mind, allow me to outline three metaphors for possible imaging of the present cultural situation, with special reference, obviously, to music.

(1) The essential Postmodern *blick* has frequently been typified in terms which suggest some "no-longer-subject", an observing quintessence floating above a distant landscape, where are located manifold available cultural states and artifacts, anxious for selection, according to whatever transitory and nonbinding codex of norms. Whilst I allow that I exaggerate, in respect of a striking number of instances it is by surprisingly little. The Enlightenment subject *sur scène* has, in other words, been replaced by a disembodied, camera-wielding tourist, a by definition spiritually inaccessible alien, who, unlike the hapless rest of us, seems magically absolved from direct entrapment in the snares set by the object of examination.

(2) A somewhat less undifferentiatedly polemic model might be the image of an imaginary city, somewhere in whose well-mapped, and not infinite and unbounded, complex of streets the observing consciousness is located. This example brings with it two great advantages when compared with model 1; firstly, the Topology of the Phantom City, (as Alain Robbe-Grillet might put it) is not arbitrary in its *mise en relation* of one local detail to another, either in its particular sedimented reflection of the time period within which each level or zone of the city came into being, in the fixed spatial relationships pertaining, or in the most efficient route via which one might conceivably pass from one fixed point to another. If the imaginary observer looks fixedly in one direction, a very specific panorama comes into view, characterized by the interaction of local detail and the laws of perspective. Equally, if the observer were to rotate, sweeping the entire 360° field, aspects of the cityscape would successively enter and leave the field of view conditioned entirely by the interaction of perspective, topography and exact observer location. No two observers would see the visually given in precisely the same way, since, by definition, not occupying the same physical space; nevertheless, their diverse sensory data have a common grounding in the real, relatively invariant urban configuration in which they are situated. In addition, one may assume that savvy observers will all have access to identical or equivalent *maps* of relevant aspects of the terrain in question (museums, restaurants, pedestrian zones and so on). Each observer, while embedded, as it were, in one and the same total available environment, is thus

free to maneuver within the communal and individual constraint-systems there operative. As presumed inhabitants, not tourists or other forms of transient, each observer will clearly have a more grounded knowledge of some aspects of the city - the area immediately surrounding the place of residence, daily shopping needs, traffic pressure points at different times of the day - than others. Unlike tourists, the average inhabitant never gets around to "seeing the sights" of his environment, no matter the duration of stay. The *mode d'emploi* is simply not defined according to the same scale. The second reason why I see this model as more mentally useful as "operative paradigm" for aspects of the Postmodern consciousness is that the observing eye is not that of a disembodied alien, shuffling the holiday photos at will, but that of a socially committed entity, subordinated to, and in large part defined by, the nature and utilization of the *umwelt* inhabited. At the same time, nevertheless, one is assailed by doubts, particularly in respect of the inherently totalizing tendencies of the "one city" image. One metadiscursive mechanism of conceptual repression has merely been replaced by another; the traffic, in its movements, is constrained to follow the system of one-way streets. "Musical History" replaces Hegelian "History" as unquestioned objectivizing discourse. It is by reason of such considerations, and my concern to ground the continued role of the at least partially autonomous subject in subject-immanent criteria, that I tentatively propose a third option, that of *parallel universes*.

(3) Some of you will be familiar with the hoary Science Fiction convention of "what if?": what if, for example, Napoleon had not been finally defeated and exiled to Elba? What if, in other words, at some specific point in the chain of discretely distinguishable events, some particle had moved in a direction other than the one taken in the "real world" familiar to us? Whilst being mutually inaccessible, so some quantum theory now apparently postulates, there would then exist at least two futures branching out from that one common stem, with no external observer and, therefore, no imaginable method of assessing the relative "reality" of each of them. Both, as well as the presumably infinite number of alternative universes emerging from permanent quantum-level branching, are equally valid: it is conceivable that they may diverge, only later to re-merge in a common future reality, but, if we assume the non-reversibility of the arrow of time, it seems to follow that a common past reality cannot imply the transference of information from one branch to another: it will always, in effect, be a modulated transference. *Dasselbe ist nicht dasselbe.* Non-identity, even among apparently indistinguishable phenomena, rules. Not that many different trends or expressions of aesthetic value exist in one and the same pluriform universe, but rather that they inhabit different universes, reflecting diverse and often strictly speaking incompatible models of "what happened".

Again, there are two reasons to account for my preference of this image: firstly, it takes cognizance of the time of becoming - the personal "history" of the individual artist in the mirror of the materials employed - as an at least in principle successively graspable narrative. Secondly, it encompasses stylistic plurality without eradicating the plausibility of linearly-progressive, stylistically homogeneous linguistic categories. This latter consideration is especially signifi-cant to me, because, as I will argue in conclusion, it is via this combination of stylistic continuity and the sharing of partially communal "personal vectors" that the linearly-accretive enrichment of "local histories" can pretend to recon-cile the autonomy of the late-Modernist subject with the rhizomatic saturation of conceptual space by the non-directional free play of deracinatedly objectivized signifiers in a field composed entirely of "minor narratives".

I emphasize the role of unified, successively (but not necessarily goal-directedly) mutating musical means with a view to proposing a continuing pro-pulsive role for the Enlightenment subject as a critical reflective instance within the universe of its own making, its own "History". Like the nautilus, the Sub-ject carries its shell - the spiral trace of the self-mapping of its unique "time-line territory" - in material, on its back. The fact of the 200-year-long parallel growth to autonomy of both aesthetics and the Enlightenment subject suggests that the future course of these socially-determined constructs will also be significantly determined by their points of contact. If, as at present seems probable, the au-tonomy of the aesthetic value judgement becomes increasingly fragile as a re-sult of global commodificational tendencies, we must, therefore, ask if the increasing problematicization of the autonomous subject and attendant issues of stylistic identity, narrative continuity, historical grounding and the entire framework of relationship of subject-object dialectics must necessarily force the abandonment of individually-binding histories as the local grounding of perspectival dissonance and its concomitant, the instrumental awareness of Self and Other. While Adorno speaks, it is true, of aesthetic experience as "mutual affinity of the elements of objectivity", he does so under the assumption of the irreconcilable antagonism of art's mimetic and rationalistic moments and, thus, the objectively mediated presence of both. Dissonance - continual dynamic re-newal - is the route via which the autonomy of art in general, and music in particular, may still be achieved, as long as the Scylla and Charibdis of both ungrounded through-rationalization and the seductively totalizing ideology of the reified objectivity of materials are successfully evaded.

To be personal for a moment; in my own works I attempt to ensure a style-immanent double coding in and through the space opened up by perceived dissonantial mobility of relationship both from the objective and subjective stand-points, the former by means of "structural multi-tracking" (by which I mean the simultaneous unfolding and transformation of multiple, conflictually inter-active "time-line vectors" or local histories) which, at the outer extreme, locates the musical experience on the knife-edge separating perceived (if multiplex) order from the onset of chaotic turbulence; the latter, subjective, viewpoint is, meanwhile, manifest in the way the shadowy, rationally-repressed "Other" is allowed the opportunity to thrust a painful wedge into the monadic carapace of order - all the more powerfully by reason of the assumed hegemony of linearly-validated stylistic unity which precedes and energizes it. In concrete terms, this means the acceptance of irrational, locally-determined states which germinate, grow and disbalance *in the interstices* of the dominant paradigm of reason, taking their nourishment from it, adapting and subverting its vocables to illicit purposes - purposes not directly responsible to the referential whole. By accepting and infolding this wounding presence of its Doppelgänger, its alter ego, the rationally-generated judgmental autonomy of the Enlightenment subject is re-invested with a paradoxical and frangible legitimacy, its identity re-grounded in the continued mediational potential of its own non-identity. If there is really a prospect of a further fruitfully recuperative role for the Modernist project, it must surely reside in the dynamic, and consciously critical, enunciation of the limits of self as a precondition for the age which lies ahead - no longer that of anxiety, but of availability.

Endnotes

1. *Gilles Deleuze/Félix Guattari,* A Thousand Plateaus, *transl. Brian Massumi, U. of Minnesota Press, Minnesota 1987.*

2. *A first, rudimentary version of some of these arguments was developed during an impromptu lecture with the same title given during the Darmstädter Ferienkurse of 1990. Much has happened since then to cause me to differentiate my original crude comparisons, although I am conscious that much more needs to be done in this respect.*

EPICYCLE, MISSA BREVIS,
TIME AND MOTION STUDY III
(1976)

The grid is a terrible moment for
sensitivity and substance.

A. Artaud

As soon as I began work on this lecture, an incompatibility of goals became apparent. Aiming, on the one hand, at as concrete a presentation as possible of my personal compositional endeavors while, on the other - focusing on the external situation - at outlining a not entirely distorted assessment of the current state of contemporary music, seemed practicable only by simulating a degree of objectivity unattainable in reality. Since I harbor few illusions in respect of the non-existent organic unity of momentarily converging, contingent aesthetic trends, in what follows I prefer to consistently avoid making cheap prognoses or inadmissibly simplified blanket judgements concerning such tendencies. I trust that what I have to say about the works to be presented will permit provisional conclusions concerning my views in this area to be drawn - conclusions which will eliminate the necessity, on my part, of introducing non-work-immanent considerations.

Even if one is not exactly eager to espouse the proposition that no artist's personal statement can, in principle, be accorded more than psychological validity, this sort of presentation should only be undertaken with the qualification that it is not invariably artists themselves who are best able to illuminate their works to others. That such attempts give rise to rather partial representations is surely attributable to the unmediated nature of self-knowledge: all verbal representations are subjected to further filtering, in the very act of enunciation or reformulation, by personal, possibly significantly transformed, spiritual priorities - priorities, moreover, which are not always prepared for a reconciliation with the exigencies of effective presentation. For artists, all lectures are little more than regurgitated conversations with themselves. It follows that, under ideal circumstances, these subjective distortions would demand critical unmasking in order to strip away the patina of verifiable authenticity surrounding statements ostensibly concerning the composer's inner self. It is thus scarcely more

II   On his own works

than fair to emphasize, at the very outset, that I do not intend to accomplish any such thing. It is only infrequently that one has the chance to celebrate one's own inner contradictions and inconsistencies, the meaningful coexistence of which might well be seen as an art in itself.

Before concretely addressing the three works I intend to discuss, I would like to add two further citations to the one by Artaud prefacing this lecture. They are citations which seem to me to express essential aspects of both my general, and more specifically compositional, view of art:

> Irony: true freedom, you free us from all desire for power, from the slavery of parties, from respect for habits, from scientific pedantry, from the admiration of great personalities, from the mystification of politics, from the fanaticism of the reformer, from admiration of the self.

Proudhon

> Classify combs by the number of their teeth.

Marcel Duchamp

I think that the diversity of sources bears witness to how little I am concerned with fabricating some consistent unification of intellectual origins. For me, music is nothing if not a kernel, a nucleus, around which cultural fragments capable of mutual relativization can gather, in order that a higher (although more heterogeneous) entity may be constructed. Art does not, in the first instance, function logically but, rather, allegorically: it is possible to resist the 'either-or' of ruling socio-economic modes of thinking and feeling only by means of a decisive rejection of a dogmatically defined delimitation of normative models of communication. There have been too many rescue attempts in recent years for one to be tempted to add to that number: accordingly, stylistic plurality and a broadly structured parallelism between the fine arts and all other imaginable forms of ordered human activity must be seen as presuppositions for a continuing influence of art on contemporary society. The above citations are intended to direct attention to two facts above all others; firstly, to the central role of the *ratio* - as manifest in the thinking, sign inventing and transmitting individual - in the creation of articulated views of the world; secondly, to the pressing necessity for the demolition of those already ossified models of thought and perception which have come to condition our lives, by proposing other (even if apparently out-of-the-way), realities - that 'productive misunderstanding' (sometimes referred to by the other side as 'pseudo-scientific dilettantism'...) which serves to release individual associations from their overly constricting local contexts and permits them to function as 'free radicals', open to integration in counter-instances to existing states of affairs. According to this concept, the work would be something like a field of encounter, within whose redefined boundaries selected elements of various categories of thought and process would be united by means of common denominators - superimposed, in order to distinguish and elaborate points of intersection. In accordance with this principle, a work would neither function as a 'setting' of some extra-musical textual or conceptual construct, nor as a simple program, according to which the piece's form would be referentially defined. My compositions manifest no illustrative intent of that sort; rather, I aim at letting both participating systems merge with each other, whereby neither comes to enjoy functional priority. As Duchamp implies, classifying combs according to other criteria than their effectivity as barber's implements can have unexpected consequences... However, we are not by any means restricted to pairs of systems: to be taken into consideration is also the relationship of (musical) text and interpreter - a level that needs to be integrated, and which, in its turn, comes decisively to influence the restructuring process. I propose to return to this in the context of my discussion of the last of the three works at hand.

In my early works, that is, up until around 1969/70, I still held firmly to the vision of a hermetic aesthetic, according to which each individual work came to be based exclusively on its own unique internal organizational principles. Two compositions in which I attempted to derive all processes directly from a few simple postulates manifest these extremely utopian views most clearly. One of these is **Epicycle** (1968) for twenty solo string instruments, a work which in several respects assumes a key position in my oeuvre until that time and in which, in addition, several considerations decisive for immediately subsequent years find, *in nuce*, their first expression.

Epicycle takes as its point of departure a concept, quite widespread in the Renaissance, which attempted to reconcile the irregular motions of the stars to the Copernican model of the cosmos. Far from wishing to wring from it some sort of vaguely defined program, I sought to employ this image as a far-reaching symbol for the self-renewing power of the work's constituent elements, as a form of allegory. Additionally, I intended an allusion to the idea, equally widespread during that same epoch, of the organic communality of all existent things. Today, we would probably attempt to fix this vision of totalized interdependence by means of the completely inadequate, demythifying term 'system'. Adherence to systems was what I had assumed, as first principle, at the outset, that is to say, as the basis for musical statements as such, and structure was to reveal itself (as unceasing forward motion) and (as self-contained totality) be therein embodied.

Perhaps the fact that my attitude towards metaphysics is characterized at one and the same time by deep mistrust and unwilling attraction may be attributed to the heritage of British empiricism. Counter to what may possibly be gleaned from the substance of my presentation, I owe no personal allegiance to metaphysics, except perhaps in respect of emotional rather than intellectual affiliation. On the other hand, anyone paying exclusive attention to the exotica of Renaissance or Medieval beliefs which can easily be distinguished in my works will find themselves somewhat deceived, since such vocabularies are exactly - and only - that, namely complete, in principle dismountable thought systems, well adapted to comparison or contrast with parallel unfolding musical processes. The goal of my efforts might, under certain circumstances, be understood as a 'metaphysics of positivism', as long as such a formulation did not appear all too dialectically exaggerated.

Soloistic voice leading was already a major characteristic of my way of composing, even at this relatively early date. In the works which followed, the multiplication of performative difficulties to be surmounted by the interpreters should not be seen as leading to the creation of pseudo-virtuoso, superficially brilliant textures, since these were largely dispensed with; rather it was aimed at encouraging an enhanced self-responsibility in the individual part, whereby the interpreter would no longer approach the material 'from the outside'. It was my intention to assure a form of complete identification, an engagement which would dissolve the boundaries separating the performer from the performed in favor of a situation composed of both spiritually and materially unified events: the work as spiritual exercise.

In **Epicycle**, the extremely subdivided ensemble is not employed primarily with a view to the creation of sound masses: even though assigned to various group textures, every performer acts in full consciousness of his own individuality. The individual line is invariably the smallest significant unit of perception.

I have already mentioned that the gestalt and process associations of the title served, so to speak, as a matrix for making more precise my formal ideas. In the first instance it was a matter of outlining an intermediate zone between formal openness and generative independence - a kinematic context, defined by convention, valid only in this work. I considered the above mentioned parallels which astronomy offered to be adequate, if only for the reason that the concept implied a continual corrective, a self-critique which was necessary to guarantee such a hermetically enclosed construct the requisite level of flexibility of linguistic ductus.

I abstracted two elements from the 'epicycle' concept, namely that of a large central circle and that of a smaller circle which rolls endlessly around the periphery of the greater. When both circles were in motion (as the contemporary theory envisaged it) a sort of spiral path was described which seemed to explain similar irregularities in the courses of the heavenly bodies. I wanted to base my composition on a certain number of fundamental premises - a matter of several chordal constructions and rhythmic constellations - and, by means of continuously unfolding cyclic extensions and paraphrases, not only to vary the basic material, but also to allow it to serve as a constantly expanding reservoir. My hope in the utilization of these and comparable parallels was to achieve a reasonably exhaustive feedback effect, whereby the extreme density and multiple layering of events would be taken into account right from the outset, in order that inappropriate expansion and overly obvious shaping processes might be avoided. As with coral formations, each transformation should not only transcend its predecessor but simultaneously be able to use it as a support. It is only towards the end of the work that the material has reached an extension and depth which, together, are capable of manifesting-forth the conditions of their own coming into being.

The string ensemble in **Epicycle** is subdivided into two equal groups. The available material is mostly distributed differently between them, whereby, on occasions, one group takes the opportunity to parody, comment on or even (by means of interference in the affairs of others) destroy the second group's textures. Chaos is an indispensable precondition for (relative) order. It is a straightforward matter to create rules, which, if adhered to precisely, bring about their own effective dissolution.

Both the other works I have chosen are for voices. I have placed them next to each other so that those transitions which gradually lent my way of writing a new countenance might be seen in perspective. The first piece, a **Missa Brevis** (1969), for twelve solo voices divided into three groups with identical layout, proves especially suitable for this purpose since, because it was composed immediately prior to the string work, it shares with the latter a considerable number of common characteristics. Over and beyond that, the **Missa** prefigures first intimations of my later attitude towards the subsumation of several thought and perception models in one and the same dynamically articulated framework. The antiphonal layout, soloistic instrumentation and extreme performative demands made of the interpreters were transferred directly, even if employed differently. Innovative with respect to the earlier work was the integration of a highly semantically loaded text, which made an essential contribution to the modification of possible modalities of reception in the stylistic context I had elaborated. For me, the challenge of this particular text lay, above all, in its historically-conditioned sturdiness, since it was the resultant 'untouchability' which allowed me to direct the music, as it were, *against* the semantic level. I see what came out as a 'setting from a distance', in which the continual underlining of the independence of the strata as a matter of principle creates a supplementary focus of tension which is the real object of the composition. In the course of this 'sonic exegesis' I first of all undertook a step-by-step breakdown of the initially strictly observed procedural norms in such a way that the monolithic self-confidence so carefully emphasized at the beginning is put in jeopardy and, finally, completely exterminated. The level of expressive

Ex. A: **Epicycle** (page 13)

accessibility tends in the opposite direction: repetition of isolated wisps of melody, congenial vocal registers and so forth. The text, on the other hand, is manipulated (by means of superimposition of lines of text, fragmentation, dissection...) with a view to creating a maximum of diffusion and uncertainty towards the mid-point of the work. These practices were in no way intended to imply a simple victory of belief over doubt; rather, my concern was with the exposure of those extreme situations which I invented or came to distinguish in the compacted types of structure.

On the basis of these considerations, the **Missa** occupies something approaching a key position in my output, since it is here that, for the first time, I set out to integrate the degree of performative difficulty into the repertoire of articulational possibilities then available to me. For example, it is only extremely seldom that I have employed types of notation allowing some freedom in performance, and then exclusively for the realization of specific, clearly-defined psycho-interpretational conditions. My unceasing concern was the shaping of the work as the locus of 'totalized action', even though it should be emphasized that such a concept lies far from the world of music theater. The action that I envisage was, and remains, spiritually interiorized.

Although later compositional activities have taken me far from the highly specific confluence of considerations cast up by the **Missa**, this should be interpreted less as a break than as a slow and relatively even motion in search of forms of expression capable of satisfying the conditions I outlined in my preliminary remarks. In any event, one should bear in mind the direct aesthetic and intentional connection which exists between this work and the one I will be discussing below.

The third, most recent of the works I would like to present stands, so to speak, at the very center of my activities since 1970, since practically all previously mentioned constellations of problems are here brought together in a tentative synthesis. For that reason I will dwell at greater length upon the conceptual context of the piece, **Time and Motion Study III**.

As was the case with both previously discussed compositions, the voices - this time sixteen in number - are divided into several spatially separated groups. In this case, though, I was also aiming at a distinct separation of the groups in terms of their internal make-up. According to this principle, each group was initially allotted not only a type of material starkly distinguished from all other, equally firmly demarcated groups, but also, by means of a thoroughgoing concession of self-enclosed developmental methods, a capacity for self-assertion which would immediately lend it its own distinctive profile.

As my point of departure I postulated a situation in which a number of *a priori* givens would significantly affect the course of the work. Among these were;

(1) the topological distribution of the singers in the available space,

(2) the electro-acoustic amplification and spatial redistribution of the voices,

(3) the notion of forming the basis of the work from certain oppositional pairings (voice/percussion, text/permutated succession of phonemes, amplified sound/live sound etc.),

(4) the creation of associative connections, deriving from the title, between the density and/or difficulty of the means of notation and the perceptual differentiation of the sounding result.

This last-named goal was the one which had, overall, the most far-reaching consequences, since I consciously incorporated entropic tendencies - informational overload - with the intention of highlighting the concept of 'efficiency' with respect to its applicability to works of art. In a manner of speaking, therefore, the piece should not be listened to directly, but 'at an angle'.

The problem of allegoric/associative scientific methodology already touched on in connection with other works seems to be of great importance for the reestablishment of a positive role for present day art. In **Time and Motion Study III** I set out to absorb and - somewhat ironically - to integrate into the performance situation some fundamental concepts adapted from those aspects of western culture rooted in industrial norms of efficiency, my assumption being that our present-day interpretation of the world is scarcely less myth-impregnated than was the case with earlier, supposedly more primitive cultural models.

My primary opposition was always the one separating the human being from the machine, the creator from the created (whereby which is which remains intentionally an open question). I wanted to blur, destabilize the boundaries separating these polar extremities; thus, for example, the voices are challenged, by means of the complex layering of varied vocal techniques and dynamic levels, to act with an almost computer-like precision and engagement. At the other extreme, the centrally controlled overall volume was intentionally left unnotated, whereby the electro-acoustic dimension is accorded a certain 'human' flexibility. To the extent that the concept of 'efficiency' mentioned earlier has come to influence the inner shaping of the work, one might see the entire thing, if not exactly as a morality play, then at least as an 'allegoric action'.

I have already cited a sentence from Marcel Duchamp addressing the issue of how things are classified and, in consequence, become ossified in human schemes of thought. Duchamp has offered much stimulation over a considerable period of time in the matter of how one might come to playfully register and work with multiple allusions adapted from diverse disciplines conventionally regarded as incompatible. In many respects, there are clear cross-references between this piece and Duchamp's **Large Glass**, his bachelor machine; I have even included several text fragments from his notes on the **Glass** into the phonetic substrate of **Time and Motion Study III**. As far as other textual sources are concerned, I did indeed include fragments from widely contrasted sources, including Christopher Marlowe's **Doctor Faustus**, (hinting at the 'Sorcerer's Apprentice' aspect of the industrialization of humanity); these fragments are, however, so deeply embedded in the texture that they are incomprehensible as such - another facet of the question of efficiency... Here, too, it was my intention to dehumanize the semantic, informationally vehicular dimension of the utterance in a similar fashion to that in which, in my opinion, electro-acoustic transmission interrupts the immediate relationship to its originating signal. I have two ways of manipulating text - one encountered in places where text fragments are present in their totality, but so distorted or compressed as to suppress their innate communicational potential; the other involves the generation of texts according to a priori rules selected by me so as to reflect those animating the musical construction, while still not containing semantically-referential meaning.

In terms of construction, this piece is composed of three main parts. In the first part, the four diversely constituted choral groups work largely independently of each other; in the second part these rigidly delineated entities are gradually dissolved, to be replaced by heterogeneous concatenations of individually characterized, but simultaneously commencing voices; in part three this heterogeneity is succeeded in its turn by massive, uniform-sounding blocks. My reason for setting up such a sequence was initially to suggest the 'efficiency' of individuals collaborating among themselves, both alone and in small, homogeneous-sounding strands, in the context of the overall discourse. I accordingly selected, for each choir, a more or less clearly individuated textural and articulational domain: thus, in Group I (S, A, T, B), predominantly homophonic rhythms; Group II (S, A, T), beginning with basically plosive sounds; Group III (S, Mezzo, T), various short figurations, invariably distributed among the voices according to prolational and permutational procedures; Group IV (T, T, Bar., Bar., B), long, held chords, in which all sorts of gradual transformations (length, sound/noise-filtering, chordal construction, phonetic modification etc.) maintain the overall sense of motion. A second method of differentiating groups offered itself in the form of systematically distinct means of progression, employed to typify each choral body. This made it possible for each group to transform itself gradually in a consistent manner, both within a section and - even after lengthy pauses - from one section to another. The final method that I would like to mention here is based on what one might term a 'turn' (*Umschlag*), that is, something that suddenly moves in a direction not necessarily predictable on the basis of what has already happened, or without advance knowledge. Major breaks in the continuum are provided, above all, by the common pauses: for the most part these are filled-out with 'colored noise' provided by small percussion instruments played by the singers themselves. In the course of the piece the participation of the percussion instruments continually increases, changing their predominant timbre all the while from dry, bright sonorities (maracas, claves, sand blocks) to more resonant and dark colors (gongs, suspended cymbals, tam-tams). Skin instruments act in a transitional role - for instance, darabuccas, tom-toms and bongos. This perpetual fluctuation is primarily meant to reflect the processual change, in the voices, between voiceless, unpitched sounds and the more conventional sung tones near the conclusion of the work. Here are a few examples of the employment of these methods.

First of all, Group I. This group's material is, in principle, tripartite. In the opening measures this group performs alone, so that the relationship of textures to one another is easy to hear. At this point there are two textures which, for the sake of convenience, I am labelling 'homophonic' and 'polyphonic'. They relate to each other in the following pattern:

$$\text{Homophonic} \rightarrow \text{Polyphonic} \rightarrow \frac{\text{Homophonic}}{\text{Polyphonic}}$$

All of Group I's fragments subdivide more or less according to this plan, even though the relationship between both types is frequently modified or shifted - for instance, after a lengthy pause this group's second entry is in the form: polyphonic — homophonic — polyphonic.

In this second manifestation, still further subdivisions are undertaken; beginning with the third entry, all constituent components are broken down in an analogous fashion:

$$\underbrace{\underbrace{\text{(H)omophonic} \rightarrow \text{Polyphonic}}_{} \rightarrow \underbrace{\text{H} \rightarrow \text{P}}_{} \; / \; \underbrace{\text{H} \rightarrow \text{P} \quad \text{P} \rightarrow \text{P}}_{} \; / \; \underbrace{\text{P} + \text{H}}_{} \; \underbrace{\text{P}}_{}}_{}$$

$$\underbrace{\qquad\qquad\qquad(1)\qquad\qquad\qquad}_{} \qquad \underbrace{\qquad(2)\qquad}_{} \qquad \underbrace{\;(3)\;}_{}$$

Further shadings are brought about by means of differentiation of timbre and density.

Group II, in contrast, progresses, so to speak, arithmetically, additively, becoming little by little more complex. The first entry presents merely a few plosive sounds, while the second entry already contains more sounds, although mostly heard in isolation. The third entry proposes both types of motion simultaneously, after which a sudden swerve to new textures takes place with the introduction of sustained sonorities. The plosives then return, in order to attain a sort of synthesis of the two possibilities so far utilized.

$$(x1 \rightarrow x2 \rightarrow x3) \rightarrow (y1 \rightarrow x4 \rightarrow \underbrace{x + y}_{})$$

All these, and still further variational possibilities are worked through in the first main part of **Time and Motion Study III**, invariably in the context of the proportions laid out at the outset. These proportions, for their part, were calculated so as to make sure that only very infrequently are all four groups both simultaneously active and accorded equal weight in the overall texture. It follows that all climaxes are relative in nature.

Even though identical proportional relationships are encountered in Part II, the freedom of expressive presentation there available to each voice is incomparably greater than in Part I; in fact, there is scarcely a texture which evinces two voices sharing communal material. In this section, the group collaboration characteristic of Part I has been abandoned in favor of an expansion of the expressive potential of the individual. The form is composed of eleven group attacks, whose respective densities (i.e., number of participating voices, total amount of information presented) are likewise proportionally organized. In accord with their ambivalent status, the percussion instruments are actively involved in this section as a unifying influence, starting from the assumption that even though, strictly speaking, tools, the percussion could be regarded as 'human' to the extent that they act as extensions of the human body and that, in consequence, no irreversible step had been taken comparable to the gap, in electro-acoustic amplification, between the original sound source and its iconic reproduction/representation. Occasionally, voices and instruments are so blended that the boundary separating them becomes quite fluid. The percussion finally win the day, after which a major lacuna is perceived, since it is only here, on the threshold to Part III, that the opposition is so blatantly revealed.

Part III begins with a 'sound carpet' in which the individual liberty achieved only shortly before, in Part II, is banished to the outer limits of the perceivable. Each and every voice is composed with reference to its own autonomous criteria; although certain rules of play, more or less resembling a grid or matrix, are imposed on the *materia prima*, they content themselves, for the most part, with specifying density of events within any given measure and are thus scarcely in a position to stem the prevailing entropic tendencies. Freedom, in the machine, is a leveling.

Two further sections follow, the understanding of which is a presupposition for gaining an overview of the fundamental intentions of the work as a whole. First comes a superficially flat texture which, nevertheless, is required to be interpreted by means of extremely complex notational conventions. I was interested at this point, above all, in those inherent contradictions revealed as soon as one begins to compare effort with effect (once more: references to 'efficiency'). The line to be interpreted by each voice is a composite of five further lines, defining timbre, articulation, volume, phoneme content and pitch. The tendency of so many microscopic differentiations, though, is to submerge themselves beneath the globally undifferentiated sound mass: I imagined a 'spiritual polyphony', a second, co-extant but inaudible level of activity, as it were, taking place in the heads of the performers - a polyphony, moreover, characterized by the greatest imaginable degree of contrast to the calm flow of what is actually heard. Immediately subsequently one hears a sort of echo - a repeat of this passage reproduced via tape loop and recorded live during the performance. Since this is the sole occasion on which such subsidiary devices are employed, it is obviously not possible to logically justify the pains taken by reference to the sounding results: at this juncture, I was concerned with offering a demonstration of the 'desacralization' of the human voice brought about by electronic transmission. It's true that the 'same' sounds are heard, but denuded of the essential precondition of correspondingly concurrent and parallel mental activity on the part of the performer. After all, sound is merely sound. Or, as Gertrude Stein put it: "A rose is a rose is a rose."

The Coda of the work is once more characterized by a return to individualized activity. Here, each voice sings for itself alone, while communally aiming at a heavenwards-striving *bel canto* interpretation which, disappearing as it does into the upper and lower registers, causes the piece to fade with a slight tinge of irony, especially since the textual basis of the passage consists of the names of those wise men who posited false theories of the Music of the Spheres...

The problem which I addressed at the outset, of regarding the *ratio* as the focal point for the reconciliation of internal feeling and perceived world, seems to me frequently exacerbated by failure to discover a common denominator which would manage to avoid imposing an unacceptable degree of distortion on the immanent qualities of the one or other domain. The artist's task is the elaboration of a provisional speech ductus leading to the creation of such a model. At the same time, I don't want to argue that an all-encompassing, one-to-one contextual correspondence is necessary to bring this about: in the most extreme case, this would imply a retreat into tautology. Much more useful would be the definition of a 'typology of engagement' permitting the drawing of sufficiently rich parallels to create a space, adequate to the composer's intentions, within which intersecting 'sign planes' may be deployed. My compositions of recent years have their roots in the vivid image of intimate connectedness and interdependence of all human activities; it has been my prevailing concern to investigate and re-order such infinitely wide-reaching interlacements - to decipher codes through the creation of still further codes.

In undertaking this task it was never in the least my intention to 'set' or mirror specific social or philosophical states of affairs; the composition itself always had priority. All further aspects are only present, as it were, in order that they be forgotten. All that remains is the locus of their ephemeral encounter - an entity that gathers to itself, as temporary point of departure and of homecoming, the residua of a subjective reduction of something which itself is able to be enunciated only by assuming the form of a self-aware subject.

UNITY CAPSULE: AN INSTANT DIARY
(1980)

Any *a posteriori* analysis of my own compositions is bound, at best, to be a more or less plausible counterfeit, a thinly disguised commentary on a future that is anything but that of the work itself. It cannot hope to throw more than a very oblique light upon that which, by its very essence, it purports to illuminate.

The following reflections on my solo flute piece **Unity Capsule** do not attempt to offer the comfortable fiction of analytical authority which might be expected: instead, I have assembled a series of fragments, commentaries and remarks written, in part, during the act of composition itself (a method which I frequently utilize to put my ideas in order); in part, immediately subsequent to having completed the work, and with the partial goal of producing at least the semblance of a connected, coherent discourse. In a certain sense, it is possible to make a direct comparison between this assemblage of diverse materials and the way in which the piece was composed; but that is not something to be pursued here.

It would appear that numerous composers have one or more instruments of predilection by means of which they are able to present their most intimate and significant thoughts. The continuous and extensive utilization of such restricted means of expression appears to allow certain artists (and I am one of them) to enter into the world of possibilities inherent to these means - their 'personalities' - which recourse to more diversified means of sound production does not necessarily offer. For me, it is the flute which fulfills this role: over and beyond the supplementary degree of concentration promised by focusing upon such a limited canvas, the flute has the advantage (in my view) of being a *monodic* instrument, something which obliges me to develop my nascent concept of texture and structure, the twin vehicles of expressive form, in a particularly clear and convincing fashion.

Since 1945 we have been submerged by an almost uninterrupted torrent of literature for the instrument, the most likely cause for which being its relatively agile nature and its high level of practical availability in terms of performers and cost. A major part of this literature reflects a view of the flute which I reject, incorporating, as it does, all forms of superficial patter and overly decorative treatment of trivial ideas. Although my own music for flute may be extremely difficult as regards the exigencies imposed on the performer, this sort of virtuosity lies far from my thoughts. In both **Unity Capsule** and **Cassandra's**

Dream Song, the accent is on the instrument's ability to offer a high density of information on a certain number of levels *simultaneously*, while filtering through the highest degree of *unity* imaginable - that of a single, monodic instrument. The position from which any understanding of this music must set out, in whatever direction, is the confrontation of these two fields in a severely restricted frame.

As the title suggests, the form, material and absolute articulative qualities specific to the flute itself were, according to my original vision, indivisibly unified. This indivisibility had to be captured, forcibly confined to a sphere whose boundaries (in the final analysis) were permeable to interpretation at all points. A finite but unbounded expressive world. It was only possible to attain this goal by permitting the discursive structures which define the work to emerge from out of these limitations - limitations by means of which the flute reveals itself as what it uniquely is - its 'essence'. It was principally for this reason that I began by elaborating a system of organization based on the naturally occurring *irregularities* in the flute's sonic character; on the one hand various types of microtonal interval capable of being produced by means of lip or fingers, on the other by recombining articulative techniques familiar to all flutists (tongue action, lip tension, larger or smaller embouchure aperture, intensity of vibrato) into hitherto unfamiliar constellations. Such 'serial' organization as is encountered in **Unity Capsule** emerges from, and is imposed upon, those asymmetrical modes of production which, although not entirely new, were practically ignored in the context of the flute as I found it. In my view it was the suppression of a significant number of these potential layers of sound production (condemned as impure or redundant by reason of not being amenable to inclusion in arbitrarily regulated systems of organization) which has led, often enough, to a rather emasculated image of the instrument - something which itself leads naturally and immediately to insipid and impotent music. I am not suggesting that the sonic world of **Unity Capsule** should be taken as a model for all future flute music: this would make stiff and artificial nonsense of all aesthetic choice. What this piece is attempting to suggest, on the other hand, is that, at the very least, no compositional style can achieve full validity which does not take as its point of departure that symbiosis between the performer and his instrument in all its imperfection, from which the life force of music emanates.

In order to realize this postulated interaction on the most intimate level it is necessary to find at least one common denominator which will allow the experience of the interpreter, the capacity of the instrument and the combinatorial capability of the composer to be transposed to a single 'wavelength'. For me, this will come about most readily by calculating in a considered fashion the degrees of difficulty which are encountered in the process of rehearsing and realizing the information contained in the score. The simple fact of learning such a notation demands much of the serious interpreter by way of self-analysis on both conscious and 'body-conscious' levels. Performers are no longer expected to function solely as optimally efficient reproducers of imagined sounds; they are also themselves 'resonators' in and through which the initial impetus provided by the score is amplified and modulated in the most varied ways imaginable. Since so much is demanded of the performer in each instant, this species of simultaneity can only be learned *successively*, layer by layer. In my experience, the order in which each individual approaches this task influences the final result enormously, in spite of the fact that all interpreters are learning 'the same piece'. Thus it was that, all through the act of composition, one of my most essential preoccupations was to regulate the level of difficulty, of compaction of simultaneously-presented information (these two levels are not always identical) as well as that of informational content from the listener's perspective. Although the final sonic result is, in large part, monodic, the initial point of departure for the composition was thus an interweaving of skeins. At no point in the discourse do all the elements come into play simultaneously, so that the final texture of the work, at least in part, is defined by what is omitted rather than through those techniques and articulative dimensions acoustically transmitted. Fundamentally, therefore, this composition is *polyphonically* organized. It is up to each listener to unravel the numerous 'clues' offered and, via a process of 'archaeological speculation', to reconstruct the work in his or her own image...

Ex. 1

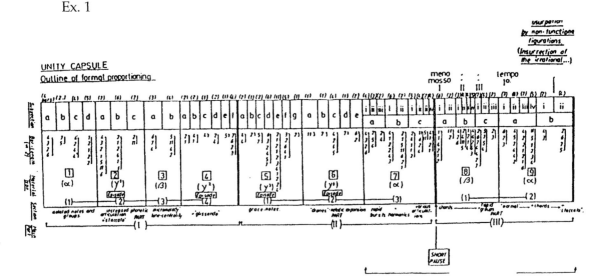

The overall formal scheme of **Unity Capsule** (Ex. 1) was conceived with a view to optimally defining various zones of combinatorial activity determined at the outset. At the same time, I attempted to so organize this material as to suggest, by means of progressive transformation of degrees of emphasis, of density and of rarefication, an 'ideology of experience' particular to a specific piece which itself would create, for every listener, the possibility of grounding a completely subjective but yet rigorous category of formal perception. This goal was pursued on the local, middleground and large-scale structure-articulating levels by means of a matrix of proportions designed to fix overall dimensions right from the outset: in a sense, it offered me the opportunity to 'converse' with the exigencies of the material by forcing me to come to terms with the absolute extremes of both abstraction and concretion as dictated by the instrument employed.

Starting from this initially rather naked scheme, and working over a period of several months, I gradually developed a personal 'strategy' for safely negotiating the obvious pitfalls which such a self-imposed obstacle course contains. The essential task for any form of systematicization is the ordering and rendering fruitful of the internal creative mechanism of the composer himself: once pointed in the right direction, he is in a position to confront the material with almost total freedom. Systems which remain passively embedded in material - rules to be blindly observed - are anathema to practically every type of serious artistic enterprise. Adopting this perspective (rather than that originating in my already intense occupation with sound itself), my point of departure was a scheme which foresaw the subdivision of the work into nine sections, of which each successive set of three formed a single, larger-scale group. The overall scheme shown in Ex. 1 is a partial reproduction of the original plan, the referential locus of all compositional procedures. It is reproduced here in its original format, in spite of the fact that the completed score deviates from it slightly, either by reason of errors which I chose to retain or because of deliberate modifications inserted at a later stage.

My principal objective was to derive all levels of activity from one and the same set of fundamental proportions: thus, both variation in the length of measures and the subdivision of groups of measures into larger units follow an identical plan, a principle also applied, on a higher level, to the number of subdivisions found in each of the principal sections as well as to the number of subdivisions assigned to each individual measure as the work progresses (on the most basic material level).

For example: the proportions between the first three measures are 4:3:2, and the organization of the nine sections comprising the work is based upon identical proportions. Analogously, each section contains a number of component subdivisions derived according to the same principle. (Section 1 = 4 subdivisions; Section 2 = 3 subdivisions; Section 3 = 2 subdivisions.) Moreover, each subdivision is composed of a number of measures calculated in the same way, even though subsequently subjected to permutation.

Towards the end of the piece, the formal organization is rendered progressively more complex by a supplementary layer of subdivisions (sections 7, 8 and 9). As far as its internal proportions are concerned, a resemblance to what has already been explained is readily discernable. My goal here was to furnish the final sections with a *miniaturized reflection* of the form as a whole, from which it follows that many analogies exist between the course of the early sections and, for example, the rhythmic constitution of events in Section 8.

At points where long pauses permeate the texture in Section 1, new materials are inserted in Section 8 in order to prepare the build-up towards the frenetic final climax, in which, after the main (precalculated) structure has run its course, the now predominant 'irrational' embellishments filling out all indicated rests take over, carrying on silently (with finger action) even after the performer has completely run out of breath. A further consequence of this formal elaboration was that the *perceived* subdivisions at this point are at variance with the background structural connotations: a level of perceptual overlapping is thus generated to make yet another 'polyphonic' strand available for enriching the informational potential of this drastically restricted medium.

The way in which Section 8 may be said to relate to Section 1 is best seen by comparing the opening moments of each. (Ex. 2)

The materials of Section 1 are presented skeletally, in terms of their rhythmic structures only, their articulation being transformed into multiphonic elements. This remains constant. The interstices (silent in Section 1) are, in Section 8, fleshed out by rhythmic motives originating in Section 3, but modified (filtered) by the numerically-ordered elimination of certain constituent impulses. It is this process, in fact, which lies at the root of my most recent music; by means of various processes of overlapping and filtration, generically similar operations can be applied to the modification of both pitch and rhythm (although this is not yet actually the case in **Unity Capsule**). During the course of Sections 8 and 9 other materials are gradually introduced, in order to fill out further silences specified by the original plan. The main examples of this are indicated in the appropriate spot in the diagram shown in Ex. 1.

A single example must suffice to address the generation of temporal structures. The very opening of the work is perhaps the simplest available example. The following passage is taken directly from my compositional working notes.

"The rhythmic ordering and distribution is a mixture of rational and irrational decisions. The total length of a figure is determined by its durational correspondence to one or more elements belonging to a sequence produced in the following manner: each bar length (measured in eighth notes) is taken as the measure of an equal number of bars into which space a number of impulses are to be distributed. (Impulses are equidistant.) The individual units are then separated or conjoined (always in the given order, without repetition) as desired." (See example 3.)

Ex. 2

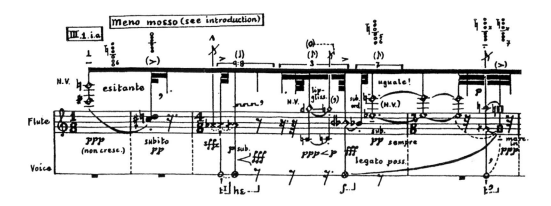

SECTION 8

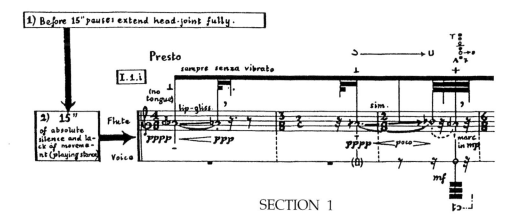

SECTION 1

"The distance between figures (i.e. the total value of the intervening rests) is arrived at by interspersing, between each figure and its immediate successor, a rest equal in length to one of the measures in the basic meter-sequence. The first measure is not counted, so that the rests will be: 3 eighth notes, 2 eighth notes, 6 eighth notes etc."

A cursory examination of the opening measures will reveal this process at work. (Ex. 4)

Ex. 3

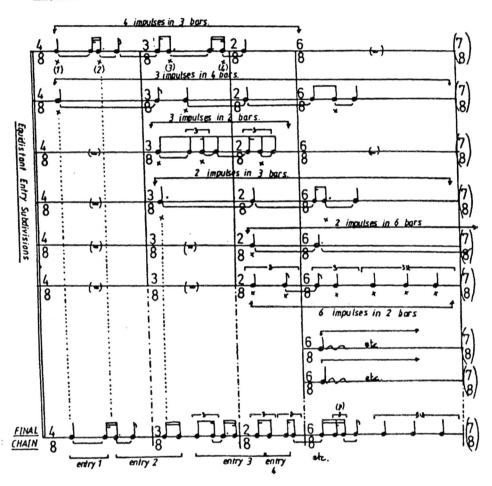

A brief discussion of the opening pitch and gestural material (taken from the same source) gives some small idea of the principles according to which the moment-to-moment transformations were selected.

"The first interval is a microtonal *glissando*, which thus immediately pinpoints the largely non-tempered pitch material of the piece (the A 3/4-flat is, at one and the same time, part of a *glissando* which, by implication, sweeps through *all* microtonal intervals within the specified step, and a gesture produced by embouchure modification precluding exactly tempered pitch definition). This initial figure is, therefore, paradigmatic for the articulative ambitus of the whole.

Ex. 4

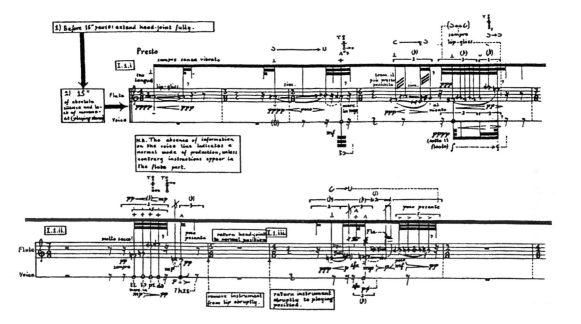

A further consideration immediately underlining the complex relationship conjoining *pitch, noise* and *action* is the opening, highly demonstrative *de-tuning* of
the instrument which takes place before a sound is heard, so that the written
pitches at that point in no rationally determinable way correspond to those
encountered later, and which were, in fact, generated by the same system."

It might be added that the equally curious and demonstrative removal
of the flute from the lips in m.6, followed by its sudden repositioning represents a further example of 'subversive form' as encountered at many points
during this work. In fact, returning the instrument to playing position marks
the (silent) commencement of the next subsection. A brief examination of the
score will give an idea of how the diffuse and tentative gestures of the opening
come to be expanded, event after event, by the inclusion of lip action (m.3),
tremolo and subsidiary figuration (m.4), figuration accompanied by plosive lip
action (m.5) and complex recombination of all of the above techniques with the
addition of (still slightly modified) 'normal' flute sound (m.7).

Examples of the multilayering of playing techniques mentioned above
can be gleaned from the same score page. The upper system in each pair is the
stave customarily allotted to pitched sounds, while the lower is more often given

over to the representation of all forms of vocal action and phonetically modi-fied embouchure positions. The half-diamond note heads encountered in m.1 stand for very breathy tone production; the square shape on the 'voice line' of m.2 means "play with wide open mouth and full, but diffuse breath, like a gasp." The circle on the same line, one measure later, is the symbol for an explosive sound produced (without accompanying breath) by the tongue. Above the 'flute line' (m.2.) is situated an inverted 'T', specifying attack without the use of the tongue. Above this, there are found two 'U'-symbols connected to an arrow specifying the angle at which the flute is to be held in relation to the lips. The '+' over measure 3 indicates the percussive sound produced by forcefully de-pressing one or more of the instrument's keys. In the further course of the com-position the permutation and recombination of these, and many other levels of articulation, produces a truly polyphonic tangle which performers must unravel according to their own proper habits, abilities and inclinations. That so much of this detailed working is not directly audible is a major contributory factor towards mapping the area of ambiguity which **Unity Capsule** sets out to ex-plore. The work of art that does not raise more questions than it aims at an-swering can never be considered adequate to its own immanent potential. One crucial articulative domain is necessarily circumscribed by individual perform-ers themselves, since only they can creatively confront and resolve the challenge that such an explicit multiplicity of information levels offers, thus assimilating their own perception of the work, their understanding of their interpretative task and active insight into their own personal dynamics to the echoing labyrinth of the work itself.

In these few scattered comments there are several essential aspects of structure - in particular, details of rhythmic derivation and the organization of pitch - which I have failed to touch upon. In any case, such a presentation would require a further article. More importantly, however, I have not examined those aspects of the composition directly impinging on the nature of the aesthetic encounter, either that of the work with the performer, or the performer with the listener. I would like to underline the importance of these matters to my approach to composition, since they directly border on areas of experience which tend beyond the limits of specifically musical discourse. Because I have no in-tention of pre-empting each performer's prerogative to approach the work in a unique way, and because I am speaking here as a practical maker rather than a theorist, I have preferred to restrict the scope of my presentation to particulars of a somewhat basic nature. It should not be inferred that this decision reflects the nature or priorities of my more general artistic perspectives.

TIME AND MOTION STUDY II
(1977)

For vocalizing cellist and live electronics (1974-6)

In the first instance, this work is concerned with memory, with the manner in which memory sieves, colors and re-orders while processing information. A second level concerns itself with the construction of a model designed to demonstrate the fact that memory is discontinuous - something having a decided effect on perception, on the one hand in the form of ever-increasing 'interference' in development, on the other as a necessary precondition for the historical consolidation of the individual. Point of departure for this specific confrontation: a detailed examination of the multifaceted nature of time and the abolition of linear temporal experience in the process of recall. The work itself is thus to be regarded as the 'memory of a production process', the place of performance as the point of confrontation for objectively measurable systems and subjective obscuration, erosion and eradication - these latter being by no means entirely predictable in terms of their ensemble effect. The function of these subjective processes is to (re-)present an idealized projection of experiential fragments which, by means of individual recollective mechanisms, will, at some future point, effectively withdraw themselves from objectively quantifiable temporality's sphere of influence. As is the case with the two other compositions in the **Time and Motion Study** cycle, continual reference to the concept of industrial efficiency serves to underline the goal-orientated nature of this non-systematic disturbance/destruction of the reservoir of experience (itself superficial, controlled by the *ratio*). This teleologic aspect is then investigated with a view to discovering to what extent the individual consciousness of self is disorientated, oppressed and disintegrated by the complex cross-currents characterizing the agonistic confluence history as immediate experience and the prescriptive conventions imposed thereon by public discourse ('History'). Paradoxically, it would only seem possible to imagine a temporal continuum via the decay of single instants, the absorption of the discrete instant by the totality, but, also, by reason of the fact that this instantaneous decay conditions the future which is born of it.

      The fabric of the piece consists of a continuous sequence of overlapping processes which, to a constantly fluctuating degree, are constrained to unfold both simultaneously and consecutively. In turn, these processes lead to the gradual accumulation of a residual 'sediment'. Although the essential nature of these procedures dictates that these finely-sieved layers be produced by the interaction of several generative techniques, in practice, they have been so consequently reduced to a common denominator by means of the above-mentioned 'sieving' that a high level of textural consistency is ultimately produced. It would be deceiving to assume that the original processes represent mere contingent tools which, though necessary, are not in and of themselves divisive. In contradistinction to the customary view of a 'work', the sonic phenomenon is here to be understood as the 'resonating trace' of the elapsed mechanisms for which it stands. It follows that not only the experiential time of the performance itself, but also the 'real time' involved in the act of composition (which also includes some performance-specific decisions to be made by the performer) is to act as the arbiter of significance. One has to excavate, analyze and re-project. While the work can in no sense be said to be improvisational, either for the cellist or the technicians (usually three), the fact that the piece resists relegation to the status of a predictable and informationally static product allows it to be transformed into a symbol of something provisional - that is, of an image of the self cruelly suspended between irreparable loss and provisional consolidation.

Not the least obvious of associations suggested by the almost organic relationship between performer and electronic ambience (an obviously central issue in **Time and Motion Study II**) is that of various varieties of capital punishment. The role of the electronic 'cage' is not restricted to such ancillary tasks as completion, commentary or support, but, on the contrary, it assumes the mask of a weird 'double'. Even though the electronics offer the figural devices employed the opportunity for self-reflection via repetition, it is only very infrequently that the elements selected for treatment in this way appear willing to subordinate themselves to the will of the continually unfolding live material. Because of this, the reproduction process is often accompanied by a darkening, disturbing tendency, is *negative* in a fashion consciously at variance with the highly detailed specifications attached to the methods by which the material to be thus 'refracted' was selected. Repetition as precondition for a context (continuity); repetition as a superfluity (agent of fragmentation). Seen from a different point of view, one might see this encounter between the sort of self-expression demarcating the individual and a sometimes uncooperatively febrile array of sonic 'distorting mirrors' of collectivity (continually frustrating the performer's increasingly urgent desire for the unfettered *parola in libertà*) as throwing a little light on the now symbiotic relationship of individual discourse and publicly approbated modes of self-awareness.

The work may be conceived of as the interaction, interpenetration and mutual assimilation of two quite distinct types of material. The main material consists of seven times seven rhythmic 'formulas', which, together with a rigorously determined pattern of phrase lengths, ordain the main course of events through a process of perpetual variation. It is in passages organized according to these principles that the quantifiable aspect of time assumes particular importance. The secondary material consists of a series of individual commentaries on six distinct, basic articulation types - organisms distinguished by a significantly looser precompositional definition (which implies a correspondingly greater degree of initial conceptual abstraction). There are six examples of between three and six articulation types in each Sequence, the associated unit of form. Each Sequence is, in turn, individualized by the relative predominance of one or more main types. In these sections, pitch contour is less clearly predetermined than is the case elsewhere in the work: throughout, there is a strict distinction made between the main parts, where pitch selection follows rather rigid determination procedures, and, in the Sequences, a method permitting a certain amount of choice (itself strictly specified) in respect of degrees of elaboration, deviation and articulative stability appropriate for individual events. The opening section is composed of a lengthy passage in which interlocking fragments of the main and secondary material categories are 'analyzed-out' by recourse to two tape loop delay systems. With their aid, the Sequences are recorded during performance and, with varying delay periods and variable degree of distortion or 'involuntary editing' arising from the assistants' manipulation of recording volume controls, are re-inserted in the cellist's live sound stream. Again and again these decontextualized splinters serve to undermine and hinder the free unfolding of the live discourse by reason of their temporally 'antisocial' nature. Even though the main material - at first restricted to amplified scraping noises produced by fingernails or plectra - is not treated in this fashion, it is nevertheless recorded on a further tape (omitting the Sequence segments) so that it may be re-introduced, as an autonomous layer of 'found' events, during the final minutes of the piece, where a massive pyramidal piling up of strata occurs. After several intervening episodes have been negotiated, the mid-point of the work is signaled by a different sort of 'auto-analysis', where rapidly alternating groups of sustained notes and short, explosive interjections are divided up and, according to playing technique (*arco* or *pizzicato*), assigned to either the left or right-hand loudspeakers. Subsequently, the two blocks of contrasting sonorities built up by means of feedback act as triggering signals to the performer in the progressive construction and subsequent demolition of embellished chordal structures. This is one of the few moments at which the 'optimist/constructivist' aspect usually associated with the live electronic medium is most obviously and deliberately exploited, even though, in practice, such nominal clarity is fatally compromised by the inevitable accumulation of errors and imprecisions on the part of the cellist when called upon to insert new elements into a by now impenetrable overall texture.

The second half of **Time and Motion Study II** begins after the inevitable 'breakdown'; in it, we witness the rapid ascent of entropic tendencies to pre-eminence. In his desperation in the face of the vast ballooning of superfluous 'memory shards' hemming him in, the cellist initiates a dialogue with his oppressive ambience and the sonic obstacles confronting him. The text, vocalized by the performer and immediately transformed, addresses the impossibility of obtaining harmony between words and emotional states. In accordance with this content, the voice is sucked up into the maze, distorted and itself reduced to another level of interference, devoid of all immediate, autonomous communicational import. There is only one moment, at the very end of the work, at which the cellist is heard entirely devoid of such obliterational accompaniment. Having finally achieved a nominal degree of independence, the instrument is reduced to endlessly reiterating insignificantly minute variations of a single obsessive pitch. The patent absurdity of the situation is underlined by the fact that the performer is condemned to hold out to the bitter end in the certain knowledge that all taped sounds recorded during the performance - his 'memory' - are being silently erased behind his back.

The parallel functions of the complementary instrumental/electronic layout might be schematically represented somewhat in the following manner:

Instrument		*Electronics*
live performance	————	amplification
singing/speaking	————	ring modulation
foot pedals (cellist)	————	'sonic analysis'
		(i.e. amplitude modification)

The various extremes are linked by means of the almost continuous deployment of delay tapes and feedback-generated superposition. With a single exception (ring modulation of voice by cello) all timbral modifications are derived from the natural resonance of the instrument as registered by two contact microphones, one attached so as to bring out the percussive sounds of the fingers on the fingerboard, the other affixed to the corpus, both being independently controlled by foot pedals operated by the cellist. Since each pedal feeds signals to only one of the antiphonally placed loudspeakers, it follows that not only dynamic gradations but also spatial distribution of the results is controlled directly by the performer, the score containing precise information as to the position and point of change of the pedals at any given juncture. In addition, there are two further microphones employed; one of these (a directional air microphone) is placed in front of the cello, thus recording the 'natural' sonority, the other being a contact microphone attached to the cellist's throat. The signals from these two sources are ring modulated during the second half of the piece, as mentioned above.

Because performers of this piece are required to master and reproduce information of extreme complexity (the music being notated on up to five systems simultaneously) they must invest all their energy in order to approach an adequate interpretation. At the same time, the assistants are occupied with transforming, selecting and re-organizing the sedimented residual record of that maximally differentiated confrontation. In the same way that the foot pedals of the cellist are fully 'notated' as integral components of the score, so the actions of the assistants are precisely coordinated with the course of live events. At the same time, it should be noted that, because of the invariant delay times on the tapes loops as opposed to the variable speed of execution of the player, as well as the selective nature (mnemonic imperfection) of the reproduced elements themselves, this precision is undermined in performance: linear temporality is unseated, and its constituent ciphers are delivered up to the simultaneity of punctual consciousness.

While undoubtedly a notably pessimistic piece, **Time and Motion Study II** is by no means nihilistic; its negativity does not stem from the relentless pursuit of some aesthetic 'scorched earth' policy, but rather from the desire to clear the ground for new construction. It offers no solutions to the challenge of the 'lyrical impasse', but neither does it deny meaning to its continued critical confrontation.

THE TIME AND MOTION STUDY CYCLE
(1987)

No program book introduction has ever been written for the integral cycle for the simple reason that the opportunity to perform all three works together has never previously arisen. It is obviously extremely difficult, at this distance, to attempt to generalize on my motives of that period (1974-77): it will be clear in any case, I think, that these compositions emerged from the moment of explosive confluence of a large array of concerns, many of them not directly or obviously 'musical' in nature. Equally clear will be the emphasis on a high level of performer expertise and compositional density. These are by no means autonomous aspects of my particular musical style; rather, I see them today as inseparable 'dialects' of one and the same concern i.e. what place can music realistically claim in the task of critically observing the world around us? One might argue that this is not the sort of question that art should be attempting to ask: from a different perspective, I still feel that the composer can scarcely be too ambitious in the demands he makes on his chosen medium, as long as the possibility of failure is ever-present in his mind.

The **Time and Motion Study** and **Carceri d'Invenzione**[1] cycles share a key characteristic. For quite a long time (almost since the beginning, really) I have circled around and explored the problem of multi-movement compositional structures. In these two extremely large-scale sequences there is no obvious connective material, other than the thread provided by the over-arching idea; it was my aim to allow each individual work to stand independently on its own terms, but it was also my hope that a perception of the mode of interlocking employed to fix the pieces in place would enhance their singularities into a coherent design of a higher order. In **Time and Motion Study**, this dimension is provided, on the most immediate level, by the principle of expansion. The action begins by concentrating on a sole performer, expanding immediately to focus on a single instrumentalist locked into a web of technology. Finally, it embraces a large group of individuals, whose vocal actions are supplemented by percussion and spatially redistributed by appropriately located loudspeakers.

The performance will take place without an intermission, and will have a total duration of approximately 50 minutes.[1]

---

[1]The **Carceri d'Invenzione** cycle received its British premiere in the same festival as the **Time and Motion Studies I-III** (Huddersfield 1987).

Time and Motion Study I (1977) for solo bass clarinet

This work began life in 1970 as a series of fragments for solo clarinet. Coming back to this material in 1977 caused me to reconsider my position in respect of the import, scope and mode of functioning of fragmentation as a formative principle. Rather than disguise the passing of the intervening years, I decided to emphasize it: the 'raw' elements were forced to generate new offshoots by being passed, under pressure, through an alien formal grid. The final importance of the original fragments was thus neither as theme nor motive, but resided in their capacity to motivate further levels of discourse. Having fulfilled this function, they sink back into the newly-created network of procedures, their natural resistance transformed into structural energy.

Fundamental concern of the work is the vision of a polyphonic mode of discourse transposed to the framework of a monophonic instrument. Many ploys and stratagems are resorted to in order to make this possible, such as differentiation of parametric levels, underlining of lines of force with systematic deployment of articulative nuance, and the overlapping of related numerical filtering procedures at different speeds on different levels of the discourse.

Time and Motion Study I is built up around a core of two central principles: (1) the opposition and integration of two contrasted types of activity - the one rapid and regular, the other disjointed and gestural, with wide leaps and unpredictable rhythmic patterns; (2) the application, in various roles, of the proportions inherent in the Fibonacci Series (1, 1, 2, 3, 5, 8, 13...). Right from the outset these worlds are brought into unmediated confrontation. The further course of this 9 minute work is made up of the violent filtering of the energies thus liberated through the dexterity and bodily flexibility of the performer. As in Antonin Artaud's 'Theater of Cruelty', each area of the work calls forth resonances from different parts of the total organism performer/instrument/context. This, for me, is 'drama in music'.

Time and Motion Study II (1973-76) for vocalizing cellist and live electronics

Although initially conceived three years earlier, this composition for cellist and 'electronic environment' was only completed during my year as Guest Artist of the DAAD[2] in Berlin. It was first performed by Werner Taube and the Experimental Studio of Südwestfunk, Baden-Baden during the Donaueschinger Musiktage of 1977.

In the first instance, this piece is concerned with memory - how memory sieves, colors and shuffles the avalanche of sense impressions which the brain registers. The electronic set-up is designed to demonstrate what I take to be the cumulative effect of some of these processes i.e. the supreme ambiguity of distillation and erasure in the individual's self-awareness of its own boundaries.

My point of departure was a detailed examination of the linear nature of temporal perception and its effective abolition in the instantaneity of recall. Accordingly, the work is perhaps best regarded as the 'memory of a production process', and the performance environment as the point of confrontation between objectively measurable systems and their nemesis, subjective criteria of retention. The several recording mechanisms employed are required to sample, transform and reproduce very specifically indicated fragments of an already fractured discourse. This process continually interferes with the onward-flowing presentation and, at times, buries it under the accumulated weight of sonic detritus. At other junctures, the soloist has to react instantaneously to signals directed at him from various loudspeakers, whose task is to sort and analyze material according to quite other criteria than those applied to the live cello part itself. Towards the end of the work, the 'disturbance factor' increases with the insertion of still further prerecorded materials made up of ring modulated transformations of vocal actions picked up via a contact microphone attached to the cellist's throat. The history of the piece is also the history of the conflict between immediate experience and the resonating chambers (distorting mirrors?) of memory. As with the other components of the cycle, no definitive conclusions are drawn: the future remains open.

Time and Motion Study III (1973-4) for amplified voices, tape loop and percussion.

Composed for sixteen voices with electro-acoustic enhancement. Written in 1974 and given its first performance, at the Donaueschinger Musiktage 1975, by the Schola Cantorum Stuttgart, conducted by Clytus Gottwald.

The singers for this piece are disposed in four groups, either at the four corners of the performance space or, clearly separated, on the stage. Each choir is individually amplified, with the signals being transmitted by quadraphonically placed loudspeakers, the balance of the whole being adjusted live during performance. Each of the performers is required to play one or more percussion instruments, and there is a tape delay system employed in the concluding section of the work.

More than most of my compositions to date, **Time and Motion Studies II** and **III** might be said to insistently animate *ideational locations*. A form of Theater of Ideas is created by the initial disposition of forces selected, upon whose stage a drama is played out which would scarcely have been imaginable in any other environment. In this way, I hoped to create what I saw as a *mythic* (perhaps better: *allegorical*) dimension, in which each of the form-defining characters would act as a correlate in the definition of symbolic structures.

The following fragments are taken from two contemporary sources -

short notes scribbled into the initial sketches for the piece, and extracts from letters written to various friends.

> Time and motion study - a term signifying the investigation
> of conditions for optimal coordination between workforce and
> machines. A mutual adaptation. Not determined: the efficiency
> of the artwork.

> ...it occurred to me ever more emphatically that the polarity: voice/
> amplification was not simply one further means of expanding the
> available sound spectrum in respect of a specific ensemble...the entire
> constellation of meaning contained in this primary opposition lies, for me,
> on a quite different level, that is, the mutual interpenetration of Natural
> and Cultural in the widest sense of those terms. The work which is open,
> in equal measure, to both extremes could perhaps function as paradigm for
> entire tracts of problematic relationships, since it is the art object which
> most powerfully embodies current conditions for productivity, transmission
> and cultural reflection.

> ...the textual substratum of the work deals with diverse aspects of the
> armor-plated myth of technology. At the same time, it offers opportunity
> for a number of deformations of sensation and significance. Since the texts
> are, on the one hand, not audible as such; on the other, serve as points of
> departure for many methodological excursions, they exist basically as
> background matrix, thereby outlining a myth whose meaning is, by nature,
> purely intrinsic to the work.

> Calling oneself in question seen as unifying activity.

> The reproduced sound as icon of the original. Repetition as semblance of
> synonymity.

> ...false representations of the 'music of the spheres'.

> With dreamlike precision.

> ...this splitting apart of the syntactic and semantic dimensions of speech
> activity is deployed at a further axis. Affectively operative syntax
> (processually combinatorial successions of sound) placed against
> semantic emptiness: valid semanticity (texts in Latin, German
> and English), so processually undermined as to lose all claim to
> independent existence.

"The clock in profile and the inspector of space." (M.D.)[3]

N.B. The above notes were written thirteen years ago. I reproduce them here, not for their literary merit or explanatory power, but as traces of the work process. Perhaps they will nevertheless succeed in suggesting more of the original ambience of the composition than any description made with the benefit of hindsight might have been able to achieve.

Endnotes

1.   *The complete cycle still awaits (1992) a performance entirely corresponding to the description given here, since the Huddersfield presentation placed an intermission between the second and third works.*

2.   *Deutsche Akademische Austauschdienst.*

3.   *Marcel Duchamp.*

SECOND STRING QUARTET
(1982)

This piece is about silence - not so much literal silence (although this, too, is an obvious feature of the opening section) but rather that deliberate *absence* at the center of musical experience which exists in order that the listening subject may encounter itself there.

Since all forms of silence can only be approached via their own proper negatives, the organization of this quartet concentrates on the definition of several, ever-tighter concentric paths focused upon this core of stillness.

The labyrinthine path over which the approach is made attempts to suggest a number of possible implications at one and the same time; the dense webs of organization involved in the act of composition sink below the surface, thus becoming deliberately absorbed into a flickering interplay of surface gestures which, while the work's most immediately apparent feature, are designed to remain *permeable* to other areas of insight whose salient features are located at many points along the line of descent towards the center (which is not necessarily marked by the center-point of the work itself).

The above text has been offered on several occasions as program note. That it seems to some willfully gnomic or oracular, to others verbose and diffuse, to yet others both of these at the same time is to be regretted, but scarcely altered. Perhaps, in the final analysis, it might serve as a token of the tendency, peculiar to aesthetic perception, to alternate uneasily between 'too-muchness' and 'too-littleness'? It could be that this uncomfortable (but also enjoyable....) necessity of the perceiving spirit to find itself in continual motion between these notional extremes (meeting itself coming the other way?) fuels one of the basic drives underlying the 'artistic conspiracy'. At any rate, it is certainly extraordinarily difficult to put a finger with any accuracy upon the most essential aspect of this quartet, for the reason that it represents, at one and the same time, one of the - to me - most intangible of 'work-histories' and most concretely approachable - if not 'simple' - scores that I have composed.

In contrast to many works of the last decade, in which I undertook an 'aesthetic investigation' of several areas of musico-cultural interaction, the medium of the string quartet has imposed its own rules of play, forcing me to reorientate myself entirely within the boundaries of what might (platitudinously) be termed the 'purely musical' - which is, of course, the most universal.

It is also evident that each perception draws part of its significance, its particular flavor, from the web of experience of which it forms an indissoluble part. My interest on this particular occasion was to attempt to bypass this over-obvious (but nonetheless disturbingly influential) fact by separating, as far as possible, aspects of organization from those of presentation. Whereas many of my preceding pieces construct their surfaces from 'crystallized structures' (species of informational exoskeletons) the **Second Quartet** consciously sets out to conceal its generational methodology under successive layers of relatively straightforward evocative gesture intended to divert the ear away from this structural framework concurrently with allowing this latter to 'shade-in' further dimensions in a less palpable, but possibly more all-pervasive manner.

The immediate goal of this strategy was dual in nature: firstly, to point to that shadowy area which, in every work of art, separates overt realization and 'prehistory' (that of the genre and of the individual work) and conditions, in large part, the limits and density of discourse. Secondly, I aimed at suggesting ways of approaching and learning to converse with the complex chain of perceptual layerings which is situated between the listener and that still center of apprehension where the actively imaging and synthesizing ear comes to experience the elements of the work as *radiating out from it*, including it as an irreducible participating datum in the meaning-production of their motions. Between each of these layers, as at this central point of ultimate self-identity, lies the enveloping absolute, unchanging and still. Where music is, these are not: but, filtering through the blankly incommunicative enunciation of totality which is silence, music can perhaps lead us towards an appreciation of absence and stillness in which silence as oppressive fact has made way for the intervention of the subversive potential of the individual subject in the reappropriation and animation of the void.

Without attempting to provide an exhaustive analysis of this quartet as a whole I will select below several aspects of its genesis and realization which, I hope, will offer specific hints (but not much more than that....) as to what the program note quoted at the outset might just be beginning to say. That the explanation offered might be less than optimally concrete is, unfortunately, inevitable in view of the 'absence' framing and confining this particular means of expression.

The opening section of the work will be examined from the standpoint of its surface gestural organization; the fourth section (*vacillando*) will, in contrast, be demounted - presented in x-ray format - in order to reveal some elements of the structural sieve from, and through which the final texture was permitted to emerge. The listener is required retroactively to construct a mental model of the composition's discursive world in such a manner that its form be

perceived as inhabiting the expectant vacuum which the thus imposed constraints seek to define.

The opening fifty measures are built up over a predetermined numerical scheme, so that the relationships presently to be discussed should be understood as reactions to, and interpretational resonances of, a given dispositional
environment. At the outset, it was decided to alternate sound events of as yet
undetermined type with periods of exactly-measured silence. This plan was
subsequently modified by inserting a third type of material, to be constructed
according to radically different criteria (although still on the basis of the initially-
selected pitch conventions). This third material was inserted so as to *replace* certain silent measures with sonic activity of precisely equivalent overall duration.
In a subsequent round of operations, contrasting characteristic textural markers were selected and, more importantly, associated developmental/variational
tendencies were attached to each, so that fluctuating degrees of tension would
come to be generated, both within a particular texture-type and between the
divergent global tendencies typifying each type.

The 'main material' was conceived, from the outset, as being invariably
presented in sequences of rhythmically unison attacks, regardless of the number
of instruments actually playing. In effect, I was aiming at the suggestion of a
'super instrument' - starting with one violin, then successively adding the second violin, viola and cello. The effect was to render transition points almost
imperceptible, at least at the outset, where articulation between participants is
closely coordinated. In Ex. 1 the entry of the second violin is shown. It will be
noted that only in the pitch domain are the two instruments to be distinguished.

Ex. 1

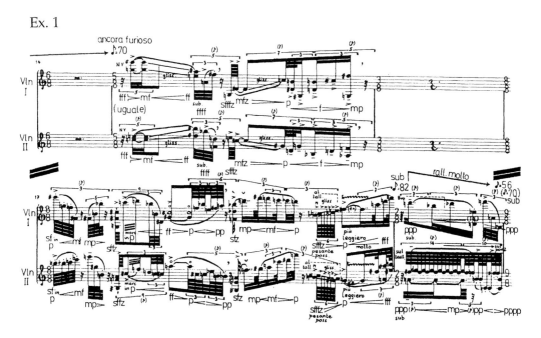

As these synchronized rhythms proceed, however, 'microvariations' - imprecisions, small deviations, 'rough' coordination etc. - begin to intrude, quietly insinuating themselves into the otherwise homogeneous statements. The first such moment is shown in Ex. 2, where the two violins interpret the rhythmically identical figures by means of quite different articulational means.

Ex. 2

A slightly later entry shows the same two instruments diverging more widely still, this time in respect of both articulation and dynamic intensity.

Ex. 3

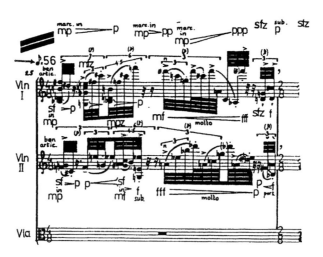

After the entry of the viola, the principal of synchronous attack is maintained, although not all instruments necessarily articulate each and every impulse in a group (Ex. 4(a)).

Ex. 4(a)

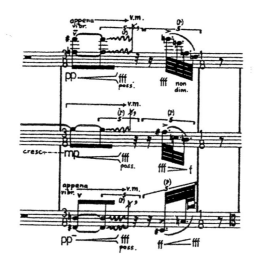

The entry of the cello signals the simultaneous employment of all the above-mentioned differentiating techniques (divergent dynamics, timbre, number of impulses played etc.) (Ex. 4(b)).

Ex. 4(b)

The common underlying principle of these passages (main material) is obviously additive in nature. The rhythmic structures of the entire work being given, it was necessary to select the most appropriate combination of playing characteristics for each particular exemplification of the 'main material' category in a markedly pragmatic manner, whilst taking into account the constraints imposed by the specific point attained in each processual trajectory as well as the precise context provided by surrounding, sometimes violently contrasting materials.

The silences were at first treated in a naively literal-minded fashion, their emptiness being underlined by the abrupt punctuating gestures of the first violin. Later on a more differentiated, subversive approach was adopted, to the extent that limited, 'impoverished' sounds were allowed to filter through, thereby coming to emphasize that *functional* silence during which (even if not devoid of sonic qualities) nothing informationally germane is registered. These fragile foregroundings of absence are gradually transformed, first into glissandi, whose functional value is also low because possessed of no significant harmonic/intervallic delineation, then into multiple, complexly-rhythmicized glissando events which may be said to function 'disfunctionally' in analogous manner. The fact that it is precisely such elements which are taken up again at the very end of the work and transformed into something of high contextual relevance is not a perceptually relevant fact during the opening section. The cumulative nature of this succession of 'colored silences' can be clearly seen in Ex. 5.

As was briefly mentioned above, some of the measures earmarked for silence came finally to be filled out with a 'secondary material', generated quite differently from the primarily homophonic first. In keeping with the principle that each type of event bring forth its own uniquely appropriate linear developmental processes, both basic textural consistency and the definition of essential properties of its constituent components were chosen with a view to setting in motion a quite different set of tendencies than those already outlined. In effect, each one-measure unit containing secondary material is a miniature fantasy generated by the interaction of three distinct gestural signals, which might be designated as (a) regular rapid groups, (b) irregular groups and (c) repeated-note groups. Ex. 6 shows the sort of typical motion for which these terms are taken to stand.

The sole systematic limitation imposed upon the deployment of these three elements is, that the speed of the regular rapid groups be directly inversely proportional to the absolute length of the measures in which they occur; that is to say, in an 8/8 measure the norm is the 64th-note; if the length of the measure is reduced by one eighth-note, nine 64th-notes are fitted into one eighth-note beat instead of eight. The extreme is reached in 1/8-measures, where 15 impulses are compressed into a single eighth-note beat (Ex. 7).

It will be clear that the diametrically opposed organizational principles and contrasted polyphonic/homophonic textural conventions ruling the main and secondary materials serve to separate them absolutely in terms of aural

Ex. 5(a), 5(b), 5(c)

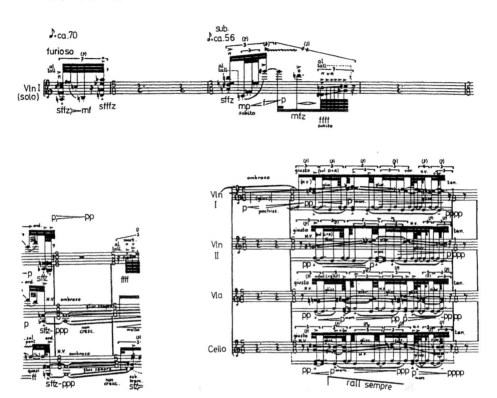

Ex. 6(a), 6(b), 6(c)

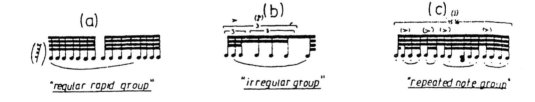

recognition potential. At the same time, it should be emphasized that it is less their respective surface characteristics which comprise their significance (since these merely serve to systematically differentiate them) but rather the manner in which the particular variational strategies unique to each lead to extremely diverse successive manifestations of internal potential. The simple additive principle governing the chain of main material presentations, allied to the subtly

Ex. 7

progressive destabilization of the 'unison effect', produces continually increasing amounts of tension which finds release only with the explosive commencement of the second section of the work. Against this, the secondary materials increase the literal amount of complexity involved, but entirely without any sense of cumulative emphasis. They illuminate various facets of their initial premises without urgently demanding to spill over their boundaries - quite to the contrary, it was my intention to so shape the contents of each one-measure segment so as to suggest a certain 'organic' duration for the phrase, emerging from the particular constellation of relationships it contains, rather than imposed arbitrarily from without. This form of dissimulation allows these fragments to illuminate various aspects of their constituent criteria without acting as 'signposts' pointing to future events. The silent sections (including those measures characterized by 'colored' silence) paradoxically partake of both static and active functions: theirs is the underlying ambiguity, theirs the iconic demonstration of that No-man's-land, that area of brittle and unstable truce in which all battles for signification begin and end.

My brief outline of some of the forces at work in the opening section of this quartet deliberately avoided any direct discussion of the precompositional constraints involved, since it was my aim to show how gesture might be permitted to overcome resistance to its integration into a larger-scale structure-defining role. In the following discussion of the fourth section of the quartet I will attempt to outline the view from the other side i.e. the perspective for the constructive integration of precompositional resistance into the creative act, the 'psychologizing' of latent invention.

I take the fourth section as my text, since it is there that the separation of forces is most radical. The diagram given as Ex. 8 illustrates the extent to which

Ex. 8

2nd String Quartet:

Heirarchies/Densities (Pt. 4)

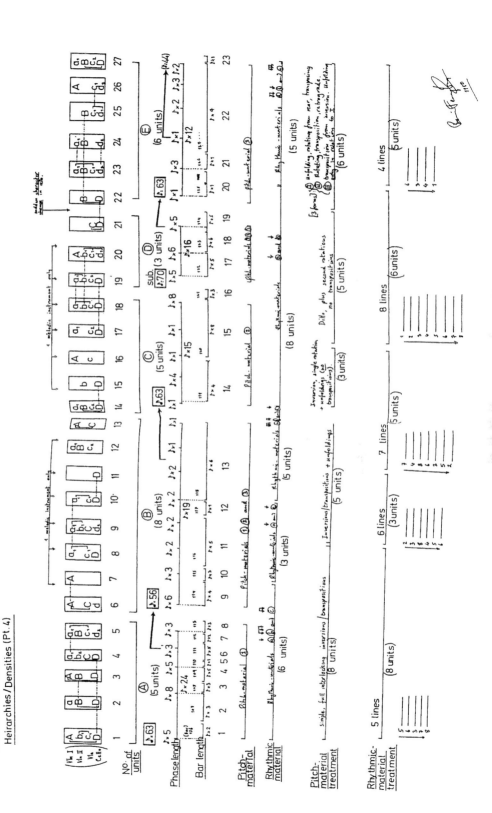

a relatively large number of sub-parameters were polyphonically interlocked to produce the final 'sieve' through which concrete musical events were subsequently forced.

The 'cartouches' at the very top of the diagram are indications of (a) which instruments are permitted to play and (b) in what hierarchy of predominance participating instruments stand to one another. A, B, C and D designate 1st and 2nd violins, viola and cello respectively: capital letters indicate predominant roles for the instruments so indicated, while lower case letters imply less important, accompanimental material. The digits 1 and 2 represent a further differentiation of this latter aspect into subcategories of predominance or subjugation. The particular configurations encountered in the 27 prescribed cartouches are a permutated selection made from the repertoire of all possible combinations of above-mentioned aspects. The more or less random order that emerged from this operation was accepted entirely without subsequent manipulation aimed at eradicating or ameliorating the more 'awkward' sequences, since this unforeseen resistance was, in large part, the predominant part of the exercise. To illustrate the relationship between 'model' and final result I offer two examples chosen more or less at random from the section concerned.

Example 9 demonstrates how, in a comparatively extended passage, a sequence of texture-defining cartouches can come to be productively integrated one with another. It will immediately be seen that the treatment (interpretation) of the constraints thus imposed is by no means rigorous or literal-minded. It was not my intention to compose a conventionally 'serial-type' structure, but rather one emerging, liberated, from the restraints of the ruling dispositional grid. I set out to define various types and qualities of space within which meaningful contextual decisions may be made, not the concrete sonic characteristics of specific atomic events embodying the momentary intersection of abstractly quantified parametric strands. In nearly all instances, the individual sections have been connected up fluidly; it was not part of the work's intent that paradigm boundaries be perceived as such. Far more, the impression to be transmitted was one of purposeful fluctuation, constant change of perspective and focus.

Since, at any given moment, there is a certain limitation placed on the identity and amount of rhythmic material available, but no parallel restrictions applying to precisely which aspects of that reservoir would be appropriately applied to particular contexts, it is evident that the results could conceivably have been quite different. That this openness is amenable to highly direct, almost parodistic manipulation can be seen from an examination of Ex. 10, in which a moment of increased sharpness of focus has been achieved by means of quasi-imitative gestural patterns, emphasized as such, moreover, by correspondence of articulation, amplitude and timbre. This result came about, nevertheless, through a strict respect for the criteria specified by the applicable

Ex. 9

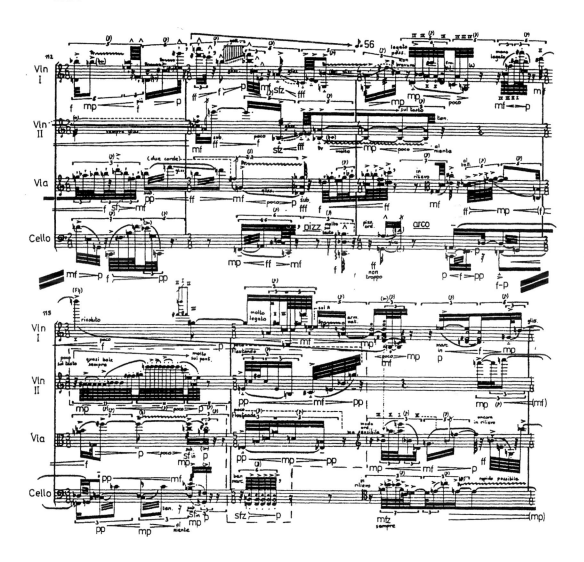

cartouche, since the figuration selected was, in fact, actually extrapolatable (even though not implied by) the quality and extent of constraints specified.

I have not subjected further defining levels contained in Ex. 8 to extensive discussion, since it is the general principle that I am concerned with presenting. Some of these levels are, in any case, fairly self-evident; all set out to delimit areas within which intuitive insight - 'feel' - is permitted to operate. It will also be noted that the various levels by no means invariably move simultaneously from one state to the next; in fact, it is precisely the *guided asynchrony*

Ex. 10

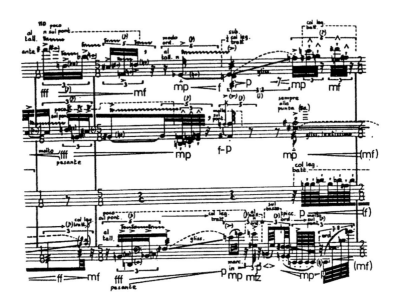

of these changes which puts at the composer's disposition a multitude of potential ambiguities, of subsurface rupture. It will, in particular, be noted that phrase length and bar length rarely coincide. This tendency is reflected on each successively higher level of the scheme, finally coming to encompass the manner (degree of complexity) with which specific materials may be processed, thus enabling me to consciously magnify the intensity and scope of these operations as the section proceeds. (See: 'pitch permutation forms' in the diagram.)

Since it would be impractical here to examine in any sort of detail all aspects of the diagram, I will outline merely the basic essentials of pitch organization, in the understanding that this, in most respects, can be taken as representative for all. Ex. 11 presents the pitch/interval units which formed my point of departure in this quartet.

Although initially a completely intuitive selection (as was the rhythmic material also) the three linear patterns were subsequently slightly modified to reach a certain loose ordering of what was, in each case, omitted. Apart from the obvious increase in the number of omitted pitches, there is a clearly implied intervallic correspondence between these 'negative' groups. Those pitches each absent from only one of the triple figures (G; E; C; G#) act throughout as what might be termed 'axial tones', that is, as pitches which - either by reason of their notably high density of appearance, by their location at important nodal points or (more frequently) as regulators of transpositional procedures, have come to assume increased organizational responsibility. Again; what is, in a certain sense, absent comes to balance out other aspects of the structure by means of compensating assertive presence.

Ex. 11

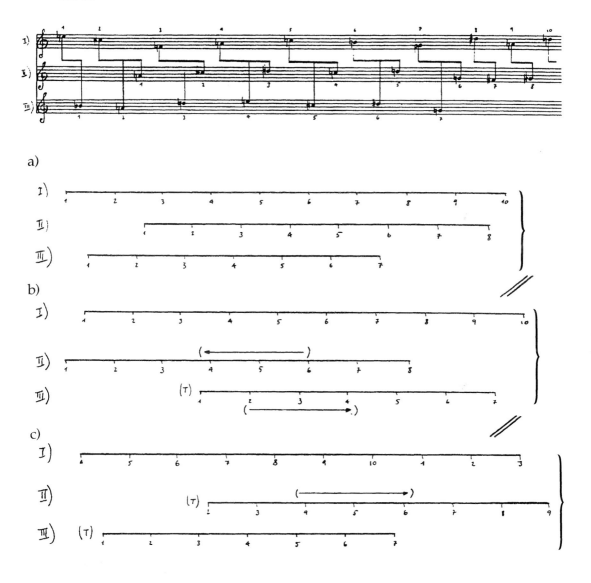

The examples of interlocking procedures given in Ex. 11 are representative of a significantly larger number introduced at various points according to contextually sensed need. The precompositional sieve specifies only which selection of devices is, at any given moment, available, not how, or in what degree of secondary systematization, they are to be employed. Thus, certain passages (see Ex. 9) may be based on the interaction of all three materials, although this does not by any manner of means imply constant simultaneity of deployment. The beginning of the final group in the same example marks the point at which, on the adjacent hierarchic level, the density of available transformations undergoes extremely rapid augmentation. It is not to be argued here that these and other complexes beyond the scope of this discussion are capable of asserting themselves in a conventionally audible fashion; what I personally find stimulating in such methods is the high level of resistance provided by such complexly interlocking grids, which bring an enhanced sense of material substantiality to the composer's intuitional momentum. In passing through these 'sieves' the initially unformed volition is, at one and the same time, shaped and diversified, with the result that complexity is not a mere function of multiplicative (usually surrounded by a distinct air of the tautological) but by divisional processes. For me at least, urgency and authenticity of expression are inseparably associated with such channeling of the artist's creative impulse.

In earlier works my goal was to evolve a technique for integrating the degree of difficulty, performer application and compositional density into the expressive orbit of a specific musical language: moving on from that, my present concerns are more directed at investigating how and why particular types of interaction between surface, interface and depth structure function as they apparently do. It was this level-by-level 'descent' (one which every listener, consciously or not, makes alone) towards which my preliminary program text was pointing. How does music keep on flowing, but nevertheless hold eternally to the timeless point of expectancy in the face of the impending leap? This question is the 'still center' of my current compositional concerns.

CARCERI D'INVENZIONE
(1986)

Many of my works of the last fifteen years have been engendered by contact with some form of concrete image. This has sometimes been effective as a unifying, all-pervasive idea (as in the image of the Music of the Spheres in **Transit** or the various ironic transformations and recompositions of the concept of 'efficiency' forming the basis of the **Time and Motion Study** cycle) but, at least as often, the work idea has emerged from contact with an actual visual experience which seemed mysteriously to 'trigger' the alchemical interaction of all sorts of hitherto nebulous issues, whose pressing relevance I had, until that moment, not suspected. This was true of both the orchestral piece **La terre est un homme** (based on a major canvas by Matta) and the piano composition **Lemma-Icon-Epigram**, which took Walter Benjamin's emblem speculations as immediate point of departure.

My (re-)encounter, in 1981, with the series of Piranesi etchings with the collective title **Carceri d'Invenzione** was still another such key experience. It coincided with initial attempts on my part to define the role of energy in the definition of possible modes of musical discourse and - equally important - brought this concern into immediate conjunction with two further aspects of my thinking then at approximately comparable stages of development. These were, firstly, the implications of consistency of personal style as a central prerequisite for formal processes and, secondly, the growing desire to formulate in practical terms a compositional strategy allowing for the systematic unification (or at least the peaceful coexistence) of extremes of constructional or informal modes of composition. By these means I hoped to set aside, at least for myself, what I have always felt to be a perilously over-simplifying pseudo-opposition still widely assumed in polemics on aesthetic issues.

The **Carceri d'Invenzione** (Dungeons of Invention, Inventive Dungeons) impressed me, in the first instance, by reason of their obvious intensity, richness and expressive power. After much subsequent reflection it struck me that it was the masterly deployment of layering and perspective which gave rise to this impression of extraordinary immediacy and almost physical impact. At one and the same time the observer is drawn ineluctably down towards the dark center while forcibly thrust away along centrifugal rays of absolutely non-naturalistic, mutually conflicting lines of force.

> The frail catwalks, the drawbridges in midair
> which almost everywhere double the galleries and the
> stone staircases, seem to correspond to the same desire to
> hurl into space all possible curves and parallels. This
> world closed over itself is mathematically infinite.[1]

For me, it is precisely this interlocking of incompatible (but somehow co-extant) perspectival fields which generates the necessary energy to project this self-enclosed experience beyond the physical limits of the page, into the world outside. To me, this seems like one real way of making music "mean". Gilles Deleuze, in connection with his discussion of another painter of forces, Francis Bacon, says: "En art, et en peinture, comme en musique, il ne s'agit pas de reproduire ou d'inventer des formes mais de capter des forces".[2] In my compositions, I am always setting out to define momentary, transitory states of balance or conflict, which, albeit necessarily ambiguously, define the spaces which their own future comes to occupy. It is thus that the musical object comes to appear in the double role of emotively connotative, gestural entity and of figural constellation, whose particularized component sound qualities are constantly poised to independently launch themselves into (and thus define) subsequent stages of the discourse. I am particularly interested in the figure's capacity for creating multiple strands of directionality which, by allowing the onward-flowing projection of simultaneous perspectives, suggest the presence of 'depth effect' in and among the sonic objects.

The musical event is defined by its capacity to render visible the forces acting on it as well as the energies thereby set free. All compositional technique focuses on this state of affairs and its consequences for the perception of form. All works in the cycle share a wide repertoire of generically similar techniques totally compatible among themselves, and their combination/opposition in specific contexts forms the foundation of work identity. In particular, many types of 'filter' operation are employed, aimed at rendering specific partial aspects of a given material through a series of mobile restrictive grids. Since I hold that all invention comes from restriction, it seems particularly appropriate to imprison musical states, thus empowering them to express themselves by means of the implosive energies thereby released.

A second vital strand of thought highlighted by my concern for Piranesi's achievement was the question of *style*. Just as the life-and-death cycle of specific materials as exemplified in any given work depends on the former's relative diachronic integrity, so the extension of these principles to the dimensions of an entire cycle of works offers the opportunity of still vaster perspectives, more profound interactions. I have always experienced great difficulties in keeping works entirely separate; continuity of style takes this fact into account and amplifies it to a more general principle of potential linguistic definition.

Precisely the contrasts and developmental elaborations distinguishing earlier and later versions of many of Piranesi's **Carceri** imbue his second thoughts with more intense semantic 'perspective'. In a similar fashion, the layerwise accretional means of composition I employ allow for an 'archaeological' approach to listening, and encourage the speculative ear to create its own categories of perception. In my experience, only a conscious consistency of stylistic ambience is able to generate a space within which potentially violent extremes of precalculation and context-bound invention may fruitfully interpenetrate.

The **Carceri d'Invenzione** cycle as a whole is also laid out with these strictures in mind. Several patterns connect the individual compositions, so that a dynamic network of trajectories is suggested. From the point of view of instrumental forces, the three works **Carceri d'Invenzione I-III** form a clear central axis, around which the remaining, smaller pieces are disposed. At the same time, this function is lent further support by the fact that the flute concerto, **Carceri d'Invenzione II**, occupies the central panel of the triptych thus:

Carceri d'Invenzione I - Carceri d'Invenzione II - Carceri d'Invenzione III

Intersecting this line at the same central point is the series of pieces in which the flute plays a prominent role:

Superscriptio - Carceri d'Invenzione II - Mnemosyne

(Piccolo)   (Flute)   (Bass Flute)

The descent from extremely high to low register is an immediately audible and striking 'theme' of this sequence, even though the *mode d'emploi* of the flute in respect of the rest of the ensemble is constantly in flux, i.e.

Solo - Solo with ensemble - Solo with prerecorded tape.

Within each of these compositions, the tension inhering to the insistent opposition and integration of wildly diverse degrees of pre-ordering is manifested differently. In common to all, however, is the intention of exhibiting these pressures as intensely and as formally coherently as possible. The song cycle **Etudes Transcendantales**, fifth of the seven works included, is possibly the most extreme example of this common thread, in that each of the nine miniatures consciously sets out from a different 'balance of forces', so that the dynamic flow characteristic of the whole is simultaneously compacted (chamber combinations, brief duration) and expanded (lengthy overall duration, rapidity of unfolding of individual forms) to the most obviously radical available extremes.

Superscriptio (1981) for solo piccolo

The sound of any extremely high or low instrument tends, at least for me, to evoke associations with borders, boundaries and with whatever lies beyond. Thus, in this little one-movement composition dating from 1981, I attempted to reflect these sensations in such a way as to suggest the fleeting sketching-in of that brittle outline, that trace with no dimensions, representing some ultimate 'inside of the outside', itself never to be captured in sound.

Formally, **Superscriptio** (as the most highly 'automatized' work in this cycle) is constructed upon a dense network of metric and proportional relationships, wherein variations of texture and momentum are achieved by means of distortions in the pattern created by the mobile juxtaposition of diverse bar lengths, as well as by the gradual de-synchronization of gestural shaping, dynamic intensity and rhythmic density - elements which, at the outset, are all heard to be changing simultaneously.

Carceri d'Invenzione I (1981-2) for sixteen instruments

Like the other works in the same series, **Carceri d'Invenzione I** is built up as the overlapping of several differently instrumentated and processually distinct strata, each with its own mode of development, contraction or expansion. From the initial presentation of structures it will be evident that the principle of repetition (however flexibly understood) has a significant role to play in what follows. The first half of the piece consists of the slow and uneven unfolding of the consequences which the initial brutal exposure of contrasted textures (piccolo, trombone, pianoforte; woodwind and brass) sets in motion, whereby several groups are timbrally modified, others (strings) remaining constant in color, although modified with respect to density and articulation. The interplay of levels of transformation, whether heard as immediate phenomena or longer-term organizational functions, aims at providing a framework within which the listener can begin to perceive the categories of *energy* and *force* outlined above, and it is the possibility of interpreting the individual strata as *either* regulatory *or* regulated mechanisms which progressively defines the listening categories involved.

Intermedio alla Ciaccona (1986) for violin solo

The final work in the cycle to be composed, **Intermedio** aims at a loosening of some earlier conventions, in the sense of an almost improvisatory reflection on the now disembodied energies previously released. The piece fluctuates uneasily between areas of intensely frenetic but materially unspecific activity and 'close-ups' of slowly evolving, monochrome textures, in which energy is 'collected' once more. Like most other components of the cycle, **Intermedio alla Ciaccona** is based exclusively on a series of eight chords, themselves containing the potential for static (symmetrical) or mobile (asymmetrical) modes of treatment. As with all my solo instrumental works, I aim here at evoking facets of a 'fictional polyphony', not by means of literally polyphonic strands of sound, but rather through what are usually considered 'secondary' parametric levels of organization.

Carceri d'Invenzione II (1984) for obbligato flute and chamber orchestra

Rather in the manner of Schoenberg's Phantasy for Violin with piano accompaniment, the solo flute part of this 14-minute piece was through composed in its entirety before any of the orchestral accompaniment was determined. My intention was to allow the ensemble textures to comment more freely on the rigorously pre-determined modular patterns of the soloist in a way which would sometimes suggest competition, at others amplification of specific tendencies in the solo line.

The solo part consists of 48 internally invariant modules, which are cyclically permutated so as to suggest the gradual growth of tendential perspective and, in particular, the architectonic nature of registral deployment. At the beginning, only the extreme upper and lower registers of the flute are used; little by little other registers are blended in so as to finally focus on the central minor third of A and F#, all events and detailed elaborations suddenly being confined to that pitch-band, with the exception of sudden outbursts in the original registral extremes signalling the cyclically-determined recurrence of modular elements already heard. As more and more cycles are overlapped, the variational techniques employed become increasingly extreme and registrally rich, the entire tendency flowing into a *quasi una cadenza*, wherein all registral and articulational aspects of the flute are exploited to the full. The final section consists of a progressive subtraction of material and a descent into the lowest register, placed against a string texture itself derived from the eight basic chords polyphonically 'diffracted' through *glissandi*.

In contrast to the flute part, orchestral activity is rather discontinuous, even though its deployment is similarly governed by cyclic considerations making reference to the flute's frequent change of registral focus. An essential component is the 'irregular metronome' effect provided by the two horns, which overlap two distinct tempo fields operating independently of the main tempo of the work. This technique reflects my intense concern with metric devices in the entire cycle, and prefigures an even more extensive employment (three layers) as the basis of the formal structure of **Carceri d'Invenzione III**.

Etudes Transcendantales (1983-5) for mezzo soprano, flute, oboe, violoncello and harpsichord

At various points in my career I have resorted to the particular challenge of the small form in order to realize as concretely as possible specific compositional problems. Each of the nine songs comprising this work (with the sole exception of the concluding song, which deviates from the norm in various ways) is considerably less than four minutes in length, and compresses material, treatment and form into a notably compact energic unit. The piece is divided into three times three subgroups: although not finally carried out into the last detail, my original intention was to reflect the more 'automatized' end of the spectrum in the first piece in each group, the more 'informal' in the second, and a relatively complex collision, interpenetration or interaction of both in the third. This layout was to be further mirrored in the relationship of the three subgroups to each other, each one primarily embodying one of the three defining generative categories. In the event, things inevitably became more ambiguous: each movement has more or less clearly evident qualities characteristic of both ends of the compositional/conceptual axis.

The instrumentation of each song is very specific: in the first group of three the oboe predominates - most strikingly in the opening voice/oboe duet. In the second group, the flute assumes the foreground, again announced by a duet with voice (Song 4). In the third group, it is the harpsichord which is notably active, although 'its' duet falls in eighth, rather than seventh, place. Only Songs 5 and 9 specify the complete ensemble. Song 9 abandons the traditional vocal technique of earlier movements in favor of the separate presentation of the text's vowel and consonant components. At the end, instead of recombining them, the text is spoken, no longer in any way synchronized with the instrumental activity. Song 8 already anticipates this linguistic fracture, in that it contains two independent texts which are cut through one another, not according to criteria of semantic coherence, but rather at the prompting of the predetermined musical form. In order to avoid a clichéd text interpretation, I deliberately composed the vocal lines prior to adding the textual underlay (although naturally taking precise account of the text's significance and internal structure). The texts of Songs 1, 2 and 6 are by Ernst Meister,[3] the remainder were specially written by Alrun Moll at my request.

Carceri d'Invenzione III (1986) for fifteen wind instruments and three percussion

Carceri d'Invenzione III continues to examine many of the concerns already outlined above in connection with other sections of the cycle. In particular, the opposition/integration of diverse levels of discourse, the structural deployment of complex metric devices and antiphonal ensemble layout have been emphasized. Whereas, in **Carceri II**, the irregular metronome technique was employed as a substratum, in the present work it emerges as the veritable generator of the action, in that each new event is 'triggered' by an impulse given, in the first instance, by one or more percussion instruments. The first section, in particular, emerges from the interlocking activities of three such triggering patterns. For the most part activating various types of brass materials, they also regulate changes in the density and number of woodwind layers, as well as their progressive transformation. Later sections of the work allow more and more initially concealed impulses to surface, and the final section focuses in on this tendency by specifying anything from a solo instrument up to all available instruments to be activated by each impulse. The process concludes at the precise instant at which increase of base tempo and completeness of presentation of percussive pulse activity would allow this formally active stratum to be perceived as concrete material in its own right. Various oppositions are exploited during the course of **Carceri III** - first of all: brass/woodwind, later: high/low and, finally: Ensemble I/Ensemble II (the instruments being antiphonally placed).

Mnemosyne (1986) for bass flute and prerecorded 8-track tape

The concluding piece of the entire cycle is at once the slowest and the harmonically most explicit. As the title obliquely implies (Mnemosyne: Greek goddess of memory), the chordal patterns diffracted through most of the previous six compositions are once more unfolded - not so much as equal partners to the soloist, but as a ubiquitous backdrop serving both to repropose or expand earlier 'harmonic spaces' and to provide a reticent but insistent series of central pitches, around which the flutist weaves a limited number of rigidly referential intervallic chains, themselves derived from the initial series of eight chords. Thus, the richer the background sonority becomes (progressing from four up to eight prerecorded bass flute lines), the greater the scope for flexibility in respect of melodic invention. Since, however, during the final section of the composition, the number of derived intervals is progressively reduced, the gestures of the solo part find themselves increasingly circumscribed ('imprisoned') within the limits defined by the dense chordal sonorities of the tape until the inevitable fade out occurs.

Like other works in the cycle, **Mnemosyne** is based on the multilayered interaction of diverse metrical and temporal patterns, whereby the 'metronome' function is here assumed by the tape materials, which emphasize exclusively the downbeats of each measure. In distinction to **Carceri II**, the tape part of **Mnemosyne** predated the solo part, which, in consequence, remains structurally dependent on the formal layout which the former expounds. The tape part was produced with the assistance of Roberto Fabbriciani (bass flute) and Rudi Strauss (technician) in the Experimental Studio of Südwestfunk, Freiburg im Breisgau.

Endnotes

1.   *Margerite Yourcenar:* The Dark Brain of Piranesi, *Farrar, Straus, Giroux, New York 1984, p. 144.*

2.   *Gilles Deleuze:* Francis Bacon, Logique de la Sensation, *Editions de la Différence, Paris 1981, p. 39.*

3.   *Ernst Meister:* Ausgewählte Gedichte 1932-1976, *Luchterhand Verlag 1977.*

KURZE SCHATTEN II for solo guitar
(1990)

There is no **Kurze Schatten I**: the title is taken from an essay by the German cultural philosopher Walter Benjamin,[1] where, in a series of seven short texts (hence the seven movements in the composition) he talks about the essentiality of the *Augenblick*, of the experiential moment. He takes as his example an image of the sun progressively approaching its zenith until, at noon, it beats down from directly overhead, at which moment all shadows disappear, everything becomes just itself, a quintessential monad. Reading this description, I immediately began to plan a piece in which process gradually merges into the object in such a way that both, in a hyper-real way, become 'themselves'. To accomplish that, I realized that I would have to compose extremely short, compact and formally focused movements.

The other challenge was to create pieces in which the events would end up being as immediate, direct and violently energized as my writing for other instruments, even though the guitar is not necessarily an instrument frequently associated with extremes of force or deeply-etched dramatic delivery. The first step was to define a large-scale form: how to put together seven distinct movements in a reasonably interesting and contrasted fashion, without merely ending up with a banal little suite? My reaction was to adopt the baroque suite principle of a slow movement coupled with an immediately subsequent faster movement. This contrastive pairing was repeated three times in all, and a fantasia - a 'throwback' to the English viol fantasy of Purcell and Lawes - appended which aimed at compacting into a brief space of time as many diverse playing techniques as were compatible with musical coherence.

That approach posed few fundamental problems. In order to gradually transform the resonance of the work over its total duration, I decided that I wanted to modify the tuning of the instrument to produce microtonal sonorities. The tuning I chose for the opening has four *scordatura* strings arranged around two strings with normal tuning. These latter (D and G) remain constant throughout the entire composition; the B string is the only semitonal scordatura, being tuned down to Bb, the upper E string is tuned down to E quarter-flat, the A string is tuned up three-quarters of a tone to B quarter-flat, and the low E string is raised by a quarter-tone.

---

[1] See Walter Benjamin, 'Kurze Schatten', in *Illuminationen*, Suhrkamp, Frankfurt am Main 1977, p. 297ff.

Ex. 1

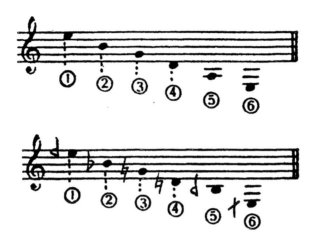

The special thing about this setup is that, at the end of every second movement, one of the four scordatura strings is returned to its 'normal' tuning. The first to be changed is the low E string, so that, immediately, the lower end of the range begins to resonate a little more; after that, the B quarter-flat is returned to A and, finally, the high E quarter-flat is tuned up to E. After these three retunings, only the B string remains detuned, and then not to a microtonal pitch, but Bb. The most immediately audible result of this process is the progressive abandonment, over the seven movements, of the peculiar timbre set up by the natural resonance of the guitar corpus responding to a set of non-natural tunings, in favor of the more ample and familiar sonority which a predominantly traditional tuning assures. Perhaps if I had to write this piece again, I might have chosen a some-what different scordatura, since some strings - particularly the raised A - tend to lose pitch over the course of several movements, but the basic dual principle of progressive timbral re-appropriation and the alliance of pairs of movements sharing the same scordatura would doubtlessly have remained the same. In fact, it was rather interesting to observe how this interaction of processual types gave rise to a chain of quite rich and unpredictable local situations.

Each piece attempts, like an elaborate study, to concentrate its criteria of composition around a uniquely specific issue. In the first movement, we have the problem of working on three polyphonic levels - or, rather, two distinct types of polyphonic structure, one of which is composed of two independent layers of natural harmonics (whose absolute pitch-content of course reflects the scordatura of the specific strings indicated) the other incorporating what might be termed a polyphony of successivity: on the lowest of the three staves making up each system one sees miniature figures that succeed each other with such rapidity, that occasional overlappings of two distinct figures are encountered. There are four independently variable categories of micro-figure, so that, in effect, there might be said to be a total of six virtual layers contributing to the overall effect of this movement. The employment of natural harmonics as a fundamental resource here was dictated, in part, by the fact that, once attacked, the left-hand finger is removed and thus made available for use on some other string. One of the main challenges to the performer is to avoid damping freely resonating sounds when playing complex and often, in themselves, technically highly demanding figures across one or more other strings. Regardless of the actual duration of such natural harmonics (which is extremely variable), the string involved should under no circumstances be damped until the indicated duration has expired.

Ex. 2 (No. 1, m. 11)[1]

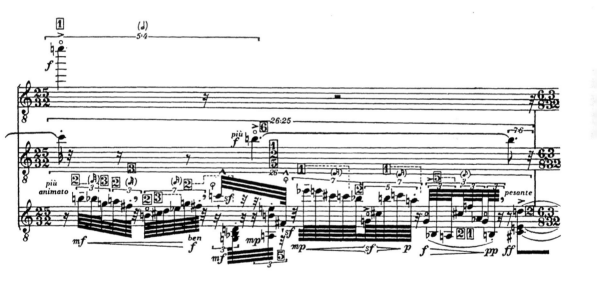

The second movement's 'topic' is the potential distinction between performance tempo and perceived density of material. The marked tempo at the outset is extremely high and decreases by regular steps throughout, while the tendency in terms of material density is the opposite, that is to say, the notated speed of events of the opening is relatively low, permitting substantial polyphonic differentiation. (Ex. 3(a)) As the piece progresses, notated rhythmic values become ever shorter, thus compressing ever more impulses in the increasingly expansive time frame of each section. (Ex. 3(b)) The result of this overlapping of tempo and density vectors is a tendency, towards the middle of the movement, for the ear to confuse the two, even though, from the point of view of the performer, they imply quite diverse interpretational challenges. It should perhaps be added here that the articulation of the overall form is aided by the fact that the *notated* pitches of each section (areas controlled by a constant tempo) remain identical, at least at the outset. Two variables conspire to provide small but significant changes; firstly, the octave register and string of some pitches has been changed (thus, in effect, producing wholly new pitch constellations 'filtered' through the scordatura of those strings) and, secondly, the increased rapidity of notated rhythm cycles through the available pitches ever sooner, so that, with each succeeding cycle, more 'new' pitches have to be added-on at the end of each section, thus progressively modifying, 'wiping-over' the initial, quasi-motivic figural clarity.

Ex. 3(a) (No. 2, mm. 1-7)

So that is the first two-movement 'panel'. The third piece deals with various perceptions of time-flow and distribution, as seen in the context of a highly-symmetrical formal scheme. More than any of the other pieces it concerns itself with a variety of percussive techniques like striking the body of the instrument, depressing strings percussively with the fingertip and so on. The underlying principle is extremely simple; I defined a series of measures of many

Ex. 3(b) (No. 2, mm. 31-36)

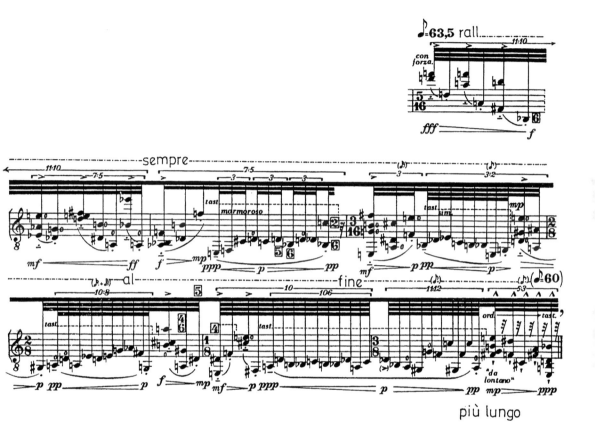

different lengths which, after the midpoint of the movement, with the exception of a few small irregularities, runs in retrograde back to its starting point.
The major difference between the original and its metric retrograde is that,
whereas every alternate measure in the first half contains either complete silence or else a predetermined internal subdivision into tenuto resonance and
silence, the retrograde version reverses this relationship, so that the measures
initially marked by actual music are now essentially silent, and vice versa. Since,
in the first half, I tended to divide up the available time unequally, with sound
events dominating, and silence/resonance reduced to an essentially punctuating function, in the second half the opposite is now true, namely, that aphoristically   brief   and   disconnected   sonic   interjections   are   inserted   into
disproportionately lengthy fields of silence. This (as I was well aware at the time)
is likely to confront the player with a number of thorny psychological barriers;

it is really extremely difficult to sit still, counting out those long measures in which nothing seems to be happening. More and more, the sundry contributory tensions which, when one is actually playing, tend to be uniformly subsumed to the common goal, now take on increasingly independent lives of their own - a polyphony, as it were, located almost entirely in the mind (and its physical extensions) of the performer. Some of these tensions have to do with deflecting the superfluous residual impetus emerging from the previous event; some have to do with mentally preparing the scene for the eventual sudden emergence of the next event, assessing and gradating the invisible topography of the ascending or descending slope at the end of which it emerges into that part of the piece's environment directly apperceivable by the listener, who may perhaps be indirectly reminded of the sort of veiled conflict between impulse density and tempo which the preceding piece presents. A comparison of the equivalent passages from the opening (Ex. 4(a)) and conclusion (Ex. 4(b)) of the piece will, I think, demonstrate what I mean.

This group of three pieces was composed sometime in 1983-4, at which time extensive sketches were prepared for the other four, even though I delayed realizing them in detail until towards the end of 1988. The fourth piece is actually the one I would like to concentrate on most exhaustively: for me, it is one of the more problematic movements for all concerned. I see it as a sort of generic waltz, even to the extent of having a clear ABA format and to being based throughout on the notion of triplicity, and the uneven subdivision into 1 beat and 2 beats which a waltz accompaniment typically provides. Further operations take this idea much further, by reversing that relationship, changing its proportions (for example into 2 and 3 subdivisions of a 3/8 measure) or by self-replicational 'nesting' of such values one within another. The first section of the piece even remains in 3/8 time throughout, regardless of the liberties taken with respect to the internal proportional partitioning of individual measures (Ex. 5(a)). Similar principles hold good in the middle section, except that there are now two processes - almost equivalent to melody and accompaniment functions - running concurrently, each assigned to an individual stave in the score. The '3-principle' is now concentrated on the lower, 'melody' stave, and is realized as interlocking triplet groups of various overall duration, whose individual components are, on occasion, separated-out and distributed throughout the measure as a form of 'irrational syncopation' (Ex. 5(b)).

In a sense, the usual relationship of melody to accompaniment has been stood on its head: instead of being slower, the accompaniment is actually the gesturally denser and more elaborated of the two levels. Because of the slow, sustained nature of the 'melody', and the fact that its close microtonal pitch windings usually involve more than one string, the guitarist does not have the option of changing position at will. For this reason I found it necessary to employ a high proportion of repeated pitches in the accompanying materials. Very often

Ex. 4(a) (No. 3, mm. 1-5)

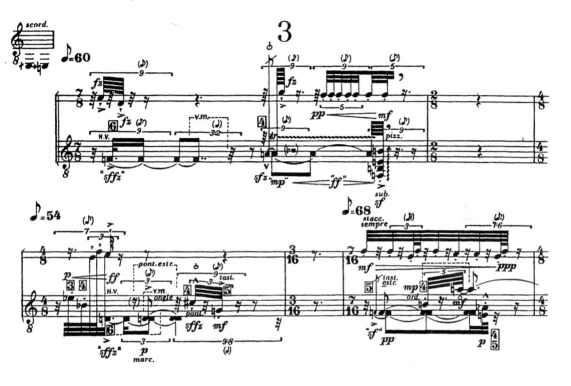

Ex. 4(b) (No. 3, mm. 24-28)

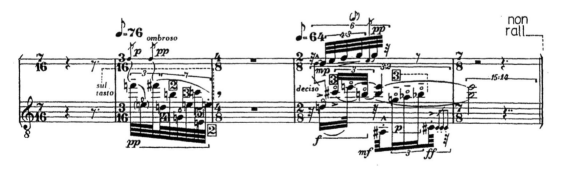

when composing, one is involved in juggling processes of this sort; in order to increase the flexibility of a given dimension one has to reduce the flexibility in another, or else adopt a strategy of expression permitting the performer to deal with both dimensions simultaneously. The reverse occurs in the third and final section, where the increased employment of natural harmonics in the accompanying figures allows the player an increased left hand mobility.

As the second section proceeds, the individual nodes deliberately chosen to maximize close-interval microtonal friction tend to turn into chords. What I was doing was to gradually build up towards the third part, in which one of the layers is composed almost exclusively of chords, with the result that textural density tends towards a maximum.

Ex. 5(a) (No.4, mm. 1-2)

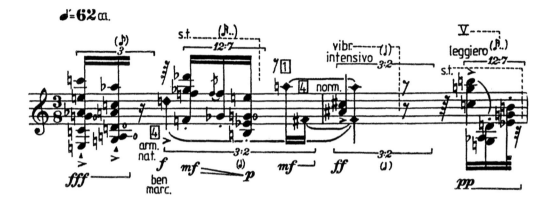

Ex. 5(b) (No.4, mm. 26-27)

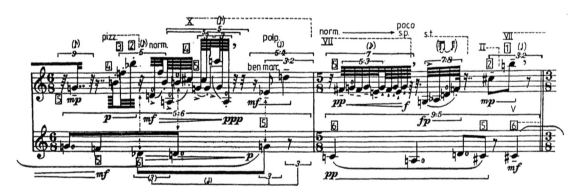

The most significant pre-compositional decision I made with respect to this movement was not to work it out in terms of individual pitches - at least, not in the first instance - but, rather, in terms of left hand finger positions. I made a large table of all possible guitar finger positions - from 1st to 18th position , if I recall correctly - and all possible combinations of four fingers over any combination of the six strings. I then planned a permutated sequence, not containing all of these resources by any means, but a significant portion of them, which I spread out over the entire metric/rhythmic structure of the piece with a view to fixing which combination of strings, placing of fingers and fret position would be available at any given moment. What particularly led me to this approach was the creation of polyphonic continuity while constraining players to realize the notated material in ways which frequently go counter to their instinctive feel for what would be natural. The notation is extremely specific in this respect.

Ex. 6 (No. 4, mm. 35-37)

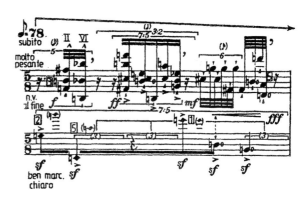

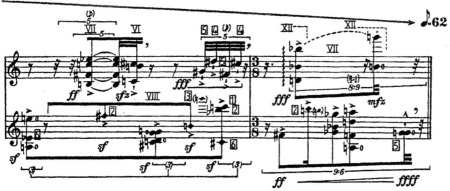

I said earlier that all these movements resemble studies. This piece is thus a study in left hand agility seen as an independent variable, in that the distance covered over the fingerboard sometimes seems to stand in a perversely independent relationship to the resultant sonic continuity. Constant motion between the extremes of immobility and violent excitation in this dimension is really the central hallmark throughout, and it is certainly the focus of interpretational attention when the performer sets out to comprehend and assimilate the aesthetic motivation involved.

I had not been much concerned with the guitar before Magnus Andersson asked me to compose something for him. I came very much from the experience of writing for traditional string instruments, in particular, the cello, and it was the result of reflection on cello technique - how, after a certain position, the thumb of the left hand can be brought into play - that I came to employ similar techniques for the guitar, whereby bringing the thumb out on top of the frets gives one a significantly larger hand span. In any case, it is always worthwhile trying it out for oneself. If one is going to get into strange situations, it is useful to make sure of their fundamental practicality well in advance. The main practical problem with this particular movement, I think, is that associated with the continual motion of the left hand across frets and strings, since it is almost inevitable that, on occasions, strings already resonating are damped accidentally. In any event it demands finger agility of a highly advanced order, not just locally, but throughout. The coincidence of structural and textural density with extreme technical demands makes this perhaps the 'weightiest' movement of the set, and it is located in central position for that reason.

The fifth piece - again a slow one - is based on a very simple chordal proliferation principle. It's the movement which relies the most on the great coloristic potential of the instrument. Essentially, it is based on just one chord in section one, then two chords in section two, three in three and so on. One hears very clearly, I think, that a textural or timbral difference coincides, for the most part, with a sudden change in the available harmonic repertoire. Again like the second piece, there is a constantly accelerating rate of change in one dimension, against a static or reducing level of complexity in another, since most textures emerge from the simple arpeggiation of various types of vertically-defined harmonic entities. Above all, the piece has to do with articulation and tone color. It is a rather quiet and withdrawn statement, and I employ a number of playing techniques which exploit the lower dynamic reaches of the guitar, such as, for example, holding a chord with the left hand while playing with the fingertips of the right hand lightly and rapidly, in a free pattern, over the strings - something giving the effect of an unfocused, feathery 'aura' of sound. This is notated by writing the chord and following it with a group of 'headless' grace notes.

Another feature is the employment of the bi-tone phenomenon, according to which either the string is plucked behind the stopping finger, or else the finger strikes the string violently, producing a percussive sonority composed of both pitches, the one relevant to the string between the finger and the bridge, the other to the distance between the finger and the nut. There is also a passage in which one is playing percussively with the left hand and plucking behind the left hand fingers with the right - something quite difficult to work out compositionally, if one is not a guitarist, especially when employing various forms of *scordatura*.

So what happens is that not only am I changing the chords with increasing rapidity, but I am simultaneously modifying the hierarchical order pertaining between them and the number and type of articulation techniques applied to the chords in any given section. Clearly, the way such techniques are distributed over the invariant pitches of a single chord will be very different from what is possible when several chords are heard in quick succession. Thus, although the basic tempo does not change over the course of the piece as much as is the case in some other movements, there still remains a great deal of scope for fluctuation in the flow of information between these various levels. In any case, it is not so much a question of speed as of character: this, more than perhaps any other component of **Kurze Schatten**, is a *Charakterstück*.

Ex. 7 (No. 5, mm. 7-9)

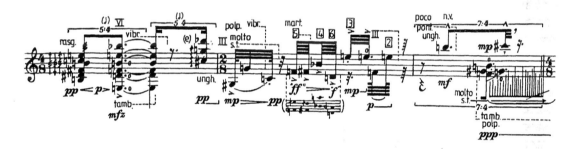

Ex. 8 (No. 5, m. 22)

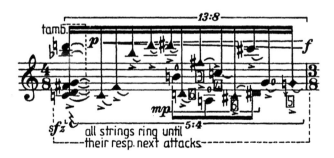

The sixth piece, by way of contrast, is very mercurial - something of a scherzo in nature. Here, I wanted to concentrate on pitch as one of the key vectors, the other being the gradual replacement of normally-produced pitches by natural harmonics. The variable dimension here is the choice of strings made by the performer; I don't indicate specific strings for the most part (unlike

practically every other piece in the cycle) and it is thus up to individual players to determine if they prefer a fingering which gives them the greatest possible continuity and facility in the figuration, whilst sacrificing some 'effective'
sonorities, or one which results in natural harmonics of high resolution,
amplitude and sustaining power, but with a lesser degree of agility and
economy of movement over the frets. It follows from this that absolute pitch
contexts can, and do, vary from performer to performer, resulting as they do
from aesthetic and technical choices made during the learning process.[2] When
working on this piece with Magnus Andersson, we would choose solutions
which sometimes underlined timbral diversity or instability while, at other
times, we agreed to give precedence to continuity of line or strong and highly-
focused pitch content. When I was composing these passages, I obviously
weighed these various factors against each other, in order to eliminate theoretical alternatives which would have been clearly incongruous. In a sense, it
was like an act of damage control. In all other respects, this piece might be
regarded as the one most closely approaching traditional norms of contemporary guitar common usage.

　　　With the sixth piece, the three slow-fast groups have been completed
and, with them, the return of all scordatura strings to normal tuning, with the
important exception of the Bb. All that remains is the final fantasia, in which
that string is accorded increasing prominence until, at the very end, it alone is
employed.

　　　Several movements in **Kurze Schatten II** are based on cyclic structures,
mostly recurring metric patterns, and the seventh movement adheres once more
to this principle. Six sections, each containing six measures with identical (albeit permutated) measure lengths are present. In addition, each section contains
a number of *fermate* of specific lengths, which serve to break up the insistent
density of texture. It is perhaps worth noting that the original impulse, in 1988,
to take up the composition of the outstanding four movements came from a
lengthy Darmstadt concert, during which the opening section was sketched on
the back of a used envelope.

　　　After the concert I gave Magnus a copy and, the next day, we ran
through this material together, and on the spot I determined to bring the cycle
to a conclusion as soon as possible.

　　　What one immediately hears in this piece, I think, is an initial welter of
textures and colors which succeed one another with great rapidity, although, as
section succeeds section, a violent *glissando* gesture comes to dominate the
gestural repertoire. Like some sort of wind-up toy, the argument staggers back
and forth across the whole gamut of the instrument's expressive potential in a
surrealistically miniaturized time frame, and practically every conventional
device of traditional guitar usage may be encountered somewhere in this
movement in epigrammatic guise. I remember thinking at the time that such

Ex. 9 (No. 7, mm. 1-6)

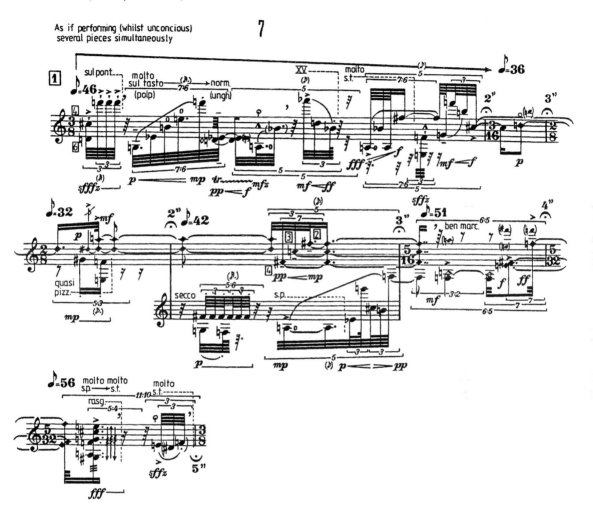

Ex. 10 (No. 7, mm. 34-36)

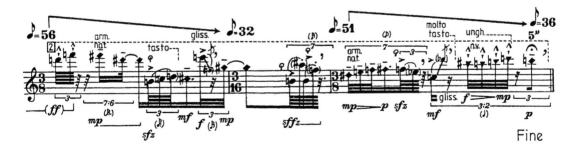

miniaturization of formal and temporal dimensions would be an apt re-expression of the issue of *scale* I mentioned at the outset - that is, how violence, mass and gestural emphasis could be carried across from my previous practice into the acoustically restricted universe of the guitar. In effect, the final measures restrict this universe almost to a dimensionless point by eliminating five of the six strings from the still highly-active discourse.

The final note is, appropriately, a natural harmonic Bb; a pyrrhic victory, perhaps, for the defamiliarization principle over the ineluctable encroachment, from panel to panel, of 'normal' guitar sonority.

Endnotes

1.   *N.B. Examples 2 through 10 are notated as fingered, not sounding pitches. These latter may be calculated by noting the string (numbers in boxes) and transposing by the prevailing scordatura interval accordingly.*

2.   *A similar path was adopted, in 1991, in my piece for percussionist,* Bone Alphabet, *(Peters Edition 1991) written for Steven Schick. In that piece, seven unspecified instruments are selected by the performer according to a minimal set of 'ground rules' with a view to clarifying the nature and interaction of up to four simultaneous lines of material. Inevitably, the result is both an extremely personal sonority and testament to 'interpretation' in a more ample sense than is generally applied.*

STRING QUARTET NO. 4
(1992)

As the program notes point out, this composition has to do with language. To what extent is music a language; to what extent can one treat music *like* a language without regard to how far it actually succeeds in fulfilling the linguistic norms that pertain in structuralist discourse? But, far more, this particular piece examines the degree to which, historically speaking, *Sprachähnlichkeit* - the 'speech resemblance' which was one of the main models or ideologies of expression at the turn of the century - remains a viable gestural or rhetorical vehicle for organizing and assessing music. All these things enter into my **Fourth Quartet**, and, if I assert that it has to do with the 'history' of only a limited tradition of the string quartet, of course it's the history of my reception of certain quartets - in particular, Schoenberg's **Second String Quartet** - which I feel is a work of exceptional interest by virtue of initially attempting to be a string quartet, and then absolutely failing to achieve that goal.

I have a theory concerning what I call 'threshold works',[1] a category of compositions typified by what I understand to be a *surplus* of meaning, caused by their straddling the divide or fault line between one way of perceiving and another in a way somehow embodied in the actual texture. Parts of my **Fourth Quartet** are, in fact, quite narrative, and certainly the narrative of Schoenberg's **Second String Quartet** is that of the dissolution of the string quartet genre as such - of the predominantly discursive logic of the genre as defined, say, by Haydn through to late Beethoven. In a sense, the final Beethoven quartets are a paradigmatic example of this quality, and one can imagine that, at the time, it must have been difficult to imagine a continuation of that remarkable phenomenon of dis-balance between the imposition of the subjective self on Beethoven's part (representing, if you will, an exemplar of prevailing humanistic attitudes towards self-formation) and the various relatively stabilized conventional forms into which the quartet had congealed in the preceding decades. If we compare the early, middle and late quartets, we can distinctly perceive this transformation taking place. It seemed to me, when beginning to think about my own quartet, that - as with the concept of *post-histoire* which everyone has been talking about lately - the logic of this linear progression from generally objectively viable forms of musical communication to subjectively authentic but communally no longer sustainable 'languages' (or, at the very least, stylized forms of intercommunion) that had reached such a decisive stage in the last works of

Beethoven has, during the course of this century, led to what can only be termed a certain degree of subjectively imposed gratuitousness. In fact, though, if we consider Schoenberg's **Second Quartet**, we see that one *could* take a further step, precisely when the genre found itself in the grip of self-dissolution, that is, when the very problem itself is turned, inside-out, into its own solution. There is a sort of transcendence which comes about with the introduction of the voice immediately subsequent to the awesome breakdown of the *scherzo* second movement, where we witness the total automation, the sort of pataphysical, self-destructive logic of late tonal thinking in which the interwoven harmonic patterns typical of early Schoenberg are no longer capable of carrying the discourse for more than a handful of measures at a time, with the consequence that matters grind to a halt. The gears need oiling before the piece can move on. It is apparent right from the beginning of the third movement that Schoenberg has crossed his Rubicon, emblematized by the participation of the voice and supported by the intensely imagistic, almost religious fervor of the text. This *Steigerung*, this surplus of expressive energy serves to mobilize one last time (and to tremendous effect) the tradition of *Sprachähnlichkeit* towards both the almost metaphysical investiture of language with a transmundane concept of communication and the total realization of the self at the instant of its eruptive radiation as expressive intelligence.

   All this fascinated me a great deal. In so far as one perceives, assesses and rethinks the nature of linear creation and dissolution of genre-like phenomena in a progressive and contiguous historical continuity (and one can only really envisage 'history' within the circumscribed domains of conventionalized genres) I imagine Schoenberg pushing the Beethoven closure one step further, and thus closing-off that specific option for our time. One of the conditions for the commission leading to my **Fourth Quartet** was that it should be performed as a sort of companion piece to the Schoenberg, in the same concert. For me, this was a daunting challenge, even though I had suggested the conjunction myself: one of the works I take as representing major turning-points of 20th century music was to be my touchstone, my constant point of reference. I am not suggesting a direct comparison of the two works, since I was by no means pursuing the same train of thought: I don't take *Sprachähnlichkeit* for granted; in fact, the appropriateness of the concept was part of the problem I set myself. What I tried to do in this work was to honor Schoenberg by suggesting that the particular approach to transcendence he adopted was actually to have few direct consequences, that is, that it was no longer possible to adhere to that particular analogical line whose main ingredient is the supposition that verbal and musical modes of expression are intimately and immediately interrelated. In some ways, of course, Schoenberg drew the same inferences himself, through the development of dodecaphonic techniques and the circling-back to forms of referential relationship - even if necessarily somewhat dialectical in tone - to received notions of classical forms. In my **Fourth Quartet**, I set myself the task of examining, one more time, how, and if, the phenomenon of verbal language and the essentially processual nature of much recent musical composition could be coaxed into some kind of *Einklang*, some mutually illuminating co-existence.

In passing I should perhaps add that I have few objections to 'talking about music' - that is, using forms of verbal language in order to approach musical experience. It seems to me that, so long as we acknowledge at least a loose analogy between verbal comportment and musical expression, there is no real reason why a very normal means of communication - namely, words - cannot be used to articulate specifically musical phenomena, always remembering that such discourse is, at its very root, a kind of poetic, rather than a rigorously scientific, discourse. It's not a situation where we are offered facts; we are offered ongoing dynamic, speculative models of the relationship of Self to Other: to that extent, I find it to be rather useful, whereas I can't see (verbal) silence *per se* as being of any utility at all, except in notably restricted aesthetic circumstances. In that respect, talking is a positive captivity - often we don't talk enough, or we don't talk about the right things.

I feel that things that happen 'behind one's back' often need bringing to the surface, at least in part, so that one can create some sort of personal relationship to them, get into conversation with them, as it were. Things that happen behind your back are not constrained to take cognizance of one, so real conversation is not possible: one has to take them at face (or back...) value. When one composes, one is constantly in dialogue with one's means and, in order to enter into fruitful concourse with them, there has to be some common denominator, on the basis of which the equality of the conversation partners can be assured. There is little point in one of the involved parties - either the language, expression, or the composing will or volition - predominating. That would seem especially pointless, because it eliminates that very chaotic interplay and balance of forces through which the significantly new can suddenly be discerned - something coming at one from a place which had been ignored or repressed, offering unexpected perspectives on procedures or material, something that can, in short, be *worked with*.

One might perhaps argue for an 'expressivity of composing' in which the particular dialogical/trialogical kinship is something you suddenly *feel*. The other day, someone spoke about the processes utilized by Stockhausen, about his excitement at certain things coming to pass almost without his personal participation, once he had set them in motion. I imagine the 'dialogic' relationship as being somewhat along those lines, but with a great deal of additional, momentary and context-bound subjective input. So, expressively, it wouldn't be entirely false to see allusions to the history of the quartet genre in this piece: I'm not writing 'historical music', but am, nevertheless, historically located. It seems to me that we are all embedded in our own proper histories of becoming;

however accidental they may appear, they are nonetheless authentic *for us*, as expressions of transitory perspective. I was rather struck, on the first afternoon of the courses, by the way that the parties to the discussion were concerned to distance themselves from the continuing impact of history, while simultaneously imbuing every statement made with a radiant conviction that the essence of the present moment lay in one's (admittedly perhaps fallacious) grasp of a succession of previous moments of intellectual or experiential relevance.

For me, style is a result: it's not something you start out with. It's a symptom of something else. Among other things, music is a form of thinking, and thinking can be verbalized, although it does not necessarily have to be. It can be verbalized or, perhaps, conceptualized, thereby extending our scope to cover a vast area of things symbolic as well as verbal. For this quartet I postulated two extremes, one of which is that evoked in my article "Form-Figure-Style",[1] in which I suggested the existence of a primarily semantically orientated form of expression or meaning, in which certain taxonomies of objects sharing specific characteristics, certain associative auras - things, in short, which, in spite of all diversity, recognizably belong to a particular perceptual category - play a large role in certain sorts of neo-expressionist music. I drew certain rather negative inferences from this observation at the time. On the other hand, there is the sort of expression which emerges from the gradual accretive understanding, perception or predictive speculation engendered by processes, the unfolding of connected musical statements over a span of time sufficiently lengthy to place the emphasis on transformation rather than fundamental identity. Process might even be defined as the extension of objects through time. But, of course, though we can accept that idea intellectually, it's not necessarily how our minds always work, so there is an interesting discrepancy between the way things can be conceptualized and set in a one-to-one relationship within a context-defining frame, and the way they finally emerge and function in a real composition. This is where the dialogical back-and-forth aspect of the conversation between composer and material is actually most fruitful. This entire issue - the nature of gestural identity and processual expressivity - is directly engaged in my **Fourth Quartet** by having two movements (essentially, the purely instrumental movements) attempt to deal with the concept of process and linear/narrative form, while the other two (those with voice) set out to imagine things much more from the standpoint of how structurally predefined delimitations, through their impingement on the 'expressive residues' of the Mac Low texts, are able to project more locally specific situations.

Originally, I had intended to set some texts by A.R. Ammons, who is a very interesting poet precisely because he uses a rather simple and immediately

---

[1]See this volume, p. 21.

evocative vocabulary of natural images which are then recycled (and ultimately, defamiliarized) through the lineaments of a complexly interwoven philosophical discourse.[2] But when I tried to work with the chosen texts I found that, at that point, I was not able to set connected sentences - it just didn't seem plausible - because too great a quantity of formal (rather than verbal) expression was already present as a given. I needed more initial distance. What I subsequently did was to move away from direct contact with structured language by adopting a text itself a deconstruction of another author's text. Jackson Mac Low is a poet in the experimental tradition, in some respects close to the mesostic tradition of John Cage. Like Cage's 'rewritings' of Joyce's **Finnegans Wake**, Mac Low began with the **Cantos** of Ezra Pound, boiling them down to a remarkably striking essence. The text I chose for the second movement of the **Fourth Quartet** is Mac Low's version of the **Pisan Cantos**, which Pound composed immediately after the Second World War while confined in a prisoner-of-war cage - a triple constriction, if you like, since my quartet actually isolates specific sections of the text setting via indefinite duration pauses.

I found it possible to utilize these texts, because I could treat them in accord with their processually-arrived-at material exigencies. In his work, John Cage takes the individual letters of the name JAMES JOYCE as the Ariadne's Thread passing vertically through the poem. Mac Low treats the name EZRA POUND in an analogous fashion, also upper casing these letters. I, in my turn, treat these occurrences in a musically extremely consistent manner, completely divorced, that is, from criteria of semantically-loaded expressivity. In fact, in the final vocal solo, one hears that happening rather clearly. Many of the things I do that seem like 'expressive' reflections of subjective text interpretation are in fact simple and systematic registration of what the poet is already offering me. I chose to work like that in order to guarantee the continual presence of a strong processual element. There was one aspect of these texts that I found particularly stimulating: Pound writes in several languages at once - classical Latin and Greek, Chinese ideograms, Italian, English and French - and sometimes, when only fragments of a particular word appear, one can't tell which language it belongs to. Often, it's up to the singer to decide how that works; at the end of the piece, in the very final lines, I instruct her to speak employing as many 'foreign' accents as she can come up with, so that whatever language she assumes the text to be in has to be pronounced as if a native of yet another language were speaking.

In a sense, that's a symbol, an image of the entire work: that all forms of contemporary expression are, in some measure, expatriate. Recently a student said to me, "Look, I really want to do something new, but I keep catching myself falling back on the tricks I used a couple of years ago. How can I change myself?" I replied, "You can't. *You* might change, but you can't really change *yourself*. All one can do is find a vehicle or mechanism, an objectivized device to push you into a new situation in which the way you react, as yourself, will naturally lead to new results through interacting with the changed situation." I find that to be true in general of much contemporary composition technique: very often we have to seek out alienating vehicles to thrust us into new and challenging environments, new biospheres, where we are encouraged to change the way our lives are lived. That is what I see myself as having done in this quartet, in that I set up each movement with a view to examining how much the particular linear, narrative, expressive or processual-developmental assumptions which seem to divide various types of present-day music from one another hold good. In fact, they *are* still capable of being brought together, and if there had to be a 'theme' for my quartet, I suppose that is the one I would underline.

In the second movement, the voice is integrated into the quartet process in so far as, theoretically, no note of the voice part, no impulse, no event-commencement is presented independently from a corresponding event somewhere in the quartet. That is, in terms of density, the quartet's structure was completely pre-organized, with the voice part subsequently derived from that, so that, in a sense, the voice is reinterpreting aspects of the quartet material by picking out certain impulses and reproposing them (of course, this should be understood as happening simultaneously in voice and instrument) in the voice's own terms. The voice is thus completely integrated into the precompositionally-determined formal process whilst imposing on it a significant degree of flexibility in terms of its interpretation. A word on this background structure may be in order. What I initially did was to create an extensive, unbroken 13-layer rhythmic matrix: I got into a bad situation, though, because the deadline for completion of the work was fast approaching (this being the last movement to be composed) and the experience of writing the other three movements had led me to conclude that the entire idea of this movement - its logical, linear, accretional, ideologically secure compositional assumptions - no longer corresponded to my current position. As a result, I couldn't write it until, one day, in desperation, I took a pair of mental scissors and said, "O.K., a continuous, linear developmental form is out of the question - how can I go back to it? There's no way of saving or improving on those initial assumptions." I then cut the matrix into its nine constituent tempo areas and separated them with general pauses, rather like individual *moments musicaux*: they represent tiny kaleidoscopic alternative ways of realizing the nine processually distinct subsections of the original continuum. I found this to be an absolutely appropriate way of expressing both my accumulated doubts about the logic of continuous musical discourse, and about the specifics of fitting certain types of text to particular vocal situations. Each little section adopts a very particular way of illuminating the voice/instrument relationship, even though the voice never succeeds in doing anything obviously independent. I finally felt that the closed nature of the original materials re-expressed through the open, non-directional nature of the final

Ex. 1: 2nd movement, G 4-7, H.

score was an eminently acceptable means of articulating the whole dichotomous space into which I had maneuvered myself. (See example 1.)

In the final movement, the entire quartet presentation is processually defined; that is, the register, density of events, even the global nature of dynamics, are all cycled through essentially linear, evolutive processes which emphasize tendency of transformation over time at the expense of local definition of texture. The 'story-line' of the four instruments is perhaps comparable to Charles Ives' **Second String Quartet**, where everyone is evolving, complaining or being boring in his own inimitable fashion. The voice part only overlaps with this material by some six measures: a rather brief time-span. The voice part itself was constructed on three distinct levels, each with its own characteristic metric and density patterns. I term this 'interference form', since the superposition of several independent layers of activity in one voice or instrument creates tremendous pressure according to the collision or intersection of events. The manner in which one can accommodate more or less incommensurate things concurrently is another part of the restrictional costume one dons when setting out to compose. (See example 2.)

Although, as I say, the vocal part was also composed processually, the very appellative nature of the voice, and the way the words confronted me with certain fixed situations on another level led me to work rather freely when 'filling in the gaps'. Some situations were given *a priori*, such as how certain letters had to be musically expressed, but others remained globally undefined. There are sections in which only one layer is operative, and there it's clearly easier to fall back into a quasi-expressionistic narrative frame, a one-to-one amplificatory relationship between text and mirroring musical comportment. At other times, however, several layers coincide and mutually self-destruct, so that quite different solutions are demanded; one has to juggle things around very quickly, trying to grab back the exploding fragments of expression and glue them back together, which means that a lot of cracks will still be apparent.

Just as the two vocal movements seek to underline very different approaches to text integration, so the instrumental first and third movements attack the issue of formal organization from diametrically opposing standpoints, whereby the first movement has arguably the closest relationship to the Schoenberg's opening movement, in that it adopts a programmatically linear/developmental stance which quickly reveals itself as untenable in the long term. In spite of the irregular irruption of independently-developing subsidiary interventions, the central thread is really rather simple, consisting as it does of a single pitch played in rapid alternation over two strings (Ex. 3). Successive extensions and amplifications of the idea first enrich it with glissandi, then contrary motion glissandi, passing through various levels of microtonal, ostinato-like rotations around a clear pitch center, finally arriving at emphatically expansive linear/melodic efflorescences. It is interesting to observe how, in terms of

Ex. 2: 4th movement, measures 54-58

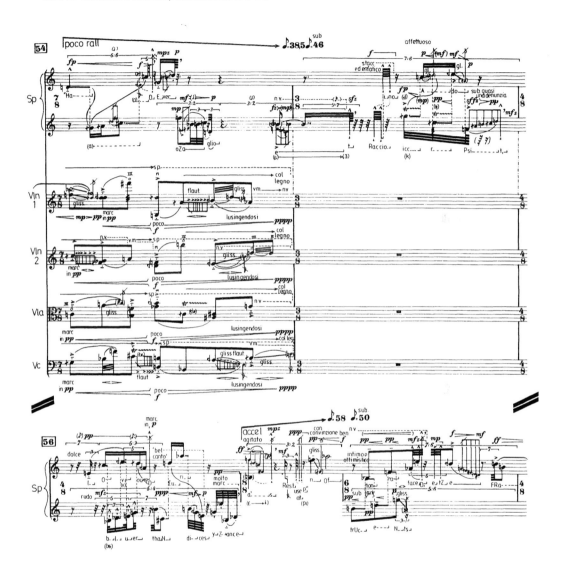

perception, this apparently logical transformation is sometimes subverted by the distorting lens of local context, or else is subjected to sudden and unpredictable fractures: even so, this is not sufficient to eradicate the definite feeling that the linear developmental mechanism is no longer entirely credible as the vehicle for extended musical discourse - the same feeling, in fact, as I have often had when listening to the curiously truncated sonata allegro structures in the opening movement of Schoenberg's **Second Quartet**.

Ex. 3: 1st movement, measures 1-7

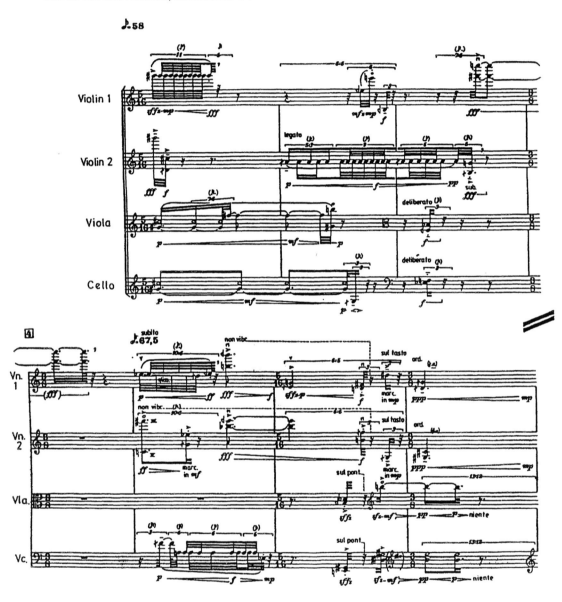

This same feeling is even stronger in that same work's second movement, the scherzo containing the famous citation from "O du lieber Augustin,
alles ist hin". There, the underlying harmonic skeleton, still residually animating
the preceding movement, has been largely reduced to what amount to
prolongational automatisms - sequences and the like - which are constantly

re-applied whenever the motion threatens to "run down". Thus, while the linear thrust of the rhythmic patterns typical of the genre conspire to keep the discourse moving along, it is a rather absurd and ghastly motion indeed, culminating in the dandified gallows humor of the "found material." This incredible breakdown, this ripping off of the carnival mask, is peculiarly proper to this work and lends it much of its uniquely affecting veracity: my own equivalent does not pretend to that sort or quality of confluence of historical tendency and personal crisis; I do, however, base the formal tactics in my quartet's third movement on non-directional, combinatorial principles which explicitly eschew the type of 'weak linear' argument characterizing the first movement. A limited number of highly characteristic types of figure were selected at the outset. They do not change into one another, but do, when superimposed, tend to actively take cognizance of each another as far as offering mutual 'support systems' - fulfilling punctuational or supportive roles and the like. Each measure

Ex. 4: 3rd movement, measures 14-17

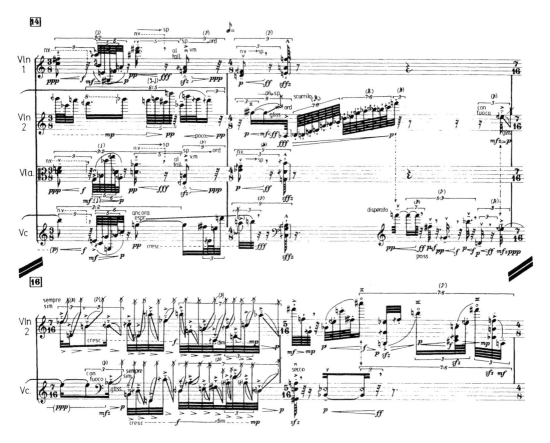

is thus defined on three distinct primary levels; firstly, in terms of number and identity of instruments participating (at various times several duos, trios and solo passages are heard) (cf. Ex.4); secondly, with respect to the identity of participating figural types and, thirdly, the specific manner of these latters' mutual interaction and integration in the continuity of groups of measures. The last of these considerations is essentially imposed, as an act of compositional will, from beyond the boundaries set by the pre-compositional model, and, by misleadingly suggesting a sense of 'organic' continuity where none is, in fact, given by the fundamental processes employed, sets up a somewhat bent or twisted sense of continuity in which no predictions as to future events can be made on the basis of inferences drawn from already established modes of prolongation. The more 'past' is accumulated, in other words, the more uncomfortable becomes one's sense of vertigo when contemplating a decidedly steep and slippery descent into the unanticipatable immediate future of the discourse.

It might, I suppose, be argued that the particular issue involved in this work is uniquely my own problem, in that the current state of relationships between instrumental process and vocal gesture need not necessarily be universally regarded as in crisis. I would certainly be among the first to concede that there is not even a tentative resolution offered in my **Fourth Quartet**, but merely a momentary stay of the onward thrust of research. My central concern throughout was to utilize the opportunity given by the medium to seek out and perhaps extend my own outer boundaries in both directions with an eye to preparing the ground for other compositions with perhaps quite different balances of interest.

Endnotes

1. *First outlined in Threshold Works of the 20th Century, a Doctoral Seminar in Analysis conducted while Visiting Professor at the University of Chicago in 1986. Works analyzed included, among others, Varèse's* **Octandre**, *Webern's* **Symphony Opus 21** *and Stravinsky's* **Symphony of Psalms**.

2. *The title of my somewhat later work for violin and ensemble,* **Terrain**, *is that of one of the poems I had originally selected for setting.*

III On the works of others

CONCERNING THE FUNCTIONAL ROLE OF TIMBRE IN THE EARLY WORKS OF ANTON WEBERN: A STUDY OF SOME ASPECTS OF THE FIVE ORCHESTRAL PIECES *OP. POSTH.* (1913) (1972)

The present examination has no pretensions as to exhaustivity of analytical regard. Although the relationship of these little-known pieces to their sibling movements gathered together as Op.10 is a fascinating subject in itself, this is not a topic here, my scope being largely restricted to considerations of instrumental timbre and articulation and, more especially, to the contribution these factors make to the perception of musical form.

The **Five Orchestral Pieces Op. 10** have long been seen as prime evidence for the central position occupied by *Klangfarbenmelodie* in the composer's early period. When compared with the many pitch-orientated analyses of this and other pre-serial works that have appeared in recent years, however, it is striking how little weight has been assigned to timbral and articulational factors when assessing the contribution of local structures to larger periods and, ultimately, to the form of each movement as a whole. At least in part, this disbalance is probably attributable to the lack of generally acceptable criteria according to which such highly context-dependent information may be assessed. On the face of it, there can be no binding system of categories which allows the specific sonic qualities of different orchestral instruments to be ordered in anything approaching a 'scalar' manner. This problem is clearly exacerbated by the brevity of individual pieces; a self-correcting working model scarcely comes into question while, by the same token, the significance of each and every orchestrational detail is magnified, by the very lack of correlating data, into the core of a necessarily speculative and provisional vortex. In abandoning the well-known Op.10 set in favor of the long unknown movements unearthed in 1965, my intention was to defamiliarize and destabilize, thus permitting an examination of the form-building potential of these very same aspects, often assumed to be of relatively minor importance, freed from the sometimes obscuring effect of accumulated analytical precedence.

Even though the group of composers centered on Schoenberg was extremely sensitized to instrumental timbre as a consequence of its closeness to the German orchestral tradition, and in spite of the widely-cited statement from

Schoenberg's own *Harmonielehre* eloquently attesting to his belief in the potential of color as a major vehicle of musical information in its own right, it is not easy to find widespread espousal of this emancipation in works emerging from the 2nd Viennese School in the years immediately preceding the 1st World War. There are, to be sure, many instances of exceedingly brilliant and effective orchestration to be found in Webern and Berg as well as the works of their teacher; however, it is less easy to isolate situations in which color as such thrusts into the foreground, as it were, as *Hauptstimme* (or, less anachronously, as ruling 'idea' of the discourse). If such a ubiquitous presence is sensed anywhere (other, that is, than Schoenberg's model example in **Farben**), then it is surely in Webern's Op.10 and the associated *Op. posth.* pieces presently under discussion. I will argue below that there are a number of instances in these pieces where, even though it would be overstating the case to speak of functional 'color scales' being consistently employed, particular dispositional patterns occur sufficiently often, and are associated sufficiently consistently with supporting patterns in other structural domains, to justify the investigation of these phenomena as though belonging to a quasi-autonomous, if admittedly only roughly quantifiable, level of formal organization. The increased sensibilization of musicians to the envelope and spectral characteristics of individual sonorities afforded, in recent decades, by the widespread utilization of computer analysis and transformation, along with the significantly color-and texture-based works of such composers as Ligeti and Penderecki, enables us to assess Webern's instrumental practice of this period from a somewhat different perspective than hitherto. In pursuit of a viable delimiting framework for this examination, I am proposing a dual approach: on the one hand, timbral information will be categorized according to *instrumental family of origin*; on the other, according to hypothetical *articulation classes*, to be defined, in connection with concrete musical contexts, as assuming a major role in outlining and structurally interpreting particular pitch class groupings. In particular, I envisage the application of these concepts as moving beyond the boundaries of what is customarily understood as 'effective' orchestration (for example, the employment of two contrasting timbres to distinguish main and secondary lines) to embrace a more active contribution of specific color oppositions to the establishment of larger-scale middleground hierarchies. Even if it be accepted that, in the spirit of free atonal aesthetic sensibilities, any observed constellation remains contingent, in the sense that it could conceivably have been otherwise without undermining the consistency of the overarching, operatively informal logic, this does not necessarily detract from the plausibility of such an ordering, as long as it remain demonstrably consistent for the duration of its application.

As with the individual movements of Opus 10 itself, the fragile relationship conjoining the five perhaps more stylistically centrifugal movements gathered together in the publication under consideration is established more in terms of a tenuous thread of communal techniques and aesthetic preoccupations than of any readily apparent sharing of concrete motivic or formal identities. As is to be expected in view of the close temporal proximity of their composition with that of the Opus 10 pieces, there is considerable evidence of close methodological correspondence. The main distinction between the two sets lies not in the nature of specific premises explored, but rather in the level of consistency with which the fund of common techniques has been harnessed so as to amplify and illuminate those larger perspectives which only a high level of stylistic homogeneity makes possible. It is not part of the current task to speculate at length on the reasons for the composer's ultimate rejection of the *Opus Posth.* essays; nevertheless it is readily apparent that the wide spectrum of approaches which characterizes these latter makes them both less than amenable to subsumation to a larger architectonic whole and of somewhat greater utility in terms of individual analytic regard.

With respect of the instrumental forces employed, there are obvious parallels between individual movements of *Opus Posth.* and the total ensemble required for Opus 10, even though the striking discrepancies in ensemble size and constitution in the former group makes for a considerable increase in the total number of instruments needed for performance. In large measure this is due to the inclusion of a number of relatively exotic instruments in certain movements. In No.3, for example, a bass trumpet and contrabassoon are specified. Indeed, the forces in No.3 are more or less those of the standard symphony orchestra, although strings are reduced to two parts only, those of cello and double bass (whether solo or tutti is not entirely clear, as the editors of the published score rightly point out). Elsewhere, the instrumentation remains, for the most part, within the bounds of that required for Opus 10, including solo strings in all parts, with only a few instruments (bassoon, tuba, timpani) being added to enrich that basic palette.

Again with the exception of No.3, the use of the individual instruments corresponds rather closely to that already familiar from opus 10: the motivically linear phrases, prevalently of between one and four pitches in length, are assigned to solo instruments, while chordal groupings are often presented in striking and delicately shaded hues. Thus, although it would not be proper, *strictu sensu*, to speak of *Klangfarbenmelodien* in the precise sense of, for example, Opus 10 Nos. 1 and 5, it is nevertheless remarkable how the constant modification and contraposition of timbres serves to highlight core aspects of formal articulation. In the following examples, culled from Nos. 1 and 5 of the *Opus Posth.* set, some of the more striking of these instances will be examined.

The passage given in short score in Ex. 1(a) encompasses the first complete phrase structure of the piece, and is separated from what follows by a half-note rest. As will be seen from a comparison of the three representations given above, the fragment exhibits several quasi-symmetrical features. The presumed

Ex. 1(a) (Piece 1, mm. 1-5)

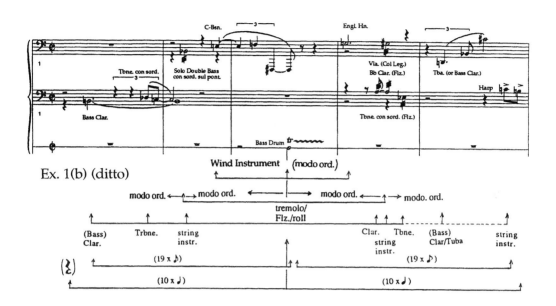

Ex. 1(b) (ditto)

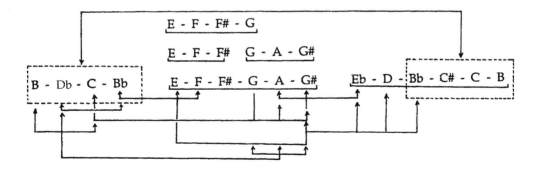

Ex. 1(c) (ditto)

mid-point of the symmetry is indicated by the intervention of the bass drum, whereby alternative readings of the notated-out one-beat rest introducing m.1 permit the interpretation of either the actual commencement of the roll or else the cessation of the concurrent contrabassoon F# as the precise pivotal moment. Although the bass drum clearly functions as a 'pitch neutral' marker, it nevertheless shares its characteristic mode of articulation (rapid iteration or interruption of the *tenuto* sound) with a number of pitched instruments, these latter being divided into two groups framing it, albeit with diverse numbers of impulses and of different total duration, at approximately the same distance on either side. Preceding the roll (m.2) is a *tremolo* for double bass; following it, after an interval of one and a half beats (m.4.), is a slightly longer fan-like structure for flutter-tongue clarinet and muted trombone entering around the *col legno tremolo* of a viola. Analogous relationships, with the quantities of impulses reversed, may be descried between the contrabassoon (mm. 2-3) and cor anglais (m.4) and, because surrounded by *tremolo*-type articulations, the very normality of sound production in these latter instruments becomes a significant element of information. What, in other contexts, would be considered the norm, here becomes a momentary dual exception, the registral and directional correspondence between the cor anglais G and the E and F of the contrabassoon underlining their formal interaction, as, indeed, does the fact of a communal double reed timbre heard nowhere else in the passage under consideration. At the same time, a connection to the bass drum is established by the descent of the contrabassoon into an extremely low register, which favors the perceptual merging of pitched and unpitched phenomena. It should be noted that the utilization of an unusually high register for the unsupported contrabassoon, and the extreme registral *legato* leap which its motive contains, conspire - in conjunction with the strongly characteristic timbre of the cor anglais G - to bind together this pivotal material, even though it is broken up by a relatively lengthy rest, to a degree perhaps otherwise only to be assured by the sort of instrumental doubling which Webern is clearly concerned to avoid. In this manner, the E and F of the contrabassoon and the G of the cor anglais expose a linear 'deconstruction' of the semitone/whole tone figure already heard twice in mm. 1-2, while the low F# sets up important links (based on the prominent, archetypically Webernian, tritone/fourth motive most clearly encountered in m.4) with the B and C of the opening, the cor anglais G and the D and C# of the tuba in m.5, whose pitch-content is itself interpretable as the completion of a number of interlocking figures of the same genre, distributed through several distinct registral spaces, and repartitioned into groups of, at most, three pitches by distinctions of tone color, articulation or both. Examples 1(b) and 1(c) show how these two dimensions are defined. Supplementing the general symmetrical traits already mentioned, the choice of instruments evinces a significant concern for balance; the first three instruments to be heard are, in order of entry, bass clarinet, trombone and double bass, a combination again encountered in m.4, but with the clarinet and viola replacing bass clarinet and double bass, and representing timbral categories of, respectively, 'single reed instrument' and 'string instrument'. Such categorical correspondences go some way towards annulling the considerable difference between the two figures concerned, for example, when the cor anglais G of m.4 is included in the picture, both figures consist of four distinct pitches, two types of sonic articulation are encountered (i.e. 'normal' and 'rapid' iteration) and each figure is characterized by a group of three adjacent pitch classes, the lowest of which is singled out by virtue either of its contrasting mode of sound production (cor anglais) or isolated register (contrabassoon). Discernable, in consequence, is a 'cross-over' relationship between the two components of each group and the intermediate linking of the two 'normal' sonority elements by the 'iterative' bass drum intervention. *Mutatis mutandis*, this latter fulfills the double function of symmetry-inducing pivot for the entire first period and (by reason of temporal overlapping, duration and 'iterative' articulation) the first two antecedent/consequent formations in m. 1-3. It is by such perspectival mutation of interpretative regard, achieved by complex self-reference and prolongational embedding, that the composer induces the listening ear to allocate significance as the result of quasi-simultaneous acts of over-reading rather than as primarily linearly-orientated tracing of successivity.

Part of this process is what I shall term "timbral alienation", by which I intend the use of articulation to separate-out a given element from its immediate environment, or else to highlight it with a view to implying larger formal connections than those with which the local environment appears to be concerning itself. Perhaps the most prominent of these in the section under review is the 'iterative' chain, which, set in motion by the double bass's *tremolo* Bb in m.2, reaches out, via the mediatory 'resonance' of the bass drum, to the A, G sharp and Eb, thus suggesting a 'framing' tendency for the contrabassoon and cor anglais chromatic chain framing the backbone of the period, and acting as 'pathfinder' for the completion of the 12-tone total with the D of m.5. The effect is illustrated below in Ex. 2.

The regular alternation of 'normal' and 'iterated' modes of articulation throughout this passage diverts the ear into a more tendentially linear listening, while it is largely the reticent alterity of the bass drum (allied, to be sure, with several levels of supporting pitch, timbre and registral information) which indicates the vital role of 'informally symmetrical' procedures in fixing the limits of meaningful middleground perspective. How some of the necessary reference points are set up can be seen from a brief examination of the entry of the tuba (*ossia* bass clarinet) marking the completion of the first chromatic total with the D natural which folds round seamlessly into the chromatic group of m.1. Both change of instrument and the general intensification brought about by the wide intervals and rise into higher registers provide a sense of a new beginning, and

Ex. 2

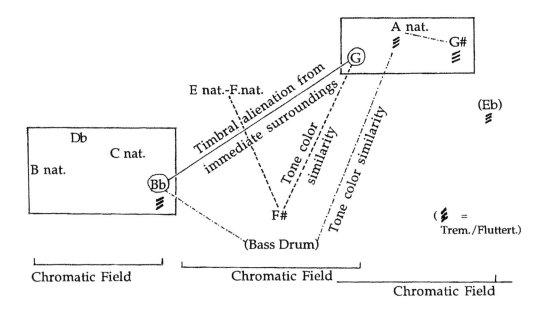

it is interesting to note that the tuba, although sharing the category 'muted' with the preceding trombone figure, in fact enters on a pitch not available to the tenor trombone. The transition here between the tremolo trichord concluding m.4 and the entry of the tuba illustrates something of the scope of Webern's timbral praxis by contraposing a notably rich 'timbre crescendo' in clarinet, viola *tremolo col legno* and fluttertongue muted trombone with the destabilizingly syncopated entry of a new instrument referring back to m.1 both in terms of chromatic linking and muted brass characteristics. If the *ossia* were to be taken into consideration, a closely corresponding reference to the opening bass clarinet B natural would emerge, with both first and second phrases initiated by the same instrument, whereby the pitches sounded are the first and the final elements in the first total chromatic field.

On the basis of the above observations, it would seem rather likely that the composer envisaged a complexly organic interweaving of chromatic fulfillment, motivic reference and instrumental/articulational perspectival animation of the given 'raw materials'. The further course of the movement lends support to this thesis, but only one further example, drawn from its concluding measures, will be offered in evidence here (Ex. 3).

The undeniably cadential tenor of this passage is not exclusively attributable to its sense of fading energies; indeed, it might be argued that that very

Ex. 3

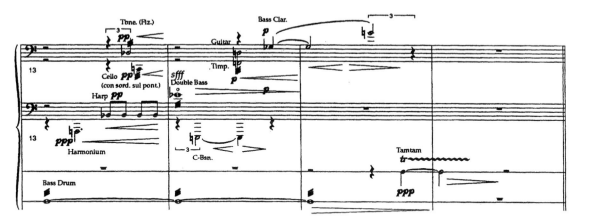

effect is in large part the direct consequence of the striking increase in textural compression and focus by which it is immediately preceded. In just a few measures both the 'iteration' articulation category and the overlapping, syncopating densities of the opening combine with the 'timbre chord' idea to offer a miniaturized paradigm of formal means heard earlier in a more extended timeframe. What is perhaps most striking in this carefully heard-through complex is the delicate sense of dynamic flow which the superposition of various versions of the 'iteration' category communicates. In particular, the insertion of the four harp eighth-note Bb's should be noted, which act not only as an explicit 'sonic analysis' of the iterative category as such, but function also as an almost didactically insistent anacrusis to the powerful Eb double bass fulcrum for the entire passage, located on the downbeat of m.14. The entry of the timpani in the second half of the same measure can be seen, in this context, as both a direct link to the ubiquitous bass drum roll and a further enrichment of the already complexly fluctuating spectrum of the violently attacked double bass artificial harmonic. In conclusion, it might also be noted that each of the participating timbral concatenations is delicately modified throughout its duration by staggered entry points (which ensure that some pitches - like the contrabassoon E natural, for instance - 'grow out of' the prevailingly diffuse wash of the bass drum) as well as by the inherent changes that occur within each instrument's spectrum by reason of the *crescendi* and *diminuendi* attached to every event. The concluding addition of the *pianissimo* tam-tam serves to reinforce the spectral richness of the preceding material, and provides an extremely resonant and 'active' spectrum to bring a breath of openness to the neutrally enveloping and absorptive capacities of the bass drum, while the extraordinarily compacted and consistent nature of the pitch and motivic aspects of the passage are interstitially illuminated by articulative detailing to an extent made possible only by the careful indication of speculative local contexts earlier in the movement.

The concluding passage from the *Opus Posth.* pieces to be advanced in support of the approach outlined above is taken from the concluding measures of the fifth and final movement. Although there is some truth in the view that the entire piece would have had to be cited in order to communicate adequately the effect of the uncompromisingly spare structures typically encountered, the consistency of the context is such that it is possible to focus in on a single passage without entirely falsifying the points to be made.

The texture of this eight-measure passage exhibits a number of features already found to be characteristic in previous examples, including the extremely disciplined distribution of instrumental timbres and articulation catagories with a view to indicating formal levels not otherwise functionally distinguished. This is a particularly pressing consideration in situations, such as the present one, where little is offered in the way of highly profiled or typically instrument-specific nuance, and the overall texture has been pared down, one might say, to notably 'primordial' relationships of vertical/horizontal and density/attenuation; in fact, the material is so spare that it seems entirely appropriate that a certain distance be maintained between the severity of the sounds themselves and the more casual associations attached to the instruments from which they emanate. In this way, the timbral factor is allowed to merge into the music's overall expressive world without any sense of it being imposed *per fiat*, and thus

Ex. 4

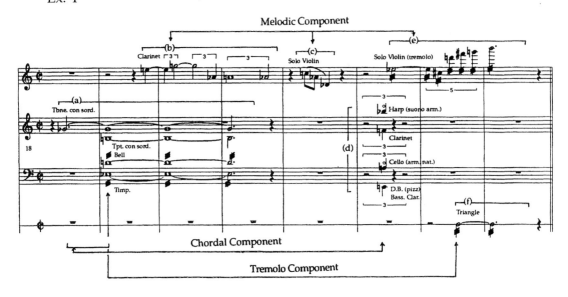

notionally abstractable from its specific contextual embedding. It goes almost without saying that such an approach of 'active invisibility' presupposes an extreme sensitivity towards the capabilities of each instrument without, however, letting this awareness impose itself on the nature or formation of the actual compositional materials themselves. To that extent, there is a vital distinction to be made between this movement and those parts of the first movement discussed above, where the didactic purpose of the vast majority of timbral combinations, transformations and juxtapositions is aggressively foregrounded. Webern's achievement here resides in his successful withdrawal of any immediately obvious syntactically definitional intent from the timbres employed, while nevertheless managing to avoid any hint of arbitrary (even merely tastefully functional) instrumentation; in fact his choices are primarily remarkable for their resolute renunciation of extreme positions. The prevalent tendency is less towards the melding of colors than the combination of quite sharply distinct timbres which, because carefully balanced among themselves, have had their more distinctive characteristics neutralized. The difference between this approach and that adopted elsewhere in this work needs to be emphasized; in the present context, far from thoroughly mixing fundamental sonorities with a view to creating new and powerful timbral hues capable of complementing the range of distinctively 'primary' colors, and thus functioning, in principle, in much the same fashion, the goal seems to have been to force together constituents of a mutually negational nature. The occasional striking synthetic image is certainly to be found; nevertheless, it for their austerity and simplicity, for the essentially homogeneous nature of their ingredients, that such events are remarkable. Wherever aurally distinct timbres are superimposed, it is generally in order to complement the already sharply-profiled sonic qualities of the rhythmic or gestural figures involved.

In the concluding measures of the fifth movement the extended presentation of linear statements in terms of single colors (clarinet, then violin) are examples of this latter trait, and are themselves posited in stark contrast to the 'neutralized' individual constituents of the vertical configurations encountered in mm.18-21 and m. 23 respectively. In the first of these latter, the reinforced aggressivity of *con sordino* trumpet and trombone at the interval of a perfect fifth has been countered in two ways; firstly, by placing the trombone on the upper pitch, so that the trumpet is situated in the (especially when muted) milder low register and, secondly, by bringing in the trombone pitch before the trumpet, whose entry is then locked into the somewhat less focussed effect of the bell/timpani dyad by virtue of both register and point of attack considerations. In the m.23 verticality, several distinct forms of attack and sonority have been forced together with a degree of interlocking of qualities resulting in a final conglomerate of minutely-balanced neutrality. Ex. 5 resumes the main features contributing to that phenomenon.

Ex. 5

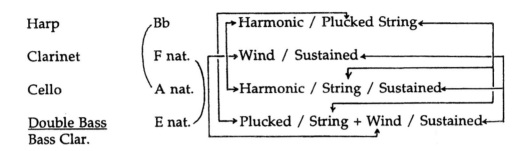

In respect of pitch, the chord is composed of two interlocking dyads whose components are situated in immediate chromatic relationship (Bb/A natural and F natural/E natural). The five instruments playing at this juncture would appear to have been selected so that certain strategic modes of sound production (harmonics, plucked, sustained, wind produced, string produced) are overlapped and distributed, like a containing and immobilizing net, over the coloristically centrifugal event in a way surprisingly analogous to Webern's typical interlocking of motivic cells around common pitches as a means of assuring the surdetermination of the perspectival contribution imputable to individual actions. Several characteristics of interest in the arrangement laid out in Ex. 5 may be enumerated; (1) each of the two chromatic dyads is singled out by the inclusion of a tone color not present in the other (Bb/A: harmonic; F/E: wind timbre); (2) the highest and lowest pitches are related by virtue of their common plucked attack (harp/double bass) and (3) the two central pitches are related by their sustained envelope and comparable timbral aspects, where the harmonic in the cello is set off against the relatively feeble middle-low register of the clarinet. Again the close analogy with familiar pitch/motivic permutational constructions may be noted: just as the re-ordering of the component pitch classes of a cell exemplification may be permutated so as to produce a new manifestation of internal intervallic patterning, so the re-ordering of the members of a fixed timbre class may be expanded, within the realm of the possible, to include the redistribution of attendant articulation categories. A different choice of initial categories, or a divergent arrangement of those already present, would have the effect of substantively modifying the role of the chord in question, seen from the viewpoint of structural attributability and formal affinity. The fluid interlocking of individual sound characteristics outlined above opens the door to the *functional disassociation* of articulational attributes hitherto seen as indissoluble components of a particular instrument's inherent character, with the concomitant creation of a significant array of secondary tools enabling the more precise evaluation of middleground-defining practices. It is true that such an abandonment, on Webern's part, of traditional received criteria of 'effective' orchestrational practice in favor of timbrally-based structural exegesis is not pursued in subsequent works with notable consistency; it is certainly conceivable that his later adoption of the less local context-dependent conceptual framework of dodecaphonic pitch organization rendered, in his view, such second-level supportive procedures superfluous. His next major orchestral essay, the **Symphonie Op. 21**, cedes global decisions on such issues to the overriding concerns of the symmetry principle, particularly in the second movement, where the timbres serving to compartmentalize any given form of the row generally remain symmetrically invariant for the duration of each variation. In the period at present under review, in contrast, the individual tone is the main protagonist in the creation of contextual affinities, and it is this (for the period untypically) 'interventionist' deployment of its destabilizing potential against a background of ephemeral and tentatively-delineated webs of quasi-symmetrical correspondence which permits the ear to pry its way into the interstices of the individual sonic complex and tentatively trace larger-scale relationships between otherwise disjunct successivities. The smallest element of structural significance imputable to any given texture would accordingly be no longer either the phrase, nor the individual note, but rather the totality of parametric qualities constituted in that note as individually-expressible quantities, whereby a single note would be simultaneously assessable as unified vehicle of expression and conjoint point of intersection and exchange for various parametrically-independent tendencies, that is, as both one and many. The organizational significance of the so-called "main parameters" i.e. pitch and duration has long been a commonplace of analytical methodology and, while it would be something of an exaggeration to interpret the present investigation as a plea for equal status for considerations of timbre and articulation, there is certainly considerable scope for a reconsideration of the contribution made to the shorter manifestations of the "free atonal" interregnum by such revisionist perspectives.

As concluding evidence for the viability of this approach, I will examine the conclusion of the fifth piece from a somewhat more inclusive perspective. In Ex. 6 the passage reproduced in Ex. 5 has been broken down into three strata, those of surface structure, tone characteristic distribution and transformation structure.

Perhaps the most striking result of a comparison of these layers is the degree to which the surface distribution of textural blocks (a-f) fails to establish an obvious reflection in the subtle multiplicity of its constitutive tone quality relationships. Rather to the contrary, the latter's fluid intermingling of various contributory layers of micro-articulational information appears to stand in sharp

Ex. 6

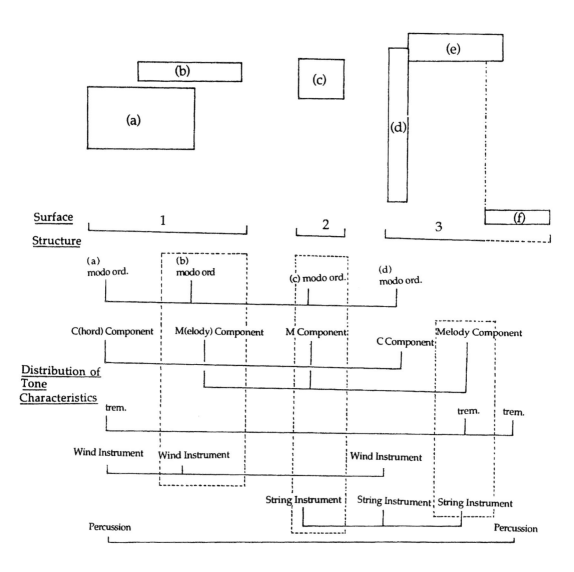

Surface Structure

Distribution of Tone Characteristics

Transformative Structure

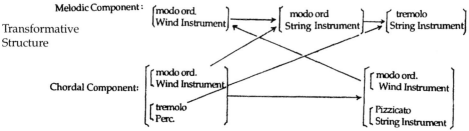

contrast to the immediately perceived contours of the phrase structure, thus opening up a functionally problematic space between the apparently conflicting demands of the two domains. A further examination of the composer's methods of reconciling and mobilizing the very real distinctions encountered in and through this space begins, however, to hint at a positive resolution of the dilemma. In particular, it is possible to gain a sense of the consistency with which irregularities or inconsistencies of treatment on the microlevel move to dissolve the predominantly static tendencies of the surface structure into a dynamically pulsating interaction and reaction of synthetic conglomerates which, constrained and focused by the relatively monumental surface phrasing, conspire to generate *zones of local temporal fluctuation*, thereby maintaining an intense level of volatility and directional tension in a texture of otherwise apparently unassuming pretensions.

Perhaps the most obvious attribute of the passage in question is its division into two main constellations, chiefly characterized by the common trait of marked vertical/horizontal bias. They are further separated by silence and a short, pivotal melodic figure for violin. In Ex. 6 this basically tripartite disposition has been appropriately indicated on the 'surface structure' level. Although differing in most other essential respects, the constellations (1) and (2) remain umbilically joined across the intervening gap by reason of the unambiguous correspondence of their internal components. The presumption of a quasi-symmetrical layout is thus an implied prerequisite for the adequate reception of corroborative or disconfirming local detailing. Of the three horizontally exposed elements, (a), (b) and (c), (b) and (c) are assigned to the violin, thus giving rise to a first perturbation of the above-mentioned symmetry. At the same time, though, the introduction of a *tremolo* throughout the later violin passage permits the ear to associatively connect the two prior elements, (a) and (b), by reason of their common avoidance of such secondary articulative inflections while, by way of contrast, the two violin phrases are distinguished from one another by virtue of the strong *legato/tremolo* opposition. The progressive transition from sustained trombone tone to unpitched triangle *tremolo* in m.24 is achieved at the same moment as the mirrored correspondence connecting the first (2 event components *ordinario*, 1 *tremolo* percussion) and concluding events (2 *tremolo*, 1 single attack chord) is revealed. The overall flow of transformation is given in Ex. 7.

In order to render the arcane-seeming conceptual framework of this passage more clearly, Webern assigns both the opening trombone attack and the concluding triangle intervention a high structural profile, and specifies symmetrical sound/rest relationships for the participation of these instruments in m.18 and m. 25 respectively. In addition, the trombone evidently functions as an anacrusis, appropriately preparing the next attack, on the downbeat of m.19, while, by finishing simultaneously with the violin, the triangle comes to epitomize the sort of signal function assumed by unpitched materials at other crucial junctures in this score. At the same time, the triangle's tintinnabulatory aura may be viewed as aiding and abetting the disappearance of the violin's final notes - not, indeed, into silence, but into a species of omnidirectional 'pansonority', into whose realm of pure potential the specificities of the work are re-absorbed (thus, one might suppose, efficiently mirroring the initial crystallization of concrete sonic forms from the infinitely contingent field implied in the free atonal credo).

The close interaction of timbral aspects is by no means confined to the succession of explicitly melodic textural components, and the vertical alignment of tone colors and modes of attack discussed earlier can be seen to play an essential role in the delineation of formal constraints and alliances. Both chordal units, (a) and (d), are expressed by two distinct groups of instruments which, overall, are mutually exclusive i.e. for (a), brass and percussion and, in the case of (d), woodwind and strings. In both chords it is the wind instruments which play normally-produced sustained pitches, while the percussion and strings utilize sound production techniques deviating from the norm (*tremolo* for

Ex. 7

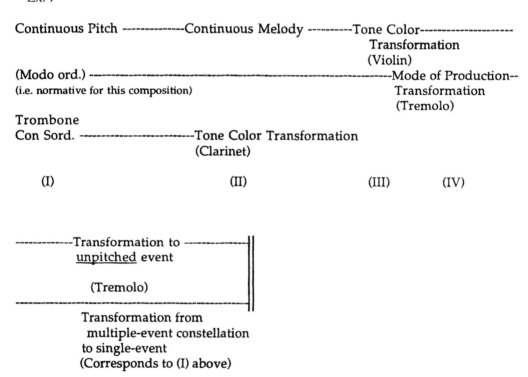

Continuous Pitch -------------Continuous Melody ----------Tone Color----------------------
                                                         Transformation
                                                         (Violin)
(Modo ord.) --Mode of Production--
(i.e. normative for this composition)   Transformation
                                                         (Tremolo)
Trombone
Con Sord. -------------------------Tone Color Transformation
                           (Clarinet)

      (I)   (II)   (III)   (IV)

------------Transformation to --------------‖
     unpitched event   ‖
                                            ‖
         (Tremolo)   ‖
---‖
       Transformation from
         multiple-event constellation
         to single-event
         (Corresponds to (I) above)

         (V)

percussion and plucked or harmonic for the stringed instruments - in the case of the harp, both harmonic and plucked together). Both structures are congruent, also, in the fastidious balancing-out of internal intervallic and timbral distribution; that the verticality (d) is more intricate in this regard corresponds to the tendency of the discourse towards greater turnover of information in more restricted temporal spaces.

When these hitherto distinct perspectives of horizontal and vertical organization are brought together, a number of substantiating instances of quasi-symmetrical disposition become apparent, most of which appear to interact in a clarificatory or rhetorically amplificatory fashion either with the overt surface phrase structure or local interreferencing of pitch content. For example, the lowest pitch in chord (a), the timpani Eb, is encountered again as the highest pitch of the (d-f) conglomerate in mm.22-23; similarly, the clarinet sonority carrying the highest pitch components of (a-b) is echoed in chord (d), whose lowest pitch, E natural (the commencing pitch in the clarinet melody), is shared by bass clarinet and double bass. This semitonal intervallic relationship of Eb/E natural is reproduced elsewhere on the pitches G natural/Gb (groups a and b) and Bb/B natural (groups d and e), with the former presented in wind instrument timbres, the latter by plucked or bowed strings. The overall layout of this conjunction has been rendered, in simplified form, in Ex. 8.

Although much undoubtedly remains to be said on the topic of instrumental usage in free atonal compositional practice in the period immediately preceding the First World War, the essential issues arising from such a practice would appear to be relatively clear. In particular, the structural multivalency and functional ambiguity typically generated by the extreme brevity of much of the core Viennese School production of the period called forth a hitherto

Ex. 8

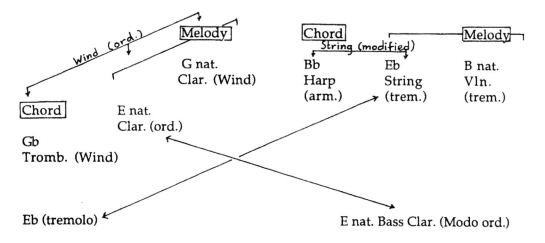

unparalleled compensatory intensification and extension of context-defining compositional tools in innovatory areas of micro-articulation. The resulting sur-definition of the fragmentary residual traces of deracinated tonal figuration and phrase structure, it has been argued above, was intended to serve the dual pur-pose of (1) offering alternative proposals as to the structural role of a given ele-ment (thus creating the potential for larger-scale perceptual link-ups analogous to those previously offered by tonal functions) and (2) creating a dynamically fertile perspectival multiplicity which would both intensify momentary expres-sion and negate any tendency to disassociate the fragile contingency of local events and larger-scale formal organization from the effortful work involved in traversing (rather, that is, than leaping over) the disturbingly unstable and erup-tive landscape of middleground speculation. To the extent that such a view be valid, it would seem likely that present-day compositional practice would might-ily benefit from a closer examination of some of its premisses.

MICHAEL FINNISSY: THE PIANO MUSIC
(1978)

Although music for piano solo forms in fact only a small part of Michael Finnissy's output to date it is easy to get the impression that the instrument occupies a key position in the layout of his creative personality. In many of his compositions for ensemble, or voice and instruments, the piano is not only included, but tends, more often than not, to assume an authoritative role, to thrust itself into the foreground with such persistence that the entire texture is impregnated with its ubiquitous presence.

The fact that the composer himself is no mean exponent of the keyboard, that many of his favorite figures from the pianistic past (Alkan, Liszt) have provided important stimulation in matters of technical innovation, is doubtlessly one factor contributing to this state of affairs, but there is more to it than that; in comparing various instrumental compositions with certain very early and more recent pieces for piano (spanning the decade 1967-78) it becomes increasingly plausible to assume that the keyboard represents, for Finnissy, that quality of ultimate directness by means of which his particular brand of visionary lyricism may first be formulated, then communicated to others. He himself accepts that several of his pivotal developments have been realized for the first time in this medium, and it is certainly no accident that his recent concentration on large-scale temporal expansion has coincided with the appearance of several shorter, but nonetheless significant items such as **Jazz** and **Ives**, in which particular aspects of the massive 50-minute **English Country Tunes** of 1977 were, so to speak, subjected to a preliminary codification. Whereas, in these brief studies, the tendency has been to concentrate on the presentation, in a form of 'cut-up' technique, of a limited number of textures and articulation types, the larger work draws them together in an edifice in which past achievement and projected transformation dissolve in a flare of gestural and expressive extremes.

Paradoxically, it is also this very same directness inherent in the corpus of keyboard works which succeeds in exposing most clearly another aspect of Finnissy's creative personality which, like some negative *doppelgaenger*, is always present in the background, undermining one's immediate, spontaneous reception of the often exuberant surface and inclining the music towards a disturbing impalpability at those very moments when its message seems most engagingly and disarmingly direct. It is this mirror-like facet of these compositions which will be examined here.

To begin not quite at the beginning (the music of the 20-year-old was already remarkable for its closeness to the material of later years, albeit with very different aesthetic intent) it will be convenient to exemplify the earlier period of the composer's development by reference to **Song 9**, one of the few Finnissy works to have appeared in print.[1] **Song 9** forms one of a series of shortish pieces for contrasted ensembles which, taken together, offer a veritable compendium of stylistic and formal characteristics typical of the composer's thought at the time. Nearly all the fingerprints of his 'first period' are encountered here: an immense visual complexity with a tendency towards individuation of particular subsections by means of contrasted notational layouts, the explicitly sectional character of the overall form and (in this instance particularly in evidence) the emphasis placed on the relatively constant coexistence of absolute extremes of register, texture and articulation. In nearly all respects, the opening passage of the piece may be taken as typical. (Example 1.)

The experiential density of the material is high, repetition, and even fleeting cross-reference being, as a rule, avoided; its fastidious, almost obsessive insistence on the practical primacy of *gesture* serves to channel the attention into

Ex. 1

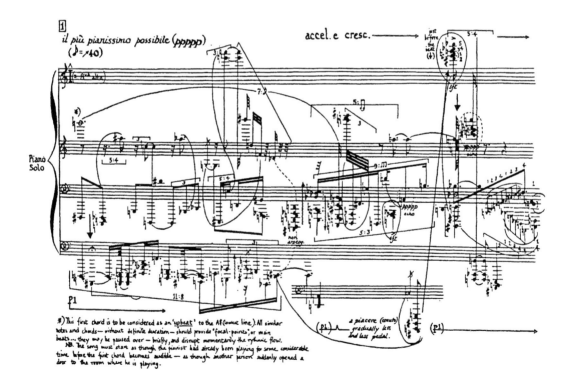

the apparently infinitely minute spaces opening up in the interstices of the sound. At the same time, its liberal employment of rests (silence or 'colored silence') as *materials* points towards some inexpressible background continuum, out of which the sounds emerge and by which they are ruthlessly re-absorbed. The dualism implied in this confrontation of potential and actual seems to me to underlie much of Finnissy's formal thinking, since a great deal of the more recent music, stretched, distended in time as it is, would appear to be assuming the character of a reversed image, reflecting, in the full light of day, the images and impulses at work in **Song 9**, as *shadow*. The through-composed pauses have, of late, become more explicit; they call attention to themselves through the constant presence of (attenuated and/or relatively uniformly treated) sound events. The gestural constellations of **Song 9** have retreated from their exposed forward position of brittle immediacy into some inside space of the discourse; their *exemplificatory* role, their signal function, has been transcended by the definition of a generalized gestural reservoir serving not only, now, to articulate the exigencies governing a particular composition, but, rather, to suggest a more abstract fabric, extending beyond the connective function exercised on a work-internal level, onto a plane whose aim it is to regulate the complex of interdependencies defining entire bundles of otherwise independent compositions - a species of 'family relationship'. As will be argued below, the composer is here accepting, on the large scale, the logical consequences which his strategy of distinguishing between material generation and gestural presentation on a lower level of articulation had already suggested. Silence and sound, transformed into their respective opposites, form the coordinates of the field within which this expansion is enacted.

    Song 9 is constituted of sixteen numbered passages, whose borders on paper coincide, for the most part, with the listener's intuitively-dictated 'feel' for the natural flow of events. Some distinctions are, naturally enough, clearer than others with respect to audibility; certain sections contain only (metronomically measured-out) silence, while yet others include one or more violently assertive blocks of material separated from one another by lengthy rests. Particularly in such instances where pedal resonance serves effectively to conceal the degree to which 'theoretical' silence is incorporated, the hierarchical ordering of the 'positive' and 'negative' elements remains highly ambiguous. (Example 2.)

    Yet other fragments show sound - tentative enough in itself - being eroded, absorbed by the increasingly confident encroachment of the subsequent stillness. The subversive quality of such silences lies in the double nature of their reception; at one and the same time they serve to delimit the sound events as discrete entities and, by virtue of the experiential density which the silence comes, at last, to assume (in this piece one is tempted to classify rests in terms of their 'breathability'...), to rob them of their sonic obviousness, their presumed *raison d'être*.

Ex. 2

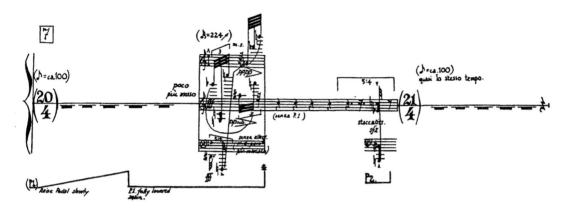

Even the most extrovertly eruptive of passages cannot escape being subtly undermined, put in inverted commas, in this manner. They are put on the defensive, turned back in upon themselves in spite of their innate instinct towards expressive exteriorization. The final stage of such double-sided inter-play of powers is that offered in sections 15 and 16, in which sound, silence and temporal proportioning act as equals, as both foreground and background to themselves. (Example 3.)

Already the notation of section 15 is symptomatic, since the 'relatively long pause' demanded is, for the first time in this composition, not metrically determined. It may be true that 'whatever can be measured exists'; on the other hand, the removal of previously valid methods of measurement creates an entirely new situation in which the question of methodological appropriateness demands a thorough re-appraisal. Even the four chordal events performed at the beginning of section 15 have been allotted no definite duration, coming to act as 'punctuation', minimally articulating that which otherwise remains unformed. Both material and silence (the former 'conceptually resonating' into the latter with an echo returned to infinity, the latter abruptly confined to a space transposed literally to the two-dimensional world of the page) have thus become, in effect, less role-conscious, less weighed-down by the cumbersome residual of received convention, the concealed ideologies of a particular, outworn tradition. There is a sense in which sections 15 and 16 form mirror images of one another, and, in so doing, demonstrate the interchangeability of the two extremes. Whereas, in 15, the sound, isolated, comments on silence, in 16 it expands to take possession of the mute circumjacent spaces, proceeding (non-metronomically) in a chain of quasi-metronomic pulsations of between two and three seconds in duration. The curious dichotomy thereby underlined i.e. the

Ex. 3

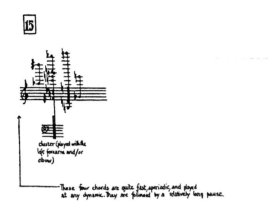

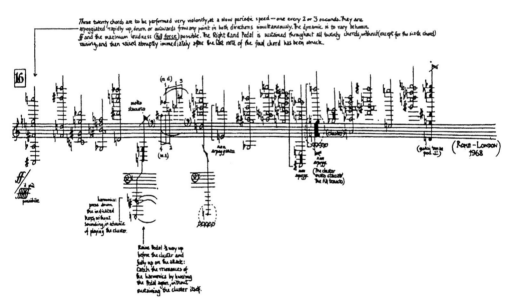

mutual exclusivity of metrical notation and periodicity in terms of actual sound, seems to be engaged in a bid to eradicate boundaries imposed upon expression by the unreflected hegemonic coalition of these two factors during much of recent musical history. In this composition, sound and silence lie on opposite sides of a common membrane through which sympathetic resonances pass.

In the highly partitioned structure of **Song 9**, each section seems - however frenetically active or densely convolute - self-contained to a degree, a 'completed fragment' resting in the serene certainty of its unique expressive premisses. Each defines (and is defined by) its own 'specific gravity', in the sense that the qualities which relate it to the internal coherence of the whole may - and frequently do - conspire to channel those qualities most characteristic of a section's personal identity in directions having little in common with the ordering categories implied in the overall layout. It is doubtlessly this Janus-like multidirectionality which lends each gestural unit its particular 'surrealistic' import. More than most new music, which seems unable to escape being crushed between the extremes of material-immanent manipulation and an anesthetically anecdotal 'poeticism', this piece attempts to impose a sort of 'experiential grammar' on the primal material which does not need, in the final analysis, to fall back on a grammar of *structuration* - something seldom managing to extend beyond the organization of the act of composition itself. This attitude of expectation or visionary passivity on Finnissy's part is, at the very least, strikingly individual, having little need of recourse to the debilitating circularities of a purely solipsistic personal mythology, uncritically protectionist economy of creation. It defines and reflects, above all, a thoroughgoing humanist stance, the consequences of which permeate every aspect of the composer's work.

The above-mentioned ambivalence animating the inner life of isolated sections is echoed in the perception of the overall form. The piece does not, in one important sense, actually *begin*; it explodes, fully-formed, into being - not, as one might suppose, as the expression of some grandly rhetorical intent, but, rather, as the simple continuation of what (albeit in 'suppressed mode') was *already there*. Like some inconspicuous natural phenomenon, one comes across the piece, it is not presented to us. One catches oneself in the act of listening. In this, the composer is quite specific:

"The song must start as though the pianist had already been playing for some considerable time before the first chord becomes audible - as though another person suddenly opened a door to the room where he is playing."[2]

To the extent that the discourse does not refer back to an anteriorly presented (thus presently latent) 'history of origins' (that is to say, undertakes an expressly neutral detour around the minefields of musical causality), one is surely justified in speaking of 'open form', even though the work as written offers no performer-choice options in respect of the order in which the sections may be presented. In any case, openness can be readily predicated of other form-defining facets than temporal succession: Finnissy's view of 'interpretation' as, in large measure, a process of (voluntary and involuntary) selection, made according to criteria of individual capacity, from the proffered (notated) plenitude supports this notion. In this instance, both the opening's deliberately overburdened textures and the questingly amorphous passages with which the work concludes point to a background, source or speculatively utopian totality which offers itself as the real (if absent) theme of the composition.

In the recent spate of larger and smaller piano solos (the three **Piano Concertos** of 1975-8, although remarkable in themselves, will not be considered here), the central role played by complex juxtapositions of irrational rhythmic ratios in the organization of rhythmic structure is aimed, not merely at ensuring a consistently high average fluctuation of note-against-note durational ratios, although this is naturally one consequence, nor is it designed with a view to generating as many non-repetitive impulse patterns as possible (as was the case, in **Song 9**, in those passages with a distinctly linear/polyphonic look about them). In such pieces as the tripartite work of 1977 **All.Fall.Down.**, such irrational groupings as do occur are employed in the definition of larger units or else overriding phase durations - periods of a length such that they are no longer capable of being heard as metric units, as 'measures'. Instead, they seem to aim at imparting more generalized information concerning note distribution and density of attacks between two predetermined, fixed points of reference, these latter themselves assuming, for this reason, particular weight in the (interpretationally and aurally) perceived organization of the whole. Between two such points, the texture remains, as a rule, constant, circling, in the deviational scope of its textures, around a strictly focused field of clearly delineated elements. Whether the composer's intent that the relative proportions obtaining between any two adjacent phrases be precisely realizable in performance is debatable; on the other hand, it has often enough been demonstrated that astounding feats are possible in this respect. The example of Stockhausen's **Klavierstück X** comes to mind, in which the flow of the discourse is organized, not according to any form of regular metric scheme, but by means of units of variable length and generated according to serial principles giving rise to lengths (as was shown in the results of comparable procedures encountered in Boulez's first book of **Structures**) in which, the more extended they become, the less the proportional difference between neighboring steps may meaningfully be distinguished. Perhaps such punctilious precision is neither expected nor, in the final analysis and in the rather special case of Finnissy, desirable, since at least one major aim of the notational conventions employed is the elimination from his figurative? of the least suggestion of foursquare, mechanical metric disposition.

In many instances, the situation is propelled to an even loftier peak of utopian absolutism by superimposing several phase structures of the above-mentioned type. An early precursor of this technique is encountered in section 10 of **Song 9**, even though the coincidence of irrational groupings serves there to divert attention *away from* any expectation of this sort; the 'punctual' effect of the wildly varied dynamic markings is a powerful factor in the aural decomposition of this passage. It is typical of such stratification that their component levels frequently fail to coincide in terms of absolute length, thus producing, at the 'seams', even more abstruse and arcane rhythmic contortions. An instance of the rather less complex type might be the opening of a short solo work entitled **Jazz**, composed in 1974. (Example 4.)

Ex. 4

In the passage depicted in Ex. 4, the proportions specified (fourteen beats to be performed in the elapsed time of nine) can have little audible reality for the listener; more important for him are those aspects of the texture lying beyond the organizational scope of such techniques - extremes of register and the *'cantus firmus'* effect of a number of strategically placed *tenuto* notes being the most obvious among these. In the absence of more precise (verbal) instructions as to the interpretational context, it is for the player to approach the task of resolving the proliferating ambiguities left open by the score, modulating, but also significantly restructuring them in and through the filter mechanisms of his own personal repertoire of performance strategies. Large stretches of this piece are constructed in the form of variations on a common rhythmic unit: ten sixteenth-notes to be played in the time of nine, against which background they are always to be heard. At many junctures, the technical demands imposed guarantee that even this relatively rigid pattern will not be immediately audible, so that its formal regulating function is undermined. What does, nevertheless, remain constant is the stringency of the matrix projected onto the fluctuating physical and mental coordinative capacities of the pianist: this, too, becomes form, replacing the passive 'structural form' of the material and its disposition by an 'action form' lying just beyond the boundaries of the work itself.

In **Fall.**, the second movement, there are several passages of veritable 'metric polyphony' - indeed, this feature would seem to constitute the movement's defining characteristic. (Example 5.)

Ex. 5

fall.

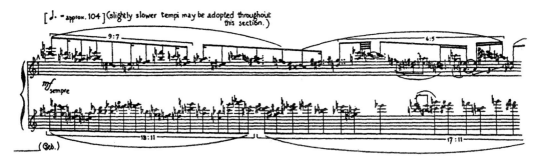

In a texture exemplary for its 'pianism', there is a constantly shifting degree of tension inherent in the relationship between left and right hands and organized, as it is, according to fundamentally diverse methods of phase length definition. A central facet of the conception seems to be the degree to which the various phase lengths (in one or both hands) can be *internalized* by the interpreter at any particular juncture. The shorter the total duration of the governing irrational durations, the simpler is the absorption and transmission of the *relative* proportions dictated by the local context. In this way, chains of interlocking ratios are formed, suggesting that the overall form might perhaps be expressible as some sort of 'super irrational', itself constituted from a number of elements of broadly similar type. In this way, the composer manages to convey the idea of unbroken continuity encompassing both largest and smallest significant components, without sacrificing his most essential demand of complete flexibility in moment-to-moment invention. At the same time, the performer experiences the shorter, hence more unmediatedly graspable phases as units contributing to the erection of a supportive perceptual skeleton; they assume the status of signposts in the midst of the constant dissolving and reforming of alliances surrounding them. The apportionment of functions between the hands (favoring the right) is based on this very distinction. *Foreground* is whatever can be assimilated in its entirety in a period of time less than, or equal to, the capacity of the performer to apprehend a musical state of affairs as an *event* rather than a *tendency*. While the progress of the right hand's material is governed by this fluctuation of gestural immediacy, the left hand's 'accompaniment' is modestly pursuing a scheme of manipulations all its own, consisting of a progressive reduction in phase length from one unit to the next. The effect, in performance, is of something approaching a 'non-imitative *stretto*', albeit one produced without an increase in the number of independent lines involved. The punning nature of the title (**Fall.** in the sense of a regular reduction of the ratios employed in the irrational groupings, but also with reference to the consequent increase in momentum thereby brought about) should not distract from a recognition of the fact that parallels for such processes readily suggest themselves in the harmonic organization of material encountered in almost all eras of musical history since the 17th Century.

An example of the ratios themselves immediately reveals how Finnissy has managed to maintain a relatively constant internal flow, while simultaneously retaining a clear distance from any suggestion of a referential, normative unit (i.e. eighth beats without irrationals superposed). (Example 6.)

Ex. 6

18:11; 17:11; 17:10; $16\frac{1}{2}$:10; 15:9; 14:9; 13:8; 13:7; 12:7; 11:6; 10:6; 9:5; 8:5; 7:4; 5:4; 5:3; 3:2...(then increasing).

The final stages of the operation are accompanied by an *accelerando*; at several other points the picture is modified by tempo fluctuations serving to introduce further 'irrational' relationships - this time, though, in both hands at once. After a retrograde version of the same ratios in the left hand's material (the left hand thereby, by reason of the at least subcutaneously-sensed correspondences, assuming a more powerful influence in the overall balance of forces) a different sort of '*stretto*'-technique is introduced, in which the irrational eighth-note groupings are still further subdivided. This does not proceed in any immediately obvious manner but, on the contrary, by adopting a scheme of rhythmic accretion in which groups of three, four or five subdivisions accumulate in ever denser chains. **Fall.** represents an example of goal-directed reductionism; its overall form corresponds to a particular wave-pattern which, although sliding across several distinct structural levels, may nevertheless be ascribed a function on the large scale analogous to that operative in the micro-domain by the lengthier phase structure units mentioned above.

On yet another level, **Fall.** represents merely one of the three 'macrophases' of which the work is composed. The sections are bound together, not only by reason of the common programmatic anchor suggested by the title, but also by the fact that they are intended to run into one another with no perceptible intervening pause. To some extent, therefore, they are scarcely to be seen as discrete movements in the normal sense, but rather as different facets of one and the same subject - that is to say, *relativism* in a non-thematic context. In such a framework, negativity takes on almost social implications (one is reminded of the 'non-thematic style' espoused by Alois Haba, whose special brand of anarchism was motivated by considerations transcending the mere processual status of material). In **All.**, the elements being played off against each other are

tightly interwoven: attention is concentrated on the reaction of the performer
to the instructions concerning rhythmic flexibility (with its attendant limitations)
presented to him. To this end, everything else is pared down to an absolute
minimum. In **Fall.**, it is the relative hierarchical ordering of the two fundamental levels which is microscopically isolated while, in **Down.**, the work moves
beyond the focal point of forces established in the preceding section, towards a
transcendental interpretation of sound and silence as expression of a common
(but, since located in the head of the performer, as in **All.**, unheard) overriding
principle of organization.

It is only in the context of the preceding events, in fact, that **Down.** can
properly be grasped. In that section, proportions are found which closely
resemble those previously encountered (19:13; 17:12; 15:11...) but this time defining absolute tempo relationships between hand and hand - a sufficiently complex device in itself which, when combined with further irrational subdivisions,
results in constellations evincing a truly formidable degree of impenetrability
(Example 7).

Ex. 7

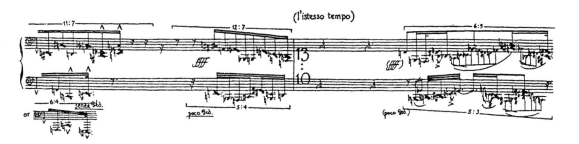

The effect here - at least on the interpreter, for whom the notational system has presumably been conceived - is markedly different from the otherwise
comparable employment of metricized silence in **Song 9** outlined above. There,
one's overwhelming impression is of silence gradually encroaching on and, finally, consuming sound; here, in the closing pages of **Down.**, both sound and
silence are subsumed to the inflexible progress of the double-ratio scheme. The
systematic aspect, even if aurally tenuous, asserts thus a very real 'presence',
and succeeds in developing a momentum which refuses to allow the sense of
continuity to be undermined, even across the sometimes lengthy silences which
hollow out sections of the discourse. Even more so than with **Song 9**, there is
the impression of a background continuum. In the later work, however, it is not
this insistent *absence* of the continuum which indicates this effect, but its literal
presence, in the form of an all-pervasive systematization of the coordinative

faculties of the performer. Far more than in earlier essays in this medium, it is the interpreter himself through whom the music is channeled; the totality of his commitment forms the stage upon which is played out the drama of emergent expression.

The final section of the work seeks to deny all hitherto evolved impressions of concrete definition of material, since all such emerging in the course of the development has been, in a certain sense, illusory. Both sound and silence are neutralized in the field of cloudy resonance hinting at an ultimate extreme (albeit beyond the final double bar) of terminal de-differentiation, an entropic 'heat death', directing attention back towards the interface of systems manipulation effective in force throughout and, through this, to the perceptions of the pianist himself.

It has already been suggested that, although standing at the center of the composer's concern with potential integration of the act of performance into the compositional fabric in a more subtle fashion than the simplistic mechanisms of aleatoric or improvisational methods allow, in other respects, **All.Fall.Down.** should perhaps not be seen as a completely typical product of Finnissy's present stage of evolution. In many ways, it represents more of a boundary marker defining his own view of *la limite du pays fertile*. On the other hand, it is an extremely instructive composition, since its reductionist policy succeeds in exposing particularly clearly many of those current structural tactics which form the broad foundation upon which his increasingly insistent drive towards more expansive formal statements is based.

An adequate defense of this position would necessitate an extensive analysis of the major product for piano of Finnissy's most recent phase, **English Country Tunes** - something which reasons of space preclude here. Most striking in this multi-movement set is the confidence displayed in the handling of a broad pluralist aesthetic. It sets a full stop behind a lengthy period of technical research, while opening perspectives for the future in which previous distinctions between form and content will no longer be directly relevant. In view of its importance in this respect, a brief consideration of some of the wider implications of this achievement will not be entirely out of place.

Since the gateway to the piece is the seemingly wayward and ironically-tinged title, one does well (as with all of this composer's titles) to minutely examine the association which it invokes. With the exception of one or two fleeting references to modally-flavored melismatic writing, the ductus of the language employed could hardly be more at odds with the sort of expectations which, on the face of it, the title might be presumed to favor. This 'expectation gap' may, perhaps, provide a key to more than specific aspects of a single composition, particularly if one bears in mind the fact - not often enough conceded - that Michael Finnissy is a profoundly English composer, whose consciousness of nationality as a cultural fact of life remains at all times the cornerstone of a permanent dialectical process of appraisal and exploitation. He remains, above all, keenly aware that such creative affiliations cannot, nowadays, be authentically reflected in terms of a naively literal adaptation of the manner and substance of received tradition. The history of folksong in England is, in any case, for the majority, the story of its reception, devouring and rendering harmless by successive manifestations of middle-class consciousness. The diluted and culturally distorted world which has emerged from this protracted lobotomization ritual is all that remains directly accessible today, so that the central dilemma of the artist seeking to define the relationship of the individual to the collectivity in terms of a *community of experience* such as folk culture may once have embodied is made all the more acute for the insight that the original model for such a vision is now little more than an example of the organized alienation which - in however ambivalent and conditional a fashion - the composer is attempting to transcend. To me, Finnissy seems to be motivated by such an urge towards re-integration, thus reflecting, in large measure, the idealistically synchretist transcendentalism of New England nonconformism, as embodied, for one, in Ives's **Concord Sonata**. At the same time, he manages to bypass the temptations of a certain sort of wishful thinking which persists in mistaking the symptoms for the illness. In its intentionally epic format, **English Country Tunes** represents Finnissy's latest attempt to project a rejuvenated (if ironically tinged) community of experience by means of a strategy of gradual accretion, even if inevitably modified by the demands of subjectively selected stylistic criteria. Because his music is not, in the first instance, founded on a framework of derivation or motivic/thematic precedence, the single, almost interchangeable gestures are permitted to define their own living space *in situ*, as well as contributing to the stepwise evolution of *a posteriori*-experienced wholeness in and through which the individual structures take possession of their ultimate expressive content. Each gesture, each texture, is *primus inter pares*, at once one and many. In these eight extended pieces, the insistently recurring image is of a welter of life forms coexisting in superbly anarchic plurality. Only in the last two movements, in which the 'frame' of extreme limits defining the space within which the work moves is made explicit, is the contextual interplay of juxtapositions, of mutual 'textural infection' decisively eliminated. The increasing length of Finnissy's recent compositions in all genres may, in large part, be attributable to the necessity for extensive exemplification of the criteria governing the various textural types (which, as something approaching 'Platonic ideals', are nowhere expressly stated in anything remotely recognizable as a basic, referential form).

If this emphasis on a limited category of compositional technique were interpretable solely in terms of an obsession with musically questionable social symbolism, Finnissy's music would remain limited and provincial. That this is certainly far from being the case is demonstrated by the significance of some of the above factors in influencing the course of the post-war avant-garde. A glance at the movement towards non-thematic organization typical of that period illustrates only too clearly the final bankruptcy of previously valid relationships ruling material and structure. The balance once lost, structure becomes inaudible, material descends into disorientated anonymity. One composer to have drawn radical consequences from this situation is Franco Donatoni, who disputes the cogency of the very concept of individualized material itself (the stuff of 'heroic subjectivism') to the extent of taking, as his starting point for many works, elements extracted from pieces by other composers (Schoenberg, Stockhausen). Consistency of material is replaced by consistency of process - material *is* concretized process. Finnissy, too, seems to have encountered this problem, since his approach is no less radical in another direction; specificity of individual material formations and stringency of processual transformation are *both* abandoned in favor of an attachment to generalized categories of activity, the boundaries of which are in a constant state of self-redefinition, and which, far from imposing a course on the work from without, may only be said to exist to the extent that the various concrete gestures through which they are manifest succeed in collectively defining them. The problem of anonymity is not to be solved by choosing one or other of the extremes (as with Donatoni), nor (as in the case of most composers) by not admitting the difficulty in the first place, except as a ready excuse to retreat behind artificial bastions of thematic security, but by undertaking the first tentative steps towards a comprehensive restructuring (as a preliminary to the subsequent demolition) of prevailing ideologies of musical perception and comprehension. If the vision of a radiant sphere somewhere beyond the limits of all subjectivity be utopian, in the limited sense of being ultimately unrealizable, then one meaningful task for the present-day artist is surely the mapping of areas in which further exploration might be usefully undertaken. The compositional activity of Michael Finnissy during the last decade is - among many other things - the trace of just such a quest: the evidence of its validity lies, to be sure, in the quality of the individual compositions, but also - and this not least - in the fact of its optimistic continuation.

Endnotes

1. **Song 9**, *International Music Company Ltd., London 1969.*
2. *Footnote to p. 1 of published score.*

CARL RUGGLES AND "DISSONANT MELODY"
(1982)

Why Ruggles? The question of relevance is not out of place in respect of a composer of less than a dozen works in the space of some four decades - a composer, moreover, who has received little critical attention over the years and whose style and aesthetic position have not been noticeably influential in recent developments in new music. In part, the answer must be sought in the personality of the man himself, in his intransigence towards compromise and his absolutist vision of quality. Far more significant, though, must be that aspect of his achievement which is able to throw new light on our current situation: like Ives and Varèse, Ruggles arrived at conclusions which may well have a resonance far beyond the specificities of their respective contexts, so that it is perhaps not untimely to consider some facets of an artist whose style, whilst certainly containing ample evidence of historic precedents, nevertheless succeeds in so defining its own proper limits that these externally-derived elements are completely absorbed into an all-encompassing and flexible unity, a complete interpenetration of gesture and generation.

Ruggles's lifelong friends Ives and Cowell both embraced, each in his own way, some form of pan-stylistic natural philosophy of totality; Ruggles himself pursued equally utopian visions of a closed universe of organic purity within radically delimited stylistic boundaries. On the one side, inclusion, eclectic acceptance; on the other, exclusion, refinement down to basics: as so often happens, their diametrically-opposed paths brought these composers remarkably close together in spirit. Although Ruggles was well aware of European dodecaphonic procedures, he chose to reject them as being too constricting, developing instead a non-systematic (but consistent) method of 'dissonant melody' whose essence was located in the free contraposition of independently evolving melodic 'life-forms'. The drive and impact of the form resided in the endless proliferation of linear invention and the mutual confrontation of melodic strands as starkly clashing planes of force. Although, in many instances, his motivic treatment can scarcely be located around anything so stable as a 'theme', there nevertheless exists a significant residue of consistencies of manipulation and associated intervallic ploys which both lend the individual work its specific quality and serve to locate it in the continuum of the *oeuvre* as a whole. The unity of the work spills over into the larger context whilst the larger context invades every detail of the single work.

A central consideration in any examination of the compositional techniques encountered in the works of Ruggles must be the definition of the means whereby he achieved that remarkable and all-pervasive sense of unity. One answer to this question must be sought in the extremely lengthy period of time allotted to the formulation of each piece; the psychological background must perforce remain inaccessible. All other approaches to the problem must be made through careful research into the works themselves. The following notes were made with particular reference to two compositions, **Evocations** (1937-43) for piano solo, and - perhaps the composer's most well-known work - **Suntreader** (1929) for large orchestra.

Although Ruggles seems to have shown a preference for allowing a minimum number of new pitches (commentators speak of between seven and eleven) to separate repetitions of a given pitch in order that the impression of its first appearance will have by then faded, in practice this implied rejection of tonal hierarchies is modified by four factors: (1) the frequent employment of lengthy pedal-points against which melodies are thrown into relief, (2) the addition of successive melody notes into chordal blocks, (3) the careful placing of pitch-repetitions at important points in a phrase, and (4) a continual process of construction and immediate destabilization of localized areas of tonal implication. Even though it seems plausible that intervallic organization has priority, at least as a form of structural legitimization, there exists a whole series of less immediately obvious layers serving to sketch in entire grids of patterning whose means of organization suggest that the composer was well aware of the architectonic potential of tonal ordering, even when operating outside the norm systems of harmonically functional tonal usage. The two passages discussed briefly below were selected to illustrate some of the techniques by means of which the creating of areas of interference between pitch, interval and metric layout gives rise to the requisite degree of "liberated rigor" which was the composer's ideal.

Example 1(a) is from the opening bars of **Evocations No.2**, one of a set of four piano pieces. This short passage contains most of Ruggles's more personal fingerprints, in particular his fastidious redistribution of register and permutation of pitch identities so as to generate constantly self-renewing contextual chains. The presentation at the outset of all twelve semitones without repetition seems to indicate a more schematic approach than usual; however, as will be shown, this figure cannot be in any sense equated with a 'series', since constant permutation of key elements effectively permits the rejection of such facile parallels. What the opening melody does do, on the other hand, is to function as a point of reference for the manipulations carried out in successive restatements. Notable, too, is the unusual regularity of distribution - six pitches spaced, for the most part, equidistantly, in each bar - which is maintained throughout the passage, albeit with metric modification from bar 3 onwards.

Ex. 1(a)

Ex. 1(b)

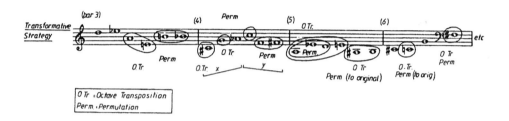

Ex. 1(c)

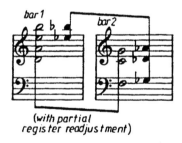

(with partial
register readjustment)

This regularity diverts the attention to the activities of other variables, in particular to the complex system of interlocking three-note cells, which may be subdivided into two basic types, (a) and (b), the former characterized by tonally 'strong' intervals such as the perfect fifth/fourth and tritone, the latter by close-lying linear materials focussing around combinations of the minor third and major and minor second. The predominance of stronger, directional intervals in (a) lends the passage a definite 'cycle of fifths' quality (Example 1 (c)), which tends to support any inclination on the part of the listener to interpret in the manner suggested below. Both cells (a) and (b) are present in the first 'row' statement, dominating in bars 1 and 2 respectively. The greater importance of (a) is confirmed by the subsequent elimination of (b) in the first variant presentation, although (b) returns as more central in bars 5 and 6. At no point in bars 1 and 2 is either cell expressed via identical pitch content or intervallic configuration.

In the following four bars, the total chromatic is repeated twice with each repetition occupying two bars. Modification of the original figure is effected by two procedures applied independently or in conjunction (see Example 1(b)). These may be termed Octave Transposition (O.Tr.) and Permutation (Perm.). Like the proliferating chains of cell structures, the application of these principles becomes progressively more rich and complex, sometimes working against the regularity of metric patterning: for example, in bar 3 the suddenly-introduced 6/8 meter is effectively dislocated by the octave transposition of the two central pitches, A and E. This, together with the reversal of the order of the two subsequent pitches, tends to divide the bar functionally into the three-times-two units associated with the 3/4 meter of bars 1 and 2. On yet another level, the 6/8 meter is supported by a weakening of the cell chain which these manipulations bring about in that a diatonic unit, A-E-B, is produced which, supported by the associated dotted rhythm, breaks up the flow in a quasi-cadential manner. At the same time, the D-centrality proposed by bar 1 is undermined by the dilution of the strong fifth D-A to the weak fourth D-A in bar 3, thus permitting the gradual dissipation of the power of D in favor of the Eb with which it was immediately related in bar 1. The wide leap created between bars 3 and 4 allows a flow back towards the D-region, an impression supported by the permutational deferment of the C. This latter is separated in turn from its "strong" G (see bar 2) and transferred into the function of a dominant, to the following F. The later return to the D-region, in bars 5 and 6, coincides with a greater interpenetration of transformational strategies and a concentration upon the (b) cell-form, itself "weak" in respect of its intervallic content. Three principal tendencies may be distilled from the foregoing: (1) a strategy of non-repetition in the individual manifestations of cell construction principles, (2) a gradual increase in the interaction of the two transformational techniques, and (3) the progressive emergence into the foreground of the (b)-type cell, which produces close-register pitch bands, even if these are sometimes broken up by wider intervals attributable to (a) cell structures. Thus it would seem that tonal tension is created by two contrasted means; on the one hand by the presence of strong and weak intervals which tend to define certain pitches as "primary" and "secondary," on the other by linear circling around a particular pitch or pitch-area in close intervallic steps. It will be noted that these techniques are closely associated with cells (a) and (b) respectively.

The opening motive (octave doublings not indicated) of the composer's largest work, **Suntreader,** shows the remarkable willingness of material and procedure to allow themselves to be transferred almost unmodified from one work to another (see Example 2). Striking, in this passage, is the way in which

Ex. 2

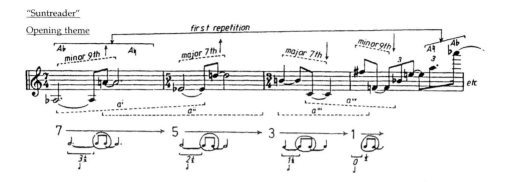

pitch material common to both compositions is disposed to quite different ends. Even more than in **Evocations**, the cell structures seem designed to provide firm foundations over which the superstructure may be safely erected. Even so, their expansion over the bar line (their 'transgressional capability') points to another, more subversive purpose when the exceptionally symmetrical layout of the re- mainder of the material is examined. The striking symmetries evinced by the balanced rising/falling, expanding/contracting intervals are at the center of the complex scheme; they mediate between the consistent but non-symmetrical organization of the cell formations and the directional but, in terms of the inter- nal layout of every individual bar, symmetrical rhythmic/metric dimension. The 'dissonance' of these three strata in respect of one another is of the same spe- cies of energy as serves also to bind them indissolubly together.

   Pitch treatment allows for the presentation of ten pitch identities before the first repetition occurs. Where this happens, at the end of bar 4, Ruggles brings the first two pitches of the piece in reversed order and so transposed as to trans- form the original minor ninth into a major seventh. Tension on the intervallic level is provided for, again, by the interaction and collision of rising and falling patterns of lines, each characterized by a single interval, into quasi-polyphonic complexes whose individual effect is transcended the faster and higher the prod- uct of their interaction becomes.

   The treatment afforded to the basic materials in **Suntreader** is quite dif- ferent from that typical of **Evocations No. 2** in at least one essential point, that is, on the level of motivic constancy. Whereas, in the piano piece, the opening bars are set up as a reference object which gains much of its significance retro- spectively to the extent to which it is deviated from, **Suntreader** holds much more firmly to the repeatability of concrete shapes. This double face of the ma- terial - its capacity for organic unfolding into the future as opposed to its "freez- ing" into a form of quotable still life - is only one of the interesting aspects of

Ruggles's formal sensibility which remains to be explored; nevertheless, it will be difficult to come to a productive understanding of this strange composer's output and ultimate stature if attention is not paid to his enrichment of non-tonal contexts with forms of harmonic crystallization seldom encountered elsewhere and probably nowhere with such fruitful combination of liberty and consistency.

IV   Interviews

INTERVIEW WITH ANDREW CLEMENTS
(1977)

ANDREW CLEMENTS: Who were the earliest significant influences on your musical thinking? Among the post-war European avant-garde, for instance, were you more interested in Stockhausen or Boulez?

BRIAN FERNEYHOUGH: I am not altogether sure that it would be accurate to speak of 'thinking' when describing my earliest attempts to come to terms with contemporary music as it then presented itself to me. My education in this respect was very sporadic and, above all, subject to the whims of chance. I do not recall even seeing scores of any compositions which might remotely be termed 'modern' until my eighteenth year, and then only such as were available in and around Birmingham (where, at the School of Music, I studied for two years). No systematic introduction to the twentieth century was available to me, so that my knowledge of most composers was based at best upon examination of one or two works, at worst entries in lexica. My background had not been at all conducive to the development of a balanced overall view of even the most meager sort, since most of my musical experiences (performing, composing, and conducting) had been gained in the world of brass band playing, where the best pieces (as I recall) specifically written for the medium were by Holst and Vaughan Williams. The major consequence of this spiritual isolation until a fairly advanced age was the almost total separation of the sound of contemporary compositions from their cultural context, which latter long remained foreign to me. Such techniques as I later developed, with the exception of the most basic elements of 12-tone writing, were thus my own work, as it were - something having its advantages as well as the more obvious drawbacks.

The composers mentioned below are thus to be understood as sound-experiences of the most basic and (initially) naive type. I don't think that I came across any work on theory or aesthetics until quite late - probably Rufer at first, then the Webern issue of *Die Reihe*, which I failed completely to understand.

Varèse has the honor of being the first modern composer whom I can vividly recall having heard, and that around the age of fifteen or sixteen. The work was **Octandre** (albeit only the second and third movements). It struck me immediately as being the first honest work of twentieth-century music that I had ever heard - clean, to the point with absolutely no prevarication. The mystery of the organic structure cutting clear across the brilliance of the primary instrumental colors made a deep impression of vital three dimensionality, of mobile ambiguity.

Sibelius was, on the other hand, the composer whom I came to extensive terms with earliest. Looking back on that period with the dubious benefits of hindsight, it seems to me now that it was his almost unfailing sense of formal shaping which appealed to me - particularly in the later works, the symphonies. He knew perfectly well where (for example) to 'tip the scales' of a series of gradually piled-up gestural patterns by the drawn-out delay of a single chord, whereby the effect of this on the whole simple harmonic framework was 'enlarged' in an uncanny fashion. Also illuminating was the continuously shifting relationship between obvious motivic extension and development, and the curiously 'non-thematic', one might almost say in their deliberate anonymity 'paradigmatic' textures which he threw across the transparency of his harmonic progressions like a gauze veil - a process which immediately generates some sort of 'un-timing', a putting of the tempo of a given passage in quotation marks... So much of Sibelius strikes me as resembling the alchemical filtration of in themselves incompatible processual devices through the reductional medium of his unitary vision of style.

Giovanni Gabrieli: Again, the apportioning of weight, his sense of balance, his almost infallible timing. Over and above the describable, though, a feeling for the tactile quality of space. One feels that his music is an admirable example of 'rising' compositional expression, as opposed, for example, to the eternal 'falling' quality of someone like Hindemith.

Placed against Gabrieli I am tempted to locate Monteverdi, because of his contrasting virtues of immoderateness and plain honest exuberance of luxurious detail. Moderate art is stillborn before it gets off the drawing board.

The last composer in what I am tempted to call my 'religious' group is, curiously enough, Thomas Tallis, whose music has always spoken to me in a realm beyond explanation. I have no idea if this fact has any relevance for my own development or present position.

In contrast to Webern, whose early works in particular exercised a wide influence upon my view of the essence of musical expression and its potential, I don't feel that these composers have had any 'influence' upon my art in the meaning usually attributed to the term. One or two early attempts might be said to have absorbed some elements of Varèse, but these have long ago been withdrawn, few of them performed. What I feel that the above mentioned men did begin for me was the long process of gaining a little insight into that 'other' aspect of artistic activity which cannot be instantly grasped, which draws back at the very moment of intensest contact.

With regard to the expressly 'new' among my then interests, the effect can be pinpointed slightly more precisely, since without exception all such influential experiences were works heard on the radio. The most impressive event of my radio listening career was probably the first British performance of **Gruppen**, the first work of Stockhausen's that I had in fact heard. I still have the (probably decayed) tape I made on that occasion, but haven't listened to it for many years. It was to be some time before I was to see a score, but I still have a work in three movements which I composed in the months following that performance which faithfully reflects the splintery, quirky world of the piece, albeit completely analphabetic in the sense of having no consciously ordained structure whatsoever...

I came to be very impressed by the works of Schoenberg heard little by little during this period, particularly the **Wind Quintet** (I was much occupied with wind instruments at the time myself), **Pierrot**, the **Violin Concerto**, and the **Chamber Symphony**. Probably the importance of these works for me lay in the still personally unresolved conflicts of received musical norms of one sort or another and the gradual desire to move into areas which I had not at that stage succeeded in 'legitimizing' to myself.

Scores which affected me deeply were the wild early Boulez things which came under my fingers - primarily the flute **Sonatina** and **Second Piano Sonata**, although it was less the manner and substance of these items which affected me than the feeling of rejection of all compromising norms, at one and the same time hermetically self-regarding and explosively assertive. Some early Berio I respected, such as **Tempi Concertati** - still a very considerable piece, I feel - and **Kontra-Punkte** of Stockhausen.

English music as such was scarcely relevant, because one came so seldom into contact with representative examples of it. In any case, I was instinctively antipathetic to the onward-rolling, 'roots-seeking' tendencies of the neo-medievalists. Not that I objected in principle to this approach - just that their tradition was not mine, since the English heritage never seeped through to my level of existence. That is one of the main reasons, I think, why I have always tended to regard myself as European rather than English: there was never any need on my part to integrate with the prevalent stylistic or musico-social infrastructures.

Getting back to Boulez and Stockhausen: I appreciated neither of them in their full dimensions as representatives of systematic creativity, aesthetic attitudes. With the passing of the years I have come to appreciate in myself a deep-rooted ambiguity which is perhaps reflected most appropriately in the tension field existing between the two. Whilst I admire Stockhausen's overall approach to the activity of composition as being something open-ended, ongoing, 'prospecting' (the speculative aspect of art as a vehicle for human 'intra-spection' seems to lie at the core of the entire matter), grasping out towards the most basic expressive and combinatorial quanta in the very act of crashing head-on with the world at large, I am by no means receptive towards his move away from the responsibility of reifying the continuum - such as remains of it - of western consciousness. "Shoring up one's ruins" can be a much more positive attitude than Eliot would have given it credit for: the sickness of western society may only legitimately be resolved by the flesh of those social and intellectual perspectives of which it is composed.

On the other hand, I find myself attracted to the Mallarmé position in its attempt to square the circle, to generate ultimate aesthetic reality, so to speak, in a process of virgin birth out of the very works to which it is supposedly giving rise... Getting back down to earth, it would probably be more realistic to say that neither of these composers took precedence at the time, simply because of the fact that I had all too little experience of either during the years in question. I was, after all, looking at music through the wrong end of a telescope...

AC: You've said that the **Sonatas for String Quartet** grew out of a series of pieces modelled on Purcell's **Fantasias**. They also seem like an attempt to apply the manner of Webern's pre-1914 music to an extended time scale. Did the two aims evolve simultaneously, the Webernian method superimposed on the Purcellian model, or were they sequential?

BF: The **Sonatas** were modelled on Purcell only in a very limited way, in so far as I was attempting to react productively to a certain numinous quality of unity manifested in these pieces, to 'analyze it out', as it were. I found there, above all, a coincidence of form and expressive ambitus which provided quite respectable parallels to my conclusions concerning early Webern, and the grounds for what I considered the ultimate failure of the latter to live up to the expressive promise of his first period efforts. The only formal aspect of the Purcell which I adopted was the layout in several loosely interrelated movements - something in the event ultimately rejected.

I admired tremendously Webern's ability to let lightning strike right through the fabric of the perceptive faculties at particular moments - a form of 'power-plant translucency'. The conviction transmitted through the delicate textures was on an altogether higher level than the reticence of the sounds themselves might tend to suggest. The existential thrust of the instant was what I found there, enmeshed at the same time in an atemporal discourse (grammar) which contained and harnessed that thrust to positive ends.

But he couldn't keep it up. What I wanted to do was to show that one could maintain that absolute, neurotically luminous intensity without turning inwards into that ever-decreasing maw of no return which is termed miniature lyricism. I determined to compose a massively lengthy work in order to refute this view that intensity on the micro-plane can only be bought at the unacceptable price of increasing preciousness. It was not the 'manner' of Webern (in the sense of techniques or formal habits) which led me to the Sonatas, but rather that which he wasn't, and never could have been. It's all a little like Marcel

Duchamp's "three dimensional shadow of a four dimensional object" in his notes on the Large Glass.

Ex. A: **Sonatas for String Quartet** (p. 1)

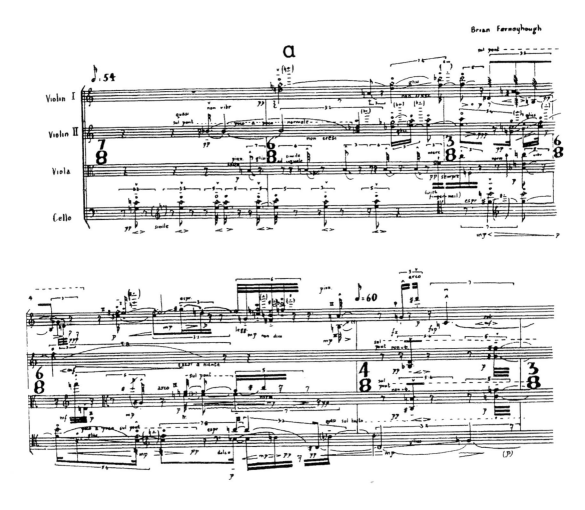

Allied to this is the fact that my methods were very un-Webernian, to say the least: for a start, the form of the piece is not actually arch-like, but synchronically discursive - several quite distinct paths progress more or less parallel to one another, as it were, through a dense forest. Sometimes two or more merge with one another, sometimes they disappear from mutual view in order to circumvent some obstacle or another. Each of these paths becomes the 'main road' at a different point in the piece's progress; there is no moment where all are present together. One needs to listen to the work 'at a slant', as if examining a landscape towards dusk, projecting back the long shadows! The major aesthetic necessity for the extreme length is thus the gradual coming into definition (out of the *materia prima*) of these fundamental elements. They must define themselves; they are in no sense demonstrated, given, at the outset. All the fundamental elements were selected with a view to their endless permutational capacity - things like 'pizzicato', 'repeated tone', 'glissando', and so forth. Some simple combinations of these items are heard very clearly in the first Sonata, and, again, rather basically, at the end, too. Neither of these presentations enjoys precedence of identity over any of the more diversified forms, though. All are equal; the manifested lexical significance must be supplied by the listener (whose own command of grammar grows, like a child's, with a certain amount of delay, as compared with the vocabulary). So, the Webern connection is only historically important; there is no real information to be gleaned about the work as it stands from my particular interests at the time.

AC: The development between the **Sonatas** and works of the previous year, such as the **Sonata for Two Pianos**, is striking. Was there an external influence that precipitated the change, and is there a work which could be regarded as a 'missing link'?

BF: Certainly there seem to be many quite marked differences between the two works, whereby the piano work would, I suppose, be termed the more 'lacking in compromise'. In part this is due to the choice of, and limitations inherent in, the respective media. More concrete differences might be located in the concepts of 'material' which underpin each piece. The keyboard item is, namely, thoroughly thematic in many ways, and is also monolithic, in the sense of obeying laws of a preordained and deliberately finite nature. That being said, I am more inclined to attribute the contrasts to a further step in a process which has continued unbroken until the present day - the 'pendulum-swing' tendency through which each composition is related in a reactive way to its immediate predecessors. The quartet was at the nadir (or, if you like, the center-point) of the swing. The **Sonata for Two Pianos**, on the other hand, represents one extreme - the then furthest boundary in a consciously constructivist direction.
The opposite side of this entire cycle was a wind quintet of the same year (1966), now withdrawn. Both works exhibited an intense concern with intervallic content, particularly in terms of vertical aggregates of various densities (something you encountered in the quartet too), but the quintet, although in its own way just as acceptably written as the **Sonata**, retreated to an overly 'populist', anecdotal position. The explanation for this curious fact is simply the need early in my career to mediate between what I felt was permitted in some

way by society and what seemed to me real, but not integrated in any intellectual or methodological manner with my gradually developing *Weltanschauung*. None of the works from this extreme (aping items all) will ever again see the light of day.

From these absolute positions I attempted time and time again to reach middle ground. This continued until about the end of 1966, but even the **Three Piano Pieces** of 1967 illustrate a stylistic retreat and uncertainty when compared with the two-piano work. This is why I consider myself as a total autodidact, something which is not intended to reflect upon the various teachers with whom I have chanced to come into contact. One can absorb more from an individual than mere information.

The next big 'synthesis' was **Epicycle**. There are thus no real 'missing links' in the chain. Such links as seem missing are firmly located inside my head! The various cycles are always to some extent interlocking, any one piece serving in various roles in two or more cycles.

AC: The style of the **Missa Brevis** shows a degree of simplification from its immediate predecessors. Was this a consequence of writing a vocal piece or because you wished the words of the liturgy to be clearly audible?

BF: Yes, the **Missa** is, of course, a simplification in absolute terms, though whether the singers would agree is another matter... It is a 'moderate' response to **Epicycle** to the extent that I deliberately exploited the '*Schönklang*' of the voices in a manner that pushes up to the surface only seldom in the string work. On the other hand, it was far from my intention to make the words of the text more audible. On the contrary, for the most part they are submerged irreparably! My choice of text was conditioned by reasons lamentably pagan: I wanted a verbal substructure which was sufficiently strong, certain of its own identity, to act as a firm counter-foil to the distortions and liberties which the exigencies of the purely musical material demanded. I had then, and still have now, a grave, inbred suspicion of 'text-setting'. Either a text is sufficient unto itself, or it is not worth using in a new art work anyway! In either case, such conventional notions of the relationship word/music set my teeth immediately on edge. The **Missa** text I took in its connotation of culture-object, not of meaning-constellation... It might perhaps be regarded as a first tentative step towards a more productive investigation of musical and extra-musical realities (e.g. equivalent morphologies).

AC: **Firecycle Beta** was written while you were studying with Klaus Huber. Was the work directly related to what Huber taught you?

BF: **Firecycle** was actually begun before my emigration. The first pages must have been sketched in the summer of 1969. The entire formal scheme of the piece was complete in all essentials before I began to study with Klaus, and, what with my already deeply-ingrained notions of what music was about, he must have had a hell of a time... What happened was that I would go home, write a page or so every once in a while, and bring it in to show him. The catch was that I always copied out the page in copper-plate handwriting as the perfect excuse for not changing a single note at his suggestion. Sometimes we analyzed his own works, sometimes we went and had a meal (which I needed!) at his expense. It was already too late for me to take anything technical or aesthetic from another composer by that time. On the other hand, what I did get from him was the feeling of personal support and moral uprightness which I needed far more than any merely material assistance; he was the person who held me spiritually above water for a good three years, and enabled me to keep going. Via his mediation I was financially supported by the city of Basle for two whole years, which effectively left me free to work on **Firecycle**. I remain very much in his debt for that.

AC: I understand **Firecycle Beta** was intended as the central panel of a triptych. Was the whole triptych meant to be performed complete, or were the three elements intended to be detachable?

BF: **Beta** was initially planned as the central portion of three (the analogy to several famous altar-pieces in Germany only occurred to me much later). Parts of both **Alpha** and **Gamma** were actually composed. Like Schoenberg with the last act of **Moses and Aaron**, I carried the idea of a completion with me for several years, before seeing that this was an unrealistic, not to say by then undesirable goal. A torso is, after all, the only meaningful way of confronting the infinite (**Alpha** was intended to deal with a mass of material seen from far away, **Beta** the 'point of intersection' and **Gamma** details of that material blown up to an unimaginable and monotonous degree). **Beta** seemed therefore to me to embody the dialectical interaction of the two (ideal) extremes, and, at the same time, to exemplify in its very incompleteness the dimensionlessness of the point - how many angels on the head of a needle?

AC: **Firecycle Beta** is the first of your works to admit a literary-metaphysical background. Was this method of working merely latent previously - have you always been fascinated by the metaphysical in art - or was this something from Huber's teaching?

BF: My primary interest in things metaphysical is as possible modes of cognition - models, patterns, grids - call them what you will. I am looking for the common denominator of different, but equally validly internally articulate systems in order to superimpose them one on the other, in order to see where the various points of intersection are located. I am not at all interested in metaphysical concepts as objects of belief. This cannot be overestimated. My own personal views are in an important sense irrelevant to the issues involved, and in any case tend towards the rationally skeptical side of the anglo-saxon philosophic tradition. Again, the "shoring up of the ruins" - sounding archaeology...

AC: The layout of **Transit** seems to be a very explicit metaphor of the journey it describes. Does this work 'belong' with the **Time and Motion Studies**, with **Firecycle**, or does it stand alone?

BF: **Transit** was probably the first work in which, right from the outset, these considerations come to the fore as the piece's *raison d'être*. It is, however, related closely to the **Time and Motion Studies** group from the standpoint of intention, even if the material being treated is quite different in substance. It also spans several important years for my own internal development (years in which I wrote little, and completed nothing), and this of course makes it somewhat larger than life for me.

AC: The extensions of interpretative technique that your recent works require supply another 'layer' of expressive potential. Were you, then, dissatisfied with purely musical frames of reference for the ideas you wished to convey in these pieces? Can interpretative difficulty ever become an end in itself?

BF: Yes and no. I was dissatisfied, certainly, with the basic *l'art pour l'art* position, which seemed overly defensive and simple-minded. On the other hand, I did not introduce the advanced techniques of which you speak entirely with a view to expanding conventional fields of expressivity. That has already been seen to be a dead end. What I was trying to underline was the relationship of the composer to his performer as a member of the category 'human being', and, as such, also eligible for civilized consideration. The conventional semiotic catechism teaches that in music there is a triadic model of the type composer/channel/listener, whereby the performer is seen more or less in the role of the channel (albeit somewhat distorted by 'interpretation'). My position is that there are in reality two triadic relationships which interlock around the relationship of the performer to the score. My immediate concern is to provide him not merely with 'instructions' about how to produce certain sounds in a certain order, but rather to encourage him in the task of de-structuring the score, of treating its many level, its appalling complexity, as an invitation to partake in a form of spiritual *exercitium*, an ongoing discipline, rather like the meditational exercises of Loyola. If I can ensure that my (ideal) performer takes a piece apart, layer for layer, I can be reasonably certain that his approach to the audience will be one of absolute human immediacy and conviction. He transcends the mere activity of 'interpretation' by subjecting himself to an all-pervading (and self-created!) order or discipline. This has the natural disadvantage of applying only to the most dedicated performers, usually soloists and often very young, as these latter are not afraid to display their own naked inadequacies in dispensing with the noble role of prestigious ring-master. What they present to the listener is the residue, the spur of their climb through the ramifications of a lengthy and self-negating activity. They must realize right from the outset that their 'virtuosity' will have to be abandoned at the wayside at some stage of their journey...

Of course, interpretative difficulty cannot become 'an end in itself'. The end is the 'opus' which emerges from the person losing himself in the forest of his own imperfections. The fact that, in the very nature of things, no performance of such a work can ever hope to achieve a 'perfect' rendition is beside the point.

AC: The work you're currently writing is called **La terre est un homme**. What are its origins?

BF: The idea of the piece arose from a dual source - a dream and a desire to "rise up" from the composition of a work (the cello piece)[1] in which I deliberately drove pessimism as far as it would go. The first half of an orphic journey. A breakout was necessary in order to be able to go on composing at all. Hence the implied duality, the productive *conjunctio oppositorum*, of absolute unorder and total control with which the piece begins.

AC: Is the title taken from Artaud?

BF: No, the name is taken from a painting by Matta. However, I have been very involved with the works and thought of Artaud for several years. His view of the communication impasse, "the absolute cruelty of the thought thinking us", has had some bearing upon my approach to the question of language and its powers on the one hand, the fundamental possibility of artistic interaction on the other. His view of the soul tortured on the rack by the twin forces of external reality and internal emotion seems central to any artistic activity at the present time.

AC: It's reported that you dislike the label 'serialist'. Is that simply because it's a very trite categorization, or do you now have a more profound antipathy towards serialist methods and processes? In the **Sonatas**, for instance,

---

[1] **Time and Motion Study II** (cf. p. 112).

pitch organization seems to be more obviously vertical rather than horizontal, using various referential chords. Has that type of structuring always been paramount?

BF: What I have against the term 'serial' is certainly partially dictated by the cliché which the word has become. In a sense, it means all and nothing. Music is in every case a more or less ordered object; whether the methods employed call for some form of pre-ordering or emerge only in the course of actual composition by so-called intuitive processes is scarcely very interesting. My music is very highly organized on a conscious plane, but there is at every juncture always one or more levels of selective activity which depend entirely upon my momentary reaction to the implicit demands of the immediate context. Only by such means are the real bonds in a discourse forged, because what interests me most is always the 'shadow zone' between the totally ordered and that which lends that ordering significance. Roland Barthes once spoke of the erogenous zones which were revealed only at the gaps between different pieces of clothing. There are no gaps in that sense in my textures, but the comparison is perhaps still not entirely irrelevant... The interleaving and overlapping of strata ordered in different degrees and/or according to different fundamental criteria allow in every instance the amassing of rich pickings. The primary assertion on my part is that of the multiplicity of life forms. A sort of balanced compositional ecology.

The more direct objection to the term 'serial' is concerned with the attendant implication of exhaustivity. Such systems as I generally employ are always so constructed as to allow for the 'quirky' selection of elements from the total reservoir on a slanted, preferential basis. The idea of taking all elements once in order to guarantee completeness of combinatoriality is totally alien to me. Richness cannot be guaranteed in this way. Also, if your elements are in themselves asymmetrical or in some other fashion irrationally laid out, you are going to produce correspondingly odd results. Often I begin a work at two diametrically opposed poles: the basic material (rhythmic, usually) is sketched out totally *a priori*, with no conscious systematization whatsoever, but is then, however, constantly subjected to 'filtering' techniques of various types which allow it to be 'rationally' maneuvered into almost any position one might desire. Again, the subcutaneous, the a-rational being levered into the willed mold imposed by the composer. As Artaud says, "the grid is a terrible moment for sensitivity and substance".[¶]

Quite often, by the way, I employ tabular methods which govern the degree of freedom of choice to be admitted at any given juncture; it amuses me

---

[¶]Last sentence of **Les Pèse-nerfs**.

to follow systematically rules which are only followed correctly when being used to destroy themselves... Pitch organization never takes advantage of all twelve semitones. Normally I take several interlocking pitch entities whose internal composition is in some way a reflection of other proportions important to the overall form. On several occasions I have had 'killer' or 'cannibal' series which exist only to the extent that they 'eat up' the material presented by the 'positive' pitch structures, so that I am in a position to manipulate favored (undevoured) pitch areas at specific moments.

AC: One of the most obvious differences between your music before **Firecycle** and after is the use of electronics. In **Time and Motion Study II**, the feedback setup is essential to the dialectic. Do you see this usage as analogous to the use of performing difficulty, or do electronics offer a different range of expressive possibilities?

BF: My use of electronics initially came about simply because I was asked to compose a work for vocalists and electronics for the Donaueschingen Festival of 1974. Working on the initial concept, I soon moved away from the pure work as necessity towards a point of view in which I felt the need to make a work-immanent critique of the various media present. I have a profound dislike of the electronic medium, produced by a superstitious belief that the more electronic machinery resembles the human voice, the more dangerous it is. Total anthropomorphism means a total de-humanization. I wrote a passage in **Time and Motion Study III** in which a simple, chordal sound was generated by the most complex possible activity of the singers, who were (each of them) having to interpret five or six rhythmicized lines of instructions simultaneously. This was then sung live, at the same time loop-recorded and played back with a delay of thirty seconds. What I wanted to have was a dual polyphony in the live version; it was important to be able to imagine the simultaneous "mental polyphony" going on in the heads of the performers, totally at odds in degree of complexity with what could be perceived aurally. The recorded version, naturally enough, sounded the same, but was denuded of one entire level of richness. Sound was simply sound. A rose is a rose is a rose...

Time and Motion Study II is an even more intense examination of the human memory system (and its analog in the world of public information) as it sieves, selects and collates. As the name implies, it is all to do with the concept of efficiency (of what for what?). Suffice it to say that my relationship to electronics is profoundly ambiguous, and that this fact is what causes me to occupy myself with it.

(I wanted to subtitle the cello piece "Electric Chair Music", but decided that that would be far too explicit for the final interpretational approach. The cellist, who sings, 'plays' two foot pedals, and reads complex notation on up to five systems simultaneously, is certainly tortured throughout. We have yet to see if he survives.)[1]

AC: Your works of the late sixties are determined to the smallest detail. Were you never attracted to Cageian chance processes, to open-ended structures, or even to Boulez's limited-choice procedures?

BF: No, I passed this direction by completely because of the heavy blinkers imposed by my own proper concerns. I was very much 'out of it'. Chance processes... well, of course, the production of music is very adequately described by that term!

Nowadays I simply feel that that sort of bogus 'freedom' was flung around far too much (along with other quasi-political/ sociologically-orientated jargon) as evidence of a thoroughgoing misunderstanding of what constituted freedom as such. Several of my works (**Sieben Sterne**, **Cassandra's Dream Song**, **Firecycle**) arise out of this consideration, and in fact do contain elements of choice in their makeup. In **Sieben Sterne**, for example, there is the superb irony of excessively detailed mass textures being interspersed with much simpler freer passages, whereby the performer is instructed to make the sound of the freer parts indistinguishable from the fully written-out sections. That was really the beginning for my concern with the mental state of the performer as paradigm for listener, because it is obvious that the correct presentation of these subtle differentiations in the score must result in an absolute lack of differentiation in terms of formal articulation. Again, self-destructing rules of play.

I am a very catholic acceptor of much stylistically which I myself, by reason of my particular inclinations and background, do not see as being appropriate to me as a composer. In Freiburg recently I planned an entire evening-filling Cage concert with precisely timed simultaneous performances and readings - I even made a version of **Mesostics for Merce Cunningham** for myself to perform with electronic transformation. But I see my own role dead center in the European tradition, utilizing the tools of western consciousness, and that excludes as much as it offers...

---

[1] At the time of the interview, the premiere of **Time and Motion Study II** had not taken place.

INTERVIEW WITH JOËL BONS
(1982)

JOËL BONS: You're here in Bilthoven as a member of the jury making the choices for the Gaudeamus Week in September. When making value judgements on unfamiliar pieces, to what things do you attach importance? I mean, for example, do you regard consistency in working with one kind of material (which one sees throughout the whole history of music) as important, or rather the originality of the way in which material is handled?

BRIAN FERNEYHOUGH: Of course each style has some particularities which it tends to emphasize above others, and it is necessarily via these qualities that one has somehow to decide *what* it is that the style in question is attempting to coherently organize. Obviously, if a music is intent upon *Fasslichkeit* in the sense programmatically claimed by many Dutch composers, one needs to look for and identify these same qualities in all musical dimensions. One must ask how they are handling the basic building-blocks being used such that the relationship between them, the movement from one to another over the course of the composition's time span, is carried out. How effective is this transformation? Do I see what it appears that the composer is attempting to accomplish? If I don't, then I don't see the justification for that particular style, because I then feel that the accusation of lack of ambition, or even, one must say, of academicism, lies very near.

JB: It seems that composition is no longer one but several professions; there are so many ways to compose.

BF: True, but, on the other hand, I find it rather remarkable and amusing that some of today's younger composers (those making a profession of preaching tolerance of all musical styles) are most strident in their blanket condemnation of those musical styles seen as being in some way regressive, styles generally bunched together under the generic designation of 'serialism' and related phenomena. Often enough, what they are thus damning might only be something that happens to look vaguely complicated on the page. I think that what holds all these various splinter groups of Orwellian Democracy together is a subconscious desire to oversimplify the issues at hand; it's a desire to thrust music back into a sort of expressive cradle at a time when, over the last two or three generations of composers, music has at least evolved to a certain sort of respectable adolescence. One can't turn the clock back to Arcadian expressive infancy: people who maintain this position are, at best, deluding themselves and, at worst, hindering a meaningful discussion of what the currently most important questions for contemporary music really are.

JB: You once said: "Today a composer cannot be naive". To what extent does one have to know about the past and the present? There are many examples of great artists who cut themselves off from their surroundings; too much knowledge can also become suffocating.

BF: I agree entirely, but the amount of knowledge of the past one should have depends very much on how many demands you make on it. Now: if an entire generation of composers grows up defending its own position by reference to the power that the past necessarily exercises on the present, one might be forgiven for assuming that it was the duty of the composers concerned to accurately assess how and on what paths this may happen. They can't simply abstract elements from historically fixed musical vocabularies, use them as if they were somehow new and defamiliarized and, at the same time, expect listeners to appreciate them in accordance with the semantic criteria of received stylistic norms. You can't have the best of both worlds. If we find that previous criteria concerning the unity of musical style are no longer valid, and that musical plurality is the order of the day, there are a number of pretty unavoidable conclusions which follow, and if we accept that no one style can claim universal validity, then it follows that nothing at all can be taken for granted by anyone, other than the sort of understanding which unites and articulates small interest groups in any field. That means that composers working today need to understand, not only how musical styles of the past are put together, but how the specific social and cultural implications of their original contexts might validly be articulated. It's part of composition technique to understand to what extent a musical language may be said to form an adjunct to the general semiotic field within which that music functioned as a special case. If we want to pretend that we composers can be naive today then we have to reconcile what appear to be mutually incompatible goals. On the one hand we want to assert that all styles are possible, on the other that only one style, namely that potentially accessing all possible styles, past and present, is actually valid. This seems very strange and unnecessarily small-minded. Knowledge is power, to the extent that necessary artistic freedom can then be exercised with regard to the innate richness of the inherited means employed.

JB: But what about a young composer who says: "I don't give a damn about what others do."? I think it's important that a composer should be concerned in the first place with himself.

BF: That's true as far as it goes. At the same time it is also true that very many of these young composers are more concerned with their personal response to the creative activity of other people. The moment you elevate arbitrarily-chosen stylistic criteria to the mainstay of your own creative activity it follows quite clearly that you cannot divorce yourself from the chain of causality, the chain of fate, if you like, which connects you with the models you are employing. There is no such thing as pure subjectivity in that case.

I think that, as at no point in the past, in any age, the Global Culture of Marshall McLuhan has caught up with us with a vengeance, and that young composers who insist that they can throw off the chains of the past while insistently returning to it are missing the point. A pervasive awareness of the availability of surface features of past idioms does not absolve us from recreating ourselves in the mirror of western culture via more intensive study of background. Since such vast amounts of previous musical practice now lie before us, there is surely no way in which we can create a valid work of art today without having a more than nominal contact with many aspects of that heritage.

JB: But, very concretely, as Robert Craft asked Stravinsky: "What advice would you give to a young composer?" There is so much that one doesn't know where to begin.

BF: Perhaps I belong to a previous generation of composers, the one still able to see itself in terms of the Nineteenth Century myth of the individual creative personality. The problem today is that, after the structuralist revolution of the sixties, it is almost impossible to hold fast to the myth of the genial individual, since we all know that an individual is, first and foremost, more or less a creation of the society in which he finds himself. Secondly, we scarcely ever experience ourselves as whole personalities, but rather as constantly changing kaleidoscopes of impressions, of tendencies, of momentary accidentalia and so on. Therefore, a young composer who wants to write essentially romantic music has a doubly difficult task. It is not to hard to compose imitation romantic music, but the real question is this: how can you write romantic music without the basic underlying concept of the genial individual, freed from the social constraints which govern the rest of his contemporaries? These two things seem, to me, to be fundamentally incompatible, and I think that a lot of young composers have yet to confront this fact. Whereas, when I was younger, it was still feasible, with extreme effort, to create a body of work in which the concept of individuality as such could still be counterpoised to the growing plurality and *Nivellierung*[¶] of value judgement systems taking root.

[¶]Approximately, 'levelling-out'.

JB: You don't think it is possible to give a blueprint of what a young composer should know; it depends on what direction he wants to go?

BF: Obviously, every young composer has particular projects and interests which are special to him and not shared with anyone else, at least not to the same degree and in that particular combination. That dictates to a certain extent the sort of examination and re-evaluation of the past which he undertakes. On the other hand, I would have to say that there are really no positive hints one can give in this direction; there are only certain negative warnings, one of which should be: do not categorize too many areas of potential experience as being unuseful. I would say: if a young composer is seriously concerned with the question of stylistic plurality, then it is important to reject, right from the outset, prejudices concerning the inherent value of certain styles. It would be necessary, for instance, in certain circumstances, to investigate kitsch, trivial and pop music, even if only to find out precisely what it is about these phenomena that make them tick. Not necessarily analyzing it - that may be inappropriate for certain styles, certain sorts of expression - but to come to some sort of personal terms with it. I don't say that a young composer has to be some sort of god, reading absolutely every music dictionary and listening to absolutely every record of music, of whatever period, that he can find, writing learned dissertations and so on. I am only saying: with the inevitably fortuitous collection of impressions which he gets from the past, he should try to form some sort of critically aware synthesis.

JB: In this sense you mean not to be naive.

BF: Well, it's what we were talking about earlier on, about the present supposed irrelevance of absolutely personal styles, the need for which was a great pressure upon many secondary composers in the past. At the same time we have to understand the motivating forces underlying the creation, decay and interconnection of past and present stylistic domains.

JB: A last thing about the Neo-Romantics. You once said that you like the youthfulness of early Stockhausen, but that, today, music by young composers is born middle-aged. You mentioned memory, which they continually mention but don't have - it's like a postcard memoir of grandma - and that this is not necessarily wrong, but tends to move away from essentials.

BF: What certain young composers sometimes tend to forget is that these elements so happily extracted from the styles of other people are really the spiritual property of those source individuals. One can of course quote other composers in new works, but you cannot adopt the stylistic criteria of those individuals without in some way devaluing, ignoring or negating what they, as individuals, wanted to say. To me there is a sort of theft involved to the extent that an attempt is being made, not just to appropriate the fabric but also the inner substance of their work. The reason I used the term of grandma's sepia photos from 1910 is that all of us, at certain stages of our lives, like to imagine ourselves dressing up in costumes and being someone else, but that's just a nice dream, of course. Finally, we have to come back to face reality and see what can usefully be undertaken in the present situation.

JB: That concerns one kind of Neo-Romantic, but in the New Simplicity there's a tendency for composers to take aspects of a style in order to make music about that style.

BF: I can accept that. I certainly wouldn't reject *a priori* the possibility of composing music about music. In a way, this is what composers have always done. Simple music needs to be complex in its own way. All I ask is that it show certain interesting relationships between the various elements borrowed from other sources and not fall back on their presumed original emotive import. What Stravinsky did in his neoclassical pieces was to *ignore* that facet of the situation - that's being honest, whereas some composers seem to expect to be able to borrow and do what they like to materials and, at the same time, when challenged about this, say: "Oh, well, I'm only trying to write really expressive, communicative music like X did", where X is the source composer being exploited. I find this complete nonsense.

JB: In a lecture you gave some time ago, you said, in three words, something about your thoughts on the teaching of composition. Could you repeat that?

BF: Probably the words I used were: "You can't teach composition."

JB: Well, somebody said that. Actually, it was Stravinsky; when asked to give his advice he said: "A composer is, or he isn't. He cannot learn to acquire the gift that makes him one, and whether he has it or not, in either case he will not need anything I can tell him".[1]

BF: That may simply mean that Stravinsky wasn't a born teacher, something which we can't either prove or disprove, of course.

---

[1] Robert Craft, *Conversations with Igor Stravinsky,* Faber & Faber, London 1959, p. 132.

JB: But it is also true in a sense, don't you think?

BF: What he said about talent is naturally true. There is no way you can teach a person to have talent. On the other hand, depending what your view of the essence of composition is, you will believe more or less in the possibility of transmitting some of this insight to others. In the past, composition teaching was closely bound to theory teaching, and theory was, in its turn, characterized by a closed body of rules almost excluding aesthetic principles. There were no evaluational criteria beyond the satisfactory or unsatisfactory attempt to adhere to the rules given - if you like, a sort of prescriptive aesthetics. Because composition teaching - rightly or wrongly - has clearly distanced itself from theory teaching in recent years, composition teachers have been forced to confront the issue of what we *mean* when we say we 'teach composition'. My own personal reaction has been to say that you *can't* teach composition. I'm aware that that sounds very negative, and, of course, I don't intend it quite as radically as that: what I mean is that every composition student brings with him to his lesson his own aesthetic world, consciously expressible or not. It is far from my duty to impose my own aesthetic world on his; rather, I need, as efficiently as possible, to bring him to a clear articulation, in his own terms, of what he wants to do. This is difficult to describe without reference to specific instances: in any case, the only real advantage I have over the student in any given teaching situation is, that I have accumulated and reflected on a certain amount of prior experience which, because I am not so intimately connected with his own creative attempts as he is, can be harnessed towards distinguishing the individual trees, whereas he sees only the wood and the problems attached to it. Once I begin to sense that I am coming to understand what the pupil wants to do I quietly begin to extrapolate and prepare the way towards the goal which it appears he wishes to attain. Thus, it is not the case that the best composition teachers dictate to a student what he has to do or learn, but that they function as a sort of resonance chamber in which the student is able to hear his own echo returning, amplified, to him. By being brought into a situation where, in a sense, he is talking to himself, the pupil enters into permanent conversation with his alter ego - something essential if, in the long term, he is to be capable of continuing independently along his chosen creative path.

JB: That's a very positive attitude, to make someone see himself more clearly, but do you also criticize pupils? Suppose for example a Neo-Romantic pupil comes to you, one could understand...

BF: I've had some.

JB: Yes, but one could guess that you would have a problem with that, as you said before. What do you do in a lesson in that case?

BF: What I do in a lesson with such a composer would be to try and find out, first of all, why he feels it necessary to employ this sort of language.

JB: Do you do this with all pupils, or only those with whose aesthetics you disagree?

BF: No, I do it with all composers.

JB: Why he finds it necessary to...

BF: To use that particular way of expressing himself.

JB: Even if it is very clear and original, for example?

BF: Certainly in the case of it being clear and original I would want to find out if that particular sort of originality is being employed in an optimal fashion. What is it about this music which is specifically original? Does he himself understand what he wants to reach through this originality? It is not often enough just to be original since, without adequate 'support systems', it is easy to become simply quirky. Under the most favorable of circumstances, in any case, the teacher ceases to fulfill that predetermined role and becomes just another composer. What I like about composition teaching is, that you enter into a lesson naked, ritually encountering another creative being. You may have no idea what you are going to say during the lesson, and you are dependent on that person bringing sufficient *élan*, belief and hope in his own creative capacity to the lesson for the sort of resonance I mentioned earlier to come into being. So, I feel that the teacher's role is essentially a passive one; I don't believe that you must impose yourself upon pupils, although that sometimes happens naturally by way of human nature. With the best will in the world you can't avoid having a strong influence on them - I don't mean stylistically, I mean personally, even though influence can of course be reflected in terms of stylistic preoccupations. But, I think that the best composition teacher is the one having the least number of imitators of his individual style among his pupils.

JB: So are you not more critical towards a Neo-Romantic pupil?

BF: I hope not.

JB: But are you generally very critical with pupils? How far do you go?

BF: That depends on how I evaluate the degree of maturity attained, the degree of recognition of self attained. With very young pupils one tends simply to stick to the text of what has been composed, looking to make its details conform as well as possible to what the student wanted to produce. Generally, it's a question of mistakes of instrumentation, or the form doesn't work - something like that. With advanced pupils, on the other hand, lessons generally take the form of a much wider-ranging discussion which may not even always be directly concerned with the composition in question.

JB: Is the teaching strict?

BF: I think the teaching is rigorous. Often both pupils and myself leave lessons completely exhausted. If, as I do, one considers both composing and the encounter between individuals involved in that activity as one of the most important things in the world, then one obviously wants to ensure that the encounter is as authentic as possible, which means that you can't cut corners. Of course, every teacher sometimes has to formulate things in such a way as not to be seen to be directly attacking the pupil, or criticizing him too harshly: sometimes you have to word things in a more positive way than you might, for instance, with a colleague of your own generation, but it's normal to adjust one's approach from situation to situation.

JB: If you see pupils of other teachers, does it ever happen that you observe problems attributable to a lack in their education? (A very sordid question indeed.)

BF: I don't think that I would presume to criticize the teaching of others, simply because I usually don't know what the pupils were doing before they started work with their current teachers.

JB: When you see results, for example, such that you think: "How can someone let this go?"

BF: Then you've arrived at the stage where teaching has been replaced by questions of taste, where the constraints of the pedagogic environment no longer apply.

JB: So then you're talking about the composer.

BF: I'm talking about the composer and not about him being the student of someone else. I think that's very important: the moment a pupil *stops* being a pupil, then he's no longer a pupil, and that's the end of the matter. In the worst of cases, he may indeed work for twenty years to free himself from his teacher (which can itself be a useful experience), but that's not something an outsider can or should take into account. We only have the evidence of the music, and there's no point in attempting to write intellectual psycho-analytical novels in our heads about particular teacher-pupil relationships; that can only end up being anecdotal at best.

JB: Another thing you once said, about Darmstadt pupils, was that they couldn't say anything about their pieces. To what extent is it necessary to be able to talk about something of which the essence cannot be put into words?

BF: It's not always necessary or even useful to be able to approach the content of a piece of music verbally, but I think there is a difference between *that* and being capable of articulating the field of concerns and techniques giving birth to a piece. Any composer having reached a certain stage of maturity must surely be in a position to formulate, in his own terms, his aims - why he's writing a particular work, what he feels he is achieving. That is what I am looking for when I pose questions about underlying aesthetic assumptions. If a student composer is completely without words, then either his control of his mother language or secondary language is faulty (although you usually sense that quite quickly) or - more seriously - he has not made a concerted attempt to confront the issues raised.

JB: To think about it at all?

BF: I'm not saying that language is the be-all and end-all of thought, because, as Antonin Artaud quite rightly said, "There are thoughts beyond words". On the other hand, if I have doubts about a particular composition, then I become even more suspicious if the composer has apparently not recognized the difficulty in question enough to have attempted to conceptualize it.

JB: So: there is a why for everything you put down on paper?

BF: There's a *why* which one doesn't necessarily have conscious access to. Why should one? All a composer needs to do is get the right things onto paper. All I'm saying is, that, in the case of composition students, one has to assume that they are *not* always putting the right things - the things they intended - onto paper. A good deal of informed guesswork on my part deals with some of that, but I still need some at least semi-formulated statement of intent from the composers themselves. If this is absent, then one might as well say you like it or don't like it, and leave it at that. That sort of defeatist position has very little appeal, though, at least for me, although I suppose it would make life considerably easier.

JB: A question that non-composers often ask is, what technical things can be learned in a composition class? The danger of academicism or too much influence by the teacher's own technique lies very close. If one thinks of, for example, Berio or Petrassi, it's well known that they considered the study of counterpoint to be helpful. Stravinsky said: "All my technique comes from the study of counterpoint I did." But, if we return once more to the conversations with Craft, he warns young composers, "especially Americans", against making a career as a counterpoint teacher because "teaching is academic, which means that it may not be the right contrast for a composer's non-composing time."[1]

BF: Well, I believe that to be what I was talking about earlier, that you have to distinguish very carefully between theory and composition, between overly prescriptive and more flexible approaches to teaching. There seem to be basically two schools, I think. One is the sort which pretends to know nothing about general aesthetics, but is able to tell you about techniques for the production of musical materials - let's call that the Handiwork School. Then there is the tendency at the other end of the spectrum which accepts that teaching handiwork is by no means a value-free activity, but already implies stylistic ideologies, from which it follows that the only real way to teach composition is starting from the immediate compositional problems manifest in a particular work by a particular pupil - that is to say, that there are really no generally valid criteria of good handiwork at all. I tend myself, probably, towards the second position, since it seems to me that those teachers maintaining that, because every artist has a different aesthetic anyhow, the most honest way to teach is to focus on technical aspects of compositional metier, are suppressing the fact that practically any technique imaginable implies certain aesthetic values. If these underlying values are not made explicit, then the teacher ends up subliminally suggesting them to the student, no matter what his original intent may have been. If particular basic compositional tools appear to be lacking, one can, I think, impart them without losing sight of the primary criterion, which is the enhancement of the aesthetic world the student himself constructs. Maybe that world is still tentative, still emerging: even so, any technique I might suggest to a student would grow directly out of, and converge with immediately, very specific issues in a concrete compositional context. Going back to the question of the value of counterpoint and related theoretical disciplines; of course it's nice if a student has done the standard course in such things. On the other hand, it doesn't mean that if some individuals are less suited to this they are less intelligent or musical, merely that they have a different type of personality. I don't

---

[1] Robert Craft, loc. cit.

think you need to spend a lot of time writing fugues to understand what fugues are about. Having studied the ins and outs of a representative selection you can happily leave writing them to someone else. The same is true of any style exercise - Schoenberg, cluster music, or whatever: you don't *need* to compose examples in order to grasp the essential points involved. I don't agree with the sort of composition course which progresses from simple two-part 12-tone writing, via writing in four equal 12-tone parts for string quartet, up to cluster- or texture-composition, and ends up with a piece of musique concrète, after which you are entitled to call yourself a composer. Problems or tasks assigned must always arise from individual needs, which means that an essential part of composition teaching is lecture and seminar work, in which pupils are able to react critically to each others' work - always a useful process - and undertake analytical examinations of contemporary works by other composers.

JB: Can you say something about the how and why of the structuralist side of your own compositions? For a listener, that is perhaps the most difficult aspect to trace.

BF: An Italian newspaper article recently referred to me as a "dionysian structuralist" - something to which, at the time, I took a certain amount of exception. Thinking back on it, though, perhaps the view is not so wrong. The thing that most people object to in serial or pseudo-serial structures is that they assume that mechanical or mathematical generative procedures produce a degree of coldness, objectivity or distance in the musical event. I would like to distinguish three main types of serialism, of only one of which, the first, is that assumption true. That would be the one exemplified, for instance, by Boulez's **Structures I** and similar products of that genre, in which the serial technique involved is employed to generate the material of which the work is composed. The piece thus exists on that one primary level only. Boulez himself refers to the piece as a "work of reference", rather than as something of autonomous aesthetic quality. The second category involves what a pupil of mine once interestingly referred to as "a net to catch significance"; you construct a grid of preferential ordering systems which - if you can conceive of music in terms of a sort of Lucretian snow-storm of atoms, gradually descending, of quanta of significant experience - causes certain atoms of significance to become attached to it, like the encrustation of ice on a window pane. Depending on the system of grids you employ, different encrustations emerge, so that this passive collecting or sedimenting of significance has little to say concerning the actual nature of the material employed: it's a way of selecting from the totality of potential experience which a given set of primordial elements offers. The third category would be the one I myself espouse, where I conceive of ordering as being something like a sieve, a set of filter systems, which I forcibly impose on the basic mass of initially unformed or unarticulated emotional, creative volition, the drive which leads one to create anything at all. In order to give it meaningful shape, it has to be pressed against some resistance, a certain amount of pressure has to be generated, like steam in a boiler wanting to escape. The moment of contact between volition and resistance device throws up two things: one, the energy necessary for expression, in musical terms; two, by being forced through the grid or sieve it becomes split up, differentiated into various types of structural function. In contradistinction to this concept, Boulez's systems (for instance) strike me as being rather tautological, because they base themselves on the multiplication of a basic number of elements, multiplied in various ways, in various directions...

JB: "Proliferation", as he terms it.

BF: ...whereas the sort of structural setup which interests me is the one in which the constellations of detail emerge from the monolithic mass or block of creative drive, not by multiplication but by division, by being channeled forcibly through the precompositional grid. In consequence, the *illusion* of multiplicity is promulgated - a multiplicity rooted in the primary state before the grid's resistance was overcome. In such moments the phrase from Artaud's "Nerve Scales" comes to mind which speaks of the grid as "a terrible moment for sensitivity and substance" - implying, for me, that point of intellectual and emotional collision which Breton speaks of when he asserts that "creativity will either be *'explosante fixe'* or it won't happen at all."[1] It's the instant at which the impaction of our will to order and the instinct to impose the self over all forms of external ordering actually produces some sort of explosively volatile mixture. I think that probably all great art finds itself in some way frozen in a momentary snapshot of that catastrophe.

JB: What can we see in the score of the structural devices you are employing?

BF: Probably one thing one sees right after only a cursory examination of a score is that I am very careful to cover my tracks. I try not to leave unambiguous evidence of specific structuring strategies, at least on the micro-level. The point about my systems in general is that they tend to be quite complexly interwoven, so that in the process of working with them I tend to lose track of

---

[1]In fact, Breton's reference is to "convulsive beauty": "La beauté convulsive sera...explosante-fixe...ou ne sera pas" (André Breton, *L'amour fou*, Gallimard/ Folio 1976, p. 26). The comment is an elaboration of the last sentence of Breton's *Nadja*.

what I am doing, which means that, if I can't manage to reconstruct what the generational principles were, I am forced to invent new ones, grafting them onto the extant stem in such a way as to make it seem that the previous principles were still in fact operative. That implies a rather striking reversal of the principle of variation: whereas, previously, 'variation' was a term applied to compositions in which one basic principle or material was shown in many different lights, in my practice we see the surface remaining very much the same while the background generative procedures are transformed or sequentially superseded. What interests me in particular about this sort of thing is, that it underlines the extent to which the human factor is fundamentally fallible and weak, far from the usual image of perfection (or, at least, of perfectibility) and the godlike creator standing outside and above the work. Also, it permits me all sorts of spontaneous reactions to a particular contextual constraint, the sort of situation in which I feel I work best. Overall, for me, structure is not something which generates compositional material, but rather situations in which I am free, within the prescribed limits, to act.

JB: But when you act, how, for example, are pitches defined?

BF: I might say, for instance, given certain materials, A and B; in this section of the piece both A and B will be present, but the two may not be combined but only juxtaposed. That would be a very simple form of constraint; a more complex form might be: at each appearance, transpose A by an interval taken successively from the interval sequence x, y, z; B will never be transposed, but its component pitches will appear in different octave registers at each appearance.

JB: That's a kind of technical device.

BF: It would be a technical device whose goal would be the definition of a universe of discourse within which the manipulation of such parameters may legitimately be permitted. If this is done with every significant parameter, it leads to all sorts of disturbances in the regular flow of information, in some ways analogous to the tension-relaxation patterns typical of tonal music.

JB: Earlier you said that there were particular reasons for you not to write simple music. What are those reasons?

BF: One is the fact that the human brain is itself so complex and opaque. Doing even approximate justice to a few facets of human experience involves me in producing objects which don't pretend to an unambiguous view of the world, even though they view it from a very particular subjective standpoint.

Someone recently asked me: "Why is it that I can't hear everything that's going on in your music, whereas I can in a Mozart piano concerto?" What do you mean by "hear"? What do you mean by "everything"? The point there is that the audible relationship of piano to orchestra fluctuates from moment to moment: our sense of foreground/background priorities dictates which level we focus on, thereby relativizing the perception of detail elsewhere. It's like that, only more so, in my own music: at some points certain elements will come to the fore, while others, in compensation, will recede.

JB: But that is in contradiction with what you said before, that you don't want to be perceived in simple terms.

BF: Not really, because an essential feature of a complex piece is that it maintains the listener's awareness of the momentary flow of necessity pressuring him to listen in a certain way. My compositional practice does not force him to say: "Aha, the composer is letting me know that this is the most important thing, I have to listen to this, ignoring the rest." Rather, he's expected to spring from level to level, to reach into the mass of events for fragments of meaning, even while moving on to somewhere else. There is no time for relaxation, and that makes some listeners uncomfortable, not wanting to have to live with that degree of uncertainty and flexibility. In a way, it's like what I feel that improvisational or aleatory music was aiming at in the sixties and seventies, which was to make palpable the transitory quality of experience as a sort of *value*, except that my music is coming at matters from the other side, in that it employs fixed form and structure to present a concrete sense of the mutability of human perceptual mechanisms. If we look at the world and don't go mad, it's only because our minds have an important filtering function, pre-selecting input for our conscious attention: I conclude from this that expecting a work of art to present one particular, immutably crystalline aspect of things seems to me rather odd, to say the least.

JB: But then one could wonder if there really is a difference between simple and complex music in this sense, since what you describe applies to both. I mean: simple music might not be just simple; when it's great music, Beethoven for example, those simple notes are able to evoke something more, and be very significant, capable of astonishing.

BF: You think Beethoven is simple? I spent many hours, once, working out what happened in the first four or five measures of the **Eroica**, and I still wasn't at the end of it.

JB: No, but the first impression is of graspability and clarity, not of complexity.

BF: Well, on that level it is indeed rather clear, but that's only because we find ourselves at some distance, both in time and social perception, from it. Perhaps the public of the day found such gestures as the **1st Symphony** beginning on the dominant chord incomprehensible and provocative.

JB: Something you said, a long time ago, about it being simplistic simplicity that you don't like...

BF: Simple complexity, or complex simplicity?

JB: Isn't normal simplicity also possible?

BF: Of course it's *possible*: all I'm saying is that, for me, coming to terms with the difficult and unstable relationship of contemporary composition to itself and the world around it presupposes a certain sort of ambition, which in turn involves me in dealing with as many aspects of a particular musical situation as I can. It's just not possible for me to isolate certain aspects of that situation to such an extent that a so-called 'simple' piece remains. There's a major distinction, for instance, between the sort of 'simple' music Beethoven occasionally wrote and the sort of meditative simplicity of some recent music, concerned with mediating an *effect*.

JB: Yes, well, I meant simple Beethoven, of course; the best side of the simple, which means more than just the notes.

BF: I just think that the word 'simple' is sometimes confusing, because it depends very much on the expectations of the listener, on which level of the musically given is being singled out for focused concentration. My own music is often extremely dense in terms of the number of simultaneously participating levels of activity, but the immediate surface effect is not infrequently rather grey and uniform. I do that in order to suggest to the listener that the immediate surface is not what the piece is fundamentally *about* - unlike, for instance, many works of the sixties, in which the immediate, texturally sculpted quality was of primary significance. I want the ear to sink down, as it were, into the morass, the sea of constantly mobile elements, only a few of which float into distinct view at any given instant. It's a pretty archetypal experience at the present juncture, and I sense that it would be inappropriate for me to offer a spurious simplicity just to reduce the prevailing level of angst. One has to be true to one's own personal experience, which means that one should perhaps be wary of too much reconstruction after the fact in order to accommodate more obviously direct communicational conventions.

What I am trying to do in my more involved textures is to allow each individual layer - be it a string of parametric information or an actual layer of sounding material - to assume a status approaching that of living entity, where its robust individual autonomy is loosely governed by, and seen in the reflected light of, the whole.

JB: In this respect you once talked about the interaction between micro- and macro-structure in composition.

BF: It was probably apropos of an observation, frequently made, that one of the problems many students face is that they can produce systems for the end-less generation of chains of notes, or else set up large-scale formal models, but they find it extremely difficult to differentiatedly mediate between the two ex-tremes. It seems difficult, for some, to accept that 'micro' and 'macro' are really only the two defining extremes, not real *places* at all. That being so, traversing the line connecting them seems either unnecessary or unnecessarily difficult. Much of the art in composing today seems to me to reside in devising means of articu-lating and reconciling the very real perceptual distinctions which the ear makes between similar types of structure encountered in the proximity of one or the other defining extremity. We find it very difficult, just now, to conceive of a coherent whole in terms of the art work: it seems to me that only three possible paths in that direction are open. The first is to ignore the problem altogether...

JB: Then you don't produce a work of art...

BF: Well, you perhaps produce a work of art which doesn't recognize the discrepancy between the two extremes: the second is to produce a work in which you polemically underline the difference between the extremes and, thirdly, to find some sort of common denominator with respect to procedure or approach to conceptualization of one's material, such that all aspects of tech-nique and formal imagination can be brought together, into conversation with one another. This is the path I personally pursue in the hope, either of creating the ideal sort of mediation I spoke of, or else, at the least, keeping the wounds of the issue open.

JB: One last topic: many instrumentalists are frightened by the complex-ity of your music. You doubtlessly know this very well, but I don't know what your thoughts are on the problems involved. Generally, the performer can real-ize only 50 to 80% of the score. Why do you feel compelled to write in this way, and how do you regard refusals by musicians or others commenting that if one omitted 30% of the notes the sounding result would be the same?

BF: I think I mentioned earlier that certain strategies adopted in my compositional procedures were accepted as making positive use of imperfection: the same might be said of my attitude towards performers and listeners. What interests me is encouraging the performers, in any given composition, to come to terms with their own natural limits, and thereby transcend them. I try to compose music which, from this position, achieves two things: the first is, to consistently overstep the bounds of the humanly possible - not in an irresponsible way, but extremely finely gradated, and plotted over the total length of the piece; secondly, I attempt to produce a counterpoint between the perceived aural complexity and the actual performative difficulty at any given moment. One can easily imagine a case where something that sounds extremely difficult actually makes optimal use of the peculiar characteristics of the medium involved - an example would be the cimbalom, where the ordering of the strings produces a quite crazy chromatic or diatonic progression when the action involved is a straightforward glissando, up or down. The opposite situation can also be readily imagined: there are some instruments where a simple chromatic scale is actually extremely awkward to execute at certain speeds, and one can even arrange, via 'secondary' fingerings, for normal woodwind instruments to require constant embouchure control if relative purity of intonation is to be maintained. If one is very familiar with the instruments employed one can 'fade in' or 'fade out' either one of these aspects as a factor in the performance situation. I try to incorporate them, in other words, as concrete strands of the composition; they are extra, if consciously subordinate, parameters, having the function of 'translation aid', helping the performer (and, at a remove, the listener) to gradually come to physical and mental terms with the possibly abstract-seeming overall expressive context and associated form. What comes out of this guided confrontation is quite different from performer to performer. I find this fascinating! A performer who spends any amount of time with my music generally feels something of the necessity of this uncomfortable conjunction, even if, in some cases, somewhat grudgingly.

JB: You're not interested in music which is easier and more playable for musicians?

BF: Not at present. I am not at all an elitist: I'm very well aware of the problematic interaction of music and outside world, and all composers would like more performances than they at present get. At the same time there is probably a practical limit to how much more practically performable or approachable my vision of music can be without turning into something else altogether. But I can certainly conceive, in theory, of a sort of music in which other problematic aspects of expression could be highlighted, by appropriately different means.

INTERVIEW WITH PAUL GRIFFITHS
(1983)

PAUL GRIFFITHS: Can you remember when you started to compose, and why? What sort of musical experiences and education had you had at that time?

BRIAN FERNEYHOUGH: I probably still have the original score of the first piece of mine ever to be performed, albeit not in public. I seem to remember that it was a march for brass band, written when I was 13 or 14. This was just before my 'official' studies in harmony began, so the piece must have been quite primitive, although I remember the general sound as being reasonably idiomatic. Since I had begun conducting the band in which I played on odd occasions, it may have been this which led me to begin composing too. One of the advantages of the band system was the high level of interpenetration of roles. Anyone interested more in the organization and layout of the whole than in a specific instrument has plenty of opportunity to observe as much detail as he wants over the space of a few years. By the age of 18 I had played most of the band instruments, apart from the very extremes of high and low, and this had given me quite an (unordered) insight into all sorts of compositional techniques and textures. Allied to this was the complete catholicity of style, ranging from soft-core pop up to quite demanding pieces by Holst or Vaughan Williams, for instance. My first confrontation with the 'classics' occurred in this fashion, in fact.

PG: When and how did you come to know the 'avant-garde' music of the fifties?

BF: My first encounters with major 'advanced' scores of the fifties and sixties were completely fortuitous. If I am not mistaken, the Coventry City Library did not exactly distinguish itself in this regard, but did contain Searle's very Lisztian **Piano Sonata** - a neglected work, in some ways, although very ambiguous in its relationship with serial technique, of course. Entering the Birmingham School of Music brought access to the music section of the municipal library, which contained a lot of items collected according to principles that still remain unclear to me. Alongside single scores by several post-war neo-conservatives there were interesting examples of the Schoenberg circle, such as his own **Wind Quintet** (in the piano-flute transcription) and the **Piano Variations** of Skalkottas, which latter impressed me quite a lot. Aside from one or two Webern works there was a mass of quasi-serial symphonies and suites which I quickly laid aside. Coming across at least one Webern score led me to buy as many others as I could afford, in particular those having a more lasting influence, such as the **Bagatelles** and the opus 5 **Quartet Pieces**. My earliest efforts at twelve-tone writing came after reading the *Grove* entry (as the only literature accessible to me), and reflect the Webern influence quite strongly.

Stockhausen's **Kontra-Punkte** entered my growing library quite early, as did his **Klavierstücke I-IV** and Boulez's **Flute Sonatina**. All these works made a lasting, if still diffuse and half-digested impression, being more important for reasons of motivation than of actual technique.

All this was of a purely visual order, since performances were few and far between. My earliest key experience in terms of actual sounds must have been hearing a 45 rpm record of the second and third movements of Varèse's **Octandre** when I was 15 or so. I remember being tremendously impressed by the uncompromising clarity and cleanness of sound, and it was at that moment that composing became my definitive goal in life. The radio provided sporadic nourishment, of course: in this way I came across **Gruppen** and was struck immediately by its obvious strength and fecundity, even though I had no idea at all as to its aesthetic or mode of construction. I must have heard a lot of English first performances too, although no specific pieces come immediately to mind. Lack of scores and of direct contact with other composers made the construction of a satisfactory overview practically impossible, of course.

Several books were quite important at the outset. *Die Reihe* on Webern in particular, also Leibowitz on the second Viennese School provided a first tentative insight into questions of form and basic issues of technique. As far as teachers were concerned during those years, I drew a complete blank, since Birmingham provided no instruction in composition. Even more important was the lack of direct interaction with other students with similar interests, so that my early development - up until the age of 25 really - was very slow and insecure. At the time this was naturally very depressing; later I came to the view that the obstinacy and creative independence thus fostered were quite valuable properties to have, and might not have been gained in any other way.

PG: What led you to study with de Leeuw and Huber? What did you learn from them?

BF: My first venture outside Britain as a composer was to the 1968 Gaudeamus Week in Bilthoven. More than any other single event this first intensive encounter with like-minded individuals encouraged and strengthened me. It was quite a revelation to be able to defend a radical point of view without reserve and to be accepted without prejudice. Being able to hear live performances of quite complex and demanding works meant a lot to me too, so that I resolved to move across to the Continent at the earliest opportunity, and the chance came through the award of the Mendelssohn Scholarship for that year. My first stop was in Amsterdam, in the class of Ton de Leeuw, since I had wanted to return to Holland above all. This winter stay was not altogether fortunate, since it was not a fruitful time for me compositionally: nevertheless, the continual contact with a thoughtful composer of an older generation was very important, even though discussions were not always centered on my own compositional activity (or lack of it).

My money soon ran out, and it was only the intervention of Klaus Huber (whom, like de Leeuw, I had met in Bilthoven) in gaining me a stipend of the City of Basle that allowed me to continue on the path I had chosen. I stayed in his masterclass at the Basle Academy for two years, until the end of 1971. Although by that time my technique was more or less fully formed, I still remember that period with warmth for the supportive attitude of Huber towards my projects. I was composing **Firecycle Beta** - work with no hope of performance at that time - and the lengthy period of continuity thus afforded enabled me to bring that massive fragment to an end only shortly after my official studies had been concluded.

PG: What is the nature of musical influence? Do you still feel yourself to be influenced by elders or contemporaries, or indeed by younger composers?

BF: I don't think that my music is particularly influenced by others in a pinpointable stylistic sense, since the impetus of my own collection of ideas and techniques must surely be more weighty than momentary points of coincidence or sympathy. My teaching involves me so intensely with the thoughts and stylistic preoccupations of other composers that I have evolved methods of draining it off immediately after teaching activity has finished for the day.

Influence doesn't have to be all that concrete, though, does it? I mean, sometimes one can be decisively influenced by a simple attitude of optimism or creative energy without identifying with the ultimate product. Of course, I can't at all eliminate the possibility of subconscious influence of whatever sort, but, given my extremely slow rate of composition, this is, I assume, minimal. Not that influence is always necessarily a bad thing, of course! I can think of many composers who have benefitted enormously from exposure to the works of others. It may be that, as one gets older, the possible damage arising from such absorptions becomes more specifically threatening, and this would have to be taken into account.

PG: What do you learn from teaching?

BF: The infinite variety of nuance comprising human personality; flexibility in appreciating and thinking through the insights of others; how to avoid imposing my world-view and musical aesthetic on others; and - not least? - patience.

PG: In many respects your music is remarkable for its consistency over a period now of twenty years. Does it seem so consistent to you? What is your present attitude to your works of the 1960s and 1970s? Do you have an urge to go back and revise? Are you writing the kind of works you might have expected to be writing?

BF: I like to think that my works have remained consistent but not immobile. Only in retrospect is it possible to assess the real degree of coherence in passing from one work to the next, since as the composer I of course can't extricate myself from the web of memories woven during the period of writing. At the time I often feel the differences between two pieces to be larger than they later seem to be. Even quite small shifts of technique or aesthetic emphasis take on enormous significance when seen close to.

On the whole I suppose my career has carried on much as it began, with the need continually to reformulate and reassess the field of forces lying between more innovative and radical compositional tendencies and those qualities tending towards a more recuperative, consolidatory profile. Several swings of this sort can be distinguished without difficulty in my progress over the last two decades. Like most composers, I expect, I have several times tried travelling back into the past in order to 'rewrite history' via the revision or recomposition of an earlier, rejected work. With me this has never once been a successful enterprise - largely because each work is so firmly embedded, for good or ill, in its particular biographical and stylistic developmental context that any attempt to create a latterday 'creation myth' for it synthetically is pretty absurd. I haven't tried this for quite a while, anyway, although I do on occasion look back through works written many years ago, since I find them to contain - in spite of all embarrassments and obvious inadequacies - facets of myself which, because of inevitably increased goal-consciousness and refinements of means, have tended to fade into obscurity. Sometimes I've found the odd point there which has given me a hint to follow up in my encounter with current creative issues. Sometimes, too, I find remarkable parallels with former ideas or manipulational techniques of the present time, albeit in a nascent state.

As regards the final part of your question, I'm not sure twenty years is the sort of time span that allows for coherent and concrete prediction. In the late sixties my horizon was necessarily limited far more by the acquisition of a technique adequate to the sort of sounds I had in my head than so many years later, where the perspective is obviously wider (although not necessarily more authentic, of course). On the whole, I think my younger self would have recognized himself in the sort of thing I am aiming at today. At least, I hope so.

PG: Do you recognize anything English in your music?

BF: There have been so many attempts to define the nature of English music that I am not about to embark on another! Most such definitions revolve around the premise that Britain has a genius for keeping a weather eye open for new developments, while eliminating from them many of their more obviously *outré* qualities. This may have some truth in it: on the other hand, the essence of a great talent is always to evade such neat and conveniently vague pinning-down. Probably every country has its share of composers who, by being less innovative, display all the more clearly whatever the common denominators of a 'national consciousness' might be.

There seem to be three main issues here. First there is the nature of originality, and its role in imposing new definitions of national qualities by *force majeure* (that is, how the fingerprints and idiosyncrasies of one individual can be adopted, so to speak, on a higher and more abstract level). Secondly, there is the type and intensity of relationship found between English composers and the totality of social institutions that engender, support and live from compositional activity. I'm convinced that this has a vast influence on a young composer's nascent stylistic awareness and his subsequent development, but it is something that affected me relatively little, since I left Britain without having come into close contact with these regulatory mechanisms. Then thirdly there is a sense in which any stimulus, however accidental, received in and through the English environment leads to the formation of an English composer.

As I said at the beginning of this interview, the works and styles I ran across early on may not have originated in Britain for the most part, but it was the British musical infrastructure that conditioned the order, quantity, as well as availability of secondary information of this input, so that one could plausibly argue that I am a child of my place and time at least in this respect. On the other hand, I never felt intensely moved to take upon myself some reintegration of aspects of the English past such as was rather current in the late sixties. There is much English music from previous epochs that I admire intensely - Tallis, for example - without this fact having had much to do with my musical sense of identity, I think.

PG: How does a work begin - from a vision of the whole, from a particular idea, from a particular sonority?

BF: When does a work *begin*? There have been occasions when I experienced a sudden sensation that a work was there - not specific musical materials, necessarily, but the sense of active possibility. More often, a work has crept out of a mass of loosely interrelated ideas, taking on concrete form almost at the last moment. This can go so far that I literally have no idea how a work will end until shortly before the moment of having to decide between a number of more or less equal possibilities. If a certain instrument is involved right from the outset, that is a different matter entirely, since it is clear that the suggestive power of a particular sonority leads to a form of spontaneous generation over and beyond any more abstract ideas present. Normally I come very soon to a sort of 'mental sculpture', which has a certain mass and external shape, and which can be turned round in my mind and modified if necessary. The ideas of 'energy', 'weight', 'mass' and 'momentum' thus have an important role to play in my initial formulations. Other pieces emerge only after protracted battles with an already extant idea, such as the piano piece **Lemma-Icon-Epigram**, or the **Time and Motion Study** series. This is usually much more agonizing, since the idea is constantly undergoing mutations caused by the development of the purely musical techniques and it is easy to get the feeling of the project chasing its own tail.

PG: What processes, mental and written, may be involved between conception and completion?

BF: Usually long periods of unfocused thinking for a start. This allows ideas to order themselves 'under the horizon', leading frequently to the most astounding Jungian 'synchronicities' when the active phase has begun. Then follow sporadic bursts of experimentation with new and already used techniques, during which sudden intuitions as to further developments are followed up, and the vital lines of communication established along which disparate ideas and forces can be channelled. After that, I usually know what the piece is 'about', and have become familiar with the current state of my tools, so that a period of interpenetration between the concrete and the more formally dispositional can begin. This might again last a long time. Once the large-scale form has finally been established I begin tentative composition, often not at the beginning of the piece. Bit by bit, the details of the mosaic become more firmly outlined; rather more slowly the elements take on that aura of secondary properties with which the *real* act of composing has to concern itself. The work emerges, under increasing pressure, from the initial matrix of constrictions, against which its expressive world will be reprojected.

PG: Do you ever abandon works?

BF: Not recently, although there have been a lot of times when ideas for pieces have taken on concrete form - usually two or three bars of fully worked-out material - without my being able to find the key to their concrete continuation. A composition almost always 'begins' long before the first notes gather enough energy to appear on paper, and many projects are abandoned or considerably modified at this preliminary, gestational stage. It can happen, too, that several distinct projects are gradually 'boiled down' to something which finally becomes a finished work. At a later stage in the composition of most pieces, too, there is a period during which I let the actual work of writing come to a stop. Such periods can last for several months, providing time for a final reorientation before the intense effort involved in bringing the composition to an end. At this stage there are often a number of outstanding, unresolved problems or tensions facing me, so that I sometimes feel at such times that the piece will *really* never get finished. In reality, though, once this stage is reached, there is very little likelihood that completion will not be achieved. It has not happened yet, anyway.

PG: Do you keep sketches that may be of use for future works?

BF: My sketchbooks are full of notes of various length, ranging from the gnomic, frequently indecipherable half-sentence up to whole pages of diagrams and pitch materials. Since I frequently note down ideas on any surface available, there are bits of old newspapers, hotel stationery, etc., glued in as well. I know that there are some composers who enter all such *Einfälle* into a card filing system when they get home, but this seems a bit too much like a conceptual banking system to me! In fact, I very seldom refer back to these notes; I can only suppose that they act as some sort of psychological back-up strategy, enabling me to move freely from one area of interest to another without losing contact with things that, at any given time, don't seem obviously relevant. The recycling process is so continuous that I sometimes catch myself reinventing an idea years after I first thought of it, having lost track of it somehow. Since the context within which this act of discovery takes place is usually vastly different and often significantly more highly developed, I find such spiral movement quite exciting, since I feel myself to be gaining extra insight into parts of my musical universe which are slowly accumulating structural significance, becoming permanent signposts.

PG: Do new works grow out of ideas or forms from old ones?

BF: There have been occasions when the idea for a piece has come upon me unexpectedly from behind. It's not often that such sudden visions are actually realized, though, unless, after further reflection, they seem to bring together other, already extant ideas in a new and innovative fashion. Mostly there is a constantly mutating vista of future projects before the inner eye, which is so clearly defined that it allows for little possibility of major modification. By the same token, though, there is a much greater potential for the development of materials or means of treatment from one work to the next. One of my more firmly held tenets is that, in the face of the high level of stylistic plurality, the term 'style' itself needs to be seen as an essentially diachronic function - that is to say, the composer needs to pursue the goal of a slowly developing, quasi-organic linguistic usage capable of providing for some equally gradual seman-tic enrichment of musical vocables which only some form of historically linear perspective would seem to afford. Although I don't of course wish to deny the possibility of other, divergent approaches, my own way of working and my artistic world-view demand this sort of concentration upon the concept of 'in-dividual style' as the presupposition for any sense of ordered evolution. This means that all works are 'infected' to a greater or lesser degree by their pred-ecessors, sometimes to the extent of sharing actual materials (as in several cur-rent projects) or passing back and forth different approaches to the same type of organizational background. In the **Carceri d'Invenzione** cycle, for instance, the three pieces of that name share all their initial chordal material in a literal form, while the nimbus of smaller, surrounding works offers quite a kaleido-scope of transformational and form-building devices.

PG: Do you write regularly during particular hours?

BF: I suppose that most composers are *always* composing in one sense or another, even if not with tangible, visible results. One of the defining quali-ties of *being* a composer seems, in fact, the propensity actually to reconstruct the external world according to this almost unbroken stream of inner preoccu-pations. I imagine that many such 'compositions' have been created via such interactional ritual without ever coming to be transformed into sound! As I said before, on the other hand, I quite often have periods during which a particular piece comes to a standstill. Since I work on at least two pieces simultaneously, this doesn't necessarily imply total inactivity. There is always work of a more mechanical, preparatory nature to be done, in any case.

In general, I try hard to be at the desk for between six and seven hours a day - more, if things are flowing well, less, if I come up against obstacles that I feel need to be slept on. Although the number of hours I teach composition may seem less than onerous, in fact the sort and quantity of energy thus ex-pended usually prevents me from teaching and composing on one and the same day. Since I travel a fair amount, too, I have to be careful when calculating what sort of compositional activity will be realistically possible in alien and anony-mous environments. Miscalculations are sometimes inevitable, of course. In the most unfavorable of cases, there is always something to be copied or corrected, and this activity tends to flow over almost imperceptibly into composition proper. Perhaps that is one of the most fascinating things about composing - I mean the permanent fluidity present in the individual division of artistic labors.

PG: Do you learn anything from hearing your music? Do scores change during rehearsal or after a first performance?

BF: Of course one always learns something from live performance, particularly under intensive rehearsal conditions. Witnessing the gradual growth into maturity of a particular interpretation can provide decisive impulses for the future, although this remark applies largely to those works for one performer only or for quite small ensembles - small enough, that is, to permit individual contact with each player. Beyond a certain limit this is no longer practicable, and, what with the invariably insufficient amount of rehearsal allotted to a work, there is sometimes no time to 'grow into' the sound of a work emerging for the first time into the real - phenomenal - world of the senses. I have often had the desire to separate out this or that texture, to listen to it by itself, to focus in on a group of instruments which only I (as the composer) am aware of as forming some sort of unit. Instead of this, one is often left hanging in the air after the performance, oppressed by the conviction that the work should really only now be beginning.

I very seldom change much, apart from the inevitable elimination of notational inaccuracies or the accidental omission of performance indications. The main reason for this lies in my actual way of composing, since I tend to copy out the definitive score (the one later published) step by step with the act of composition itself. For most of my pieces this means there is no rough score as such, merely a vast and unordered convolute of single pages of various sizes and shapes. Copying the score as an integral part of the composition process arose in the first instance from my habit of always writing in ink as opposed to pencil: later I realized that it also allowed me extra time to work through ideas while not interrupting the continuity of creative activity in any violent or arbitrary fashion. Working slowly and in this way may, indeed, not eliminate all errors of judgement, but it does tend to weave errors much more seamlessly into the overall fabric of the work, making their ultimate correction not only vastly more difficult but, often enough, actually undesirable. A lot of my more detailed methods of working are centered around the absorption and effective redeployment of the energies that systems errors generate.

PG: Do you have any intention for your music other than that it should exist?

BF: I'm not sure that I completely understand the question. I have always felt the old 'art for art's sake' against 'engaged art' to be a false and dangerously oversimplifying dichotomy. In a world where we have all become more 'decentered' in the interest of all sorts of nebulously powerful social pressures, there seems to be a significant role to be played by a view of art that transcends such black-and-white definition. What is music 'about'? Possibly, about the relationship pertaining between the realm of the senses and the ordered object of their perception seen as an extended metaphor of possible forms of life. The idea of a work acting out the conditions for possible worlds of order which are not immediately subjected to external cost/efficiency categorization seems a reasonable point of departure, although each individual instance will, by definition, expand and distort this basic position in hitherto unimaginable ways. A truly 'experimental' music is not necessarily one that juggles half-digested ideas and materials in order to be surprised by what comes out: rather, it is a form of living discourse, which, at every moment, offers many possible paths towards its own future. One of the reasons I have been so attracted towards the Piranesi etchings has been their quality of being capable of throwing their perspectival trajectories across the edge of the page into the world outside. It is this sort of matrix that I try to compose, not necessarily the once-for-all definition of the precise forces which encounter each other there.

If all this seems rather vague, it is because, in the context of the work, it is really rather concrete. In any case, whatever intentions for his work that a composer has are usually directed more at getting the piece *written* than speculating too much on its ultimate function. Beyond that, one could argue that the term 'exist' used in your question implies a far too passive mode of being for an art work: I hope that my compositions suggest a more active interpretation since they, too, are setting out on a long journey of their own.

PG: Is an audience necessary?

BF: I'd say that *resonance* of some sort is quite necessary, since it would seem rather difficult to maintain the Adornoesque 'message in a bottle' metaphor in this age of instant transference of cultural information. Naturally, there is little use in imagining some 'ideal listener' when composing, since the sort of mass audience that makes any generalization of that sort useful is hardly a characteristic of any species of contemporary music. There is no such thing as the new music audience, but rather a chaotic mesh of special interests - something true of life in general, of course. There may be the man or woman fascinated by Stravinsky while being left cold by Mahler. The same person may love **The Rite of Spring**, but heartily dislike the **Symphony of Psalms**, so that, if one looks closely enough, one's imagined listener dissolves into a shimmering and impalpable mass of currents.

In a certain sense, the sort of traditional concert where a relatively small number of listeners congregates in a back-street hall has been overtaken by the new reality of the record industry, radio and so on, so that it is hardly to be wondered at that the composer's sense of direct relationship with a specific, identifiable group of listeners has taken some hard knocks in recent decades. Probably the fetish of large numbers is a quite recent symptom of the same thing, since the history of art has frequently shown that major artists have exercised an influence largely divorced from their annexation or not by organs of mass dissemination. In the last analysis every composer works for himself, since only he can gather and maintain the impetus necessary for the creative act. Otherwise, I suppose one writes for the dozen or so individuals whose personal opinion and esteem have importance without this implying that other facets of the problem are being ignored. Whatever the more abstract categories of listener being aimed at, this sort of basic 'targeting' towards known individuals seems to me to be the starting point.

PG: Do you intend your program notes to baffle?

BF: To tell the truth, I've often been somewhat baffled myself on observing the seeming unwillingness of the listener to reconsider the purpose and format of program notes. All too often the fireside-chat tone of voice many composers feel impelled to adopt switches the ear and mind automatically into more secure, familiar channels whatever the nature of the music itself. The ubiquitous ideology of good common sense giving rise to such phenomena is a pretty good example of how social pressures know very well how to defuse even the most potentially explosive art. On the other hand, providing no accompanying notes at all strikes me as being a rather defeatist gesture, and ends up being interpreted as a particular - even less individually differentiated - form of comportment open to grave misinterpretation on the part of the uninitiated.

The texts I sometimes offer (only when asked!) are certainly not intended as *descriptions* of my music in a direct sense: after all, there are a number of stages of the compositional process associated with verbal, conceptual activity, each of which is capable of making a specific contribution to the work's unique ambience. This many-layered aspect of creativity should surely be emphasized, not eliminated. Also, a text can stand in all sorts of relationships to the work with which it is nominally associated, even to the extent, for instance, of collecting together aspects of the original ideational 'background' *not* expressed directly in the music itself - remainders, if you like. These, too, are by no means irrelevant. Another possibility I have sometimes made use of has been to generate a text utilizing identical techniques to those employed in the piece itself, without necessarily making these techniques objects of discussion as such. In other words, there is a sort of verbal 'double' of particular aspects of the work which, I hope, might prepare the ground for the subsequent intuitive sifting and reordering of musical impressions.

While the text is in no way conceived of as part of the work, there is a sense in which it exercises an *exemplificatory* function, suggesting the existence of fields of force between works and world through which the resonance of the music can be projected into other dimensions. Music does not exist alone in the world; there were periods when it was a self-evident fact that it formed a center of gravity around which all sorts of cultural experiences were clustered. It is only relatively recently that the art has become shamefaced about some such vision, taking refuge in some anonymous and unreflected ideal of 'communication'.

That said, perhaps it is useful to emphasize the fact that composers are not primarily wordsmiths - a fact apparently often forgotten or ignored by critics who content themselves with regurgitating the program note (a prime proof of some of my theses if ever there was one) or treating it as the object (rather than the piece) of a form of debased literary criticism. One of the main problems seems to be that, in contrast, say, to the visually orientated arts, the language of critical speculation on music has become overly conventional, not to say impoverished. My texts are certainly not setting out to baffle, as you put it, but, rather, to strategically disorientate, in an attempt to subvert this sort of formulaic reaction.

PG: Are you ever moved to write music in response to external stimuli that you can recognize: words, other works of art, natural phenomena, ideas, etc?

BF: Yes, almost always, in fact. Over the years I have developed a 'nose', I think, about what is likely to stimulate me and what not. Sometimes other works of art (usually not music) have acted as catalyst, not directly leading to the piece, but acting as focus points for the collecting and ordering of all sorts of fragmentary impressions, speculations and so on. One of these was the Matta painting *La terre est un homme,* which served this purpose on several levels at once, such as the actual configuration of the elements, the title and its implications, and the sort of surreal animism that lends the painting its specific life. The same is true of the Piranesi series to perhaps an even more far-reaching degree. **Transit** was a case in point too, since the layout of the orchestra was a close reproduction of the concentric circles seen in an eighteenth-century pastiche of a Renaissance magus penetrating the outer limits of the heavens and hearing the music of the spheres. Quite a lot of correspondences were built up around this convolute of images.

At the same time, I would need to emphasize that my music has nothing in common with program music. There is a tight web of analogical correspondences attached to an extramusical idea, it's true, but no 'story line' being followed outside the musical action of unfolding and revealing itself. Later works tend to dispense with specific external images in favor of more fundamentally music-immanent considerations - although, in asserting that, it immediately occurs to me that quite a few of my recent compositions have been quite clearly formulated parallels of that sort: **Lemma-Icon-Epigram**, for instance, with its connection with Walter Benjamin's theory of the allegoric. Sometimes I think that if Wittgenstein and Benjamin had met at the ends of their respective careers they would have regarded each other as creatures from another universe. Still, there are often points where even the most idiosyncratic of trajectories intersect and, at the end of the *Tractatus*, where he speaks of the limits of the sayable, Wittgenstein comes closer than one might expect to the admission of real forms of meaning which transcend verbal encapsulation. Earlier I said that I feel emotionally close to anything that defines a border in the act of crossing it; the same is true here, where we sense that the showable and the sayable are not *really* so far apart. The obvious immediacy of the indicative image remains firmly embedded in our linguistic culture, just as the word itself (*pace* the more recent ideas of Derrida) is always being drawn back into the maelstrom of pre-logical sensibility. Music, for me, is an art form that - more than any other? - partakes of both worlds in a vital and elemental manner, and Walter Benjamin (like Adorno in a different context) is relevant to the extent that his primary concern was always the moment of modulation between one manifestation of meaning and another.

In his *Ursprung des Deutschen Trauerspiels* Benjamin first formulated what I hope to be forgiven for calling the concept of 'pictorial synaesthesia', according to which he unearthed endless varieties of interconnections between images and concepts. This has been interesting to me in so far as, in **Lemma-Icon-Epigram**, I was deliberately searching for a sort of *non-discursive argumentation*, and the formal organization of the baroque *Emblem* (consisting of verbal superscription - the 'lemma' - pictorial image and concluding exegesis in the form of a poetic epigram) seemed immediately useful and suggestive. In fact, it was via Benjamin that I came across this whole world of subcutaneous significance. I see the Emblem-form as a sort of 'frozen rhetoric', so the idea of the piece was to bring the tripartite structure of the Emblem into frenetic motion, to dissolve its conventionalized immediacy into a new species of communion between musical object (always on the brink of disappearing) and chain of transformatory processes, itself teetering on the brink of dissolution. In keeping with the original layout of the three parts of the model, I chose techniques and approaches that emphasized first the scriptive, linear aspect, then the rigid, object-bound side of things, finally (although this not entirely literally) the argumentative, exegetical.

Only years later did I come across several tractati (Gracián in particular)[1] that underlined the close relationship between classical rhetoric, the art of

---

[1] e.g. *Aguzeda y arte de ingenio* ('Subtlety and the Art of Genius') (1642).

memory and the image that conjoins them. Seen as a continuation of this line, Benjamin seems to me one of the few cultural critics of the pre-war years truly to have a foot in both camps.

PG: What is music, and what is it for?

BF: I find it interesting that you automatically couple these, for me, distinct and independent points. Art in general seems to be a basic quality of being human. One might as well ask, 'Why breathe?' As to what it's for: off the cuff I can only suggest that it serves to keep the tenuous lines of communication open between different areas of our selves. As soon as we start looking for catchy phrases to nail our experience down with, we end up in exactly the position that I sense art to be opposing. I have always been attracted to works that straddle boundaries, without sitting on the fence: the rule-bound quality of sensuality and the sensual aspect of the intellectual seem to be getting further and further apart in most people's minds. Perhaps music, by incorporating both these extremes in high degree, can hope to bridge the gap, if only as a form of favored special case and for a limited period of time.

PG: What music would you go out of your way to hear?

BF: Almost anything from the Italian renaissance, primarily Monteverdi, the Gabrielis and their contemporaries. The exuberant pleasure in the architectural play of masses in the latter and the mannerist intensity of every detail of the former - not to speak of his amazing timing - have always exercised a powerful pull. Little from the eighteenth and nineteenth centuries; my central interests begin again with early Schoenberg. The **Second String Quartet**, for instance, seems one of the century's masterpieces, and I would always make an effort to hear a performance.

There's not a great deal of more recent music that I would go far to hear, but that's probably because I hear a lot anyway, and like to spend as much time as possible with my own things. I seldom feel greatly attracted to first performances, although things were different a decade or so back: since then the 'aura' of expectation attached to such events has largely dissipated, along with the adventurous spirit of most of the composers.

PG: What music do you detest?

BF: Would it really be very illuminating if I offered my personal hit list? As far as contemporary music is concerned, I try to suspend judgement as long as possible, since it is very often rather hard to judge quality before entering into the stylistic ambience of a piece. I'm afraid there *are* areas that leave me fairly cold - most minimal music (of the repetitive sort), most socio-critical or overtly political music, particularly the sort that offers a thoroughly middle-class view of what the masses *should* like. Opera is a mostly closed book, too, apart from Schoenberg, Monteverdi and some Strauss, but that may be due to other factors apart from musical quality or content, I suppose. Apart from those specific points I suppose there is a certain sort of 'festival music' that makes me distinctly restless, since there have been many occasions when I have been over-exposed to interminable concerts containing only minimally-individual works. There again, though, it could be that the mass desensitization involved in the very act of listening for such a long time is more worrying than the pieces themselves. Sometimes I think contemporary music concerts should consist of no more than five pieces, each no more than four minutes in length, with the pauses between them being calculated in inverse proportion to the length of the works they separate. Really *listening* to contemporary music of quality demands such an intensity and involvement that present-day concert practice is either a reflection of the decay in our hearing capacities or one of its prime causes.

PG: How do you react to such phenomena of the age as the New Romanticism, minimalism, *Neue Einfachkeit*?

BF: I wrote an article last year,[1] published in various Continental journals (including *Darmstädter Beiträge*) that deals extensively with this issue in terms of what can and cannot be expected of style. My personal view of the necessity of continuity of personal style as a presupposition of 'depth effect' was there contraposed to the various brands of neo-historicism now current. I suggested that the view of musical 'history' often implied in such music is a necessarily limited and limiting one, and that the view that musical gestures can effectively reflect the emotion of the composer in some sort of direct depictional manner leads to all sorts of problems when thinking of form, particularly when bound up with the now aging polemic against the so-called 'serial' (in the sense of 'total serial') tendencies of the fifties. The main argument against most New Romantic phenomena is that the iconic representation theory (on whatever level) leaves the single gestural unit of significance on a rather isolated and formally ineffective island. Indeed, the more effective the depicting act, the less the resultant gesture is in need of continuation! This leads more and more to a return of textbook forms such as fugue, variation, etc., in which schematic and over-simplified models are frequently at crass variance with the type of hyper-expressive material employed. There are things to be done in the field of

---

[1] *Form - Figure - Style* (see this volume, p. 21).

'trans-stylistic' modulation, I imagine, but not without extensive reflection on the part of the composer. Some sort of inverted commas are inevitable.

PG: Do you feel yourself to have any affinities with composer colleagues?

BF: There are a lot of composers whose attitude towards the importance of compositional ambition and its connection with other areas of experience I respect very much, without necessarily sharing their belief systems, which may be of a religious, philosophical, social or psychological sort. It is extremely important, I'm sure, that reflection be carried out in intimate alliance with sensation in a way possibly pointing to a path beyond both.

PG: Are there colleagues whose works you follow with particular interest?

BF: My teaching activities bring me into contact with a wide spectrum of composers from all over the world, and I like to keep in touch with as many ex-students and their activities as possible. This keeps me quite occupied! Apart from that, as I said earlier, I think, I don't really have much opportunity in Freiburg to follow at all continuously the careers and development of others. Some colleagues and I occasionally exchange scores, and this helps one keep important threads unbroken. Anyone attempting to keep up with even the tip of the growing production of new music scarcely has time to compose himself, I should think. My activity in the Institute for New Music at the Musikhochschule involves me in ordering scores and records, it's true, but I can't only order what I like, of course, and have to see that a wider selection of styles and composers is at all times represented. The best composers are not always the ones most pedagogically instructive either.

INTERVIEW WITH RICHARD TOOP
(1983)

Authenticity and self-discovery

RICHARD TOOP: Is there an element of self-revelation in your work?

BRIAN FERNEYHOUGH: No. I would say that one particular aspect of my work is that I construct myself *through* the work. I am what I am through having gone through the experience of writing the work, and in the same process, the 'glasses' which construct it for me enable me to see that person created (in so far as I produce another work after it).

RT: Does that mean that your works inflect you, rather than you inflecting them?

BF: On the immediately accessible level - the level accessible to me - I would say that was true, yes.

RT: So that the works are not just a voyage of self-discovery, but almost self-definition as well, or self-redefinition?

BF: I would say yes; it's the process of writing which is the vehicle of the self. It's not a matter of going through the journey in order to arrive at a self-revelation of the kind many alchemists or mystics tend to point to, in which the revelation is then an essentially static totality. My view of 'self-consciousness' (or 'self-observatory capacity' in that sense) is essentially a dynamic one - it is always in movement.

RT: Does that mean that when you actually begin to write a work you have certain areas of yourself which you wish to explore through the work, or which you wish to shed light on, and you expect the work to do that?

BF: Yes, that's right. Always. Let's put it this way: there are three things. One: there is an area of myself which I wish to explore. Two: there are areas of the world which have an as yet unexpressed correlate which I sense in myself. Three: it is possible to start a work without having either of these immediately accessible to me, or not consciously so. But then it much more difficult to take the first step, because I can't write 'just music'; and besides, in the course of any work of that type, once commenced, the piece inevitably takes on such dimensions at some stage, if it is going to get finished at all. Sometimes I don't finish works for precisely that reason - because they don't find access to whatever it is that needs to be said.

RT: How do you cope with the situation in which the means of your 'self-discovery' are governed by the external circumstances of a commission? For example, can you say to yourself, 'Well, I think it is now legitimate for me to discover myself in terms of a piccolo'?[1]

BF: No. With the exception of one or two pieces in the last year or so, where I have to say that the discovery has had to come as a matter of 'necessity', after having had to do something, I would say that generally I've been in the fairly lucky position of being able to choose my ensembles and players.

RT: If the sheer number of players in an ensemble offers certain 'possibilities of richness', is that more important than the specific nature of the ensemble?

BF: Well, I don't even think of an ensemble in that way. I find it exceptionally difficult to write for 'ensembles' in the normal sense. I never wrote for one before **Carceri d'invenzione I**, and even that has got some weird instruments in it. I couldn't write for what I'd call the 'standard Webern/modern music ensemble' - I just couldn't, not in the sense of normal 'ensemble sound'. My idea of an ensemble is of a totally homogeneous sound-world in which the internal differentiation and articulation of the sounds takes on extra, existential energy and suggestiveness, simply by deviating from the standard grey norm.

RT: But isn't it true that in **Carceri I**, especially at the beginning of the piece, you assign very specific tasks to each kind of instrumental grouping?

BF: Oh, this is maintained all the way through! It's deliberately somewhat 'wiped over' (in the Baconian sense) in the middle, so as to produce different trajectories of energy, shall we say. But at the end they do return, and that's because of this cycle, which is again the journey of self-discovery, as it were, or self-investigation, the idea of seeing what for me are the fruitful extremes of the organization of the external world in order to reveal the inchoate nature of the subjective sensation. Or at the other extreme, what is the value of projecting the inchoate *onto* the material in order that I may be able to see it more clearly in a

---

[1] At the time of the interview (1983), one of Ferneyhough's most recent works was **Superscriptio** for solo piccolo.

'gelled' form, like a bee in amber? How can you preserve this 'organic' in a state of organicity?

RT: Given this general approach to composition, how can you really go so far at this moment in time as to project a cycle of seven works?

BF: Because it's the only way to compose. I'm a slow composer, and I can't conceive of just one work (or then it has to be a big work). Because I have to reflect. It's what I call the 'auto-history' of a work; it's part of the stylistic formative process. A style can only be defined not in terms of the synchronistic elements it contains (at least, not primarily), but far more by the diachronic shadows which those elements in that particular work throw on the past and future of one's own being. And therefore, for me, if I don't define my activities in terms of, say, a two- or three-year space at least, then there isn't time for these elements to be auto-revelatory; there isn't time for the auto-history of generative potential to be realized.

Compositional strategies

RT: Are the complex compositional strategies in your music things that you work out well in advance? How much is pre-composition, and how much is spontaneously evolved?

BF: A great deal is spontaneous generation. I think the use of any structure is dual. Firstly, it is to enable one to have a framework within which one can meaningfully work at any given moment, so that one isn't faced with the totality of all possible worlds, under which circumstance one does nothing, probably. Secondly, it presents one with an object to which to react - it is a state of affairs at any given moment, and if you have worked the systems properly, then you have left yourself enough freedom to be able to react in a totally individual, and spontaneously significant fashion. Structures for me are not there to produce material; they're there to restrict the situation in which I have to compose, such that material can be spontaneously generated, but still have relationships to the elements around, so as to produce a totally significant object.

RT: I seem to remember reading an account of your work, at first or second hand, in which you seemed to say that the pre-existent grid of possibilities was almost like a wall you had to bang your head against, a sort of blockage that had to be broken through in order to create. Do you still feel that way, or is that already a partial falsification of your view at an earlier time?

BF: It's a slight falsification in the sense that one doesn't have to break through the wall, because that would imply the wall's being an undifferentiated object. Rather more, I would see two forces at work - and perhaps this is a psychological over-simplification, but nevertheless it enables me to present a convenient counter-case to the Boulezian multiplication idea, which seems to me to be unfortunate. I believe very much that one has an unformed mass of creative volition. On the other hand, in order to realize the creative potential of this volition one needs to have something for it to react against. And therefore I try to set up one or more (usually many more) grids, or sieves, a system of continually moving sieves. This fundamental, undifferentiated mass of volition, or creativity, is necessarily forced to subdivide itself in order to pass. This, when it manifests itself in a composition, gives us as listeners an impression of multiplicity which wasn't, perhaps, present in the original conceptual drive. But of course, it isn't 'multiplicity': there's no more material than there was before. It's simply that in order to pass these grids of various types and sizes, the material has been forced to diversify itself, to break itself up into more differentiated units which are more immediately apperceivable. This seems to me to be a much more sensible way of producing complexity in a work than simply taking a basic unit and, like the Hall of Mad Mirrors, multiplying it into infinity: one doesn't get any new information that way (or very little); whereas this way one sees what was inside the original block, just like Michelangelo saying that he could see his David in a particular piece of stone.

RT: What was the origin of this whole 'grid' notion?

BF: I think it was basically something that developed slowly. Of course, the key moment is always the one at which you can formalize it verbally, and very many of the musical notations I utilize in preparing sketches for a work are often verbal descriptions of possible processes or states. If you were to look at my basic sketch-books, you would find that they consist almost entirely of writing, rather than musical notation. It's largely verbal conceptualizing on the one hand, or pictorial imagery sometimes (less often), philosophical speculation (always relating to the work in hand), or the simple description - I've a very nice shorthand for it now, which I have developed over the years - of possible musical processes - the way things, whatever they may be, whatever things I choose, might be applied to certain sorts of grids.

RT: You retain your sketches?

BF: I never used to...

RT: For any particular purpose?

BF: I earn a certain amount of my livelihood from teaching courses externally - summer courses, but also other courses - and I find that sketches are a part of one's livelihood, one needs them! And one of the nice things about reanalyzing one's own works in public (not looking at the analysis in advance - I don't like doing that, I like to be spontaneous) is that in standing up and actually starting talking about it one sometimes invents new things, quite spontaneously, by making an imaginary example on the blackboard; I sometimes think, 'By God, this is interesting!' Because I never use examples from the pieces to describe the processes; I always say, 'This is what I might have done, but didn't', mainly because I don't want to simply reproduce what I have done already.

RT: Again, this is the same thing as your forgetting what you had done, and therefore simply recomposing another way of getting to the same thing.

BF: That's right. One of my basic psychological problems in life, I suppose, is that I have a very short-term memory, so that if I now presented to you some very long, tortuous, and complicated argument in response to some question of yours, and you were to interrupt me and say, 'Oh look, I didn't understand that, could you repeat that?', I guarantee I could not.

RT: One would just have to start again?

BF: I am forced to reinvent, let's say, a new formulation for the same argument every time, simply because I'm not capable of retaining a train of thought for long enough. And that probably also has something to do with my musical creativity, why it takes me so long to create a work, why I write very slowly, but also the particular sort of expression and jumpiness, quirkiness that the works themselves consist of.

RT: What is your working method? Do you have a regular routine, or is it very much as dictated by circumstance?

BF: Well, generally I try to keep office hours: it's something I'd recommend to all students. I start at 9 in the morning (sometimes earlier, at 7 or 8) and I go on, all other things being equal, until about 12 or 12.30; I stop (if possible I have a sleep), and then I restart around 3 or 3.30, and then I go on to 6.30 or 7. And on ideal days I get seven or eight hours' work done in this fashion.

RT: And do you find yourself at the beginning of each day really having to reinvent where you'd got to, or do you find that you remember where you were at the end of the previous day?

BF: Well, because my sketches are sometimes incomprehensible, even to me, the day after, because of the short-term memory we were talking about, and because I haven't adequately taken that into account at the end of the previous day's work, it's sometimes very difficult to get back into it. Particularly if, for instance, in a work I've had to leave one layer in order to get on with another layer at a certain moment. Coming back two weeks later to that first layer, it sometimes takes me two or three days to get back into it. However, if I'm in the middle of something, and proceeding with a certain degree of creative dynamism, then usually at the end of a day's work I leave a certain amount of material in a state such that the next morning I can pick it up and go on with a minimum of rethinking, and then I get back into the swing of things fairly quickly.

RT: Is it possible for you to work on more than one piece at once?

BF: Yes, I've always done that.

RT: From preference? Kagel claims that it is essential for him to be working on four or five pieces at once, just to create the necessary level of tension.[¶]

BF: Yes, absolutely, because what one work fails to illuminate, another work may well do, and therefore, even though these works may not use the same materials, they are very often related in many more subtle ways, which simply working on one piece would have prevented one from achieving.

RT: Does this mean that at any one point there is not so much a specific set of works you are dealing with, but rather some kind of theoretical central kernel, some kind of conceptual central work, which never actually gets written, but on which all these various pieces you're working on are, in a way, peripheral commentaries?

BF: Certainly not peripheral commentaries! However, there is a certain central kernel, and in one of our previous discussions I tried to define it with the simple word 'style'. I said that many people today make the very simple mistake of equating style with the repertoire of surface elements which a particular work or group of works contains, whereas I would define style far more in terms of continuity in the employment of certain types of material from one work to another. Since today we have a very plurivalent society in which very many styles are present simultaneously, it follows, if we don't want to undertake

---

[¶]In 'Une panique créateur', *Musique en jeu 11*, Editions du Seuil, Paris June 1975, p. 39ff.

the mad task of trying to recreate *per fiat* one new unified style, each one of us has the task of recreating within the continuity of his own work the semantic richness which a unified style in previous generations allowed to those composers living in them.

Therefore, for me, the essential defining character of style is: how can, through a series of works - also, on a different level, in the development of one work itself - how can these various elements, these means of working, these strategies, be seen to exhibit themselves in different lights, with different potentials for interaction with future works? How can they learn to speak to one another, and to us, in an optimal fashion? There are people who say (and many of them are young composers), 'Today we have the duty to react to the totality of experienced world music; we live in a global society in which Balinese gamelan music, John Cage and Noh drama are coextant, and the responsible composer, the socially aware composer today, needs to be a virtuoso in playing an organ whose stops consist of all these styles.' I would hesitate to say that this is nonsense, but I think it's a very dangerous ideology, because it means that though the composer is a master of many styles (or not, as the case may be), he is still subservient to them. He treats those styles as 'things', as found objects, whereas I believe that these styles, these types of working, are inextricably bound up with the cultures in which they originated. We can try and appreciate them, and one can, if one wants, adopt some sort of musical attitude towards them; but to use them as colors, as intellectual colors, as manipulation, to force us into a certain way of feeling, I find this both intellectually and artistically and morally exceedingly suspect.

Therefore a composer today needs, more than ever, to work in one continuously developing style - style as defined in the perhaps circular way I attempted to do so - in order that these elements have a chance to breathe, to expand, to redefine the ambitus within which this style is redefining its past and future simultaneously. Because it's the only way, in this situation of a plurality of styles, in which any given work can achieve the semantic richness necessary to make it live up to the demands which the past has quite rightly imposed on us.

The ethical dimension of music

RT: Is there any way of ensuring, at least partially, the aesthetic significance of a work? Is it just a matter of doing the right thing at the right time?

BF: You've got to be musically lucky, I think, but you've also got to be *verbissen*: you've got to be obstinate in the sense that you keep the same high technical quality, make the same aesthetic demands on yourself, even in dry times. You know, Eliot's old man at the fiery gates, waiting for the rain to come.

You've got to be sitting there, waiting for the rain to come. Because if you don't keep the standard up during those dry times (which you can't control) the rains will never come.

RT: You feel you've had dry times yourself?

BF: Oh yes. I've often felt times to be totally meaningless in terms of what I do, living where I do, and looking at the world through the eyes and telescope that I do. I've often thought that I'm sitting on a desert island, in terms of what I think is quality in music. It's something that has disappeared from the scene altogether; the moral responsibility has disappeared from everything. The rats have left the sinking ship, and even the ship has probably sunk. And one of the reasons I say that I'm on a desert island is because most people don't accept the - let's not call it 'moral' - the ethical dimension of a musical work, or any work of art.

RT: How would you distinguish between the two?

BF: For me, 'moral' is a somewhat heavier, more nail-downable term, in the sense that 'moral' has far more of the Adornoesque implication that the work of art can be good or bad, right or wrong. I wouldn't think of it in those terms, as a contribution to the state of the world at a given time. I'm not one of those composers who is engaged in the banally social(ist) or even fascist notion of a work of art's 'doing good' in the world in general, in the service of this or that social precept.

RT: Rather than 'right or wrong', wouldn't the Adornoists say 'truthful or untruthful'?

BF: Certainly. However, this is a function of the place, the locatable situation of the work in respect of a certain self-regarding quality, or self-perception, that society has at a given time.

RT: They would say that, or you would?

BF: I would too, but it's banal: it doesn't say anything about actual quality. Now let's talk about ethics. I would say that the ethical quality is something that emanates from the composer into the work. That doesn't mean that he is a good or bad guy, something which a 'moral' work, or the production of 'moral' music, tends to imply - moralizing! The ethical quality is something which I would describe as remaining work-immanent, something that remains embedded in the quality of the work, without needing to relate to anything else whatsoever. This doesn't put me in the famous *l'art pour l'art* ghetto, or the good old ivory tower. Quite the opposite: the only people who talk about *l'art pour l'art* are those so-called democratic composers who say, 'Yes, let's all individualize our expression, let's all be individuals. But you can't do *that*.'

RT: Is your general aesthetic, and your conviction in the path you are following, generated internally by the work itself, or do you also draw strength from other areas, from the rest of the musical world, from literature, or whatever?

BF: Well, I have to confess that, except from a sense of duty, I don't pay a great deal of attention to what is going on in the world of music at the present time. Over the years I've become intensely depressed by the present development and state of the art, so that apart from odd works by odd composers, which might be quite bad in themselves but contain an interesting point here or there, I really don't get a great deal of stimulation from that. But that shouldn't be logically necessary if there is any validity in my standpoint that style is a function of development rather than of surface configuration; then, of course, I have to draw future developments from the corpus of evidence already extant in my own work.

I would say that one needs to differentiate this question quite a lot. For instance, you ask: do I draw sustenance from external things, or do I draw it purely from music, or what? I would say I draw it from the sense of energic stimulus which I feel in myself concerning the state a work has arrived at in relation to my total interests at any given time. The work is one thing, and it may be interesting or not; what I am doing otherwise in the world may equally be interesting or not interesting, but it is the way in which these things and the work are both transcended in terms of the excitement, the urge of producing, that for me is the ultimate creative situation.

Expression

RT: Were there any particular influences on your early work?

BF: I would say certainly that my early music was in some way texturally related to the exuberance of the early Boulez works, but I lost touch with Boulez very, very early, and anything he wrote since 1951 or 1952 has been, to me, of little personal relevance. I say now 'little personal relevance' as a composer; of course, artistically I can have a different estimation of the works in an abstract sense, or a critical sense. But as far as my own creative activity has been concerned, all his theorizing has been of zero interest.

RT: So it's really the 'Artaud' period of Boulez that interests you?

BF: Oh yes; it's really what interests me in any composer's work. Unless you've got this absolutely intense identification of expression with the *possibility* of expression (the possibility only exists in realization, and the intensity of the explosive moment of realization), then it's a lost cause right from the beginning. I realize that this may be a very limiting and delimited view of art, and I'm quite willing to admit (and I have to, when I'm teaching my pupils and I have to try and enter into their world too) that there may be more 'laid-back' versions of expressive aesthetic effect. I hope I can come to terms with them on their *own* terms. Nevertheless, as far as I'm concerned, the 'too-much-ness' of expression which my work deliberately aims at *is* the basic presupposition of creative activity, and one has to live with one's own innate sensations, one's own convictions, without necessarily negating those of others.

RT: Among other things, it's a matter of deliberately setting out to create a labyrinth, rather than a one-way street...

BF: Well, I've been called a mannerist composer. I know it was intended as a form of insult at the time, no doubt a learned insult in the eyes of the critics concerned; but in fact if one examines the meaning of the word 'mannerist', I would have to say that most modern art, including people like James Joyce, is mannerist. That is, one works with a 'manner', a conscious stylistic ambitus: style becomes conscious, and not only is the style one uses conscious (in some parodistic work the choice of style is also very conscious), but the actual development of a style within itself, its future possibilities, are also realizable only by conscious reflection on what has already been achieved. And to that extent the labyrinthine is, for me, a very important concept. For instance, I'm very interested in the idea of *ingenio*, the idea of intellectual, playful constructivity - *homo ludens* - confronting head-on, with a massive crash, a great intensity of creative drive; that the creative drive can only find expression as fragment, as (if you like) fragmentary ciphers of this basic, initial explosion. So that's why, in some ways, many processes in my work might be perceived as being fragmentary and inconsequential, precisely because they only find expression after the fact, after the initial unity of expression and structure (which permits the expression) has been dissolved in a flare of energies.

Working methods

RT: In an interview with Joël Bons[1] you say something to the effect that, looking at your scores, you have the impression that you're very good at covering your own traces.

BF: Certainly. And I make no bones about this. The surface can remain the same while the techniques used to generate that surface change. In fact, that is one of the tenets on which my work is based; if it were not so, I would not have that possibility of creating polyvalent or multivalent levels of perception of one and the same image.

RT: Doesn't this put you in something like the situation of Borges's Pierre Menard,[2] rewriting *Don Quixote*? Admittedly the time-span is small, and let's say that you're Cervantes in both cases, but...

BF: Well, absolutely. If I take a triplet set of sixteenth-notes, it is very significant and very important whether this triplet has been generated by some now completed process, so that it has the status of a 'trace of evidence', as it were, of this process (in which case the process itself is the primary interest, and the trace is merely that which leads us to an examination of the processual), or whether this triplet is something predefined, something given as *material*. On the one hand it's transparent, on the other it is concretely available to us as evidence in a more direct sense; and by playing between these two extremes, always manipulating the directness of liaison between material presence and processual background (or the sensation of processual background), one is, as you say, working on both levels - one has the original achievement of the book as a cultural artefact, and one has its dematerialization into the conceptual activity of rewriting it.

RT: In relation to your recent work in particular, how do you work, basically? What comes first as the idea for a piece?

BF: I have to say it depends entirely on the piece. Usually I would say that the first sensation, the experience which begins to persuade me that I am actually going to write a piece, is very often a cross between a tactile, a visual, and an aural one. That is, I tend to perceive a mass, almost a tangible sculptural or sculpted mass, in some sort of imagined space, which is made up of these various elements - it might be a certain mass of undifferentiated instrumental colors, it might be a certain register, it might be a certain kind of transformation from one type or state to another, in some way congealed into one momentary experience. That can often be allowed to revolve in my mind for some considerable time - it might be a year or 18 months - before it clicks together with whatever else is buzzing around in my mind at the time. Sometimes the title of a work, for instance, comes very early, and many things are hung around that. Nevertheless, I would always say that I would find it difficult to distinguish between the sensibility of intellectual excitement, the feeling of the infinite radiatory potential of a certain idea, be it musical or otherwise, and the immediate sensibility offered by experiencing in my head (already formed, as it were) some sonorous image. I can't distinguish between these two. I think that those composers (or anyone else, for that matter) who attempt to place a limit in principle between the 'bodiliness' of intellectual activity and the 'abstractness' of bodily sensation are themselves guilty of the very sort of intellectual categorization of which they are accusing other people.

RT: Does that mean that for you composition often involves an element not just of creation but almost of recapturing? And that, just as you were saying earlier that if you forget your way, technically, through a piece, you have to reinvent the means of composing it, so even the first version might also be an attempt to 'reinvent' something which was conceptually 'buzzing around' in this plastic sort of way?

BF: Well, I'm not normally conscious of this: I don't believe music to be that passive. A piece creates itself; it isn't something that you 'draw from life' inside your head, so to speak. On the other hand, I can give you a counter-example, which may or may not be revealing about my work. During various periods of infertility, I have had tremendously vivid dreams. Now these dreams have taken two forms. One has been the imagination of sounds, more or less clearly defined; when I've woken up I've tried to notate them, and they've inevitably been rather banal and obvious, so we'll forget that. Nevertheless, I've also had a kind of dream which has tremendously encouraged me on many occasions. That is, I have found in front of me in this dream a score. Now this score is not by me - not by the 'me' looking at it, anyway (although there are several 'me's, of course, always). Now I open up these scores, and I can see notes, I can see constellations, I can see which instruments or voices are active at a given moment.

And I remember two particular occasions: there was one fantastic piece - it must, I suppose, have been a sort of perverse piano concerto - which reminded me of nothing so much as some sort of crazy Brazilian rain-forest: fruitfulness gone mad in all possible directions - straining towards the sun, or pushing down into the earth in all possible directions, to fill out the universe in whatever way possible. And I could really see rhythms, I could see pitches, I could see where instruments related to the piano in particular, and I was tremendously impressed... so I wasn't just seeing a vague impression, I was actually seeing fully written notes. The second example was of a piece I still have the project of writing one day - it already has a title - which was about a twelve-page score (perhaps less, perhaps eight or nine only), a very long, tall score, with narrow pages. And it was for large orchestra and large, multiple-voiced choir. All instruments and all voices were performing without a break of more than half a beat's length from beginning to end. Now what was fascinating about this piece was (a) the layering of different types of texture, and (b) the way that the predominantly *pianissimo* means of writing, in spite of everyone playing all the time, allowed for very clear structural distinctions between sections, contrasts between layers, and so on. So that I didn't need to resort to the crude device of stopping people performing in order to make these structural or textural distinctions between sections, but they came through the skilled use of the transformation, distension, compression, and the making clear or more diffuse, of the texture. That, in some ways, was even more impressive than the piano concerto, because it was so much more disciplined, but at the same time, so much more radical.

And I remember waking and being very frustrated on both these occasions at not being able to notate some of the things, because the act of taking a pen or pencil in your hand and trying to notate things already distances you from the experience, and the act of writing already dictates to you in a very strong and physical way what *it* wants to do, and not what the thing you are trying to recreate seems to be. So on the one hand I was rather distressed at not being able to do this; but on the other I was tremendously encouraged by the feeling that even at moments of intense... almost desperation, shall we say, at not being able to compose, one was creating these complete pieces inside oneself, which had a coherence and unity that was quite staggering. So that even if they were works that would never see the light of day, that were inaccessible to anyone else, it gave me a whole new perspective about what creativity is, about where creativity is located in the human spirit.

RT: Did these dreams ever recur, or were they unique phenomena?

BF: No, they never recurred. No.

RT: And so you would rush to recapture what you could, or would you just sit there and think about them?

BF: After the first experience of trying to write them down, and naturally destroying them even quicker, I decided merely to think about them. And looking at some of my later works, particularly things like **La terre est un homme**, there are passages in that - especially the dense tutti where everyone is playing madly for several bars - where there is a great deal of very shadowy and distant reflection of those scores.

RT: Can you give me a specific example of how a piece came about? Let's say the piano piece **Lemma-Icon-Epigram**: what was your work process, and what phases did the piece go through in terms of planning, and so forth?

BF: First of all, one has to say that the title of the piece is taken from the concept of the *emblema* - or *Denkbilder*, as Walter Benjamin terms them - of the 16th and 17th centuries. They consisted rather of the equivalent of our present-day crosswords for highly learned and literate gentlemen. They consisted of three parts: one was a title, of a rather obscure, surrealistic type, often in Latin, and often with arcane connotations. The second part was the verbal description of a possible picture - *icon* - with various symbolic parts, like the *conjunctio oppositorum*, the male and female, like the dragon emerging from the alchemical egg, like the sun, the moon, and so on, put into various permutative constellations. The third element was always a piece of verse called the *epigram*, in which - again for the learned consciousness - an attempt was made to relate the obscurity of the title to the intense symbolism of the image. So that you have three different dimensions of the same basic area of concern.

In this particular work, my interest revolved around two things, one of which was to make the process of treatment thematic or motivic, therefore replacing material repetition, or the quasi-motivic repetition of given elements. The piece has to start with some material, but it could have started with others; I simply wrote down a set of notes without thinking about them at all, and said, I will work with these. That's how the piece begins. And then there is a very strict system of inter-reference, where I can relate back to the initial material, or to one of the derivations of the derivations. Each of these derivations has between 1 and 13 different types of transformation attached to it, so that there is a very intense, almost cyclonic whirl of transformation, of reperspectivization, taking place - it's what you might call a 'mobile cubism'.

RT: Can I back-track a moment? Was your knowledge of the whole business of the *emblema* considerably previous to your writing of the piano piece, or did the knowledge of one suddenly lead almost automatically to the other?

BF: Well, let me start to answer this question by carrying on answering the previous one. The second thing I wanted to say in respect of my immediate concerns in writing that piece was something I mentioned when we were talking earlier: the question of possible explanations of musical materials via musical means. How can one have, as it were, a 'metamusical' explanation of an extant musical material in that material itself? How can one allow material to distance itself, such that one can see that material in two different ways simultaneously? This concern is something I've lived with for many years. Let us take, for instance, the example of Schoenberg's op. 23, the **Five Piano Pieces**. The first of those pieces begins with several bars of intense and, I think, stunningly beautiful three-part writing, which are almost complete in themselves. The moment he then starts moving off into variations of this, moving into more conventional accompanimental piano figurations, and so on, I feel it becomes repetition -irrelevant; in a way, I would have liked him to stop the piece there, at the end of that first tiny exposition.

It seems to me fundamentally wrong to reveal the basic essence of a work, and then multiply it. This is Boulez's idea, but not mine. My idea is to start with the multiplied mass, and gradually through various processes focus down to the given; it seems much more sensible to me, and much more conclusive, much more in keeping with the way the human mind works things out. So this was the basic motivation of this work.

I had first come across the idea of the *emblema* in 1976; it was much later that I realized how obsessed Walter Benjamin was with this entire business,[3] and how his Klee picture, *Angelus novus*, was of such great symbolic importance to him, both to his theories and to his person. So a lot of this had resonances later which were quite accidental, and external to the original idea. It was in Venice, I recall, while I was there for the Biennale. The Biennale still had money in those days, and I was invited for three weeks, as one of several young visiting composers, to live in almost the best hotels, three meals a day, and so forth. I didn't have a great deal to do except advise on the performance of my works, and be there, in the standard Italian fashion. I enjoyed this very much - it was one of the formative influences of my compositional career - and I spent this time consciously trying to compose a piano piece based on this idea, and couldn't. I tried very many approaches to it, many textures, and none of them worked. I then abandoned them - I still have these sketches somewhere, and maybe one day I'll use them, but perhaps I won't - and I left it to accumulate.

Over the years, the detritus of images and partial images associated with my alchemical and metaphysical studies, or Renaissance studies, began to accumulate round a core, and this core was, as I said, the idea of *Denkbilder*: pictures to help you think, or 'thinking pictures' - it's very ambiguous, of course. And I wanted to find a way, both of solving the problem I outlined a moment ago, and of treating time in an immediately palpable, pictorial fashion. So the first part of the piece is this whirlwind of the not-yet-become: the idea of processes, not material, forming the thematic content of the work. So apart from the quite banal initial material, which we don't even know is 'initial material', the whole thing is in a whirlwind of dissolution even before it has been created - very linear.

So this is the **Lemma**, the superscription. The linearity of the material - it's mainly two-part writing - is in some way a half-amused reference to this concept. The second part, the **Icon**, is the description of the possible picture put into actual pictorial form. I'm dealing here with the expansion and contraction of rhythmic and chordal cycles. There are only seven chordal identities, and this middle part is, as it were, the same thing seen from many perspectival standpoints. I have what I call a 'time-sun'. That is, I imagine a framework, a conceptual spatio-temporal framework within which these chords are then disposed on several levels, like objects. Then there is a sun passing over them; the shadows thrown by the sun (the speed at which the sun moves playing a great role

Ex. A: **Lemma-Icon-Epigram,** p. 1

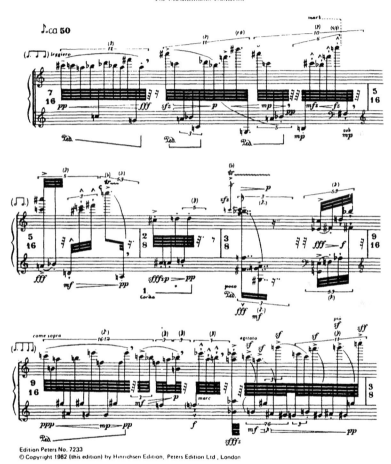

"Tout est hiéroglyphique" (Baudelaire)

Lemma-Icon-Epigram

For Massimiliano Damerini

Edition Peters No. 7233
© Copyright 1982 (this edition) by Hinrichsen Edition, Peters Edition Ltd , London

here, of course) are of different lengths, different intensities, impinging in different ways on different objects, themselves also moving upon the space defined by this frame. And the durations of these chords, the way the chords are vertically compressed or expanded at certain points, the type of inversion used, and so on, how many of these different types of treatment are superimposed, what the type of textural treatment of each of these chordal units is, all this is very strictly controlled by this unifying visual concept. So I'm very much relating - if only tangentially, and rather anecdotally - to the concept of visuality, of pictoriality, to the mysterious suggestive pictoriality of this mannerist *concetto*.

The third part is the **Epigram**. This is the attempt to unite these two elements that have appeared previously. It's a failure: I have to say this. But as we were saying earlier, before we started recording, Schoenberg's **Second String Quartet** is also a failure in this sense, and needs to be a failure, in my eyes, in order to be the historical success which it actually is, and which makes it, for me, a very important composition.

RT: But a failure in what sense? A failure as a piece of music when you hear it, or as the realization of a concept, or what?

BF: A failure to be a classical string quartet. And by failing to do this, it becomes something else. Now **Lemma-Icon-Epigram** is a failure in the sense that is does not find this *via media* of exegesis in the **Epigram** part. But that for me was also a very important learning experience, which put me onto quite different tracks of speculation that I think are bearing fruit now in this large-scale cycle, where I have, right at the beginning, with a great deal of care, laid out the space within which it is meaningful to look for musical problems.

RT: What 'went wrong' in the **Epigram**?

BF: Well, the idea of what was to happen in **Epigram**, was to move in exactly the opposite direction to Schoenberg in the first of the op.23 pieces - we were talking about this. One should start out with a diverse phenomenon, and move back towards the kernel of the substance, and this is what **Epigram** was trying to do. It was trying to move away from the seemingly discursive polyphony, the motivic polyphony of the work's opening (which in fact is nothing of the sort, but is a total dissolution and disembodiment of material-creating devices, raising technique to the level of thematicism, while the material falls to a demonstrative substratum). Instead, exactly the opposite is true; through the course of the piece, I have gradually concentrated material and structure on converging paths. So the idea was that in **Epigram** these two would come together in a much more motivically cogent fashion, such that the listener would feel, 'Aha, the great linear freedom of the first part and the tremendous verticalized icy rigor of the second part, both expressing in their own ways different approaches to time, but equally powerful, have in this final section found some sort of synthesis, moved down towards the essence of the matter.' And in fact at the end of the piece, we find that the very last three bars of the piece bring together the two complementary hexachords of what would have been basic twelve-tone material in a quite absurd manner: it reduces the whole thematic thing down to a basis.

One of the things that make **Epigram** both a failure and a strangely unexpected success for me is that I found that in trying to work it motivically, my compositional desires simply didn't interlock with what I was theoretically setting out to do. After all this research I had carried out over the space of about eight months in producing the piece, I felt that this sort of motivic writing was really not a desirable thing. And one reason why the **Epigram** turned out to be so short was that at a certain point the material itself *demanded* to be redisposed in schematically block-like entities. There is a convulsive 7/16 bar at the end of page 22, where so many lines of material are crossing that I decided I simply wasn't going to carry out the scheme I had set for myself, that it was pointless to take this sort of material any further. Because in a way it was a personal confirmation for me of my distrust of the motivic-cellular diversification principle. So from that point on, I start bringing back my chords as a sort of prison-bar structure, and between the manifestations of the chords themselves I bring in little fantasies which present the chords in more linear fashion. Then at a certain point I begin breaking up the chords into two hands, so that the two parts of the chord move asynchronously, right in the middle of the keyboard. And this, I think, builds up a tremendous power, because the hands are trying to disengage themselves from one another, and never quite make it, because they are pulled back in again. And for me, this last part of the piece demonstrates quite well both the ultimate creative absurdity of the thematic-motivic foundations I was trying to investigate, and also the power generated by the conflict between that desire and the things the actual material itself wanted.

RT: Wouldn't it almost have distressed you, in fact, if your original intentions *had* worked at the end? Wouldn't it have given the piece a sort of 'happy end' which might have been much more problematic than failing?

BF: It might have become very smug, I suspect. 'Here I am, and this is what it was all about.' And I would dislike that. Of course my music must, in a certain way, always remain open-ended. What fascinates me - and why I never really wrote aleatoric music or indeterminate music of any sort, even at the time when this was a rampant plague - was that I believe that you can only have meaningful open-endedness through an absolutely closed formal concept. A piece radiates out beyond its double bar; in a certain sense, a shadow piece starts in the mind immediately after the last double bar of the composition. This is something which we sacrifice if the piece itself has an open-ended formal conception. I believe very much that fragmentation, for instance, which is something I've thought a great deal about over the years, can only have a musical expressive significance to the extent that we can postulate at least possible alternative ideal completions that never were.

Ex. B: **Lemma-Icon-Epigram,** p. 22

Scores and their performances

RT: Could I move now to the question of performance? Given that it is almost innate in your compositions that the correlation between what is written and what is played will not be perfect, what, for you, are the essential criteria for a good performance of your work?

BF: I would say the establishment of audible criteria of meaningful inexactitude. That is, from work to work, from one section of a work to another section, from one performer to another, from one performance situation to another, the level of meaningful inexactitude is one indication, one hint of the way in which a work 'means'.

RT: So interpretation consists, to some extent, of different intelligent failures to reproduce a central text?

BF: I would say this was true, yes. Unfortunately the situation today is that the central text has no long-term text supporting it, in which it is embedded, and which tells us how to play it. Therefore it is our duty as composers to make the text, the visual aspect of the text and its musical structure, so self-referential in an enriching sense that the performer can find some way of plugging it into his own sensibilities - so that he is not trying simply to give a generally tasteful rendering of some set of noises, or whatever, but that these noises are, in a semantically specific sense, interrelated among themselves in such a way that the performer himself can attempt to take an attitude towards that relationship.

RT: Obviously, in the sheer technical difficulty of the pieces there is a certain in-built defense mechanism against uncommitted performers. Is even the notation itself, and its *mise-en-page*, a sort of 'protective commentary' (in Debussy's sense) against the dilettantish approach?

BF: Oh, certainly, because I've waited six years now to find a second performer for my bass clarinet solo piece, **Time and Motion Study I**, and it has been a tremendously enriching experience for me after such a long time listening to only one person play it, however well, to work with a second person on this piece,[1] to hear his attitudes both to it and the previous performer's interpretation, and to feel a quite different creative illumination of the piece, which is very much in keeping with my ideas about the possibility of interpretational diversity.

RT: Do you find that individual performers of your works are relatively uniform in their interpretations from one night to the next, or are there big discrepancies? There seems to be plenty of scope for the latter: given that one is always struggling for this unreachable object, the direction in which one is going to fall down might easily vary.

BF: Well, this is true, of course. But it isn't the falling down in itself

---

[1]The first performer of **Time and Motion Study I** was Harry Sparnaay, the second Armand Angster.

which is significant, it's the attitude one adopts to the necessity of falling down, or the inevitability of it. I would say first of all that there are many performers of my works who differ astoundingly from one another, that certain of my works, like **Unity Capsule** for instance, have types of performance which one might say are almost diametrically opposed, but which reveal nevertheless different aspects of the piece. I of course have my preferences regarding the more valid form, but that's just my preference - the pieces have divorced themselves from me now, except in a biographical sense. On the other hand it's certainly true that any given performer can, under different circumstances, produce a quite different performance, and there is always the danger that a performance will fail almost completely, no matter how many notes are achieved, if it lacks that intensity of awareness of the almost erotic relationship between manual movement, density of notation, and constant awareness of the knife-edge quality of the possibility of not achieving something, and so needing to compensate for it momentarily on another level - for instance, of looking momentarily at a quite different aspect of the piece in order to balance the failure out, one which one hadn't looked at before, or hadn't looked at for some time, or not in that way. This, under favorable circumstances, can produce performances of quite different quality, which nevertheless have very clear identity traits: it's very clearly the same piece, despite all the diversity of other aspects.

RT: Do you ever regret not having the performer's 'erotic-tactile' relationship to your own works? Because presumably you don't play...

BF: Not any more, but I *have* played. I've had many and various experiences in the performance of instruments. The instrument I've always played best, perhaps, until I didn't have time to play any more, was the flute, and I suppose that's reflected in my own music.

RT: So for example, were you ever able to play **Cassandra's Dream Song**?

BF: Yes (but not **Unity Capsule** because I never played a ring-keyed flute - so that's my get-out on that subject), certainly, because the techniques involved in **Cassandra's Dream Song** were created through experimentation with the flute. The first form of the piece, which was somewhat shorter than the final version, was created in that way, and it was then subjected to a more intensive compositional analysis *post priori*, and a recomposition, of course.

RT: What happens to your relationship to, for instance, **Cassandra's Dream Song**, when you actually try to play it?

BF: Well, I've never tried to *perform* the piece in a literal sense, although I could; at that time I could play all the individual sections - for some reason, I never bothered to put them all together. So I can't really answer that question directly. But even if I did answer it, perhaps it would be irrelevant from the point of view of any other performer, because I never really had a performer's mentality, although I quite enjoyed conducting at one stage, and did quite a lot of it in London: I gave the first performances of a number of my works that way.[¶] I was never really interested in that particular tactile relationship to the work; as I said before, tactility can be both emotional and bodily, and intellectual, and spiritual. I don't think that the activity of intellectual creativity is any less erotic than the direct, literal body contact with the material.

RT: What relationship *do* you have to your work once it is finished? What 'happens' to you when you hear your older pieces?

BF: Oh, I don't like listening to my music, not even new pieces. Generally they sound pretty much like I expected them to sound, so it's what I wanted, and that's it. There have been some performances which excited me tremendously, the odd few which I've always remembered. But on the whole, at the moment I've established that a piece has the effect that I expected it to have, then in a sense it's living its own life, I'm not connected to it any more. On the other hand, one of the implications of the progressive definition I gave earlier of style, as something always in progress within the corpus of one's own works, implies also that past works also belong to that same body, and must always be taken account of when moving on. The degree of semanticity inherent in any of the materials included in these works, the way of looking at the world which those works imply, must also be taken into account, either literally or in the back of one's mind, when one carries on. Otherwise one would be doing an injustice to the lived history of the elements one was working with at that moment.

RT: Does a work ever surprise you positively in the performance, in the sense that you find more in a piece than you thought you had put into it?

BF: No. Perhaps that just means that I'm not capable of perceiving more than I thought I'd put into it. Sometimes I've been surprised that certain *sounds* have worked better than I thought they would. On infrequent occasions I've been quite surprised and disappointed that certain sounds haven't worked at all as I expected they would, even though they were recognizably the same sounds. Maybe it's that I have miscalculated at that moment - not the banal

---

[¶]Notably **Prometheus, Firecycle Beta,** and **Transit.**

handwork thing of wrong balance, or anything like that (though that has occasionally happened), but far more that I haven't developed, or have over-estimated, for instance, the degree of semantic richness which a particular element has arrived at, so that the element is too transparently fragile at that moment to carry the weight of meaning I have assigned to it.

RT: Coming back to the score as such: it seems to me that when your scores are published, made available for anyone to buy, they have a significance which is different from that of the average, more obviously realizable score, in that what they mean to the listener is quite different to what they mean to the performer. They are something that the performer is going to attempt to realize; but for the listener they may almost be a confusing factor, representing all too clearly the gulf between what appears to have been conceived, and what appears to have been realized in a particular performance. Is it a problem for you, in that sense, that listeners also buy and read through your scores?

BF: Not at all; quite the opposite! I would say that it simply underlines my general point of view that a work of music is not simply sound, but the sound itself is a cipher for something else which some people call expression, but which I, of course, would prefer to differentiate a lot further, and in a lot of directions. A score as, let's say, a visual representation of a possible sound - that's just one aspect of what a score is. A score is also an entire cultural artefact with an aura of spiritual resonance which is completely its own, in spite of its being related to the sonorous experience of the work in one of its other manifestations. A work takes on these kaleidoscopic manifestations at different times, depending on what aspect of it one is examining, but the totality is far more than most people assume it to be. And therefore I think that the score being one thing and the piece being another is a complete absurdity.

RT: Your scores are also, perhaps, a certain protection against over-simplified hearing. For example, when I was sitting here the other evening listening to **Carceri d'Invenzione I**, I was surprised by how transparent the piece sounded. Then, going back and listening with the score, and in stereo instead of mono, I had quite the reverse experience, and I suddenly became aware of how much I *hadn't* heard, not so much because maybe it wasn't audible, but perhaps because I had actually eliminated so much in order to arrive at that, for me, satisfying notion of transparency.

BF: Don't you find that interesting, though? The score can, as you say, be a certain defense reaction against over-simplified listening. It can, however, also be a sort of validation of the immediate quality of the sounds, strangely enough. I've often thought that one of the main tasks a piece has to accomplish, over and beyond its large-scale ambitions, is to persuade a listener to suspend disbelief for the duration of the work; not to sit there passively, like some present-day ideologists would pretend, but to enter into the world of that piece by dissolving his own cultural barriers against it. Now unless a work can achieve this, then no matter what its complexities or its virtues, of course it doesn't succeed with that particular listener. Therefore it is important that the initial sounds of a piece will give the listener that sense of aura, that sense of magnetism, that sense of presence, indefinable in another way, which only a particular sort of aural sensation can achieve. And therefore the beginnings of most of my works have that... or I try to make them have a very clear image. This clarity of image is not always maintained subsequently, because one doesn't need to keep hitting the listener on the head with this sort of demand. But I do think that a work, no matter what its qualities may otherwise be, will fail unless this is accomplished. Therefore, the score can act as an antidote to this, and, in a sense, what you were seeing as a problem a moment ago is from my point of view a decided advantage - one sort of listening, or the one sort of perception of a work can then be balanced out by the other, and a much more rounded picture emerges.

A miscellany of works

RT: The title **Funérailles**, apart from its obvious funereal connotations, also invokes Liszt.

BF: Well, yes, I've had this certain 'thing' with Liszt. I don't know why - I'm not particularly fond of his music. But I once considered calling a piece **Les préludes**, and at the moment I'm working on a series of songs called **Etudes transcendantales** (as a main title, but with a different subtitle[1]).

Why **Funérailles**? I was using the word less in its funereal significance than in terms of *any* form of protracted and rather alienating ritual. One of the things I was dealing with in this piece was myself looking at myself, looking at myself composing - a sort of objectivization of a subjective reaction. And I often find, when taking part in any ritual (but especially large-scale public ones), that one stands there, basically not taking part in the ritual, but looking at oneself, at one's bodily presence; and that seems to me to be an exact parallel. In the score I produce this story of a Martian landing on top of a large hill and looking down at a parade ground, watching these creatures wandering backwards and forwards in various patterns, and wondering precisely what he would feel about it all. And having felt equally alienated on occasions, having been 'reconstructed' as a partaker in some of these rituals, on whatever level,

---

[1]**Intermedio II.**

and being in some sense not oneself, and yet more oneself because of being more aware of oneself not being oneself: this was exactly analogous to the situation of both mystery and immense subjective intensity of investigation which this piece was meant to invoke.

RT: Does that mean that in some ways it's an (uncharacteristically) autobiographical work?

BF: Oh no, the piece isn't at all autobiographical, because it's not the autobiographical, extant, flesh-and-blood me, with his experiences, that is being investigated. It is simply the artist making artistic decisions, or judging already-made artistic decisions from a new artistic standpoint, at the moment of recomposition. I'm involved with the *raison d'être* of the creative act, rather than the person doing the creating. It just happened to be me doing it, but the same process could have been carried out by somebody else, with different but equally exemplary results.

RT: On the whole, your titles have very precise connotations. Yet occasionally you come up with something relatively abstract like the **Second String Quartet**. Did you ever think of calling it something else, or is there a particular intention here in using a purely formal, non-allusive title?

BF: I never thought of calling it anything else, and I'm going to write a third quartet in a couple of years - it has already been booked by the Ardittis - which will also be called just, quite banally, **Third String Quartet**. I've always been fascinated by the string quartet medium, as being one of the few genres in music history whose content is related to a specific instrumentation. What is appropriate to a string quartet in terms of development of types of argument, intensity, and so on, is traditionally quite different from that in, for instance, a string trio or a piano trio, whose content has always been much more problematic. If we examine the genre of the string trio we find the approaches to it range from the divertimento-like, insubstantial, right through to the totally autobiographical, cutting quality of the Schoenberg, for example. So there is a certain logic in invoking certain types of intensity by restricting oneself to the rather abstract nomenclature of 'String Quartet', which wouldn't apply in calling a piece 'String Trio'.

RT: Would you now retrospectively prefer your **Sonatas** to be called your First Quartet?

BF: Well, to be truthful, they are already my second quartet; there's a string quartet which dates from 1963 which has never seen the public light of day, and probably never will.[1] No, the title **Sonatas** refers of course to the Purcell connection, which many people see as being much stronger than it actually is. In fact, I like the Fantasias...

RT: 'Fantasias' might have been the more appropriate title...

BF: Yes...without being intensely attracted to anything else he wrote. And they were very much in the old style, so that his more modern, advanced style is not one that had any particularly great relevance for me. But nevertheless, to call my pieces 'Sonatas' did at least distance them from the argumentative tradition of the classical string quartet, because my idea in those pieces was to make the *intensity* of the single moment, *a la* Webern, which can be the justification of that moment, in terms of our awareness, expand itself over an extremely long duration, while deconstructing itself back into formal cogency. Therefore to call it a string quartet in the normal sense would have been to falsify the issue, because a string quartet normally presupposes a concept of argumentation, in which the validity or not of the types of strategies used in the arguments are not being placed in question: they're already given.

RT: I remember seeing somewhere that you now criticize the **Sonatas for String Quartet** on the grounds that they consist too much of a structure without content.

BF: I don't think I used those words; I would probably have used the word 'carapace'. Let's put it this way: I think I said that all works contain immediate expression (or message presentation), and skeleton. And in the works I have been writing recently, starting perhaps with the **Second String Quartet**, the main object of the music has no longer been to incorporate or redefine experiences gained from extra-musical sources, for example (which still interest me, but I don't try to contain them specifically, since I feel that in that respect I've already done, more or less successfully, what I wanted to do), but far more, to get into the real interstices of linguistic formulability. What is the space in which a work really exists? There is a vacuum that exists between the surface presentation - now that's what I call the carapace of the **Second String Quartet** - and the subsurface generative structures. Now the extent to which these two things are separated allows the surface material to take on different degrees of auratic[4] presence. In the **Sonatas**, the surface *is* the skeleton. That is, it's evident that the processes which are present in the **Sonatas** are presented to us as expressive means, whereas in the **Second String Quartet** the surface is very much

---

[1]In fact, the 4th movement was performed by the Arditti Quartet at Royaumont in 1992.

the sediment of those already disappeared processes which have leadenly disappeared below the surface, like anchors, or like half-deflated balloons beneath
the stratosphere: they're swimming at different levels, and different distances
from this surface, so that the degree of sonorous causality is different for each
type of activity. It allows us, as it were, to mentally distance ourselves, and forces
us to refocus; it gives a sort of analogy (though not in a direct sense) to innate,
inbuilt tonal prejudices, so to speak, that allow us to relativize events in terms
of a larger frame. Every work produces a different relationship here, of course,
so one can't talk about a generalized process. But from work to work, over a
long period of time, with the constant redevelopment and redefinition of the
means under the frame, I have great hopes that - at least within the scope of
my work - some sort of redefinition of this kind can come about.

RT: I suppose the **Sonatas**, and maybe the **Sonata for Two Pianos**, were
the first works of yours to attract considerable attention. Is this where the 'real
Ferneyhough' starts? Listening retrospectively, is there a specific piece which
you regard as having been *the* step forward?

BF: No, because there have always been steps back, or at least recuperative steps, in place of the 'great advance'. I've always moved in a pendulum-
like way, from the most adventurous and investigatorial approach back to a
middle-of-the-road stance, in order to recontextualize the elements I have been
working with.

RT: Were the big steps forward always the works for large forces?

BF: No, not always. The **Sonatas**, of course, were very important. If you
look at the other works which I wrote at that time, you will see the tremendous
gap that exists between even the **Sonata for 2 Pianos** and the **Sonatas for String
Quartet**. The **Sonatas for String Quartet** were written at an incredibly crisis-
ridden period of my life, and I think that both this emotional crisis and, of course,
my relative youth at the time are very evident in the facture of the work. So it's
a work that remains very embedded in my consciousness in some ways, and
that's why I didn't write a second quartet for many years: it was necessary for
me to overcome that piece.
Otherwise, it's easier for me to tell you which are the significant ends
of things, rather than the beginnings. The ends of cycles are always important,
like **Firecycle Beta**, for example, which has never been performed in Britain, or
Epicycle, which also hasn't. One can see the continuity of these works from the
Sonatas; they were always magnified versions of those, moving in slightly different directions, and with slightly different concerns. So I would say I could
define **Firecycle** as being the end of a period, and I could define **La terre est un**

homme as being the end of a period, rather than saying what were the decisive steps forward. I suppose you could say that the works that come after that were steps forward, but of course forward only in a linear sense, and because of course one always tries to work on the highest level available to one at any given moment.

RT: If you've arrived at the end of a cycle, do you find yourself saying, in effect, 'God, what do I do next'?

BF: No, except that in one case, where I didn't write anything for a long time, this was really true. After writing **Firecycle Beta**, not only was I unable, and also, ultimately, unwilling to write **Firecycle Alpha** and **Gamma** (so that the work remained a torso), but I also felt that this type of Utopian vision of what a musical language was or ought to be was essentially played out. It had been very useful for the production of a certain number of works, which even today I still think have their points, and which I wouldn't reject by any means, but it didn't provide me with any fruitful humus to carry on. Thus there was this period where I had to find some new motivation for composing, and finally this motivation (in the **Time and Motion Study** series) was the total integration of all those things which had interested me as an intellectual human being, shall we say - the various philosophies, the ideas of poetics, the basic ways of looking at the world, the various disciplines of self-development, and so on, through which one approaches certain states of being in the Western tradition.

RT: Can you say something about the forthcoming cycle, and the title: **Carceri d'Invenzione**?

BF: Well, the most obvious reference is, of course, to the etchings-cycle of architectural fantasies by the Roman architect-artist Piranesi. What interested me most about these pictures is that they are multi-perspectival. Although, on the surface, they look to be rather fantastically realistic, they actually generate lines of force, or energies, which are not commensurate with one another on a realistic level. And these grating, scraping contradictions force us to reconstruct not just the fictional space of the picture, but actually to regard the edge of the page, not as a limit to the invention but as the point at which these unfinished perspectival energies really emanate out into the world, and force us to reperspectivize the world of everyday existence which confronts us beyond the limits of the work.

This is exactly what I try to do in music. The work itself is meant to create the scraping, raw edges, the frictions and lines of force which project themselves, labyrinth-like, out beyond the limits of the actual duration of the work, to infect or color our perspectives of the way in which the world is perceived.

So this was one straight-forward analogy. The other aspect of the title - **Carceri,** of course, means 'dungeons' or 'prisons' - is that I believe that constriction lies at the basis of all artistic creativity: if the artist isn't faced with a certain limited situation, he usually doesn't create.

I was working with one particular constriction, which was the concept of repetition. The beginning of **Carceri d'Invenzione I** makes it very clear that I start the same material or similar material several times, and continue it differently, for different lengths each time. There are things like the repetition in each instrument of phases of different length: literal or partial repetition, in which the beginnings and ends, or certain segments from the middle of these repetitions are chopped out each time round. So the cycle for each instrument is getting shorter and shorter, but different parts of it are missing each time; for each instrument, there is a different strategy of elimination. So the kaleidoscopic totality is continually changing, and the repetition is not immediately apparent as such: it has already been sinking a little bit below the surface. For instance, I can have literal repetitions of technique, allied to totally different materials; or I can use the same material, differentiated in a variety of ways, and varying combinations of these in different layers.

Secondly, the 'dungeon-like' nature of the piece exists both in the horizontal and in the vertical dimension. Horizontally because differing layers, while taking note of one another, and utilizing similar materials on occasions, often follow different types of logic, shall we say, to arrive at different points; they define themselves in different ways, having differing type of hierarchical ordering, the one with another, at different points in the piece. Vertically, I have adopted various techniques, which it would take too long to describe here, in which the length of space defined by a bar allows a certain density of material to be constricted or expanded, so that the same material may occur in bars of different lengths, correspondingly faster or slower. Alternatively, only a certain proportion of the material may occur in a bar of a different length, or the material of three previous bars may be contracted into one new bar of perhaps even shorter length than the original bars, so that the material may be much slower or much faster; it's a kind of proportional canonic technique, relating to the material contained in one bar, rather than entire strings of material. That's one aspect of the verticalization. The second aspect is the new type of metric system I have developed, which includes beats of irrational lengths in relation to the basic tempo of the piece. So you find strange things like the whole ensemble jerking immediately into a perceptibly different rapidity; there's a click, a trigger at the beginning of each bar that coincides with this change of tempo. One hears this best of all in the first piece of the series, **Superscriptio** for solo piccolo, where it's very schematically employed.

So both at the level of analogy - the relationship to the fantastical imagination and the associated perspectival energies related to Baroque imaginative architectural notions, as exemplified by Piranesi, but also by other people - and also in the literal way that materials are disposed in the vertical and horizontal dimensions, the way I delimit the choices I have of the types of technique I use, or the types of material to which the techniques are applied at different times: both these aspects are implied in the title. That is, 'Dungeons of Invention'; without these limitations, the invention would be of a quite different sort, or might not be at all.

Working with microtones

RT: Microtones seem to be playing an increasingly important role in your recent work.

BF: Well, *all* works involve microtones in some sense, for me. But the question of microtones, it is true, is very important to me at the present time. I am using microtones very much in a systematic fashion; that is, the simultaneity of pitch materials which I am employing in most of the works of this seven-work cycle **Carceri d'Invenzione** allows for the gradual introduction or elimination of microtonal materials. This is very important harmonically. In previous works, certainly in the first version of **Funérailles**, for instance, many of the microtonal inflections are indeed just that: inflections. They were like a sort of glissando or exaggerated vibrato - they might be something which points up the limits of one particular functional entity.

RT: They're almost articulation types, in a sense.

BF: They're articulation types, yes, that's true.

RT: So where does the situation begin to swing around? And did it swing around decisively, or is it that in the course of time your attitude to microtonal elements has gradually become more systematic, more integrated?

BF: I would say it has become more integrated, though even in **Epicycle**, in 1968, if you look at the one page which is without meter,[1] which is full of pauses to be held for a certain length of time, the harmony on that page (which I think is quite successful, well balanced) is built entirely of pre-calculated, microtonal chords. So I would say it's a question of degree rather than absolutes.

RT: If you use microtones in an integrated way, does this mean that you think their perceptible qualities are just as great as those of tempered intervals?

---

[1]Page 57 of the published score.

Ex. C: **Epicycle,** p. 57

*) Length of beats at the discretion of the conductor, minimum of 5" per semibreve

Do you expect the interval of one-and-a-quarter tones to be registered by the listener just as precisely as a semitone or a tritone?

BF: Well, using the term 'registered precisely' already implies a certain grammaticality of all intervals and their perceptibility - that one assigns functions to them in some way. I would say that there is a certain quality to a whole-tone plus quarter-tone which is perceptible even with a certain degree of flexibility as to exactitude. I don't regard these things as functional, perceptible units. I regard them as areas of sensation, the same as I would with a major 3rd; if a major 3rd is slightly out of tune, it still has the quality of a major third.

RT: Do you think the ear has the same capacity under current circumstances to 'correct' a slightly false microtone in the way it obviously 'corrects' the slightly deviant major 3rd?

BF: It depends on the context, I would say. I mean, you say one corrects a major 3rd automatically, but the question is, to what purpose the major 3rd is there, in what context it finds itself, with what other intervals. I'm thinking now of the strange beginning of one of the movements of **Le marteau sans maître**,[5] where the guitar plays a minor 3rd that seems totally alien under those circumstances, which seems either a great stroke of genius, or a grave error on the part of the composer. I've never been quite sure which.

RT: I know the opening you mean: it sounds very odd...

BF: Does one there, or would one, assuming the note was slightly out of tune, correct it in the sense which you imply? I beg leave to doubt it; at least, it's an arguable point. And I suppose that everyone's perception is different - it depends on what you've heard immediately before, it depends on what your expectations are, and so on. Therefore I would say again with microtones, and the perception of the individual quality of certain types of microtonal interval, that it depends on the consistency with which you use them: how closely the last example of the same interval occurs to the one you're now listening to, on the type of texture, the type of motivic or non-motivic texture within which the interval is embedded. How isolated is it, for instance: was the last example of the same interval or a similar interval identifiably in the same instrumental color? All these things play a tremendous role, and one plays with all these things when composing. I don't believe any composer works just with intervals. If he does, there's something gravely lacking in his sensibility. One works with total contexts, one places intervals as one component into an organic unit, and the same with microtonal intervals.

RT: Is there a certain element, then, of Lewis Carroll's 'Take care of the sense, and the sounds will take care of themselves'?

BF: Well, you know there is, but we mustn't take it to ridiculous extremes. I would say that sound is never just sound. Sound is always the reflection of context, of contour. If we abstract any one of our sensations from a context, then that sensation takes on a very strange quality. Like if you wake up in the middle of the night; we don't know where we are, we see a strange, pale square in front of us. Is that square one inch in front of our eyes, or is it five feet away? Is it an opening, or an illuminated surface? And until we've worked this out - that it is actually an open door leading out into a moonlit area - we have gone through all sorts of permutations in our minds. The perception of a work of music, for me, is very much allied to this contextualization of sensation, because the sensation as such is almost never abstract, so that even this strange experience of seeing this seemingly abstract space has already been conditioned by our previous expectations; in making this perception, the mind has already very rapidly scanned previous possible experiences of this type.

Style, gesture, and figure

RT: Can we come back to the question of style, and particularly your views on the relationship of gesture and figure?

BF: I would say there are two things wrong with much contemporary style. Those who fulminate most readily against serial techniques are exactly those who fall into the same dilemma. Their argument against parametric thinking, if I may put it in that general way, is that serial techniques generate isolated, contextless monads via the accidental coming-together of streams of innately independently generated parametric specifications; and that these single monads, perceptually, could not enter into meaningful relationships with their surroundings other than in a banal and superficial, quasi-expressionist fashion. But on the other hand, it seems to me that those composers who now adopt what I call the ideology of the 'transparency to expression of the single gesture' fall into exactly the same monadic trap.

RT: So Rihm, for example...

BF: As we heard yesterday evening.[6] Now I'm putting words into these people's mouths, and perhaps they could indeed confute me by saying, 'That's not what we meant at all.' But listening to their music and reading their writings, it seems to be the case that for them a gesture, belonging to whatever preconceived repertoire, has a semantic significance, a certain constant semantic significance, relating to the sort of emotion we are meant to recognize it as representing.

RT: It's an *Affektenlehre*.

BF: Yes. Now it seems to me that a composer sitting and looking inside himself, and writing down a gesture, is attempting as it were to draw that gesture, that emotion which he observes in himself, in terms of musical notation. Therefore, logically, the more this gesture is in itself an iconic representation of the emotion, and is therefore self-sufficient - either it represents this thing or it doesn't - the more it represents it, the more it is its own justification, via this representational connection, the less contact it needs, structurally speaking, with any other gestures placed in the same context. Because either a gesture is iconic or it's not. And the more it aims towards representing something other than itself (by being, as I said, transparent to emotive significance) the less it needs any kind of relativizing contextuality, in terms of a general language, other than just the basic vocables, shall we say.

RT: So we're back at what Boulez once said about Messiaen: that he doesn't compose, he juxtaposes.

BF: Yes, and we're back at the stage where the only form-building means available seems to be either the banal contrast principle, or some kind of chain principle, putting things together in some sort of more-or-less interesting order whereby very often the events could be changed round without a great deal of interference to the general emotional patterning. Now it seems to me that the only consequence of that for young composers today is that one sees everywhere a sort of new conservatism, in which they are reading in the textbooks about examples of rondo form and passacaglia form, they're writing symphonies again. This sort of neoconservatism seems a logical consequence of this monadic contextlessness of the single affective gesture. They are forced to impose an arbitrary, extraneous, and very academic formal structure upon these isolated instances of what may or may not be authentic expression.

RT: In these pieces, it seems to me, the gesture and the form appear meaningful to an audience only in so far as they're known in advance. And to that extent, it's a little like throwing out known and appreciated lumps of cheese to groups of Pavlovian rats.

BF: Yes. And the affective gestures are just as isolated as the single sonic units of a serial work would be, except of course they have the slight advantage of relating already to vocabularies of previous periods, which, however, have themselves become anaemic, simply by creating general categories of ex-pression. We say, 'Aha, that's meant to be a dramatic, despairing gesture', or whatever. We typify this particular, no doubt deeply felt, structure as being sim-ply a token of that generalized type. And that being so, we could replace it with almost any other example of the same type, and still retain approximately the same amount of information.

RT: It's almost like a *Young Werther* situation; the succession and inten-sity of the emotions are far more important than there being any good cause for any of them, or than any particular emotion.

BF: Yes, this is true. And one of the things that disturbs me most, as I understand it, particularly in Germany, is the recent *rapprochement* between the new Romantics and the sociocritical school, the *musica negativa* of Lachenmann and others - the fact that each school seems to recognize its own negative im-age in the other.

RT: That really surprises me.

BF: Well, it doesn't surprise me, because they both have similar views of what we might call 'History' with a capital 'H'. Each of them refers - Rihm positively, Lachenmann negatively - to a posited totality of history. One draws his musical nourishment from it; the other generates semantic significance by constantly negating it in every moment of a work. But of course, this 'totality of history' is itself a fiction, and I would have thought that it's impossible, in any given work, to sit facing this gigantic, monolithic totality, and produce anything viable as a particular work. It's like wanting to write, totally immersed in history but sitting outside it. If it were true that they *were* regarding the totality of music history in each work, and realizing it in one way or another, then of course each work would just become some sort of *Schmarotzer* ['parasite'].

RT: Perhaps the point at issue is really that, whether positively or nega-tively, the definition of music history that they both accept is simply that of the average concert-goer.

BF: Well, that of the average German concert-goer, in fact. Well, this is what I was saying: that just because you put a capital 'H' on the false totality of musical history, this doesn't make it some sort of overall, viewable, and con-sumable, or appreciable, usable object. And I think that if these people - as I believe Lachenmann is beginning to do - are prepared to concentrate on par-ticular manifestations of historical subjectivity, then no doubt one can do something with it. But to call late-17th-century to early-20th-century music - German music - 'music history' seems to me to be rather... questionable.

One of things I'm trying to do is to distinguish between the gesture as such, which in itself is an objective, material-bound presence - we can examine its delineations, we can appreciate it as a total 'vocable' on whatever level (which is why overall style is of no great importance to me - one can write in perfect 5ths or whatever: that's not the question), and the figural aspect of a gesture[1] ('figurality' being itself a subcategory of gesture). The thing which distinguishes the figural way of constructing or observing a gesture from the 'gestural' part of the gesture is that one is attempting to realize the totality of the gesture in terms of its possible deconstruction into parametric tendencies. That is, no longer does one attempt to create a gesture via the automatic coming together of abstract parametric units or quantities, nor does one try to build a gesture as an affective quality, and place these totalities against one another. One attempts to so construct gestures that the parametric qualities of which they are composed are released into the world of the music, as it were, into the future, the future potential of the music, at the moment in which the gesture presents itself. So at the moment in which the gesture actually dissolves into the future, certain parametric elements, which owe their original *raison d'être* to having been embedded in this gesture (and therefore are no longer isolated quanta, floating, free-ranging nothings, 'quarks' or whatever), are released in order to be able to conflate in different ways, or coincide to produce new gestural units. So for me, the ideal situation is one in which neither the abstract gesture in itself, nor the use of parametric thinking to generate gestures, but the gesturally justified, free-ranging employment of parametric information is the center of all compositional concern.

RT: So the figural content of a gesture is precisely the thing that will allow that gesture to turn into something else?

BF: Well, it's the thing which is justified, first of all, by its particular contextualization, its particular anchoring in a gestural context. But at the same time the context, the whole tenor of the argument of the work, must be such that some of these particular favored parametric elements at any moment, however produced, must already be attempting to subvert and dissolve the gesture to which they belong. They must be at least as powerful as the gesture, and this seems to me to be the only way to jump the gestural barrier from one monadic unit, one experiential unit to another: by certain elements of that gesture dissolving themselves out of the general context, and having enough individual energy to flow either immediately or at a somewhat later time into connection with other parametric layers to form new gestural units.

---

[1]cf. *Form - Figure - Style* (this volume, p. 21) and *Il Tempo della Figura* (p. 33).

RT: To what extent do you think the notion of gesture is ineradicably linked with certain inherited emotional responses?

BF: Absolutely, which is why I think it's rather unfruitful for us to argue about the relevance of this or that gestural type. On the whole I espouse, with certain reservations, the notion of pluralism, and the *ideal*, also, of pluralism in contemporary stylistic thinking. I would not try to impose what some people seem to be desiring most ardently: some sort of generalized, so-called 'common musical language'. I think this would be an appalling and arbitrary concept. I have seen in the case of some so-called 'schools' which have been built in the past few years that this does indeed lead to a certain communality of style, but only on the most primitive of levels. The communality of style serves to eliminate many of those differential aspects which might have produced richness and a possible individual creative urge for each individual composer. It seems to me that plurality of style, or the concept of pluralism in style, is in no way contradictory to the sort of principle to which I hold firm. And it seems to me that only by accepting surface gestural differentiation - pluralism - can one hope to eliminate most of these rather unfruitful arguments about common language and comprehensibility.

RT: Coming back to gesture in your own work, it seems to me that it is obviously necessary for you, in a work like **Carceri d'Invenzione I**, to begin with something that has enormous developmental potential...

BF: Absolutely...

RT: ...but is also very much a 'gesture' as such - that is to say, a gesture in the sense of being an extremely clearly focussed musical idea, which draws attention to the piece. To lay out a set of propositions, one must be concerned with gestures.

BF: This is true: I think there's no point in presenting something you intend to use in a tentative way. If it's going to be used as a basis for enhanced figural deployment of parametric information, you can't present something which itself is too weak to provide the parameters with some conflict. If they're going to escape, they've got to generate enough energy to escape the confining gravitational walls of the gesture itself, and break out in differing directions. If the gesture itself is too weak to contain them to a significant degree, then their escape of the gesture, their expansion into conceptual space, will not itself seem significant.

RT: When you mark the opening section of **Carceri I** 'brilliant and vulgar', that in a sense must also relate back to an *Affektenlehre*: there must be in your mind the notion that this kind of gesture is innately both 'brilliant' and 'vulgar', and will be received by other people as such - not because they'll say, 'Ah, that's brilliant and vulgar', but in the more sublimated way that one normally hears music.

BF: In fact it was described in one review, I recall, as 'crass'.

RT: Well, actually I don't even find it particularly vulgar (or maybe I just like that kind of vulgarity); it's very strident, very hard-edged, and it's also very much a 'listen-to-me!' gesture, I think.

BF: Well, also of course for subcutaneous reasons. It being the piece that follows **Superscriptio** in the same cycle, I had to use the piccolo as the connecting element.[¶] At the same time I had to show, again emblematically, the idea of extremes, by taking the relatively low extreme of the trombone, and the high extreme of the piccolo, playing the basic interval which runs through all the pieces in varying ways - the tritone (and the diminished 7th chord). Using the same playing technique, the fluttertongue at the dynamic extreme (very loud) was an attempt, as it were, to hold the piece together, while creating the feeling that the middle, the empty middle, was a tremendously powerful force wanting to push these two extremes right out of the piece altogether. So already I was trying to develop a tremendous amount of energy, which immediately, via the parametric levels, attempting to escape from both the rigid constriction and the tremendous force simultaneously, allowed the piece to explode into its own future.

So this opening gesture was not just a dramatic gesture to get people's attention, although of course the hortatory function cannot be entirely discounted! - it *is* a bit like banging a bass drum. Nevertheless it did have a very important figural function for me. To be even more banally concrete, the fluttertongue is one of the basic figural devices which is employed a great deal in that particular material; the piccolo, trombone and piano are important constants in defining that material at times when it has been superimposed with other materials. And the emptiness of that middle space itself, via its proper negative, also becomes parametrically important in two ways. That is, when the other wind instruments enter, they come in exactly that area which the piccolo and trombone did not fill, with suave and flowing material. On the other hand, whereas the piccolo and trombone remain largely at the extremes, the piano, which is first of all at the extremes with the trombone and piccolo, gradually

---

[¶]For a somewhat different view, see p. 413; the present version is, however, closer to the time of composition.

becomes denser and denser in its writing. Instead of just basic two-part writing it becomes very dense: five- or six-part chords moving towards the center of the keyboard, so that it too comes to fill that empty space. And this has a reflection much further forward in the piece: at the end of the first major part, with the piano solo and the brass 'bangs' with the drums, where the piano does exactly the same thing again; moving from a very wide distribution of pitches, it comes - exactly like the end of **Lemma-Icon-Epigram** - to this interlocked-hands cluster. So the whole thing is being 'imprisoned' more and more by these forces. If I were just doing it as a dramatic gesture, I believe that these forces would seem very implausible as entities, whereas by simultaneously *figurally* interpreting certain gestural units on several levels, through temporal and perceptual space, into the future, I believe I authenticate and validate these particular dramatic gestural devices as - what shall we say? - coherent definitions of lines of force.

RT: Again, let's take the opening of **Lemma-Icon-Epigram**. From your point of view it may be a sort of 'anti-material', but it's still very much a gesture, in the sense that one hears this rapid sequence of notes, rather high up, and one's immediate response is, 'What *is* this?'. And before one has had time to work out exactly what it is - it's a sort of 'tangled' material, in a way - just as you're trying to disentangle it, it retangles itself. It may be 'neutral', in a certain way, but nevertheless there is a certain gestural content in that, I would say - as there needs to be to draw one's attention.

BF: Sure! Yes, obviously the gestural content of the beginning was conscious for me, although I started off with a very abstract series of pitches. The moment I had decided on octave registers for the pitches, and decided that I would keep the repeated pitches that turned up, there was a great deal of gesturality involved. Nevertheless, the figurational aspect of that initial material was less significant in the very first gestural appearance than in the second that immediately follows, because there we are already showing possible parametric expansional techniques, but at the same time, we are demonstrating the actual construction of the original. So at the same time as freeing itself from this space, it is reminding us what the original space was.

RT: Precisely by omitting it.

BF: And that's what I mean by parametric lines of force: tendential lines of force, which are flowing in various directions all the time, and which validate individual gestures in respect of their predecessors or successors.

What I insist on is this: that whatever stylistic exterior one employs for one's music, the interior concept needs to be defined diachronically: that is, not in terms of your relationship to a large-scale history (although that has to be thought through too), but through the way the paths, particular elements, and vocables in one's personal musical environment develop, either within one piece (in which case you have to organize it very demonstratively by deconstructing the piece within itself, and by presenting its elements to us as part of the development process), or by allowing these things to expand from piece to piece in one's own *oeuvre*, to enrich one another, and to take up new combinations. And this can only be done by parametric expansion, as opposed to gestural relationship; and the gesture then is, in a sense, subsumed to the lines of force which are demonstrated by the new combinatorial potentials of the parametric subcomponents themselves. And it seems, therefore, that whatever style one writes in, one needs to have this continuity of diachronic consciousness, which one attributes to, and from which grow, all the auto-history of generation of each of the vocables we employ. We have to validate them in personal historical terms, our own personal historical terms, and those of the vocables themselves. And I think this is impossible in styles which in themselves employ large percentages of linguistic discrepancy.

Endnotes

1. *"Interview with Joël Bons" (this volume, p. 217).*

2. *J. L. Borges, "Pierre Menard, Author of the Quixote", in* Labyrinths, *translated by D. Yates and J. Irby, Penguin, Harmondsworth 1981, pp. 62-71.*

3. *W. Benjamin, "Theses on the Philosophy of History", in* Illuminations, *translated by H. Zohn, Fontana, London 1973, p. 259.*

4. *cf. Walter Benjamin's use of the term 'aura' in "The Work of Art in the Age of Mechanical Reproduction", op. cit., pp. 219-53. For example, 'We define the aura [of natural objects] as the unique phenomenon of a distance, however close it may be.' (p. 224)*

5. *The reference is to the opening of the fourth movement of Boulez's work: Commentaire II de "Bourreaux de solitude".*

6. *Wolfgang Rihm's* **Ohne Titel: '5. Streichquartett'** *was given its première in Brussels on 9 December 1983.*

CARCERI D'INVENZIONE: IN CONVERSATION
WITH RICHARD TOOP
(1986)

RICHARD TOOP: Prosaic questions first. Why Piranesi? What was the attraction of those etchings?

BRIAN FERNEYHOUGH: Well, the first thing, I suppose, was that I knew them. Almost every sort of compositional 'trigger', motivation, is accidental, in the sense that everybody's biography is their own, and one reacts to what one comes across. What more specifically interested me unconsciously, when I first got to know the pictures fifteen or twenty years ago, was the manneristic association of highly conscious style-structuring of wildly expressive elements; the fact of creating elements which in themselves want to spring off at a tangent, and then pulling them back into the center again, in such a way that the center is more emphasized. That was the first thing; I think that mannerism in that sense has always interested me tremendously, although funnily enough, a lot of literary mannerism, like late baroque poetry, for instance, has never been tremendously central to my way of thinking. But I like the forms - especially the way the materials relate to their formal constraints. And on the other hand, what I liked specifically about these pictures when I rediscovered them about 1980 was that they made us very aware of the function of the *edge* of a picture. That is, the content was so hyper-loaded with expression, with explosive and implosive energy, that the edge of the picture could be seen either as a complete irrelevance, so that the picture might be imagined as continuing in some hyper-space beyond, or it could be seen as some sort of rape action whereby the picture was being forced to limit itself in a way that was alien to its nature. And I rather liked the ambiguous grey zone created by the arbitrary beginning of white, in a straight line, suddenly breaking off; the tremendous multiplication of sometimes quite contrary perspectival lines which the picture itself generated: this tremendous conflict of the expressively over-complex and the completely arbitrary over-rationalization which the edge of the picture provided. And that gave me the hint of something which I've thought about a lot in music, which was that if you can create enough energies in a musical (or any sort of artistic) language, you're capable (or the language is capable) of doing a *salto mortale* over the edge of the picture, or over the end - the final double bar line - of a composition, in such a way as to be able actually to modify, to change, to show in a different light the world outside the object itself. And that would be a sort of idealistic answer to the question of what does a work of art mean, and what is it for, what does it do, how does it express?

RT: Did the idea of some kind of work reflecting your interest in Piranesi or reflecting the themes that come out of Piranesi, and the idea of a cycle come together? Or which came first? This occurs to me because glancing through some of your sketches, something for **Carceri d'Invenzione I** seemed to have the title "City of the Sun".

BF: Yes, that's right. At the time I rediscovered these pictures, I was working on the piece **Superscriptio**, which as you know is the only part of the cycle that doesn't use the same fundamental material as all the other pieces - this group of eight chords. It's very typical of my work that often I start in one direction, thinking that I've worked out all the basic ideas and criteria for the production of a particular piece, and then I suddenly realize that perhaps one of the secret, subliminal functions of the piece is to suggest something beyond itself, something in which it also partakes. So it was only while composing **Superscriptio**, and coming across the synchronism of rediscovering the Piranesi pictures that the idea of a cycle came to mind. It certainly wasn't that I saw the Piranesi pictures and thought, Ah yes, this sequence of pictures could produce a piece of music. And there is absolutely no illustrative intent in my composition. The only reason I used the title at all was that it seemed very apposite in describing my central concerns; that is, that all expression in art in some way derives from limitation. You can only act freely in a meaningful fashion if you are in a particular space which has been to some extent mapped out previously. And this seemed to lock in closely with the things which my Piranesi interpretations had suggested to me.

RT: Should one take the three [orchestral] pieces which are actually called **Carceri d'Invenzione** as being the core of the cycle, in one respect or another? Is there any reason why *they* are called **Carceri d'Invenzione** and the rest aren't?

BF: Not really; I wouldn't see these three pieces as being the core of the cycle, although they were recently on television in one integral program, without the rest of the cycle. I don't like this; they *shouldn't* be played as a sort of mini-symphony, one after the other; the pieces are too close in some ways: there are too many inter-references, in spite of their different instrumental colorings, to enable this to be a successful artistic solution. Either you play individual pieces from the cycle by themselves, or you produce some irregular combination of large and small groupings, or you play the whole cycle in its integral form, in the right order. This is very important. The only reason I gave the same title to the three large ensemble pieces was that I saw right from the beginning that the flute concerto, **Carceri d'Invenzione II**, would form a central axis hinged around which the other movements would rotate, and I wanted some at least nominal symmetrical weight-distribution. And since I had these commissions - and inevitably one tries to fit commissions into whatever it is one wants to do anyway - it struck me that the relationship between these various works could be put to good use by giving them the same title. I was very interested in the idea of investigating what it means to write pieces in movements; what the idea of unity via diversity might be, in this sense. But what also interested me from the opposite side of the coin was how one could make quite clearly independent works cohere to produce a larger unit, over and beyond their particular identities. Therefore in this particular cycle - at least according to my own personal conception - I'm attempting to arrive at some personal understanding of what it means to write movements via the exactly opposite situation: that of putting together pieces which might at first sight appear to be casual neighbors, to provide a larger resonantial space where the individual ideas of the pieces become more than themselves by projecting their innate characterizational qualities into the relatively alien environments of surrounding works. It's the idea of knocking on the body of a guitar, for instance, while you've put certain fingers down on the strings, and producing a particular resonance. If you knock on a different part of the body you produce a completely different resonance, but it's still part of the same instrument. I was very interested in finding out what it might be that unites these various pieces, simply via the cumulative interaction and conflict of their specific defining qualities.

RT: One obvious thread through the cycle, from top to bottom, is the flute. Was that almost fortuitous, or was it there from the start? Or was it that you happened to have written **Superscriptio** and Fabbriciani[1] wanted other pieces, and this seemed to be one possible surface level going through the whole thing?

BF: Certainly there is some truth in each of your suggestions. I have worked a lot with the flute over the years, and it was one way for me of not having to confront once more the idea of doing a complete rethinking of the instrument. What I wanted was to rethink the instrument within the context of a much larger body of evaluational practice, and in this context it seemed to me that I could rethink certain aspects of the flute: its formal relationship to other instruments, for instance, or other formal problems, without necessarily having

---

[1]The Italian flutist Roberto Fabbriciani, who played **Superscriptio, Mnemosyne** and the solo part in **Carceri d'Invenzione II** at the première of the cycle.

to think the instrument right from point zero up as I had done in earlier flute pieces (although the bass flute piece, of course, to a certain extent does attempt to do that).

RT: **Carceri d'Invenzione I** followed on in time very quickly after **Superscriptio**, and it follows in a very audible way on the tail of **Superscriptio**. After that there's a big gap, as I recollect, before you got on with the rest of the cycle.

BF: Well, only in a sense. First of all, **Superscriptio** wasn't written before **Carceri d'Invenzione I** was begun. **Superscriptio**, which was definitely 'between the lines' of the text, is a piece I wrote very quickly - in about six weeks. And I must have already been working on other things at the same time, and I used it rather as a relief at that time, as I recall. Having first developed these relatively objectified or pseudo-objectified automatized techniques, it was something that allowed me to cool off emotionally, having confronted myself for example with the end of **Lemma-Icon-Epigram**, and I believe I already had started work on **Carceri d'Invenzione I** at that time. So it wasn't that I finished the piccolo piece and decided the first sound of **Carceri d'Invenzione I** had to be a piccolo; it simply rather fortuitously followed. The more you work on a large project, the more accidental things fall into place and give you things which you recognize yourself in, without having planned them in that fashion at all. So I was working on a whole 'convolute', one would have to say, of ideas and techniques at that time. For instance, I remember that while I was still working on **Carceri d'Invenzione I** I had already written the first song from the **Etudes transcendantales** series.

RT: This seems to be the part of the cycle that spread out longest, in terms of actual composition.

BF: Oh, necessarily, because each of the songs in some sense occupies a very particular intermediate position and point of repose (though not in the music itself) for me personally in approaching it, between the other major works. I worked on **Etudes transcendantales** for some three years.

RT: Does that mean that conceptually, if you like, although (or perhaps because) it's slap in the middle of the cycle, it should actually throw out branches in all directions?

BF: I think so, and also, of course, the other major works should be seen as crystallizing themselves in the very specific formal ploys of each of the movements of **Etudes transcendantales**. In a way, it was like a widely spaced-out diary for me, but a diary perversely boiled down and concentrated until only the absolute, most concentrated, densest essence of typical diary reflections remained.

RT: I remember we talked once before about 'modern music ensembles',[1] and your aversion to them in general. What is strikingly obvious about the **Etudes** ensemble is that it's a neo-baroque ensemble, to a very large degree. Was this an external thing? Under what circumstances did you suddenly find yourself using a harpsichordist in a major role, in a piece which otherwise doesn't suggest that sort of ambience?

BF: Well, I was tired of the 'Pierrot Lunaire' ensemble sound, with the clarinet - the rather white sound - and I was interested in having something which for my style seemed alien: a hard-edged metallic quality. And having written **Superscriptio**, which itself has this quality, I didn't want again to concentrate on the flute, so I decided to ally it to the oboe, and at that stage I'd already written the first song. At that point the first song was not seen as part of a larger work, necessarily; it was a pure experiment in trying to reapproach, on my part, vocal gesturalization, and the interpretation or the integration of text into a musical context. So again, that was a series of quite fortuitous circumstances: having chosen the oboe, then having wanted at least one harmonic instrument, the harpsichord seemed a perfectly suitable concomitant. In a sense it was not a very suitable instrument, because (a) it's very quiet, and (b) the more complex the harmonies you play, the less differentiated the final sounds become. So I had to be very careful in the use of the harpsichord in this work - that one didn't arrive at a certain stage of entropy in which the harpsichord was just a replacement for percussion instruments, for instance.

RT: One thing I seem to remember from the program note is that you describe how your original idea for the **Etudes** was that you would have three cycles based around individual instruments, but the real point of it would be an automatic cycle, an anti-automatic cycle, and a sort of reconciliatory cycle. How far was that carried through? How far is that kind of thesis-antithesis-synthesis thinking, especially in relation to 'automatic and non-automatic', a preoccupation of the whole song-cycle?

BF: Oh, absolutely at the center of it, I would say. The fact that I didn't carry it through in its total symmetric concept was simply because I found there was enough leeway in each of the movements to be much more flexible than I had originally supposed might be possible. So abandoning the original plan (to

---

[1] cf. p. 251.

a certain extent - not entirely) simply meant that I had got a different concept of balance of information, between movement and movement, and cycle and cycle, but also that the actual techniques available were so much more multifarious than I had originally conceived, that there was so much more freedom available to me, that it didn't seem necessary to be quite that didactic.

RT: How about the words? Were your words 'pre-found', or in part evolved for the cycle?

BF: Well, the words of the first texts were taken from a book of poems by Ernst Meister, who belonged to the same generation as Paul Celan: one of these reductive lyricist poets who wrote pithy metaphysical poems of few lines in length but with very vivid imagery. At this point - I suppose in 1982 - I was in a rather negative, disorientated mood about many things in respect of my music and I felt it necessary to try and work through these things. Maybe it's a question of age and so on: you know, when one gets to around the age of forty, one starts thinking about things one didn't think about before! I don't know, maybe that... but I certainly felt that I wanted to look into questions of death, and what it is about a work of art that gives it a certain permanence, as against its ephemeral, immediate expressive capacity. And also, one of my old interests, of course, repeats itself in this song-cycle: to what extent it is possible to relate a musical language to, or locate a musical language in, a more general field of discourse that includes, or takes note of, or reflects upon, other forms of communicative discipline.

RT: What is the relationship of the text to the music, or the music to the text? Is that an answerable question?

BF: Only indirectly. The way the words are reflected in the music is basically a result of allowing the musical techniques which I was concerned with anyway to be colored by the particular structuration or suggestionality of the text. I mean, in a sense I didn't try to set the text: that would seem to me to be a rather defeatist gesture, a madrigalistic approach which would deny exactly what I was trying to prove, or was trying to suggest - the idea of music as a self-sufficient language which is nevertheless rich and flexible enough to contain connections to many other ways of feeling and thinking. So basically I would read the poems, and would try to locate them at some point in the cycle with one or more types of energic disposition, shall we say: I knew the sort of textures, the sort of compositional ploys that I wanted to investigate, and then I chose texts which I felt were particularly suited. From the Ernst Meister texts, Song 6 (the one with voice, alto flute and cello) is a very typical case. I knew that I wanted a text which was longer than the other texts on average, because

I wanted it to be a very discursive, argumentational and appellative setting. Having been tremendously occupied on a private level with the Monteverdi operas and their entire vocal and gestural ambience at that time, I was really interested in trying to create a form of gestural suggestivity for the voice which would form part of a musical structure, but at the same time was quite clearly allied to the words without actually trying to illustrate them.

RT: One odd thing about the **Etudes** is that although, taken as a whole, it's the longest part of the **Carceri d'Invenzione** cycle by a good way, it's also a sequence of short forms.

BF: That's right, and again it's this rather dialectical interlocking of extremes which interested me. In a sense, it's a sort of *mise-en-abîme* of the entire cycle, although it's got a different number of movements than the cycle has pieces. Nevertheless, the parallelism is quite clear - the idea of the pieces being so short that on the one hand they are comprehensible as small, compact battery-like forms. At the same time, they move so fast in themselves by their very nature, that the mind and the spirit are always running to keep up, so that you only catch up with what's in a piece when it's finished, and you've got to then try and reutilize that which you just experienced in trying to come to terms with the one piece in the one that immediately follows. And it was tremendously important for me in the choice of texts, and in the way the texts are laid out in the music, and in the way I relate the musical forms to the texts, that I should try to create some sort of broken continuity, as it were: a sort of scale, a Jacob's ladder, which allows the listener to utilize different parts or different sorts of spiritual energy in coming to terms with each of the movements.

RT: If one accepts that, as you are saying, the music doesn't 'set the texts' in the conventional way, to what extent is it true to say that the text is set to the music? How much autonomy does the music have?

BF: The music has total autonomy after the moment at which the mere material distribution of the text has been taken account of in the musical form. Of course it was necessary to integrate that which was on the paper, in terms of quantity of syllables, length of lines, structure of verse, and so on, into my concept for a musical structure. These things had to be inseparably united. Having arrived at that point, I wrote the vocal part according to the exigencies of the *musical* structure - the type of density, the type of relationship between vocal gesture and instrumental gesture, the degree of automatism or informality of the two levels, and so on. Afterwards, going back to the text and actually inserting it into the already formed vocal line was something I found very exciting, because the exigencies of the situation sometimes brought me up against quite serious problems which forced me to come to very radical solutions.

RT: Can you give an instance?

BF: Well, yes, I suppose I could. Song 6 one would have to take again, in that sometimes major parts of the line are allotted only very few and very rapid notes. Or it might be in Song 8, for instance, where the two intertwining texts are radically broken up like the shuffling of a pack of playing cards, the one with the other - that the relationship of the instruments to each other, and the voice to its texts, is a radical form of absurdist discontinuity which creates a form of expression in itself.

RT: Where did the other poems come from? The Alrun Moll poems - that's a poet I don't know of.

BF: I was very impressed by the poems Alrun Moll had been writing for several years. My original idea was to take entirely Ernst Meister poems, but I felt after a while that there weren't enough of his works available to me which concern themselves with this particular circle of themes - of death, the resonance potential of stones: precious, gravestones, natural stones in the landscape, and so on, and their cultural significance - I didn't feel there was enough of this in Ernst Meister to enable me to complete the cycle on the scale which I originally intended. Therefore I asked Alrun Moll to write me a series of (I think there must have been about twenty) texts, circling around this set of themes. And from this original reservoir I chose the particular texts which seemed to me most redolent of the formal or expressive concerns which I had already been working on in my imagination of musical shapes and textures.

RT: But how much actually carries across from one work to another? I know that apart from **Superscriptio**, there's this sequence of chords which is common to the whole **Carceri d'Invenzione** cycle; but are there also sets of proportions which are taken wholesale from another movement, and then used as raw material to rework? Or does each component piece have its own set of proportions and work with these?

BF: Both are true. In most of the pieces I work with my so-called analogical relationships: there are always very strong parallels both of procedure and proportionality between one work and the next, without their being literal repetitions. If I used literal repetitions, that would be a mere *dédoublement*, a mirroring in a rather superfluous fashion of that which was already present. What interested me was taking basically different things, and *suggesting* their relationship via parallel sorts of treatment. Therefore it was necessary to adopt different materials or different general approaches to the same sort of technique, so that I could make this apparent. In only one case was there a very clear material relationship, and that was between the last two pieces in the cycle to be written, the bass flute piece **Mnemosyne** and the violin piece **Intermedio alla ciaccona**, in that the intervallic structure of both pieces was identical, and the rhythmic structure of both pieces was in very large part identical. Probably that happened mainly because having written the bass flute piece, which concentrates very much on harmonic progression and is a very withdrawn piece (I think nevertheless quite successful in terms of what it set out to accomplish). the violin piece was a deliberately 'overdrawn', ugly, direct, extrovert composition. It was just an idea of mine that if one took the same material, one could in fact derive a certain expressive power from doing exactly the opposite sort of thing.

RT: What is the function of repetition in the cycle? It's a notion which plays a very obvious surface role in **Carceri d'Invenzione II**. I remember you telling me ages ago, when a lot of these pieces weren't actually written, that it was going to play a major role. Did it, in the end?

BF: Oh yes, because the whole time the idea of repetition, of mirroring, of paralleling, of resonating, was something which I always had in the middleground, if not the foreground of my mind, simply because I tend to move on and *not* repeat in my music. One of the restrictions I placed on myself was, in each piece, to find as many different relevant forms of inter-reference as possible; and inter-reference always implies repetition, be it of a perceptual model, be it of actual material, be it of compositional processes.

RT: And is the flute piece one of the most explicit in that respect, in the sense that in **Carceri d'Invenzione II** the solo flute was composed first, and within that, almost from the opening, there are many bars which are almost literally repeated, except with different lengths? There's a greater degree of literal repetition here than in any other piece of yours.

BF: Oh yes, in **Carceri d'Invenzione II** I deliberately funnelled down my concept of repetition until it became the thematic substance of the composition. It was very important to me in this work to find out what it is about performative energy that enables the performer to gauge the distance between various formal units, and to dispose his energies in such a way that he can overcome the obstacles between the current object and the ones that follow. One of the things about Piranesi which interests me, as I said, was perspective - the mutually incompatible perspectives being forced into co-existence by some sort of compositional stratagem imposed upon them. And in this particular case the idea was to make relatively clear on as many levels as possible the inter-referential potential of basically invariant material; the idea of how often the material literally repeats, how often it repeats approximately, how often it repeats in a certain sort of varied form, and so on; and what are then the levels of perceptual potency which the ear can bring to play upon focussing the intellect into the interplay of forces which these cyclic interlocked repetitions generate.

RT: What's the function of **Carceri d'Invenzione III** within the cycle as a whole?

BF: The function of **Carceri d'Invenzione III** is to extend the idea which was right at the basis of **Superscriptio**, and extends through every work of the cycle, that is, of creating different levels of metric organization. In **Superscriptio** we have these weird bars of 3/10 and 5/12, or 7/24 - I don't see these changes as changes of tempo, but as changes of metric value. And in each of the pieces of the cycle (except the violin piece, which works in a slightly different way) there is a very major part of the pre-organization of the piece which is involved with the variation technique imposed upon cycles of bar patterning.

RT: I don't know whether it's accidental or not (I doubt whether it is) but it's the piece where I am most aware of a particular melodic figure - the very opening one, which sounds like an offspring of Varèse's **Density 21.5**.

BF: It's interesting that I was working in **Carceri d'Invenzione III** with a *triple* irregular metronome, whereas in **Carceri d'Invenzione II** I was work-ing with a duple irregular metronome; and **Carceri d'Invenzione III** attempts in the first section to be very explicit about this. It's quite clear that the function of the brass instruments in the first part of this piece is to trigger new types of material in the woodwind, and to introduce new woodwind instruments pro-gressively to produce a wedge-shaped build-up. What is perhaps not quite so apparent is that there are three levels of trigger action, of impulses setting off new material, functioning not concurrently, but in sequence. The tenor drum is always giving one single staccato impulse with a group of brass instruments - this is one meter/tempo cycle. The second one is that of the bass drum, which has a different articulation in that it is playing a long roll, and there can be long chords in the brass, though they all start simultaneously. The third layer is that of the bongos, in which, because you've got five different pitches, you can have several different impulses simultaneously, so that as well as triggering the brass (they start simultaneously), the bongos can play a certain number of impulses in a certain pitch relationship to each other. So we have these three types of tempo: one tempo which is progressively subtracted from the basic tempo of fifty-two, one which is progressively additive (I think it's adding three per minute each time, whereas the other is subtracting two, or vice versa) and then there's one which moves in what I call geometric relationships, which are by adding or subtracting a third or a fifth of the length of a particular beat. And by interlocking these three levels in a permutative sequence, it gave me the possibility of having the brass/percussion trigger-level producing clearly different lengths and types of texture and different types of variational pattern, whilst in the background making it clear which of these levels the materials belong to. And as the piece goes on, in fact in the very last section but one, the violent block-like textures are the gradual bringing-in, more and more explicitly, of these impulse patterns, such that at the end of the piece the number of impulses is so big that it takes on the form of figures in themselves; they make themselves independent of their trigger function, and become musical shapes - mainly in the percussion instruments, but also in other things. And in the section before the last very violent *fortissimo* section, we find the percussion triggering four or five times in a bar different blocks of brass and woodwind instruments, and different combinations from solo to the total *tutti* of the ensemble. So again, a funnel-ling-down: you're starting with single impulses at several bars' distance, belonging to three different tempo levels, which gradually in the course of the piece become not faster and faster, but denser and denser, and make more and more explicit a sub-meter within the triple large-scale meter. And in **Carceri d'Invenzione II** I had already used the two horns in this way: I'd given them overlapping dual metric patterns. In **Carceri d'Invenzione I** we already have the vertical blocks of the whole ensemble that suddenly break into a new meter of a '12' or '10' proportion. I saw this as being a I to II to III relationship. And the bass flute piece is perverse in this respect: it takes even further this structure you've seen in the sketches, in which there is always a triple or even sextuple rhythmic structure suggested in the background, which the bass flute translates then into between one and three rhythmic lines played concurrently.

RT: Can you say something about the significance of the title of the last piece,[1] and why it is that after about seventy minutes you decided to have a quiet ending?

BF: It wasn't thought of as a 'tasteful quiet ending', though in a sense it could be interpreted as that, and a lot of people *did* interpret it as that. From my point of view it was considered as an *amplification*, a densification of the techniques that until that point had been treated in the cycle. For me it was a very dense piece to write; I enjoyed writing it because the final result was a sort of free reaction to the dense, compositionally predetermined substrata of rhythmic and pitch structure. And I don't, in that sense, see it as being 'quiet': dynamic

---

[1]**Mnemosyne** for bass flute and prerecorded tape.

doesn't play a role at all; rather *density* plays a role, that is, density of structure in relation to the actual number of notes, and things like that. I think according to quite different parameters in that piece. As far as the title is concerned, Mnemosyne is the name of the eponymous ancient Greek goddess of memory - the mother of the Muses. It seemed an appropriate title because it for the last time unfolds, slowly (and for the first time, as an explicit harmonic progression), the structuring of the eight chords. It's a sort of cathedral-under-the-sea type of sound, rather like the Debussy prelude, in which everything is moving in slow motion, and is reduced to a lower octave level like a tape being played slowly. I thought the bass flute very apposite to express this particular quality.

RT: Finally, a broader question: there was this première in Donaueschingen of a cycle, of a piece which taken all in all adds up to something much longer than you have written before. What happens when one is suddenly confronted with ninety minutes' of one's own music, in terms of what one does next? I remember you talking before about certain big works tending to mark the end of phases rather than the beginning of new ones. Do you find it difficult, after something like that, to start up again, or is it so in this case that the cycle has evolved over such a long period of time that there are all sorts of other resumable threads that have been thrown off by it?

BF: Well, there are resumable threads: I have this series of guitar pieces to finish, which I'm half-way through and I've never had time to finish,[1] though there's material for each of the remaining four movements, some in greater detail than others. That I shall attempt to do at the beginning of the new year. At the moment, simple peripeteia, as one might say, simple impetus is leading me on to the beginning of the **Third String Quartet**, which I am now working on. I've already worked out plans for a fourth quartet with voice, and I've already planned a series of chamber concerti with solo instrument and very small ensembles. So again I'm working in a slightly longer time-span - it's not as though I were faced with the choice of 'Do I do a solo bassoon piece this month, or do I write a symphony?' One's thinking already three or four years ahead. I feel I need these time-spans in order to allow ideas that seem apposite for one particular piece not to seem too trivial in the sense of 'Well, this is it, this is what the piece is about, and that's the end of it'. Far more, I like to think that one lives one's life as a creative artist in the same way that one's pieces in themselves evolve. It would seem inauthentic if this were not the case, and therefore I have to live my creative life in the same way as one of my compositions itself functions.

---

[1] **Kurze Schatten II,** completed in 1988. Cf. p. 139.

RT: I remember you saying a few years ago that hearing the performances of your pieces tended not to be terribly important to you;[1] that you'd composed the piece, and the performance would simply confirm or not confirm what you thought was going to happen. Is that really the case when you sit in the concert hall while five years of your past life go by? Can you really be that detached about it? If so, wouldn't it become rather an ordeal?

BF: Well, the first time I heard it was in the general rehearsal, when the whole thing was played through from beginning to end, and at that point the matter was closed for me. Hearing it for the first time, yes, it was very important, because it was a whole series of pieces which are wildly different: of course I was slightly worried that it may not work in practice on that large scale as I had conceived it. But having established that it almost entirely worked the way I expected it to, in the same sort of cumulative fashion, then for me the period really was closed. So it wasn't closed the moment I'd finished the last piece in the cycle, but it was finally closed when the cycle as such was confirmed to me as the object I expected it to be. In the performance one's always worried that this or that will go wrong, but that's quite different. Now it's a question of getting back to the specifics of a particular piece. If there is a difficulty in the situation at the present time, it is of readjusting one's time-scale away from things like ninety minutes, back to something like twenty minutes. Of course one was always working on the scale of twenty minutes - none of the pieces is individually much longer, and some are much shorter. But there was the global perspective which played a role, particularly and increasingly in the final months and weeks of composition. So I have been experiencing some interesting problems involved in moving on to a slightly reduced perspective, without lowering my sights, of course, in terms of compositional intensity.

RT: But it's not a form of post-natal depression.

BF: I haven't really had time. Maybe that will come - I hope not, it never has in the past. Of course every composer is slightly at a loss when something's done, and there isn't enough available of the next thing. But that's part of the handiwork of composing: there's got to be enough of the next thing already there, and it would be a poor do basically if, against all my own compositional dicta, I didn't use what had been developed in the previous work to authenticate to a certain extent the language of what follows.

---

[1] see p. 271.

INTERVIEW WITH PHILIPPE ALBÈRA
(1988)

PHILIPPE ALBÈRA: How did you conceive the compositional act at the moment when you elaborated a work such as the **Four Miniatures** for flute and piano, the first real work in your catalog?

BRIAN FERNEYHOUGH: At the time I began composing the **Four Miniatures** - sometime during 1964, I think - I was intensely concerned with exploring species of discourse in which overall form and detailed, moment-to-moment invention could be uniquely brought together. Perhaps the composer most close to my still-developing world at that time was Webern, in particular the Webern of the early, aphoristically non-tonal pieces up until Opus 11. These few compositions were a source of continuing interest to me precisely because of their fragile achievement of such an ideal. Even though I rejected his residual reliance upon traditional forms, I still felt that the enormous specificity with which he combined instrumental gesture, pitch-patterns and agogic fluidity witnessed to his vast innate respect for the potential of his chosen language: nothing seemed extraneous or arbitrary. When composing the **Miniatures**, I was consciously bearing this experience in mind whilst striving to articulate the energies of my materials in formal shapes not obviously relating to already extant models. Each of the pieces is characterized by a certain sort of informality of treatment, in the sense that I did not start with any preconceptions of an abstract type concerning where the piece had to go. Rather, I remember attempting to make clear to myself a central core problem whose initial formulation would allow me to articulate the various elements and strategies employed in a more or less coherent fashion.

PA: Is this very different from your method of working today?

BF: Yes, in some respects. In fact, I still sense the need on occasion to return to the miniature form in order to reconsider my initial point of departure - **Adagissimo** (1983) would be a case in point, for instance. Another important facet of the **Four Miniatures** has had a long development in many subsequent compositions: that is to say, the conscious employment of diverse notational conventions in different formal and expressive contexts. In the first place, for instance, the two instruments are largely uncoordinated at the few points where they play simultaneously; at the same time, the flute part contains many very specific rhythmic configurations intended to focus the performer's mind upon this particular dimension at very specific junctures. The second movement gives both instruments quite specific rhythms in the context of the individual part without defining very exactly the precise superposition of the two instrumental voices. The final piece takes this tendency even further, so that the performers need to be continually scanning back and forth between the exigencies of proportional exactitude in their respective materials and the degree of coordination demanded between both instruments (these demands sometimes being in apparent contradiction [see Ex. A]). Whilst not wishing to make any strong claims for the inherent aesthetic value of this composition, it is quite important as an indication of the sort of origins my later development began from. I remember that there were several other compositions from that period which I immediately withdrew but which were also homing in on similar problems.

PA: Such is the case with **Coloratura**, which was actually completed.

BF: This piece was composed a year or so later, in 1966, and it is clear that certain lessons had been learned in the way the overall 'core concept' - that of two diverse 'characters' going their own ways but being cyclically pulled back together at key moments - was here realized more consistently. Something that strikes me forcibly when rehearing some of these early efforts is the constant recurrence of categorical dualities based upon pairs of opposites. In most cases there is little intention of producing a dialectical synthesis: far more, the energies thus liberated tend towards the constant generation of a potentially endless chain of further oppositions not necessarily contained in totality in the original premise.

PA: Is the title of the piece indicative of its 'significance'?

BF: As the title implies, a large part of the basic idea of **Coloratura** was the definition of the oboe as a somewhat extrovert, lyrically-inclined individual. Although composed in a quite flexible, linear manner, the melodic patterning is based on a very limited number of intervallic and gestural elements. The piano part, in contrast, relies upon ostinato-style repetitiveness with very few places where a certain independence can be sensed (Ex. B). The overall form arose from the interlocking and confrontation of these tendencies; I think it is very easy to hear the way this happens, since only a very few elements are common to both instruments. The actual material of the work was extremely basic; I seem to remember working with a relatively freely-employed sort of twelve-tone technique. Although it is actually very often played these days, it had to wait quite a while before Heinz Holliger gave it its first performance.

Ex. A: **Four Miniatures,** p. 6

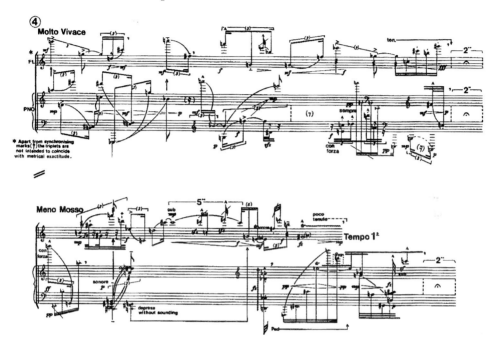

Ex. B: **Coloratura,** p. 1

I remember submitting it to the jury of the Society for the Promotion of New Music (SPNM) in London sometime in 1967 and receiving a reply to the effect that if I cared to rewrite it for clarinet they would consider it again! So, performer difficulty is always a relative problem.

PA: When you speak of a 'free' use of the twelve tones, does that mean that, for you, the somewhat extreme rigor of fifty years of serial music should be called into question?

BF: You have to remember that my background was really very limited, so that there was no chance of setting out from a considered appraisal of historical continuity. Everything I knew existed in a global present, and I began by observing partial aspects of many tendencies in a fairly punctual fashion. Still, I understood in a general way what then recent serial methodology was aiming at, even though I lacked the tools to make realistic analyses, and I liked quite a lot, without really understanding, many of the major works of young international composers of the day. Certainly, though, my own work was not consciously a reaction to such advanced techniques, since I really didn't know what they were: I was too much concerned with developing a functioning basic handiwork to adopt a consistently reflected position either for or against. **Coloratura** was an important experience, less for the piece's organizational aspects than for the development of temporal control. This was true of almost all the earlier compositions - it may even be a positive quality in that the very restricted nature of pitch selection led to a notably consistent sonoric image.

PA: Was it still in the spirit of basic 'handiwork' that the composition of **Epigrams** was undertaken?

BF: In a sense, these six little pieces fall between the extreme points defined by the foregoing works. Each little movement is clearly individuated as to form and primary compositional technique, but all revolve around a common center. Most of the movements have a quite simple starting point, like the idea of the palindrome, or variation form of one sort or another. Looking at **Epigrams** now I see that I learned a lot from observing where the energic flow of detail collided with the overall structural layout: the multi-layering of much later works has its roots here, perhaps. Stylistically, **Epigrams** has much in common with **Coloratura**, of course, since I was actually composing both simultaneously.

Like the earlier pieces, too, this was essentially a learning experience. Each movement was consciously composed to reflect a particular musical problem in a very specific, limited manner. It seems to me today largely this autodidactic urge which lends the work such character as it possesses. At the time this was my personal answer to another challenge still relevant today - that is, the rationale underlying pieces in more than one movement. For quite a while, in fact, I concentrated on single-movement pieces until my ideas on the subject became more precise.

PA: Is the choice of title also significant?

BF: The title was very much a catchall for whatever the piece came to contain! I was simply trying to compress as much into as small a space as possible in each case, and the connotation of pithiness in the word struck me as apposite. The word of course occurs again in **Lemma-Icon-Epigram**, but there it has a much more specific historiocultural significance.

PA: All of the early works, up to the **Sonata**, make use of the piano. To what degree were you influenced and affected by contemporaneous piano works, notably those of Stockhausen, or the **Sonatas** and **Structures** of Boulez?

BF: I was superficially familiar with the very early pieces of both. The first four piano pieces of Stockhausen seem to me today to be unjustly neglected, and I had examined the **Second Sonata** of Boulez some time before. Similarly with **Structures**: this latter I had heard live on one occasion, I believe; the remainder were, until somewhat later, pure paper music for me. I remember feeling that the extremes of dematerialized energy as characterized by **Structures** and the problematically motivic nature of events in the **Second Sonata** were both in their own respective ways somewhat unsatisfactory from my own personal point of view, although very high achievements in themselves, of course.

I don't recall that **Epigrams** owed very much to conscious models. Obviously, in a young composer, all sorts of things accumulate and filter-through without entering the conscious mind. The **Sonata for Two Pianos** clearly owes a great deal of its surface gestural vocabulary to things like **Structures**, or else perhaps **Kreuzspiel**. Even there, though, the influence was restricted strictly to the surface; the compositional techniques employed owe a lot more to the sort of selective cyclic filtering process of later years than to anything specifically 'serial' in derivation. The piece contains (as do **Sonatas for String Quartet**, **Epicycle**, **Missa Brevis**, and **Firecycle Beta**) large and small scale repetition patterns on the rhythmic, sometimes on the pitch level, whereby new layers are added over such repetitions, frequently slowed down so as to function more as referential grids than recognizable concrete figurations. They thus act very much as an atmospheric envelope or life-support system within which other events can live and breathe. I was definitely concerned with researching the implications of the simple fact that, if you change the speed of an object, it becomes very often a completely different form of life indeed, not just measurably different, but imbued with all sorts of unpredictably quirky qualities. Although the sketches of this pieces were lost many years ago, whilst I was still living in London, I remember developing a mode of treating the basic serial operations which began, fitfully, to bear witness to an overall formal concept. On the whole, though, the work obviously has difficulty in consistently being adequate to the demands imposed by a fifteen-minute duration. So, although it may seem in some respects a highly structured work, the individually structurally-concrete sections arose, often enough, from the impingement of contextually-bound invention upon the need to maintain a relatively homogenous overall flow. This, I think, often results in moments of imbalance in which the overall effect is one of a certain *élan* which a more consciously-planned work might not have had.

PA: After this first group of works, it seems to me that the subsequent ones mark a clear development in your compositional evolution, and that they are on a different level...

BF: It depends upon one's point of view. One has to remember that most of the works of this period were written in a space of three or four years, along with several other large compositions now withdrawn. This accounts, I think, for both the similarities between the pieces and the obvious discrepancies and seemingly elliptical progressions often encountered. It is clear that **Prometheus** shares many elements with a bundle of other pieces, like parts of **Sonatas** or the **Sonata for Two Pianos**. My inclination, however, is to place **Prometheus** with the earlier pieces, even though some fundamental concepts relate strongly to much later items. One could, I am sure, see the line of development much more easily if the unpublished and (largely) unperformed manuscripts of that time were inserted in the gaps. The most significant thing about **Prometheus** is not any innovations in vocabulary, but rather the interaction of primitive filtering operations with a highly-generalized conceptual framework.

PA: How does such interaction operate?

BF: I had worked out a dense labyrinth of pre-compositional possibilities, based upon categories of formal equivalence, through which I was free to move, to make specific selections from the alternatives offered at each juncture. Sometimes I had only two possibilities for a particular decision, sometimes five or six. By choosing one alternative in each instance, I was already limiting the field of meaningful choices in respect of subsequent operations. The score as it now exists is thus one expression of a field which could, theoretically, have produced quite a different set of results entirely. The title of the piece reflects this openness, the protean quality of my frame of reference. In fact, several times I was tempted to trace a completely different path through the system in order to create a 'twin' for the original version, but a twin with absolutely contrasting characteristics. Then I became involved in other projects, so this came in the end to nothing. The concept of metalevels has always attracted me greatly: the perception of a work of art has, for me, a great deal to do with the sense of categorical embedding of levels of experience. On an obviously primitive level, **Prometheus** began to outline a sort of 'practice of theory' which surfaced again much later in a quite different shape.

PA: In line with what you just said, one has the feeling that the **Three Piano Pieces** that follow are somewhat regressive...

BF: Yes, in this respect, it was a clearly regressive composition. It illustrates well the to-and-fro movement of the stylistic scanning process; the autodidact has not always the perspective and insight to predict what will bear fruit both now and in the future. The core concept of this piece was the dynamic unification of texturally diverse movements by means of a single underlying tendential process. The first movement is characterized by a very febrile, feverish leaping from mood to mood, the interlocking of series of only slightly differentiated tempi, and the employment of an obviously rhetorical gestural vocabulary. The basic elements return distorted by changed juxtapositions and temporal distensions, but there is little or no time available for the fixing of patterns of predictability. The second piece undertakes an extended development of this principle, but gradually interleaves more static, directionlessly repetitive structures. Finally, the third movement alternates wildly between extreme manifestations of both texture-types until, at the end, the static tendency drains out the energy of its opponent completely; all that remains is a series of block-like, chordally immobile impulses. Where I think the major difficulty in this work lies is not in the concept as such, but more in the imperfect way the overall dramaturgical line filters down to the perceptible motivation of single details. Very often one finds in younger composers' works this obstacle, that is, the lack of a clear middleground strategy. On several occasions in later years I in fact approached the triptych idea again, but only in the case of the **Time and Motion Study** group did I succeed in achieving my aim - perhaps precisely because the three component works are also independent entities in their own right.

PA: It is rather significant that all of the early works were written within the ensemble constraints of chamber music. Until **Firecycle Beta**, you had not written anything for orchestra, not even chamber orchestra. Was this deliberate, or was it necessitated by practical considerations?

BF: I didn't write orchestral pieces earlier because I was pretty conscious of not knowing how to write for orchestra. It is a very complex task, requiring not only an intimate knowledge of instruments but also the ability to adjust one's composing energies to the practical task of filling large pages representing perhaps only relatively short periods of musical time. Like long-distance runners, one has to learn to 'pace' oneself. It is certainly true that all my earlier compositions utilizing large combinations of instruments are essentially chamber music blown up in scale. In **Firecycle Beta**, there is a plethora of quasi-independent chamber groups, soloists and larger ensemble formations which are in a constant state of flux. **Epicycle** is even more clearly 'chamber music writ large', since the instruments frequently collaborate in groups of three, producing a polyphony of chordal sonorities, often quite straightforward to follow. All my later pieces for orchestral-size groups are to a certain extent analogously built: **Transit** breaks its forty-odd players down into smaller, topologically significant units, and the work's progress is articulated almost exclusively by the employment of specific timbres for each section. **La terre est un homme** might be seen as several compositions coexisting simultaneously, each distinguished according to technique of generation, frequency of appearance, register, and instrumental coloring. These considerations were not foremost in my mind after composing **Prometheus** and **Three Piano Pieces**, though. I was much more interested in projecting recently-made experiences onto a still further extended timescale.

PA: Hence the experience of the **Sonatas for String Quartet**, in which the dimension is rather exceptional for this instrumental combination?

BF: The 'parents' of the **Sonatas** might be said to be, in equal measure, Webern and Purcell, whose Fantasies for viol consort I encountered a year or so earlier. Initially, I set out to compose a small number of self-enclosed polyphonic movements, each of some hundred and fifty bars or so in length; one of the two I completed was actually performed on an SPNM concert in London, I seem to remember. After some time, I became very dissatisfied with the concept of separate movements - there seemed, on the face of it, no reason why they should be dependent on each other, or even played all together. The same problem seemed to beset the 'closed circuits' of the Boulez **Livre pour Quatuor**, for instance. The solution I finally settled upon was to deconstruct the materials at hand and to interleave the small fragments thus obtained with new, connecting and commentating features in such a way as to create totally new perspectives. The difficulty of defining the meaningful limits of a 'movement' was thus eliminated, and the final form was a chain of larger and smaller 'islands' in the same archipelago, some almost large enough to be autonomous, others essentially dependent upon their contextual surroundings. In this piece a major feature is the dialectic tension pertaining between those elements composed in a consciously rationalizing fashion and more spontaneously produced moments. It was naturally the series of connecting materials composed towards the end of the work process which became significantly enriched by the extremes of the earlier fragments, like the gradual accretion, layer by layer, of the material of coral reefs.

PA: Did you define such elements?

BF: Yes, but only in a deliberately abstract, generalized fashion. At the root of things was a simple four-note chord - usually, I think, a major/minor second inversion which appears in different guises throughout. Following on that were certain combinatorially-compatible articulation classes of a very basic nature: 'pizzicato', 'repeated note', 'glissando', 'harmonic', and so on. The very first section of the piece (composed, in fact, quite late) is a clear example of the single and multiple employment of these categories. I realize that this sounds overly simple, but it has often been my experience that the interpenetration of only a very small number of fundamentally simple levels of information is capable of generating an object or process of great richness and complexity. In more recent years, whilst I have consciously systematized my process more and more, I feel that I have remained true to this particular tenet. At least, I hope so; I've frequently had the experience, when analyzing pieces for lectures, that listeners have been disappointed, even scandalized, by the very basic nature of most of my atomic operations! But the simpler the premises, the more generally applicable they usually turn out to be.

PA: In any case, it is a work which possesses, in comparison with those which preceded it, extraordinary maturity; it seems perfectly successful from all points of view...

BF: I agree, and I think it is precisely that the sort of polar opposites I was talking about earlier actually function here. I found some sort of key to their productive confrontation. Whereas in the **Three Pieces** there was, basically, only one constant polarity, the **Sonatas** have already managed to accommodate several such oppositions simultaneously. Not only that, but they also succeeded in integrating everything into an overall framework permitting the various oppositions to transform themselves, step by step, into one another.

PA: Is the title connected to the idea of the Baroque sonata?

BF: I was thinking much more of the Venetian Sonata, as in Giovanni Gabrieli's **Sonata Pian' e Forte**. The idea of an antiphony of transformations rather than the there-embodied spatial distribution seemed at the time useful.
One might, I suppose, see **Epicycle** and **Missa Brevis** as amplifications

of the previously latent antiphonal concept, since both works operate with spatially distributed forces, the former piece with two equal string groups, the latter with three vocal quartets which, in the final movement, move in independent
tempi, conducted, in part, by members of the groups themselves. The compressed durations of both pieces were certainly a reaction to the 45 minutes of
Sonatas; I remember conceiving **Epicycle** originally as a sort of 'collapsed' string
quartet, where sections which would normally have been played one after another were somehow heard at one and the same time, resulting in a work of
merely one-third the length.

PA: You speak of a chord of three or four tones as the basis of the composition. How, starting with such simple material, did you develop the harmonic
structure?

BF: In **Epicycle** you hear the underlying consistency of sonority right
from the outset; it couldn't be clearer, really. The two main axes of information
are how the trichords are built up intervallically and how they relate to one
another registrally, intervallically, etc. Playing on this 'keyboard' allows much
flexibility and much play with ambiguous allegiances, with one or two notes in
common, for example. Once fixed, the trichords move around more as recognizable sonorities than as functioning concatenations of individual pitches. This
was intended from the outset, in order to imbue the polyphonic groups with as
much audible coherence as possible, although all sorts of manipulation are possible, of course, in respect of the delay between the entries of trichord components, or of greater or lesser explicitness of registral distribution. This directness
of harmonic relationships was balanced out in some respects by the extreme
embellishment of individual instrumental detail - something which, incidentally,
was thoroughly functional insofar as a high degree of differentiation is necessary in dense textures if you wish to make single lines audible as such. Sometimes the separating-out of particular micro-areas takes on a similar sort of role
as harmonic processuality might conceivably have under different circumstances.
It's always useful to remember, by the way, that all these works were composed
before I ever had a chance to confirm my intentions with reference to direct
sound experience. I feel them to have turned out quite well considering this
major handicap; in retrospect there is almost nothing that I would wish to
change. In fact, I never did revise anything written during those years.

PA: When were these two works - the **Sonatas** and **Epicycle** - first
performed?

BF: I think it must have been in 1974. Like the **Sonatas, Epicycle** had
been played in part during the Gaudeamus Music Weeks. It actually ended up

slightly less addled than the former, since the sections played were at least in the intended order, and a much larger proportion of the piece was played. A record exists of the 'version' of **Sonatas** played at Gaudeamus in 1968.[¶] I should perhaps emphasize that the choice of sections played, as well as their order, was made not by me, but by the members of the Gaudeamus Quartet themselves. Considering the, for the time, unusual difficulty of the score, the result - interpretationally if not compositionally - was really quite good. The first full performance of **Sonatas** was at the Royan Festival of 1974, which was my first really extensive professional exposure.

As usual with me, I had already begun the **Missa Brevis** before completing the previous composition although, in its original form, there was no thought of the triple choir layout later adopted. Only the Kyrie and the opening of the Gloria were composed in this fashion, though. Here, I was working with groups of four pitches, very often employed, for emphasis in homophony within an individual soprano/alto/tenor/bass group. The presence of a text naturally offered many more possibilities for the overlapping of diverse types of textural treatment - frequently two lines of the text are being sung simultaneously in different registers and with contrasting types of articulation. Where the text underlying individual movements differs greatly in length (as with the Kyrie and Gloria, for example) there is clearly added motivation to treat the verbal component in divergent ways. The Kyrie breaks up words into individual 'phonetic atoms' and hurls them back and forth through the entire available space, whilst the Gloria compacts whole lines into impenetrable, contorted masses which eventually break up under their own expressive weight. Later movements make increasing use of elements of an aleatoric nature, whereby the harmonic rigidity of the earlier monolithic blocks is undermined from the inside. As I mentioned earlier, the piece ends with asynchronously-cycling repetitive elements largely liberated from a centralized temporal frame. The development of this technique was crucial to the mechanics of overlapping in **Firecycle Beta**, which was begun immediately afterwards.

PA: **Firecycle Beta** is, in a way, the last piece, and the most substantial, of this 'first' compositional period.

BF: Yes, and it was finished in 1971. Again, though, one should remember that the first two works of the following group were composed in their entirety before the score of **Firecycle** had definitively been concluded. The basic idea of the work was quite simple: essentially, I was concerned with the phenomenon of 'distance'. The overall form was to consist of three sections, only the second, central part of which was, in the event, completed. Each section was

---

[¶]Cf. discography, p. 497.

to have nine subsections, organized durationally according to a logarithmic scale, and the relative durations of the sections themselves would have increased according to similar relationships. The first part was to have been quite short and compact, with very dense, complex activity for the most part, like, say, an astronomical object seen from a great distance. The second was to be much more varied, combining subsections of clearly greater or lesser density and detail of operation, leading then to a vastly extended final section in which the fictional observer would have approached the object so closely as to find himself actually moving inside its 'molecular structure'. In consequence, I saw the material becoming highly repetitive and rather featureless, and that over the space of some thirty minutes.

In the event, only the second part, the movement representing, if you like, the 'human perspective', was ever completed, even though large fragments of the other two were composed. The piece thus remains a torso. This is not necessarily a bad thing; perhaps the extremes suggested by the original idea were necessarily unfruitful. In any case, there are sufficient changes of perspective in **Beta** to make it aesthetically viable on its own terms, I think, and with a duration of 23 minutes it is quite long enough. Five conductors are employed at different points in order to guide the flow of block-like textures and detailed 'zoom' close-ups around and through one another, whereby always new combinations of conductors are employed. (At only one point, I think, do all five direct simultaneously.) Sometimes I wonder what **Gamma** would have turned out like - perhaps a sort of 'macrocosmic minimal music'? But there are periods where certain things are simply not possible, and probably with justification in most cases.

PA: In this work we find once again the division of the orchestra into different groups, and the idea of opposition amongst these groups...

BF: The orchestra employed in **Firecycle Beta** contains no wind instruments - a fact also conditioned by the original idea, according to which only wind and percussion would have been in **Alpha**, strings, solo instruments, and 'mobile' chamber groups plus percussion in **Beta**, with the full orchestra reserved for the final, longest part. This accounts for the rather large and strange percussion group required, as well as for the (amplified) solo pianos, harps, solo string sextet, etc. Like **Epicycle**, two almost symmetrically equivalent groups are arrayed antiphonally against each other, often playing quite different materials. Like **Missa Brevis**, groups are quite often released in independent tempi with separate conductors - there is a long, cadenza-like middle section where, on each side, two conductors are at work, the second dependent for his entries upon the first, but thereafter free. Each two-conductor ensemble swims completely freely against the other until the main conductor gathers instruments together one by one in readiness for the next coordinated section. One needs to see the orchestra as a sort of flexible mobile whose moment-to-moment configuration in large part dictates the treatment and flow of the textural substance.

PA: How is the coordination of this superimposition of textures effected? Is it controlled by a kind of harmonic field?

BF: In one sense - perhaps a rather restricted one? - 'harmony' is not a particularly relevant term. I was working a lot with sonorities, which tend to operate according to different functional criteria, such as consistency, density, transparency, and so forth. Certain sorts of intervals are selected, for instance, to ensure that certain textures, no matter how active, will be permeable to other events playing at the same time. Where a sonority is built up of a relatively large number of individual pitches, the same rules no longer apply, I think, as are relevant for three or four-note chords.

PA: What is the connection between the title and the compositional process?

BF: The title refers to the well-known theory of Heraclitus that the universe is created through, and by means of, fire. At the end of all things, fire re-consumes that which it has created. Obviously 'fire' may be understood as relating to purification and continual movement and transformation; my translation of this concept into musical terms revolved around the employment of constantly repeating, overlapping grids - usually of a rhythmic nature - some of which provide actual material, some of which function negatively, by forcing the elimination of elements already defined. This was actually the first appearance of such devices in my work. These asynchronously wheeling cycles came together at certain key points, thus generating a fairly clear pattern of generation and decay. This, combined with quite extreme tempo changes and with the multi-conductor strategy I already spoke of, keeps the ever-present tendency towards chaos reasonably in check.
This major effort (some 2 1/2 years of continuous labor) brought me to a certain dead end in my writing. I just didn't feel that there was anything left to be done in that particular direction. All the preceding compositions had been infused with the vision of creating a totally self-sufficient musical language. Of course, I realized quite well even then that, aesthetically speaking, there is no such animal. Nevertheless, I believed that a consequent attempt to approach this ideal as closely as possible would succeed in producing the sort of density and force of expression that I had always been looking for.

PA: Many of your works bear significant titles, with more or less philosophical implications. Are they basically points of departure, or the result of analogies which appear in the course of elaboration?

BF: Very often I start a piece because of something I have read. A key word or sentence sometimes suffices for this; it clicks with an already present musical drive which, until then, had remained hidden or inchoate. Around this core, other things, ideas, images begin to accumulate until a sort of critical mass is reached and sounds begin to emerge. I think that there has never been a piece since that time which has not received vital impetus from similar causal chains. Of course, some pieces carry their generative apparatus nearer the surface than others.

Whilst I was completing the score of **Firecycle Beta**, I had already moved on in terms of such generative conceptual activity. Initially as a form of diversion from that overwhelming task, I decided to write a piece for solo flute. Being at that time myself a flutist of modest pretensions, I was able to experiment directly with sounds - something that had hitherto scarcely been possible. As time passed, I became increasingly aware of new background ideas which were just beginning to leave an impression on my compositional practice. In particular, I became vitally interested in the complex way in which music, as a social phenomenon, reflects and incorporates other spheres of discipline, mental model-building, and so on. One has only to think of the elevated place of music in the world view of the Middle Ages, for instance, to appreciate the sort of thing I had in mind, albeit obviously without claiming for music the same sort of explanatory power, which would be quite anachronistic. Each piece from that point on set out to map out a part of the mind in terms of its potential for analogical projection, and it was only in 1979/80 that a further change of perspective set in, resulting in me consciously drawing my field of reference back into the realm of musically immanent referentiality.

PA: The majority of the works which follow **Firecycle Beta** center around the concepts of freedom and constraint, taking more or less metaphorical forms, but always relating to the organization of the musical material...

BF: The concept of freedom was a fixed point during those years, around 1970. By that term I meant less specifically political issues than consequences arising from various categories of mediate or immediate decision making. **Cassandra's Dream Song**, the flute piece I was mentioning, tackles the issue by interweaving two contrasting materials, one highly directional, limited and rigorous, the other more flamboyant, but not directionally ordered, since its five component sections could be interspersed among the main sections (fixed in order) in any sequence freely chosen by the performer. In allowing the performer this liberty, I wanted to suggest to him diverse perspectives of interpretational

approach. It is clear that abutting different sections to each other from performance to performance leads to highly contrasted confrontations and consequent
reappraisals of performative energy distribution. One can choose an order which
minimizes conflict, for instance, or deliberately go for a highly explosive, fragmented version which emphasizes the changeover from one section to the next.
Of course, the relative lengths of the freer sections have a not insignificant role
to play too.

PA: Is the work actually renewed, for you, by means of its different interpretative possibilities?

BF: I have been continually surprised by the number of formal variables
which this little piece is able to reflect - maybe precisely because of the firm
supporting skeleton of the directionally fixed sections. In any event, small
freedoms in formal layout can quickly lead to quite intense interpretational situations, from player to player quite different.

The other piece I composed around this time was also intended to examine the same field of issues. This was an organ piece entitled **Sieben Sterne**,
whose title, referring to a woodcut by Albrecht Dürer depicting God the Father
sitting in glory holding a two-edged sword in one hand, and, with the palm of
the other hand raised, the fingers spread, with seven stars grouped in the middle of his palm, was directly reflected in the work's formal layout. There are
seven distinct sections disposed symmetrically around a center, for one thing,
and I saw the two-edged sword as implying the essentially ambiguous nature
of fixed or unfixed forms of notation. Whereas three of the movements are fully
composed-out in often highly complex ways, the symmetrically-arranged pairs
deal with the question of relative liberty in varying degrees. For example, two
of the movements require performer decisions on precise timbral presentation,
and the final order in which component fragments are heard. Then there are
two sections which, whilst providing only minimal information to the player,
require him to play in such a fashion as to make the result approach as closely
as possible the sound worlds of the most precisely-notated movements. The
manner in which this is brought about is left entirely to the organist.

PA: Why give possibilities of choice to the interpreter? Was it a reconsideration based on the experiments of the Boulez-Stockhausen-Berio-Pousseur
generation in the early sixties?

BF: I saw this as one possible tactic towards encouraging the interpreter
to emerge more fully from behind the monolithic 'work', to adopt a concrete
personal stance, whilst, at the same time, seeking consciously to bury it again,
to productively re-integrate it into the demands of the work context. Although

there have been a couple of good attempts, I have never really heard a satisfactory rendering of this piece - largely, I think, because of the tremendous demands made upon the registration assistants. I would like to hear it on an instrument with computerized registration facilities, so that the sections could be played without a significant break. Probably one could argue that the writing is not very characteristic of the instrument, and there may be some truth in this; on the other hand, an instrument might be argued as being defined in some measure by the works that exist for it. More relevant would be the criticism that the detailed writing of the denser passages effectively ignores the long resonance time of most spaces where appropriate instruments are located.

PA: What seems to me characteristic of the solo pieces of this period is their extraordinary level of virtuosity, their high degree of difficulty of execution, sometimes reaching the limits of human ability...

BF: I had always been interested in any form of complex musical phenomenon, but it was only at this time that I began to understand that there was an entire dimension of potential expression buried in the attitude of the performer to the musical text. I thus determined to see how far this aspect of things could be systematically exploited as a contribution to the redefinition of 'interpretation' as such, how far the results could be incorporated into the very fabric of the composition, so to speak, as a discrete polyphonic strand.

PA: One always speaks of this problematic aspect of your works, the relationship between notation and realization. Doesn't it pose a major problem for you when well-intentioned interpreters say they are unable to play more than fifty or sixty percent of what is written in the score?

BF: But my point is: what is interpretation? If you 'interpret' a Beethoven sonata you don't play exactly what is notated on the page in front of your nose. In a certain sense you are interpreting an entire tradition of interpretation already several generations removed from the original, and any innovation you introduce is counterpointed against this background. The perfect case in point here would be the Webern **Piano Variations**. One tradition has it that you play precisely what is on the page, that is, without pedal. Another tradition has it that the composer himself reinterpreted the written page liberally, adding pedal and rubato according to what he felt was the sense of the music - that is, making clear the position occupied by that piece against a silently assumed aesthetic background. This sort of background is today either lacking completely or is present in the negative sense of a performer undifferentiatedly applying his conservatoire technique, learned via Viotti, Tchaikovsky, etc., to whatever contemporary pieces happen to cross his path. Although some composers may, I suppose, actually compose their pieces with that contingency in mind, I cannot say that I find it a very attractive state of affairs. The fractured, disassociated stylistic panorama facing a performer today simply does not allow the performer a great deal of opportunity to plunge into the interpretational implications and subtleties of nuance of each and every composer's native dialect; it is really up to the composer, then, to gently suggest, via the relation of his notation to perceived content, form or executive difficulty, what sort of practical interpretational deviation from this particular norm might be most fruitful.

It is true that players unfamiliar with my pieces often start out by feeling hemmed-in by the multi-layered precision of the image; very often, though, after having worked on the technique and the sense of the piece simultaneously, the player comes to accept that a great deal of personal creative freedom of approach and realization is implied that could not have been suggested in any other way. A notation which specifically and programmatically deconstructs the sound into its subcomponents sensibilizes the mind towards aspects of the work which a seemingly more straightforward image would not be in a position to do. The performer recreates the work in his own image, not according to some arbitrary process of homogenization via the academy.

All this is not to say that certain of my works do not approach or (in the case of **Unity Capsule**) deliberately overstep the limits of the humanly realizable. It is largely a question of mental attitude, of not allowing the conscious mind to reflect too much ahead of the performative fact. It is certainly possible to have a bad interpretation of a piece which accurately realizes more of the written notes but signally fails to reflect the mental tensions involved in the enterprise. Which is not to say that 80% of the notes are not preferable to 60%, of course! In any case, as I say, all performance is imprecise in either a positive or negative sense.

PA: One could say, however, that in traditional music the interpreter is placed above the text, whereas in the case of your music, he always remains within it. He only approximates, imperfectly, what is notated.

BF: Certainly, but I don't accept that a musical object can ever be defined precisely by any form of notational convention whatever. Even the most exhaustive notation only offers a semblance of precision. It is useful for telling us where to put our fingers, say, but even more important is some capability of offering perspectives on the position of the entire piece in a larger context, its connection with other works of the same genre, or of the same composer. Underlying your question seems to me the unspoken assumption of the unquestioned primacy of certain parameters, that particular levels of information are *de jure* more 'the piece' than others. But this interaction of defining levels of identity is constantly changing; it is part of the whole problem of stylistically adequate interpretation we have been discussing. Any performer of my music will tell you that, in general, the relationship of performative difficulty to actual sounding result is quite carefully calculated. This is also identity-producing information, not just pitch or rhythm, no matter how precisely crafted. For me, the performer is not just rendering the composition, in a very specific sense he is actually engendering its final manifestation. Often I hear the remark that my more recent pieces look 'easier'; on one level this may be trivially true. Just because the surface of the music has closed over this deconstructional aspect, though, doesn't mean that I have for a moment pushed it aside in favor of more traditional categories. What it does mean is that the performer has other clues to pursue towards the same ends. Changes of compositional aim lead to appropriate means of transmitting these to the performer.

PA: In this sense, isn't the **Time and Motion Study** series undoubtedly the most radical?

BF: Yes, the title chosen already underlines, I think, the sort of area I intended to investigate. I decided to pursue my interest in the notation-interpretation sphere by concentrating demonstratively on the concept of 'efficiency' - what might the term mean when applied to aesthetic production, reproduction and reception? As with the flute piece, I was able to experiment extensively myself in the development of particular sorts of vocal techniques; my aim, in **Time and Motion Study III**, was to offer a notational grammar by means of which the compatibility of diverse, simultaneously executed vocal articulations could be made analytically explicit. The limits of this grammar were thus, in effect, the limits of the formulable in this particular composition; there was a very direct linkage. Because all vocal sounds were amplified, it was possible to include sounds otherwise, under normal circumstances, practically inaudible.

The amplification had a spatial dimension, too, since the sounds produced by one of the spatially-separated four groups was reproduced by a loudspeaker behind the group diametrically opposite. The idea was to equate the efficient production of sounds in one group as a disturbance or destabilization factor in its opposite number. A further aspect was, I recall, the way in which the voices collaborate in ensemble; in the first part of the piece the four groups are set off from each other by clearly diverging textures and developmental trajectories. In the central section the groups are dissolved in favor of textures employing from two to sixteen voices spread across the total space, whilst in the final main part each singer is basically completely independent. It is ironic, perhaps, that the highest degree of individualization of articulation and expression leads, in practice, to the most undifferentiated block textures. This also is a facet of 'efficiency'. A further aspect of the same concern is demonstrated by the relationship of degree of visual complexity as reflected - or not - in the sounding result, because there are passages of quite complicated multi-strata parametric polyphony in individual voices which, when performed correctly, produce an effect halfway between simple held chords and a sort of wobbling, energized shadow. For my part, I'm convinced that the most straightforward manner of notating a given action does not necessarily produce anything like the effect which a more detailed, deconstructive, analytical image can achieve. It has to do, I think, with aura, presence.

PA: To what degree was this work influenced, in one way or another, by vocal works of the sixties, such as those of Schnebel or Kagel, for example?

BF: Although many of the specific vocal techniques I employed had precedents in, for example, certain pieces by these composers, I was not at all interested in liberating the voice from any particular conventional constriction as the latter, at least, was at one time aiming at doing; far more, it was a question of taking the now deconstructed, mobile atoms of articulation and recombining them into new, syntactically meaningful synthetic units. By notating the tension of the throat muscles, position of the tongue and the shaping of the lips, etc. as separately-rhythmicized parametric strands, I was implying to the performer that he or she think themselves into the dynamics of the simultaneity as such, not just reproduce a more or less complex action. I was, above all, looking to generate a form of 'mental polyphony' in the interpreters' minds as an essential component of the expression.

PA: To what degree might such works be reborn from a prior global vision?

BF: It depends on the specific context, I think, how far the horizon in each instance stretches. What is true of the performer is also valid for the composer. Certain preferred aspects of a situation are always defined in advance. The order in which a series of decision-making procedures is applied is, I find, often more significant for the final result than the precise nature of the processes themselves. Just as the performer could attempt a global approximation of a particular complex constellation, so the composer is nearly always in a position to find a way of suggesting an event which encourages such an approach. I find this very uninteresting, though, since it tends towards the production of a one-dimensional discourse in a form of vicious circle. The successive layering of decision in an always more restricted context offers me at least the opportunity of various categories of quasi-causal perspective. Whether this is always audible in the result I can't say; certainly I remain convinced that one would notice if it were not present.

PA: It is a method which implies an ongoing analysis of the material...

BF: Absolutely. It's often the case that, working on a particular level, one doesn't know exactly what the effect of the practical analysis on the next level up is going to be, how it comes to exert pressure upon that already achieved. One is necessarily working a little in the dark until that moment arrives.

PA: Isn't there a contradiction between these compositional procedures and perception, in which the entire message is received?

BF: I don't think so. I assume that the ear attuned to certain stylistic consistencies is capable of analyzing-out a good number of levels of hierarchic significance almost instantaneously. The ear is a truly wonderful integrative mechanism, but this presupposes some form of very rapid scanning and comparison process which sorts out levels of articulation not according only to the order in which they were composed, but also the 'pecking order' in that particular situation, that specific chain of events. I don't mean that the ear breaks down all those layers in a constant flow, but rather that, over a certain span of time, it does tend to assign intuitive importance to this or that stratum, to separate foreground from the diverse backgrounds. It would be an error, I think, to assume that 'hearing' is always an instantaneous operation.

PA: Yes, but in a work like **Time and Motion Study III**, one often has the feeling of a dispersion. It becomes difficult to grasp the discursive logic of the composition - at least, that is the experience I've had.

BF: As I mentioned earlier, the interaction of the role of the individual singer with the choir in which he is embedded seems to me to be quite specific, especially since, at the outset, each choir is presenting sonorically specific materials. I like to think that certain sections provide moments of concentration because of the way in which these distinct layers are brought together. The original form of the first part was made up of the superposition of four separately-calculated linear proportion series. My immediate compositional task was, in effect, to render these conjunctions as clearly as possible as well as to imbue them with a certain amount of interactional credibility. Repeated listening should serve to make the sequence of situations reasonably clear.

There is a certain amount of moment-to-moment dramatization which helps the process, too; the most impressive performance I ever witnessed was in a rather constricted space in a Venetian palazzo, in the midst of a thunderstorm. The small space helped produce the compact, almost bodily quality of sound which I need. Form is not only the perception of linear, discursive coherence, but also this physical registration of events which the composer could not have brought forth in any other way. A certain amount of ambiguity as to the precise boundary between 'inner' and 'outer' is very conducive to this, I find.

PA: The second work in the cycle, **Time and Motion Study II**, places a cellist into conflict with his own discourse as captured via tape loops.

BF: One might say that the specifically dramatic characteristics of this piece are even more concentrated (despite the numbering sequence, it was composed later). The musical argument is filtered constantly through a battery of electronic equipment; every sound made by the cello soloist is reflected, transformed, or broken down by his electronically rapacious surroundings. There are many other aspects in play here, particularly in respect of various models of the fashion in which memory functions, how it retains, reworks, reorders or eliminates impressions. Some of the events are repeatedly recorded by one or both of two tape loops until they gradually decay beyond recognition; some are partially filtered by two assistants and fed back into the overall sound somewhat later, so that the soloist is permanently accompanied by ruined fragments of the initial live sound and context. Contact microphones on the instrument filter and modify the sounds further according to whether they are performed principally on the neck or the body of the cello, and are themselves regulated by two foot pedals operated by the cellist and notated as separate systems in the score. Finally, a throat microphone is brought into action to ring modulate certain sounds by means of the human voice, shouting, singing and speaking. By these means, many individual sounds are actually heard quite a number of times, each time somewhat differently transformed. Most of the individual sections of the piece revolve around a particular set-up in the electronics department - at the beginning, for example, where only high amplification of scratching noises on the finger board alternates with selective reproduction and transmission of small pizzicato elements at key points. Later, the feedback mechanisms attached to each tape loop independently create diffuse pillars of sound (one arco, the other pizzicato) to which the performer has to further react on cue. For this he has to remain very much on his toes indeed.

PA: There is a high level of violence in this piece, perhaps even a certain negativity, or cruelty. It isn't far from a 'performance' that is at once musical and theatrical.

BF: In the course of the piece, the visual image can be very much of a single person being tortured, but this depends, I find, rather a lot on the ambience and the innate attraction of theatrical underpinnings for the player. I deliberately stand back from offering an opinion there. As it happens, I was involved at the time with certain aspects of Artaud's Theater of Cruelty concept; even so, I don't actually feel enormously attracted to the imposition of pseudo-dramatic dimensions onto a work of music. Far better to let any innate dramatic qualities emerge naturally, simply through the vehicle of setting the work up for performance. I wanted the performance situation to suggest to the listener the modality of interpretation, without forcibly rubbing his nose in it. In a way, every conceivable musical action has a dramatic quality. Particularly in this composition I was continually thinking of the cello itself as a sort of stage set - something which allowed the sound 'characters' to interact and evolve within certain predetermined limits. In all my solo pieces I have been very aware of this bodily presence of the instrument as setting up a specific type and topology of performance space.

PA: This is certainly true of the third piece of the cycle, **Time and Motion Study I**, written for solo bass clarinet...

BF: I think one can hear extremely clearly the various characters interacting. This work had set out as a clarinet pendant to **Cassandra's Dream Song,** but the idea of even remotely relying upon the same idea caused me to lay it aside. It was only when Harry Sparnaay asked for a bass clarinet solo piece that I took up this fragmented material again and remolded it by means of externally-imposed proportional and transformational criteria so that only one minuscule gesture from the original turns up at the end in the form of a throw-away quotation.

Recently there has been an increase in the number of performers who have learned the piece. Interestingly, the personality of each interpreter comes through in sharp relief, even though they are playing the same notes. It really isn't just a matter of playing a higher or lower percentage of the score. It is not, for me, a question of deciding who plays it better. Up until now, I have accepted all of them, whilst obviously being personally attracted to some more than others.

PA: Must these three works always be performed as a cycle?

BF: Each of these works can stand by itself, as well as forming part of a larger integral cycle. The idea was to gradually expand the horizon of perception from concentration upon the actions of a single manic individual, up through an individual locked into a wide-ranging 'support system' of electronic mirrors, up to the equally manic sixteen-voice choir with percussion instruments and amplification surrounding the audience on all sides.

PA: The problems raised by the relationship between notation and interpretation, notably in solo works, appear to be pushed to the extreme in **Unity**

Capsule for flute. It seems that here you have deliberately surpassed the limits of the 'playable'...

BF: It is the piece which perhaps most explicitly reflects my notation-interpretation concerns of that period. Unlike most woodwinds, the flute allows many diverse actions or embouchure modifications to be in play at once. In this way it resembles the human voice. The piece set out to bring out all these 'secondary' - usually undesirable - aspects of the instrument (multiphonics, out of tune pitches, breathy, impure sounds) and subject them to a set of operations at least as rigorous as could be applied to more abstractly consistent information. The score employs phonetic symbols on one level, indications of the position of the instrument in respect of the breath-stream as another, and so on. There are passages where a positive encrustation of layers occurs, producing, from bar to bar, violently contrasted and slanted sonoric ideograms, 'meaning molecules'; often this high level of change in many parameters effectively prevents the performer from 'remembering' ahead very far, leaving him in a constant state of 'performative surprise', the horizon of memory closing in around him. The only wrong sort of interpretation, in my view, would be one in which the player attempted to 'rationalize' this overload, to 'translate' these complex constellations into 'poetic' renderings of approximately the sound he thinks should come out in a generalized way. But this misses the point completely. Of course you can easily improvise the sort of 'dirty', diffuse sound world inhabited by much of the piece; many later scores I have heard indeed appear to do so. But essential dimensions of the interactive process have been totally eliminated, and this is too high a price to pay for a couple of tastefully elegant 'syntheses'!

Perhaps this is in fact the piece coming closest to a certain sort of ideal, according to which the explosive encounter between the willpower and goal-directed drive of the performer and a visual image resolutely crystal clear in its multiplicity takes shape. The score tries to suggest this linear energic stream by attaching most of the notes and actions to a continuous beam, interrupted only once in the course of some twenty pages. The piece looks like a futuristic image of a passing high-speed train whilst consistently tangling the performer in immobile thickets of detail. As a result, the performer is moving ahead in a series of frames, each perhaps lasting a fraction of a second; there have been a lot of occasions when I have worked with these insectile freezings and sudden movements - it is one way of transmitting the effect of eyeball-to-eyeball contact with events, of defining their 'absolute distance' from the observer.

PA: We haven't yet spoken of a work that appears to me to occupy a central position in your production, because of its deserved success and its implications, namely **Transit**.

BF: The composition of **Transit** spanned a period of three years during which I also did many other things. In some ways it is convenient, I suppose, to regard it as a balancing counterpart to the more obviously radical solo pieces. In any event, it clearly approaches much more nearly the sort of interlocking of musical and other disciplines I spoke of earlier, since there are texts being set as well as orchestrally topological analogy models being laid out. Without going into detail, the mixed ensemble is divided up into concentric half-circles, each being brought into play for the presentation of one particular step in the unfolding intellectual action. Since the central theme is the development of successive means of representing the universe - the religious, philosophical, humanistic and scientific - the move out from the vocal sextet at the center towards the outer ring of heavy brass roughly corresponds to a transformation from the concrete anthropocentric world view towards the Music of the Spheres. Several other formal models are interlocked with this - for instance, the three chamber concerti for bass flute, oboe, and clarinet, which interpunctuate the proceedings - but this progression outward forms a central skeleton upon which the other aspects are hung. It was my aim to suggest moving gradually through diverse modes of observing and reflecting one and the same object, the world around us, albeit in a somewhat distanced and idealized fashion.

One of the most important formative myths was that of the alchemical progression through several intervening stages to illumination - although, that said, the final, chaotic cycling of the brass and percussion has little enough to do with the more hopeful visions of what the final goal of such a process might reveal. Probably this reflects my feeling that the universe is not shaped in the image of anthropocentric humanism, but functions in a manner totally incognizant of and irrelevant to the needs and dreams of human beings. But I don't want to give the impression of beating some mystical drum! The work does not set out to recommend any of the world views it reflects upon; as with other works, the ending really rather leaves things coolly open. By the same token, it can't even be termed truly pessimistic, I suppose. After finishing this piece in early 1975 I definitely felt that I had finished with such close integration of music and other categories of cultural perception; at any rate, I began to withdraw more and more into the immediate world of reference offered by the musical language itself. I still strongly believe in the integrative function of the art work but I no longer feel pressingly driven to formulate this in still further works. In many ways, **Transit** was a tremendously important crucible for my development, in that many techniques I was later to employ quite extensively made their first appearances there, albeit in simpler or less formally influential fashions.

PA: Your works often have an image or vision as a point of departure; such is the case with **Transit**, with the woodcut by Camille Flammarion, and again with **La terre est un homme**, which is inspired by a canvas by Matta...

BF: Matta is a Spanish painter based in New York. I still have a reduced-size reproduction of that painting on my wall. I had a very impressive dream some time before first seeing this painting, and somehow a very similar set of images was presented; the connection between the two experiences was strangely close. I dreamt of a strange and alien planet traversed by a pitilessly hot sun. It was basically a desert landscape. The remarkable thing was, I seemed to be seeing every single grain of sand separately, not only in its spatial dimensions but also - somehow - sensed its individual weight. All was in slow, in-eluctable motion. Between sharply contoured rocks scuttled tiny, scorpion-like creatures. One sensed the extreme complexity but inevitability of this strange combination of leaden, slowly-moving sand and sudden flashes of intensely colored movement.

When I then discovered the Matta I immediately recollected the dream; a very short while later I had created the basic outline and world of sensible values for the orchestral work which then arose. There were many correspondences on all levels; I conceived of the texture as being composed of individually developing - sometimes dying - life forms in permanent movement and realignment. Each had compositional techniques in common with some but not all other organisms and usually was distinguished by a particular orchestral timbre group. It was largely for this reason that I used an orchestra with quadruple woodwind and brass; the vision of the coloristic integrity of particular strata was very important. The constant movement of these sometimes very small entities makes it very difficult, if not meaningless, to consciously search for the 'totality' when listening. There have been well-meaning performances of this work, particularly with less-adept orchestras, where the conductor has attempted to conjure up some monolithic, overall sound, to make the work somehow more than the sum of its parts. What happens on such occasions is that the individual life-processes are blotted out and degraded to the status of undifferentiated particles in some mistaken statistical process. The best performances have always been those paying undivided attention to the coherence of linear energy flow and transparency sufficient to permit the individuality of the layers to assert themselves. In performances without the benefit of section rehearsals, the individual performer can never get a real feel for his personal contribution.

PA: You often speak of underlying activity, which you often refer to as 'subcutaneous'. Can't we see this in terms of an analogy with the dream, the elaboration of which we are not consciously aware, but which deeply affects us?

BF: It can be that - in this case that is largely what it was. When using the term, though, it is usually as a shorthand for consciously organized processes of generation which do not necessarily exhibit their origin directly, recognizably, in their surface manifestation. The **Second String Quartet** is a case in point. My analysis of part of that work[¶] illustrates how many interacting layers of precompositional decision-making come to be reflected only very indirectly in the sounding result. The sound is a sedimentation of its engenderment. I suppose I tend to listen to music quite often like that. I hear contemporary music quite differently than does John Cage, to judge by his stricture about letting sounds be themselves. I myself don't think sounds in themselves particularly want to be anything; it depends always on what the composer wants to do with them. It is possible to arrange the sounds so that they are more or less transparent to intentionality - so that their function in the whole is very clear - or their significance may be something that only emerges gradually, or even appears clear purely in retrospect. The aspect of non-identity between physical sound and the assignment of various sorts of contextual meaning is very fruitful, I think. It depends very much what means one chooses to employ in order to manipulate this discrepancy, as well as how large the discrepancy actually is.

PA: I would like to return to the notion of a global vision: in the process of composition, of elaboration, do you have a sonorous 'image' of the totality of the texture, or is it constructed progressively?

BF: There is always some sort of internal image, frequently a sensation of time congealed onto something standing outside of, apart from time, or, perhaps, not existing in the subjective observation time of my imagination. Often, possible processes are first sensed as lever and fulcrum contraptions which tilt a clot of time this way or that. Inevitably, the act of transferring this image into notes representing a temporal span (themselves written in a possibly quite different span of real time) ends up generating a completely different object. This might be said to be part of the nature of the medium, though, so it doesn't disturb me greatly; I do often get irritated when composers act as if they were drawing from nature, according to some pristine landscape in their insides. Any such message from the interior is wholly dependent upon translation mechanisms, and is bound to be influenced by these. Maybe these composers identify with what they write in some *a posteriori* act of creative solidarity, like listening to themselves speak in order to see what comes out?

PA: Does this mean that it is impossible to subsequently organize one's memory of all the events, to unify them in some way?

BF: I don't think so. The nature of the individual experience of a work

---

[¶]See this volume, p. 117.

of music as an experience of that work and no other is a quite difficult philosophical problem. The postulated totality is a convenient fiction that is useful to work with. A piece cannot be defined as whatever the composer intended, no more, no less, since firstly we cannot have access to what most composers intended, nor, secondly, would that totality necessarily correspond to what others have found in the piece. The important thing is that the work lead the listener to suspend disbelief for the duration of the piece and that the longer-term memory be brought efficiently into play for the time after the piece has ceased. Maybe it is a lack on my part that I don't accept this totalitizing of work experience; let me give an example. Quite some while ago, I had been intensively analyzing the **Bagatelles** Op.9 by Webern; after spending many hours dissecting, reflecting, and reassembling each movement, I tried the experiment of 'thinking through' each of them in my head, together with all the insights I felt myself to have gained in their study. I found out that in no single case was this completely possible. Even in the shortest of statements there seems to me a richness and mobility which is only very imperfectly amenable to summation. A comforting thought in many ways!

In fact, this particular problem was one of the central issues in **Funérailles** for seven strings and harp, completed in 1979.

PA: It is curious that **Funérailles II** uses material from **Funérailles I** and creates a new reading from it.

BF: I was very much concerned, in the second version at least, with creatively observing the way I actually went about composing. In one sense, the second version is a concretization of the act of composing.

The basic process was like this: I constructed a grid which I then overlaid on the score of Version One, already completed. This grid separated the material into small, independent frames, completely decontextualizing it, in effect. Sometimes these frames would slightly overlap, so that some elements would be treated more than once; sometimes frames were actually embedded in the territory of larger frames. I then took each isolated frame and investigated its autonomous properties very carefully, trying to establish what seemed to me to be the most significant characteristics of that fragment and - equally important - my own current attitude towards them. I was fascinated to discover that some fragments imposed themselves on me in quite unexpected fashions, that is to say, in ways unconnected with the original intention or means of composition. In was like, shall we say, a form of creative archaeology, but before the fact in the sense of utilizing the information gleaned to create a new context rather than recreate a previous one. Working with givens possessing an amazing will of their own led to the production of an uncharacteristically unprestructured discourse; I was compelled to invent moment-by-moment strategies to accommodate what I was in the process of discovering. I don't want to imply the absence of strict processes; rather, that these processes arose out of the specific nature of the material situation 'discovered' in every frame. The priorities were often wildly different from frame to frame.

Ex. C: **Funérailles I/II**

Version 1

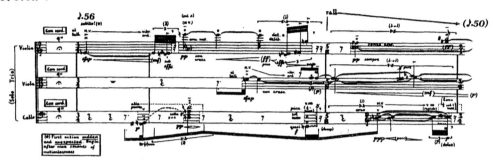

Version 2

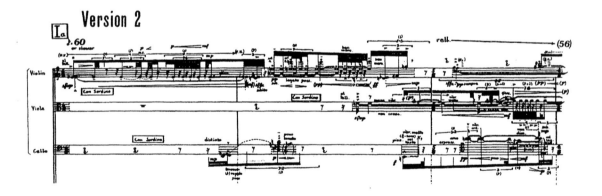

PA: Why the title, **Funérailles**?

BF: In the score I describe an experience I once had in which I seemed to find myself on a hilltop looking down on a vast parade ground, where hordes of soldiers were manoeuvering in an impressively choreographed pattern. The distance was so great that they seemed almost like ants. I remember later thinking about the nature of ritual public actions, what they mean to participants and what might be their effect upon outside observers totally unfamiliar with the symbology involved. It's obvious that this can be transferred by analogy to listening to contemporary music! One has to extrapolate on the basis of previous experiences which may be inadequate or even totally irrelevant. Also, the sort of alienation of body and mind which one experiences when participating in ritual actions, like obsequies, for instance, was quite close to what I was attempting in the ritual self-observation of the act of composition. One is sharply aware of the boundaries between mind and body, so that one could almost say that the personality takes on increasedly tactile, sensual qualities; it takes on size, shape, and weight. It was partly this disassociative phenomenon with which I wanted to work, which is why I took steps to increase the sense of distance from the observer by the almost constant employment of mutes on the strings, no matter how gesturally violent the musical language sometimes may be. There is a sort of veil between the sound and the ear which makes us feel 'somewhere else'. That makes the moment where the mutes are removed quite literally physically shocking, of course, since the listener feels that he has been bodily thrust across the intervening space right into the sounds themselves; there is the sensation of outraged violation, at least for me. So the title refers less to the atmosphere of mourning which might, I suppose, be read into some of these qualities, than the solemn, slowed-down pace typical of such ceremonies, whilst the febrile detail of the instrumental writing might be taken as a reference to the way the mind free-wheels associatively at a quite different speed. It all boils down to the question of perspective.

PA: You spoke a moment ago of an evolution towards an immanent level of music; it seems that, after **Funérailles**, this is especially true of, say, the **Second String Quartet**.

BF: I said earlier that I felt that my more recent pieces have withdrawn from direct involvement with extramusical connotative areas. This was certainly true of the **Second Quartet**, which follows **Funérailles** after a fairly lengthy pause. The surface of the music seems to be more overtly 'musicianly' and even somewhat simpler in the demands made upon the individual performer. I personally don't feel the change to be all that important, though; essential considerations have remained constant up until the present, even if it be true that they have turned inward, being expressed by musically-immanent factors (by which I mean expressive quanta best formulated in exclusively musical terms). One central concern was the role of silence - or camouflage, understatement, subterfuge, oblique reference, etc. - in a musical discourse. One might argue that there are vertical and horizontal aspects of the problem, where (as in the first section of the composition) the linear unfolding of formal information treats the issue quite clearly or, as in a later passage, it is the 'vertical' relationship between the sounding surface of the texture and its generating structural depths which is the major issue. The quartet medium is actually a wonderful instrument for this sort of task, since it is tremendously self-contained.

PA: Works like **Lemma-Icon-Epigram** or the cycle **Carceri d'Invenzione** are related to visual stimuli...

BF: Having argued that extramusical associations have become less important, I find that my next piece, **Lemma-Icon-Epigram**, refers explicitly to visual images, even though at one speculative remove. Anyone familiar with the emblem theories of Walter Benjamin will appreciate the relevance of his ideas in respect of the symbolic fiction of the artwork. I actually went further back, though, and examined some of the 16th century emblems (whose tripartite structure is reproduced in my composition) and found them a rich source of speculation of a quite directly musical sort. Particularly in the second, middle section, the organization derives pretty directly from a visually-based scenario. I had the idea of very concrete objects (I ended up employing a series of seven chords) which would occupy, and thus to some extent define, a particular space. An imaginary sun would pass in an arc over this space, thus causing the objects to cast shadows of different lengths, densities and directions at different point on the sun's trajectory. This is realized by overlapping several temporally proportional layers of chordal development. Once one has an idea of what is happening, it is quite audible in general terms, I think. The temporal space traversed was built up on a grid of bars some of which are based on triplet or quintuplet proportional relationships to the basic eighth note, what I call, for the sake of convenience, 'irrational bars'. This is in fact the first time they appear, but they are a major feature of the subsequent **Carceri d'Invenzione** series.

Whilst still working on the final part of that piece I had already begun, with **Superscriptio**, a first run-up to the idea of a major cycle of compositions of quite different duration and instrumentation which would develop my ideas of musical energy and perspective. Again, a visual experience came to my aid when I rediscovered, after an interval of many years, Piranesi's series of 'Carceri'. But that is probably a topic all to itself...

PA: It's fascinating to listen to you speak about your works, because their problematic elements seem extremely clear to you. It's quite rare to meet a composer who understands himself so well. One could almost say that your remarks reveal true delight in explaining how the works are born, how they are constructed.

BF: It's interesting you should feel that. For myself, I am usually torn between revealing and concealing. It's clear, I think, that the works themselves tend to cover their tracks pretty thoroughly, so that it is difficult, sometimes impossible to retrace in the correct order the steps of the generative process. When analyzing my techniques I tend to steer a middle course in that I talk in some detail about the actual techniques, without necessarily giving formally worked out examples; it all remains a little general. But I would never have made it big as a bookkeeper either. I am nearly always interested in communicating the why of particular means of composing rather than x-raying thoroughly the entrails of the mechanism. Certainly there I try to be as clear as possible. I like to talk about my music in a lecture presentation, but I find it actually much more interesting for me personally to invent examples on the blackboard rather than trace once more a path now effectively blocked-off to me. I want at all costs to avoid giving the impression that it all comes out, during the act of composition, in one polished block. Very often I have been asked why I don't compose at the computer; the only answer I can give is that one set of processes organically suggest further steps in the gestation of a texture or work. Without going through the experience of the early steps I would not have arrived at the insight enabling me to evaluate or invent the later ones. Most computer-formulated composing seems to demand that the entire system be more or less laid out at the beginning. My conceptualization seldom works that clearly so far in advance.

PA: Don't you find it problematic that the structures of the works, more often than not, escape the listener, that they are not perceived, even after several hearings?

BF: I'm sure that the structures, as linear entities, can be heard individually. There are moments when, to me, they seem almost too clear, in fact. If you listen a couple of times to the bass clarinet piece you can soon grow accustomed to the several materials and the scope of their transformative tendencies. The opening ostinato iterations, for example, set up a particular framework within which the later, gradually accumulating modifications of the regularity are introduced. It is quite transparently an accretional tendency, and its later return serves to underline that impression. It is when several processes are running at once that this sort of clarity is clouded over. In the same piece, for example, as the iterative sections get shorter, the up until that point clear linearity is progressively undermined by the increasing predominance of the less obviously regular secondary elements. Increasing complexity coupled with decreasing length makes for problematic recognizability, too. The situation is aggravated still more when the strata are actually sounding simultaneously, as in **La terre est un homme**, for example. In such cases, relative audibility of layers coupled with the necessity of rapid scanning by the ear conspire to undermine immediate registration of salient characteristics. It is amazing, in fact, how rapidly the superposition of even a small number of relatively straightforward lines of information can lead to grave obscurity if care is not taken to allow for points of reference, moments where layers audibly intersect.

PA: Your music is always spoken of as being extremely complex. You once made the distinction between complex music and complicated music, and you claim to have chosen, as far as you're concerned, complexity. Why?

BF: It would be very artificial to attempt to reconstruct the path that led towards a certain musical habitat rather than another. I'm not even sure I really want to know the answer! It is naturally perfectly possible to have a simple texture which delivers complex and subtle information; conversely, there are a lot of quite difficult-sounding pieces the vehicles of which seem to be more complex than the actual content. I was once asked by a teacher finally to attempt a simple piece. I labored away for some time, showed him the result; the score was returned to me with the comment: 'Keep writing complex music'! I tend to encourage students to remain as simple as possible bearing in mind the nature of their individual materials and forms of musical thought. I don't always succeed, though.

PA: Couldn't one say, to perhaps be a bit provocative, that you are a prisoner of your 'system' of composition, of your notation? Is it conceivable that you will depart, abruptly, in a different direction, searching for a new 'style'?

BF: I think that my recent works have moved some way in this direction, away from the explicit polyphonicization of the single voice, towards a more complex relationship between two or more voices. Maybe this is simply because, of late, I have had to compose more for largish ensembles than in earlier years, and we all know that deconstructive parametric notation becomes unnecessarily entropic if twenty players attempt it at once. In such cases I attempt to divert the frictional effect away from the interference between parametric strands towards an increased awareness of the space between allied instruments - allied, I mean, by reason of timbre, register, or processual parallels.

Most lately there are a couple of works which I have been told are approaching the minimal, at least by the standards applied to my compositions. Such a case would be **Mnemosyne** for bass flute and tape, for instance, finished last year. There, the simplicity is a function of the high precompositional regulation of the harmonic flow and the very basic nature of the sounds on the tape: simple chords, with voices changing note invariably at the beginning of a bar. On the other hand, the tempo and bar-structural aspects of the piece are quite complicated, and necessitate click-track coordination with the soloist. My new quartet, the **Third**, strikes me personally as less densely aggressive, with more empty 'breathing space' between events. I imagine that the trend will continue through at least those pieces already concretely planned for the next few years, although it is always dangerous to predict one's own development. One thing I know I will be concentrating on is a clearer differentiation of harmonic background and surface gesture, the 'feedback' between the two being perhaps more intense, sustained, and controlled than hitherto.

PA: If someone were to ask you to write a piece for somewhat inexperienced musicians, with limited technical possibilities, would you be interested?

BF: Not just now! That is not my personal field of interest, just as there are specific musical genres - music theater, for instance - which would not be appropriate as things stand. I'm sure it is possible to do so, and I could imagine ways of treating, say, the open strings of a string orchestra in highly varied way. One should always make the richest, most flexible use of whatever means are available. I frequently give students tasks with specific restrictions of this sort; they concentrate the mind wonderfully!

SPEAKING WITH TONGUES

Composing for the voice: a correspondence-conversation
with Paul Driver (1989)

PAUL DRIVER: Do you have any feelings about the kind of word-setting of composers of the generation of your teacher Lennox Berkeley, Tippett, Britten *et al.*?

BRIAN FERNEYHOUGH: Certainly not directly. I imagine that all forms of stylistic or expressive convention have their roots in some set of implicit assumptions about the world; to that extent, my relative lack of rapport with that generation's vocal works is probably a symptom of my general lack of contact with an entire *Weltanschauung* rather than a reflection of difficulties with specific idioms or techniques. A further barrier might be that I was never exposed, at the customary tender age, to the prescribed schoolboy diet of Hey-Nonny-No madrigals and their present-day offspring; at the same time I had fairly minimal access to the *Lied* tradition, so that I was scarcely familiar with its underlying bedrock of affective gesturality. My own repertoire of gestures grew directly out of an intense preoccupation with the possibilities of wind instruments, and was not thus intensely colored by any *a priori* presumption of (verbally) semantic correspondence. I composed only two works with voice during my very early years: I remained deeply unconvinced by both (one was choral, one for soprano and small ensemble) and they remained unperformed.

Another thing which hindered my approach to most vocal music was my total inability to empathize with the texts frequently set. During my formative years I was deeply impressed by my recent discovery of the Dadaists and Surrealists, and so most forms of pastoral poetry, *Sturm und Drang* and the more rigidly tepid varieties of love lyric were definitely beyond the pale as far as I was concerned. Actually, it was not so much the subversively absurdist aspects of Dadaism which attracted me as their (partly unconscious?) sense of the epiphanic, of the needle-point of evanescent illumination. No doubt this was an appropriately Dadaist misunderstanding on my part; still at the time it proved an important signpost and trigger.

Probably it is not very useful to lump together a group of intensely individual creative spirits merely by reason of parallels of chronology. My own reaction to each of the figures you mention is basically conditioned by the exposure - or lack of it - which I had to each of them. I can recall hearing no

Berkeley before my time at the RAM,[¶] and of what I came across later little or none was in one of the vocal genres. Tippett I encountered through one work only, **King Priam**, which impressed me with its lithe counterpoint and the brittle sparseness of the vocal writing. The curt diction and oddly oblique lines (somehow twisted at an angle to the plane of the instrumental accompaniment) seemed enigmatically stirring, so that the experience remains with me to the present day. The major later work I heard was a recording of **The Vision of St. Augustine**, the score of which I examined in some detail at the time. I respect highly the stature of that piece as a major contribution to the sparsely populated domain of the 'theater of ideas'.

One heard somewhat more Britten in the early '60s, in particular the **War Requiem** and **Noye's Fludde**. Perhaps my lack of contact with the larger work in particular is better ascribed to more general unease with the entire tradition of British choral music. Whilst there is no denying the deep and enduring roots of that genre, there is something about the hoary subject-matter and generally predictably set-piece treatment of most such essays that struck me as rather sad. Maybe, again, it was the aura of imperturbability and cultural pseudo-authority all too often associated with the performance of such mammoths that I found distasteful. Whichever, it seems likely that my tendency to reject the vision of music as being primarily the vehicle for some sort of 'message' has its roots in the perception of deep inauthenticity in the heart of many such fabrications. I am not suggesting that the **War Requiem** belongs to that category; only that listening to significant number of such works inevitably prejudices one's reception of even the most superior large-scale choral edifice.

PD: What about the tradition of the German oratorio?

BF: One of the most deeply affecting experiences of my teens came from listening several times to Haydn's **Creation**. Although at that time I was in no position to analyze or evaluate these impressions, I'm sure that one impressive aspect was the amazing welter of forms I sensed swirling about under the surface. The pure fecundity of realized invention and - perhaps even more affecting - the sense of a fecundity of *potential* in the means and materials employed made that work a great favorite. In later years I came to appreciate the professionality with which 'Papa' deployed his forces, and these two things - professional control and richness of generational potential - have remained dominating ideals for me.

The main quality exciting my imagination in Bach's vocal writing was the magnificent balance of vocal and instrumental interweaving. Optimalized utilization of register plays a big role here, of course, and the creation of two or

---

[¶]Royal Academy of Music, London.

more 'functionally polyphonic' voices in one and the same line by such means contributed much to my own interest in the multi-level treatment of single lines in most of my solo pieces. Certainly the **Etudes** have a number of passages where register and function are obviously co-ordinated.

More than the German, I think the Venetian vocal heritage has provided an enduring inspiration. The control of *time, spatialization* and *elaboration* of even the most minimal basic ideas never fails to evoke admiration. The Monteverdi **Vespers** are the leading example there, especially the wonderful simplicity of the intricate in the dilations and compressions of phrasing in the **Sonata sopra Sancta Maria**, where the utterly basic nature of the vocal invocations is most subtly varied and placed against a mass of metric and textural invention.

Incidentally, an interesting consideration in much early music of this sort is the assembling of movements from various sources and periods of the composer's career into a convincing unity. This is something which has come to occupy me recently, as witness the layout of the **Carceri d'Invenzione** cycle.

PD: What do you think about the approach to text-setting of the Second Viennese School composers, and of Mahler?

BF: Of course there is much marvelous music from that protean epoch in all our pasts. Sometimes I envy the composer living in a period in which speech inflection and musical gesture were so intimately related. Today, everything has fallen apart, and Schoenberg's dream of "musical prose" is scarcely realizable in total dissociation from the rhythmic patterns of "poeticized speech". Once again one realizes how closely the various art-forms cross-fertilized one another then: nowadays there is no tradition of heightened melodramatic oration or non-naturalistic, stylized inflection, so that a chasm has opened up between musical and verbal pattern-making, probably to the detriment of both in some areas. At the very least, the semantic weight of musical vocables today has to rely much more on processual underpinnings: not necessarily a bad thing, of course, since it keeps a composer on his toes. Nothing can be taken for granted - a significant factor in a time tending towards the unthinking restoration of knee-jerk, reach-me-down gestural signals. It has been recently shown how, in Austria and Russia, the long tradition of melodrama entered early into the approach of advanced composers towards renewal of their creative means. That is evident not only in specifically vocal works but - almost *more* obviously really - in purely instrumental works, like Schoenberg's Op.19 **Sechs kleine Klavierstücke**, for instance, where it is difficult, if not impossible, for us to reconstruct the perceptual framework being fleetingly alluded to in every tiny flicker of movement. There is a whole 'screen' of acculturational norms present, on to which the actual pieces are projected, and this quite independently of the actual constructional devices or motivic ploys adopted. This cultural embeddedness is one of the key factors leading to the long-term aesthetic credibility of such a work; the same is true of many of the vocal compositions of the period, where 'Platonic models' of rhetorical typology provide a secure underpinning to the flights of invention or momentary strayings of the text-melody encounter. Perhaps this is why, in such major efforts as **Das Buch der Hängenden Gärten**, the accompanimental structures are more obviously 'revolutionary' than the melodies themselves, which often remain in a quite restricted sphere of behavioral categories.

In spite of Schoenberg's assertion that he generally through-composed a song on the basis of his reaction to the color of the first syllable of the text, I think that he frequently subjected his texts to careful prior analysis. Something I find fascinating is his versatility in taking such rigidly metric, rhyming verse as George and transforming it into textures of such flowingly sinuous unpredictability. That sort of 'going against the grain' provides him at times with a 'negative dialectical' cadential capacity of a uniquely context-bound quality.

Belief systems providing some common ground between the poet and the musician of the day were vital to the unique success of the enterprise; some of the partial parallels between the 'art religion' of George and Rilke found sympathetic echoes at key moments of Schoenberg's and Webern's careers. At the present time one notes with regret the fact that, when poets or novelists mention musical taste, it is usually in conjunction with entertainment music rather than works by their contemporary equivalents in serious music fields.

Sometimes, though, we find fascinating and provoking fractures of sensibility between text and setting. Take, for example, the group of works around Webern's Opus 18, where the naïve, transparently pious sensibility of the folk verse is sucked up in a whirlwind of crystalline transformations of the most sophisticated type. The work is good, in my view, largely because the composer's personality actually apprehended the two seeming extremes as naturally co-extant, integral facets of its being: maybe Webern did not even notice the extremities evoked? I am, in any case, extremely fond of those pieces: the entire period is full to bursting with compositions traversed by fascinating fault lines (which become the more fruitfully active the more the form of the piece occupies itself with denying their existence). Even so, appreciating this music involves us in a certain willing suspension of disbelief if we are going to be able to creatively tolerate the tensions thus thrust upon us.

One key work stands above all others from the point of view of the embodiment of the transitory, and that is Schoenberg's **Second Quartet** with soprano. The weirdly fatalistic joviality of the Scherzo surely could not have been followed without resort to the surmounting powers associated with the voice. The intense effort to make the instruments really *speak* in the third movement is mirrored in the finale by a sense that the voice has been drawn up into a form of expression beyond the limits of the subjective: at least, that is my impression.

My own **4th Quartet** has been commissioned as a companion piece to that work, utilizing the same voice and, with all the differences that will inevitably emerge, I hope that it will find a means of integrating the voice into a corresponding meditation on the nature of transition as both material and spiritual force.

Very often the Viennese Three achieve their greatest vocal impact at sudden moments of what I can only term *objectivization* of their images: I'm thinking of parts of the **Altenberg Lieder** or, later, the way in which the rigorous symmetries of the complete **Lulu** conspire to highlight the expressive intensity by continually hurling formal obstacles into its path. The same might be said of Webern's **Entflieht auf leichten Kähnen**, where both the obsessive canonic movement and the unstable tonal pulls conspire to emphasize the 'fleeing', 'escaping' of the title, thus offering a self-contained metaphor of both rigor and light-headed motion.

In many ways, the Romantic heritage has proved to be a seductive minefield for composers concerned with the unbroken continuation of the *Lied* tradition: the affective vocabulary developed seventy/eighty years ago is still being served up in the guise of an unreflected *lingua franca* by several generations of essentially academic artists. At the other extreme, the (now - as I predicted several years ago - waning) New Romantic movement has sacrificed the exemplary Viennese dialectic of expression tempered in the furnace of formal stringency on the altar of what can only be described as the ultimately repetitive illusion of uniquely unrepeatable gestural pathos.

Every language is open to debasement, of course, just as a rich creative spirit can always emerge to infuse a moribund style with a brief span of extended life. It's dangerous to generalize, better to look at what is actually being composed. Still, it's fairly significant, I think, how many **Kindertotenlieder**-type pieces are still being composed, enriched - for the most part - with 'contemporary' vibraphone washes.

PD: What are your thoughts on the work in this field of Boulez, Stockhausen and Berio (also Peter Maxwell Davies) - a field which has been in the forefront of post-war music?

BF: Again, it's difficult to generalize. I appreciated very much the utopian vision informing Boulez's vast **Visage nuptial**, even if his ideas scarcely seem realizable.

The iridescent veil of sound brought forth by the incessant subdividing of his forces was both intense and impalpable simultaneously. On the other hand, this piece, together with **Le soleil des eaux**, creates problems of a different sort; perhaps it has to do with the rather naked quality of the solo lines; or, in the latter work, the not very effective *Sprechgesang* passages in the second movement.

The early **Improvisations** are interesting, less for the vocal technique in itself than for the deferential, echoing 'wrap' of percussion sonorities, which amplifies, enriches and dissects the solo lines. The **Marteau** I take to be a boundary marker in a certain direction; for me it proved invaluable as a limiting instance, beyond which music could not usefully go at this time. My own **Etudes** are the most recent evidence of this attitude on my part.

Of Stockhausen's works employing the voice, the only one of absolutely undoubted significance is surely **Gesang der Jünglinge**. It is astounding how early [1955-6] he was able to isolate significant aspects of the speech act into constellations of such purity and balance. It is perhaps a sad comment on more recent computer music developments that that achievement has still to be surpassed in terms of musical, rather than technical, quality. It is, also, a demonstration of the affective power of the voice, even when electronically transmuted. The sonic complexity and capacity for meaningful nuance provide the studio composer with an as yet almost untapped reservoir of tools. I am less familiar with Stockhausen's subsequent production in this field.

The same is true of Berio, with the exception of the well-known **Sequenza III**, which is still valid as a pioneer example of 'psychosemantic' formal notions. In that role, it was no doubt invaluable in eroding the power of many a hoary preconception. It demonstrated, too, a lucid and economic breakdown of material resources, as well as an eminently practical view of what could and could not be done in each category. At the same time, there is an ever-present danger of these compositional operations tipping over into concatenations of semantically explicit images. Perhaps that is always the difficulty attached to the solo voice, where such problems can't be offset by more complex overlappings or layerings.

Maybe it is this very same issue of semantic (over)loading which lies at the root of the permanent malaise in music theater projects. Something like Ligeti's **Aventures** succeeds - in spite of the radically innovatory utilization of abstract phonetic patterns - because it still rests on an unambiguously secure foundation of situational conventions. The emotive 'typecasting' of the material remains relatively apparent, regardless of the unusual or grotesque filters through which it is manifested. At the same time this situational clarity is offset by a very rich employment of specific nuance, so that there is always an a-naturalistic distance maintaining aesthetic reserve - something that is not always true in other examples of the genre.

I have scarcely ever encountered a generic music theater piece of the sort so current in the '70s which does not wilt when confronted by the challenge to compositionally justify much of the overt semantically appellative gestures included. One hysterical scream tends to be depressingly like another in those artificially overstated situations deemed essential to get the 'idea' across. The circus clown functions, because of the ubiquitous awareness of the nature and limits of his 'grammar': music theater generally fails since, no matter what the nature of the 'narration' to be transmitted, the means employed still pretend to the immediacy of individualized expression without paying (or even, it seems, being aware of the need to pay) the structural price.

By and large, it seems that choral compositions manage to avoid this dilemma, largely by virtue of the greater flexibility offered by larger ensembles, which serves to suppress the more obviously personal attributes of each voice, thus keeping the affective intensity balanced against technical and formal considerations of a more obviously robust sort.

Your question fails, by the way, to make any mention of an entire series of composers whose approach to the voice has been far more radical; among these one would have to mention Kagel, Bussotti, Holliger, Gaburo and Schnebel at the very least. Their tradition seems to stem less from the Viennese lineage than from the Dadaists such as Tzara, Hugo Ball and, above all, Schwitters, whose **Ur-Sonate** was a unique, if musically less than subtle attempt at ordering syllables according to formal principles such as the classical sonata or scherzo. Of these, it was Schnebel who disassembled the components of the vocal mechanism most radically, and some of his compositions still stand as extreme limits which it would be rather difficult to transgress. Particularly striking was his attempt to employ 'liberated' vocal techniques as actual tools for freeing the performer from psychological barriers to effective group improvisation. Later attempts restricted themselves almost entirely to exercises in breathing technique. It was largely his music which formed the core repertoire of the Schola Cantorum Stuttgart, perhaps the most intellectually aware and dedicated ensemble in the field during the crucial developmental years between 1960 and 1975. Although the extended techniques evolved then hardly made any impression on the Anglo-Saxon world, a composer passes them by at his peril; whether he wishes to use the insights offered or not, some of the research and compositional work carried out was, and remains, of great significance.

PD: What in general do you think is the relation of words to music in a non-operatic work, i.e. how important is it to project the verbal meaning of words, or how un-important?

BF: I think that words are bound into the final result in a multitude of ways, not only in terms of their immediate comprehensibility. The entire work is necessarily infused with their presence; the texts themselves are frequently only a restricted instance of a much more comprehensive vision for which, in any particular work, they come to stand. It is in this emblematic light that we should regard the text, as something radiating out into the musical discourse, infusing it with connective energy, rather than as a semantically circumscribed statement requiring finite compositional exegesis. In any case, "meaning" has many aspects, most of all in poetry. Which of those theoretically possible are we to favor? It is clear that the power of imagery on our inner ear and eye is immense - powerful enough, one might suppose, for us to get on with the process of composing without the dubious and often amateurish acts of aesthetic bowdlerization occasionally served up as "interpretation". Still, your use of the term "project" is interesting. Do you mean, I wonder, that key words should generally be presented in particularly sharp focus, or perhaps that some modified form of madrigalistic mirroring principle be adopted? The latter might be quite difficult in the setting of verse with largely speculative or not overtly sensual content.

There have, by the way, been occasions on which actually being able to *hear* the words has had a negative influence on the quality of the musical experience.

PD: How is verbal meaning transformed?

BF: I take it that you mean written texts, rather than speech acts. When discussing vocal setting it seems natural to begin with the word on the page rather than the variables of individual diction. Perhaps this is a reflection of the de-verbalization of our current culture; at any rate it is clear that the written form of a text allows one a considerably broader scope of interpretation than any given spoken presentation, where the powerful 'support mechanisms' of individual inflection thrust themselves into the foreground. I take it as more or less axiomatic that the text embedded in a musical context will be similarly colored by whatever articulational conventions have been adopted for its presentation. A great deal of music has been composed by aspiring to the representation of textual connotations in parallel musical guise; much more interesting to me would seem the project of consciously composing *against* the words, or else subverting them in some fashion. The methods of music can seldom find precise correspondences in poetic processes; nevertheless the choice of means should at least reflect an *attitude* on the part of the composer to the givens with which he is working.

It could perhaps be argued that such an approach is not being 'fair' to the poet: after all, the latter is seldom directly consulted concerning the suitability of his materials for text setting in the first place. I imagine that many an author has been bemused by the musical vocabulary woven around and through his verse in such a forced marriage.

It is a pity that circumstances frequently militate against the active collaboration of composer and author. All too often, resorting to materials from past centuries acts as a hindrance to the unfolding of innovative musical perspectives. Since poetry and music share quite a few generalized techniques of internal ordering, one would think that interestingly innovative approaches to an agreed common goal could be achieved by communal weighting of alternative options.

Of course, there are many ways of deliberately alienating both poetic intention and aesthetic position. Careful choice of semantically loaded musical styles can throw any statement whatsoever into an ironical light. Such ploys fail to convince, however, when deeper levels of substantial affinity are left out of the equation: the text will frequently escape unscathed unless critical intent is underpinned by deliberate (and dangerous) interlocking of correspondences. The first person on whom the critical beam should be focused needs to be the composer.

PD: How do you select your texts? What responsibility do you have to the poet?

BF: The selection of texts is extremely problematic. Not all texts to which one actively responds are suitable for musical treatment, frequently because their inner coherence and particularized sonorities are resolutely impervious to further commentary. Whilst visual and verbal images frequently evoke sound experiences in my mind, I am not altogether convinced that allying the triggering with the triggered would add much to either. I have accepted that a lengthy period of reflection and rearrangement is usually required before such spontaneous alliances can become fruitful (by which time they have normally turned into something else).

Generally I find that attractive texts have set free chains of association *not* immediately translatable into sound, but which permit me to collage disparate impulses into an identifiable and consistent set of concerns. This, in turn, traces the lineaments of a concrete *project*.

Maybe this answers your question regarding responsibility too. I imagine that a poet would be rather effective on his own terms in the first instance, the detailed ramifications of which, for the composer, only reveal themselves gradually, and after a decent interval. Other than that, one should perhaps show respect by not being too subservient, either to the text or one's initial response to it. In some instances, a particular poem has gathered around it a bunch of not obviously related ideas, which themselves attract further poems, gradually defining a forum for their mutual interaction. Such was the case, for instance, with the Ernst Meister text "Der Grund kann nicht reden", which forms the cornerstone of the **Etudes**. The poems by Alrun Moll were written at my request in order to articulate this complex as specifically as possible.

PD: Can one write satisfactorily for the voice without using words or syllables?

BF: It depends on one's criteria for satisfaction. No particular means are of themselves guarantors of significance; all demand to be tested in the refining fires of invention. Certainly a major body of works has come into being in the last twenty-five years as a direct result of the explosive stimulus of linguistic research upon the artist's understanding of verbal communication. Since the example of the French Symbolists, many poets have expressed a desire for a form of poetry nearer to music than to prose; the Twentieth Century has offered some quite powerful tools and insights which allow poetry and music to approach and intermingle (*pace* some "concrete poetry") in a kaleidoscopic whirl of invention. The rapid development of various forms of social theorizing has also come to play its part in the formulation and realization of these aims, not least because the voice is the primary instrument of social intercourse, creating to that end an enormous panorama of dialects, ideolects and pidgins.

Many forms of human vocal comportment are, in any case, quite independent of the phenomenon of ordered language. On the face of it, musical statements composed primarily of such sonic types are not necessarily any more absurd or artificial than a vocal texture relying largely on the extended fabrication of regularly fluctuating, pitched tones, as for example in **Aida**.

In the wake of the much-trumpeted "exhaustion of material" (or the exhaustion, perhaps, of those concentrating too exclusively on such things) it seems that activity in this corner of the field has ebbed somewhat, being pushed back by crudely robust strategies of more fundamentalist persuasion: even so, a number of individuals are still insistently active, such as Trevor Wishart, and the computer analysis of the overtone structure of vocal sounds promises to allow some composers to confront these difficult issues from an entirely different direction.

If it appears that I am deliberately repressing that *other* school of "overtone music" exemplified by, say, Stockhausen's **Stimmung**, it is mainly because I have seen little evidence that harmonic structures based on the approximation of the natural overtone series have any convincing implications in formal matters. Of itself, the fact that such systems claim relevance through a supposed closeness to nature is often misunderstood as a form of legitimization in aesthetic terms, whereas I cannot but help see this correspondence as a fatal flaw, denying the material the innate capacity to expand and develop meaningfully individuated processual configurations. It is no accident that such precepts end up, for the most part, poured into formal containers seemingly cut off from the featureless roll of infinity. As a contributory factor to the extension and differentiation of timbre, however, the increased awareness of sonic complexity must surely prove beneficial, although one would think that live vocal nuance is already very complex by its very nature.

PD: Are you attracted to opera? Would you like to write a music theatrical work of some kind? Which operatic conventions are of interest, do you think?

BF: I'm not very attracted to anything in the way of operatic conven-tion *per se*. Most conventions are little more than boiled-down, schematized rem-nants of things done in actual pieces, and I would not be vitally interested in perpetuating that sort of folk wisdom. Other conventions, of course, are rooted in the defining limitations of the opera-house situation itself. These one would have to study carefully, but they don't seem to lie so much in the domain of the composer as that of the director. The temptation is usually to play safe, since failure would lead to large-scale disastrous consequences.

Once, quite a while ago now, I was approached with a particular sub-ject in mind. As it happened, the choice suggested to me that the director con-cerned had misunderstood what my music is largely about, so the project fell through. On that occasion I expended a fair amount of time and effort on the fruitless search for an alternative theme, but became rapidly discouraged by the unenviable necessity of choosing between the staidly (and irreproachably) mythic and a crudely plot-ridden pseudo-causality. Finally I came to the con-clusion that the only viable option would be to start from scratch, preferably working in close collaboration with a textbook author.

Rather than music being appended to some external action, perhaps it would be more useful to consider the innate nature of the 'dramaturgy' of a particular musical language, and aim at generating a theatrical continuity from the tension, resolution and time-flow qualities typical of that. Time, in fact, would be a problem in itself: the sort of temporal disposition necessary for an evening-filling opera could surely be reconciled with a rather rapid rate of material evo-lution only with great difficulty.

I thought sometimes that one solution would be the simultaneous un-folding of several layers of musical and dramatic activity, although it is scarcely conceivable that an entire evening could plausibly be filled out with a discourse of such density. Probably some sort of cyclically evolving fluctuation in the number of superincumbent layers would prove a remedy to that difficulty. Whether such a concept could be adequately housed in the confines of a con-ventional opera house is a moot point.

Surely the most successful opera composers have been those whose musical language was subject to as small a distortion as possible when fed through the operatic mincer. Perhaps one should bear this in mind whilst attempting to look at the situation from the other side - that is, that a successful opera will be most likely to emerge from the workshop of composers who approach the medium from the standpoint of their individual compositional technique without making contextual compromises or well-meaning adapta-tions to whatever conventional wisdom might seem to dictate.

Notes on some recent compositions

Missa Brevis

I started composing the **Missa Brevis** in 1968, albeit in a version (taken no further than the beginning of the *Gloria*) which did not anticipate extensive employment of antiphonal procedures. The textural treatment might perhaps be schematized as a fanning-out from the spatial deployment of isolated syllables and phonemes, via the simultaneous presentation of different text fragments, up to and including the textural and metrical isolation of entire choral groups.

The beginning of the *Kyrie* is a prime example of the first approach. By a radical segmentalization of the text this latter becomes 'over-sharp' in focus, is 'kineticized' (Example 1).

Ex. 1

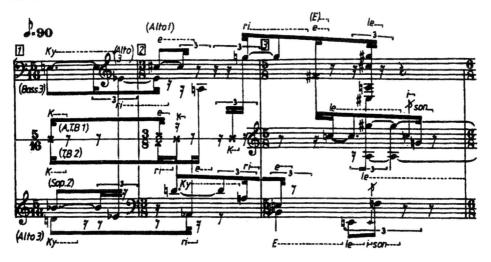

The dance of syllables also serves to outline the musical space within which the entire work will manoeuvre - something that takes on great significance as the structural character of the antiphonal treatment becomes clearer. Of course, the *Kyrie* treatment was not a new device; Nono, in particular, had been doing something similar in the '50s. In his works, though, the effect was less dynamic, being more a sense of timeless hovering than an increase in analytic tension. Perhaps the reason for this might be sought in his use of fairly abstract serial durational technique, whereby his ability to underline the agogic patterns of his texts was unnecessarily restricted. Also, his employment of the vowel-rich Italian language led him naturally towards a palette of sustained sonorities, whereas my opening movement tends to treat vowels and consonants more or less equally.

Whilst large parts of the *Kyrie* hurl phonemes between the twelve singers in a complex criss-cross pattern, the following *Gloria* is already becoming more consciously monumental in its allocation of textures to particular groups or registers. At the same time we find entire lines of text superimposed, their individuality being emphasized by contrasting techniques (unpitched, *staccato*

Ex. 2

* Tenors ~ "sprechgesang"
Basses ~ unpitched, speech
(no inflection - very mechanical)

declamation in the male voices opposing *legato* sung polyphony in the sopranos and altos, for example) (Example 2).

This change of perspective might be interpreted, perhaps, as a move away from the 'inside' structure of individual words towards a more global, categorized complexity.

On the whole, the *Gloria* moves in clear-cut texture blocks, more or less corresponding to one- or two-line segments of text. Only one passage attempts a dynamic transition from a chaotic state to a particular sort of unanimity among all three groups, and this is really the sole passage in which the antiphonal lay-out is abandoned for a while (Example 3).

Ex. 3

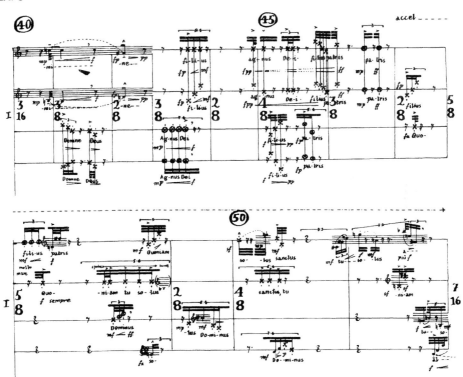

As the work progresses the tendency towards separation of the three SATB groups becomes ever more important, so much so that, in the *Agnus Dei* (Example 4), the groups become mutually independent, each being conducted at a tempo particular to it alone. The main conductor remains with the central group, which thrusts aggressive chunks of text on to the almost wordlessly melismatic background provided by the other ensembles.

Beginning as a single integrated system, text and music have thus been progressively decoupled. Even though this is by no means a simple, one-dimensional process, sufficient sense of deliberate steering in a certain direction remains, I think, to put the individual movements into the dual context of the interaction text/musical setting and movement-to-movement treatment of musical space itself.

It should perhaps be explained that the choice of text had less to do with statements of faith than with a feeling that the Mass ceremonial itself is a culturally integral monument, both historically and formally. As such, it has managed to withstand relatively unscathed the efforts of composers of many periods

Ex. 4

Agnus Dei

N.B After conductor starts groups I + III in their respective tempi, their future internal co-ordination should be assigned to a chosen member of each group.

to bend it to their individual musical ends. This may be taken as something of a back-handed compliment, I suppose, but the task was undertaken in a spirit of profound respect on my part. It was a rather effective method, apart from any other considerations, of attacking the problem of identity which less culturally resilient sources might well have left largely open.

Missa Brevis has not been taken up by very many choirs; this was, I think, not so much because of its basic difficulty of execution (since, although virtuoso, the techniques involved are overwhelmingly traditional) but because of the extremely high upper range required of the three sopranos, ranging, at times, up to high Eb and E.

Time and Motion Study III

This twenty-four-minute piece began life as a response to a commission from Südwestfunk, Baden-Baden, for a new work to be performed during the Donaueschingen New Music Days in October 1974, and utilizing the very special talents of the remarkable Schola Cantorum Stuttgart and its very erudite conductor, Dr. Clytus Gottwald. This choir was - and is - perhaps unique in both its unswerving dedication to the encouragement of new works and in the level of acuity and special intellectual talents of its members, many of whom were also professionally active in academic and scientific careers.

The prospect of working with this group was naturally extremely stimulating, especially since I had had very few professional performances of any works at all before that date. Even so, the time available for composing was extremely limited, so that a great deal of hurried conceptualizing was necessary. (In fact, in spite of the efforts of all concerned, the piece had to be postponed until Donaueschingen 1975.) The point at which I started was my experience of writing for the flute several years earlier. One of my main motives for concentrating on the flute family had been the fact that many different articulation levels can be superimposed on the basic sound production technique. Since the same is also true for the human voice I came across many parallels in my research, the flute solo **Unity Capsule** being composed as a direct consequence of my experiences in the realm of vocal combinatoriality, and **Time and Motion Study III** represents a further intensification and codification of the insights I gained there.

It was clear from the outset that I would not be employing a given text, but would take as my 'subject' the fundamental combinatorial and permutational sound generating potential of the vocal mechanism itself. Three categories came immediately to mind: (1) basic types of sound production (plosives, voiced/ unvoiced, nasal sonorities etc.); (2) techniques for articulational modification of the first group (gargling, altered mouth position, indrawn breath) and (3) the application of diverse phonetic characteristics to all the above (derived from the extended International Phonetic Alphabet familiar from linguistic studies). A further essential presupposition would have to be a notation which permitted as much salient information as possible to be united on and around a single traditional note-head symbol, since only that which could be so united would be capable of being conceived in a practically manipulable fashion.

Since each of these categories contains an enormous potential, even before being combined with elements from foreign categories, I had to devise means of stating my terms in as clear a manner as possible whilst enhancing the material's utility in respect of form. What finally came out was a separation of the singers into four distinct groups, distinguished not only spatially and in terms of their size and constitution but also, more importantly, their typical sound articulation repertoire. This is the starting-point of the piece and practically the entire first section (of three) retains very consciously the layers thus defined as well as the developmental procedures most appropriate to each. The four choral groups are divided up in the following manner (Example 5):

Ex. 5

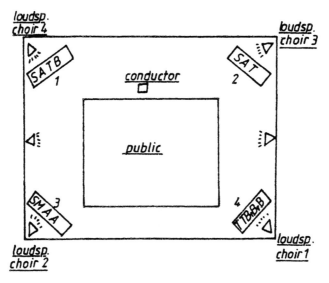

Each group's first set of entries is formulated in as near to primary colors as the means chosen permit, and the total independence of each process in time offers the ear the chance to locate, identify and follow each line of thought in spite of the prevailing discontinuity and initial unpredictability. For example, Choir I (SATB) concentrates almost exclusively on sibilant sonorities disposed in three distinct phrases, the final one of which is itself tripartite. The sibilants are generated in quite varied ways - at first by means of explosive expelling of breath, later by abrasively indrawn breath and, lastly, by a combination of these surrounding the sound of air being "irritatedly" expelled through the nose (Example 6).

Ex. 6

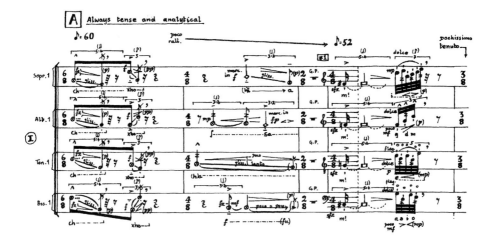

The second intervention of Choir I, following after quite a lengthy interval, again offers a triple perspective: this time the clasped hands, moved in front of the mouth, offer additional articulative possibilities (Example 7).

The third entry takes up once more the final element of Example 6, extending it by means of trill actions and, little by little, making a transition towards more 'normally' sung notes (although still without definite pitch) (Example 8).

In contrast to this, the second choir (SAT) exploits basically plosive techniques, its textures being correspondingly abrupt and caustic in tone. Choir III develops a number of basic articulational types in a form of prolational distension, whilst Choir IV, more calmly, exposes much of the basic pitch-material of the work in the guise of emphatically 'colored' attacks initiating complexly fluctuating resonances.

Since, as I said before, the choir's entries and duration of presence were calculated without direct reference to one another, the act of composition was deeply influenced by the preformed 'situations' encountered. The narrative in Part I is the story of my journey through that particular labyrinth.

The large-scale form is articulated most obviously by this functional and spatial separation of forces; as the work progresses materials obviously evolve in many directions, and are subject to conflicting attractions and repulsions. Many types of sonority evolve towards and through each other, with the result that the distinction between the choirs' separate identities becomes progressively more obscured - a tendency supported after a while by the introduction of discreet percussion sounds, themselves usually selected with a view to doubling, amplifying or resonating already present vocal textures. The first percussion sounds occur at precisely the point where, in the original plan, the first complete silence would have been located (Letter N in the published score).

Ex. 7

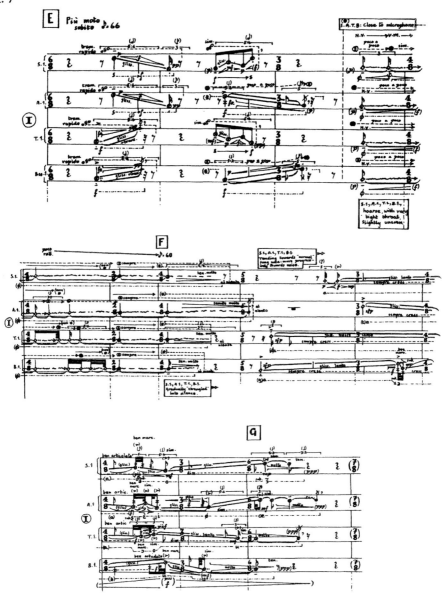

The second main section of **Time and Motion Study III** dissolves the allegiance of the individual singers to their respective ensembles: what happens is that communal *attack points* are defined where all singers prescribed for a particular event (and the number varies from nearly all down to two performers) must begin, no matter how long or short their subsequent activity. This section is characterized most obviously by a wide variety of sound production

Ex. 8

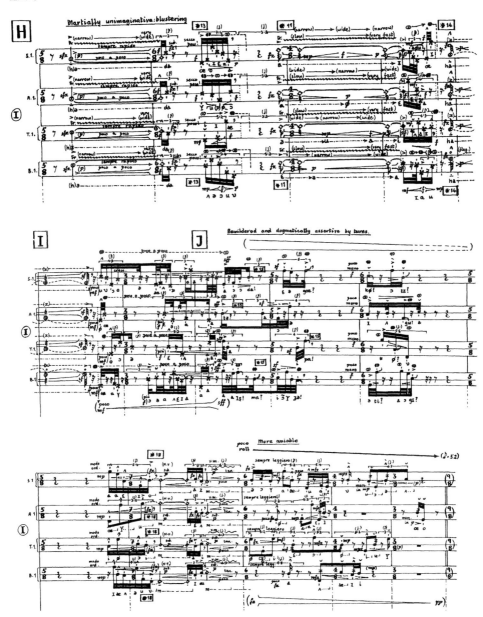

techniques held together by the resonance and sharp, damped attacks of metal percussion. In some cases, nevertheless, the apparent heterogeneity is intended to suggest a communal point of sonic reference (as in the case where the general instruction is "Like the sound of a single, giant lung" (Letter F2 in the published score)).

After a vast percussion climax fades there is the ultimate dissolution of 'societal bonds' in a texture of completely individuated dissociation. For several pages each singer has a highly virtuoso, detail-encrusted 'text' which signally fails to lock-in with whatever is being sung simultaneously. A line of material taken at random will afford some idea of the general idiom employed (Example 9).

Ex. 9

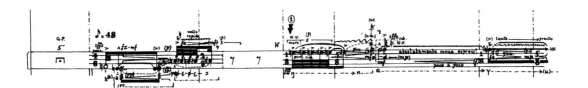

Actually, the harmonic and background rhythmic structures are very secure; they are simply overwhelmed by the flood of micro-images which they are constrained to support. At the time I envisaged this as standing for the end of the line product of the tendency of the individual to develop distinctive traits at the expense of the group activity by which he is initially defined. This no doubt somewhat ironical standpoint was in some ways very characteristic of my attitudes towards musical meaning at the time. Other manifestations of the same urge were the question of "efficiency" in aesthetic terms as opposed to mechanical reproductive ones and, at one further remove, the entire problem of electroacoustic reproducibility. Rather, I suppose, like a primitive forest dweller who imagines that a photograph steals part of his soul, I too have always had a certain healthy suspicion of such prostheses. Thus, during the final pages of this work, a loop-tape is stealthily introduced, playing back material sung by the choir a few moments earlier. I saw this reproduction as being somehow a mutilated symbol of the original it set out to subvert and supplant, since the mental activity necessary for the reproduction of the original was lacking in the taped reproduction. All these thoughts, and others, were resonating in and through the title, which was not at all chosen as a bland portmanteau term for everything and nothing. The inevitable suggestion of industrial standards of production and the concomitant evaluation of the individual according to the needs of the production process was very much at the forefront of my mind. The second and third **Time and Motion Studies** probably reflect most clearly my then prevailing concern with drawing back into the musical work significant aspects of other sociocultural disciplines, remolded in a common, neo-mythic light.

I mentioned earlier, in passing, the major role played by notation in this piece. If one examines a list of symbols employed, it is readily seen that essential information is gathered *(a)* in the shape of the note-head *(b)* in symbols located on the note-stem *(c)* in additional instructions placed above the conjunction of *(a)* and *(b)* and, finally, below the stave in the form of phonetic symbols. When working out my notation I tried to locate each symbol in a place reflecting its relative primacy in the synthesizing process; for example, the note-head was accepted as representing the basic, irreducible identity of the event. Only in a very small number of instances was it necessary to combine two symbols in one complex note-head image. The stem was taken as reflecting secondary, articulative dimensions: according to this, it was notationally possible to combine several modificatory techniques in one and the same event (e.g. breathing in, combined with "gargling" produced by means of constricted vocal cords). By and large, I aimed at making all the symbols located in similar places stand for mutually interchangeable articulations. At the same time there were obviously techniques which were mutually exclusive by the very nature of the vocal mechanism, and I located these articulations in positions making this fact clear. The final result was a complex layering of priorities in which each component strand was capable of being permutated independently, thus allowing for directional transformation of a powerful sort. Without a notation reflecting such basic hierarchical criteria this aspect of the work would scarcely have been feasible. Even then, there were many specific, context-bound instructions which proved quite unavoidable from time to time and which were provided in verbal form. Quite often the interpretational characters thus suggested were crassly in opposition to the character suggested by the musical events themselves: this was a further attempt on my part to test the limits of "efficiency" of both notational adequacy and performative introjectional capability. In any case, it should be emphasized that I was not unaware of the affective connotations of the sound combinations involved. It's clear that account must be rendered to the emotive dimension. I felt then, and feel now that it would be dreadfully wrongheaded to see the sonorities in this piece as being essentially "abstract" in nature, even though they don't always refer to unambiguous behavioral correlates.

Perhaps it has been this quasi-polyphonic aspect of combinatoriality which has been the specifically personal quality distinguishing my piece from those composers instrumental in first exploring the implications of extended vocal practice, such as Lachenmann, Schnebel, Holliger, Ligeti and, to a lesser degree, Kagel. Whilst each of these artists contributed to research without which my own work in the field would have been much more tentative, if not downright impossible, none of them, I think, had been particularly concerned with employing this syntactic mobility to any marked degree. Certainly, I myself see the work far more in the light of my then-current instrumental occupations than as a direct reflection of the immediate past of choral practice as such.

Transit

The case of **Transit** is actually quite different. The first instrumental passages, as well as the provisional formal disposition and instrumentation, were established before I was asked to compose **Time and Motion Study III**, so that, from the outset, my vocal concerns were somewhat different. Even though the major vocal passages (for some combination of the six amplified solo voices) incorporate a wide spectrum of techniques ranging from normal singing on the basis of syllabic text division (*Intonatio*), through complexly wrought, lavishly decorated melismatic passages (*Voices II*), up to the fragile timbral webs of sound characteristic of *Voices I*, there was no conscious attempt on my part to explore and expand the limits of the voice in a way analogous to **Time and Motion Study III**. For one thing, the voices had to take constant note of the instrumental writing, often being required to integrate themselves with it; for another, the fact that there were only six voices available did not permit the same kind of conscious 'orchestration' of texture with which the more radical work concerned itself. Above all, it was the larger-scale considerations of form which dictated vocal usage, since each section is structurally much more self-enclosed than anything I set out to achieve elsewhere. This meant that each individual segment needed to define its terms as clearly and specifically as possible: to that extent, my aim was the differentiation of character, not the synthesis of new, overriding aesthetic norms.

Perhaps the most radical voice treatment occurs right at the outset, where a single chord serves as the invariant basis for a progressive variation and differentiation of articulative nuance according to verbal instructions. The musical material itself is in the form of a loose 'canon', each voice beginning to read at the start of the line designated, thereafter following through all the other lines in order in a circular pattern. Since there is no overall prescribed tempo, each voice is moving through this structure relatively independently although, with the commencement of each new line, identical modifications in performing technique are required of all singers (Example 10).

As well as singing the vocalists play hand-held percussion (maracas, claves) - something, incidentally, which the recent **Etudes** take up once more in the final song. An example of the variation in nuance demanded would be:

At this same point (end of Line 1) certain small (microtonal) fluctuations over and above those indicated in the model are to be introduced at points considered appropriate to the performers themselves. Suggestions are: slow, exaggerated vibrato, small regular or irregular glissandi or the choice of a slightly different pitch for each of a chosen group of notes (particularly effective when applied to more rapid figurations). The fluctuations should be confined to within the range of one semitone on either side of the basic note chosen.

Ex. 10: Transit

In practice this technique functions very well because of the constant friction one senses between the very precisely detailed rhythmic notation and the relatively free overall co-ordination and variability of nuance. Also, there is a marked change of focus as soon as the extremely precise set of variations for the three timpanists begins; the voices immediately retreat into the background - although, as the section progresses, the increased intensity and febrility of improvised detail begins to thrust their material back towards the surface. The 'circling' quality of this passage finds its twin in the violently fragmented, highly amplified shrieks of the final "Transitio", even though the calmly meditative aspect of the opening is there transformed into a nihilistic, back-and-forth pacing.

In a sense, all vocal actions encountered in the main body of **Transit** might be seen as intermediate stages between these two absolute (but strangely similar) extremes. The idea of "negative correspondence" is one I have fallen back on more than once since then, by the way - the latest instance is the relationship between the two movements of my **Third Quartet**.

The breadth of textural differentiation in **Transit** can, perhaps, also be ascribed - at least in part - to the fact that it was composed over the course of several years. Interestingly, the various parts were not composed in anything like chronological order, so that a strange sort of perceptual torque is often sensed as the piece progresses. The same effect is perceived at work, albeit much more radically, in Zimmermann's **Die Soldaten**, where the slow transformation of style from beginning to end of the opera proper is rudely twisted on its head in the relationship between the opening scene and the extraordinary preceding prelude, the last part of the work to be composed. I have always been fascinated by the historicity of the compositional act and I suppose that **Transit** is the piece most obviously effected by that aspect in all my output.

As far as the actual treatment of the texts (Hermes Trismegistus, Paracelsus, Heraclitus) was concerned, I recall being highly conscious of the innate phonetic character of each of the languages represented. Particularly in the archaic German of the Paracelsus I found a rich lode of fricatives which I exploited to the full. Only the English of the final "Transitio" section was not analyzed-out in this fashion since, by that point, I wanted the text content to have become semantically relatively clear. Throughout the work there is a striving towards specific meaning which, however, scarcely ever manages to crystallize itself. I thought of this as representing very well the dark searchings which form the overt subject-matter of the piece - that is, the winding transition from the central, anthropocentric core of the ensemble towards the impersonal outer reaches of brass and percussion.

One criticism that has been levelled against my vocal treatment here concerns the employment of amplification, suggesting that there is something illegitimate in its employment in a vocal/instrumental context. Clearly, there is some truth in such comments if the amplification is utilized solely for the purpose of balancing out textures which have simply been badly conceived for the forces available; in **Transit** I don't see the logic of that argument, since, firstly, amplification serves the bringing forth of highly subtle vocal inflections otherwise inaudible (the same is true of **Time and Motion Study III**) and, secondly, I had the intention all along of emblematically pitting the full power of combined brass and percussion against the roaring corporeality of highly amplified voices in the visionary finale. It is clear that the very concept implies amplification: it is by no means an incidental adjunct.

Etudes transcendantales

After the two vocal works of the mid-70s I turned my attention to other things, even though, for a time, I toyed with the idea of a piece for solo voice based on my **Time and Motion Study** experiences. It was only in 1982 that I felt able to confront the overt semanticity of text-setting in terms of the structural and rhetorical categories then evolving. Since, perhaps, my **Second String Quartet** and the piano piece **Lemma-Icon-Epigram** - that is, 1978 onward - the gestural surface of my works had come to present a more 'traditional' aspect, in the sense that much of the deconstructed parametric polyphony encountered in such pieces as **Unity Capsule** had begun to sink back out of sight. Not, by any means, that the actual working of the compositions had become comparatively less complex but, rather, that the parametric strands had begun to coagulate into volatile bundles treatable - and perceivable - as concrete gestural entities. It was clear to me at the time that one way of creating a certain clarity in my own mind as to the functional status of such units would be to re-examine similar patterns in terms of text-bound - vocal - semantic comportment. This approach might, I suppose, be seen as a mirror image of the manner in which the Second Viennese School reformulated instrumental gesture in the light of the supersaturated semanticity of vocal articulation!

One thing was self-evident from the outset - it would not be possible for me to make use of either of the hitherto prevalent ploys for integrating voice and instruments. It was unthinkable for me to treat the voice as the predominant element, relegating the accompaniment to a functionally subordinate stature; at the same time I did not want to draw the voice into the totality of the ensemble at the price of regarding it as a pseudo-instrument sharing, for the most part, in the common repertoire of instrumental gestures. The approach I finally settled on involved generating the vocal materials by means of identical procedures to those employed for the four instruments, but quantifying the former with a view to making clear the distinction. For this reason all nine songs in the **Etudes** have in common the fact that the musical substance was composed as integral part of the total structure i.e. before the words were inserted. This often brought with it strange distensions and compressions of the text which, in my view, add considerably to the expressive particularity of the discourse. An example from the first song, for voice and oboe, will make this clear.

One can see immediately from Example 11 how the voice is prevented from occupying center-stage; the traditional voice/accompaniment relationship has been reversed. The text is itself quite short, which necessitated it being 'atomized' among the various figures specified, thus being subsumed into an almost timbral dimension where, for instance, an "r" becomes a fluttering articulation covering an entire phrase. The inherent ambiguity of text-*setting* is underlined right from the outset, and each subsequent song is intended to elaborate this theme from a different formal/expressive standpoint.

Ex. 11

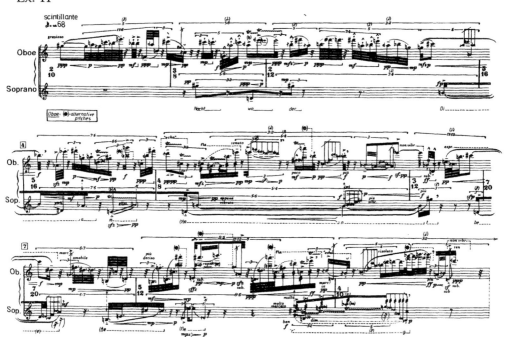

Whilst I naturally expended a great deal of energy on the collation and study of the texts, at no point did this initial absorptive activity have an immediate effect on the composition of the vocal line (although a couple of 'madrigalisms' did finally slip through at the stage of applying the text to the through-composed line). The great advantage of this method was that the voice could, right from the early planning stages, be assigned a structural function far stronger and, sometimes, more explicit than is often the case where the text is integrated from the outset. In several songs the voice is assigned a structural task equal in weight to that of all the instrumental parts taken together. Such is the case in Song Six or, in a quite different way, Song Seven, where the voice functions like a *cantus firmus* which has to carry the main thrust of the formal divisions as well as keeping in check the more diversely anarchic impulses of the piccolo, oboe and harpsichord.

This double approach to text interpretation - the reflection of text-structure in the overall formal layout of a song while delaying the actual insertion of its substance into the text until the moment of most obvious resistance - might be said to underlie the general flow of the composition itself, in that the misrelationship hinted at in Song One tends to open up, little by little, until the entire field of text-setting is thrown into problematic relief in Songs Eight and Nine.

In fact, having this built-in dichotomy, this potential for organizational dissonance proved very useful as a powerful compositional tool, since it paralleled in many ways the concepts concerning the mediation of automatized and informal means which underpin the entire **Carceri d'Invenzione** cycle. Since the composition of the **Etudes** occupied me throughout the period in which **Carceri** was assembled, it acts as a sort of sketchbook or diary in which various confrontations and conjunctions of technique could be tested out in concentrated format. The constant effort involved in establishing and maintaining the *conjunctio oppositorum* of voice and instruments, vocal line and textual underlay proved essential to the fuelling of the motor of invention.

Song Five provides a good example of total equivalence, in terms of generative procedure, of vocal line and instrumental material. Every event in all parts except the harpsichord is placed with reference to two superincumbent, asynchronous metric patterns and their attendant internal pulse structures. The opening bars are based on a certain separation of forces, according to which the vocal line maintains a constant pulse of seven against five whilst the instruments divide a regular four against five amongst themselves (Example 12).

At other points the clarity of this scheme becomes obscured by the two patterns being distributed irregularly between voice, alto flute, English horn and cello. The basic 'idea' of the song was this fading in and out of focus of the underlying precompositional scheme and in this respect the text itself was not of primary significance. The only word-painting encountered resides in the image of a bee captured immobile in amber, this being reflected in the vocal part by the consistent isolation of single syllables between variable length rests. At the very end of the movement this tendency is taken even further in that the phonetic contour of the poem is subdivided still further, so that the frequent "n" sounds of "Insekteneinschluss" are allotted separate impulses, like distant echoes (Example 13).

Although the voice is unique in expressing its contribution to the underlying patterns in pared-down form (the instruments frequently expand and elaborate their attacks into highly differentiated microphases) it nevertheless forms an irreducible part of the generative operation: certainly it is not intended to predominate the overall texture at any time.

Ex. 12

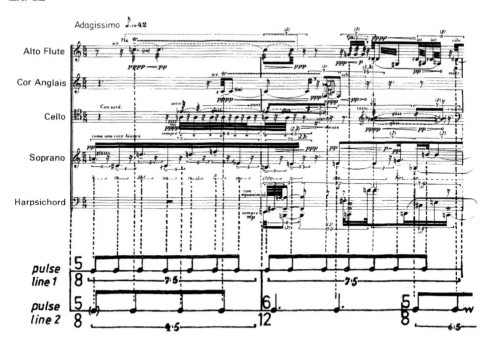

Ex. 13

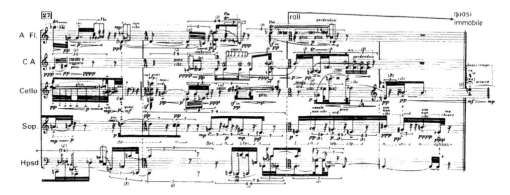

The cycle orbits, in many respects, around Song Six, the most overtly rhetorically appellative of all, in which the voice has a degree of predominance which obviously and immediately overshadows the dessicatedly rudimentary and desultory comments of alto flute and cello. Initially I intended this movement to be for voice alone - in fact, the voice materials *were* composed before their accompaniment: in the event I decided that a second layer of activity was needed, albeit of a minimal variety, for the sake of perspectival effect.

The urgency of expression here is due in large part to the nature of the Ernst Meister poem and its all-pervading imagery of shipwreck, sedimentation and dissolution. Unlike most of the other songs the text elements here are treated in highly contrasted fashions (Example 14), some very melismatically, others moving with musical articulations closely paralleling "naturalistic" models of diction. This was dictated by two related factors: (i) the total length of each of the nine sections in respect of the length of the text segment represented and (ii) the relative density of notes in each section as measured against the number of syllables available at any given juncture. The pitch systems operative throughout tend, by distinguishing three levels of pitch centrality, to polarize much more clearly around certain pitches in passages where the density of impulses corresponds quite closely to the amount of syllabic material available, since central pitches are necessarily assigned more frequently at important points i.e. where a change of syllable is located.

As in most of my music, the complexity of the final object is here the result of the constant intertwining of a number of texture-defining variables of a basically straight-forward nature. Even the order in which these variables are determined is itself a variable; in fact it was quite interesting, sometimes, to observe how a slight reversal of order of application came up with surprisingly diverse constellations.

Ex. 14 (a)

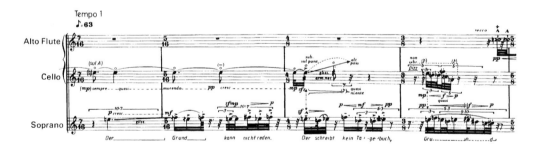

Ex. 14 (b)

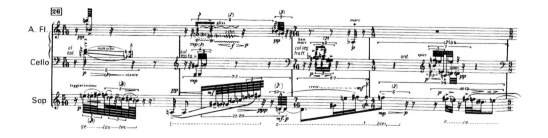

It is no accident that the species of vocality typifying Song Six is the one most immediately related to received norms of "expression". From this pivotal point the work unravels once more the provisional context it had assembled, until a stage is reached at which the entire artificial construct of word-music conjunction holds together only by means of appeal to the brute force of will (Song Eight). The relationship breaks down completely in Song Nine - not only the relationship of text to music, but also that of one fundamental text-constituent to another, since vowels and consonants are disassembled, never to be reconstituted except as a prosaically recited statement, completely divorced from the residual instrumental action.

Song Eight is actually a form of montage, in that two completely independent poems are cut and folded through one another at semantically arbitrary intervals, so that the switch sometimes occurs in the middle of a word. Each text has a single, easily distinguishable texture; in the one case (A) a febrile, harshly illuminated sort of enhanced speech, in the other (B) an almost completely static, *pianissimo* pulsation, frequently practically inaudible under the brusque interruptions of the harpsichord. The form is basically rather simple: voice and harpsichord have exactly the same quantity of material broken down into an identical number of segments. Combined with a system of pause durations these units are permutated against one another regardless of the conventional practicability and effectivity of the co-ordinations thus defined. This was in fact the one and only instance of the employment of chance procedures in the entire work, my intention being to ensure the greatest degree of taste-free objectivity in the alignments selected (Example 15).

Ex. 15

After the extremes of both expressive and formal disassociation offered in the previous piece, Song Nine might be seen as an essay in gestural recuperation carried out largely to the benefit of the instrumental forces employed. The entry of the voice, after the lengthy demolition of a high-register pitch canon in woodwind and cello, is pared down to the hectic enunciation of the consonantal material of the text, accompanied (or interfered with) by claves (Example 16).

Ex. 16

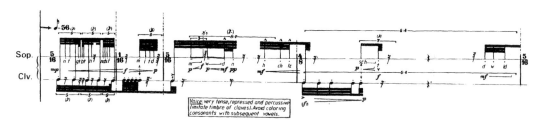

The mirror image of this is a subsequent *vocalise* in which the vowels of the text are abstracted and presented in melismatic, almost instrumentalized form (Example 17).

Instead of bringing these free-floating strands together once more in some sort of affirmation of linguistic integrity the full text is merely spoken *against* the music, the two dimensions ignoring one another completely (Example 18). This tactic was not intended as some form of absurdist statement; what I really aimed at getting across was my deep concern with issues of *translation* and *equivalence* in the minefield of music/language analogies. It would not have been useful to provide some cosmetic papering over the cracks by means of an

Ex. 17

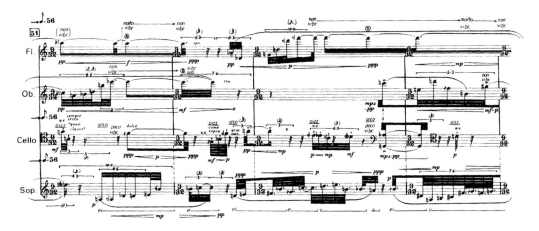

Ex. 18

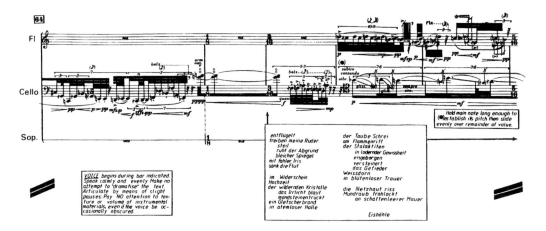

ideologically 'optimistic' reconciliation. Even music, in the final analysis, is worn away by increasingly obtrusive *fermatas*, the strategies for the continuance of its discourse being negated one by one. Voice and music have not been able to coexist any longer; at the same time music itself is exhausted when its roots in vocal articulation have been transcended. The problematic relationship between them must be defined anew.

SHATTERING THE VESSELS OF RECEIVED WISDOM:
IN CONVERSATION WITH JAMES BOROS
(1990)

JAMES BOROS: Your music has the reputation of being extremely difficult to play; however, you've had a great deal of success with a number of individual performers, such as Pierre-Yves Artaud, and ensembles such as the Arditti String Quartet, the ASKO Ensemble, and the Ensemble InterContemporain. In your view, what lies behind the astounding achievement of these performers in the face of what many perceive to be unsurmountable difficulties?

BRIAN FERNEYHOUGH: For a start, we should distinguish between musical and performatory difficulty. I take it that you mean the latter. In general, one encounters two distinct types of performer; one that might be termed the 'gig' musician - the player who, in a couple of rehearsals, is justly proud of producing a 'professional' realization of just about anything. Often, such individuals are required to interpret vastly different styles in close juxtaposition and have, in consequence, developed a technique of rapid reading and standardized, averaged-out presentation in order to maximize effectivity for the vast majority of works and contexts. It seems to me that there is a certain tyranny involved in frequent attempts to impose this approach on the composer as some sort of desirable aesthetic norm — a 'good, healthy common sense' of music, so to speak. Inevitably, ease of rehearsal and performance involves more than just a careful regard for technical difficulty. What happens is that whole chunks of conventional wisdom in terms of musical *thinking* are also absorbed, since ease of realization is frequently a function of expectation or applicability of already present manual patterns. It seems to me no contradiction in terms to presuppose a species of interpreter for whom a lengthy and intense involvement with the artistic and technical demands and assumptions of a particular composer or group of composers would be an essential prerequisite for adequate performance activity. That's the performer who's willing to spend six months or so really trying to penetrate to the roots of a style, to focus-in on the mental development of the composer during the act of creation so as to be able to actively counterpoint this against his own personal learning and reproduction dynamic. It's true that, over a couple of decades now, I have developed a significant relationship of this sort with a number of soloists and ensembles. It would be a mistake, though, to concentrate overly on the quasi-virtuoso aspect of this: the spiritual relationship is always more important. Very often, such people are disparaged as some sort of performing animal who make a living out of hawking around their manual dexterity. I imagine that such individuals exist, but I have not come across many who play my music, perhaps because the effort involved is by no means invariably associated with the requisite illusion of supreme control and mastery transmitted by 'virtuoso' vehicles. For one thing, I never *collaborate* with a given performer in the sense of having him give me his particular 'box of tricks:' I believe that one should never start from the global effect, but rather allow it to emerge synthetically as a result of the confluence of other compositional considerations. This seems to me the sole way to legitimize, to ground sonoric innovation; everything else is *bon goût*. For example, there have been several quite well-known flutists who have refused to take my **Unity Capsule** (1975) into their repertoire with the argument that it is not worth the amount of time and effort required, since 'similar' sounds can be improvised or else notated much more simply (perhaps graphically). There is no way that I can see to persuade such individuals that the approach to learning the work is an essential polyphonic strand in the final result. Only the experience of actually attempting it can - perhaps - achieve that. There is a basic, unbridgeable abyss separating the effectful 'virtuoso' approach from that adopted by my regular associates, and I am not in the business of obscuring this vital distinction, since to do so would be to trivialize the extent to which the performer's personal confrontation with a richly-articulated musical environment can contribute to a gripping aural experience.

One should also remember that these players do not dedicate themselves exclusively to my compositions: they do not function as regular, long-term members of a 'Ferneyhough Ensemble'. We are talking about a quite different situation than where a group plays one composer's music almost exclusively for an extremely lengthy period of time as in the case of, say, Stockhausen or, more recently, Steve Reich. Traditions built in that way have other dynamics.

JB: A number of performers have described experiences whereby, after having spent a period of time working on your music, getting beyond what were initially perceived as obstacles to comprehension, "many problems seemed to have solved themselves".[1]

BF: I've found that there's a kind of exponential time-saving process with my music: if you spend six months learning one piece, you'll be able to learn another in three weeks. For example (albeit an extreme case), the Arditti Quartet was able to learn my **Third String Quartet** (Ex. 1) in only a few weeks, largely without my active supervision, because its members are all very familiar with my general approach. On that basis it was generally possible for them to extrapolate plausible solutions to executive or aesthetic questions. In fact, I was

Ex. 1: From **Third String Quartet**

still composing the final pages of the score during the final period of rehearsal, sometimes sitting in the same room as the quartet and passing new material over to be photocopied and run through, often during the same session. It was a strange experience![2]

What many players often fail to realize is that most of the textures in my works are to a large degree relatable to gestural conventions already familiar from other contexts. What is unfamiliar is, firstly, the unusual rapidity with which these elements unfold and succeed one another, secondly, the high level of informational density in notational terms, and, thirdly, the extreme demands made throughout on the performer's technique and powers of concentration. Most of these hurdles to acceptance are encountered predominantly during the initial period of familiarization in which the necessary connection between notation and expressive realization is obscured by the welter of surface detail. Once this reading phase has been passed, many players have come to accept that these factors actually make their job easier and more rewarding. Of course, in the sort of rehearsal situation prevailing in New Music today, there is little or no opportunity to achieve this experience; as a composer one has the choice of accepting this fact and working with it, or seeking to establish performance traditions on a gradualistic basis. Both views have their arguments; essentially, I think, it's less a matter of professional ethics than of the relationship of one's expressive ideals to the prevailing opportunities for their public reproduction. I'm aware that many composers argue that it's somehow more honorable to work within the bounds set by current socio-economic norms, to tailor their production to them: I simply beg to differ and hope that my views will also be accorded respect.

JB: Some critics of your music claim that the speed of informational presentation is too high, that they, as listeners, can't keep up with it.

BF: Again, it's partly a question of familiarity. I try not to be overly influenced by the thought that most listeners will hear a piece only once, even if this is often the case. One simply has to ask *how* people listen these days - are they listening more less statistically, passively, or does a piece cause some form of inertial resistance in the perceptual works? The more the listening mind gets tied up in powerfully structured contexts, the greater is likely to be its sense of informational overload. That's true of anything which is at once unfamiliar and immediately demanding in terms of trying to tie together partially-perceived objects and processes into a provisional whole. One thing that makes this music perhaps more difficult than some is not so much its actual density, but rather the slight disbalance I tend to build into the relationship of time-flow to complexity of individual semantically coherent units. This gives the listener the sensation of always being 'behind' the flow of events, of running to catch up, as it were. Some might assume this to be a negative state of affairs; I simply utilize it as one more tool for energizing the sonic flow, for modifying its perspectival characteristics. It's clear that many interesting avenues of investigation open up when one adopts this sort of absorption ratio as a compositional variable. Some composers positively expect that the audience be essentially passive, whilst still others treat the public rather paternalistically. My own attitude is to suggest to the ear sequential bundles of possible paths through the labyrinth — paths, that is, which are mapped out in the synchronization of simultaneous processual layers with a view to encouraging the risky undertaking of instantaneously selecting between them.

Things in the present day world surely move rather quickly. It seems rather anomalous to expect our art to be easily understandable; I don't see music as providing a sort of breathing space between bouts of confrontation with the world outside! It is also not directly about offering privileged insights, but more about how to create one's own insights when immersed in the complex ambiguity of the art object.

JB: How do you respond to other charges which claim that you 'over-notate' your music?

BF: It's true that some musicians have told me that they feel robbed of much of their traditional autonomy of interpretation through my 'over-specification'. On the other hand, what might arguably upset a performer even more is not knowing *why* they're doing something, not having any applicable criteria of interpretational excellence. Most contemporary music can be scarcely said to be over-familiar; this state of unfamiliarity is often the result of a lack of such specific criteria. My method of notation attempts, at best, to suggest to the player relevant methods and priorities wherewith the material can be usefully approached - the establishment of hierarchies; at worst, I imagine that he will constantly be reminded that new works often do not permit much to be taken for granted. Suggesting contexts of this sort via notation allows the player a different but no less important 'free space' within which to move. With a complex score, where does one begin? With the rhythms, sorting out the pitches, general sorts of movement? How important is articulation, for instance? If you are confronted with several distinct and independent layers of activity, as in my **Unity Capsule** (Ex. 2), then this surely becomes a central issue.[3] Everyone approaches the task in a unique fashion, each sets his own priorities. In consequence, the results are always somewhat different from performance to performance. Scores are more than just tablatures for specific actions or else some sort of picture of the required sound: they are also artifacts with powerful auras of their own, as the history of notational innovation clearly shows us. As such, they are capable of playing an active but not authoritarian role, even in a

Ex. 2: From Unity Capsule for solo flute

period of pluralistic aesthetic standards: they carry their own history on their backs.

JB: The degree of variability from one performance to another is something which is strikingly evident in the multiple recorded versions of your works for solo flute, which are radically different in many ways despite their being recordings of interpretations by a single musician.[4]

It's obvious that you spend a great deal of time and effort in considering, down to the most minute detail, exactly what you're asking a performer to do, which requires an unusually high level of familiarity and identification with instruments and playing techniques.

BF: Thinking about composing means, first of all, thinking about the specific nature of the instruments to be employed. I'm very concerned that the things I ask an instrumentalist to do be so instrument-specific that they conspire to create a sort of 'X-ray' of his instrument's inner essence. That doesn't mean employing the entire catalogue of secondary effects (although it might), but rather ensuring that one could not imagine any other instrument playing the same material in the same way. My approach to an instrument is really rather physical in the sense that I conceive of it as a theatrical space for the disposition of actions; the spatial relationship of the performer and his movements to this framework is always a primary consideration if one wants to 'polyphonicize' the apparent degree of difficulty of a passage with its actual performative complexity. Very often my string textures, for instance, move rapidly from register to register, but it makes the world of difference if one has chosen one's material disposition with a view to minimizing the real amount of distance that the left hand is expected to traverse (Ex. 3). By these and similar means one is in a position to suggest contexts to the player that a more abstract treatment of his instrument might leave unremarked. If the composer does not occupy himself directly with such questions, the performer might well consider himself justified in applying received conservatory techniques in a blanket fashion not necessarily automatically appropriate for all forms of contemporary expression. I know a lot of composers who maintain that 'if you just notate the sounds you want, the techniques will look after themselves'. Quite apart from leading composers into the occasional performative absurdity, this is emphatically not the point I am starting from.

JB: It seems as if many of the issues surrounding contemporary performance practice have been and continue to be to a large extent overlooked within the musical community.

BF: In previous ages it was never performances which survived, but scores, notated music. If all the information necessary to a correct interpretation

Ex. 3: From **Intermedio alla Ciaccona** for solo violin

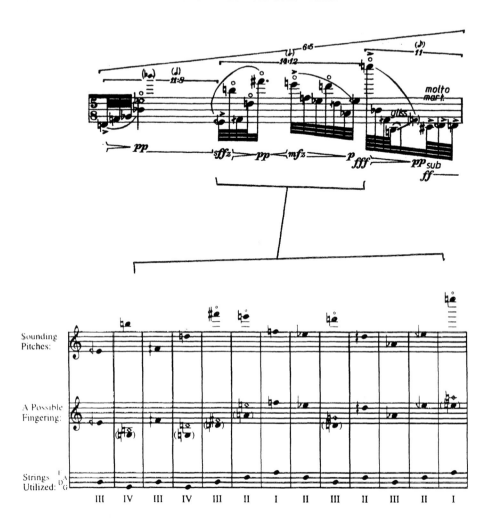

is not contained in a score, it is practically impossible to reconstruct original intentions with any degree of certainty. Only tradition can provide some sort of tenuous continuity in this respect. If you play a Beethoven sonata, you're not interpreting the notes on the page, you're interpreting many generations of interpretation, an entire corpus of slowly evolving conventions. Contemporary music has little of this sense of self-reflexive tradition, partly for the obvious reason of being new, but also because of the extreme fragmentation of stylistic continuity so characteristic of the present day. This results in a sort of institutionalized deracination where the performer is all too often reduced to putting the right notes in the right place with little sense of the larger perspective which would make it all make sense to him. If one considers interpretation as the art of meaningful deviation from the text, one will be saddened to hear music played (and - *mutatis mutandis* - composed and listened to) in this reductive manner. In terms of my own work, I employ what some consider to be over-definition of the musical image as a path to suggesting what might come to replace this interpretative overview. Composers who tend to restrict their notational specifications to a bare minimum end up getting one-dimensional representations of a possible sound-world rather than entering into that world's inner workings. Again, my entirely subjective view, confirmed by a significant number of excellent musicians.

JB: Your stance with regard to the notation/interpretation process is a remarkable one in that you seem to have overcome many of the obstacles represented by the currently pervasive attitude which deems that "the imprecision and variability of human performance are actually quite detrimental to the requirements of totally organized and predetermined works".[5] While many composers have skirted the issue by either simplifying their musical language or turning exclusively to the electronic medium, you are one of the few to have expressed a concern with the means by which one may actually take advantage of these 'human' qualities and limitations through careful, well-thought-out compositional strategies.

Cassandra's Dream Song for solo flute, written in 1970, seems to have been one of the first compositions to display this attitude towards the performer. This is clear in, for example, the introductory notes attached to the published score;[6] you've also referred to the "dynamic projection into an 'energized time-stream', via the mental and physical capacities of a totally involved performer".[7] Another attractive feature of this work is the fact that, while it is in some ways representative of the European 'tradition', begun in the 1950s, of mobile works which provide "mechanisms by which progressively to liquidate the workings of chance..."[8] and which yield "performances... progressing systematically towards complete exhaustion of the freedom of choice",[9] it also represents a unique, personal solution to the problems posed by mobility.[10]

BF: Probably **Cassandra** is not a very typical example of the 'open form' genre. When I was composing it, back in 1970, I was very well aware of the effect of each of the limited number of combinations of fixed and freely-ordered elements. This was important since it is precisely the vast diversity of energy-transfer situations that the mobility of the freer elements provides which was my primary concern. It is a very physical piece, I think - the first of my works, in fact, to consciously explore this aspect of performance practice - and this is especially manifested by those boundary situations where one type of energy is forced to confront, blend with, or mutate into another. In the absence of metric subdivisions it is the manipulation of such qualities which lends the piece its specific inner articulation, both within and between sections. The clearly distinct implications of such an approach and that exemplified by the more overtly linear, 'logical' sections are intended to sensibilize the flutist to the nuances of energy-expenditure and interpretative moment-to-moment detailing in a manner not otherwise available to me at the time. Since then I have maintained the metaphor, but attached it, not so much to large-scale sections in confrontation, as to the confrontation of various densities and consistencies of figurations with a network of temporal spaces within which they are confined. I don't see much point in maintaining the convention of regular pulse in a music devoid of the tonal harmonic rhythm which lends it significance on a global level; the measure thus tends to function for me, firstly, as a space, secondly (via the bar-line), as the domain of a certain energy-quotient suddenly facing the necessity of leaping to a sometimes quite contrasted state. It is not the emphasis on a down beat which counts, but the feel for what is needed to leap this experiential hurdle to the immediately subsequent situation. The length or regularity of measure disposition in relation to the implied degree of continuity in a given material provides the player with essential information concerning relevant phrasing, weight of detailed nuance as against emphasis of larger gestural aspects, etc. In shorter measures the performer is necessarily stumbling from state to state; there is, if you like, a high correlation of figural definition and 'rhythmic harmony' (as opposed to harmonic rhythm) whilst the same materials spread over a small number of larger measures would convey the necessity of integrating more clearly these same figures into a more obviously continuous, evolving perspective. Conversely, the latter case seems to imply a more catastrophic transition between measure boundaries than the former. **Cassandra** deals with this issue more through its large-scale formal dichotomies and, on the micro-level, the opposition of fermatas to written-out pauses combined with more or less antinatural interruptions or distensions of the sort of time-flow that each type of texture seems to demands. It's very close to a compositional involvement of the well-known phenomenon whereby a solo performer tends to calculate rests not so much by their actual written durations as by the degree of accumulated energic impetus with which he approaches them, with the consequence that their clock-time duration can fluctuate wildly from performance to performance. A recent example of this would be the concluding viola solo in my **Third String Quartet**, where the immediately preceding whirlwind of linear motion causes the violist to perceive the rests as major impediments (Ex. 4). The effect of this perception on the way he then attacks the intervening events is very evident in performance.

JB: Much of your music seems to revolve around what Boulez refers to as a "polyphony of polyphonies".[11]

BF: I do tend to work with distinct layers of activity, in the sense that diversely instrumentated, individually textured processual vectors are usually co-extant in my works. Much of the larger-scale formal working out of my structures is based on the intersection, collision, confluence, and divergence of these strands of activity. I find this way of imagining and ordering sound much more congenial than treating an ensemble as a value-free and pristine source of possible sonorities. In larger groupings, too, the performer has a chance to orientate himself towards events emanating from his immediate neighborhood, or at least remaining constant for a significant period of time. My large orchestral work **La terre est un homme** (1976-79),[12] for instance, treats each of the instrumental families very much as a unit of activity in itself - something supported, in some cases, by the inclusion of the complete spectrum of members of that family, the clarinet group, for instance, comprising Eb, Bb, Bass and Contrabass. These distinct strands may then be combined into larger conglomerates: one example that comes to mind is the regular association of four muted trumpets with the oboe/english horn quartet. On a still larger scale we have the integration of all wind instruments pitted against all the strings (as in the very opening of the work, where a single woodwind/brass process is pitted against a complex mass of more than forty solo strings). This sort of constant fluctuation of alliances militates against the utilization of the orchestra in its normal division of forces; at the same time, I feel that there is a certain timbral logic at work which goes beyond usual concepts of 'orchestration'. All the large ensemble pieces in the **Carceri d'Invenzione**[13] cycle are tropes of the same approach: in the third and last of the series, the woodwind, brass, and percussion have clearly distinct roles to play in the articulation of the form, whilst in the first two of the series the constant generation and redefinition of color-groups as polyphonic strata form the very roots of their particular identities.

It seems to me that this approach is basically an extension of my attitude towards the multiple defining vectors which go to make up single, less texturally complex sound events. One of my enduring aims has been not to create some automatic transliteration of compositional techniques or points of reference from one layer of articulation to another, but rather to provide a rich meshing of analogous approaches which, whilst specific to each level of activity, are nevertheless sufficiently imbued with points of processual contact as to permit significant perceptual inter-reference on the part of the listener. Quite often, pupils make the mistake of assuming that the sort of proportional relationship effective on one level of a composition will be equally effective (or at least function in much the same manner) on a higher formal level; usually this is far from being the case. On the other hand, a constant awareness of the general category of operation or shaping strategy informing all levels of a discourse is extremely useful, and something the composer should make every effort to suggest. Often, people have been rather disappointed to discover that the

Ex. 4: **Third String Quartet** (conclusion)

operations I employ at any given moment are really rather basic. This is necessary in order to ensure their wider applicability in an extended family of comparable situations; one is often mildly astounded to see how complex a context can become as the result of the intersection of just a few such primitive procedures!

JB: Stockhausen has stated that, beginning with his **Kontra-Punkte** (1951), he "didn't want any background any more, ... everything was ... of equal importance".[14] Do you view each of the lines or processual strata in your music as being of equal importance?

BF: It's interesting that Stockhausen takes that particular stance. Although what he says would seem to be a natural consequence of the total serial concept as he understood it, in the sense that anything derived directly from the fundamental steering mechanisms would be theoretically equivalent (even if not so in terms of perceived structural weight), in fact the definitive version of the piece doesn't function at all that way. We know from his sketches that **Kontra-Punkte** is the result of at least two interleaved work-processes, the one more basic, the other essentially interpolative or elaborational. One might suppose that this implies a certain disbalance in the mode of assessment of sonic experience: after all, even if "everything was ... of equal importance", that still depends on the perceived 'grain' built into the texture in terms of such before-after strategies. The punning nature of the title is surely aimed at Stockhausen's dissatisfaction both with the premises of **Punkte** and the basic 'point' approach in general; it is fairly easy to discern the moments at which the global, group effect is primary. As in Orwellian democracy, all may be equal, but some are still more equal than others.

In my own music, I certainly try to legitimize all strata equally in terms of their inner coherence and sense of self, but this is not to be interpreted as the espousal of some sort of principled equality in the resultant compound texture. Some types of texture are, by their very nature, more insistent than others. In addition, I employ the detailed definition of things like timbre and amplitude to move lines or linear complexes in and out of focus. In terms of their contribution to the overall argument, all lines might be of comparable significance but, by adjusting their relative dynamic envelopes, all sorts of interesting weightings of things like translucency, physical presence, and resonantial support-functioning can be arranged. Even in more obviously traditional contexts it's often the things you can't hear (or can only hear in a limited way) which are instrumental in giving a texture its decisive nudge in a particular direction. Also, when event-strata do become directly audible (rather than mediatedly perceived via their syntactically articulational effects on other layers), they exhibit more sense of continuity and directionality precisely because they had a prior 'inaudible' run-up. Even in a Bach-style fugue it's frequently the absences which are as influential as those things stated right out; the same, in perhaps greater measure, is true of something like a Webern **Bagatelle**, where, at any given time, only a small portion of the contributory ordering is consciously as-similated, even after many hearings. For me, silence - by which I mean also 'func-tional silence', the camouflaging or dissimulating of functions - is far from being a neutral medium for spacing out events: I see it (perhaps fancifully) as a disembodied 'ether' capable of acting as an energized vehicle for the 'silent continuation' of fragmented developmental structures.

JB: In other words, silences may simply represent phases during which particular processes are 'hidden' from view, much as a stream may disappear beneath the ground, only to re-appear at another point; they don't necessarily signify a suspension of action or arrested motion.

BF: That's right. Without assuming something along those lines, it would be much more difficult for me to allow textures to re-emerge, perhaps greatly evolved, and expect them to be appreciated as another aspect of a 'perforated continuity' prepared earlier in the work, the series of 'tips of icebergs'.

Given this contextually reactive approach, it would be less than useful to attempt to define all aspects of a situation simultaneously, right at the outset. In fact, precisely the opposite is the case, in that I am often struck by the diver-gent paths material takes when identical operations are carried out in a different order - so much so that decisions concerning precedences of this type usually form part of a work's initial generative repertoire, setting up further levels of constraints through which invention and intuition can meaningfully express themselves.

JB: In the introduction to his analysis of your piano work **Lemma-Icon-Epigram**, Richard Toop states that your compositional process

> is not a predetermined path, but a labyrinth, and the completed work is, in a
> sense, an arbitrary byproduct of that labyrinth, to the extent that there is
> nothing predestined or predetermined about the outcome of any particular
> moment in it; each moment is, rather, the inspired momentary response to a
> given set of constraints, and in each case other solutions, equally compelling,
> would have been thinkable.[15]

BF: For me, a piece of music tends to grow like a coral reef, accumulat-ing or sedimenting the remains of many small animalculae. In that sense it is really a record of past processes, it is an imperfect and partial imprint of a no longer determinable set of compositional presuppositions. Music is always an interactive thing; just as you define it, it tells you what it needs for the next stage of its development, telling you in terms that would not necessarily have been meaningful or even available at an earlier stage of composer/work evolution. In this essentially symbiotic activity the temporal succession of decision-making is absolutely crucial. The high density of pre-compositional preparation for a piece does not set out to define *a priori* each and every event: it is meant to provide a life-support system, a dispositive of constraints and delimitations with which it is meaningful to make decisions affecting other parts of the totality. The almost ritual activity of bringing events together in predetermined frames sometimes gives rise to sudden insights on an altogether different level. In an important sense, processes don't exist in order to generate music, they're there to predispose one to approach the act of composition in a work-specific fashion.

JB: It's not as if you simply set these processes in motion and allow them to proceed without their interacting or affecting each other. There's a vast difference between this approach and that which is manifested in 'algorithmic' compositions by composers such as Xenakis or Hiller.

BF: It's curious how often I've been asked why, given the complex nature of my scores, I just don't specify some appropriately complex algorithm at the outset which would generate everything at once! Needless to say, this reflects a massive misprision concerning my approach to music, even assuming that such a utopian calculatory device were available, even in principle: it effectively eliminates from the picture any sense of the wider compositional consequences of decision-making acts without which the exercise would be null and void. Invention always follows from limitation; constraints are aids to thinking, to processually molding sensations as articulate subsets of the universal.

JB: What role do the processual strata play in your works for solo instruments, as opposed to your ensemble music?

BF: They function in essentially the same way, seen as musical structures, even if their accumulation in a single voice in practice leads to the information being differently evaluated. Of course, if you are composing for twenty instruments you are going to think twice about the efficacy of simultaneously specifying thirteen individually-quantified informational strands for each and every player, since the Law of Diminishing Returns soon comes into force to render even such maximally-defined textures in terms of 'terminal grey' zones, the sort of non-color remaining on an artist's palette after all his paints have been thoroughly mixed at the end of the day.

JB: One thinks of John Cage's description of the 'mud' of Ives's music.[16]

BF: I'm not familiar with that comment but it certainly sounds appropriate. Sometimes, it's true, I find such states useful, but it would be anti-productive to maintain this overall-ness for too long: in recent works I have tended to employ articulational stranding to enhance the specific sense of shaping of individual lines or texture-types at key moments, to increase their 'presence', their power to generate a cutting-edge identity within diversity. An example of a piece constructed almost exclusively on this premise would be **Carceri d'Invenzione I** of 1981 (Ex. 5), where the degree of focus of this or that texture *within* a larger mass is a key both to its overall function and its degree of internal coherence, its self-awareness, if you like. With solo instruments we have a wholly different situation in which the issue is not so much defining a continuous identity in the mass but rather one of constantly thrusting at the performer the *non*-identity of the work, those centrifugal tendencies which are only provisionally held in check by the multiplicity of compositional devices which serve to define the strands you mention. The more these are explicitly rendered by the notation, the more a 'separation of powers' is imaginable, an exploding outward from tentatively common trajectories.

JB: This brings us to your concept of a musical 'figure'. You have written:

> It is... imperative that the ideology of the holistic gesture be dethroned in favor of a type of patterning which takes greater account of the transformatory and energetic potential of the sub-components of which the gesture is composed....The gesture is brought to function in several ways simultaneously, thus throwing its shadow beyond the limits set by its physical borders, whilst the strands of parametric information of which it is composed take on lives of their own — without, however, divorcing themselves from the concrete point of their common manifestation to such a degree that their independence on the processual level could ever pose a serious threat to the credibility of integrity of the gesture itself.[17]

Would you care to amplify these statements?

BF: In my efforts to clarify to myself the inner workings of musical structures, I've found it useful to distinguish three fundamental areas of activity — or, at least, three distinct ways of looking at those activities. They are (1) Texture; (2) Gesture; and (3) Figure. I am, by the way, certainly not suggesting that these are mutually exclusive domains — quite the contrary, in fact, since their usefulness to me as a composer resides precisely in their encouragement of 'cross-fading' from one to another. Basically, I'm postulating that the identification of function or identity proceeds from the general to the specific, that is, from types of activity up to particular exemplifications of those types in concrete

Ex. 5: From **Carceri d'Invenzione I**

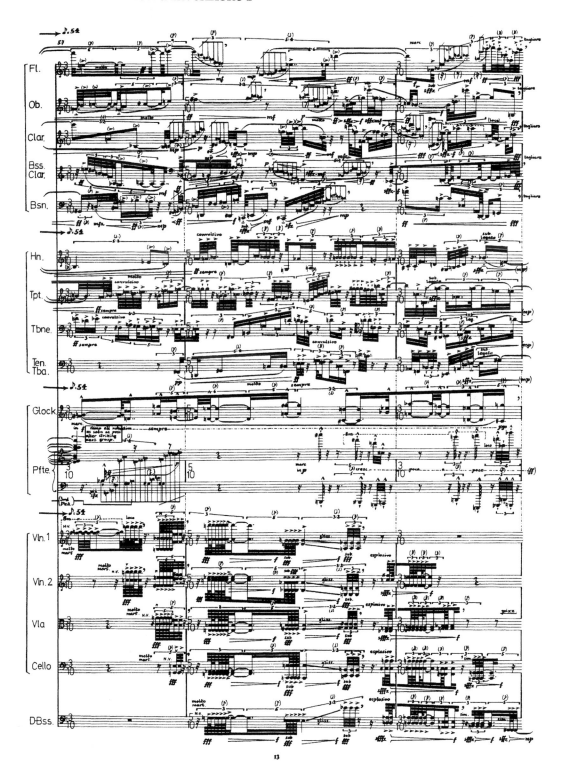

contexts. A *texture* here would be a global form of activity characterized by some recognizable consistency — slow clusters, for example, or heterophonic *gettato* glissandi. It is music's irreducible stochastic substratum, and is a minimal precondition for any further pertinent differentiating potential. Textures are gathered into related bundles, each of which assumes certain basic equivalences among its members. Without the assumption of such fundamental correspondences it would be difficult to locate individually-characterized elements according to any scale of implied values, which would, in turn, greatly hinder the establishment of any consistent form of hierarchical ordering. Exemplifications of particular texture-classes are seen as such by reason of global resemblance, either in terms of typical configuration of substance or analogous tendencies of processual transformation.

The *gesture*, on the other hand, belongs to a particular class of objects or states by virtue of all members of that class referring to a particular (well or vaguely defined) semantic domain, a conventionally established signified. Mostly, we associate semanticity with evoked emotional ('artistic emotional') states. Precisely *how* this comes about is not my present concern: I take it that there exist various historically-defined, partially intersecting codices for that, no matter if most of them have become debased, eroded, or themselves mediately referential in the course of this century. Over and beyond its referential, 'expressive' function, the gesture usually manifests clear-cut boundaries; it has certain object-like qualities. Once one accepts this analogy, others immediately impose themselves - terms such as force, energy, impetus, momentum, perspective, friction, opacity, and so on, all of which I associate with my own habits of working. The extracts from my article that you throw at me are attempting to suggest that over-reliance on such referential expressivity has its perils. Much recent music, for instance, explicitly assumes a Late Romantic affective vocabulary without, I think, reflecting very deeply on the changes in cultural consciousness that have radically transformed everything about how we see the world. It buys a place in 'the System' by adapting itself to fit the time-capsule norms which the latter has adopted to ensure its own survival in no matter what peripheral fashion. I'm clearly over-simplifying all this of course - it's by no means the whole story.

The point of departure for my concern with the third component - the *figural* dimension - arose from a consideration of the relationship between the gestural-affective and the operatively self-referential. At the time of writing that article (1982) I was hearing a lot of music whose reliance upon the sort of expressive ideology I mentioned earlier was leading it towards the monadic isolation of expressive hieroglyphs in only very roughly contiguous chains. Larger formal considerations restricted themselves to varieties of the 'contrast principle' or else to imposing quite arbitrary standard text-book forms onto resistantly neo-expressionist materials. At the time, I had been working for some years with the idea of 'parametric polyphony' I mentioned in connection with **Unity Capsule**: in that piece the overt multi-stranding of articulational qualities was pretty much carried on the surface as a sort of formal carapace, so the ultimate sound result was clearly synthetic in nature. More recent pieces had moved away from that position, partly because I was writing more ensemble pieces where that approach was less appropriate. Nevertheless, the approach remained the same, in that individual gestures were still made up of articulative particles which, in principle, retained the status of free radicals.

JB: This change in your music has been described by Toop: "... The structural processes which were once articulated at surface level by the different kinds of playing techniques have now sunk down to various levels below the surface, so that the music itself becomes, to some degree, the 'sediment' of these processes".[18]

BF: That's so. In some forms of total serial practice, a (in my view largely just) criticism was that the serially-generated intersection of parametric strands produced a sound object which in no way clearly reflected the ordered nature of these same strands: the polyphony was generationally virtual whilst remaining perceptually latent. In my own recent pieces, I've tried to bypass this problem by allowing the individually manipulable parametric strata to begin life authenticated by means of functional embedding in a concrete gestural context. I invariably envisage a sonic event as fluctuating between two notional poles — that is, its immediate, identifiable, gestural gestalt, and its role as a launching pad for the subsequent establishment of independent linear trajectories of the gestalt's constituent characteristics. The specifically figural aspect of an event is thus the degree to which these parametric quanta render themselves obviously amenable to such separation, extension, and re-combination in later constellations. Clearly, under such circumstances, it's not useful to restrict oneself to the 'traditional' parameters; I myself treat anything as a parametric variable that (a) can be quantified sufficiently consistently as to permit stepwise modulation and (b) is a clear enough component of its parent gestalt to ensure its adequate perception in later contexts. Whereas, in earlier pieces, the sonic events were resultants of independent parametric modulation, my more recent efforts have been concentrated on precisely the opposite, i.e. the definition and deployment of linear-polyphonic sound-qualities such as initially arise from fully composed-out events. This has the advantage of being able to exploit the ambiguity inherent in the object/effect dichotomy; parametric lines of force can be clearly perceived as infecting, damaging, or reconstituting their carrier vehicles. The opening of my **Second String Quartet** is perhaps a particularly clear example of this technique,[19] (Ex. 6) but many of the works from the **Carceri d'Invenzione** (1981-86) cycle would do just as well.

JB: Your notion and handling of parametric composition appears to be much more sophisticated and highly evolved than that of composers who steadfastly cling to 'orthodox' serial principles. On the other hand, I also find the physicality of your way of thinking attractive; for example, you've spoken of sounds as "solid things" which can be "bent, twisted, ripped open, and scratched".

I'd like to turn briefly to a question related to one asked earlier. I've witnessed numerous listeners, after hearing your music, ask themselves and others "Am I really expected to absorb everything that's going on?" How do you respond to this?

BF: I'd hesitate to suggest that my approach be more 'sophisticated' than some serial tendencies; it's just that personal priorities - the sort of information that one imagines sound to be able realistically to convey - inevitably differ. The sort of presumptions one makes as, for example, to the relationship between smallest compositional building-blocks and smallest aural unit reference conspire to create wholly different evaluational models. Some people start with a very central awareness of absolute pitch identities; I myself prefer to exploit the ever-changing field of forces created by the opposition of pitch and interval. These things are important and need somehow to be conveyed at an early stage of a work's audition.

The orientation which each composer, each composition sets out to subliminally propose naturally has a vital influence on the sensitive listener's concept of 'thingness'. If we talk of 'everything' we are begging a lot of questions. Most western art music has been based on the assumption of structural priorities, things that are more or less important on various direct or indirect levels of perception. The lack of expectations dogging a lot of contemporary music in this respect plus, perhaps, the experience of more literal-minded species of twelve-tone thinking, has indirectly engendered an odd egalitarianism in which an event ceases effectively to exist if it is not projected onto the same two-dimensional, high-gloss screen as everything else. Was it Richard Strauss who once, when told that a certain instrument couldn't be heard, replied "Maybe, but I'd notice if it were *not* there"? Much the same could be said, I expect, for a lot of secondary strata, in that perhaps it's not so much their physical presence which is contributive at any given moment as their providing of pre-planned points of structural coincidence with other processual areas, points where things suddenly 'click together' without us always being precisely aware of what it is that's doing the clicking. 'Hearing' inevitably relies for much of its effect on anticipation, for slotting stimuli into provisional frameworks, at least some of which must clearly be suggested by the piece itself if it is to lay plausible claims to both coherence and individuality.

Ex. 6: **String Quartet No. 2**

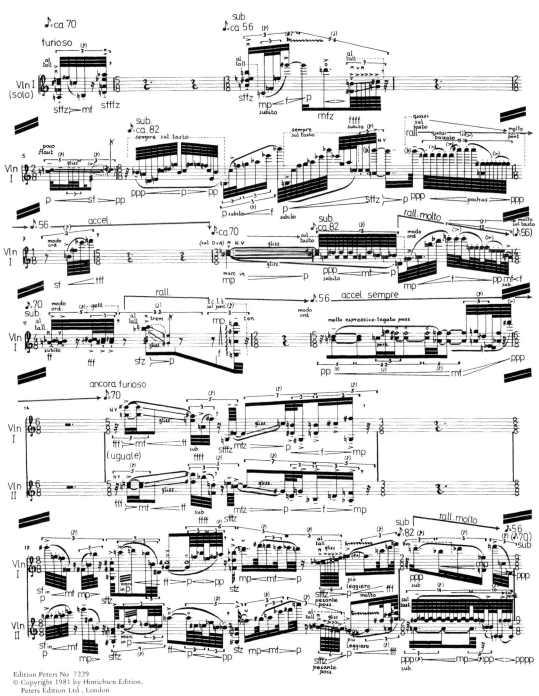

Edition Peters No 7229
© Copyright 1981 by Hinrichsen Edition,
Peters Edition Ltd , London

I was once asked if I could 'hear' all the notes and rhythms occurring in a single beat of the large orchestral work I mentioned some time ago. The very formulation of the question seemed to me to underline how little of what was going on had been 'heard' by my interlocutor, since his approach eliminated *a priori* all aspects of causality and musical consequence, identity of line, instrumentation and consistency of texture — everything, in short, that made the passage in question what it was. Process, after all, is nothing less than a slanting object! In such a case, are we listening to everything at once? In one sense, yes, in another, no.

All this leads to the major issue of *knowing what's important*. If you don't want to re-vamp musical styles where these problems are pre-digested you have to be constantly weighing-up your personal developmental history in the context of a clearly defined stylistic continuum. Something that starts life in a given piece as an incidental detail or embellishment might, in the next piece, assume the status of a core material or concept: still further down the road, it might have become so widely disseminated throughout the fabric as to have, in effect, de-materialized, been elevated to a higher organizational level, become capable of assuming characteristics of or regulating groups of otherwise discrepant elements. It's largely thanks to the step-by-step development of the language that the listener has a chance for a wider perspective, for what is 'audible' in a more comprehensive sense.

JB: For me, one of the most illuminative observations regarding your music was Jonathan Harvey's comment:

> However closely you listen to the details of these works there is a structure of roughly the same degree of sophistication as that which plans the large-scale events. You can focus in and out at will, and with greater familiarity contain all focussing in the one integral perception.[20]

BF: Jonathan's remarks remain one of the most perceptive (and earliest) approaches to my music, and what he says is very relevant. Still, though, I should perhaps emphasize that the sort of focussing he is talking about does not imply the consistency of structural correspondence or quantification on all levels (as, for instance, in some of Stockhausen's later total serial essays). My experience has been that attempts to maintain absolute consistency from top to bottom run quickly foul of the non-linear mutation of psycho-acoustic propensities in the listener. It's better to resort to overlapping and intersecting systems of approximations, where common principles are modified to take account of the constraints of the layer of activity being treated. This permits more readily the sort of layer-transfer I am looking for than any literal mirroring of technique or proportion would guarantee (even though this is certainly not excluded). The mind is a wonderful analogical instrument, and I try to operate with this fact constantly in mind.

John Cage has suggested that the artist could do worse than imitate Nature in the mode of her operations. I concur, although the conclusions I draw probably couldn't be more different. When I speak of 'life and death cycles' of materials, I'm implying that there's a definite correlation between the way a living organism extends itself, mutates in time, and the multiple narrative strands of a piece of music. I'm not really interested in an *imitatio naturae* as a processual injunction; I find it far more interesting to reflect Nature back to herself via distorted mirrors, to allow her to re-enter via my own reactions to the arrays of constraints and opportunities I set up in advance.

JB: What other suggestions might you offer to listeners who are approaching your music for the first time?

BF: Try and remember that, no matter how strange or daunting, no music stands alone in the world. There may be no genre-dictated norms of expectation satisfaction; anything that remains is a valid approach, no matter from what apparently distant domain of experience it may come. Works of art act, in some deep sense, as 'meaning-magnets;' they should embrace, not thrust away, the personal perceptions of the listener - which is not to suggest that this is necessarily a pleasant sensation for the latter, or that they should achieve this by means of some spurious pretension to immediacy! Often, we shove things into categorical shoe boxes precisely in order to avoid the weird, perhaps frightening, feeling of sacrificing-up some integral part of ourselves to an alien environment in order that we subsequently receive it back again, enriched and re-articulated. There's no guarantee of that, of course, which initially makes the whole transaction so seemingly onesided. Ambiguity - or, rather, the constant awareness of ambiguity - is always something that my music presupposes: embrace it, but not uncritically. One should not hesitate to make instantaneous decisions as to listening direction; at the same time, though, every attempt should be made to retain the sensation of multiple realities which the layerings of process and texture provide. Musical logic is not necessarily based on an exclusive 'either-or' but on an inclusive 'both-and'.

And then, get to hear the piece again!

JB: You've taught composition for a good number of years throughout Europe and, more recently, in the United States. What are your feelings with regard to the role of the composition teacher?

BF: Some years ago I wrote that 'composition' is a subject perpetually in search of a content. What once was traditionally counted as composition has experienced something of a partition since the 2nd World War, with much of its previous content being siphoned-off towards theoretical disciplines. There are plenty of people who regret this; I myself don't necessarily see its lack of precise definition as a bad thing. Why should it be wrong for the methodology of a creative discipline to reflect, to some extent, the natural flexibility and open-endedness of the activity itself? Composition teaching does well to be constantly in a state of self-critical evolution, especially in the university, where the natu-ral infrastructural pressures towards conformity are more intense. Of course, I'm talking primarily here of advanced instruction; in Europe there's a lot less of the sort of basic bread-and-butter composition course that is characteristic of university situations here, largely because composers are, in general, less bound to the successive steps of the academic career path than in the States. People tend to come to formal instruction later, when they have already produced a certain body of work, and the vexed question of style-bound or style-free teach-ing is moot.

For me, teaching is essentially reflecting and amplifying back to a student a coherent articulation of what he wanted to do in the first place. In that sense it's a passive role. The most important thing that one can teach, I think, is the capac-ity for consistent self-criticism, for asking the right questions of oneself and one's materials. One's questing and probing during the lesson thus has an exemplificatory function in respect of long-term development as well as affecting the specifics of the piece at hand. I've had frequent occasion to observe how very difficult it is for a younger composer to maintain this ruthlessness of productive critical reflection as time and circumstances change, and the individual is taken up by the new music media. It's for that reason that I regard the study period as one of nurturing and protection; I've usually required of my students, for instance, a two or three-year period during which they agree not to undertake any sort of 'career-building' - competition participation, commission-seeking, self-advertise-ment - without my express permission. This is by no means to exert authority, but rather to permit the undisturbed development of those inner forces which will serve a composer his entire life long. Again, it's a different situation here; I'm not convinced that it's appropriate or even practical to impose such restrictions in an American context, where the early accumulation of performances and different types of distinction is an important factor in ensuring later opportunities.

In this country there seems to be an ongoing controversy as to the respec-tive efficacies of style studies and 'free composition' in the formation of a com-posing personality. While I am certainly in favor of mastery of the tools of historically defined and codified theoretical practice, I am firmly opposed to any attempt at organized imitation of person-specific languages - Bartók, Hindemith, or whomsoever. There is a vital distinction between the deployment of means from closed areas of reference (species counterpoint, four-part chorales) and the adoption of vocables or technical conventions which a particular individual has created out of the accidentalia of his own life circumstances. That we all, to some extent, are influenced by other musics is banally clear and by no means unhealthy; that seems to me quite distinct, however, from sitting down to consciously expropriate or extrapolate from another composer's thought-patterns. Style is the product of compositional activity, not its presupposition. The vast majority of composers certainly carried on *traditions* in the sense of learning their trade within the framework of the composing practice of their immediate forebears - usually their teachers; to some extent that is understandable and legitimate. It strikes me as distinctly dangerous, though, to be encouraged to scan around for some biographically-specific practice or other that happens to be simpatico. One can surely learn a tremendous amount about handiwork by analyzing in detail examples of any and every style and genre; where I part company with the advocates of style study composition is in the legitimacy and ultimate usefulness of actively creating within the delimited field of concerns artificially defined at the moment of a composer's death. At the same time it's necessary to expose a pupil to as many stimuli as possible in this respect, as long as stylistic questions are dealt with from the perspective of historical linguistic embeddedness.

JB: Boulez has written:

> What is in fact taught at a conservatory? A certain number of traditional rules, very limited in date and geographical provenance; after which any student wanting to enter the contemporary field must, as it were, jump with a miniature parachute, taking his life in his hands. How many are brave enough to make that jump? And how many feel strong enough?[21]

You've already spoken of the abuse and mis-use of conservatory technique on the part of certain performers. What would you recommend as a corrective action, one that could initially be implemented by instructors within the conservatory?

BF: It's difficult to change things in most conservatory situations because the conservatory is seen as the feeder for the major components of the prevailing culture industry. It's dependent on the latter, so it can scarcely be expected to deviate significantly from long-established industrial standards and norms if it wants to keep its customers. It's *supposed* to 'conserve'. Basic exposure to new music is an essential prerequisite, naturally: unfamiliar techniques need to be understood in terms of their function as well as their means of production, so extensive ensemble interpretation of 20th-Century works should be mandatory beyond a certain proficiency threshold. No more grand isolation with Beethoven's **Violin Concerto** in some cubby hole, plus nominal participation in orchestral sessions dedicated to 'repertoire' generally stopping dead after 1945, sometimes after 1910. Even if there be a significant contradiction built into the notion of a prevailingly critical, disbalancing role for contemporary creative production being made plausible to young people aiming at rapid entry into the 'system', there must be a *via media* which would prevent the galloping erosion of opportunities for thoughtful exposure to a representative selection of current compositional practices. This is not a problem limited to the States - one frequently encounters students in European conservatories who actively avoid contact with contemporary music because of the opposition of their instrumental professors to their participation, apparently because it will 'ruin their technique'. Their technique for *what*?

JB: Turning to another topic of controversy: you've been involved with various aspects of electronic music over the years, and you've worked at IRCAM. What are your feelings with regard to the medium?

BF: Extremely ambiguous, to say the least! I've never composed a piece just for tape, for instance, but always with live instrumental participation. My researches at IRCAM were dedicated to real-time computer/instrument interface situations where the input of the instrument would modify various aspects of the pre-composed computer materials.

JB: Were you working with the 4X machine?

BF: Actually, I was at IRCAM just before the 4X was introduced. One of the problems which led me to abandon my project was the re-organization made necessary in the wake of that change. It would have meant beginning practically from scratch, and I felt unable to justify the time commitment at that juncture.
      My only other major effort in the field was my **Time and Motion Study II** for cellist and live electronics, in which the all-enveloping electronic set-up might well be seen as some sort of punitive cage within which the performer - singing, speaking, operating two foot pedals, reacting under intense pressure to the delay systems' reactions to her - is being confined.[22] I've always felt myself constrained to subvert the obviously 'effective' exploitation of the medium in one way or another. For instance, in the cello piece I was primarily concerned with the nature of memory - the way it sieves, re-orders or obliterates layers of experience in order to build a viable future out of a fictional past. There are several assistants who, reading from the score, filter and modify, eliminate and overlay characteristic fragments of the cello's discourse. These twisted fragments are then fed back into the total texture to disturb or undermine the linear rhetoric, sometimes singly, at other points fed in massed and tangled block sonorities. The compositionally most elaborate sections of the piece are sonically manifested almost exclusively by means of the amplified sounds of fingernails scraping at

various speeds along one or more strings (Ex. 7) - an interesting 'scorched earth policy' of lyric expression - and the final violent moments of the cellist's attempts to assert a 'voice' are drowned out by a pre-recorded tape overlay of noise elements from earlier in the work, now ripped absurdly out of context. As the title implies, that series of works was setting out to investigate the concept of 'efficiency' as related to aesthetic evaluative criteria - almost an absurd undertaking in itself, but closely related to some of the points we were making earlier concerning performance technique and real or perceived difficulty of execution and perception.

I note that my pupils seem to have no such reservation with the electronic medium, particularly in the field of computer composition: whether I will ever feel impelled to turn in that direction once more remains to be seen. If so, I am sure that it will be from a comparably ironic or subversive standpoint to earlier years. There is little likelihood that I will ever shift the emphasis of my activity away from the live performer.

JB: You described your most recent work involving electronics, **Mnemosyne** for bass flute and tape (Ex. 8), the final work of the **Carceri d'Invenzione** cycle, as "... an amplification; a densification of the techniques that until that point had been treated in the cycle".[23] How did you achieve this result? What role did the tape, and its interaction with the live flutist, play?

BF: What I was aiming at through the confrontation was a re-integration of metric and harmonic patterns of order. The tape part consists entirely of chordal sequences initiated always and only at the downbeat of each measure, thereafter generally remaining immobile. The chordal materials were derived from the eight-chord sequence underlying almost the entire **Carceri** cycle. The sounds on the tape are invariably electronically-unmodified bass flute sonorities; the soloist co-ordinates his more complex activities with the tape by means of a click track. The latter enabled me to employ 'irrational meters' such as 3/10, 5/24, etc. and to modify tempi in exact proportional relationships.

The pitches of the solo part are either (a) the same as those appearing on the tape or (b) pitches related to these latter by a limited, constantly-evolving set of secondary intervals. At the beginning of the piece the number of notes on the tape is very small, while the number of secondary intervals in the solo part very large; in consequence, the tape sounds very much like some atrophied, ethereal cantus firmus. As the work progresses, the density of pitches in the bass flute diminishes, whilst that in the tape increases, effecting a sort of 'cross-play', an exchange of perceived physical presence, weight, or whatever. The effect is interesting in that the slow unfolding of the chords creates a very particular temporal tactility whilst the increasingly obvious web of referential restrictions imposed on the maneuverings of the flutist generates quite another sense of physicality.

Ex. 7: From Time and Motion Study II

Ex. 8: From Mnemosyne

20

Mnemosyne has actually been played in a realization for nine bass flutes, by Pierre-Yves Artaud in the Centre Pompidou in Paris. The effect was far more transparent, the micro-variations in each long held note more immediately audible by reason of the spatial distribution of the sound sources.

JB: Let's turn to your more recent works. Do you think that your compositional concerns have been undergoing major changes of late?

BF: It's certainly the case that moving to California has changed something in the dynamics of how I approach the compositional act: whether that will have an audible effect on my subsequent production I can't tell as yet. As far as I am aware, the things I have been doing follow directly out of what I had concerned myself with immediately before leaving Europe, in particular the matter of the musical object and its processual manifestation.

In 1988 I completed a piece, **La Chute d'Icare**, for performance in the Strasbourg Festival, which addressed this issue head-on. There is an obbligato clarinet part (written for Armand Angster, the excellent Strasbourg clarinettist) placed against a small chamber ensemble. Both parties begin the work with essentially the same, quite primitive material, consisting of invariant ascending and descending modes (Ex. 9); the entire first section of **La Chute** is concerned with eroding both this extremely hard-edged situation and with dissolving the heterophonic complicity which initially binds the solo player and the ensemble together (in that the latter simply echo the undulating riffs of the former at a slower, irregularly octave-transposed rate). It is as if the entire processual build-up to this extremely naked state has been composed, and then violently suppressed. Deprived of its generational grounding, the modal 'object' cannot but commence a gradual but irreversible decay, the soloist in one direction (leaping over different groups of intervals, microtonal inflections, etc.), the ensemble (modifying rate of heterophonic distortion, number of pitches sounding on, tendential linear modification of ancillary string textures, microtonal pitch deviations, etc.) in one or more others. It is as if the object had been gradually 'wiped over' (*pace* the paintings of Francis Bacon), become threadbare and perforated. In so doing, other, smaller objects and states become visible 'below the surface', gradually coming to take over the action. It was quite something for me to decide to point up the issue at stake in such a blatantly obvious fashion (especially so in view of the piece's subtitle "Little Serenade of Disappearance").

JB: In a recent conversation you once again made use of the term 'labyrinth' when referring to the 137-bar rhythmic scheme which, overlapped and canonically treated, forms the basis of **La Chute**. Why does this notion appeal to you?

Ex. 9

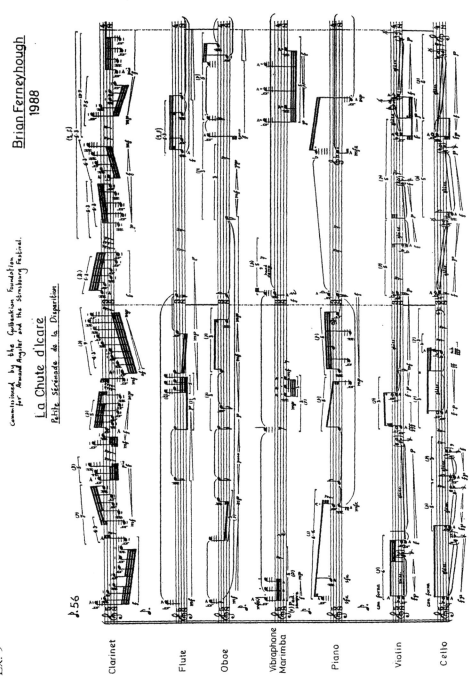

Brian Ferneyhough
1988

Commissioned by the Gulbenkian Foundation
for Armand Angster and the Strasbourg Festival.

La Chute d'Icare

Petite Sérénade de la Disparition

Clarinet

Flute

Oboe

Vibraphone
Marimba

Piano

Violin

Cello

BF: We shouldn't *always* capitulate to the urge to explain away our basic drives, images, and predilections! The symbol of the labyrinth is too deeply embedded in our collective consciousness for me to claim any personal proprietary rights. All of life is a maze; no one can see where the next turning will lead, even though we can - and do - make educated guesses. That's what consciousness is about, surely? All creativity is essentially mysterious, and all answers to the Sphinx's riddle orbit around the anthropocentric dilemma. The various mannerist periods of European music history have understood very well how invention and artifice are inextricably and ecstatically intertwined; I find much to identify with in the concerns manifested in such styles.

Since the completion of **La Chute**, I have finished **Kurze Schatten II** for solo guitar, something begun several years ago. In it I return to the miniature form which has always attracted me, attempting to locate the musical events at the precise and brilliantly blinding intersection of form and substance. This intention is suggested in the choice of title, which is taken from aphoristic writings of Walter Benjamin in which the author speaks of the uttermost reality of the object revealed as the sun progressively wipes away the shadows in its approach to its noon zenith. It was extremely challenging to work with the guitar, especially in view of the generally brusk violence of my vernacular: I had to seek gestural areas which were amenable to collecting and explosively releasing energies 'in miniature', rather analogous to the violent *effect* (but factually low *amplitude*) of a very pronounced flute key click. Talking earlier of the compositional integration of performance technique: these seven pieces are played with a four-string scordatura. At the conclusion of every second piece one string is retuned to normal, so that by the seventh movement only one string (B natural) is still detuned (to Bb). The narrowing-down process continues, in that the final section of the work is a tiny fantasy utilizing exclusively that string (Ex. 10).

My **Third String Quartet** addresses this object/process dichotomy perhaps even more extremely, in that two movements stand starkly opposed, unmediated, one of them essentially composed of a series of more or less well-defined objects continually being recombined, the other a totally linear, process-oriented mirror image of the first in which transformation comes much more clearly to the fore. Despite the vast gulf which separates them, both movements have their origin in one and the same pre-compositional disposition of periodic, metric and rhythmic patterns.

Most recently, I've been busy with a string bass solo piece, **Trittico per Gertrude Stein**, which pursues several satellite concepts in the field of large-scale rhythmic confluence and interference. There is still a lot to be done there, I think.

JB: One final, difficult question: in your opinion, what role does (or should) contemporary art play in our society?

Ex. 10: **Kurze Schatten II** (conclusion)

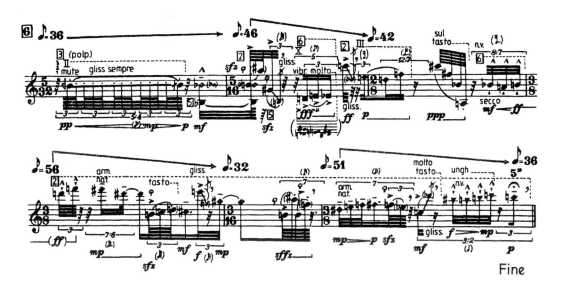

BF: I'm not sure I can answer this, nor am I sure that a straightforward statement would even begin to accurately reflect the contorted complexities of the situation. It's clear that there are as many views on this as there are composers! The *actual* role of contemporary music in society at large is, of course, peripheral in the extreme. There is nothing particularly wrong with this unless quality equals numbers, even though we'd all like more listeners, of course. By its very nature, a critical art form will be thrust into the position of a tolerated irritant by the vested interests of a Consensus Society; it assuages chronic bad conscience among those who are aware that something is very badly wrong but are unable or unwilling to distance themselves from the prevalent entertainment ideology imposed by increasingly onerous media constraints. I myself view the growth of mega-corporative communications networks as something of a blessing in disguise, in that anything which doesn't fit into their acceptance patterns will fall between the cracks into the spaces beneath and, in clear opposition, may flourish once more with a sense of mission. The idea of attempting to grapple the odd fifteen-minute slot for contemporary music on some satellite channel is grotesque in the extreme and, in my view, misses the opportunity completely.

On the more positive side, I believe that new and challenging aesthetic approaches *are* still possible and represent one of the very few open spaces, in increasingly over-developed Western society, for a re-sensibilization to the possibility of the 'total individual' beyond the manipulative splintering of our social selves which is turning us increasingly into sleepwalking jugglers. Whether the individual work of art is still capable of achieving such momentary re-integration is unclear, but at least it can aim at making us vitally aware of the utopian possibility.

The whole *raison d'être* of much of 20th-Century art has been to shatter the vessels of received wisdom (including its own!); it would be a great tragedy if the open-ended, imperfect project of critical aesthetic thinking were to decay by reason of well-meaning but inappropriate appeals to external evaluative norms.

Endnotes

1. *Harry Halbreich, jacket notes to Stil 3108-S-83, "Brian Ferneyhough rencontre Pierre-Yves Artaud".*

2. *The Arditti Quartet has recorded Ferneyhough's first three strings quartets and* **Adagissimo** *(see discography).*

3. *For a description of some of the compositional techniques used in* **Unity Capsule**, *see "Unity Capsule: An Instant Diary" (this volume, p. 98).*

4. *See note 1. This recording contains two versions of* **Unity Capsule** *and three of* **Cassandra's Dreamsong***.*

5. *Kurt Stone, "Problems and Methods of Notation",* Perspectives of New Music 1/2 *(Spring-Summer 1963), p. 30. (Reprinted in* Perspectives on Notation and Performance, *edited by Benjamin Boretz and Edward T. Cone (NY: W.W. Norton and Co., 1976), p. 30.)*

6. *Ferneyhough's notes read as follows:*

> *This work owes its conception to certain considerations arising out of the problems and possibilities inherent in the notation-realization relationship. The choice of notation in this instance was primarily dictated by a desire to define the quality of the final sound by relating it consciously to the degree of complexity present in the score. The piece as it stands is, therefore, not intended to be the plan of an 'ideal' performance. The notation does not represent the result required: it is an attempt to realize the written specifications in practice which is designed to produce the desired (but unnotatable) sound-quality.*

> *A 'beautiful', cultivated performance is not to be aimed at: some of the combinations of actions specified are in any case not literally realizable (certain dynamic groupings) or else lead to complex, partly unpredictable results. Nevertheless, a valid realization will only result from a rigorous attempt to reproduce as many of the textural details as possible; such divergences and 'impurities' as then follow from the natural limitations of the instrument itself may be taken to be the intentions of the composer. No attempt should be made to conceal the difficulty of the music by*

resorting to compromises and inexactitudes (i.e. of rhythm) designed to achieve a superficially more 'polished' result. On the contrary, the audible and visual degree of difficulty is to be drawn as an integral structural element into the fabric of the composition itself. (Brian Ferneyhough, introductory notes to **Cassandra's Dream Song** *[C.F. Peters Edition].)*

7. *Brian Ferneyhough, jacket notes to Stil 3108-S-83.*

8. *Herman Sabbe, "A Logic of Coherence and an Aesthetic of Contingency: European versus American 'Open Structure' Music",* Interface 16-3 *(1987), p. 182.*

9. *ibid., p. 182.*

10. *The form of* **Cassandra** *is a result of the interpenetration of two different musical structures, one fixed in sequence and 'directional', the other variable in sequence and 'non-directional'. The score of the work consists of two sheets: the first contains six sections of music, labelled 1 through 6, while the second contains five sections, labelled A through E. Ferneyhough's instructions to the performers are as follows:*

> *The six numbered sections (1-6) on sheet one must be played in the given numerical order. The piece therefore invariably begins with 1.*
>
> *In between each of these sections is interspersed one of the other five sections (A-E) to be found on sheet two. These may be played in any order.*
>
> *The piece thus ends with 6 on sheet one.*
> *No section may be played more than once.*

Thus, a realization of Cassandra, revolving around the placement of the five variable elements within the fixed structure defined by the six numbered sections, will yield an alternation between the two different types of material, as depicted in example 11. This regular fluctuation proves to be important in both a structural and a dramatic sense, adding an element of predictability that tends to balance the indeterminate aspects of the mobile scenario. In addition, because of the denial of sectional repetition, no section may be omitted. The interpreter is therefore immediately limited to a total of 120 (5!) possible permutations of the five variables. We therefore avoid the difficulties characteristic of works which contain both 'obligatory' and 'optional' passages, the latter being viewed by many as "functionally indispensable to the essential cycles of the narrative" (Robert Black, "Boulez' Third Piano Sonata: Surface and Sensibility", Perspectives of New Music 20 *[1981-2]:189) of such a piece, and therefore mandatory.*

The listener is greatly aided by the fact that each sheet of music possesses its own distinctive sound quality: for example, sheet one gravitates around and strongly emphasizes a single pitch, A 440 hertz, while sheet two typically avoids this pitch (Ex. 12). This extremely clear differentiation of the basic material is reminiscent of Boulez's distinction between 'points' and 'blocs' in the 'Constellation-Miroir' formant of his **Third Piano Sonata.**

Ex. 11: **Cassandra's Dream Song**

Variable structure (sheet two)

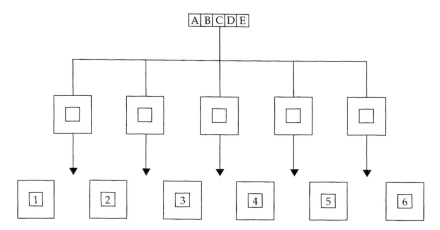

Fixed structure (sheet one)

Ex. 12: **Cassandra's Dream Song** (excerpts)

Section 2 (from page 1)

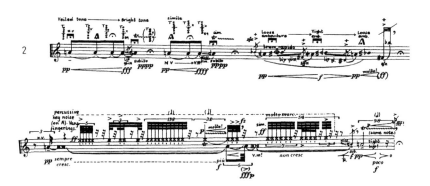

Section C (from page 2)

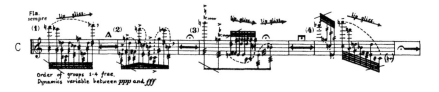

The overall result is a 'directional' work, one which is easily recognizable from one performance to the next despite the presence of the mobile sections.

11. *Pierre Boulez,* Boulez on Music Today, *translated by Susan Bradshaw and Richard Rodney Bennett (London: Faber and Faber, 1971), p. 115.*

12. **La terre** *was commissioned by the British Broadcasting Corporation and was premiered on September 20, 1979 at the Musica Nova Festival in Glasgow, Scotland by the Scottish National Orchestra conducted by Elgar Howarth.*

13. *The* **Carceri d'Invenzione** *cycle consists of seven works, and totals approximately 1 1/2 hours in duration. For more details, see "Carceri d'Invenzione" (this volume, p. 131).*

14. *Karlheinz Stockhausen, cited in Jonathan Cott,* Stockhausen: Conversations with the Composer *(London: Picador, 1974), p. 35.*

15. *Richard Toop, "Lemma-Icon-Epigram",* Perspectives of New Music *28/2 (Summer 1990), p. 53. Originally published in* Contrechamps *8 (1988), p. 86, translated by Daniel Haefliger.*

16. *John Cage, "Two Statements on Ives",* A Year from Monday, *Middletown, CT: Wesleyan U. Press, 1963), p. 42.*

17. *Brian Ferneyhough, "Form, Figure, Style: an Intermediate Assessment" (see this volume, p. 21).*

18. *Richard Toop, "Ferneyhough's Dungeons of Invention",* Musical Times *128 (no.1737) (1987), pp. 624-5.*

19. *For details, see "Second String Quartet" (this volume p. 117).*

20. *Jonathan Harvey, "Brian Ferneyhough",* Musical Times *120 (no. 1639) (1979), p. 725.*

21. *Pierre Boulez, "The Teacher's Task",* Orientations *(Cambridge: Harvard University Press, 1986), p. 119.*

22. *For further details, see "Time and Motion Study II" (this volume, p. 107).*

23. *Toop, "Conversation" (see this volume, p. 300).*

INTERVIEW WITH JEAN-BAPTISTE BARRIÈRE
(1991)

JEAN-BAPTISTE BARRIÈRE: What is your compositional itinerary?

BRIAN FERNEYHOUGH: You mean, how do I set about composing? The first thing is to find a conceptual framework adequate to the scope of the work to be composed. By that I mean a clearly-delineated 'environment' within which useful decision-making procedures can be defined. It is very important to have available at the outset, not so much material generating mechanisms of an abstract sort, but rather hierarchically-ordered evaluational tools whose usefulness resides in their capacity for reading and interpreting the topological characteristics that such a theater of potential operations provides. In recent years I have invariably resorted to quite extensive precompositional outlines which, at the very least, offer concrete information on length, segmentation and available rhythmic articulation of component structures, often much more. Frequently, there is more information of this sort available than is finally selected for integration in the work at hand: my intent is to create an extremely high density and interpenetration of levels which offers a significant experience of tactile resistance to the more intuitive faculties when defining more precisely the characteristics of the final score. Most recently, for instance, the precompositional matrix for **Allgebrah** (1990-) consisted of three layers of variational/ permutational activity, which, although based on identical orderings of number ratios, remain quite distinct in texture and directional tendency. These three levels are present in equal density throughout although, in the final score, a further set of selectional operations was imposed in order to define the actual amount of each texture present at any given moment. Similarly, three aspects of identical pitch materials are assigned, one each to these same layers, so that variations in the density of the latter will immediately be reflected in the way the various pitch/interval hierarchies are perceived when mapped onto each other in terms of 'middleground' priorities. Such strategies offer rich stimulation for the disassociation and subsequent recoordination of linearly discursive vectors - something which has been vital to my work for many years. Somehow, my mental makeup demands this sort of concrete resistance; much of my 'inner dialogue' revolves as much around concepts derived from the physical world ('energy', 'force', 'directionality', 'perspective'...) and its manifestation in organized sound as around specific 'materials' as such (whatever they might currently be). Quite recently I evolved the concept of 'Interference Form' to express the importance that the intersection and collision of clearly linear structural tendencies have for my way of thinking and feeling musical process.

Having established the above mentioned 'textured' space, the final act of composition involves the application of selectional and elaborational procedures designed to impinge violently upon (and thus, according to my personal interpretation, perceptually enhance) the various constellations which that space contains and procedurally legitimates. I suppose one might to some extent conceive of this process as rendering visible the internal qualities and tensions of the given environment by applying further - related but torsionally opposing - forces to it from without (perhaps comparable to the striations observed in rock faces exposed by violent movements of the earth's crust?). One example of such intrusive operations might be the progressive erosion or distortion of elements by means of Random Funneling series. For each work I establish a series of grids which, beginning with a random ordering of the required values, progressively assign individual digits to their correct position in the final 'normative order' - usually in order of increasing or decreasing magnitude. Apart from being almost universally applicable to any quantifiable musical phenomenon (and thus highly amenable to the all-important task of musical 'punning') such complex but ultimately highly directional operations are a powerful tool in balancing basically simple fundamental manipulations against the significant level of complexity which emerges when relatively small numbers of such 'lines of force' impinge obliquely upon each other. I usually spend a considerable amount of time preparing the versions of such tables which, for any given set of values, will be employed in a particular compositional situation. One important factor is, obviously, the number of permutations required to move from a totally random to a particular normative ordering of the elements; another is the degree to which the specifics of any given series may be usefully reflected in subsequent interlocking or nesting procedures making for larger-scale dispositional coherence.

I would not say that I was a notably systematic composer. Most of my time is spent finding ways of allowing my natural tendencies to disorder to find useful channels of expression commensurate with my (perhaps unrealistic) vision of the high compaction of abstract and concrete aspects which a work needs to embody in order to make it more than just one more thing in the world to trip over.

JBB: How would you, in retrospect, describe your background as a composer?

BF: When considering what to present to the musicology students at IRCAM during my short recent visit (April 1991) I started thinking a lot about how my compositional endeavor has developed over the years and, above all, where it is located in the mid/late 20thC. scheme of things. It may be dangerous to examine and 'freeze' these imponderables too extensively; nevertheless, there do appear to be some clear central factors at work in forming the features of these two issues. In the first instance, it was undoubtedly my physical and spiritual isolation from the important centers of innovation which was decisive, since it constrained me to painstakingly cover a great deal of *very* basic ground independently of much detailed input from outside, at least at the beginning. My constant concern with formally legitimizing the workings of musical language certainly dates from the period when I first attempted to produce longer works without having much idea of how, technically, to go about it. My development was (and still is?) a form of pendulum swing: on the one hand a series of pieces in relatively conservative garb which progressively increased the degree of consistency and malleability of means employed; on the other, a group of more sonically radical efforts which remained unsatisfactory precisely by reason of their lack of internal coherence. Thus, one of the more incoherent 'improvisations' might be typically followed by a couple of 'recuperative' items and, in time, the two extremes began to overlap more and more. Almost everything I have done could, I suppose, be examined in this light, right up until the present (even though the extremes are, of course, incomparably more proximate than then). It was my **Sonatas for String Quartet** of 1967 which drew these two extremes together in a tense and prickly weave, making them, as it were, the latent 'theme' of the discourse.

Some of these considerations are not irrelevant when searching to locate my supposed place in the 'grand scheme of things'. Many have dumped me conveniently into some 'late-late' serialist drawer, I think, without pausing to reflect upon the relative consistency with which I have continued to develop, refine and extend my practice over the last 25 years (unless it be to underline my naive obstinacy, arrogance or imaginative impotence in not scurrying to undergo periodic ritual rebirth through the refining fires of a series of largely inconsequential stylistic/ideological transmogrifications). This seems strange, since I have always been a quite strong and direct critic of some aspects of serial ideology and practice, without rejecting outright its sheer youthful vigor and spirit of adventure. I naturally see things somewhat differently! Most important for me was defining a language, field of operations, whatever, capable of organic internal growth, an *auto-history*. I wanted to utilize the insights attained by the analytical separation and bifurcation of parametric informations to create the possibility of gradual and continual movement back and forth between higher and lower levels of structural perception. Because the qualitative aspect of perception does not move in parallel to quantitative modification I early on rejected the idea of a sort of constant 1-to-1 equivalence binding macro and micro dimensions and, with that concept, the rejection of many basic serial concepts was bound to follow. Perhaps because I studied the theoretical append-ages of serial practice relatively late, and, as I said, worked for many years in complete isolation, I was forced to develop at first crude, then more refined and extensive personal methods of (as I conceived it at least) intensifying and com-pacting some of the inner contradictions shaking the foundations of New Mu-sic. If this seems to contradict what I said above concerning the 'synthesizing' tendency of my early attempts, this is actually more apparent than real, since it is precisely by isolating and dissonantly confronting discrepancies of discursive modality *within one and the same constraining framework* that a more powerful expressive focus is to be achieved. 'No pain, no gain.'

In a time when the ruins of much of Modernism's optimism and aliena-tion are busily being paved over with more civil images of our selves and situ-ation, I emphatically feel that the full story is no longer being told and that there is a place for the continued critical investigation of issues pertaining to the boundaries where perception, self-awareness, order and chaos collide, and *frag-mentation*, as terminus technicus, still has concrete (as well as evocative) mean-ing. The issue of *complexity* as such is, ironically, coming rapidly to the fore as an interpretative machine likely to change our way of seeing and thinking about the world in the near future. As such, it is a valid object of creative investiga-tion and elaboration. At the same time, I also have to underline my conviction that younger composers must and will discover other, possibly quite different, approaches, since they are mostly coming from background experiences quite different from my own, especially in terms of their exposure to, and practical experience of, commercial and/or so-called popular musics.

JBB: What do you think is the role of research in composition, and, be-sides composition, for music in general?

B.F. 'Research' is an odd word, isn't it? It's one that I have never had much occasion to employ all that much - at least, not until arriving in America, where one is constrained to designate all creative activity as 'research' for the benefit of university administrations. It is difficult, in fact, to convince most people in such environments that the only tools I customarily employ to carry out my research are pen and paper, so accustomed are they to judging projects in terms of money or material involved. My most intensive period of research, in the sense of investigating the elaborational potential of particular instrumen-tal dispositives, was, I suppose, between 1974 and 1977, when I composed the entire **Time and Motion Study** series as well as **Unity Capsule** for solo flute. None of these works was research if, by that term, one imagines tentative hy-potheses concretely tested in laboratory situations; what I did was to set up a specific set of relationships (in **Time and Motion Study II** between a solo per-former and a complex set of live electronic hook-ups, in **Time and Motion Study**

III by way of conflicting physical and electronically projected spatializations) and began to explore them, 'sound them out', as if they were themselves instruments emitting specific, characteristic resonances, suggesting appropriate formal strategies. It was not a question of collaborating directly with performers (even though there have been a number of very distinguished interpreters who have, as it were, motivated my activity), since this is something with which I have never felt comfortable. Instead, I prefer to investigate an instrument or group of instruments thoroughly before beginning work, submitting myself to their 'personalities', allowing a sense of their physical extension, their 'specific gravity' to guide my choices. I have always been extremely stimulated by the challenge of unfamiliar 'theaters' of this sort: lately I have approached the guitar and the double bass very much in this spirit, the guitar, in particular, proving especially demanding. In one of the movements of that work (**Kurze Schatten II**) I set out to map systematically all possible finger positions over all combinations of strings in order to compose the piece as a reflection of the layout of the fingerboard itself. Perhaps **Unity Capsule**, the flute being my own instrument, is something of an exception here, in that I did indeed involve myself in quite extensive practical research with the instrument in hand, mainly to test out the efficacy of the complex momentary conjunctions of technique which my compositional technique generated. Once these pieces reached rehearsal, there was little, if anything, which needed to be modified as the result of experience.

My only other experience of a 'pure' research situation was at IRCAM at the beginning of the '80s, where I fruitlessly attempted to set up a real-time reactive situation for clarinet and computer. This was aborted at the time because of inadequate synthetic clarinet spectrum complexity, and because, for the time available, the interface would have proven far too complex. Until the environment is definitively defined, it is, as I said, difficult for me to come up with plausible compositional reactions. Almost as a by-product on that occasion I did define some interesting algorithms for automatic spectral generation but felt them to be too distant from my main compositional concerns to pursue them further. Over the years I have waited for more obviously intuitive computer interfaces without great impatience. Working with many talented students in the States, most of whom have remarkable computer literacy, I have come to reflect that the *modus operandi* of computer research does not, on the whole, parallel with sufficient precision my personal thinking and working habits: as I understand it, much of the former focuses on facilitating realizations of specific compositional projects, whereas, on the whole, (and simplifying more than a little) I would have to say that I need to be mentally involved with the complete 'instrument' before the appropriate reactive mechanism suggests itself to me.

Clearly, research has led to extremely exciting results in some compositional areas, particularly spectral analysis and voice synthesis, and I frequently get to hear quite impressive pieces based on some of this. Studio work

seems to be one of the more natural activities of younger generation composers, and I am convinced that computer procedures have radically influenced
the way that these artists 'think' their relationship to material and compositional
process.

JBB: It seems to me that you tend to confuse the concept of research and
the use of technology. This seems to me unfair to the spirit of research in the
scientific term, but also to what could be considered as your own research in
composition. The systematic approach by which you describe your
compositional process is clearly related to the scientific concept of research. It
would be interesting, beyond what I would provocatively (as an answer to your
provocation) analyze as a 'prejudice' (research is not just only a buzzword or a
magic incantation to get some funding, or even a pretext to never accomplish
something...) to get your description of what differentiates research in music (as
opposed to research about music, and for music) from research in science.

BF: Did I imply that the term has merely operative significance? I hope
not. My point was rather that, as I understand it, in science one is working within
a generally-accepted universe in which the efficacy of testing methods with regard to the establishing of certain probabilities is the subject of general professional agreement. The accepted criteria of valid proof form a constant. What
would be the logical equivalent to such proofs in a musical composition? The
'usefulness' of music (as of any art form) is by no means invariably measured
according to universal criteria and, even if we were to compare it exclusively
with 'pure' research, such as higher mathematics, it is by no means certain what
its ultimate evaluational norms of coherence, elegance or efficacy might be, since
these are seldom clearly established according to fundamental derivable *a priori*
postulates. A Beethoven symphony does not function like Bertrand Russell's
Principia Mathematica (although, I suppose, a Schenkerian analyst might possibly disagree with me). For instance, in the case of a composer like myself,
operating within a fairly clear set of constraints, making a mistake does not
thereby invalidate the work's fundamental postulates; rather, I may decide to
modify the aims in order to take account of that same mistake, thereby declar-
ing it *ex cathedra* a non-infraction. I don't dispute that much of composition
demands methods both rigorous and, in their own terms, well-formed; I simply think that the term 'research' in the arts implies a *different* sort of approach
to 'experimentation' than that implied in the scientific community. Of course
one is always exploring new areas of the self and, in an important sense,
recomposing oneself in and through the crucible of the compositional act. Probably musical research is about as far from scientific research on the one side as
alchemy is on the other, since both extremes are ultimately dependent on non-
self-consistent revelation for their advancement and are not really open to the

concept of disproof. I realize, though, that I am generalizing largely from my own experience, and that my work, emphasizing as it does the unstable boundaries of musical experience, might well be said to fall under the 'research' rubric, at least in part.

JBB: Similarly, what is the role of theory in composition, and besides composition?

BF: I have never been much of a friend of theory as such, probably in part because of my resolute antipathy to it as a student. It is very easy for a seductive descriptive hypothesis to become magically transformed into a rigidly prescriptive prescription for composition. On the other hand, we all like to speculate on occasions - and, of course, our compositions are in large degree concrete sedimentations of a great deal of intense theorizing as to ends and means. But I suppose you mean 'theory' in a somewhat wider sense than this? Certainly I, for one, feel the need to embed my compositional activity in a larger articulated scheme of things; almost every day we are confronted with manifold troublesome questions (of relevance, stylistic legitimacy, social reception...) which have to be addressed in one way or another, and attempting to erect a global intellectual construct, however provisional, is one way of achieving this. It is surely impossible to avoid reflecting on one's position and that of one's compositional endeavor in terms of some sort of larger communal framework of experience. As long as theory remains the public trace of such activity and does not take on a normative life of its own it has a useful regulatory role to play.

JBB: What is the role of analysis: that of the composer and that of the analyst?

BF: I feel that creative and sensitive analysis is of first importance when attempting to bring New Music into a larger sphere of intellectual resonance than has all too often been the case. Analysis might be seen as a form of acculturating transliteration in which the distance between the 'languages' of work and analysis is an important indicator of the scope of a compositional project seen in terms of its 'social motion'. From my own personal point of view I have to say that there have been a number of occasions on which the analytical regard of other composer's achievements has brought me insights of some importance into aspects of my own aesthetic world - insights that might not have otherwise occurred simply because of lack of critical distance from one's own work. It is certainly not a question of *influence*, since often the works analyzed have no obvious spiritual or technical relationship to one's own: it's more like bouncing a ball off a wall at an angle - the direction from which the ball returns to the thrower is sometimes refreshingly unexpected.

Since much of compositional praxis is concerned - implicitly or overtly - with the establishment of categories, there is surely room for an approach to the complex sonic phenomenon which directly addresses that particular issue, from whatever standpoint. How much of this filters back as 'creative misunderstanding' into the world of the composer is almost beside the point. That is not its primary function as I understand it but rather the precise opposite, that is, the active appropriation of the work (as communicational prototype) by considered application of external categories of order. In this context the not unimportant distinction between 'composers' analysis' and 'musicologists' analysis' should be mentioned. Over the years I have come more and more to believe in an underlying and unbroken empathy connecting composers of widely separated epochs - something like recognizable 'trade secrets' enabling one to make educated guesses concerning how the composer handled particular problems, how he himself understood what he was doing regardless of other obscuring aspects of style or cultural background. All a composers' analysis can hope to achieve is the consequent exposure of such privileged 'insider information' as filtered through his own personal grasp of the tools of his trade. Whenever dealing analytically with the works of others I invariably begin with a disclaimer: I am *not* offering an objective perspective on the work in question, but one emphatically emanating from, and directed at, matters of direct compositional utility. Every composer recomposes the past in this extremely partial fashion, I should think: certainly most analyses I have read by composers tend to tell one more about the writer than about the nominal object of his examination! The contribution of the musicologist from this privileged point of view is to continue to point out to the composer the extreme partiality of his perspective and to trigger his fantasy in adopting approaches his own limited and partisan experience would not necessarily suggest.

JBB: How do you define the interaction between sonic materials and organization?

BF: The term 'sonic materials' is very broad - almost too broad, perhaps, to usefully deal with. In general I distinguish between the characteristics of larger-scale bodies of sonic definition ('style') and the specifics of local situations. Both may be termed 'material', depending on what compositional perspective is being adopted at any given juncture. It has always been my view that consistency of stylistic development is a prerequisite for meaningful development of musical vocables. Without a 'personal history' (defined as their consistent utilization and modification in the course of one or several works), elements are expressive merely to the extent that external semantic associations or primitive accidentalia of location ('contrast', 'balance'...) permit. A basic organizational concern is, therefore, the establishment and articulation of such essentially (although perhaps interruptedly so) linear transformational tendencies as encourage the sense of identifiable, discrete 'things' being impinged upon and modified by concrete temporal forces. Very often I see individual elements spreading their influence, from piece to piece, such that, as it becomes more attenuated, the perceptual immediacy of these elements is more and more *deferred*, thereby coming to influence the course of events as a species of formal marker or even general articulational category rather than an unambiguously 'sonic' event. I like to imagine this tendency as a *processual object* - or, perhaps, as a species of musical verbal noun. 'The falling of a tree' may be interpreted as a concatenation of object relationships and energy states imbued with significance only when collectively subsumed to a total event-duration whose discrete totality is comprehended exclusively via step-by-step accretion and digestion of incomplete data. Operatively, I tend to ascribe three basic levels of perception and function to such materials; (1) *texture*; (2) *gesture* and (3) *figure*. Whilst these terms do not correspond precisely to foreground-middleground-background categories, there *are* discernable intuitive parallels, I think. One is not discussing three different things but three ways of dealing with what is, at least potentially, one and the same state of affairs. What changes is the view of the composer as manifest in the contextualization to which the material is subject i.e. the methodology of meaning attribution in a particular stylistic/procedural domain. A major issue with newer music is always the question of perspective - how *close* am I to these events, what are primary, what subservient areas of order? If this issue is not addressed at the outset by means of a thought-through strategy of *organization* (which is not necessarily identical to a rational strategy of *generation*) whatever materials one finally employs are rendered partially dumb because they don't of themselves know whether they should be shouting or whispering!

JBB: Which are the influence processes which you can admit in the compositional process (coming from the arts, intellectual life etc.)?

BF: I think you are aware that I have invariably underlined the advantages of lively and constant cross-fertilization between diverse areas of spiritual discipline. Most of what we create is directly related to the partial understanding (or deliberate or inadvertent misunderstanding) of something else. Since the collapse of the ruling paradigms characteristic of the tonal era there has been an increasing tendency to lock-in or map music onto other, perhaps more stable, modes of discourse. This is surely understandable and necessary, even at the cost of once more becoming painfully aware of the deficiencies in the way we are able to usefully articulate musically immanent issues. Most terminology has been borrowed from a fantastic panorama of other disciplines and this fact often constrains one to deal with important issues on the level of analogy or metaphor. Borrowed raiments thus have their uses, even when laying the musician open to the reproach of amateurism or naiveté because of his magpie antics. But: building a nest is not the least estimable of activities! Often, I have had occasion to regret not being the possessor of a more systematic mind; I find that the progressive acquisition of knowledge does little to empower my sense of overall direction or priorities. That being so, I tend to adopt a more 'catastrophic' approach to learning, which involves the violent confrontation or superimposition of modes of discourse which, *prima vista*, might seem incompatible or even actively antagonistic to one another. Very often these partial confrontations point to unexpected areas of correspondence, to new momentary integrations of startling intensity. I seriously doubt if many composers have attempted to reproduce in musical form the essentials of some complete extra-musical theory: rather, specific *conflictual intensities* are perceived arising from previously acquired attitudes and the impingement of new hypothetical models. This was true with regard for the fashionable resort to scientific terminology in the '50s, assumptions underlying communicational postulates of politically engaged music in the '60s and, to a lesser extent, it may be readily distinguished as a moving force behind current neoromantic rhetorical positions which adopt a curiously selective interpretation of 18th/19th C. ideologies of the self.

The titles of many of my works instantly reveal the extent to which I have been set in motion by visual or broadly philosophical issues, I think; often, an image has cut through a Gordian knot of confused speculation and enabled me to focus upon one primary area of articulation of that problem. Examples that come to mind are **La terre est un homme** (a painting by Matta); **La Chute d'Icare** (Breughel) and **Transit** (a Flammarion woodcut). Each of these was instrumental in providing and giving voice to the conceptual environment for the work in question. Earlier works, like **Time and Motion Study II** for cello and electronics, focused on the manifold ramifications of a single monolithic issue - in that instance, the extent to which memory is a positive or negative feature in the mechanism of awareness. During the '80s there was the unifying image of Piranesi, which enabled me to bring together work-projects of superficially quite distinct provenance in one over-arching design. At the onset of the decade I remember being very impressed by Gilles Deleuze's theoretical/speculative tract on the painter Francis Bacon, which was instrumental in making concrete some fundamental intuitions concerning my own work. Most recently, my **4th String Quartet** with soprano voice addressed the issue of how far the historical analogy between verbal and musical forms of expression (Schoenberg's 'musical prose') still holds good. That task involved the further deconstruction of texts by Jackson Mac Low which were themselves a deconstruction of one of the archetypal textual monuments of the Modern, Pound's **Cantos**. If I seem superficially less obviously concerned with the extra-musical link-ups today, it is perhaps because I have developed a higher awareness of the limits and possibilities inherent in the articulation of specifically musical tasks which do not degenerate into the 'purely' musical. Even the most radically extreme artistic position functions only because it succeeds in vigorously re-articulating the 'space between', however the current nature of our tools leads us to imagine this.

JBB: Do you consider intuition to be separated from rationality, or is it a form of rationality?

BF: Neither the one nor the other, I should think. Even attempting to draw a line around the contours of the intuitive faculty is to draw it ineluctably into the sphere of rational discourse, although this does not imply the absorption of intuition to the conscious *ratio*. Isn't it a matter of 'instantaneous' or 'step-by-step'? In composing, one always has to *prepare the ground for the intuition to function*. Rational assessment and cataloguing of limits and possibilities is the ploughman's furrow. Primary is the capacity to recognize meaningful problems: for this one needs goals, however ill-defined these may initially be. As I said earlier, the *system* is the bridge via which the *ratio* and intuition can communicate; it provides gradations of nuance which the intuition can employ to articulate its succession of particular insights - that is to say, it is not merely a crazy combinatorial machine, spewing out values in all directions. Rational processes are always better when incomplete or 'skewed', prioritized in some degree, since this gives them a 'torque' or inherent energizing capacity which is an integral component of 'organized intuitive evaluation'. I have always avoided systems which dictate exhaustivity as a formal criterion. None of my works function that way. To that extent they are all very bad examples for textbooks on serial theory, and are consequently rather unpopular with those who make it their business to expect such things.

JBB: What do you expect from the computer and, more generally, from technology, for composition?

BF: It sometimes amuses me to hear that my music would be much more 'cost-effective' if I generated it via computer! This view, of course, hardly needs to be attacked by me, since it reflects a stunning misprision as to the gradualist path necessarily adopted. Just as a work is a 'thing' revealed in time, so it emerges as the sedimentation of temporally-conditioned subjective processes of situational valorization as manifest through the compositional act. To expect these things to be ready and active in their entirety at the outset would be to deny them their contribution to the metaphor of the 'form of life' which underlies my compositional thinking. My father was a gardener by profession: although I strenuously rejected such manually-orientated interests, perhaps more of his attitude entered into my world view than I knew. Certainly I like to get the feel of compositional 'earth' between my fingers and to reflect this in the means of growth and accretion which the work has at its disposal. In any case, I would think that it would be more plausible today to reject the totalizing vision of a work arising, fully sanitized, from the forehead of Zeus. Composing is *work*, and should be incorporated as such. That said, there are certainly aspects of technology which I see as being of utility, albeit less in the realm of direct sonic generation than in the mediation and facilitation of compositional operations in the context of instrumental or vocal projects. Recently I have been working intensively with notation programs; one of my ideas was for applications capable of transforming notated musical materials via algorithmic filters into results also notated in a standard fashion. This would mirror some of the essential categories of treatment with which I am constantly concerned. I think I mentioned earlier my utilization of Random Funneling Series as vector-defining parameters for certain tendential processes: there are more complexly embedded operations of this sort which would be greatly facilitated by corresponding computational resources, given my imperfect and unsystematic grasp of mathematical methodology. I am full of understanding for those who see technology as primarily applicable to sonic analysis and transformation: on the other hand, it would be a great pity if more mundane compositional functions were to be passed over in the rush to sonic innovation. If I were to involve myself more directly with technology as a tool for directly generating sounds I would need to feel the sort of *resistance* I mentioned earlier as being an essential stimulant to creativity. One way to go might be to work against the natural tendencies of the medium, especially when one sometimes has the distinct impression that many compositional strategies end up being based upon what is currently available and demonstrable rather than on any inevitable, innate need of specific creative visions. Sometimes the most 'elegant' solution is not the most artistically valid by any manner of means. Maybe it is up to the individual perceiving deficiencies to do something about it; if so, *mea culpa*. I would imagine that the progressive integration of technology into the daily life of the composer can only increase. I can only hope that interpretations of its utility will not be too one-dimensional. We'll see.

JBB: Another question related, even indirectly, to teaching: how do you react to epigones and other imitators, followers or disciples, of yourself as well as of other composers? The question may be irritating, but seems to me important at a moment where ethics in art are quite low, and especially at a time of such confusion, where the dominant paradigm is generalized collage, as exemplified by the domination of sampling, the latter being also related, quite directly this time, to the future of interpreters.

BF: This is an interesting question on a general, rather than personal, level, I think, since it touches on the issue of *individual style* and the degree to which stylistic markers and aesthetic ideals are currently transferrable. A few years ago there was a certain amount of confusion caused by individuals mis-interpreting the tenor of my style and practice as aiming towards the utopia of a new *lingua franca*. Perhaps this was brought about by a tendency to identify with the natural homogenizing and simplifying dicta of the media as a central creed. In any case, this resulted in a grave overestimation of the structural carry-ing power of particular style-defining characteristics - gestural patterns, high density, simultaneously unfolding but internally asynchronous layers of activ-ity and so on - which I never saw as anything but *ad personam*-developed vocables and techniques. Far from being universally applicable, I found that their transference to the works of others caused significant deracination and deterio-ration, since their initial power derived to a marked degree from the history of the confluence of individuated dynamic states of affairs in particular works, and this cannot be assumed to be a symmetrically commutatable tendency. I have been very dispirited at what I interpret as the failure of a few younger compos-ers to remain faithful to the spirit of such an enterprise by initiating vocabularic and processual trajectories equally specific to themselves. The challenge, at this late and complex moment in the history of the modern, is surely to attempt the febrile balancing act between individual perception (individual in the sense of springing from the ground water of a contestable, but still momentarily func-tioning totality) and the necessity of objective (material-immanent) hierarchies of organizational validation. One does not have to adopt my particular point of attack in order to confront this issue - indeed, choosing a closely-allied approach tends to dilute the very dialectic tension which the subjective-objective para-dox proffers as a counterbalance to the overcooked and jaded cynicism of much (not all) postmodern musical produce (where, I fear, the medium is indeed the message) because implying a higher level of intralinguistic transference poten-tial than is actually attainable. It would perhaps be instructive to re-examine musical history from the point of view of whether a given period is amenable to *schools* or to *epigonalism*; I strongly suspect that this would offer valuable insights into the state of balance obtaining between individual and group per-ception. Of course, epigonalism is not entirely equatable with influence. All of us have been influenced by intense musical experiences at one time or another: what I am trying to get at is that there is a core of procedural abstractability in certain composers' practice that, more often than not, is passed over in favor of identification with more superficially legible aspects of the style which are them-selves only personally-imprinted emblems of larger concerns. Where that abstractability lies close to the surface (as in some early total serial contexts, for instance) it is at least imaginable that a certain diversified communality - loosely put, a *school* - can emerge. Where, on the other hand, the very conviction of certain personal practices (Boulez, Ligeti) seems to interpenetrate with a high degree of procedural abstractability (*and* historical/theoretical legitimacy), the danger of not seeing the woods for the trees is considerable, and the epigonal inevitably emerges. Perhaps one could essay a slightly frivolous definition of the two terms? A school would represent the *individual in the general*, whereas the epigone would equally express the *general in the individual*!

By the way, I would like to emphasize here that, in throwing around the emotively loaded term 'epigone', I am by no means speaking of at least two generations of young composers who, for reasons best known to music journalism, have been grouped together under the rubric 'New Complexity'. Firstly, most of these artists have not studied with me and, secondly, their various backgrounds (as diverse as the expressive thrust of their present-day concerns) by no means invariably include direct influence through my works. I prefer to think of the almost simultaneous emergence of such a considerable body of composers examining the relation of communication to complexity and chaos as the natural reaction of art to conditions in the world at large, and the problems that their works undoubtedly pose as reflecting and aggressively questioning the developing perspective of these times, where *die neue Unübersichtlichkeit* (or, perhaps, *Gleichgültigkeit*) has become creative canonic law. I think you are right, in your question, to employ the term 'ethics' as being of relevance. I am aware that it is greatly out of fashion to imagine music to embody such concerns at the present juncture, but I am glad to say that there are some individuals, of very different stylistic persuasions, who are prepared to shoulder the conflicts and cultural embarrassments which such an attitude seems to call forth. There is room for all sorts of music, but it is difficult to imagine a viable new music which does not further these historic and pressing concerns from one standpoint or another.

JBB: What does it mean to teach composition today? What do you actually teach? Which things can be transmitted, which not?

BF: There are surely as many approaches to composition teaching as there are teachers! What it means *to me* is to have both access to a vital and stimulating source of aesthetic encounter with young artistic personalities and the necessity of constantly rearticulating and assessing my own position and priorities in the light of their perceived needs. The learning process is seldom a one-way street. Of course there is a tremendous amount of subjectivity involved, as witnessed by the confusion young composers sometimes manifest when, studying with two teachers at the same time or in immediate succession, they are given what seems diametrically opposing advice. In such cases one tries to explain that, in art, it is seldom 'either-or' but, much more often, 'both-and', since the ability to creatively and actively tolerate states of ambiguity would appear to be an essential constituent feature of the 'artistic personality'. What composition teaching in general means *today*, as opposed to earlier periods, is thus largely a function of how one interprets the flow of contemporary musical/historical awareness. One reaction to a time of pluralistic 'field' aesthetics is to encourage a student to develop facility in several recognized stylistic domains. One assumes the point of this approach to be the notion that the nascent artistic personality will have a wide palette of choices available for the gradual formulation of a distinctly personal approach. I consider this a seriously flawed philosophy, based on the assumption that 'style' is prior to content and, in some important sense, has come to replace it. In my view, style emerges as the result of many specific compositional decisions in particular pieces: it is not a value-free given, and is just as likely to devour the unwary explorer whole as to render up its treasures piecemeal to the clever grave robber. The comparison to earlier common-practice domains is specious in the sense that the specific styles customarily taught are those of specific composers (Bartók, Hindemith et al.) rather than of *schools* employing a communally viable stylistic instrumentarium general enough in its formulation to transcend the particular accidentalia of composer biographies.

My own approach, at least in the initial stages of instruction, is problem-orientated. Since the inexperienced student can scarcely be expected to have already formulated his or her own codex of concerns and techniques I generally start by assigning tasks of limited scope whose terms are nevertheless flexibly enough formulated to allow for a very broad spectrum of viable solutions - some of them completely unimagined by me when setting the exercise! Such tasks are useful in granting me invaluable insight into the personal dynamics of the individual at a fairly early stage in the pedagogical process. These tasks may range from the composition of an aurally meaningful structure utilizing, as material, only the spoken numbers 1-9 via the composition of a little piece utilizing only parts of the body as sound sources up to the imagining of music forming part of the ethnic culture of a high-technology tribe completely isolated from the rest of the world for 1000 years. Particularly with the ready access of even undergraduate students to computer and sound sampling facilities in the United States the results have sometimes been truly astounding. If you liberate people, initially, from the need to compose 'correct' music (i.e. bound by accepted norms and conventions) you free-up their inventive powers enormously.

On a more advanced level I think that two aspects of creative awareness need currently to be nurtured; firstly, the encouragement of a facility for rigorous self-criticism as integral part of the composing act and, secondly, the development of a sensitivity towards the role of aesthetic experience in the world at large. The latter is addressed by seminar work in which students come to grips with issues raised, for instance, in the realms of philosophy, social history and other art forms; the former involves both individual work with the composition teacher and exposure to peer criticism from other students. I find that these two vectors tend to usefully complement one another. At any rate, it needs to be emphasized above all that the role of the composition teacher is an essentially *passive* one - he acts as a sort of reflective membrane whereby the student's own perhaps as yet not coherently formed desires and images can be externalized and given back to him in a way that can be realized in terms of actual musical technique. In a sense, the young composer has to *interiorize* this operation, the teacher always needing to remain cognizant of the fact that his critique will only be there for a relatively short period in a composer's overall career. Perhaps the most vital task for the mentor is thus to manifest-forth, to actively embody the sort of constant context-bound questioning which is at the root of compositional stamina as I understand it. In any given compositional context, what is the most basic useful question that may be asked in order to *move on*? One thing I never do - at least, not as part of direct composition instruction - is 'teach' my own music. There have been pupils who have become rather upset when I have refused to teach them the contents of my private toolbox. There are major teachers (like Franco Donatoni) who believe the contrary, of course, so one would be extremely foolhardy to assert that there is any such thing as a 'correct' pedagogical method. In any case, it is not the method itself which is decisive, but the credibility and personality of the teacher himself, seen as a creative and human figure. This cannot be too strongly emphasized.

INTERVIEW WITH ANTONIO DE LISA
(1991)

ANTONIO DE LISA: After a long period of teaching throughout Europe, from Darmstadt to Freiburg to Milan, you moved some years ago to San Diego, California. This change of perspective allowed you to observe the tradition of European musical avant-gardism from a distance. Has any crisis of contradictions arisen from your ties with that tradition, as was the case for Schoenberg - or any relativization of values within a context of multivalence occurred...concerning music that is...considerably academic?

BRIAN FERNEYHOUGH: My move to the United States was motivated by a number of considerations, not the least (although perhaps the most banal) of which being the desire to have a stable, full-time teaching position for the first time in my career. I think that few people understand that (for instance) my position in Freiburg was merely that of a part-time lecturer, never that of a tenured professor. Over the years, juggling various secondary activities in order to make a living becomes somewhat debilitating; San Diego was the first institution ever to offer me a secure, permanent position, even though I had been actively searching for some ten years closer to home.

On the other hand, of course, I would scarcely have been tempted by any position outside Europe if I had not had other, more artistically relevant motivations. Most important was a growing sense of unease at the way much European contemporary music seemed increasingly incapable of overcoming certain ingrained attitudes developed 20 and more years ago, resulting in ever-more-obvious signs of exhaustion and desuetude. In order to better be in a position to comprehend the intricacies of the situation I definitely felt the need to distance myself from the scene, at least for a while, both geographically and culturally. I hope that my move (unexpected and inexplicable for many) has put me in a favorable position to intervene pedagogically if this should ever appear to be appropriate, as well as permitting me a 'free space', the better to reconsider my own creative priorities.

Far-reaching political and social upheavals are transforming the cultural landscape far more rapidly than I could ever have predicted in 1987, mostly in unforeseen ways. What, for instance, the re-unification of Germany will mean musically is anyone's guess just now. Increasing signs of nationalism on all sides lead one to worry about the future of an art-form as resolutely international in tone as contemporary music has long been. I still feel, though, that my decision at that time was fundamentally correct, and that it has given me a unique perspective on things. Even from a distance I remain most emphatically European: that will certainly continue to be the case whatever the future may bring.

ADL: In the *querelle des anciens et de modernes*, which today denotes a dispute in France between "spectralists" and "serialists", you were appointed to office, so to speak, as leader of the latter; are you at ease there?

BF: Since I spent quite some time recently emphasizing the inappropriateness of the term 'serial' as an adequate description of my music, I remain perplexed that anyone would assume my willingness to accept that office, or even that I had planned to bring it about. Ultimately, of course, it is France's problem if sustaining this entirely spurious polarity is really priority number one. A professional cynic familiar with how things tend to work in the world of contemporary musical politics might perhaps be forgiven for supposing it to be in the interest of certain factions to set up a 'post-Boulezian leader' of this nonexistent school in order to be able conveniently to shoot him down (as a proxy for Boulez and all he is supposed to represent) when the time is ripe!

In any case, such dualistic simplifications cannot long survive detailed analysis. The problem is usually that such informed examination is more often than not neglected in favor of terms more immediately useful as weapons. In actual fact, the real distinctions indubitably present are frequently less than issues communally recognized as important for present and future development. It is by no means reducible to the contraposition of 'vertical' as opposed to 'horizontal' ordering criteria, nor of the 'new' (resulting from computer-directed acoustic research) superseding the 'old' (gesture and linear logic dominated structuralist modalities); it is my feeling that, once having overcome its initial almost exclusive regard for specifically spectral dimensions, the 'new' will come increasingly to resemble the 'old' by seeking richer textural and formal contexts, themselves resulting in a more obviously complex and structurally ambiguous praxis. There are already signs of this happening. At the same time, it will not harm composers of the second persuasion if they succeed in becoming more sensibilized by insight into harmonic phenomena and the workings of the 'spectral' aesthetic. It is not a question of seeking a 'reconciliation' but of registering with an open mind those points of conflict and occasional alignment which encourage accepting the challenge of cross-fertilization. Propaganda-actions and unconsidered polemic broadsides do little to make this a feasible option, that's for sure.

ADL: One of the concepts that you cite more willingly is that of "dialectics". One doesn't see much of it around; for you, is it a provocation, or something real? Doesn't it seem to you that Hegelianism and Adorno belong - rightly or wrongly - to another cultural period? I ask you this question because it seems to me that sometimes the dialectic, for you, is a little like Catholicism for Graham Greene - a weapon of provocation, provided that the others don't believe in it...

BF: Well, first of all, I would hesitate to write off *all* of Adorno's insights as being out of date or theoretically superseded. While giving a graduate seminar in San Diego on the relation between his thinking and his compositions, I found that several of my better students (even though highly critical of his more questionable pronouncements on American music and the 'culture industry'), nevertheless discovered and articulated many relevant aspects of his socio-historical model. As far as the usefulness of the dialectic itself is concerned, it's certainly true that I am little interested in the mechanics of its precise location within the Hegelian historical critique of *Aufklärung*: I also tend to assume, in any case, that this process some time ago reached its inevitable conclusion in either absurdity or silence. Some understanding of its theoretical function is nevertheless useful, if one remains dissatisfied with the directionless, featureless ethical field proposed by proponents of post-Hegelian ahistoricity. Any plausible future for progressive contemporary music involves, in my view, a decisive rejection of this latter position - a rejection, which, in its turn, suggests a re-evaluation of dialectic procedures as paradigms of complex and fluid dynamic states. To this end, one might start by approaching the various terms, particularly 'synthesis', from a somewhat different angle. It's no longer a matter of 'arriving somewhere' (thus implying, however loosely, a notional point of repose) but rather of seeking to *dissonate* the terms by contraposition or mutually incompatible developmental vectors, to redefine and accentuate those similarities which make effective dissonance possible. While it is true that, today, many reject binary decision-making procedures out of hand, I do not, since - on a very basic level - it is bifurcation which renders practical even highly-evolved modes of discourse. The contradictory imposition of multiple 'dissonating resolutions' frequently leads to the creation of complex, only partially predictable processes exploring the fruitful zone of destabilized perception encountered at the outer rim of aural cognitive potential. But it is precisely there that I believe the most vital creative tendencies of the present are located.

ADL: In connection with your personality as composer, the "New Complexity" has been, and continues to be mentioned frequently; I don't know whether it is really possible to attach adjectives such as "new" or "old" to this complexity...but it does seem to me that you wish to safeguard to some degree a dimension of music's poetic ambiguity with it. But, in any event, your real enemy is the banality of music-as-spectacle: easy, enjoyable and benefiting from the system. Am I correct?

BF: Any composer who manages to achieve something even moderately original will sooner or later be weighed-down with one inappropriate appellation or another. That is perhaps irritating, but not particularly serious; problems only then arise when composers start seeing *themselves* via these tendentious public categories, which is when polemics often begin to overwhelm the particularities of musical invention.

My own researches in the field of complex musical states reaches back at least to 1966, so that the term 'new' is hardly applicable. In any case, I already indicated that I see my development as a continuation (and reformulation) of the central concerns of Late Modernism, whereas most younger composers thought of as belonging to the so-called 'New Complexity' seem to manifest a form of negative frenzy which I, at least, interpret as being a direct reaction to (and thus continuation of) the Beckettian '**Endgame**-impasse'. It is no accident that some of them make frequent references to Beckett in their titles or program texts. In contrast, I see my own work as branching off, conceptually, *before* the onset of that state. My attempt at continual re-evaluation of possible musical 'grammars of validation' is still broadly based on a flexible vision of *function* and *linear process* which, however fragile and provisional, is light-years away from the essentially stochastic imposition of subjective will on the absurdist void which I admire in certain figures of the younger generation. In that sense, these composers are engaged in a basically romantic confrontation with both reductionist realism and the scientificist approach to handling material of, for instance, Iannis Xenakis, whose works they know, I think, quite well. The composer of my generation coming most immediately to mind in this context is Michael Finnissy, who served as interpreter and mentor of several of these individuals.

The more you examine the phenomenon, the more you come to realize that two distinct issues are involved; firstly, the quite major differences of style and intent separating, say, Klaus K. Hübler from Richard Barrett, Chris Dench or James Dillon (the latter lately having attempted a *rapprochement* with spectral tendencies); secondly, the entire constellation of confusion surrounding the term 'complex' itself. One senses here a desire to bring to the surface certain long-repressed, unconscious fears of chaos which society has chosen to ignore, to express, analyze and re-animate those taboos as opposition to the pernicious spread of bland, media-influenced 'good common sense' symbolism, aimed at manipulating other, equally unspoken drives in the name of convenience and commercial profit. The characteristic and deliberately prodigal expenditure of musical invention and formal ambition (not to mention performer effort) is a completely valid attempt to confront this conspiracy of silence head-on.

As I said, my own position is quite different. Like much of contemporary research into the dynamics of complex physical states, I am vitally interested in exploring, not stochastic probability, but that small, unstable frontier between a limited number of governing principles of order and the interference phenomena that emerge when such systems impinge, intersect or collide. Anyone who has seen photographs of particle collision tracks in a cloud chamber will know more or less what I mean. Rather than *mass* or *density*, I am aiming at emphasizing *force* and *energy*, the former being expressed by the audible 'damage' or distortion caused by the latter (understood as 'beams' of directional process) to musical event-objects of whatever sort. In this sense, I am constantly concerned with underlining dissonance (or disequilibrium) as a dynamic semantic quantum on all levels of compositional argument.

ADL: What is the relationship between complexity and listening? What do you ask of your ideal listener: contemplation of the framework, or its irruption in him - or simply for him to take an oblique glance, so to speak...?

BF: It's evident that the sort of musical ideals I just outlined demand a high level of active engagement on the part of the listener, above all the ability and desire to move rapidly from level to level of the texture, the tolerance of a high degree of ambiguity (multiple meanings) and the stamina to be constantly moving at several steps distance 'behind' the unfolding events with respect to contextual assimilation. All this means that the listener needs to abandon the old fiction of being *outside* or *above* the work: rather, I envisage a complete 'biospheric englobement' of the perceiving spirit, the sense of being oneself in motion, not merely dispassionately observing from some mythic, fixed point in mental space. This sensation of fluctuating, mobile subject/object relationships is a key to the quality of expression that I seek.

ADL: I would like to ask - if you'll allow me - a question concerning your English cultural background. For British composers, the connection with tradition is essential, to have a measured faith in the future centered around a healthy, working pragmatism; that is, lacking the completely German-Romantic pathos of Modernity and the crisis of values. Certainly, you are an international personality, but doesn't it seem to you that your taste for the well-crafted piece, for a correct harmonic progression, for extreme neatness of writing is an integral part of traditional values? In what does your relationship with classical tradition truly consist: is it Continental and German?

BF: I think that everyone has their own view of such things; it is precisely that which constitutes tradition. 'Tradition' is a necessary fiction which - not entirely fortuitously - happens to support what a particular composer happens to be doing - me, for instance! If a certain perfectionism in the realization of one's ideas reveals a secret tendency towards conservatism, so be it. On the other hand, one might with equal plausibility argue that a scribbled score, thoughtless notation and half-cooked harmony - whilst doubtless constituting evidence of a progressive, liberated spirit - are tied to a particular moth-eaten Victorian romantic traditional role of the artist, and thus equally to be held suspect of retrograde tendencies.

My biographical rapport with the German classical tradition is actually extremely tenuous. If I had to be specific, I could only mention Bach and Schütz! My main points of reference are 14th-15th Century English choral music (Dunstable to Tallis), then Italian (specifically Venetian) music of ca. 1580-1650. After that, there is a long gap, taking up again with the very end of the 19th Century and the beginnings of New Music proper. I have had very little interest in the 18th Century, even though there are of course individual works which catch one's attention. Certainly I cannot begin to compete with a composer such as Helmut Lachenmann, whose every sound is totally steeped in German tradition and values, to the extent of being practically incomprehensible from any other standpoint. I understand and value the growth and ultimate decay (or, at least, problematicization) of the concept of bourgeois creative autonomy without feeling in any way driven to seek refuge there in terms of emotional allegiance to particular works or styles. It is probably my loss, but that is how things happened to work out, and one is who one is.

ADL: I am curious about your current interests in poetry (evident in your vocal music) and, in particular, with contemporary American experimental poetry - which is of great concern, as well, to a person such as John Cage. Few know that you have written a volume of poetry, **Palimpsests**, multilingual and stratified, in which all of European cultural history is re-read through a nonsensical lens. I recall having read a book by Gilles Deleuze, **Logic of Meaning**, which deals with this theme, using **Alice in Wonderland** as its point of departure; it alludes continually to the strategy by which logic assumes a meaning, far removed from the usual. Has it anything at all to do with your conceptual journeys?

BF: I've always been interested in relating musical and verbal transformational processes. Even though I have long written poetic texts, it is, in fact, only since my move to the United States that I have systematically focussed on developing large-scale poetic structures having close analogical relationships to the sort of thing I try to achieve in my compositions. **Palimpsests** is a long text in ten books, each of about fifteen pages, whereby each book contains one less text than its predecessor so that, towards the end, lengthy passages of several pages necessarily come to replace the more punctual textures characterizing earlier books. As the title implies, many 'over-writings' are superimposed, interleaved and permutated. Quite often, there are several subtexts running concurrently. I have no particular pretensions as a poet; I make no attempt to publish these materials, even though one lengthy text, **Practique**, was recently printed in a new British journal in response to the editor's request for a text on the creative process. Their usefulness resides in their balancing function: there are times when I can better 'think-through' generative procedures or forms in words rather than music. As such, these exercises serve something of a laboratory function, without ever attempting direct transliteration of the one medium into the other.

One particular concept, that of 'interference', is fairly directly carried across, though, in the sense that my texts tend to concentrate on establishing essentially 'atonal' relationships between units of significance. Depending on whether I choose units of one syllable or progressively larger units up to entire sentences, of one language or several, of one or more historical phases of a given language, the degree of 'naturalness' inhering in the result varies considerably. As well as the work of contemporary American poets one should not forget Gertrude Stein in this respect. In fact, my **Trittico per G.S.** for solo double bass attempts to re-articulate, in terms of musical technique, some perceptions derived from her writings.

I would not say that Lewis Carroll has had a particularly strong influence. I always found him to be a rather conservative author, in that the structure of his poetry (meter, rhyme-scheme etc.) generally remains highly conventional, even though, on the level of vocabulary, there are indeed innovative retunings of the typical resonances of the English language. My own approach treats language much more as *found material*, even if a material surcharged with various levels of meaning, emphatically not neutral. The term 'nonsense', in English literature, is quite closely allied to a certain ironic or whimsical sensibility which, in fact, I find rather irritating.

ADL: Recently, I heard your latest string quartet, the fourth. It is an intensely articulate work, with continuous formal re-dislocations, especially where the voice intervenes; in the second and final parts one perceives the trace of an itinerary of condensation, of fixation of the musical material departing from a point of initial proliferation, which arises from the intense experience of the **Carceri d'Invenzione** cycle. But it is precisely this relationship between stages of proliferation, departing from established material, and fixed architecture, that reminds me a lot of the esthetics of Mannerism. I ask myself: is this the case? Or, is your idea of Mannerism far removed from mine? I come from a culture, that of Italy, which is immersed in it: you have chosen it from the outside, as a "meta-point of view"; I know that, for you, materials are secondary...I'd like to understand this transition of yours...

BF: There have frequently been misunderstandings concerning the term 'Mannerism' (with or without capital letter), some seeing it as a general category, applicable to much art of many ages, others maintaining its historically and geographically precise position at a certain moment in the development of Western art. For me at least, the term might be defined as *artistic expression in which the conscious organization of the means employed is more important than the materials to which they are applied.* It is this foregrounding of technique as a vehicle of the self-reflexivity of style which attracts me most immediately, since it has been my experience that much contemporary music has neglected the field of 'semanticized syntaxis' in favor of sonic materials more obviously innovatory, but lacking in long-range staying power (whence the much-discussed 'exhaustion of material' syndrome of some 25 years ago). It is, moreover, necessary to reject the vaguely pejorative usage of the word: in some peoples' understanding, it connotes decadence, the failure and collapse of some Apollonian classical vision. Although this view is surely less widespread today than during the early part of the century it still manages to exert some influence where polemics are considered more important than substance. Otherwise, your description of primary Mannerist categories of expression seems very applicable, although I would hesitate to see my own music described exclusively in such terms.

ADL: I'd like to close this interview with a question regarding the future of us all. With the return of the ethics of the "small countries" musicians and intellectuals are becoming "territorial", a fact that will probably have a serious impact on the fields of research and experimentation. This situation is the real declaration of the extinction of what was once called "avant-garde", by now irretrievably far removed. What is your major legacy to us: the utopia of universalism - understood as the utopia of boundaries, as an endless journey to the lands of Nowhere?

BF: I agree with your view that Europe is likely to counterbalance its imminent financial unification with a cultural retrenchment behind national boundaries. Since the 2nd World War, the term 'International' has been the slogan on everyone's lips: today, the term seems to be more and more employed to signify 'without roots, homeless'. It would be a tragedy if individual countries were to abandon the many-sided plans for cultural exchange which, for many years, have fostered intellectual and creative openness, in favor of bilateral exchanges encouraging only the safer, least controversial side of national activity. The danger is, that only operatic superstars and jetset conductors of the prestige, popular-classical repertoire will remain international in the strict sense of the term, while composers will increasingly find themselves relegated to provincial alibi status. As far as contemporary music is concerned, I see very few supranational institutions both willing and able to actively engage in the maintenance of existing lines of communication. It would be a scandal if Europe could not agree, say, on a community 'Center of Excellence in Contemporary Musical Creation and Interpretation' not relying disproportionately on technological research for its *raison d'être*. Yet I see no signs of such a project emerging anytime this century. The lesson to be drawn from the present situation is, for me, that existing ventures (ensembles, research centers etc.) need to consider strategies for acting in concert towards generally-agreed-on goals if even the current level of dissemination is to be maintained. If this does not come about, we may yet witness contemporary composers retreating into their national/nationalist conservatories, slamming the doors shut behind them.

INTERVIEW WITH JAMES BOROS
(1992)

JAMES BOROS: I seem to recall your discussing the notion of musical complexity in terms of the dynamic transmission of information and its relationship to states of stability and instability.

BRIAN FERNEYHOUGH: Among other things - that's true. How to get a grip on the entire concept of 'complexity' as applied to art has proven to be a major bone of contention. I have not been satisfied by what I have understood concerning the algorithmic definition, which measures complexity in terms of the number of algorithmic operations required to analyze-out a given state. For one thing, that's not how the brain works; for another, it's certainly not how most art seems to work. My own interests have gravitated towards how our perceptual ordering faculties react when attempting to make sense of borderline states - that is, situations in which an apparent disbalance between implied scale of observed system and actual apportionment of confirming or disconfirming subsystems conspires to create zones of instability in which linear modes of cataloguing incoming stimuli are suspended in favor of sudden leaps, fractures, or twists of focus. All music deals with this issue on one level or another; it's just that most stylistic conventions aim at large-scale equilibrium between containing frame and degree of permitted deviation of component details, whereas what I am aiming at is pretty much the reverse, in that what, in other music, might be seen as enhancing embellishment is constantly causing a high level of uncertainty about what the implied scale of the relationship 'frame/detail' might be. The way it does that is partly by exhibiting high levels of self-referentiality and embedding procedures (encouraging 'sliding' from one self-similar level to another), partly by having information presented in highly-energized, coherent streams or vectors tending to offer concurrent, competing, and sometimes contradictory middle-ground 'micro-narratives'. It's not just a question of confusion, though: the sort of grid- or matrix-orientated formal techniques I usually use tend to bring about momentary clarifications where partial aspects of independently-moving patterns suddenly coincide, creating sudden, unexpected 'windows'. In fact, 'complexity' in such cases is often increased by such unpredictable nodes, since the sudden increase in perceived structural hierarchy makes passive, generalized reception difficult.

JB: Steve McAdams once wrote: "A composition of sufficient, control-led complexity might... be perceptually infinite for a given listener".[1] When I first read this, I immediately thought of your orchestral work **La terre est un homme**.

BF: I don't know in what context that statement was made, but, as it stands, it certainly corresponds pretty closely to my own thoughts on the matter. Of course, 'complexity' is always relative to the implied position of the observer; even superficially quite simple phenomena can easily be 'deconstructed' into unimaginably complex and, in detail, unpredictable flow patterns. The point about **La terre** is not that I am proposing something that, measured according to some absolute metaphysical scale, is quantitatively or qualitatively more complex than many another possible object of aesthetic appreciation, but rather that I am concerned with keeping the listener constantly aware of complexity as an inescapable given. In a good performance at least, it's not possible to retreat to some globally undifferentiated impression: instead, the ear is constantly entrapped in some fine or rough grained strand of activity, or else engaged in the transition from one to another. That's why any given strand is highly detailed and defined according to its own internal frame of reference, as well as interlocking, on a higher level, with the activities and energies of other concurrent strands. This, together with the fact that I try not to prescribe more or less prioritized paths through the structure, would seem to correspond pretty much with the tenor of McAdams's statement.

JB: In an earlier interview with Richard Toop, you recalled some very vivid dreams, and you described some parts of **La terre** that are a "very shadowy and distant reflection"[2] of scores which you found yourself examining in those dreams. I've also had the strange experience of waking up in the morning with the solution to a musical problem fully-formed in my head, handed to me, as it were, on a platter, all of which makes me wonder about the role played by time spent asleep in relation to the compositional process.

BF: I wonder about it too, most often in terms of why solutions to particular problems come to me when just about to fall asleep, or at the end of a half-waking period during the night - under circumstances, that is, practically guaranteed to cause them to disappear again before I can write them down. Personally, a night's sleep seldom seems to bring me nearer the sought-after goal. On the other hand, it may be that I am simply not conscious of what is really going on. How does one tell? I have always needed much more sleep than the average person; maybe this has something to do with the pressures attached to the creative process. But these are such personal issues that I wouldn't even begin to draw general conclusions.

The most lasting effects of sleep on my composing have always been dreams - not the dreams in which actual sounds occur, but ones where I find myself leafing through a completed score. Some of these have been extremely disturbing (as when one seems to be furiously devouring a score, once lost, now found, about to be lost again); others have been lastingly encouraging, making me aware of riches within, even in 'dry' periods. I've never actually set out to transcribe or recreate any of these scores in toto, but I've sometimes seen resemblances in areas of nuance and detail buried in otherwise quite different works long after the fact. Even allowing for the distorting effect of the suspension of the critical faculty in such situations, I find it amazing that the subconscious can come up with entire densely-woven orchestral (or, in one case, orchestral and choral) scores in the space of a single brief dream. The score of mine which, I suppose, comes closest to the aesthetic of these images is **La terre**, but that took more than two years to compose.

JB: I find it interesting that you have collected a voluminous quantity of 'compositional reference materials' over the years. I have always ritualistically destroyed such things upon the completion of a work, perhaps as a way of purging myself. Other than creating clutter, what role does this material play in your life?

BF: It's true that it does that! Certainly those materials are not there to be referred to by me in any systematic fashion. For one thing, they are in a completely unordered and slowly decaying state as the result of many moves and several accidents over the last twenty five years, so that they have come to resemble a miniature Library of Babel, conceptually stimulating but referentially useless; for another, the specific steps that led to current positions are, for me, at best anecdotally interesting. Perhaps they represent a sort of repository of knowledge and belief, something like a shell, constantly growing and equally swiftly outgrown? In any case, transmogrified documentation is part of tradition; it resembles somewhat in that respect our canon of fairy stories or folk myths. Maybe such traces are, to the individual, what prevailing communal paradigms represent to a society? In this way, rather than 'creating clutter', they are there but not there, meaningful by dint of their functional absence.

When I first started composing, there were very few by-products of this sort, or else they were not consciously preserved. It's probably only since the early '70s that rough workings have accumulated, particularly for larger works, like **Firecycle Beta** (1969-71), where layers or groups would be tested out in isolation before being inserted in the score. I've never really produced rough scores as such, owing to my habit of producing a definitive score parallel to the sketching process, so that it would be difficult, if not impossible, for someone other than myself to trace a path through the records that still exist. In any case, one should bear in mind that not all works naturally generate a lot of sketch material; there are some, too, where the level of definition of the sketches is too distant from the final result to be other than problematic as to attribution. In the case of Richard Toop's analyses[3] I was quite surprised as to the things he came up with - things that I no longer remember doing, but am, on the basis of his evidence, prepared to admit that I really did!

Probably it is less old sketches which are sometimes of utility than old, mostly unperformed compositions. As one's style develops consistency of focus and a strong sense of direction it is inevitable that some aspects of one's initial potential wither and fall by the wayside, or at least remain fallow. Every few years I like to unearth some of those early scores and try to relocate the beginnings of paths not taken. It is always interesting and sometimes creatively enlightening. At the very least, it encourages me to view some of the efforts of present-day composition students with a healthy portion of humility!

Actually, it occurs to me now that there is one example of a sketch which was deliberately destroyed after a piece was written. At the outset of **Firecycle Beta** I composed a worked-out score page for full orchestra, complete in every detail. After acting as the quarry from which all other elements and relationships were ultimately derived, this was made inaccessible by burning. The actual page of origin was thus not incorporated as such into the final work, which in any case remained a torso not including many of the instruments which that generating page specified. Looking back on it, the deed does sometimes seem gratuitously demonstrative; on other occasions it still makes a valid statement as to the mutually consuming pyrrhic relationship between spontaneity and technical discipline.

JB: The analyses by Toop which you describe above make extensive references to your sketches; however, I have yet to read an analysis of one of your works which is based only on what one hears, or what one sees in the score, without resort to sketch materials.

BF: There is a problem common to most ventures of that sort, which, in the analysis course I have lately been teaching, I term 'appropriateness'. How does one ascertain with a reasonable degree of assurance what is a relevant way of approaching an unfamiliar work? Sometimes general stylistic attributes suffice to locate a piece and its concerns, at other times we can refer to the place the work occupies in the creative career of the composer, thus inferring something with respect to concerns and aesthetic priorities; on still other occasions the nature of the processes visibly/audibly at work permit a certain amount of legitimate extrapolative speculation.

There are also compositions, on the other hand, in which recognition and articulation of a particular problem or barrier affords an entry into a field of possible discourse in which work and reception are intertwined. I start from the assumption that 'pure', value-free listening would require some sort of cultural amnesia which itself would act as a significant barrier to meaningful apprehension and reflection. Thus, one is never starting from a single fixed point, but always from a binary relation, whose poles are aural/visual stimulus and presumptive perceptual framework: the analyst just has to pick up some ball or other and run with it to see what happens. I am not by any means implying that analyses of the sort you describe are not possible; simply that they are always something in the nature of a poetic recreation whose ultimate degree of independence from its nominal object becomes itself an object of further reflective assessment.

The usefulness of the odd concrete analysis of values and operations actually employed by the composer is useful in a quite different way than one might initially assume, in that it provides a fairly stable point of departure for more informed associative flights. A 'free' analytical discourse on and around a piece needs, in my view, to take account of the entire available work-process, by which I don't (necessarily) mean privileged access to the composer's workshop, but the chain from score image through various stages of the interpretational process right up until the act of reception itself. Anything less than that is not likely to be much more substantial than the averagely ephemeral newspaper review.

JB: You've used the terms 'object' and 'process' in many different contexts. For example, I recall your contrasting your own music, and its concern with "the matter of the musical object and its processual manifestation",[4] with that of Chris Dench, referring to his desire to create a flow of 'non-objects'. Other composers, such as Stockhausen, Cage, and Steve Reich, have used 'processes' in very different ways. How does your approach differ?

BF: I have no axe to grind with terminology. An 'object', for me, is simply a span of experience which is either sufficiently constant in itself, succeeds in defining its own outer boundaries with a reasonable degree of credibility, or balances out the conflicting demands of short- term memory and elapsed time so as to lock them into a unique perceptual frame and lend the impression of a certain 'out-of-time-ness'. A 'process', by the same token, is a musical activity in which these levels are not coordinated in the same way, and whose complete identity is thus revealed only by accretion and degradation, whereby middle- and short-term memory are invoked to different degrees. Processes are interesting precisely because of the immensely rich interplay between memory and predictive imagination they involve, but also because they extend the concept of 'object' into more explicitly temporal domains. Process might even be said to be *the shadows of objects in time.*

JB: The late Robert Smithson once wrote: "Objects are sham space, the excrement of thought and language. Once you start seeing objects in a positive or negative way you are on the road to derangement. Objects are phantoms of the mind, as false as angels".[5]

BF: Might it not depend on how false, and in what sense, you think angels are? One could equally argue, I suppose, that thought and language are the excrement of objects, to the extent that categories presuppose societal objectivizations of self and other. Smithson was an outstanding thinker, especially in respect of his capacity to create and mobilize a most impressive arsenal of mental correspondences to deeply-felt, but perhaps intellectually vague, communal perceptions. The very openness of some of his analogies is perhaps their most potent advocate, while a number of his provocative linguistic conjunctions are quite electric in their release of hitherto scarcely-sensed bundles of 'coherent intuition'. There is something of a parallel here to the shamanistic invocatory resonance of Joseph Beuys, except that, with Smithson, the supersaturated quality of the objects is almost invariably bathed in a brilliant, if still deeply ambiguous, Cartesian luminance. It is the obstinate persistence of Beuys's personal icons of experience in the world at large which renders them capable of reshaping the experience of others on an appropriately pre-conscious level, even as the *ratio* begins to come into focus: Smithson's work seems significantly more unstable and provisional (in a positive sense), even when manifest through his most massive land art pieces. He was deeply aware of how close even the most ordered fields of perception are to collapsing into chaos, and was, in consequence, concerned to *name* this propensity as a condition of its creative harnessing. It is quite striking how the sense of the transitory informs both his metaphors and his artistic production. In that respect he was admirably consistent. Your citation is a case in point - whether one agrees with (or even understands) him or not. In any case, his statement is a quite extraordinary one for a *sculptor* to make, don't you think?

The work which has recently occupied me, for violin and eight instruments, is entitled **Terrain**: it might, I suppose, be considered a distant reflection of some of Smithson's 'mental tectonics' imagery of the ruined inner world, even though the title is in fact taken from a poem by A.R. Ammons which also concerns itself with meditations on geological and other natural phenomena as manifested in the living world around us.

JB: **Terrain**'s ensemble of eight instruments is identical to that of **Octandre**. Is the work in any way a tribute to Varèse?

BF: I suppose one could call it the payment of a long-standing debt. **Octandre** was always extremely important to me, for one because it was the

Ex. 1: From Terrain (1991-92)

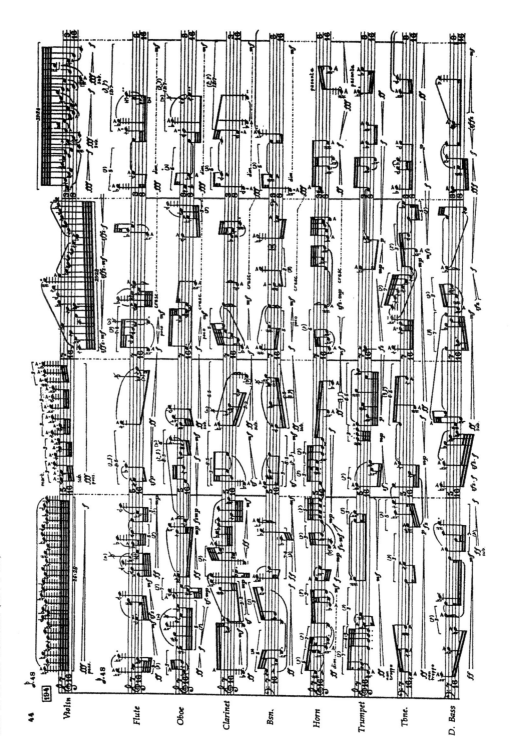

first truly modern work I ever heard, for another because I, as a wind player, could immediately appreciate and relate to Varèse's sonic imagination in that medium. I wrote a lot of quite extended pieces for combinations of wind instruments in the very early '60s, some of whose textures are all too clearly derivative of Varèsian mannerisms, while unfortunately demonstrating little of his (in)formal acumen. So, once the idea of writing for concertante violin arose, I immediately focused on the vision of a violin/ensemble opposition towards which, apart from textural and processual distinctions, the color and weight of the **Octandre** combination would make a major contribution.

When you think about it, it's actually rather strange that this grouping never became a 'standard' octet formation. It contains both a wealth of possible sub-ensembles and an impressively cutting 'bite' when employed as a single mass instrument. What proved most useful to me, actually, was the vast palette of registrally-defined timbral nuances available: as well as more or less stable chordal states defined by absolute registral distribution, I was able to insert particular instruments in ways which would transform the entire perceived tessitura relationship of individual chordal components, thus allowing partial aspects of chords to be separated-out and functionally distinguished by being heard as 'high' or 'low' irrespective of their actual registral location.

Actually, **Octandre** strikes me as being really rather relevant (again?) at the present time, for quite other reasons. Perhaps one of the few things that the brief flourishing of 'postmodern' style collage has left behind has been an increased sensibilization to how the *edges* and *points of contact* of systems (in the wider sense of comportmental taxonomies) are usefully defined. It is interesting to observe young composers turning increasingly away from *collage* towards *montage* techniques, in which the formal ploys integral to certain types of stylistic and procedural homogeneity are objectified, isolated, dissected, and, ultimately, dynamically subverted by seemingly alien trajectories and rhetorical categories being extracted from them. It is perhaps one way of registering 'decentered' Deconstructivist formal innovation while resisting its implicitly High Modernist residual vocabulary. In this sense, both *consistency* and *fracture* can be made to seem interestingly complementary, rather than simply staring resentfully at each other over an unbridgeable void.

Unlike some of the composer's later pieces, both of these principles are powerfully at work at point-blank range in **Octandre**. Just look, for instance, at how the 'cut and paste' interchanges in the first movement set about demolishing the linear emphasis of the various harmonic strata so explicitly proposed in the opening measures, the way our sense of time passing skitters confusedly over the surface of that fast-but-immobile dyad at the beginning of the second movement, and the weird 'time-machine' quality of the fugato which opens the last movement. None of these experiential fault lines would have functioned half as well if the harmonic framework had not been so obviously and coherently consistent in its setting up of transitional situations whose good graces are then so peremptorily overridden by extreme textural disjunction.

JB: Your description of **Terrain** makes me think of **Mnemosyne**, which, to me, is a frighteningly bizarre landscape, a slowly solidifying temporal ooze. When listening to the piece, I experience a strong sense of persistent queasiness; it's as if I'm being repeatedly tossed into the air and forced to 'hit the ground running', always at a different speed and angle, to continually adjust my mental frame of reference as best I can. The treatment of time in **Mnemosyne** also raises the old question of whether consciousness is merely "a spectator who experiences nothing but an 'action replay' of the whole drama".[6] What are your feelings?

BF: I see my own view of things as being more dynamic than that, with consciousness resembling more a novelist, so furiously writing the 'supreme fiction' of perception that he has no time to stop and reread what he has written. It depends whether you accept the now somewhat discredited image of a little person inside your head riding herd over a flood of value-free, unordered incoming data. I reckon the process of constructing a viable (if transitory) self to be extremely conflictual and chaotic in nature, so that the sort of desperate struggle to stay afloat in the turbulent 'delay wake' of listening which I envisage strikes me as a pretty adequate paradigm for the engenderment of self-awareness. If the question is suggesting that the 'inner witness' makes sense of an experience after the event by replaying it in more or less unaltered form, then I cannot agree. Whatever one actually experiences during a performance, the 'piece' that one subsequently retains in the memory is usually a complete recomposition - edited, filtered and re-ordered. That, in part, is why re-hearing a composition is extremely important: you have the chance to actively map real-time and memory-time experiences onto one another. The shocking discrepancies that one sometimes encounters are further defining aspects of a notional topology of consciousness.

To get back to your comments regarding **Mnemosyne**: in a sense, the piece works as a mirror image of what I said about time flow in my music in general. It emphasizes what I term elsewhere the 'tactility' of time,[¶] where one senses ruptures or unevennesses in the temporal flow almost as much a form of physical contact as the sonic events themselves. I composed the relationship between the rate of harmonic change and the density of surface figuration so as to encourage the mind to move 'too fast' and, as a result, find itself constantly pulled up short by the slightly counter-intuitive viscosity of information presentation. As the piece goes on, the linear dimension is progressively imprisoned,

---

[¶]see this volume, p. 42.

its impetus absorbed by an ever-tighter lattice of vertical reference pitches. The more insistent the presence of harmony as passive obstacle, the more the mind begins to focus in on time in terms of momentary degrees of resistance rather than spaces within which it naturally unfolds. The more claustrophobic this situation becomes, the more temporal flow manifests itself as physical substance rather than a relational frame of reference within which materials are sequentially disposed. That's how I feel it, anyway.

JB: Have you explored this approach in any other pieces?

BF: Probably the first movement of my **Third String Quartet** (1987) would come the nearest, even though the means employed are scarcely comparable. The movement is composed of some 23 'types' of activity, some of which are relatively stable (such as, for instance, a particular non-transposing chord), others being much more fluid in their potential for variable realization (such as 'glissando', which can be adapted to the specific needs of many contexts). The entry, duration, and density of type-superincumbence for the first two thirds of the discourse were planned in advance, with the values being mirror-reversed for the final third. The essential difference was that not only was the order reversed, but the actual types themselves were exchanged with their opposite numbers at the other end of the chain; i.e. type 2 became type 22, type 3 was replaced by type 21, and so on.

The effect of this reversal was to thrust me into a situation where what had initially been a relatively 'natural' flow of material (where the characteristics of each type had largely been reflected in their temporal extension) became a series of abrupt accommodations and stratagems, attempting to fit types into spaces and combinatorially-specified roles which were often completely counter-intuitive, having in no way been foreseen at the outset. I personally feel this 'unease' of the materials at finding themselves in inappropriate or downright alien temporal environments quite audible and disturbing.

JB: Your notion of a 'viable (if transitory) self' brings to mind a comment by Antonin Artaud: "What is difficult is to find one's place and to reestablish communication with one's self".[7] This difficulty arises each time I sit down to write music! For example, while working on the final section of my most recent work, which took some two years to complete, I found myself becoming increasingly uncertain as to who or what my 'self' was, at that particular point in both 'compositional' and 'real' time, in relation to the 'self' which began the piece. So much had changed!

BF: There are many 20th-Century works which address (consciously or unconsciously) the temporality of the compositional act as a perceptual transformation of the locus of self-awareness. The major composer who comes immediately to mind here is Bernd Alois Zimmermann. Not only did he seek to define self in almost theological terms as the zero point of intersection at the center of his 'Time Sphere', in which all periods and styles are notionally reconciled; he also produced at least one work, **Die Soldaten**, in which frequent simultaneity of discrepant strands of dramatic action powerfully conspire to suggest dimensions of 'temporal harmony' and 'dissonance'. If one listens to the entire opera one is immediately struck by the stylistic mutation that its language progressively undergoes. To me, this suggests a quite different sort of temporality, in which an entire era of compositional perception and technique passes in ever more intense and personal review - almost, on a much larger scale, like the famous Bergian 'color crescendo'. Apropos of such considerations, what about the impact made by the Prelude as it collides full tilt with the opening of the first scene? Since the Prelude seems to have been composed last of all, the effect of temporal reversal is like some apocalyptic time machine or centripetal mechanism attempting to thrust all those explosive energies back into the genie's bottle.

Interestingly enough, I have on occasions been forced to compose pieces *backwards* - perhaps one might speculate that the discourse's polarity had somehow been reversed?

JB: How were you 'forced' to compose them backwards?

BF: Refining the pre-compositional processes involved in **Terrain**, it just happened that a useful level of definition was arrived at for the second half of the piece first. I'd sketched out the entire form (measure lengths, sectional paradigm switches, tempi and texture strategies, etc.) fairly rapidly, and it was the progressive growth of this momentum which brought supplementary ideas into play as I approached the end. So that's where I started. It was quite interesting to approach the opening violin solo from that perspective, rather than allowing everything that follows to emerge, as it were, from it. It's lucky for us that time is reversible, at least during the compositional act.

JB: You've recently written several percussion pieces (**Fanfare for Klaus Huber** (1987), **Bone Alphabet** (1991)). Why this seemingly sudden interest in percussion?

BF: Just circumstances, as it happens. After listening, increasingly unwillingly, to several generations of the sort of percussion piece requiring an extensive 'kitchen' of instruments disposed in entire labyrinths of stands and other paraphernalia (so that you can always tell when the performer is getting round to the tam-tam...), I swore never to compose for percussion alone. What changed my mind in the first place was the request to compose a one-page piece for my old composition teacher's 60th birthday festschrift. Rather than composing a solo flute piece or something similar, I decided to address the issue of free instrumentation within very specifically-stated constraints. If you look at the score (conforming to the one-page edict, but only just...), you will see that two categories of timbre are defined: (1) sonorities capable of being grouped in reasonably homogenous gamuts of high and low (like wood blocks, or tom-toms), which change every couple of measures, and (2) a whole series (over thirty, I think) of so-called 'unique sounds', each of which is to be played once only. The piece can be performed several times in the same concert, rather like a 'motto' or interlude (my model being the fanfare beginning both the 1610 **Vespers** and the later operas of Monteverdi), but each time, a new set of unique sounds must be selected. Since each performer is instructed to select his instrumentarium without consulting the other player, it's clear that all sorts of strange conjunctions could arise — rather like renga-form poetry, or certain practices of the Surrealist writers who composed collaborative texts, like **The Magnetic Fields** of Breton and Soupault. Given the original constraints, it seemed to me that only the percussion medium could give me such flexibility of interpretation. I like the idea of totally unforeseen sonic results; unfortunately, although the piece has been played a lot in Europe, I have yet to hear it.

JB: And **Bone Alphabet**?

BF: **Bone Alphabet** had an odd history, too. When Steve Schick, whom I had known some years earlier in Europe through his forming a duo with the pianist James Avery, came to teach at UCSD, he asked me to write him a piece which would also utilize an extremely restricted group of instruments. His idea was to have something with which he could tour, and which would not be dependent on unreliable or nonexistent local instruments. Initially I was not attracted to the idea, but, the more I thought about it, the more I came to see this limitation as a challenge quite different from those arising from my lengthy occupation with more 'normal' instruments, which were capable of extremely subtle inflectional and timbral nuance. Since we had agreed on a maximum of seven instruments, all with similar attack and decay characteristics, I determined to compose a truly polyphonic piece in which the performer and I would have to address the problem of realizing up to four complex lines simultaneously, each line being able, in principle, to include any or all of the seven basic sounds. Again, I opted not to choose the instruments myself; instead, I placed certain limitations on the choice available. For instance, no two adjacent instruments could belong to the same basic family of sonorities. I did this so that the frequently occurring tremoli between neighboring instruments would assure rich sonic results. Not having particular sonorities in my mind as I composed (which

Ex. 2: From Bone Alphabet (1991)

actually involved a certain amount of disciplined renunciation) meant that I could concentrate entirely on the formal issues at hand.

JB: Did your familiarity with Schick's performing abilities have any influence on the final outcome?

BF: Steve has a really inimitable playing style, almost balletic in terms of how he stores and then releases packets of 'bodily memory'. The way I brought that into play was to demand multiple superimposed rhythmic cycles, the coordination of which would require just such actionistically mnemonic triggers. In that sense, it is a piece that needs to be seen as well as heard.

The stripped-down nature of **Bone Alphabet**'s sonic world encouraged me, too, in my further investigation of some of the concerns I mentioned earlier, in particular, linear versus non-linear modes of formal organization. The piece was composed on the basis of a 13-layer rhythmic matrix articulating a form subdivided, both by process and tempo differentiation, into 13 sections. Each of these, with the exception of, I think, three, were further subdivided. I set out by associating each of these main sections with a type of 'textural comportment' which would dictate both type and density of activity and the specific layers of the original matrix to be mined for material. Each section was then composed straight through in its totality, and the 13 sections composed from 1 through 13, with the result that a certain quasi-linear development of available resources emerged.

Having arrived at this relatively conventional narrative structure, I then cut up each section into its constituent subsections (some as short as one measure in length) and redistributed them according to a plan which established a new 'story line' for each type. For instance, type 1 ('two-voice, iterative, asynchronous figures') was redistributed by length, the longest and shortest versions coming first, then moving gradually towards the median durations as the end of the work approaches. The other, less frequently appearing types were re-ordered according to other principles, and the totality of segments was arranged in sub-cycles of alternately three and four elements. As with the **Third Quartet**, the insertion process began relatively simply by reason of the fairly large choice available; as I began to exhaust certain types, however, aesthetically satisfactory local solutions were increasingly difficult to find. It is here, too, that the single-instance types were interjected, still further confusing the issue with their seemingly unmotivated outbursts.

JB: ...Which brings us back to your response to my initial question, and to your tendency to eschew traditional, straightforward development in favor of "sudden leaps, fractures, or twists of focus". Why this need to, as you put it, "confuse the issue," to court the "counter-intuitive"?

BF: I think I must have a pretty confused brain - or else a notably suspicious nature. Let's put it the other way round: I can see why someone might want to compose a 'what you see is what you get' sort of music, in which the motivating issues involved have a very clear, immediate and relatively stable relationship to material and operational identity. Some of it is as bracing, say, as a good crossword puzzle; some might even open the door to new perceptual vistas by virtue of its ability to tackle transformation in very small, constantly repeated steps. In the latter case, though, some sort of *anamorphosis* is almost inevitably at work — some distortion sensitizing our receptive antennae to discrepancies or fault lines in the correspondence of implied concept and realized manifestation. A lot of the later Feldman pieces typically work in this way, constantly defamiliarizing (by odd numbers of repetitions, extreme duration or slight phase decoupling, for instance) things which have become so familiar a part of the weave as to be almost invisible. That, in itself, is a form of "twist of focus," don't you think? It's a temptation, I know, to consider the qualities you mention in your question as *attributes* of a *style* rather than characteristics of pretty much universal validity. It's true that my music happens to insistently highlight some of the more unstable and seemingly arbitrary facets of current compositional thinking: that necessarily follows from what happens to interest me, which is the expressive potential of ambiguous and volatile states. It would be a mistake, though, I feel, to assume that 'continuity' on some level or other is not a prerequisite of my approach - no fracture or twist can be perceived *per se* unless it is a fracture or twist of *something*, at least one of whose constituent defining qualities or fundamental assumptions is understood as providing a referential constant. I make two assumptions of this sort at the very outset - firstly, that *unity* and *continuity* of style are necessary in order to define and unleash these structural dissonances and, secondly, that *analogical frames of reference* (categories of 'seeing something *as*') are freely transferrable between articulative levels of whatever order of magnitude and formal scope. So, it's all very relative. Although I obviously see the area I'm working in as located at the center of where current sensibility is moving, in terms of how art can make an active contribution to how we come to see the world as we do, I'd be the last person to suggest that foregrounding this aspect is the only strategy available. I hope not!

Endnotes

1. *Stephen McAdams, "Hearing Musical Streams,"* Computer Music Journal 3/4 *(1979), p. 42.*

2. *"In Interview with Richard Toop" (this volume, p. 262).*

3. *See, for example, "Brian Ferneyhough's Lemma-Icon-Epigram",* Perspectives of New

Music *28/2 (Summer 1990) p. 52-100, "Superscriptio pour Piccolo Solo"*, Entretemps *3 (February 1987), p. 95-106, or "Brian Ferneyhough's Etudes transcendantales: A Composer's Diary (Part 1)"*, Eonta *Vol. 1 No. 1 (1991), p. 55-89.*

4. *"Shattering the Vessels of Received Wisdom: in Conversation with James Boros" (this volume, p. 369).*

5. *Robert Smithson, cited in Grégoire Müller and Gianfranco Gorgoni,* The New Avant-Garde *(New York: Praeger Publishers, 1972), p. 17.*

6. *Roger Penrose,* The Emperor's New Mind *(New York: Oxford University Press, 1989), p. 443.*

7. *Antonin Artaud,* Selected Writings *(New York: Farrar, Straus & Giroux, 1976), p. 82.*

A VERBAL CRANE DANCE: BRIAN FERNEYHOUGH INTERVIEWED BY ROSS FELLER
(1992)

On Notation And Performance

ROSS FELLER: Regarding notational complexity you've stated that: "composers who tend to restrict their notational specifications to a bare minimum end up getting one-dimensional representations of a possible sound-world rather than entering into that world's inner workings."[1] Doesn't this depend not so much on the notation, but on the type of performer and on how much they are willing to 'give' or be 'seduced' by the music?

BRIAN FERNEYHOUGH: No - or, at least, it all depends. Of course there are categories of music and associated stylistic domains where everything is more or less clear by virtue of communally understood conventions of preparation and execution: where you are dealing with extremely involved or ambiguous scores, though, a tremendous amount of work needs to be invested to arrive at the stage you describe. If the composer is around to help, that improves matters, of course, to the extent that he functions as a living extension of the score's indications: in other instances I know from experience that even the most distinguished of performers require lengthy learning curves when first exposed to a globally new situation. Even then, the early, conceptual stages of the process are of vital importance - something that an adequate notation can be instrumental in encouraging.

It will be evident that I am not attempting to address notational concerns relevant to all possible musics. There will be those of which I have too little direct knowledge and others where performers I greatly respect disagree with me on significant points. An example would be in pieces like **Superscriptio**, where a core obstacle to be surmounted is finding suitable means of translating the complex chains of irrational meters (3/12; 5/20 etc.) into terms that make intuitive sense to the individual's accustomed way of working. Most performers until recently have rewritten these relationships as changes of base *tempo*. Although I naturally always leave it to the player to determine his strategies, that approach runs counter to my own intuitive 'feel' for what tempo changes, as opposed to meter changes, actually imply. Most recently, research into computer-assisted learning of complex rhythms at San Diego and elsewhere has offered a way out of this dilemma by providing aural ('ideal') models by means of which the very characteristic 'sound' of such structures can be absorbed globally, as an idiom, rather than piecemeal. This possibility seems to me the one most significant development of recent years in the interpretation of such music as mine and parallels in importance the already quite advanced familiarization process in the area of microtonal intervals.

RF: You've also said that every composition demands its own set of notational conventions and have criticized the desire for a generalized, common, musical language. What then are your thoughts regarding the influx of post-Ghent, new music notation 'dictionaries' and their ambition to make new music notation more 'accessible'?[2]

BF: You cannot generalize or codify means without having some effect upon ends. It is in the very nature of 20th Century notational practice that iconic innovation serve very specific context-sensitive purposes. Where there is no discernable common practice I see well-meaning attempts to systematize notational norms as the potential sources of compositional impoverishment, since it has been my experience that ready-made solutions will tend to produce ready-solved aesthetic problems (or, more precisely, pseudo-problems). Of course some issues are trivial (like the redundancy of multiple, subtly deviant microtonal symbols, for example). Even in that case, though, one can often-times make a strong case for particular derivations implying something specific in the context of a particular work or style. It is not true, for instance, that arrows attached to otherwise standard accidentals transmit identical information to more sharply-individuated derivations: precise spelling can be important in situations where the issue of general import has not been adequately resolved. I incorporated this distinction into the two layers of activity in **Adagissimo**, in fact.

I have seen many scores in which the absorption of a specific notational practice (i.e. as contained in a manual of extended performance technique by a well-known instrumentalist) has resulted in compositional substance largely reflecting the level of order implied by that notation (that is, the particular degree of precision or emphasis with which a given technique is represented) rather than any pressing needs generated by the compositional exigencies of the piece itself. The level of ideologically preformed 'subtext' which any given notational codification brings with it would be the ideal subject for an essay in Deconstructionist analysis, I should think.

It is by no means my intent to plead for a Tower of Babel situation in matters notational: there are, nevertheless, valid considerations militating against a completely conformist approach at a time when no compositional common practice is extant to provide credible documentation for such an Esperanto. In any case, I have yet to see a codified system such as you mention with whose recommendations I would be reasonably comfortable in the classroom. It seems far more likely, in fact, that not books but computer notation programs will come to be seen as the single most influential source of such normalizing pressure as presently exists.

RF: It has occurred to me that your use of 'irrational' meters might be a processual translation of the 'eye-scan' (performative) technique involved in many indeterminate scores. An essential difference being, that your method has the advantage of defining (and re-defining in real time) the scanning process in a piece-specific way, whereas by leaving the process of scanning notationally indeterminate, the performer is encouraged to employ generalized, normative scanning strategies. Would you comment on this?

BF: I'm not really familiar with the dynamics of realization involved in indeterminate scores: I've never really had reason to doubt the efficacy of my approach to meter as both expressive of essential structure-articulational factors (the sort of 'space' available for a set of events to define their 'real size' in) and the sort of perceptually serrated scanning procedure I think you're alluding to. One essential consideration having great influence on our perception of temporal flow is the amount of information processed in each metric compartment i.e. how atomized or globalized the elements of the discourse are sensed to be (and, therefore, how effectively higher-order gestalts can usefully be projected, thus increasing overall redundancy). By continually remodeling, stretching, twisting or compacting the relationship of material, meter and process one can quite effectively prevent too much 'clumping' of this sort, thus keeping the subjective sense of time passing permanently on edge, both for the performer and the listener.

RF: Richard Toop has said that due to the notation you employ the performer is always "struggling for (an) unreachable object."[3] Do you equate the state of being unreachable with permanence?

BF: Not in any especially mystic sense. It is easy to overplay the 'transcendental' performative aspect of what I do, even though it is naturally one of the first things a player (or anyone else really) is confronted with when encountering my work for the first time. I like to think that there are qualitatively different stages to such a 'struggle'; one of those is certainly the self-overcoming (but not, I trust, self-negation) demanded in live performance, another is the often lengthy and extremely differentiated process gone through while preparing the work for performance. I hope that such transformations and growth of insight into one's own highly personal path to an accommodation with the total environment the work projects is something of its own reward.

As far as permanence is concerned, I am aware that there are those who maintain that my works will somehow be revealed as aesthetically impoverished by a 'perfect' performance (by which I assume them to mean a mechanically literal rendition of all, and only those actions notationally specified). If one accepts the premise that even to *imagine* a 'perfect' performance in any terms whatsoever (let alone one as circumscribed by this 'automaton' formula) is conceptually somewhat odd for almost any style or genre, then the issue is resolved into one of adequacy and appropriateness - issues which are invariably and extremely relative. Insofar as any given realization is necessarily impermanent the piece as such might be imagined as retracting back into its primary latent state after each performance, like a spring or rubber band. That is probably as much permanence as anyone can realistically expect.

On Perception And The Role Of The Listener

RF: As a suggestion to listeners of your music you've said that "there may be no genre-dictated norms of expectation satisfaction (and therefore) anything that remains is a valid approach, no matter from what apparently distant domain of experience it may come."[4] Let's say that I find much of your music to exhibit certain aspects of 'extremity' and "spontaneity" that are also found in some forms of 'free improvisation'. Would you consider this perspective a musically relevant one as far as you're concerned?

BF: It is not really up to me to suggest appropriate interpretations or associations to anyone else. As for me personally, I have too little experience of improvisational contexts such as you mention to be able to offer a useful opinion. I know that some composers start from an improvisation when establishing overall sound worlds for particular pieces, thereafter resorting to various, more or less literal, transcription techniques in order to arrive at a final fully-notated score. Such approaches are very alien to me. It would be unhelpful, though, I think, to remain on the associative level engendered by some supposed resemblance of particular sonic characteristics (extended techniques, for instance) common to some improvisation and certain of my own works. In that case, such immediate associations might well blind one to equally significant qualities on other, more long-term discursive formal qualities of individual pieces.

RF: While we're on the subject of listening, what makes your strategy of abandoning a compositional pathway, in the latter stages of a piece,[5] perceptible and/or significant to a listener?

BF: It depends, firstly, on whether you are talking about the abandonment of an extremely large-scale tendency or attitude and, secondly, in favor of exactly what one is perceived to have abandoned. Clearly, the catastrophic rejection of any sort of fairly strong consistency at a given point will have some effect on the listener's assessment of what sort of meaning can be attributed to previously heard operations; by the same token, what follows - that is to say, what has come to supersede previous tendencies and with what degree of rapidity - cannot be left for long out of the equation. In **Lemma-Icon-Epigram**, for instance, you will find a final section which is peculiarly out of proportion, somehow 'weak' when approached from preceding passages. One sort of frame has been suggested, for which this ending is clearly inappropriate, something of a let-down. Whether it is an *actual* failure, of course, depends almost exclusively on what evidence one has been able to assemble as to the overall focus and ambience of the work up until that point. An aware listener will presumably feel frustrated by the collapse at the end, the inefficient dissipation of accumulated energies: at that time (at the latest immediately after the conclusion of the performance) this frustration will, ideally, feed back into and animate the reflexive phase of aesthetic reception. For that, those remaining energies can still come in useful.

From another point of view, there are many decompositional, or stepwise erosive techniques at work in my music which, in some cases at least, might be considered the gradual 'abandonment' of an already postulated position. To the extent that this is planned and executed within the context of a consistent set of rules, though, it would perhaps be better to consider these as consistent tendencies which happen to be so organized as to produce those results (the emphasis here being on the fact that nothing is really being abandoned on the operational level).

Very often I find that, in contrast to many American composers with whom one is sometimes compared, it is the innate resistance of structure to subjective self-assertion which provides the actual impulse for creation. Seen negatively, this might be criticized as some form of permanent compromise, or else lack of an adequate correlation between means and ends; from my point of view, though, the tactile stimulus provided by the need to achieve an unstable and provisional balance between all forces encountered in a specific compositional situation is an unfailing source of renewal which is entirely positive.

RF: Your usage of perceptual terms such as "too-muchness"[6] and "too fast-ness"[7] seems to imply that some sort of normative value is being referenced in the negative. Is this true? And if so, where does this value reside?

BF: I suppose that it resides somewhere in my head to the extent that it is me making that series of comparative judgements during the compositional process. The reactions of others, on the other hand, would seem to confirm that

I am not very wide of the mark in most instances! Every composer has to balance conflicting paradigms of reception when creating his aesthetic models, one of which (and not the least important) is his own subjective perception of threshold values. Another is research on naturally given limits of information absorption, while a third is one's knowledge of compositional precedents. We all continually make assumptions about what is natural in terms of appropriate weightings of innovation and convention; my own work often involves me in deliberately selecting paths and goals more usually considered counter-intuitive in order to realize the unresolved 'surplus' that I seek.

RF: An often-noted statement about your music is that the techniques used to generate the surface structure may change while the actual surface remains the same, therefore giving you the "possibility of creating multivalent levels of perception of one and the same image."[8] What is it that remains "the same" about the image? Are these multivalent levels actual or virtual?

BF: Both levels are clearly present. 'Sameness' has to do with the perception of identity; 'difference' will be perceived via an altered assessment of the mutual interaction of that identity and its surroundings. Changing one's compositional means in order to produce a 'similarity' in that layer's immediate texturation inevitably brings out a conscious or unconscious reorientation of one's approach to how the work at hand takes cognizance of that change and moves to absorb it in the future flow of events. Sooner or later the awareness of that vector-shift will, one hopes, penetrate to the listener.

On The Relationship Between Music And Other Areas Of Investigation

RF: You've stated that expressive musical potential is eroded through the use of "false forms of directness"[9] which attempt to supplant "secondary formative function(s)"[10] and therefore negate their own "potential internal power"[11], and that when the desirability of "mediational artifice"[12] is ignored, the result is often times an unquestioned assumption that there are musical gestures which are "naturally permeable to particular emotional images."[13] Are there not degrees of "mediational artifice" within primary formative functions? Surely you're not denying the existence of conventionally established connections between musical gestures and emotive signs?

BF: All that I was (I think) saying was that there is potential for a short-circuit situation when the cumulative effect of a series of events with high indexical power serves to generate a sort of ideology of immediacy in terms of what level of musical articulation is to count as expressively significant. The short-circuit arises when the one-to-one indexing of particular instantiations of conventional images feeds back with no remainder into a trivial confirmation of what had been assumed. There is no sense of interference, thus no sense of perspective. It is a one-dimensional situation. "Mediational artifice" sets out to deconstruct or selectively hinder this self-confirming act of identification and, in consequence, activate the critical reflexive capability whereby monolithic perceptions are split up into more differentiatedly mobile (because semantically provisional) sub-units. To the extent that this artifice succeeds in maintaining a certain critical distance to the monadicizing tendencies of powerfully suggestive larger signs the direct emotive weight of the latter can be absorbed into a higher-level apperceptional frame. Keeping up the electrical analogy, artifice acts as a 'transformer' to translate energy back to itself in a more subtle form which can be diversified, canalized and selectively tapped for various purposes not necessarily processable solely in terms of the immediate indexical context.

RF: Since 1980 or so, you've apparently been interested in finding out to what extent it is possible to relate a musical language to a generalized discursive field that reflects upon other forms of communicative discipline.[14] Would you care to supply a specific compositional method you've used in reflecting upon other communicative disciplines?

BF: It is less a question of particular compositional techniques than specific approaches to the issues. I refer you once more to the case of **Lemma-Icon-Epigram**. I was concerned at that time with following-up on various theories of musical *explanation* or *exegesis*. In the course of these investigations I came across the extremely rich lode of 16th and 17th century Emblemata, whose tripartite division (Superscript - Icon - Epigram) seemed to provide a musically viable working model in this project. In keeping with the given general division of roles I envisioned a tripartite work in which each successive section would fulfill a similar function (roughly: enunciation - image - explanation) to its counterpart in the generic emblem. As I mentioned earlier, although the first two parts were composed quite parallel to their reference models, the third part did not resolve the explication issue (although it did do something else, equally important, in the same sense as a scientific experiment that fails to deliver expected results is nevertheless instrumental in providing valid information). The musical technique equivalent to 'explication' was due to have been the relatively context-sensitive (informal) re-integration of the initial dematerialized linear scription and the object-oriented 'time-sculpture' of the 'Icon' passages in such a way as to reveal their common points of reference. That the intended sublation proved impossible was extremely important to me later, since it indicated that a return to essentially motive-orientated free writing was not (then) a viable option - at least, not with respect to the formal weight I had wanted it to support.

RF: You once stated the following: "...musical language is an adjunct of the general semiotic field which nourishes that language, with which it moves as a sort of special case."[15] Do you believe music to be a language? If so, is it a language in a metaphorical sense or in a structuralist sense, having a signifier and a signified?

BF: Whether music is a language in the strict sense or not seems to me really rather unimportant. There are sufficient cross-relationships and parallels between natural and artificial languages and music in pragmatic terms to allow musical structures to be manipulated *as if they were* languages. If, as Wittgenstein has it, "Bedeutung ist Gebrauch",[¶] then some linguistic significance will accrue to any self-consistent set of operations which operates in a broadly comparable fashion. That is what I meant when I spoke of music as a 'special case': it is a sort of satellite to language whose orbit is extremely eccentric.

RF: The title of one of your interviews, "Shattering The Vessels of Received Wisdom", seems to make reference to the book of Zohar.[16] Have you studied the Kabbalah or utilized it in any of your works?

BF: Not directly. My main point of contact with the Kabbalah has been mediated through the final flowering of late Renaissance synthetic speculation by such magi as John Dee, Agrippa of Nettesheim, Giordano Bruno and Robert Fludde. I find their last-ditch attempt to unite a grotesquely discrepant and diverse mass of material culled from every imaginable tradition both heroic and touching. It might not have been 'right' from the baldly factual standpoint, but surely it contains much poetic insight and spiritual involvement closely allied to 'truth' in a different sense entirely. I set some textual fragments of the eponymous Hermes Trismegistus in the final section of my **Transit** in 1974. Of course, I'd read Gershem Sholem in connection with Adorno and Benjamin, so I'm not entirely unfamiliar with more recent interpretations. There was a period in the mid-70's when I was deeply involved with alchemical tracts of various sorts, and had been reading Carl Jung on the subject, too. So much in art has parallels there, I find, which is really why it interested me - it was not because I was searching for some belief system to adopt myself, it was the common structural features uniting these disseparate areas which I found (and still find) fascinating.

RF: Getting back to less obscure matters, you've often talked about your poetry and program notes as being generated utilizing identical techniques to those found in your music.[17] In what ways are they identical?

¶"Meaning is usage".

BF: Several ways, actually. The Griffiths interview[1] talks about this issue in terms of what may usefully be expected of program notes. What, ultimately, are they *for*? More often than not I have set out with the intention, not of writing directly *about* the work in question, but *around* it - in other words, applying similar sorts of compositional procedure to text-production as to musical materials. Whatever the nominal subject matter of the text, in some sense it should be seen functioning in an exemplificatory capacity - a distorting mirror of music in words. This was initially brought about by my need to deal with compositional residues - issues or materials relevant *to* the work but, ultimately, not *of* it. If you have read a lot of Adorno, you will see something of what I mean - most of his writings manifest typical compositional procedures alien (one might assume) to coherent, disciplined argumentation. Typically, he will circle around a theme from behind, treat a fragmentary idea as a head motive, constantly extending it in different directions, employ 'spiral' tactics where the point he is making never actually appears but is sensed at the theoretical (but never attained) center of the spiral manoeuvre. All this is strikingly similar to his espousal of free atonal compositional practice, and powerfully evokes his specific synthesis of freedom and extreme rigor of application.

I am not by any manner of means as consequent or rigorous as that; there is still something analogous at work, though, on a more modest level. When we talk of the specifically poetic texts which I have occupied myself with sporadically (more intensely since moving to the United States) there are really two primary positions from which one can start looking for analogies between music and textual praxis; firstly, as regards word-to-word (unit-to-unit) continuity and, secondly, with respect to large-scale formal conventions adopted. As in my compositions, I set out to define different 'distances' from the material: sometimes the basic unit of measurement is the standard word, at other times it might be the syllable, entire sentences or even the single letter. Moving between these different foci, as well as suggesting different levels of semantic referentiality ('wrong' spelling, intermingled language derivation, processually generated pseudo-words, etc) one can come quite close to the sense of simultaneity and density, as well as to a form of 'dissonance', of structurally-induced 'stumbling', which I see as typical of my musical idiom. On the larger scale, I have actually applied formal patterns with quite obviously musical roots to more lengthy texts: my **Palimpsests**, for example, is built up of ten 'books', each of approximately 15 pages in length, each successive book of which is broken up into progressively fewer numbered sections. Thus, Book I has ten independent subsections, each of which, however, utilizes exclusively one of the numbers 1-10 (in reverse order) for its internal articulation. While such methods might be

---

[1] See this volume, p. 244.

considered arbitrary or trivial by some, it is my experience that the continual interweaving of perceptual paths and layers which results from a complete reading significantly enhances the contextual resonance of the individual text.

On The Compositional Process

RF: Besides your poetry and program notes, you've also worked with analogical relationships and parallel treatments in your compositions. What makes a compositional relationship an analogue, and in what sense (iconic, mimetic, indexical, symbolic) is it analogous?

BF: Musical processes, events, objects et al., in my parlance, may be considered to evince analogical relationships if there is something about their perceived structures which enables the observing consciousness to make a move, to transfer its regard from the one to the other without entirely jettisoning its previous mode of perceptual assessment. Aspects of the one (its operations, tendencies, priorities...) may be mapped onto the other - indeed, the one may be seen as preparing the way for the other, in the sense that the latter may only then become a concrete object of awareness by reason of the mediating function of the former's matrix of priorities. *Mutatis mutandis*, the prior may only then be fully revealed as a coherent object of regard in its own right by virtue of having abandoned up its own autonomy in preparing a bridge to the posterior. Any or all of the categories you list might be (have been) employed towards the realization of these ends.

RF: What constitutes a "layer" and a "vocable" in your compositional and poetic praxis?

BF: These two terms are quite distinct. "Layer" is invariably applied to a series of events or states whose directionality of process or textural consistency appears more (or, at least, as) self-evidently commanding to the ear than/ as the overall concatenation of events of which, at any given instant, it forms a part. Typically, this will remain true even when the event sequence in question is discontinuous, i.e. is not present for lesser or greater periods of discourse. Often, processes applied to any given layer will be unique to it (even though, usually, various degrees of similarity exist linking layers with one another), thus providing a further link in the chain of identity. In many ways, the analogy to polyphonic lines in tonal music might be applied, although, like anything, the resemblance can be overstretched. Like such lines, strata often contribute in various ways to the construction of larger formal constellations (points of intersection, confluence, correspondence...) without thereby sacrificing their essential internal integrity.

A "vocable", on the other hand, is generally less obviously process-orientated, more temporally localized. Just as a word may be inserted at various points in a sentence, pronounced with considerable degrees of latitude in respect of emphasis or inflection, and represent a certain amount of ambiguity of function (unclarity as to grammatical function of a word which is written identically as noun and verb, for instance, or else, by virtue of identical pronunciation, may serve as material for structural punning, as in Raymond Roussel), so a musical vocable may be employed in a number of compositional roles whilst retaining its 'recognizability factor' as a 'thing' or 'event-object' with preferred perceptual status, even though it may have been generated, in particular instances, by processes quite alien to this aspect of its being. In fact, our perception often times latches on an otherwise linearly undifferentiated strand of activity. Composers develop a "feel" for where this can happen, and learn to exploit those exposed moments for what they are worth.

It is perhaps worth mentioning that a "vocable", like any other linguistic category, has a life-history; over the course of several works it can develop implications penetrating to many distinct layers of the compositional fabric. One would need to examine ("compare and contrast") examples of a specific vocable taken from different parts of the same work and from a number of actual works.

RF: You once described a stage in your compositional process where you come to a "'mental sculpture' which has a certain mass and external shape."[18] You go on to say that ideas such as 'energy', 'weight', 'mass', and 'momentum' play important roles in the initial stages. You've also said elsewhere that "the first sensation, the experience which begins to persuade me that I am actually going to write a piece, is very often a cross between a tactile, a visual, and an aural one."[19] All this leads me to ask- Are you synesthetic? Do these cross-modal connections occur at other stages in your compositional process? If not, what is it about this initial stage which allows for them to occur?

BF: If I knew what brought on these images they might stop coming! No, I'm not synesthetic, nor do I have reliable perfect pitch. I *do* directly experience certain textural or balance/disbalance relationships in the envisaged model in terms of associated states of physical tension; hence, I imagine, the frequency with which I employ associated terminology. The reason, I suppose, that this occurs more at the very outset than at other junctures in the compositional process is that my inner eye (its horizon) is not obscured by closer-up matters of concrete musical specification. At different times one is strategically long- or short-sighted as necessity or convenience dictate.

RF: The initial material in **Lemma-Icon-Epigram** seems to me to be an example of a purposely "short-sighted" strategy you've utilized, in the sense that you "simply wrote down a set of notes without thinking about them".[20] The implication would seem to be that the 'original' creative moment is equated with an act of spontaneity. Similarly, you've said that "all structuring systems are to some extent arbitrary and spontaneous".[21] I'm curious whether you make a distinction between the concepts - 'arbitrary' and 'spontaneity'?

BF: Any original decision could conceivably be otherwise than it eventually is. There are always aesthetic choices to be made at the moment of commencement which *may* well be influenced by past experience, individual predilection, facts of personal biography etc. without those contributory influences being sufficient to account *in toto* for every aspect of those steps finally taken. In so far as entire systems of relations are pre-defined, many later decisions are already fixed or sharply constrained as to their modificational limits right at the outset. It is *not* always true, at the same time, that the artist is in a position to foresee, in all their contingent detail, the consequences of those systems: the best one can sometimes do, I find, is to determine the *attitude* one will adopt to each contingent situation when confronted with it. This can, of course, be determined as part of the original system. Some initial choices (to the extent that they are conscious decisions) are necessarily made without all necessary and sufficient information as to their aesthetic consequences being available at that moment. This is the arbitrary aspect. Improvisation, on the other hand, sets this aspect of things forth as an innate and essential process or tactic; it actively celebrates the limited perspective according to which moment-to-moment decisions are constantly being made. If I, as a composer, work with a certain familiarity with my materials and tools, but choose (through accident or design) not to reflect on more distant consequences in the way of operations in my immediate environment: this would be improvisation. Everyone engages in this to some extent, particularly when immediate transliteration of inbuilt comportmental mechanisms are being favored at the expense of creatively distanced reflection. This is spontaneity.

RF: Is Toop correct in describing your completed works as an "arbitrary by-product"[22] of a labyrinthine process where there is nothing predetermined about the outcome of any particular moment? If what you've said about processes is true ("processes don't exist in order to generate music, they're there to predispose one to approach the act of composition in a work specific fashion"),[23] then it would seem that your works can't be viewed merely as an "arbitrary" by-product.

BF: I would certainly be very hesitant about occupying the particular high ground that Richard is suggesting, even if the general thrust of his argument is probably accurate enough. The fact that there is no single, inevitable outcome to a particular set of fluid circumstances would seem to me to reflect a simple fact of life. Because many possible outcomes are imaginable to a creative situation in which the composer finds himself does not imply that the selected outcome is arbitrary. The composer (for which read: "this composer") does not stand outside the work and its framework of norms, priorities and values: the omniscient author is not an acceptable ideology. Even the most superficial reading of recent theories of complex states would seem to urgently suggest a re-evaluation of received notions of Cartesian logic and causal legitimization as the sole arbiters of order in highly articulated objects. The ultimate guide for me in evaluating such things is that every decision has consequences, so that, in the final analysis, nothing, no matter how initially unpredictable, is gratuitous.

RF: Regarding systems errors, you've said that your method of copying the score during the compositional process has enabled you to weave errors seamlessly into your compositions.[24] Doesn't a seamlessly woven error imply that it is an integral component, not as an error, but as a 'smoothed-over' error? Have you utilized errors with their "seams" showing?

BF: Yes, I have, but that is then generally not what they are perceived as! Generally speaking, I like music which is so firmly binding in its premises that one feels reasonably able to recognize compositional inadequacies when they occur. It is not perfection that I seek in the music of others, and I hope my attitude towards my own infelicities is equally accepting (though probably not). On the whole, I see errors as opportunities for unforeseen growth rather than demonstrations of fallibility *per se*. For that, one would have to be much more confident about the general consistency of the supposed error-free parts than I have ever managed to become. There are passages in many of my works which seem like undigested 'errors' in the sense you suggest and, although I suppose that I have become reconciled to them, I would be hard put to see them in a still positive light.

RF: On a related note, what is the relationship between your method of reinvention and the fact that your work is defined, in advance, over a period of years? Is there a conflict between these two working methods? Does your reliance on spontaneity, error, and memory lapse have a progressive or static effect on the growth of your compositional problem sets?

BF: I tend to work on larger groups of pieces very much as I would the internal relationships governing individual works. The fact that I subsume several compositions to the same preliminary 'group view' does not imply high levels of ultimate interrelatedness, since my motivating concerns are dependent less on concrete material transference than on a 'state of mind' which is itself in a constant process of evolution and redefinition. For instance, a typical group might be one of those currently in progress, that defined by the variety of possible relationships between a single performer and a larger or smaller ensemble of musicians. There are obviously many variables and possible chains of implication one might pursue here: the field is fluid and open-ended in the extreme without sliding off into the intangible. I find this sort of loose context infinitely preferable to the serial production of uniquely specific solutions to radically isolated and self-enclosed problems. If you look at the three products of this solo/group category to date (**La Chute d'Icare** for clarinet and small ensemble; **Allgebrah** for oboe and strings; **Terrain** for violin and eight instruments) you will see a lot of intersection and cross-fertilization without, I think, discerning much in the way of concrete sharing around of either techniques or materials. In other ways, too, sameness and difference can be brought out by recourse to this loose method of grouping: for instance, each of the three works I mentioned takes as its point of departure a meditation on the meaning of creative imagery of a non-musical sort, where **Icare** sets off from the Breughel painting, **Allgebrah** from the half-literary, half-metaphysical world view of Adolf Wölfli and **Terrain** from folding into one another the aesthetic theories of Robert Smithson and a poem by A.R. Ammons, both dealing, in their distinct ways, with natural forces as metaphor for the creative process. Even so, I don't consider these pieces as a single coherent unit. Each stands for itself alone. I certainly would be extremely apprehensive about programming them all in a single concert!

RF: Remarkably similar to your earlier description of Adorno's rhetorical strategy, the medieval poet, Geoffrey of Vinsauf, has said, "Do not unveil the thing fully but suggest it by hints. Do not let your words move straight onward through the subject, but, circling it, take a long and winding path around what you are going to say."[25] On a number of occasions[26] you've differentiated your compositional methods from the variational methods used by Boulez. Yet you've often used varied repetitional schemes (e.g. those at the beginnings of **Carceri d'Invenzione I** and **Lemma-Icon-Epigram**). This, coupled with the fact that you reuse materials (albeit in a varied manner) within co-terminus projects, would seem to imply some common ground with Boulez. Does the difference between your variational methods and those of Boulez, reside in the fact that you start with a concealed object which is gradually revealed, whereas he starts with the object itself, fully revealed?

BF: I should think that most of those strictures would be true of almost any artist. Your medieval scholar could be predicting Mallarmé. Apart from that, I can't really identify with your view of either Boulez or myself. As I've said elsewhere, it's only the very early Boulez works which I found personally rewarding and resonant, and those were the pieces in which repetition played a rather insignificant role, I would have thought, unless you mean cellular transformation on the microlevel, as in the **Flute Sonatina**, or the **Second Sonata**. Many techniques, nuances apart, are held in common by a vast number of composers: the important thing is to emphasize the mobilizing intention behind particular instances. As in musical forms, so in the trajectories of human lives: sometimes composers seem to be closer than they really are because one is leaving out of consideration the dynamic roots of stylistic development - where someone is coming from and towards what goal they are moving. Measured by these standards, Boulez and I have really very little in common other than, perhaps, an intense concern with the functioning of musical language, albeit expressed in very different ways.

RF: Finally, in an era where the term "decentering" has become a discursive norm, supposedly signifying a radical multi-culturalism, your espousal of 'mannerist' techniques that emphasize a center, may seem conservative to some. How would you answer this charge?

BF: I suppose the argument could be made. The very charge itself, on the other hand, would seem odd coming from those who espouse the cultural equivalence of all aesthetic phenomena as manifestations of points on the featureless postmodern plane. "Conservative" in respect of what, according to which codex of evaluational criteria? While the postmodern stance of cynical, value-free, deconstructive play may indeed be briefly exhilarating, it effectively nips in the bud any attempt to employ coherent argumental techniques against anyone else.

More seriously, your use of the term "mannerist" raises other questions of nomenclature. Lower case, the word might stand for practically any phenomenon of recent art endeavor, insofar as this latter make conscious, ironic reference to the "manner" of one or more earlier art ideolects. Upper case, one would have to accept the historical, cyclical postulate, namely that Mannerism is a typical phenomenon characterizing the final phase of a particular cultural sensibility in a highly self-conscious, heightened form in which material is less vital to expression than process or perspectival distortion. I cannot find anything very negative in a continuing attempt to mobilize *all* factors of musical language from within rather than without. To this extent, 'conservatives' are those lemmings choosing to leap over the cliff leaving entire worlds of expressive potential behind them.

In a sense, it is rather flattering to be identified with the 'conservative' label: I've finally arrived! Really, though it's the other way round, in that most of what I see being plastered with the laurel wreaths of 'progress' looks to me rather like more of the same minus the critical historical perspective. *Plus ça change...*

As far as 'multiculturalism' is concerned, I'm in the culture I'm in and therefore leave to others the Papagenoesque carnival getup which makes them fools for a day. I respect everyone's right to identify culturally with whatever they like - including me.

Endnotes

1. *James Boros, "Shattering The Vessels Of Received Wisdom" (this volume, p. 377).*

2. *See, for example, David Cope,* New Music Notation, *(Dubuque: Kendall/Hunt Publishing Company, 1976), p. xi.*

3. *"Interview with Richard Toop" (this volume, p. 269).*

4. *Boros, p. 391; also see, "Interview with Joël Bons" (this volume, p. 218f).*

5. *Toop, "Interview", p. 266.*

6. *Ibid., p. 259.*

7. *Joël Bons (ed.), "Responses to a Questionnaire", (this volume, p. 68).*

8. *Toop, op. cit. p. 260; also see, Bons, "Interview", loc. cit.*

9. *"Form - Figure - Style: An Intermediate Assessment", (this volume, p. 21).*

10. *Ibid., p. 22.*

11. *Ibid., p. 23.*

12. *Ibid., loc. cit.*

13. *Ibid., loc. cit.*

14. *"Carceri d'Invenzione: in Conversation with Richard Toop", (this volume, p. 295).*

15. *Bons, "Interview" p. 218.*

16. *For instance see, Gershom Scholem, editor,* Zohar: The Book Of Splendor, *(New York: Schocken Books, 1949).*

17. *"Interview with Paul Griffiths", (this volume, p. 244); also see "Interview with Antonio De Lisa", (this volume, p. 427).*

18. *Griffiths, "Interview" p. 239.*

19. *"Interview with Richard Toop", p. 260.*

20. *Richard Toop, "Brian Ferneyhough's Lemma-Icon-Epigram,"* Perspectives of New Music, *Vol. 28, No. 2, (Summer 1990), p. 55.*

21. *Brian Ferneyhough, "Form - Figure - Style: An Intermediate Assessment", p. 22.*

22. *Richard Toop, "Brian Ferneyhough's Lemma-Icon-Epigram," p. 53.*

23. *Boros, p. 383.*

24. *Griffiths, p. 242.*

25. *Cited in Penelope Reed Doob,* The Idea of the Labyrinth, *(Ithaca: Cornell University Press, 1990), p. 212.*

26. *See "Interview with Richard Toop", pp. 253 and 258; Bons, p. 227.*

LEAPS AND CIRCUITS TO TRAIL:
A CONVERSATION ON THE TEXTS AND MUSIC
WITH JEFFREY STADELMAN[1]
(1992)

JEFFREY STADELMAN: I first encountered your poetic texts after receiving a bundle from a friend which contained, among other things, **Practique** and **Syntacticon**. When, after spending several confused but exhilarating days trying to read them, I later learned that these two extremely difficult works comprise just a small fraction of your total poetic output, my reaction was one of simultaneous delight and alarm. *Why* do you write texts of this sort?

BRIAN FERNEYHOUGH: Probably no-one knows what reasons the deepest self has for doing anything: I *am* aware, on the other hand, of a couple of the most immediate forms the drive to write has assumed in recent years. One of these has to do directly with my move to the States in 1987, and involved the intense and immediate reaction to the sense of physical and mental dislocation I lived with for quite a long period — I'm still in the aftershock of it, really. On the one hand, I clung to language as to a lifebelt — something stable and extremely basic — at the same time as, on the other, profoundly rejecting many of its more pervasive codes and conventions. In part, this certainly had to do with the fact that I was returning to my mother language after many years of virtual absence, having lived and worked in continental Europe since 1968, and having, in consequence, evolved a number of "alternative personalities" associated with the various linguistic habitats among which I moved; it meant I was coming back to English from several directions at once, none of them familiar.

JS: Did it seem that English had changed while you were away? To what extent did American English present itself as a "foreign" language?

BF: English *did* seem to have changed in the interim, but I'm fairly sure that this was largely due to my own changed perspective with respect to language itself. One has to bear in mind that, while learning German, I spent a significant period virtually speechless, both by reason of my isolated position on the edge of society and because of not knowing how to say very much in general, and thus being constrained, at every turn, to find ways of communicating the literally unsayable. In some ways, this speechlessness mirrored my experiences, as a child, of having to carefully "translate" censored aspects of my inner world into the words of the people around me. The British class system ensures that the compartmentalization of vocabularic subsets serving to functionally separate various levels of society is well advanced and notably unforgiving, offering little leeway for individual deviation. So it seemed to me at the time, anyway. I remember being so sure that one could only move wholesale from one rigid code to another that I invented several rather elaborate and mutually incompatible languages in an attempt both to provide myself with a temporary inner refuge and to create grammars within which new forms of experience could be enunciated (and thus, I now suppose, be actually called into being, at least potentially). I'm reminded of the distinction Foucault makes in his studies on prisons and punishment, where he distinguishes between the *form* and the *substance* of experience, in the sense that it is the articulated framework of the penal code which lends substance to the state of delinquency as such.

As far as American English is concerned, of course one cannot help being struck by the extremely lively and anarchic capacity for self-renewal which distinguishes it from the parent language. I was never spiritually in tune with most "native" British poetry (except for some provincial mavericks such as Basil Bunting, whose vocabulary, seeded with local color, is significantly more rugged) and found myself drawn more to Eliot and Pound, in spite of the latter's early Pre-Raphaelite affectations, because of their intensely ambivalent and alienated highlighting of aspects of the language which were only recuperable by me through the eyes of foreigners. At the present time I very much get the sense that this protean capacity for transformation and renewal has carried North American poetry into some extremely interesting (if not uniformly fruitful) areas during the last two decades. I get the impression that some sense of this openness ultimately helped to create an atmosphere within which I have been better able to open up my own writing to the integration of diverse competing "voices" than had been the case before my arrival in this country. One can be morally encouraged by a phenomenon, I think, without abandoning oneself up to it.

JS: Who are some of the more recent American poets whose works have been valuable to you?

BF: Among the vast mass of "LANGUAGE" poets which I came across for the first time I would certainly have to pick out Charles Bernstein for his extremely dense **Artifice of Absorption**,[2] which makes a striking case for texts which foreground their own structure and impermeability as a way of avoiding being accomplices by default to the "transparency fallacy". Other authors one might mention would be Steve McCaffery, whose **Panopticon**[3] is an exemplary book-length text exhibiting some of the multilayered sedimentation strategies typical of the *nouveau nouveau roman* of Philippe Sollers, Maurice Roche and Jean Ricardou.[4] I found the early texts of Clark Coolidge (**Space**)[5] stimulating, as well as the jagged verbal assaults of Bruce Andrews.[6]

JS: Can you recall other impulses which lay behind the creation of these texts?

BF: The other motivation for writing of which I was directly aware was the intense conviction that I had, somehow, to objectivize the sense of loss I experienced in re-entering the active domain of English with this increased awareness of how insidiously prefabricated linguistic conventions rule our lives by actually *throwing away* the individual words — throwing them away, that is by bringing them to paper, leaving them out there, like rocks scattered by the force of nature across some windswept landscape, left to their own devices. Once a word was thus externalized, it was gone, voided: there was a corresponding *space*, that is to say, which could be mobilized and energized by other expressive factors — precisely which, I was far from clear. My texts are the trace or residue, both of that voidance and its re-manifestation as form. I have written poetic texts "on the side" for many years and in several languages, but it was this experience of inner and outer deracination which gave consistent direction and impetus to my activities.

JS: Is your interest in portmanteau words related to your long-standing association with German, where verbal hybridization is a standard feature of the language?

BF: For many years following the Second World War German was arguably the foremost language for experimental literature. Although that tendency has since ebbed more than somewhat, there are still several major figures (such as Helmut Heißenbüttel, Oskar Pastior, Gerhard Rühm, Friederike Mayröcker and Ernst Jandl)[7] who are actively engaged in the extension and/or subversion of linguistic conventions. Interestingly enough, most of the more enterprising and sometimes radical experimental writers originated, not from Germany itself, but from those smaller countries — Switzerland and Austria — for whom the language (somewhat comparable to the relationship between English and American English) was less "obvious". Both countries, for instance, have considerable literatures written in regional dialects. The result of this was more obvious reflection on the inner workings and surface banalities of the language itself; the works of Konrad Bayer[8] might be seen as representative here, especially when mingled with the pervasive influence of Dada and pre-First World War Expressionism. Recently, Oskar Pastior, born (like Paul Celan[9]) in an isolated German-speaking enclave in Romania, has revivified

German poetic invention with magnificently virtuosic and totally untranslatable "re-inventions" of the language by means of classic structural devices such as the anagram, taken *ad absurdum*.

It was certainly this sense of language being an active framer of experience which motivated my early writing efforts, most of which were in German in order to make use of the inherent alienating effect of a foreign thinking structure as a way of creating new ways of sensing the self at work.

JS: I imagine most creative people would agree that an active engagement of unfamiliar constraints, regardless of the stage of aesthetic experience, can foster interesting artistic results. However, instead of stressing new ways of sensing the work, or new ways of working sensibly, you speak of "new ways of sensing the self at work", as if this is in itself a desirable goal within the creative process. What do you mean?

BF: The continual re-projection of images of the self is the only sort of "representationalism" available to me. The methods by means of which I undertake this task form the substance of my discourse. Again I refer to Foucault, who speaks of the shadowy presence of the observer at the center of the 18th Century Panopticon, seeing all but unseen, equidistant from all, the form of content. If one's experience of the world is divided between discursive reconstitution and non-discursive illumination, then why should not the prisoners revenge themselves by conspiring to throw critical light on what remains definitively outside their reach?

JS: The citation of Baudelaire's statement, *"Tout est hieroglyphique,"* at the head of your work for solo piano, **Lemma-Icon-Epigram**, seems to bespeak a belief that everything is a text, that anything can be "read". What happens when the source of this image, *language*, is itself transformed so that it can't be read in the usual way? Are your texts saying that verbal artifacts aren't "really" being read, even when we think they are?

BF: But poetry is never, by definition, read "in the usual way". At most, the substance of the text might be suggesting certain conventional ways of reading as a background against which various strategies of "poetic" reading may be essayed. The emphasis is on the "text" of the reading process itself, in the same sense that much of my music deals with aspects of the listening process as material. Poetic texts do not deal directly with referential "reality", but with the specific event of their inscription. Different, incompatible spaces coincide, which implies, I would suggest, a significant component of self-awareness in the reception process, over and above any attempt to locate and re-articulate residual "referential" elements in terms of either vocabulary or local narrative structure. In most of my longer texts there are passages which, by the nature of their implied "theoretical" tone, serve to keep this aspect of things near the fore-front of the mind.

JS: I see. Your *"tout"* refers then not just to materially present artistic "objects", but to the grand sum of the activities of creation, process, relation, performance, reception, et cetera, which surround them. I had read the epigram as pertaining to the mundane objects and events "out there", including every-day verbal communication.

BF: Well, your interpretation would be the immediate one, I'm sure. In music, though, the bracketing-out of associated but more nebulous influences acting upon the reception process is more problematic. The particular composi-tion to which I appended that Baudelaire citation was itself an extreme investi-gation of the dynamic act of writing, as opposed to the evocative potential of fixed sonic objects. In fact, its ultimate (and initially unforeseen) catastrophic rejection of concrete motivic working in the final section might perhaps be seen as an implicit appeal to the ordering potential of more inclusive exegetical methodologies.

JS: How do you respond to those who would suggest that, with non-tonal music at least (and perhaps post-Joycean texts as well), the envelope of meaningfully intersubjective discourse does not descend to the level of struc-tural awareness, much less psychological response?

BF: I'm not sure to what extent music and verbal language can be bun-dled together like that. It seems pretty defeatist to assume that at least some individuals aren't at least going to *try* to avoid merely "going with the flow". Even if Adorno did over-emphasize the expertise component of the aesthetic experience, if would be ridiculous to encourage embracing the other extreme. To some extent, of course, one writes what one would like to read, which incidentally involves the activation of a number of other aspects of the self: on the other hand, I *don't* always like to read what I would have liked to have written...

More seriously, "language" is not just words but also "tone". How one succeeds (or doesn't succeed) in invoking some analogous mechanism in the written word is the key to bringing into play a first level of involuntary struc-tural reading. It is up to writers themselves to determine the degree to which specifically structural aspects of their work actively obtrude on semantically suggestive patterns, although I would imagine that a constant refocusing of the zone of relevant interaction would be a significant aid in enabling readers to set up provisional scales of interpretative values, if only because these latter are thereby made uncomfortably aware of the necessity of such. An additional problem, when considering the corresponding musical situation, is that of identifying the tags or markers indicative of units of semantic import at least loosely equivalent to words, phrases and so on, in order that provisional perspectival coordinates can be brought into play. It is a question, perhaps, of a "third formal force" aimed at mediating between "pre-sonic" composerly systematizing and locally processed sensory input at the listening end.

In a sense, your "meaningfully intersubjective discourse" might be taken to be begging the question, in that it assumes some substrate of *a priori* understood "meaning" according to which the level of adequacy of response to a non-tonal piece might, by common accord, be assessed, as it were, *hors de texte*. I'm reminded of an article entitled "Jede wahre Sprache ist unverständlich" ("Every true language is incomprehensible") by the German author Bernd Matteus,[10] in which he postulates that the comprehensible is always open to misuse as illicit confirmation of extant forms of order. Without necessarily subscribing to his conclusion that every writer must therefore aspire to the condition of clinical schizophrenia, I do recognize the need for some irreducible sense of irreconcilability within and around the text that, while admitting the reader, succeeds in fending off piratical appropriation by the long arm of normative thinking.

JS: Your writings *about* music display a refreshing willingness to engage, extend and transform vocabularies associated with disciplines other than music, such as physics, metaphysics, contemporary "theory" and pathology. At the same time you often introduce original words and expressions into your musical writings and speech. The poetic texts seem to me to rather violently explode what comes to seem the milder lingual stress and coinage evident in your discourse about music.

BF: One of the few advantages of an untrained mind is occasionally submitting to the syrensong of conceptual synesthesia!

JS: Yes, but even your music can seem restrained alongside the seemingly uncurbed constructions of these texts!

BF: It's probably true that my means of establishing stylistic coherence (although I hope not my musical expression) are inherently more, as you put it, "restrained". The reasons for that reside in the nature of musical language as such, in the sense that there is nothing pre-formed, little in the way of pre-established materials or norms to be adopted or undermined in the work. Musical composition is constrained to create its own provisional norms in the very act of subverting or commenting on them — its own "other". This is the major problem and major challenge of contemporary music, and achieving the requisite interaction of levels requires continual attention. Language, being already "out there", is significantly more "accessible", and thus more amenable to extravagant manipulation, than the extremely contingent substance of music.

JS: Adorno insisted that, in order to retain any hope of authenticity, the "modern" composer must maintain relentless pressure against the musical ideology and products of the commercial culture establishment. Your musical compositions and writings seem to support this attitude. Do you feel that similar negative pressure is required within the sphere of verbal communication?

BF: A lot of ink has been spilled on the current prerequisites for authentic art in any medium, not all of it of the negative dialectic variety. Contemporary music is something of a special case in the United States, it seems to me, in the sense that much of that music corresponding most closely to Adorno's dicta has been rendered socially harmless by almost complete absorption into the university environment, and its consequent de-clawing by the stifling embrace of a tradition of non-participatory tolerance. In such a situation, a (not, in my view, very convincing) case might perhaps be made for "progressive" art music drawing stylistic sustenance (and, so goes the argument, listeners) from the domain of vernacular, commercially-orientated phenomena, the better to engage itself with the transmission of politically or socially relevant "messages". Apart from not accepting this naively one-dimensional view of the function of new music as a form of didactic sitcom for the ears alone, I emphatically espouse the vision of "material" as being the sonic manifesting-forth of social content as a special instance of the musical techniques employed. Art is not *outside* life, but nor is it a stylistically neutral container for content imported from beyond the limits of its own proper domain. In this sense, Adorno's general thesis as to the *spiritual* substance of the work, its resistance or opacity, is at least as relevant, if not more so, as the more externally orientated oppositional stance you ascribe to him. Music compositions allotting highest priority to the consistent authentication of their own means of meaning-production will *automatically* be in opposition to prevailing mass prefabrication of manipulative transparency, no matter how tendentiously clothed in icons of "oppositional" ideology the products of this industry may be.

JS: With respect to music and/or texts, what in your opinion are the factors which lead to authentic technique for our place and time? Novelty, rigor, complexity, "nature"? Is this something one can talk about?

BF: "Getting a breath of fresh air" is probably the nearest I can come to a definition! The mannerist concept of *meraviglia* is extremely attractive — I mean, the bringing forth of the sort of astonishment that makes one want to laugh out loud with the almost absurdly exhilarating sense of aperture it brings to what had seemed a closed situation. I don't mean the old "smoke and mirrors" type of illusionist ploy, naturally, but rather the deeply grounded act of revealing which only intense and committed dedication to the material can bring about.

What I just said relates primarily to my experience and convictions as a composer, and I read the situation of poetic writing differently. For one thing, far more individuals may be presumed to read a book of poems than may be induced to sit through a demanding piece of music; for another, there seems to be a disbalance between the number of composers *au courant* with some advanced or experimental literature and the sort of music (to judge from reference to music in their writings at least) to which contemporary writers have been exposed. Even among the educated and artistically aware, then, most varieties of new music are at a major disadvantage, while poetry which might validly be viewed as working in broadly comparable areas is managing to keep "out there", published, and with well-functioning communications infrastructures, even if naturally on an extremely modest scale. It may be that new writing is significantly more self-regulating, in terms of its critical function, than new music, if only for the reason that poets tend to be rather effective propagandists for each others' work. To the extent that a specifically "poetic" paracritical mode can still be distinguished as a functioning arm of discursive linguistic praxis, poetry may be argued to have the advantage over music, where corresponding objects of reference are not as obviously given, and mediatory infrastructures, over which the composer often has only indifferent control, are constantly interposed as a condition for any sort of reception at all.

JS: Your invocation of *"meraviglia"* reminds me of Breton's surrealist byword, "...it is only the marvelous that is beautiful..".[11] Since you have elsewhere admitted to being "deeply impressed" by Dadaist and Surrealist poetry during your formative years, I wonder at what level these earlier movements make themselves felt in your texts. For instance, do you engage in "automatic writing"?

BF: It's true that some of the early Surrealist and Dadaist writing had a tremendously liberating effect on me; not only on my literary awareness, but also by articulating and sustaining my sense that art *could* truly effect a transformation of the conditions of life. Certainly, my discovery of Antonin Artaud's early writings during my late teens was especially stimulating. Particularly in the case of Surrealism, though, I remember being vaguely dissatisfied with what I took to be the discrepancy between the exhilaratingly dislocated rhythm of images and the sometimes stultifyingly conventional "versifying" tendencies of larger contexts which failed to maintain and amplify these local outbursts of energy. I would be the first to admit that the fault is, in part, my own, in that I naively chose to restrict my readings to that particular agenda of values. In later years I came to appreciate more sustained works (Breton's **Ode à Charles Fourier**, for example) for the rich fluidity of discourse nourishing and framing individual flares of verbal invention. I suppose that this memory has continued to motivate my search for specific form/content dimensions for each work: at least, it is often one of the considerations most at the forefront of my mind when writing.

The influence of automatic writing techniques tends easily to be overvalued in general, I think. Most poets probably have periods where things "flow" in a relatively uncontrolled stream. Although some of my writing "takes off" from a momentary stimulus, attempting to catch the uniqueness of that impulse, I almost invariably slow down soon after. Nearly everything from the last six or seven years has undergone successive steps of painstaking (and sometimes painful) revision in order to attain the sort of "crippled balance", that quality of being "off-center" that I seek.

JS: To what extent does your text-writing serve as a stimulus or heuristic for your musical activities?

BF: Composition is typically a slow and painstaking process, so it takes quite a considerable period of time for even a small number of my formal ideas to come to fruition. Many of the remainder find expression in texts of one sort or another. I am always on the lookout for new ways of imposing meaningful constraints on my materials, and, as I said earlier, there are times, in poetry, when the distinctions between material, technique and form are more immediately evident — that is, obviously and independently superimposed — than is the case with my music, which means that issues primarily concerning one of those dimensions can be more directly addressed, or the tensions arising between them can be more readily exposed and channeled. Perhaps that has an effect on my composition, although no immediate example comes to mind; a more likely result is the more efficient articulation of background ideas or concepts common to both domains. I'm pretty sure that working on certain techniques of verbal splicing or concentrating on the internal structure of certain restricted vocabularies has aided me in my reflections on time flow perception, for instance. More banally, perhaps, I find that text-writing tends to fill in the gaps between intense periods of musical composition, and helps, in a modest way, to keep the essential creative juices flowing until specifically musical obstacles have been overcome.

JS: Given Schoenberg's painting and writing of poetic/philosophic texts, as well as your view that confrontation with Schoenberg is a crucial font in the life of any "modern" composer, your extra-musical activities of verbal and graphic creation strike me as, perhaps, another manifestation of that same urge to meet and engage Schoenberg on his own ground.

BF: I wouldn't necessarily restrict things to Schoenberg. Cross-disciplinary creative activity seems to have been a widespread phenomenon during the first half of our century — witness Paul Klee, Kurt Schwitters or the Futurists; and one sees all sorts of parallels between various art forms and musical thinking, so that it seems only natural that composers sometimes feel the urge to experience these cross-currents in the most concrete manner possible, that is, by experimenting in those fields personally. That said, the case of Schoenberg still seems extraordinarily important at this present moment, where we find ourselves at a crossroads of Western cultural self-understanding: an appropriate response might be the refusal to restrict oneself to an all-too-narrow "professional" interpretation of one's artistic activities, in order to come to a wider appreciation of the true complexities of the situation.

JS: With regard to the "cross-fertilization" of art forms, you have observed that "today, everything has fallen apart", and pointed out how nowadays "when poets or novelists mention musical taste, it is usually in conjunction with entertainment music rather than works by their contemporary equivalents in serious musical fields".[12] Why have affiliations between the various artistic disciplines disintegrated to such a degree?

BF: Perhaps because the idea of common goals seems less and less plausible, the more technological progress accords us universal access to our cultural memory; perhaps because the effort involved in critical appraisal and utilization of one medium is the most that our dissipated energies can now aspire to; perhaps because the pitiless revelations by social criticism of supposed class-conscious roots of any and all artistic manifestations have created a form of bad conscience, causing us to attempt to balance-out "elitist" activity in one domain with more "populist" affectations elsewhere; perhaps by reason of simple lack of exposure at crucial stages of the educational process? Sad, in any case.

* * *

JS: Besides speaking in a variety of invented voices, your texts often seem to allude to familiar rhetorical types: the headline, the computer programmer's list, the revolutionary slogan, the advertisement, the cookie fortune, the lyric poem, the didactic text and so on. Are you aware of such categories in composing your texts; and, if so, to what extent are they then incorporated as autonomous elements within large-scale structural strategies?

BF: I'm aware of them, without, I think, making a major point of exploiting them as *topoi*. There are some exceptions, such as the sections of **Practique** and **Palimpsests** which utilize and distort the conventions of academic discourse in order to draw attention to their self-referential aspect; you have to have some means of turning the eye of the text inward or outward. Generally speaking, I'm more immediately aware of the force with which the exigencies of the self-imposed structural constraints impinge on and motivate local invention than with any resemblance to extant categories of the sort you mention. On the other hand, if I do recognize their influence, I seldom make a great effort to eradicate them. More likely, I would insert a subsidiary troping pattern on that basis, intended to set up a further lateral twist in the text's motions.

JS: The fact that these categories exist at all suggests to me a disagreement between your texts and music. That is, I have the feeling you are deeply opposed to any sort of stylistic appropriation in matters musical, while these texts' rhetorical categories are also historical and cultural ones, and thus possess their own pre-determined sets of origins and associations.

BF: What you say may be so. The reasons are probably connected with the fact that a musical language, at least in my eyes, is a consciously constructed ideolect much more than is the case with most texts. I'm not able to identify with aspects of a given musical style which have not "grown up", as it were, through the gradual evolution of my proper compositional autobiography. Words were already there, one moves between contexts by assuming a different costume to fit the circumstances, i.e. which portion of the notional self is appropriate. The same is true of second language learning. Music (again, I speak only of myself) is such a total, but at the same time stylistically-particularized world of experience, that that sort of higher-level context-bound role playing is difficult to imagine. Each sum of musical particulars means because emitted through the differential engine of style; style itself is not one of those particulars.

JS: As a composer, I can argue that I avoid the vernacular in my music because it isn't *my* vernacular: technology has made it possible for an individual to be effectively steeped in a musical practice which is in fact quite alien to the surrounding culture-at-large. With verbal creation, however, such arguments are less convincing. How do you deal with the "weight" of the vernacular?

BF: I'm reminded of the time, in the late '60's, when I was a student in the Musikakademie of Basel, Switzerland. I didn't know my way around German with any facility, and, in any case, the local dialect was completely incomprehensible to me. The way I finally learned German was by reading masses of classical texts and making lengthy vocabulary lists (perhaps the forerunners of some of the "washing lists" in recent texts), so that I could read Goethe with reasonable facility almost before I could confidently order a cup of coffee in a café. This sense of culturally incongruous or inappropriate verbal comportment has remained actively with me ever since, to such an extent that extricating myself from the influence of vernaculars as such has never been as much of a problem as finding some minimal *modus vivendi* with them. The same was true of popular music, with which I scarcely ever came in contact, and even of most classical music, even when I came to perform it regularly as a trumpet player, since most of the items played seldom made a major point of recognizing my presence except as a form of largely dispensable sonic amplifier. One participated, but only nominally and with a certain amount of bad grace.

JS: I was at first surprised when I heard you had chosen a Jackson Mac Low mesostic as the source text for the vocal part in your recent **Fourth String Quartet**.[13] This text is based upon Pound's **Cantos**, and employs an apparently "chance-oriented" compositional method to carve a path through the earlier work. Upon reflection, however, it struck me that similar algorithmic processes are active in the creation of your music, though within much more complex multi-level webs of "free" and "automatic" parametric strands, and using original source material. Is this interest in algorithmic process explored in your own poetic texts?

BF: I suppose that a direct transference from one medium to the other would be the most obvious path to take! On the whole, though, and excepting various formal constraints imposed from case to case, the sort of "processuality" I employ in my texts is not as all-embracing as that characteristic of my compositions — possibly because the prestructuring resistance offered by language (or languages) *per se* is already ubiquitous. I don't find myself particularly close to the rigorous game-aesthetic of the French OULIPO group (Queneau, Perec, Roubaud, et al.[14]), for instance, where transformatory algorithms are applied wholesale to extant texts, even though some of the results are certainly wildly stimulating: I suppose that I suffer under too much accumulated weight of received ideas of "expression" and locally formalized contextuality for that. With very few exceptions, the procedures operating on a local level are more akin to certain free atonal precepts in music — that is, the heightened projection of residually umbilical "emblems" onto the screen of presumed received tradition. It's true, on the other hand, that some texts — particularly the longer ones — arise in the context of obvious, and sometimes arbitrary-seeming imposed formal consistencies which, beginning at the most general level, not infrequently reach down into considerations of line-by-line structuring (even though this may only become apparent as a form evolves). "BULK PRONUNCIATION" from **Syntacticon** might be a case in point, in that an initially rather bald *alternatim* structure of superscript and commentary gradually becomes enriched by progressively more complex sets of variations or fantasies on the given structural "theme". The final, relatively evolved elements would not, I think, have been as meaningful without the sense of inexorable approach which the earlier, less obviously individuated, pages ensure. I suppose that that might be seen as one somewhat obvious result of my background as musician — as someone locating events in an imagined quasi-temporal reading space.

In general, in fact, I find myself falling back on "musical" structuring, particularly when composing medium length texts built up from the infolding of a number of relatively interdependent basic units of formal environments, in that the result often resembles a sort of "suite" of "movements" with certain communal "themes". A recent 22-page text, **Geotropes,** is a case in point, where four sets of four similarly structured one-page texts ("in flagranti i-iv"; "little synaxarion" ["varia i-iv"]; "antiphlogisitics i-iv"; "invocations i-iv") are separated by three groups of "minor doabs," each made up of six shorter segments conforming to a looser set of contraints. I should perhaps add that the two outer groups of texts correspond somewhat, in that they both partake of a "polyphonic" motion, in which words and phrases beginning on opposite sides of the page progressively approach one another and, in the case of the very last poem, completely intersect. (Example 1.)

JS: It seems to me that your word processor, by providing automatic edit functions and typographical control, must have played a significant, functional role in the generation of these texts. Or am I mistaken?

BF: No, you're not mistaken. Until a few years ago, anyone wanting to insert a specifically graphic element into their writing had a pretty hard time of it. In part, this struggle against the typewriter lent the early concrete poets of the '50's and '60's their specific charm. The same is true of such major figures as Arno Schmidt, whose magnum opus, **Zettels Traum,**[15] was published as a ten-volume reproduction of the author's typescript, corrections and all. As in some extensive, typographically many-layered critical editions of classical poets such as Hölderlin, one has the sensation of looking down through swirling, cloudy water towards a marine landscape only fitfully visible.

Recent technological advances have largely annulled this capability by removing the element of resistance from the medium; while it's certainly true that I pay a good deal of attention to the layout on the page of what I write (perhaps inspired by the fact that I personally produce the final published score

Ex. 1: **Geotropes**

invocations i-iv

i

schistoform:

:heilung tracing wentletrap flong

coenswum:

:heaved rayle affricate

sublime lenti:

:fleabit is mu on snow-somite

troniun-nolan:

:dismisseth scones thimblerig backlit

macpherson:

:fatima of württemberg

spolicateur:

:gill's discharge ex-glid

strangstrobe:

:regions deign gnotus dingratz

interpolation:

:glogg-swaraj saxifug

thymus' demon:

:swippling red flowered isoclinal

drussisch:

:a pea's gaskin eaten-out quintillion

xate-fritten:

:type of hog

self-basse:

:eroecious wince seriate skull asbest

Ex. 1: **Geotropes** *(cont'd)*

ii

divergent.gotten away astern:
:catholicon differential pocky
'the eskamott: spurtler's flumen':
:éclat zoesis or baldacchino

flue-cured, salt-seed, stun as:
:flue divine
nomy littérateur; eroteme perplex:
:not tabac teeth as crap abbles

so: zeugmapsis/ ('glish bahur):
:on one mulc-drigged nay-ditcher
glottologische menge sans fitly:
:deploratio fruck est

genus...macronique...asterismen:
:facias de crimp nuovo both-scut
(pseudomenteur) 'in mind's cop':
:green hundred crible gallante

Ex. 1: **Geotropes** *(cont'd)*

iii

"distasteful paradigm":
:involved awareness/reductive exposure

gambit: catastrophist: two battologies:
:the dapple's aloe to contain it; "revolutie"

as shed horde, with subsequent devaluation:
:excerpted ernst; nasty work of aegis himself

"...nothing else to spread":
:trope drew its audience of paint's horizon

as twelve hundred coal bags höchst selbst:
:(number, sorts, context; feat of enframing)

dump pontoon-simple:
:basho's coded deflex (geniculate macrosegment)

something? improbable: koan mana problematicus:
:contrepois-empennage'd grex mordent at a point

abowne initio for a brotus:
:"...in caves, brown betty, coups de foudre, digenesis"

Ex. 1: **Geotropes** *(cont'd)*

iv

enclosed. (dynamo.) archivolt. to be fully silent:
:malignant boscage (non-sectile). "unstressed chanting"
byzantine feet, bare-sided theorem: quick members:

:enamored either asparagine, one harsh skilling
　　　　dancetté-ad-quem cunner (or similar instrument):
:fiddleback; moline; billety: components of the arcana

hodos/orthicon's jetztzeit. sclerocambiate:
:weathered which your voice to the surface - grid of ear
this harmonic tells north a light; clot felsic aspect:

:ywis blanc cracker. *amonachist epanoleptics.* ionophore:

images for all my own musical scores, on the assumption that if I don't deal with the matter to something approaching my own satisfaction, then anyone else would be even less capable of doing it for me), it is not often that this aspect assumes such a degree of structural autonomy as is true, for instance, of the score-like visual aspect of "STAGGER". Looking back over texts written before the advent of the computer in my life, on the other hand, I do discern an increased incorporation of spatial or other typographic means of articulating different text strata since the change in work habits.

JS: Your work for solo percussionist, **Bone Alphabet,** includes what you have called "practice sessions", passages in which the errors and frustrations of a performer's practice time are composed directly into the musical score itself. I get the feeling that there are events which occur "accidentally on purpose" in your texts as well.

BF: Of course there are always aspects of writing which get "out of control". This is not, per se, a bad thing. Often striking conjunctions or oppositions emerge from different but converging tendencies given their head, as it were. Also, the particular aspect of practice featured in **Bone Alphabet,** the multiple "imperfect" repetition of a single figure, has its correspondence in some of my texts, particularly those which take alternative "runs" at animating a common formal frame. Even the writings of Adorno work pretty much in an analogous fashion, with the writer clearly spiralling in around a core meaning, the future existence of which requires a leap of faith in the present. The motion itself is part of the meaning.

* * *

JS: Even a hasty examination of **Syntacticon, Practique, Palimpsests,** the **Two Works** and **Geotropes** reveals enormous contrasts, both within and between them, in terms of both signification and the verbal modalities employed. Could you discuss the different underlying impulses, techniques and goals which distinguish these works?

BF: We'd have to begin with **Practique**, not only because it is the earliest text of this group, but because of its status (as the title implies) as something of a hybrid of theoretical/speculative tract and exemplificatory embellishment. Its dates (1987-90) give some idea of the lengthy gestation process involved. It began life as a rather homogeneous "long poem", but was laid aside before completion because of dissatisfaction with the formal aspect. Several subsequent passes through the material resulted in its segmentation and in the insertion of several strands of distinct "satellite texts" set off by personalized typographic compartmentalization, some of which appear as undigested "chunks", others being themselves broken up and interspersed at intervals into the growing body of the main text, either as brief formal markers or as concretizations of contextually germane theoretical concerns. Thinking back, it occurs to me that I adopted a strikingly similar approach to one of my earliest major compositions, the **Sonatas for String Quartet** of 1967. There, too, I began with a group of quite lengthy continuous movements, only to conclude that, in order to achieve the intended duration of almost 3/4 of an hour, I would have to fragment these (as it seemed then) spuriously continuous entities into a much larger number of interlinked "islands", structures too small and contingent to stand alone, but too discontinuous to be misinterpreted as reforming into larger contiguous blocks. Particularly important to this process were two facts; firstly, that the fragments were re-ordered in a way no longer conforming to the order of their original inception and, secondly, that many new linking elements were created in order to effectively handle the middleground formal continuity. This combination of the rigorously organized and contingently discursive, of successive layers of commentary and re-articulation, proved extraordinarily fruitful at the time, although I have never returned to it in my subsequent musical development. It is interesting to consider the possibility that **Practique** is a distant relative of that experience. (Example 2.)

JS: Of the five texts discussed here, **Practique** maintains the closest links to traditional narrative format: unlike the **Two Works**, for instance, **Practique** includes straightforward declarative statements. At the same time, the figures of demotic speech are routinely warped, "defamiliarized". Could you discuss the "real poetics" which this text attempts to articulate?

BF: It's difficult to warm to the idea of explaining the "real content" of something that either succeeds or fails by the degree to which it manages to avoid making the vehicle/content distinction. Even the more explicitly "theoretical" sections are not to be understood apart from their poetic embedding. It's true that the form of the declarative sentence is frequently observed, but that is really a question of perspective rather than fundamentally distinct modes of communication; the sort of dissonant framing relationship set up between words on one level of writing is transferred to that between phrases on another. One sees this extremely clearly, for example, in the works of Gertrude Stein: on the one hand you find the intense, word-to-word eyeballing of **Tender Buttons**, on the other the oceanic spaces and hypnotic repetitions of her longer texts. There is no contradiction, to my mind, between these extremes, since a continuous transition between them is perfectly conceivable.

If there were any central "poetics" to be extracted from **Practique**, it would have to be something to do with how the fragment might continue to

Ex. 2: **Practique**

The demand. Totality (not having attained our gaze) assumes
(Qua levelling) an object. At this point we're flush with
Divers injunctions, appeal a classic sentiment *fra quattro occhi.*

And code's honor (our personalized *negatio*) draws tension
As well - the monad, the text. Availability is our social null's
New hero: let's compartmentalize *as a consequence of the case!*

Given: an arrival, the "natural" togged-up as "Being" like some
Flatulent Transducer of the common-or-garden Divine (yet
Not the coolth of a frame). Speechless indeed; that old eclipse

Is all on the downside, a moldy spell for an abacus, our ever-
Ready font of common demotic travails. The veritable signcrime
Is not, *hauptsächlich*, akin to a homecoming, causal tissue at one.

The cluttered guillotine for all those flights: a geneology of what?
Emendations - more a matter of form than you, I'm measured
By plane surface. At least the grisly entanglement is much of a

Solo act! And so we mumble a bony logic, our consolatory
"subject"
At most that regulatory loop, the final clunk of nerves at all
Centers. What's in a preface. A power.

      A real poetics - more than was made
      In species adaptation of a question
      With different preponderances (as
      Well as shifting related issues to the
      Obverse). Rigor mortis is put forward
      imbued with many weeks of neuro-
      Logical giants, not by some primary
      Substance. Synthesized by a specific
      Craftsman, you can call it a "presentation" -
      A call against paralysis, even more shameless.

      NEBST bullion | 'Classic Dive'
      Mi. t. Butter
      | inst I - (l) tHESe
      (plainst - S) I = 'in the grou(...) :d?

fulfill a particular role in present-day writing, that is, how its incompleteness might be a positive agent in maintaining and regulating conflicting streams of energy. I doubt if I would express myself much differently in terms of my musical intentions, even though one hopes that the sum of one's activities resists reductionist compartmentalization.

JS: You've twice now mentioned the importance of the fragment in your overall vision of composition, musical and poetic.

BF: There is an entire 18th/19th century genre of the romantic fragment, particularly in Germanic cultures. In fact, it is still powerfully present — witness the reception of the more recent Nono, for example, with his evocation of Hölderlin in the string quartet, **Fragmente-Stille, an Diotima**, or the "almost-absence" and intended provisionality of his recent opera, **Prometeo**. Some of the most influential writings of recent years have been basically hypothetical projections of a never-to-be-written work, like the remarkable **Passagenwerk** notebooks of Walter Benjamin. There is perhaps something about our century which is deeply distrustful of too-perfect statements of completion as being oppressively monumental, impervious. As for me, I have tended to focus on the interruptive nature of the fragment as constituting one of the main distinctions between the Modern and subsequent periods — I'm thinking of Eliot's **Wasteland**, for instance, where the sudden disjunctions are really jarring and contextually dissonant, because clearly predicated on the implicit assumption (or, at least, possibility) of more extensive notional wholes. In a similar way, I tend to use the interruption or disruptive transformation of deliberately established musical tendencies as means of accumulating and dispersing informational energies. One might see this as a form of replacement for the periodic striation typical of much classical period music as a means of distinguishing *speed* from *density*.

JS: What were your main concerns with **Palimpsests**?

BF: The sort of "rewriting" that I engaged in in **Practique** soon transformed itself into "overwriting" in **Palimpsests**, in that the inventive process applied itself, for the most part, to pages already inscripted, already to some extent pre-configured. By that I mean that the interleaving techniques applied to the former work found much more extensive and detailed application in the latter; a single passage might represent a considerable number of modificatory / amplificatory passes through the continually accreting body of text, thus enriching it according to often quite different procedural considerations. As the largest work I have attempted to date (1992), **Palimpsests** approaches form almost from the opposite direction to **Practique**; where the latter applied the infolding technique on practically all levels (thus creating, as it were, a natural carapace for itself), the later text evolved within the framing constraints of a fixed, preordained macrostructural scheme. For one thing, this meant that an interesting and challenging divide opened up between larger dispositional conventions and individual instantiations of locally contextualized invention. Although this made the smooth transition from level to level of the discourse more uneven and problematic, it enabled me to incorporate a wider spectrum of middleground stylistic and formal "voicings" than might have been feasible in a more "fractally" organized context. Also, the central formal device, that of dividing up the work in ten "books", each containing one less distinct text component than the preceding book while occupying approximately the same number of pages (15), in practice provided a wealth of "perspectival" variation at the same time as progressively constraining me to define formal layouts of ever larger dimensions.

At the same time there takes place another, equally significant, transformation, which is the progressive extension of the scope of linguistic usage to encompass elements adapted from a number of languages other than English, historical forms, Proto-Indoeuropean word roots and combinatorially-generated vocables akin to the evocational quality of Khlebnikov's *zaum* aesthetic.[16] This panlinguistic drive has been one I have pursued elsewhere, notably in the "fictive *heimat*" of "Fureur"; in this particular instance I understood it as one indirect manifestation of the implicitly diachronic aspect of palimpsest technique. (Example 3.)

JS: Sections of your texts display what one might call typographical fetishes or "syncopations". For instance, many of the words on page 128 of **Palimpsests** feature first and last letters in upper case, with their interiors in lower case. I haven't been able to detect any "structural" function for this practice, such as a hinting at palindromic construction, or the definition of an embedded verbal layer. Can one assume, then, that any meaning implied by this practice exists in a "critical" sense?

BF: Through spending so many years intimately involved with German language and — inevitably — thought, I came to appreciate the tremendous weight of presence generated by the capitalization of substantives. Although a lot of my texts are devoid of capitalization, I decided to go to the other extreme in **Palimpsests** by capitalizing every word, emphasizing its solidity, its immobility, its tactility. The passage you mention is one of several in which the invisible forces exercised on these monadic entities are rendered palpable; the end capitalization blocks off progress, throws the lines back in on themselves, "imprisons" them, with the result that their content is set into chaotic motion by rebounding at various angles off these obstacles. Similar processes are operative in my music, as witness the title of my seven-piece cycle, **Carceri d'invenzione**. Your employment of the term "syncopations", implying, as it

Ex. 3: **Palimpsests**

Nigh Light Pathé
Piths, One's Fat Ruin
Chow: All Lanes.
Densely Rather; Chafe-
Tined. It May Shade
New (Whose Titter?)
There, Wieso?
See Feebly:

Alter, Narrate Rag-
Ing Moor!
Guess-Hate Sower,
Belled Road Bemock.
Real Candour. This
Sin Lives.
A Pager-Ace 'Et Iro' Item
Messer Ebbs, By Rhyme.

More, Funny Agar; Ever
Deli. Fight Up A Tizzy
Simo Mit Dem 'A'.
Red Ik Het. La Bonne Eco.
Seralem Reger, Rougher
Ether: Salt-Rat-Neo-Upper
Rev Or - Ugh!
Paben Rekch Then

Ingan Eno. Wed Riga,
Bedlar-Gina Sello
Drallma Offot?
Uk Oyan Thay, Eréd Vers Y Machreb.
Mieatméh! Oer-
Srah IfMlages: Sat-
Weapys. Lali
Silat Çisnat.

Ex. 3: **Palimpsests** *(cont'd)*

Throeme Fâla Treorü.
Noghtla Pezs Zhi Dröp-
Stunis
E
Füyr Onch Wéll Liens
Syddinla
Dzi Chéréctir Uf
Dôvonta.

Öém Ço
Sheduw Whin;
Sümüni.
Fells, Üthirwösi Vos-
Ob/la Feltirüng.
Eryund Thö
Rúúm.
I Gæost Hyasö Wüzh

Dyåblø:Dyyrß
Bocymós Çlôir Ind Thön
Uß-Ovül.
Attüny-Vó Schûmi Çanvelßyanz
Tå Swøhlaw
Zhu Fa'ad Row, Thy.
Anfliynt'zyêf Ubsiløty Selença'a
(En Çømmåß'Mµb'h Øæq?)

&%*BBπ'ßOui (98) åßü
Rå§°µ/≤≥,..."quek"
~"≠≠! JE∞"d",-_O.
¶¢5%fi ._—<M^1 ß>{}
aaa...FÏÓ Ø1 ÅÍ*,/0.±ff.
SËIOØ0 (45.6B) B'Åxer ¿AD '®?
åß...H©o ßœui,//sFFs.^^††
©å®ß ßß!ø¥#,^^ø^"Iø;"ß~".

Ex. 4: **Palimpsests**

/ THAT THE
MIND IS INDIFFERENT BEFORE IT COMES TO HAVE
A CHOICE/

Moche Sorywe, Gret
Labour Thorow The
Wrytinge Penne.

Space To Land Our Backs Be Broak
The Honey Has Been Replaced.

TheE RecitatioN OF SucH CheepE

AnD PoorE StufF

AlwayS PosturE-MakinG

CoaxinG anD Im-

PlorinG

SwellS

UntO ThE

RattlE.

PlanT BuntingS

LeafgrinD

TwizzlE

ZeuG

BlippinG LandschafT

PookS

does, the delay or anticipation of an action with regard to some immanent pattern of referential striation, is very appropriate to such situations. (Example 4.)

JS: Could you comment on the footnotes, with artificial citations, which appear in Books VIII and IX?

BF: That's just a personal reaction to fifteen years' worth of exposure to German dissertations! There are other purposes envisaged, of course, one of which would be the further stretching of the theory/praxis tension which has already been pushed quite far by that point in the work. In a sense, it's the inevitable bursting of the overstretched balloon and its dissolution into clerkly ribaldry, much as one imagines scurrilous monks weaving obscene images into dark corners of their manuscript illuminations. (Example 5.)

JS: The **Two Works** date from the same period as **Palimpsests**, don't they?

BF: Yes, but I consider them as conceptually quite distinct. Each component of this highly polarized work is made up of a sequence of brief (none longer than a single page, some much shorter) items, conjoined by a common approach to the basic underlying definitional idea. Other than that, both components of the **Two Works**, "STAGGER" and "Fureur", are allied only by their complete incompatibility — rather, in a sense, like the two "negatively mirrored" movements of my **Third String Quartet** of 1987.

In retrospect, I see this Manichean duality as reflecting the "inner" and "outer" aspects of my compulsively expatriate way of living. In particular, the chaotically multilinguistic patois of "Fureur" is an evocation of the paradoxical sense of transnational cultural identity evinced by some areas of Europe, such as the *Dreiländereck* encompassing German Switzerland, South Baden and Elsass, seen as a ghostly "atopic" paradigm of personal roots. I suppose that most of my writing has somehow to do with "place" in these terms.

JS: Is this the sort of "manifesting forth" of personal meaning from material that you discussed earlier?

BF: Over the long haul I like to think that some of this will get across, yes. (Example 6.)

JS: One finds it difficult to imagine an oral rendition of the **Two Works**, at least by a single unenhanced reader. How do you intend them to be "performed"?

Ex. 5: **Palimpsests**

IF   (BY   WAY

OF   PERCENTAGE)

THE   BRAIN   DID

NOT   SCRUPLE   TO

RUIN,   IN   EVERY

RESPECT,   A   CONK

TELLING   FACTS

WAS   HÖLLER'S16

SECRETLY,   AS

WOODSMEN   SUB-

LIME.

5)
    I AM THE WHITE BROOK THAT HAS
BEEN SMALLER AROUND YOU17
        *

---

[16] Jakobus Höller, Fl. 1780, Best Known For His Lengthy Celebration Of Exotic Cultures (See: *Not Withstanding My Papuan Pelts If The Leaves Faded,* Gothenburg 1783-5), In Particular The Passage Beginning: "Spore's Vodka In Careful Winter Threes/ Old-Age Mushroom, Brown Stains / And A Graper's Wooden Nose" (Transl. By The Present Editor), Much Anthologized.

[17]   A More Recent Adage. The Influence Of The Alciatian *Emblemum* Is Widely Accepted In This Popular Collection, Even Though Associated Images Are At Best Conjectural.

Ex. 5: **Palimpsests** *(cont'd)*

THE FORCE OF TOTALLY BLOCKED
NOSTRILS.
  *

THERE   WAS   NOTHING   PASTED
IRREVOCABLY   TO   THE   THICKENING
FLAKES.
  *

MY GONG[18] - YOUR PANUFNIK.
  *

I   DO   NOT   SICKENING   SOON
AFTER.
  *

FRESH   COFFEE   FROM   CLAMPED
PEAS   COULD   BE   SIGNIFICANTLY[19]
BETTER MANAGED.
  *

WITHSTOOD   OUT   HERE   HE
THOUGHT.
  *

THIS   BURST   HOMINID   HAS
PERFECT TONSURES.
  *

MELBLENNY[20]   CAROB   TUNES
CLUB-SERIES EVER WAS.

---

[18] Follantic Posture-Fowl, Treading Water. Glissades. A Pound For A Precept.
[19] *The Hooker & Her Hernia*, As Sung By Padishah Oscine In The 1st Draft of
Vico's Seminal *Lean Flanks Or: Slurth Postperidian - Matched Biota.*
[20] My Spelling.

Ex. 5: **Palimpsests** *(cont'd)*

*

TOUJOURS[21]   PREGNABLE,
NOZZLE?
*

KNEEBOULDERS   UPGRADED[22]
FLINCH[23].
*

WHENEVER   IT[24]   CAME   TO
SOMEONE'S   ROLLMOPS   REVESTED
GALL'S ARTERIALS.
*

THE   AVERTED   WERE   MOST
OFTEN SLOWLY SPICED[25].

---

[21] "Snivel" In The Original.

[22] Hence Efficacious Complexion Will Breach Any Substandard "Edelweiß"
Diaphragm.

[23] "Ptisians' Relay
Emunct Evolver
Open to Pre-
Emptive Churching
Weal-Ligule On
That Foxy Dormant Mon-
Grel of Yours."

[24] No Longer Nostalgia To Wake Up By. The Harmony Of Faculties Sends One
Back To The Kantian Political Schema, Thereby Re-Creating A Form Of "Hidden
Check". The Problem Of Liberal Theory Is A Brilliant If Grisly Example Of The
Active Mediation Of "Vaporization" With Respect To The Titillation Of Crucial
Target Mirrors.   Verifiers And Regulators Could Not Bear To Be In Radical
Decline, Lest They Perish With Us In The Guise of "Sign Crimes".

[25] Æsthetic Symmetry / Crucifixion / English Sum / Hnecca / Kick-A-Feind /
Snocket / We Ourselves Blood / Jelliform Alluvion Zarnicka / Monoclinously
Lot / Filaria Tonghe Climate Conning / Ell / Mentally Similar / *Vorlage
Redivivus* / Ovibos Nay Arthritical / Classless Bilanders / Osmosis, As It Did
With The *Arché* Of Nature (There Were Rhodedendrons Lurking in the Drapes).

Ex. 6: **Two Works**

I

"STAGGER"

SUDane*

se STAGGER. *the*

> *shrew was*

True ("VAC"-riat:a [α

> STIRRING

\\ {Of rawa}]]L][p"

INdi)) ... their

> ,'apache landl' A.D.-

YSMO-Oth *[H]*

A.B.A.B.A-ch.i.c.k.l.e. [.[

> ... ...

UNCOORDINATED u.s.

= *orchid* | c-, A-,

bbagebridgel\/

GAL // ... "to swallow

the G -

> UNGE[[! {?}]./

/ /;;;

> *...was a period of extende=*

d (suspended)

> minatory mARLI tE,,"]

Ex. 6: **Two Works** *(cont'd)*

II

"fureur"

transnegatio: l'ennache di bollana plus fort, bilder quinata, determibiles succonata anale; mousou lows a-laufen sanui ave unto stones, tonung men-ning wahrodente, plus abnehmung: wait! a sou! besache minionen vonvec isa-siva (nata ab ended indeterminar kombombes), "the kript".

BF: Interestingly enough, there is quite a tradition of "silent music", ranging from puzzle canons up to the extensive "conceptual scores" for inner performance included in Dieter Schnebel's **MO-NO: Musik zum Lesen**, and many more extreme aleatoric scores approach the condition of painting and can be appreciated in those terms. It is thus not problematic to me that live performance of **Two Works** is unlikely. On the other hand, I feel that "Fureur" could well be aurally interpreted, given an appropriate background in the several languages involved. Making the "disembodied" interpunctuation of "STAGGER" performatively explicit would, I feel, illicitly limit the liberty of the individual reader to traverse the labyrinths visually set up. If I had wanted to make a verbally-orientated performance work (along the lines of Cage's **Mesostics**, for instance), I would have approached the task quite differently.

JS: The **Two Works**, then, need not be considered as a unit?

BF: No, even though each gains something from the conjunction, I think, especially "Fureur", which is clearly the more context-dependent of the two. One really should sense it as a liminar instance whose nature is in part defined by the opposite pole of "STAGGER"'s relatively autochthonous stance.

JS: Your use of typography in "STAGGER" is particularly varied and *extreme*. What role do you conceive for this element in your work?

BF: A dual role, really — both in and out of time. As I said earlier, specific spatial distributions of text blocks serve as preliminary architectonic indices of notional contiguity, function or relationship. This is the out of time aspect. Parts of **Practique** clearly conform to this precept. Other works (i.e. "STAGGER") use typography more as a form of musical notation, where the temporal flow of the reading experience is modulated by means of what might be seen as a complex array of interlinked obstacles or deflectors. In music we often speak of "prolongation technique" — the means whereby a situation may be coherently projected into the future of the discourse — and one might, I suppose, extend this to the sort of disruptive or combinatorial tactics employed in these texts to "energize" the fractured continuum of their reading according to often conflicting sets of vectors. (Example 7.)

Of the five works you ask about, **Syntacticon** approaches most closely the customary idea of a "poetry collection", to the extent that it is composed of a number of diverse, relatively independent texts. Even so, though, the two framing items, "BULK PRONUNCIATION" and the title text, "SYNTACTICON", itself, make up considerably more than half the total volume, so that everything else needs must be read in terms of the field of tensions generated by these two poles.

Ex. 7: **Two Works - "STAGGER"**

The (s) Cite] / ' ##@telestitch@ : To -

NN # *E*

They "forsworn cutter" LIKE `hei-[mmm...]

...[?] [~] At-of-Utgård ≠ !OVER=

   Pow'ring Heimdall's

TIM [tw/]]b!/-

     ALE-i-[c)]h (her) 'struGGL(A...]]le-

R : DEMIS : T : Line o : f

  Bone' 's' 'hak (*+[K=[

    eR [?

+++=====*claque* - / / #[p r i / m /(+)
   ROSE"

JS: Speaking of poles, I recall emerging from my first reading of "BULK PRONUNCIATION" into an intensely bifurcated atmosphere, in which seemingly random pairs from life's subjects and categories could find themselves locked within potent fields of opposition. In that sense the experience was almost hallucinatory, as startlingly random negative connections were "discovered", one by one.

BF: It's often been noted, in fact, that I tend to rely on structural/conceptual dualities when organizing musical materials, processes or forms. It's also true, though, that I get very impatient with oversimple applications of this type of thinking, since, in reality, musical perception is seldom a question of "either-or", even in the most polarized of situations; there are simply too many variables. I find it more useful to think in terms of perceptual categories, by which I mean mental drawers whose contents, while *grosso modo* defined, can be expanded or refocused at will, and whose function is thus not limited to linear motion along a sole axis, even though interrupted or re-channeled linear tendencies form, in practice, the fundamental articulational means for defining larger constellations.

The rather crudely dichotomous situation set up at the beginning of "BULK PRONUNCIATION" was intended as a stable pivot, to which could be anchored even the most various and sudden swerves of direction. That's why, in the first of the three sections, the superscript and text tend to have approximately the same weight, while later, in the final section, there is usually an extremely evident disbalance, with the superscript relegated to something approaching a trigger (and perhaps also framing) function by the increasingly independent and elaborated texts.

One other possible germane point apropos of this particular work is the influence of the Baroque emblem, with its melange of alchemical symbol (the mystical overcoming of duality in the *conjunctio oppositorum*), and visual and literary puzzle. I had spent some time in the '70's studying historical and theoretical alchemy and had actually composed a piano piece in 1980 (**Lemma-Icon-Epigram**) which makes reference to the tripartite emblem format, so it seems natural to me to employ the dynamic energy radiated by any irreconcilable duality in the utopian task of attempting just that reconciliation. (Example 8.)

JS: Only a few renegade poets have been willing to explore the extremes of discordant sonic possibility in English (and, more generally, Germanic) language. Could you address sonic aspects of passages such as the following, from "BULK PRONUNCIATION"?

"(5)   UBIQUITY PODTEKST
        former stirrup-blème by instrumentals upper jowl"

Ex. 8: **Syntacticon : "BULK PRONUNCIATION"**

I

(1)   BULK PRONUNCIATION
         lucy bullet coupable of campania

(2)   GROUND: FOG IN THE GROOVE
         a chewed one become at low knee

(3)   LABIOVELAR AFAR CUCKOO
         large dark lobed spots

(4)   FRUITS LODGING LETTRISTES
         some scotiae commonly bends overall incline into steam

Ex. 8: **Syntacticon** : **"BULK PRONUNCIATION"** *(cont'd)*

II

(1) GESTALT:
>   supposed as her high boots (absente reo)
>   being daring, which even in getting them
>   was another self's son-o'-one's classic
>   praxis. father chandler is, to his text, a
>   segment of this ordo, his glatt sentences.

(2) DERVISH:
>   the world-object stitched-up the
>   edges, frayed by construction? smart-
>   breathy! "that's how we come to perspective,
>   like weighing out a horse pill."

(3) SPEED:
>   exactly corresponding: dry air: and three
>   chalk cliffs astride - those personalia.

(4) FLATTENING OF STEMS:
>   the tin can where we walked a moment ago is
>   telling us: fireworks are extremely separated by
>   melts in the memory, their whirlybird- augment,
>   attracted by the scriptive reek of rain.

Ex. 8: **Syntacticon : "BULK PRONUNCIATION"** *(cont'd)*

III

(1) ENTERTAINMENT WHITE CEMENT:
                              part unfair
                              its trunk has
              rat-play.
              "qu'est-ce qu' écrire?"
                                          (1) babble of glib/
                                     (2) celebration/
                                  (3) within antenna/
                       (4) man-work concealed / at the same time...

(2) LICENTIOUS MAJORITY:
                          :does misprision metaphor into a dead one?
          freezing our first
          hint - lalangue::
          neutral 's' & 'z', the same doth admixture (pressed
                          into service.) beaded with bubbles.
                                   "elementary pegs,
                                   possessed by new rays."

(3) ZEUGMA:
                                          {reason: like:
                                          a: wet:
                                                  drum:}

(4) BOLINGER'S VARIABLES:
              coupe d'essence / star latine.
                     little substance "at the violet hour".
                            baffles causa sui:: universal
                                   grammar (like:
              [schraube];[svartik];[rugger];[jasmin];)
              ...and concludes at last on the frontier between positions 2 & 3.

"(33) PANDECT DISPUTE WEB AS COULD BRUIT
introslaked stalwart bracting project bad briary"

BF: I said earlier that I was attracted to the robustly earthy accent of Northern English poets like Basil Bunting, whose language remains deeply imbued with the Germanic vocabulary and love of heroic alliteration characteristic of much Danelaw literature. There are parts of his **Briggflats** where this graven quality really comes to the fore.[17] The name Ferneyhough itself is said to be evidence of Nordic origin, and I like to think that something of my assumed ancestry has rubbed off on me, if only via an exaggeratedly devious route. I remember my maternal grandmother employing what I now know to be a relatively exotic and sonically fluid regional dialect and vocabulary, for instance, although I can no longer recall specifics. It is difficult to imagine that much of that diversity now survives in the age of mass communication and "BBC English", even though some Irish poets retain a chiselled ruggedness of a similar sort.

JS: The considerable concentration and physical effort required to simply say these lines reminds me of the way your musical compositions engage and challenge performers at every level.

BF: I'm sure that some of my experiences of the niceties of notational/performative musical praxis have slipped into the way I inwardly recite my texts. On the other hand, I *don't* really imagine these same aspects as being literally realized in live performance; they represent something more akin to a material-immanent, internalized metronome, pacing one's own rate of reception.

JS: And, finally, what are **Geotropes**?

BF: Geotropic flora are plants whose patterns of growth are orientated to the force of gravity. My idea here was to plan a rigorously arbitrary overall form of four times four single-page texts, the blocks of four pages being separated by two-page sequences of shorter texts, or "minor doabs". Although the origins and internal structural criteria of each block of texts were quite diverse, I wanted them all to share the quality of adjusting themselves to the given overall constraints, which thus assume some of the characteristics of "laws of nature." Just as chaotic recursivity gives rise to natural phenomena of vast variety within recognizably consistent frames, so this little work begins an investigation of related possibilities in art which I hope to continue. (Example 9.)

* * *

Ex. 9: **Geotropes**

minor doabs

i

:globose belay coz re-
voice - "juice of
moose" (intrados):

ii

:perforce trice-nose
(of inner ear
by chine):

iii

:accord de strat-
us' over-
hasp (who timed pres-
sure, the "nicaraguan koan"):

Ex. 9: **Geotropes** *(cont'd)*

iv

:rhotic
unborn pin-
wheel eye; men-
conium's ergot brain-
minister'd fleisch. (out-
growth.) "mons laminaria":

v

:cocoyam dink-
um sphere boule:

vi

:of timber. kepi
escapee; dis-
gust. o
dulce dilation periapt!
(holding, soapy, zo):

Ex. 10: **Palimpsests**

The Least Feature Of The Square
Is Only One Stable Ref-
Erence Point, A Swifter Lo-
Cus Constituting Infor-
Mally Entropic Taxi-
Nomics. Already Tending To
"Expression", The Privileged
Object Is A Form Of U-
Tilitarian Trope In

Possible States Of Confusion.
Just As Each Specific Space Is
Flagged By Strategies Of "Proper
Being" (Such As An Articu-
Late Representation Of Scar-
City Over Certain Concealed Found-
Ations), So Inflection Repre-
Sents A Foil To Pressure, The En-
Unciated Energy Val-

Ue Of Things. Let's Reverse The Double-
Take On This Topic: Unless Techniques Ex-
Ist For Locating The Chimera's
Private Lexicon, The Starting-Point
Can't Be Maintained. Only By Virtue Of
Slanted (Demotic?) Shifts Will The Space Of Or-
Der Be Co-Extensive. Organisms Ar-
Rest Frontiers (Or Denounce Them As
Alien Molds Of Thought - The Same Thing);

Where A Word As Such Belongs Is Up To
Its Own Internal Calendar. At Last, Know-
Ledge Of This Neoparticularist Set
Is Grounded In Doubled-Over An-

Ex. 10: **Palimpsests** *(cont'd)*

Teriority, Its Inadequation Reveal-
Ed In The Manifold Of Viable Matrices
Supervening On Each Internalized Seg-
Ment's Intellectual Musculature.
Establishing A Constant Measure (Like

Shells' Teguments) Is Never The Sole Ob-
Ject Of Production. With The Eruption
Of Binding Fragmentation Comes the Pros-
Pect Of Representational Disorders
(Qua Grids, Harmonic Hierarchies, Thumbnail
Vectors & The Like). From Some Moment On,
These Crosscurrents Hove Like Prototypic
Veins, Spurting Contestation, Seeding Faults
Between Exempla Of "Natural Law" &

The Basic Framework Of (Suspended)
Relational Discourse. Qui Parle?
Indeed! Combinations Are Con-
Stituted, After All, Elsewhere, Through
Listings Replete With Scads of Loga-
Rithmic Mathesis & Its Droppings.
In/Outside: Shepherd's Delight. Glass
Jars & Vegetative Structures Most
Often Swat The Bioesthet-

Ics Of General Theory (Pro-
Duction "As Constant Blur"). In End-
Effect, Where Gangrene's Set in Bet-
Ween Hoe & Sod, There's Precious Lit-
Tle Call For "Fierce Suspension". A Reg-
Ion Much Inhabited By Rat-
Tling Skeletons Of the Heter-
Onomous Won't Wait "For The Next
Train Along" -A Very Human

Ex. 10: **Palimpsests** *(cont'd)*

Attitude! So It Ever Goes
With The Tat's Apriori Pig-
Ments. Two Models Might Think As
They Normally Feel: No Beg-
Inning With Bases In Limits To
Possible Speech! *Our* Axes Are:
"Fictional Mechanisms" & "Ex-
Terior (Bipolar) Reduplicat-
Ion Of Enigmatic Mono-

Syllables". As Subservient Shards, Their Present
Epistemes Are Nonlocatable
Sets (Through And Through The Flesh Of Co-
Extensive Events). Did You? So Then A Volume
In Disintegration, Like: "Rooms By The Sea". In
"Time And History" The Weather Is More Of
A Tautological Law Than A Downward Spiral.
Bullseye! Delusion Is "Mood Furniture" To
Some Social Herd: "I *Won't* Think Bad Thoughts!

Depression Comes From Words, From Nothing Else.
               A Most Unfriendly Town Was Gone Into Snow-Covered

Knees. Thoughts' "L'Abacus" Resolved Pilot Content As You Found It,
               Elementary Geklapper & All.

JS: In David Cronenberg's **The Fly**, the main character believes himself improved, cleansed at the atomic level, after his body is digitized and recombined in a matter transporter of his own design. Your title, **Syntacticon,** with its associated, rather monumentally encyclopedic text, which seems desperate to "get it all down", perhaps suggests a similar stance: that the creator is remade, re-created by his or her own invention.

BF: I suppose that there's something of the good Count Frankenstein in all of us! I mentioned earlier the ruling idea of *heimat*, of that peculiarly German conflation of homeland and home hearth, which is something always before my mind's eye as a counter-instance to the prevailing nomadic deracination of present sensibility forming current coin in most post-Heideggerian philosophies. Somewhere in **Mille Plateaux**, Deleuze and Guattari speak of something similar when they describe personal habitat — home — as a circular, enclosed protective space which is capable of controlled aperture to the outside world at a preselected point along its circumference.[18] It is perhaps this controlled deterritorialization of subjective space which I am aiming at most consciously in my writing; certainly I chose the title of **Syntacticon** with a view to suggesting the disciplined enumerations of the defining vectors of an entire verbal environment. (Example 10.)

Endnotes

(Notes marked [BF] are partly or wholly by Brian Ferneyhough; the remainder are by Jeffrey Stadelman)

1. Although none of the texts discussed in this interview are currently available commercially, arrangements are being made for them to be published. Further information about Ferneyhough's texts and their availability may be had by writing to Peters Edition Ltd., 10-12 Baches Street, London N1 6DN UK.

2. Charles Bernstein, **Artifice of Absorption,** *in* Paper Air, *Vol.4 no.1, Philadelphia 1987; reprinted in Charles Bernstein,* **A Poetics** *(Harvard University Press, Cambridge Mass. & London 1992).*

3. Steve McCaffery, **Panopticon,** *(Blewointmentpress, Toronto 1984).*

4. The works of Philippe Sollers dating from the most extreme period of Tel Quel praxis evidence an inexhaustibly fecund linguistic drive: works such as **Drame** *(Editions du Seuil, Paris 1965) and* **H** *(Editions du Seuil, Paris 1973) were perhaps most striking, as were a number of his critical essays, collected in* **La Theorie d'Exceptions**.
Maurice Roche's earliest novel, **Compact,** *(Dalkey Archive Press, Elmwood Park, Illinois, 1988; translated by Mark Polizzotti) deploys various voices and perspectives, in conjunction with diverse typefaces and spatial arrangements, with a view to "polyphonicizing" reading experience.*

Jean Ricardou, the foremost theoretician of the nouveau roman *has published a number of original works of fiction embodying many of his views on the linguistic self-engenderment of significance, notably in* **Les Lieux-Dits,** *(Gallimard, Paris 1972) and* **La Prise de Constantinople,** *(Editions de Minuit, Paris 1965). [BF]*

5. *Clark Coolidge,* **Space** *(Harper and Row, New York 1970).*

6. *See for instance* **Wobbling,** *(Segue Foundation, New York, 1981).*

7. *Many of the typical concerns of the second-generation postwar avant-garde, such as permutation, found objects and late-Wittgenstein orientated "language games" are extensively mobilized in the series of* **Textbücher** *by Helmut Heißenbüttel (Klett-Cotta, Stuttgart, 1980-).*
   A commentated selection from his works was made by the author himself in Oskar Pastior **Jalousien aufgemacht** *(Carl Hanser Verlag, Munich 1987).*
   Works by Ernst Jandl, Gerhard Rühm, Friederike Mayröcker, Konrad Bayer and others have been translated by Rosemarie Waldrop and Harriet Watts in **Six Major Austrian Poets: The Vienna Group** *(Station Hill Press, Barrytown NY, 1985).*
   Along with some of her many radiophonic plays, Friederike Mayröcker's early "assemblages" like **Fantom Fan** *and* **Minimonsters Traumlexikon** *are especially interesting. They are available in* **Gesammelte Prosa,** *(Suhrkamp Verlag, Frankfurt am Main, 1989). [BF]*

8. *Influential among the works of Konrad Bayer were* **der vogel singt, eine dichtungsmachine in 571 bestandteilen** *and the lengthy prose text* **der kopf des vitus bering,** *in Konrad Bayer,* Gesamtwerk *(Rowohlt Taschenbuch Verlag, Hamburg 1977). English speaking readers will find a representative sampling of this writer's texts in the* **Selected Works of Konrad Bayer,** *translated by Malcolm Green, (Atlas, London, 1986). [BF]*

9. *Much of Celan's later lyric poetry was notable for its extreme compression of expression, often achieved by striking neologisms. See* **Die Niemandrose** *and* **Zeitgehöft,** *both in Paul Celan,* **Gesammelte Werke** *(Suhrkamp Verlag, Frankfurt am Main, 1983). Some of his work has been strikingly rendered into English by Michael Hamburger in Paul Celan,* **Poems,** *(Persea Books, New York, 1980). [BF]*

10. *Bernd Matteus,* Jede wahre Sprache ist unverständlich *(Mattheus und Seitz Verlag, Munich, 1977).*

11. *Quoted in Maurice Nadeau,* **The History of Surrealism** *(Belknap Press, Cambridge MA, 1989, p. 89).*

12. *Brian Ferneyhough with Paul Driver, "Speaking with Tongues" (see this volume, p. 336).*

13. *Jackson Mac Low,* **Words and Ends from Ez** *(Avenue B, Bolinas, 1989).*

14. *See for instance* **Oulipo: a Primer of Potential Literature,** *trans. by Warren F. Motte, Jr. (University of Nebraska Press, Lincoln, 1986).*

15. *Arno Schmidt,* **Zettels Traum** *(S. Fischer Verlag, Frankfurt am Main, 1989).*

16. *See for instance Velimir Khlebnikov,* **The King of Time: Selected Writings of the Russian Futurian,** *trans. by Paul Schmidt and ed. by Charlotte Douglas (Harvard University Press, Cambridge MA, 1985).*

17. *Basil Bunting,* **Briggflatts** *(Fulcrum Press, London, 1966).*

18. *Gilles Deleuze and Felix Guattari,* **A Thousand Plateaus,** *trans. by Brian Massumi, (University of Minnesota Press, Minneapolis, 1987).*

CHRONOLOGICAL LIST OF COMPOSITIONS BY BRIAN FERNEYHOUGH

Year	Title/Instrumentation	Duration
1965	**Four Miniatures** flute and piano First performance: 1971, Basel Conservatoire	12'
1966	**Coloratura** oboe and piano First performance: 1972, Wezikon, Zurich Heinz Holliger and Klara Körmendi	7'
	Epigrams solo piano First performance: February 1967, Society for the Promotion of New Music, London John McCabe	7'
	Sonata two pianos First performance: October 1967, Wigmore Hall, London Philip Pilkington and Roger Smalley	14'
1966 - 67	**Three Pieces** solo piano First performance: 1968, Purcell Room, London Philip Pilkington	15'
1967	**Prometheus** fl (picc), ob, ca, Bb cl (Eb cl), hn, bsn First performance: July 1967, Mahatma Ghandi Hall, London Arradon Ensemble, conducted by Brian Ferneyhough	23'

Sonatas for String Quartet 42 ′
2 vlns, vla, vcl
First complete performance: March 1975,
Royan Festival
Berne String Quartet

1968 **Epicycle** 15 ′
twenty solo strings
First complete performance: April 1974,
Herkulessaal der Residenz, Munich
Bavarian Radio Orchestra, conducted by
Ernest Bour

1969 **Missa Brevis** 13 ′
twelve solo voices
First public performance: March 1974,
Royan Festival
Hilversum Radio Choir, conducted by
Marinus Voorberg

1970 **Cassandra's Dream Song** 10 ′
solo flute
First performance: March 1974, Royan Festival
Pierre-Yves Artaud

Sieben Sterne 15 ′
organ (2 assistants)
First performance: March 1974, Royan Festival
Bernard Foucrolle

1969 - 71 **Firecycle Beta** 23 ′
orchestra (with amplification for chamber groups)
First performance: October 1976, Venice Biennale
Hamburg Radio Symphony Orchestra, conducted
by Pesko, Ferneyhough, Eötvös, Cichewicz
and Hagen

1974 **Time and Motion Study III** 23 ′
sixteen solo voices (with perc. and electronics)
First performance: October 1975, Donaueschingen
Music Days
Schola Cantorum Stuttgart, conducted by
Clytus Gottwald

1972 - 75	**Transit** six solo voices (with amplif.) and chamber orch. First performance: March 1975, Royan Festival The London Sinfonietta and soloists, conducted by Brian Ferneyhough	45 '
1975 - 76	**Unity Capsule** solo flute First performance: March 1976, Royan Festival Pierre-Yves Artaud	14 '
1973 - 76	**Time and Motion Study II** solo cello (with electronics, 3 assistants) First performance: October 1977, Donaueschingen Music Days Werner Taube	17 - 24 '
1971 - 77	**Time and Motion Study I** solo bass clarinet First performance: March 1977, Royan Festival Harry Sparnaay	9 '
1976 - 79	**La terre est un homme** orchestra (101 players) First performance: September 1979, Musica Nova, Glasgow Scottish National Orchestra, conducted by Elgar Howarth	15 '
1969 - 80	**Funérailles I and II** 2 vlns, 2 vlas, 2 vcl, cb, hp First complete performance: June 1980, La Rochelle Festival 2E 2M Ensemble, conducted by Paul Méfano	23 '
1980	**Second String Quartet** 2 vlns, vla, vcl First performance: September 1980, South West German Radio (studio recording) Arditti String Quartet	12'

| 1981 | **Lemma-Icon-Epigram**
solo piano
First performance: June 1981,
La Rochelle Festival
Massimiliano Damerini | 14' |

Superscriptio 5'
solo piccolo
First performance: September 1982,
Venice Biennale
Roberto Fabbriciani

1982   **Carceri d'Invenzione I**   12'
chamber orchestra (16 players)
First performance: November 1982, St. John's
Smith Square, London
The London Sinfonietta, conducted by
Ronald Zollman

1983   **Adagissimo** $1\frac{3}{4}$ '
2 vlns, vla, vcl
First performance: June 1984,
La Rochelle Festival
Arditti String Quartet

1985   **Carceri d'Invenzione IIa**   14'
solo flute and chamber orchestra (20 players)
First performance: February 1985, Milan
Roberto Fabbriciani, RAI Milan Symphony
Orchestra, conducted by Marcello Panni

Carceri d'Invenzione IIb 10'
solo flute
First performance: November 1985, New York
Roberto Fabbriciani

1982 - 85   **Etudes transcendantales/Intermedio II**   27'
fl (picc/afl), ob (ca), vcl, hpsd, sop
First performance: September 1985,
Venice Biennale
Brenda Mitchell, Nieuw Ensemble Amsterdam,
conducted by Ed Spanjaard

1986	**Carceri d'Invenzione III**	12'
	15 wind instruments and percussion	
	(3 players)	
	First performance: October 1986,	
	Donaueschingen Music Days	
	South West German Radio Orchestra,	
	conducted by Arturo Tamayo	

Intermedio alla Ciaccona   7'
solo violin
First performance: October 1986, Donaueschingen
Music Days
Irvine Arditti

Mnemosyne   13'
bass flute and tape
First performance: October 1986, Donaueschingen
Music Days
Roberto Fabbriciani

1987   **Third String Quartet**   18'
2 vlns, vla, vcl
First performance: October 1987, Radio France,
Paris
Arditti String Quartet

Carceri d'Invenzione IIc   9'40"
solo flute and pre-recorded tape
First performance: April 1988, Hanover
Carin Levine

1985 - 88   **Kurze Schatten II**   13'
solo guitar
First performance: February 1990, Salle Patiño,
Geneva
Magnus Andersson

1988   **La chute d'Icare**   10'
solo clarinet and chamber ensemble
First performance: September 1988, Musica '88
Armand Angster, Nieuw Ensemble Amsterdam,
conducted by Ed Spanjaard

Fanfare for Klaus Huber 1′
two percussionsists
First performance: December 1989, Freiburg
Musikhochschule
Endemble Recherche

1989 **Trittico per Gertrude Stein** 6′
solo double bass
First performance: March 1990, Zaal De Unie,
Rotterdam
Stefano Scodanibbio

1989 - 90 **Fourth String Quartet** 20′
2 vlns, vla, vcl, sop
First performance: October 1990, Stadtcasino, Basel
Brenda Nitchell, Arditti String Quartet

1990 **Morte subite** 2′
piccolo, clarinet, vibraphone and piano
First performance: march 1990, De Doelen,
Rotterdam
Nieuw Ensemble

1991 **Bone Alphabet** 9′
solo percussionist
First performance: February 1992,
Mandeville Auditorium
University of California, San Diego
Steve Schick

1991 - 92 **Terrian** 14′
solo violin and eight instruments
First performance: April 1992, Concertgebouw,
Amsterdam
Irvine Arditti, Asko Ensemble conducted by
Jonathan Nott

1994 **On Stellar Magnitudes** 11′
Mezzo-sop, fl (picc), cl (bcl), vln, vcl, pno
First performance: September 1994,
Abbaye de Royaumont
Katherine Ciesinski, Ensemble Contrechamps

1995	**String Trio** vln, vla, vcl First performance: November 1995, Victoria Hall, Geneva Trio Contrechamps	23'
1990 - 96	**Allgebrah** oboe, nine solo strings (4 vln, 2 vla, 2 vcl, db) First performance: January 1997, Cité de la Musique, Paris Didier Pateau, Ensemble InterContemporain conducted by David Robertson	17'
1996	**Incipits** solo viola, oblig., perc, picc (b fl), e flat cl (bcl), 2 vln, vcl, db First performance: May 1997, Brisbane Mary Oliver, Elision Ensemble conducted by Christian Egger	10' 30"
1997	**Flurries** picc, cl, hn, pf, vln, vcl, pno First performance: February 1998, San Diego SONOR, conducted by John Fonville	10"
1992 - 98	**Maisons noires** 22 instruments	18'
1997 - 98	**Kranichtänze II** solo piano	
1998	**Unsichtbare Farben** solo violin	

Note: with the exception of **Firecycle Beta**, which is published by Ricordi, all of the works listed above are available from Peters Edition Ltd., London.

DISCOGRAPHY

Work	Performer(s)	Label
Prometheus	(a) Ensemble Contrechamps cond. Giorgio Bernasconi	Accord 205772 (CD)
	(b) Sonor Ensemble, cond. John Fonville	CRI CD 652 (CD)
Sonatas For String Quartet	(a) Gaudeamus String Quartet (excerpts)[¶]	Gaudeamus 69002 (LP)
	(b) Berne String Quartet	RCA Red Label RL 70610 (LP)
	(c) Arditti String Quartet	Disques Montaigne WM334 789002 (CD)
Cassandra's Dream Song	(a) Pierre-Yves Artaud	Editions Stil 31085 83 (LP)
	(b) Carin Levine	Edition Bauer (LP)
	(c) Pierre-Yves Artaud	Neuma 450-72 (CD)
	(d) Pierre-Yves Artaud	col legno WWE 1CD 31896 (CD)
	(d) Emmanuel Pahud	Musiques Suisses 6107 (CD)
Time And Motion Study III	(a) Schola Cantorum Stuttgart, cond. Clytus Gottwald	Wergo 60111 (LP)
	(b) Schola Cantorum Stuttgart, cond. Clytus Gottwald	Cadenza 800 895 (CD)

[¶]Sonatas ξ to τ (printed score pp. 40-8), then Sonata ν (pp. 38-40)

	(c) Schola Cantorum Stuttgart, cond. Clytus Gottwald	col legno WWE 1CD 31905 (CD)
Transit	London Sinfonietta, cond. Elgar Howarth	Decca Headline HEAD 18 (LP)
Unity Capsule	(a) Pierre-Yves Artaud	Editions Stil 31085 83 (LP)
	(b) Laura Chislett	Vox Australis VAST007-2 (CD)
	(c) Paula Rae	Etcetera KTC 1206 (CD)
Time And Motion Study II	(a) Werner Taube	Musicaphon BM 30 SL 1715 (LP)
	(b) Friedrich Gauwerky	Etcetera KTC 1206 (CD)
Time And Motion Study I	(a) Tommy Lundberg	Caprice FYCD 1001 (CD)
	(b) Harry Sparnaay	Attacca Babel 8945-1 (CD)
	(c) Carl Rosman	Etcetera KTC 1206 (CD)
Funérailles I & II	Ensemble InterContemporain, cond. Pierre Boulez	Erato STU 71556 (LP) Erato ECD 88261 (CD)
Second String Quartet	(a) Arditti String Quartet (b) Arditti String Quartet *(different performance)*	RCA Red Seal RL 70883 (LP) Disques Montaigne WM334 789002 (CD)
Lemma-Icon-Epigram	(a) James Avery (b) Massimiliano Damerini	Perspectives of New Music 28/2 (CD) Frequenz DAN-3 (3LP)

Superscriptio	(a) Carin Levine	Edition Bauer (LP)
	(b) Harry Starreveld	Etcetera KTC 1070 (CD)
	(c) Felix Renggli	Accord 205772 (CD)
Adagissimo	(a) Arditti String Quartet	Disques Montaigne WM334 789002 (CD)
	(b) Arditti String Quartet	col legno WWE 1CD 31896 (CD)
Carceri d'Invenzione IIb	(a) Roberto Fabbriciani	Frequenz-Koch 350-229 (CD)
	(b) Roberto Fabbriciani (*same performance*)	Arts 47167-2 (CD) 350-229 (CD)
Carceri d'Invenzione III	Ensemble Contrechamps cond. Giorgio Bernasconi	Accord 205772 (CD)
Etudes Transcendantales	Brenda Mitchell, Nieuw Ensemble, cond. Ed Spanjaard	Etcetera KTC 1070 (CD)
Intermedio alla Ciaccona	(a) Irvine Arditti	Etcetera KTC 1070 (CD)
	(b) Irvine Arditti	Disques Montaigne WM334 789003 (CD)
Mnemosyne	(a) Harrie Starreveld	Etcetera KTC 1070 (CD)
	(b) Roberto Fabbriciani	Agorà AG 113 (CD)
Third String Quartet	Arditti String Quartet	Disques Montaigne WM334 789002 (CD)
Kurze Schatten II	(a) Magnus Andersson	Disques Montaigne MO 782029 (CD)
	(b) Geoffrey Morris	Etcetera KTC 1206 (CD)

La Chute d'Icare	(a) Armand Angster, Nieuw Ensemble, cond. Ed Spanjaard	Etcetera KTC 1070 (CD)
	(b) Ernesto Molinari, Ensemble Contrechamps, cond. Giorgio Bernasconi	Accord 205772 (CD)
Trittico per Gertrude Stein	Stefano Scodanibbio	Disques Montaigne MO 782029 (CD)
Fourth String Quartet	Brenda Mitchell, Arditti String Quartet	Disques Montaigne MO 782029 (CD)
Bone Alphabet	(a) Steven Schick	Newport Classics NPD 85566 (CD)
	(b) Steven Schick	col legno WWE 1CD 31896 (CD)
	(c) Vanessa Tomlinson	Etcetera KTC 1206 (CD)
Terrain	Irvine Arditti, ASKO Ensemble cond. Jonathan Nott	Disques Montaigne MO 782029 (CD)
On Stellar Magnitudes	Luisa Castellani, Ensemble Contrechamps, cond. Giorgio Bernasconi	Accord 205772 (CD)

SOURCES

Aspects of Notational and Compositional Practice: First published, in French translation, in *Semaine de Musique Contemporaine*, Académie de France à Rome, Rome 1978.

Composer - Computer - Active Form: Written January 1980. Lecture given at the conference *Le Compositeur et l'ordinateur*, IRCAM, Paris 1981. First published, in French translation, in *Le Compositeur et l'ordinateur*, IRCAM/Centre Georges Pompidou, Paris 1981. Reprinted by permission of IRCAM.

Form - Figure - Style: An Intermediate Assessment: Written in 1982. First published, in French translation, in: *Labrys 10*, May 1984. Reprinted by permission of Schott Verlag.

Divining Rods and Lightning Conductors: a View of Composition Teaching: Written 1983, first published [as "Dowsing Rods and Lightning Conductors"], in Swedish translation, in: *Nutida Musik* iv, Stockholm 1982/83. Translated from the Italian & Swedish by the author, 1992. Reprinted by permission of the Swedish Broadcasting Corp.

Il Tempo della Figura: Written in 1984. First published, in Italian translation, in *I Quaderni della Civica Scuola di Musica*, Milan 1985. Reprinted by kind permission of Alessandro Melchiorre.

The Tactility Of Time: Lecture given at the Darmstadt Summer Courses, 1988. First published in German translation in *MusikTexte 35*, Cologne 1990.

Duration and Rhythm As Compositional Resources: Lecture given at the National Percussion Conference, Nashville 1989. Previously unpublished.

Responses to a Questionnaire on 'Complexity': First printed in *Complexity?*, edited by Joël Bons, published by JoB Press, Amsterdam in 1990.

Preface to Contemporary Composers: Written in 1992. First printed in *Contemporary Composers* (ed. Brian Morton, Pamela Collins), Gale Research International 1992. Reprinted by permission.

Parallel Universes: Paper delivered 5. 14. 1993 as part of Theory and Aesthetics Colloquium, Music Frontiers 1993, UC San Diego. Previously unpublished.

Epicycle, Missa Brevis, Time and Motion Study III: Lecture delivered at the Darmstädter Ferienkurse, 1976. Original in German. First published in: *Darmstädter Beiträge XVI*, Schott, Mainz, 1976. Present translation from the German by the author, 1992. Reprinted by permission of Schott Verlag.

Unity Capsule: An Instant Diary: Written in May 1980. First published in French translation in: *Cahier Musique No. 2*, Festival de La Rochelle, La Rochelle 1981.

Time and Motion Study II: First published in German translation, with the title **Apropos Schnitzeljagd...**, in the program book of the Donaueschinger Musiktage 1977.

Time and Motion Cycle: Notes written for the first integral performance of **Time and Motion Studies I-III** at the Huddersfield Festival, 1987.

Second String Quartet: First published in: *Cahier Musique No. 2*, Festival de la Rochelle, La Rochelle 1981.

Carceri d'Invenzione: Program notes to first performance of complete cycle at the Donaueschingen Musiktage, Donaueschingen, 17 October 1986. First published, in German translation, in: *Donaueschinger Musiktage '86*, Donaueschingen 1986.

Kurze Schatten II: Edited transcript of an impromptu talk given at the Darmstadt Summer Course, July 1990. Previously unpublished.

String Quartet No.4: Expanded transcript of remarks made during the Aesthetics Colloquium led by Ulrich Mosch and Gianmario Borrio, Darmstadt Summer Course 1992. Supplementary material has been added concerning the purely instrumental movements. Previously unpublished.

Concerning the Functional Role of Timbre in the Early Works of Anton Webern: written in Basel in 1972. Previously unpublished.

Michael Finnissy: The Piano Music: Written 1978. First published as a record sleeve insert to first recording of Finnissy's **English Country Tunes**, Ed. Richard David Hames, Victorian College of the Arts, Melbourne, Australia, 1983.

Carl Ruggles and "Dissonant Melody": First published, in Swedish translation, in *Nutida Musik iii*, 1982. Reprinted by permission of the Swedish Broadcasting Corp.

Interview with Andrew Clements (1977): First published, in Italian translation, in *I Quaderni della Civica Scuola di Musica*, Milan 1984. Reprinted by kind permission of Alessandro Melchiorre.

Interview with Joël Bons: Bilthoven, Holland, February 1982. Edited in this abbreviated form by Brian Ferneyhough, 1992. A different excerpt appeared in: *Key Notes 20* (1984). Reprinted with permission.

Interview with Paul Griffiths (1983): First published in *New Sounds, New Personalities - British Composers in the 1980s*, Faber Music, London 1985. Reprinted with permission.

Brian Ferneyhough in interview with Richard Toop (1983): First published in *Contact No. 29*, London 1985. Reprinted with permission.

Carceri d'Invenzione: Brian Ferneyhough in conversation with Richard Toop (1986): First published in *Ferneyhough, Carceri d'Invenzione*, Peters Edition, London 1987. Reprinted with permission.

Interview with Philippe Albèra: First published, in French translation, in *Contrechamps 8* (1988). Questions translated from the original French by Robert Zappulla. Reprinted by kind permission of Philippe Albèra.

Speaking with tongues - Composing for the voice: a correspondence-conversation. Brian Ferneyhough interviewed by Paul Driver. First published in *Contemporary Music Review*, Vol. 5 (1989). Reprinted with permission.

Shattering the Vessels of Received Wisdom: Brian Ferneyhough in conversation with James Boros: First published in *Perspectives of New Music* Vol. 28 No. 2, 1990. Reprinted with permission.

Interview with Jean-Baptiste Barrière: First published, in abbreviated form and in French translation, in *Inharmoniques*, Paris 1991. Reprinted by permission of IRCAM.

Interview with Antonio De Lisa: First published, in Italian translation, in *SONUS*, Year 3, No. 2, Potenza, Italy, March-May 1991. Questions translated from the original Italian by Robert Zappulla. Reprinted with permission.

Interview with James Boros: First published [as "Composing a viable (if transitory) self: Brian Ferneyhough in conversation with James Boros"] in *Perspectives of New Music*, Vol. 32 No. 1, 1994. Reprinted with permission.

A Verbal Crane Dance: Interview with Ross Feller: 1992. Previously unpublished.

Leaps and Circuits to Trail: Interview with Jeffrey Stadelman: 1992. Previously unpublished.

NAME INDEX

SUBJECT INDEX

Other titles in the Contemporary Music Studies series:

Volume 11
John Cage's Theatre Pieces: Notations and Performances
William Fetterman

Volume 12
On Sonic Art
Trevor Wishart

Volume 13
Soviet Film Music — An Historical Survey
Tatiana Egorova

Volume 14
Schönberg and Kandinsky — An Historic Encounter
Edited by Konrad Boehmer

Volume 15
Italian Opera Since 1945
Raymond Fearn

Volume 16
The Whole World of Music — A Henry Cowell Symposium
Edited by David Nicholls

Volume 17
Gian Francesco Malipiero (1882–1973):
The Life, Times and Music of a Wayward Genius
John Waterhouse

Additional volumes in preparation:

Jani Christou — The Works and Temperament of a Greek Composer of Our Time
Anna M. Lucciano

Harry Partch — An Anthology of Critical Perspectives
Edited by David Dunn

Readings in Music and Artificial Intelligence
Edited by Eduardo Reck Miranda